[See page 22

"'RUFFO—THAT'S A NICE NAME. IT SOUNDS STRONG AND BOLD'"

A SPIRIT IN PRISON

BY

ROBERT HICHENS

AUTHOR OF
"THE GARDEN OF ALLAH"
"THE CALL OF THE BLOOD" ETC.

ILLUSTRATED BY
CYRUS CUNEO

NEW YORK AND LONDON
HARPER & BROTHERS PUBLISHERS
MCMVIII

ISBN 13: 978-1-4344-8266-2

ILLUSTRATIONS

A SPIRIT IN PRISON

A SPIRIT IN PRISON

CHAPTER I

SOMEWHERE, not far off on the still sea that held the tiny islet in a warm embrace, a boy's voice was singing "Napoli Bella."

Vere heard the song as she sat in the sun with her face set towards Nisida and the distant peak of Ischia; and instinctively she shifted her position, and turned her head, looking towards the calm and untroubled water that stretched between her and Naples. For the voice that sang of the beautiful city was coming towards her from the beautiful city, hymning the siren it had left perhaps but two hours ago.

On his pedestal set upon rock San Francesco seemed to be attentive to the voice. He stood beyond the sheltered pool of the sea that divided the islet from the mainland, staring across at Vere as if he envied her; he who was rooted in Italy and deprived of her exquisite freedom. His beard hung down to his waist, his cross protruded over his left shoulder, and his robe of dusty grayish brown touched his feet, which had never wandered one step since he was made, and set there to keep watch over the fishermen who come to sleep under the lee of the island by night.

Now it was brilliant daylight. The sun shone vividly over the Bay of Naples, over the great and vital city,

3

over Vesuvius, the long line of the land towards Sorrento, over Capri with its shadowy mountain, and Posilippo with its tree-guarded villas. And in the sharp radiance of May the careless voice of the fisher-boy sang the familiar song that Vere had always known and seldom heeded.

To-day, why she did not know, Vere listened to it attentively. Something in the sound of the voice caught her attention, roused within her a sense of sympathy.

Carelessness and happiness make a swift appeal to young hearts, and this voice was careless, and sounded very happy. There was a deliberate gruffness in it, a determination to be manly, which proved the vocalist to be no man. Vere knew at once that a boy was singing, and she felt that she must see him.

She got up, went into the little garden at the edge of the cliff, and looked over the wall.

There was a boat moving slowly towards her, not very far away. In it were three figures, all stripped for diving, and wearing white cotton drawers. Two were sitting on the gunwale with their knees drawn up nearly to their chins. The third was standing, and with a languid, but strong and regular movement, was propelling the boat forward with big-bladed oars. This was the singer, and as the boat drew nearer Vere could see that he had the young, lithe form of a boy.

While she watched, leaning down from her eyrie, the boat and the song stopped, and the singer let go his oars and turned to the men behind him. The boat had reached a place near the rocks that was good ground for *frutti di mare*.

Vere had often seen the divers in the Bay of Naples at their curious toil. Yet it never ceased to interest her. She had a passion for the sea, and for all things connected with it. Now she leaned a little lower over the wall, with her eyes fixed on the boat and its occupants.

Upon the water she saw corks floating, and presently one of the men swung himself round and sat facing the sea, with his back to the boat and his bare legs dipping into the water. The boy had dropped down to the bottom of the craft. His hands were busy arranging clothes, or tackle, and his lusty voice again rang out to the glory of "Napoli, bella Napoli." There was something infectious in his happy-go-lucky light-heartedness. Vere smiled as she listened, but there was a wistfulness in her heart. At that moment a very common desire of young and vigorous girls assailed her—the desire to be a boy; not a boy born of rich parents, destined to the idle, aimless life of aristocratic young Neapolitans, but a brown, badly dressed, or scarcely dressed at all boy of the people.

She was often light-hearted, careless. But was she ever as light-hearted and careless as that singing boy? She supposed herself to be free. But was she, could she ever be at liberty as he was?

The man who had been dipping his feet in the sea rested one hand on the gunwale, let his body droop forward, dropped into the water, paddled for a moment, reached one of the floating corks, turned over head downwards, describing a circle which showed his chocolate-colored back arched, kicked up his feet and disappeared. The second man lounged lazily from the boat into the sea and imitated him. The boy sat still and went on singing. Vere felt disappointed. Was not he going to dive too? She wanted him to dive. If she were that boy she would go in, she felt sure of it, before the men. It must be lovely to sink down into the underworld of the sea, to rifle from the rocks their fruit, that grew thick as fruit on the trees. But the boy—he was lazy, good for nothing but singing. She was half ashamed of him. Whim-

5

sically, and laughing to herself at her own absurdity, she lifted her two hands, brown with the sun, to her lips, and cried with all her might:

"Va dentro, pigro! Va dentro!"

As her voice died away, the boy stopped singing, sprang into the sea, kicked up his feet and disappeared.

Vere was conscious of a thrill that was like a thrill of triumph.

"He obeyed me!" she thought.

A pleasant feeling of power came to her. From her eyrie on the rock she was directing these strange sea doings. She was ruling over the men of the sea.

The empty boat swayed softly on the water, but its three former occupants were all hidden by the sea. It seemed as if they would never come up again. Vere began to hold her breath as they were holding theirs. At last a dark head rose above the surface, then another. The two men paddled for a minute, drawing the air into their lungs. But the boy did not reappear.

As the seconds passed, Vere began to feel proud of him. He was doing that which she would have tried to do had she been a boy. He was rivalling the men.

Another second slipped away—and another. He was more than rivalling, he was beating the men.

They dived once more. She saw the sun gleam on their backs, which looked polished as they turned slowly over, almost like brown porpoises.

But the boy remained hidden beneath the veil of water.

Vere began to feel anxious. What if some accident had happened? What if he had been caught by the sea-weed, or if his groping hand had been retained by some crevice of the rock? There was a pain at her heart. Her quick imagination was at work. It seemed to her as if she felt his agony, took part in his struggle to regain his freedom. She clinched her small hands and set her teeth. She held her breath, trying to feel exactly as he

6

was feeling. And then suddenly she lifted her hands up to her face, covering her nostrils. What a horrible sensation it was, this suffocation, this pressing of the life out of the body, almost as one may push a person brutally out of a room! She could bear it no more, and she dropped her hands. As she did so the boy's dark head rose above the sea.

Vere uttered a cry of joy.

"Bravo! Bravo!"

She felt as if he had returned from the dead. He was a wonderful boy.

"Bravo! Bravissimo!"

Serenely unconscious of her enthusiasm, the boy swam slowly for a moment, breathing the air into his lungs, then serenely dived again.

"Vere!" called a woman's voice from the house— "Vere!"

"Madre!" cried the girl in reply, but without turning away from the sea. "I am here! Do come out! I want to show you something."

On a narrow terrace looking towards Naples a tall figure appeared.

"Where are you?"

"Here! here!"

The mother smiled and left the terrace, passed through a little gate, and almost directly was standing beside the girl, saying:

"What is it? Is there a school of whales in the Bay, or have you sighted the sea-serpent coming from Capri?"

"No, no! But—you see that boat?"

"Yes. The men are diving for *frutti di mare*, aren't they?"

Vere nodded.

"The men are nothing. But there is a boy who is wonderful."

"Why? What does he do?"

"He stays under water an extraordinary time. Now wait. Have you got a watch, Madre?"

"Yes."

"Take it out, there's a darling, and time him. I want to know—there he is! You see?"

"Yes."

"Have you got your watch? Wait till he goes under! Wait a minute! There! He's gone! Now begin."

She drew into her lungs a long breath, and held it. The mother smiled, keeping her eyes obediently on the watch which lay in her hand.

There was a silence between them as the seconds passed.

"Really," began the mother presently, "he must be—"

"Hush, Madre, hush!"

The girl had clasped her hands tightly. Her eyes never left the sea. The tick, tick of the watch was just audible in the stillness of the May morning. At last—

"There he is!" cried the girl. "Quick! How long has he been under?"

"Just fifty seconds."

"I wonder—I'm sure it's a record. If only Gaspare were here! When will he be back from Naples with Monsieur Émile?"

"About twelve, I should think. But I doubt if they can sail." She looked out to sea, and added: "I think the wind is changing to scirocco. They may be later."

"He's gone down again!"

"I never saw you so interested in a diver before," said the mother. "What made you begin to look at the boy?"

"He was singing. I heard him, and his voice made me feel—" She paused.

"What?" said her mother.

"I don't know. *Un poco diavolesca*, I'm afraid. One thing, though! It made me long to be a boy."

8

"Did it?"

"Yes! Madre, tell me truly—sea-water on your lips, as the fishermen say—now truly, did you ever want me to be a boy?"

Hermione Delarey did not answer for a moment. She looked away over the still sea, that seemed to be slowly losing its color, and she thought of another sea, of the Ionian waters that she had loved so much. They had taken her husband from her before her child was born, and this child's question recalled to her the sharp agony of those days and nights in Sicily, when Maurice lay unburied in the Casa del Prete, and afterwards in the hospital at Marechiaro—of other days and nights in Italy, when, isolated with the Sicilian boy, Gaspare, she had waited patiently for the coming of her child.

"Sea-water, Madre, sea-water on your lips!"

Her mother looked down at her.

"Do you think I wished it, Vere?"

"To-day I do."

"Why to-day?"

"Because I wish it so much. And it seems to me as if perhaps I wish it because you once wished it for me. You thought I should be a boy?"

"I felt sure you would be a boy."

"Madre! How strange!"

The girl was looking up at her mother. Her dark eyes—almost Sicilian eyes they were—opened very wide, and her lips remained slightly parted after she had spoken.

"I wonder why that was?" she said at length.

"I have wondered too. It may have been that I was always thinking of your father in those days, recalling him—well, recalling him as he had been in Sicily. He went away from me so suddenly that somehow his going, even when it had happened, for a long time seemed to be an impossibility. And I fancied, I suppose, that my child would be him in a way."

"Come back?"

"Or never quite gone."

The girl was silent for a moment.

"Povera Madre mia!" at last she said.

But she did not seem distressed for herself. No personal grievance, no doubt of complete love assailed her. And the fact that this was so demonstrated, very quietly and very completely, the relation existing between this mother and this child.

"I wonder, now," Vere said, presently, "why I never specially wished to be a boy until to-day—because, after all, it can't be from you that the wish came. If it had been it must have come long ago. And it didn't. It only came when I heard that boy's voice. He sings like all the boys, you know, that have ever enjoyed themselves, that are still enjoying themselves in the sun."

"I wish he would sing once more!" said Hermione.

"Perhaps he will. Look! He's getting into the boat. And the men are stopping too."

The boy was very quick in his movements. Almost before Vere had finished speaking he had pulled on his blue jersey and white trousers, and again taken the big oars into his hands. Standing up, with his face set towards the islet, he began once more to propel the boat towards it. And as he swung his body slowly to and fro he opened his lips and sang lustily once more,

> "O Napoli, bella Napoli!"

Hermione and Vere sat silently listening as the song grew louder and louder, till the boat was almost in the shadow of the islet, and the boy, with a strong stroke of the left oar turned its prow towards the pool over which San Francesco watched.

"They're going into the Saint's Pool to have a siesta," said Vere. "Isn't he a splendid boy, Madre?"

As she spoke the boat was passing almost directly beneath them, and they saw its name painted in red letters on the prow, *Sirena del Mare.* The two men, one young, one middle-aged, were staring before them at the rocks. But the boy, more sensitive, perhaps, than they were to the watching eyes of women, looked straight up to Vere and to her mother. They saw his level rows of white teeth gleaming as the song came out from his parted lips, the shining of his eager dark eyes, full of the careless merriment of youth, the black, low-growing hair stirring in the light sea breeze about his brow, bronzed by sun and wind. His slight figure swayed with an easy motion that had the grace of perfectly controlled activity, and his brown hands gripped the great oars with a firmness almost of steel, as the boat glided under the lee of the island, and vanished from the eyes of the watchers into the shadowy pool of San Francesco.

When the boat had disappeared, Vere lifted herself up and turned round to her mother.

"Isn't he a jolly boy, Madre?"

"Yes," said Hermione.

She spoke in a low voice. Her eyes were still on the sea where the boat had passed.

"Yes," she repeated, almost as if to herself.

For the first time a little cloud went over Vere's sensitive face.

"Madre, how horribly I must have disappointed you," she said.

The mother did not break into protestations. She always treated her child with sincerity.

"Just for a moment, Vere," she answered. "And then, very soon, you made me feel how much more intimate can be the relationship between a mother and a daughter than between a mother and any son."

"Is that true, really?"

"I think it is."

"But why should that be?"

"Don't you think Monsieur Emile could tell you much better than I? I feel all the things, you know, that he can explain."

There was a touch of something that was like a half-hidden irony in her voice.

"Monsieur Emile! Yes, I think he understands almost everything about people," said Vere, quite without irony. "But could a man explain such a thing as well as a woman? I don't think so."

"We have the instincts, perhaps, men the vocabulary. Come, Vere, I want to look over into the Saint's Pool and see what those men are doing."

Vere laughed.

"Take care, Madre, or Gaspare will be jealous."

A soft look came into Hermione's face.

"Gaspare and I know each other," she said, quietly.

"But he could be jealous—horribly jealous."

"Of you, perhaps, Vere, but never of me. Gaspare and I have passed through too much together for anything of that kind. Nobody could ever take his place with me, and he knows it quite well."

"Gaspare's a darling, and I love him," said Vere, rather inconsequently. "Shall we look over into the Pool from the pavilion, or go down by the steps?"

"We'll look over."

They passed in through a gateway to the narrow terrace that fronted the Casa del Mare facing Vesuvius, entered the house, traversed a little hall, came out again into the air by a door on its farther side, and made their way to a small pavilion that looked upon the Pool of San Francesco. Almost immediately below, in the cool shadow of the cliff, the boat was moored. The two men, lying at full length in it, their faces buried in their hands, were already asleep. But the boy, sitting astride on the prow, with his bare feet dangling on each side of it to the clear green water, was munching slowly, and rather seriously, a hunch of yellow bread, from which he cut from time to time large pieces with a clasp knife. As he ate, lifting the pieces of bread to his mouth with the knife, against whose blade he held them with his thumb, he stared down at the depths below, transparent here almost to the sea bed. His eyes were wide with reverie. He seemed another boy, not the gay singer of five minutes ago. But then he had been in the blaze of the sun. Now he was in the shade. And swiftly he had caught the influence of the dimmer light, the lack of motion, the delicate hush at the feet of San Francesco.

This time he did not know that he was being watched. His reverie, perhaps, was too deep, or their gaze less concentrated than it had been before. And after a moment, Hermione moved away.

"You are going in, Madre?"

"Yes."

"Do you mind if I give something to that boy?"

"Do you mean money?"

"Oh no. But the poor thing's eating dry bread, and—"

"And what, you puss?"

"Well, he's a very obedient boy."

"How can you know that?"

"He was idling in the boat, and I called out to him to jump into the sea, and he jumped in immediately."

"Do you think because he heard you?"

"Certainly I do."

"You conceited little creature! Perhaps he was only pleasing himself!"

"No, Madre, no. I think I should like to give him a little reward presently—for his singing too."

"Get him a dolce, then, from Carmela, if there is one. And you can give him some cigarettes."

"I will. He'll love that. Oh dear! I wish he didn't make me dissatisfied with myself!"

"Nonsense, Vere!"

Hermione bent down and kissed her child. Then she went rather quickly away from the pavilion and entered the Casa del Mare.

CHAPTER II

AFTER her mother had gone, Vere waited for a moment,
then ran lightly to the house, possessed herself of a dolce
and a packet of cigarettes, and went down the steps to
the Pool of San Francesco, full of hospitable intentions
towards the singing boy. She found him still sitting
astride of the boat's prow, not yet free of his reverie
apparently; for when she gave a low call of "Pescator!"
prolonging the last syllable with the emphasis and the
accent of Naples, but always softly, he started, and nearly
dropped into the sea the piece of bread he was lifting to
his mouth. Recovering himself in time to save the bread
deftly with one brown hand, he turned half round, leaning on his left arm, and stared at Vere with large, inquiring eyes. She stood by the steps and beckoned to
him, lifting up the packet of cigarettes, then pointing to
his sleeping companions:

"Come here for a minute!"

The boy smiled, sprang up, and leaped onto the islet.
As he came to her, with the easy, swinging walk of the
barefooted sea-people, he pulled up his white trousers,
and threw out his chest with an obvious desire to "fare
figura" before the pretty Padrona of the islet. When he
reached her he lifted his hand to his bare head forget-
fully, meaning to take off his cap to her. Finding that
he had no cap, he made a laughing grimace, threw up
his chin and, thrusting his tongue against his upper teeth
and opening wide his mouth, uttered a little sound most
characteristically Neapolitan — a sound that seemed

15

lightly condemnatory of himself. This done, he stood still before Vere, looking at the cigarettes and at the dolce.

"I've brought these for you," she said.

"Grazie, Signorina."

He did not hold out his hand, but his eyes, now devoted entirely to the cigarettes, began to shine with pleasure. Vere did not give him the presents at once. She had something to explain first.

"We mustn't wake them," she said, pointing towards the boat in which the men were sleeping. "Come a little way with me."

She retreated a few steps from the sea, followed closely by the eager boy.

"We sha'n't disturb them now," she said, stopping. "Do you know why I've brought you these?"

· She stretched out her hands, with the dolce and the cigarettes.

The boy threw his chin up again and half shut his eyes.

"No, Signorina."

"Because you did what I told you."

She spoke rather with the air of a little queen.

"I don't understand."

"Didn't you hear me call out to you from up there?" —she pointed to the cliff above their heads— "when you were sitting in the boat? I called to you to go in after the men."

"Why?"

"Why! Because I thought you were a lazy boy."

He laughed. All his brown face gave itself up to laughter—eyes, teeth, lips, cheeks, chin. His whole body seemed to be laughing. The idea of his being lazy seemed to delight his whole spirit.

"You would have been lazy if you hadn't done what I told you," said Vere, emphatically, forcing her words through his merriment with determination "You know you would."

A SPIRIT IN PRISON

"I never heard you call, Signorina."

"You didn't?"

He shook his head several times, bent down, dipped his fingers in the sea, put them to his lips: "I say it."

"Really?"

There was a note of disappointment in her voice. She felt dethroned.

"But then, you haven't earned these," she said, looking at him almost with rebuke, "if you went in of your own accord."

"I go in because it is my mestiere, Signorina," the boy said, simply. "I go in by force."

He looked at her and then again at the cigarettes. His expression said, "Can you refuse me?" There was a quite definite and conscious attempt to cajole her to generosity in his eyes, and in the pose he assumed. Vere saw it, and knew that if there had been a mirror within reach at that moment the boy would have been looking into it, frankly admiring himself.

In Italy the narcissus blooms at all seasons of the year.

She was charmed by the boy, for he did his luring well, and she was susceptible to all that was naturally picturesque. But a gay little spirit of resistance sprang up like a flame and danced within her.

She let her hands fall to her sides.

"But you like going in?"

"Signorina?"

"You enjoy diving?"

He shrugged his shoulders, and again used what seemed with him a favorite expression.

"Signorina, I must enjoy it, by force."

"You do it wonderfully. Do you know that? You do it better than the men."

Again the conscious look came into the boy's face and body, as if his soul were faintly swaggering.

"There is no one in the Bay who can dive better than I can," he answered. "Giovannino thinks he can. Well, let him think so. He would not dare to make a bet with me."

"He would lose it if he did," said Vere. "I'm sure he would. Just now you were under water nearly a minute by my mother's watch."

"Where is the Signora?" said the boy, looking round. "Why d'you ask?"

"Why—I can stay under longer than that."

"Now, look here!" said the girl, eagerly. "Never mind Madre! Go down once for me, won't you? Go down once for me, and you shall have the dolce and two packets of cigarettes."

"I don't want the dolce, Signorina; a dolce is for women," he said, with the complete bluntness characteristic of Southern Italians and of Sicilians.

"The cigarettes, then."

"Va bene. But the water is too shallow here."

"We'll take my boat."

She pointed to a small boat, white with a green line, that was moored close to them.

"Va bene," said the boy again.

He rolled his white trousers up above his knees, stripped off his blue jersey, leaving the thin vest that was beneath it, folded the jersey neatly and laid it on the stones, tightened his trousers at the back, then caught hold of the rope by which Vere's boat was moored to the shore and pulled the boat in.

Very carefully he helped Vere into it.

"I know a good place," he said, "where you can see right down to the bottom."

Taking the oars he slowly paddled a little way out to a deep clear pool of the sea.

"I'll go in here, Signorina."

He stood up straight, with his feet planted on each

18

"HE LIFTED HIS BROWN ARMS ABOVE HIS HEAD, UTTERED
A CRY, AND DIVED CLEANLY BELOW THE SURFACE"

side of the boat's prow, and glanced at the water intimately, as might a fish. Then he shot one more glance at Vere and at the cigarettes, made the sign of the cross, lifted his brown arms above his head, uttered a cry, and dived cleanly below the surface, going down obliquely till he was quite dim in the water.

Vere watched him with a deep attention. This feat of the boy fascinated her. The water between them made him look remote, delicate and unearthly—neither boy nor fish. His head, she could see, was almost touching the bottom. She fancied that he was actually touching bottom with his hands. Yes, he was. Bending low over the water she saw his brown fingers, stretched out and well divided, promenading over the basin of the sea as lightly and springily as the claws of a crab tiptoeing to some hiding-place. Presently he let himself down a little more, pressed his flat palms against the ground, and with the impetus thus gained made his body shoot back towards the surface feet foremost. Then bringing his body up till it was in a straight line with his feet, he swam slowly under water, curving first in this direction then in that, with a lithe ease that was enchantingly graceful. Finally, he turned over on his back and sank slowly down until he looked like a corpse lying at the bottom of the sea.

Then Vere felt a sickness of fear steal over her, and leaning over the sea till her face almost touched the water, she cried out fiercely:

"Come up! Come up! Presto! Presto!"

As the boy had seemed to obey her when she cried out to him from the summit of the cliff, so he seemed to obey her now.

When her voice died down into the sea-depths he rose from those depths, and she saw his eyes laughing, his lips laughing at her, freed from the strange veil of the water, which had cast upon him a spectral aspect, the likeness of a thing deserted by its soul.

"Did you hear me that time?" Vere said, rather eagerly.

The boy lifted his dark head from the water to shake it, drew a long breath, trod water, then threw up his chin with the touch of tongue against teeth which is the Neapolitan negative.

"You didn't! Then why did you come up?"

He swam to the boat.

"It pleased me to come."

She looked doubtful.

"I believe you are birbante," she said, slowly. "I am nearly sure you are."

The boy was just getting out, pulling himself up slowly to the boat by his arms, with his wet hands grasping the gunwale firmly. He looked at Vere, with the salt drops running down his sunburnt face, and dripping from his thick, matted hair to his strong neck and shoulders. Again his whole face laughed, as, nimbly, he brought his legs from the water and stood beside her.

"Birbante, Signorina?"

"Yes. Are you from Naples?"

"I come from Mergellina, Signorina."

Vere looked at him half-doubtfully, but still with innocent admiration. There was something perfectly fearless and capable about him that attracted her.

He rowed in to shore.

"How old are you?" she asked.

"Sixteen years old, Signorina."

"I am sixteen, too."

They reached the islet, and Vere got out. The boy followed her, fastened the boat, and moved away a few steps. She wondered why, till she saw him stop in a sun-patch and let the beams fall full upon him.

"You aren't afraid of catching cold?" she asked.

He threw up his chin. His eyes went to the cigarettes.

"Yes," said Vere, in answer to the look, "you shall have one. Here!"

She held out the packet. Very carefully and neatly the boy, after holding his right hand for a moment to the sun to get dry, drew out a cigarette.

"Oh, you want a match!"

He sprang away and ran lightly to the boat. Without waking his companions he found a matchbox and lit the cigarette. Then he came back, on the way stopping to get into his jersey.

Vere sat down on a narrow seat let into the rock close to the sun-patch. She was nursing the dolce on her knee.

"You won't have it?" she asked.

He gave her his usual negative, again stepping full into the sun.

"Well, then, I shall eat it. You say a dolce is for women!"

"Sì, Signorina," he answered, quite seriously.

She began to devour it slowly, while the boy drew the cigarette smoke into his lungs voluptuously.

"And you are only sixteen?" she asked.

"Sì, Signorina."

"As young as I am! But you look almost a man."

"Signorina, I have always worked. I am a man."

He squared his shoulders. She liked the determination, the resolution in his face; and she liked the face, too. He was a very handsome boy, she thought, but somehow he did not look quite Neapolitan. His eyes lacked the round and staring impudence characteristic of many Neapolitans she had seen. There was something at times impassive in their gaze. In shape they were long, and slightly depressed at the corners by the cheeks, and they had full, almost heavy, lids. The features of the boy were small and straight, and gave no promise of

eventual coarseness. He was splendidly made. When
Vere looked at him she thought of an arrow. Yet he was
very muscular, and before he dived she had noticed that
on his arms the biceps swelled up like smooth balls of
iron beneath the shining brown skin.

"What month were you born in?" she asked.

"Signorina, I believe I was born in March. I believe
I was sixteen last March."

"Then I am older than you are!"

This seemed to the boy a matter of indifference,
though it was evidently exercising the girl beside him.
She had finished the dolce now, and he was smoking the
last fraction of an inch of the cigarette, economically
determined to waste none of it, even though he burnt
his fingers.

"Have another cigarette," Vere added, after a pause
during which she considered him carefully. "You can't
get anything more out of that one."

"Grazie, Signorina."

He took it eagerly.

"Do tell me your name, won't you?" Vere went on.

"Ruffo, Signorina."

"Ruffo—that's a nice name. It sounds strong and
bold. And you live at Mergellina?"

"Sì, Signorina. But I wasn't born there. I wasn't
born in Naples at all."

"Where were you born?"

"In America, Signorina, near New York. I am a
Sicilian."

"A Sicilian, are you!"

"Sì, Signorina."

"I am a little bit Sicilian, too; only a little tiny bit—
but still—"

She waited to see the effect upon him. He looked at
her steadily with his long bright eyes.

"You are Sicilian, Signorina?"

"My great-grandmother was."

"Sì?"

His voice sounded incredulous.

"Don't you believe me?" she cried, rather hotly.

"Ma sì, Signorina! only—that's not very Sicilian, if the rest is English. You are English, Signorina, aren't you?"

"The rest of me is. Are you all Sicilian?"

"Signorina, my mother is Sicilian."

"And your father, too?"

The boy's face suddenly clouded.

"Signorina, my father is dead," he said, in a changed voice. "Now I live with my mother and my step-father. He—Patrigno—he is Neapolitan."

There was a movement in the boat. The boy looked round.

"I must go back to the boat, Signorina," he said.

"Oh, must you?" Vere said. "What a pity! But look, they are really still asleep."

"I must go back, Signorina," he protested.

"You want to sleep, too, perhaps?"

He seized the excuse.

"Sì, Signorina. Being under the sea so much—it tires the head and the eyes. I want to sleep, too."

His face, full of life, denied his words, but Vere only said:

"Here are the cigarettes."

"Grazie, Signorina."

"And I promised you another packet. Well, wait here —just here, d'you see?—under the bridge, and I'll throw it down, and you must catch it."

"Sì, Signorina."

He took his stand on the spot she pointed out, and she disappeared up the steps towards the house.

"Madre! madre!"

Hermione heard Vere's voice calling below a moment later.

A SPIRIT IN PRISON

"What is it?"

There was a quick step on the stairs, and the girl ran in.

"One more packet of cigarettes—may I? It's instead of the dolce. Ruffo says only women eat sweet things."

"Ruffo!"

"Yes, that's his name. He's been diving for me. You never saw anything like it! And he's a Sicilian. Isn't it odd? And sixteen—just as I am. May I have the cigarettes for him?"

"Yes, of course. In that drawer there's a whole box of the ones Monsieur Emile likes."

"There would be ten cigarettes in a packet. I'll give him ten."

She counted them swiftly out.

"There! And I'll make him catch them all, one by one. It will be more fun than throwing only a packet. Addio, mia bella Madre! Addi-io! Addi-io!"

And singing the words to the tune of "Addio, mia bella Napoli," she flitted out of the room and down the stairs.

"Ruffo! Ruffo!"

A minute later she was leaning over the bridge to the boy, who stood sentinel below. He looked up, and saw her laughing face full of merry mischief, and prepared to catch the packet she had promised him.

"Ruffo, I'm so sorry, but I can't find another packet of cigarettes."

The boy's bright face changed, looked almost sad, but he called up:

"Non fa niente, Signorina!" He stood still for a moment, then made a gesture of salutation, and added; "Thank you, Signorina. A rivederci!"

He moved to go to the boat, but Vere cried out, quickly:

"Wait, Ruffo! Can you catch well?"

"Signorina?"

"Look out now!"

Her arm was thrust out over the bridge, and Ruffo,

staring up, saw a big cigarette—a cigarette such as he had never before seen—in her small fingers. Quickly he made a receptacle of his joined hands, his eyes sparkling and his lips parted with happy anticipation.

"One!"

The cigarette fell and was caught.

"Two!"

A second fell. But this time Ruffo was unprepared, and it dropped on the rock by his bare feet.

"Stupido!" laughed the girl.

"Ma, Signorina—!"

"Three!"

It had become a game between them, and continued to be a game until all the ten cigarettes had made their journey through the air.

Vere would not let Ruffo know when a cigarette was coming, but kept him on the alert, pretending, holding it poised above him between finger and thumb until even his eyes blinked from gazing upward; then dropping it when she thought he was unprepared, or throwing it like a missile. But she soon knew that she had found her match in the boy. And when he caught the tenth and last cigarette in his mouth she clapped her hands, and cried out so enthusiastically that one of the men in the boat heaved himself up from the bottom, and, choking down a yawn, stared with heavy amazement at the young virgin of the rocks, and uttered a "Che Diavolo!" under his stiff mustache.

Vere saw his astonishment, and swiftly, with a parting wave of her hand to Ruffo, she disappeared, leaving her protégé to run off gayly with his booty to his comrades of the *Sirena del Mare*.

CHAPTER III

"I can see the boat, Vere," said Hermione, when the girl came back, her eyes still gleaming with memories of the fun of the cigarette game with Ruffo.

"Where, Madre?"

She sat down quickly beside her mother on the window-seat, leaning against her confidentially and looking out over the sea. Hermione put her arm round the girl's shoulder.

"There! Don't you see?" She pointed. "It has passed Casa Pantano."

"I see! yes, that is Gaspare, and Monsieur Emile in the stern. They won't be late for lunch. I almost wish they would, Madre."

"Why?"

"I'm not a bit hungry. Ruffo wouldn't eat the dolce, so I did."

"Ruffo! You seem to have made great friends with that boy."

She did not speak rebukingly, but with a sort of tender amusement.

"I really have," returned Vere.

She put her head against her mother's shoulder.

"Isn't this odd, Madre? Twice in the short time I've known Ruffo, he's obeyed me. The first time he was in the boat. I called out to him to dive in, and he did it instantly. The second time he was under water, at the very bottom of the sea. He looked as if he were dead, and for a minute I felt frightened. So I called out to him to come up, and he came up directly."

26

"But that only shows that he's a polite boy and does what you wish."

"No, no. He didn't hear me either time. He had no idea I had called. But each time I did, without hearing me he had the sudden wish to do what I wanted. Now, isn't that curious?"

She paused.

"Madre?" she added.

"You think you influenced him?"

"Don't you think I did?"

"Perhaps so. There's the sympathetic link of youth between you. You are gloriously young, both of you; little daughter. And youth turns naturally to youth, though I'm afraid old age doesn't always turn naturally to old age."

"What do you know about old age, Madre? You haven't a gray hair."

She spoke with anxious encouragement.

"It's true. My hair declines to get gray."

"I don't believe you'll ever be gray."

"Probably not. But there's another grayness—Life behind one instead of before; the emotional—"

She stopped herself. This was not for Vere.

"They're close in," she said, looking out of the window.

She waved her hand. The big man in the stern of the boat took off his hat in reply, and waved his hand, too. The rower pulled with the vivacity that comes to men near the end of a task, and the boat shot into the Pool of the Saint, where Ruffo was at that moment enjoying his third cigarette.

"I'll run down and meet Monsieur Emile," said Vere.

And she disappeared as swiftly as she had come.

The big man who got out of the boat could not claim Hermione's immunity from gray hairs. His beard was lightly powdered with them, and though much of the still thick hair on his head was brown, and his figure was

erect, and looked strong and athletic—he seemed what
he was, a man of middle age, who had lived, and thought,
and observed much. His eyes had the peculiar expression of eyes that have seen very many and very various
sights. It was difficult to imagine them looking surprised, impossible to imagine them not looking keenly intelligent. The vivacity of youth was no longer in them,
but the vividness of intellect, of an intellect almost fiercely
alive and tenacious of its life, was never absent from them.

As Artois got out, the boat's prow was being held by
the Sicilian, Gaspare, now a man of thirty-five, but still
young-looking. Many Sicilians grow old quickly—hard
life wears them out. But Gaspare's fate had been easier
than that of most of his contemporaries and friends of
Marechiaro. Ever since the tragic death of the beloved
master, whom he still always spoke of as "mio Padrone,"
he had been Hermione's faithful attendant and devoted
friend. Yes, she knew him to be that—she wished him
to be that. Their stations in life might be different,
but they had come to sorrow together. They had suffered together and been in sympathy while they suffered.
He had loved what she had loved, lost it when she had
lost it, wept for it when she had wept.

And he had been with her when she had waited for the
coming of the child.

Hermione really cared for three people: Gaspare was
one of them. He knew it. The other two were Vere
and Emile Artois.

"Vere," said Artois, taking her two hands closely in
his large hands, and gazing into her face with the kind,
even affectionate directness that she loved in him: "do
you know that to-day you are looking insolent?"

"Insolent!" said the girl. "How dare you!"

She tried to take her hands away.

"Insolently young," he said, keeping them authoritatively.

A SPIRIT IN PRISON

"But I am young. What do you mean, Monsieur Emile?"

"I? It is your meaning I am searching for."

"I sha'n't let you find it. You are much too curious about people. But—I've been having a game this morning."

"A game! Who was your playmate?"

"Never mind."

But her bright eyes went for the fraction of a second to Ruffo, who close by in the boat was lying at his ease, his head thrown back, and one of the cigarettes between his lips.

"What! That boy there?"

"Nonsense! Come along! Madre has been sitting at the window for ages looking out for the boat. Couldn't you sail at all Gaspare?"

Artois had let go her hands, and now she turned to the Sicilian.

"To Naples, Signorina, and nearly to the Antico Giuseppone coming back."

"But we had to do a lot of tacking," said Artois. "Mon Dieu! That boy is smoking one of my cigarettes! You sacrilegious little creature! You have been robbing my box!"

Gaspare's eyes followed Artois' to Ruffo, who was watching them attentively, but who now looked suddenly sleepy.

"It belongs to Madre."

"It was bought for me."

"I like you better with a pipe. You are too big for cigarettes. And besides, artists always smoke pipes."

"Allow me to forget that I try to be an artist when I come to the island, Vere."

"Yes, yes, I will," she said, with a pretty air of relenting. "You poor thing, here you are a king incognito, and we all treat you quite familiarly. I'll even go first, regardless of etiquette." And she went off to the steps that led upward to the house.

Artois followed her. As he went he said to Ruffo in the Neapolitan dialect:

"It's a good cigarette, isn't it? You are in luck this morning."

"Si, Signore," said the boy, smiling. "The Signorina gave me ten."

And he blew out a happy cloud.

There was something in his welcoming readiness of response, something in his look and voice, that seemed to stir within the tenacious mind of Artois a quivering chord of memory.

"I wonder if I have spoken to that boy in Naples?" he thought, as he mounted the steps behind Vere.

Hermione met him at the door of her room, and they went in almost directly to lunch with Vere. When the meal was over Vere disappeared, without saying why, and Hermione and Artois returned to Hermione's room to have coffee. By this time the day was absolutely windless, the sky had become nearly white, and the sea was a pale gray, flecked here and there with patches of white.

"This is like a June day of scirocco," said Artois, as he lit his pipe with the air of a man thoroughly at home. "I wonder if it will succeed in affecting Vere's spirits. This morning, when I arrived, she looked wildly young. But the day held still some blue then."

Hermione was settling herself slowly in a low chair near the window that faced Capri. The curious, rather ghastly light from the sea fell over her.

"Vere is very sensitive to almost all influences," she said. "You know that, Emile."

"Yes," he said, throwing away the match he had been using; "and the influence of this morning roused her to joy. What was it?"

"She was very excited watching a diver for *frutti di mare*."

"A boy about seventeen or eighteen, black hair, Arab eyes, bronze skin, a smile difficult to refuse, and a figure almost as perfect as a Nubian's, but rather squarer about the shoulders?"

"You have seen him, then?"

"Smoking ten of my special Khali Targa cigarettes, with his bare toes cocked up, and one hand drooping into the Saint's Pool."

Hermione smiled.

"My cigarettes! They're common property here," she said.

"That boy can't be a pure-bred Neapolitan, surely. And yet he speaks the language. There's no mistaking the blow he gives to the last syllable of a sentence."

"He's a Sicilian, Vere says."

"Pure bred?"

"I don't know."

"I fancy I must have run across him somewhere in or about Naples. It is he who made Vere, as I told her, look so insolently young this morning."

"Ah, you noticed! I, too, thought I had never seen her so full of the inner spirit of youth—almost as he was in Sicily."

"Yes," Artois said, gravely. "In some things she is very much his daughter."

"In some things only?" asked Hermione.

"Don't you think so? Don't you think she has much of you in her also? I do."

"Has she? I don't know that I see it. I don't know that I want to see it. I always look for him in Vere. You see, I dreamed of having a boy. Vere is instead of the boy I dreamed of, the boy—who never came, who will never come."

"My friend," said Artois, very seriously and gently,

"are you still allowing your mind to dwell upon that old imagination? And with Vere before you, can you regard her merely as a substitute, an understudy?"

An energy that was not free from passion suddenly flamed up in Hermione.

"I love Vere," she said. "She is very close to me. She knows it. She does not doubt me or my love."

"But," he quietly persisted, "you still allow your mind to rove ungoverned among those dangerous ways of the past?"

"Emile," she said, still speaking with vehemence, "it may be very easy to a strong man like you to direct his thoughts, to keep them out of one path and guide them along another. It may be—I don't know whether it is; but I don't pretend to such strength. I don't believe it is ever given to women. Perhaps even strength has its sex—I sometimes think so. I have my strength, believe me. But don't require of me the peculiar strength that is male."

"The truth is that you love living in the past as the Bedouin loves living in the desert."

"It was my oasis," she answered, simply.

"And all these years--they have made no difference?"

"Did you think they would? Did you think they had?"

"I hoped so. I thought—I had begun to think that you lived again in Vere."

"Emile, you can always stand the truth, can't you? Don't say you can't. That would hurt me horribly. Perhaps you do not know how sometimes I mentally lean on you. And I like to feel that if you knew the absolute truth of me you would still look upon me with the same kind, understanding eyes as now. Perhaps no one else would. Would you, do you think?"

"I hope and believe I could," he said. "You do not live in Vere. Is that it?"

A SPIRIT IN PRISON

"I know it is considered the right, the perfectly natural thing that a mother, stricken as I have been, should find in time perfect peace and contentment in her child. Even you—you spoke of 'living again.' It's the consecrated phrase, Emile, isn't it? I ought to be living again in Vere. Well, I'm not doing that. With my nature I could never do that. Is that horrible?"

"Ma pauvre amie!" he said.

He bent down and touched her hand.

"I don't know," she said, more calmly, as if relieved, but still with an undercurrent of passion, "whether I could ever live again in the life of another. But if I did it would be in the life of a man. I am not made to live in a woman's life, really to live, giving out the force that is in me. I know I'm a middle-aged woman—to these Italians here more than that, an old woman. But I'm not a finished woman, and I never shall be till I die. Vere is my child. I love her tenderly; more than that—passionately. She has always been close to me, as you know. But no, Emile, my relation to Vere, hers to me, does not satisfy all my need of love, my power to love. No, no, it doesn't. There's something in me that wants more, much more than that. There's something in me that—I think only a son of his could have satisfied my yearning. A son might have been Maurice come back to me, come back in a different, beautiful, wonderfully pure relation. I prayed for a son. I needed a son. Don't misunderstand me, Emile; in a way a son could never have been so close to me as Vere is,—but I could have lived in him as I can never live in Vere. I could have lived in him almost as once I lived in Maurice. And to-day I—"

She got up suddenly from her chair, put her arms on the window-frame, and leaned out to the strange, white day.

"Emile," she said, in a moment, turning round to him,

33

"I want to get away, on to the sea. Will you row me out, into the Grotto of Virgil?* It's so dreadfully white here, white and ghastly. I can't talk naturally here. And I should like to go on a little farther, now I've begun. It would do me good to make a clean breast of it, dear brother confessor. Shall we take the little boat and go?"

"Of course," he said.

"I'll get a hat."

She was away for two or three minutes. During that time Artois stood by the window that looked towards Ischia. The stillness of the day was intense, and gave to his mind a sensation of dream. Far off across the gray-and-white waters, partially muffled in clouds that almost resembled mist, the mountains of Ischia were rather suggested, mysteriously indicated, than clearly seen. The gray cliffs towards Bagnoli went down into motionless water gray as they were, but of a different, more pathetic shade.

There was a luminous whiteness in the sky that affected the eyes, as snow does.

Artois, as he looked, thought this world looked very old, a world arranged for the elderly to dwell in. Was it not, therefore, an appropriate setting for him and for Hermione? As this idea came into his mind it sent a rather bitter smile to his lips, and Hermione, coming in just then, saw the smile and said,—

"What is it, Emile? Why are you smiling?"

"Perhaps I will tell you when we are on the sea," he answered.

He looked at her. She had on a black hat, over which a white veil was fastened. It was tied beneath her chin, and hung down in a cloud over her breast. It made him think of the strange misty clouds which brooded about the breasts of the mountains of Ischia.

* The grotto described in this book is not really the Grotto of Virgil, but it is often called so by the fishermen along the coast.

34

"Shall we go?" she said.

"Yes. What is Vere doing?"

"She is in her room."

"What is she doing there?"

"Reading, I suppose. She often shuts herself up. She loves reading almost more than I do."

"Well?"

Hermione led the way down-stairs. When they were outside, on the crest of the islet, the peculiar sickliness of the weather struck them both more forcibly.

"This is the strangest scirocco effect I think I have ever seen," said Artois. "It is as if nature were under the influence of a drug, and had fallen into a morbid dream, with eyes wide open, and pale, inert and folded hands. I should like to see Naples to-day, and notice if this weather has any effect upon that amazing population. I wonder if my young friend, Marchese Isidoro Panacci— By-the-way, I haven't told you about him?"

"No."

"I must. But not now. We will continue our former conversation. Where shall we find the boat, the small one?"

"Gaspare will bring it—Gaspare! Gaspare!"

"Signora!" cried a strong voice below.

"La piccola barca!"

"Va bene, Signora!"

They descended slowly. It would have been almost impossible to do anything quickly on such a day. The smallest movement, indeed, seemed almost an outrage, likely to disturb the great white dreamer of the sea. When they reached the foot of the cliff Gaspare was there, holding the little craft in which Vere had gone out with Ruffo.

"Do you want me, Signora?"

"No, thank you, Gaspare. Don Emilio will row me. We are only going a very little way."

A SPIRIT IN PRISON

She stepped in. As Artois followed her he said to Gaspare:

"Those fishermen have gone?"

"Five minutes ago, Signore. There they are!"

He pointed to a boat at some distance, moving slowly in the direction of Posilipo.

"I have been talking with them. One says he is of my country, a Sicilian."

"The boy?"

"Sì, Signore, the giovinotto. But he cannot speak Sicilian, and he has never been in Sicily, poveretto!"

Gaspare spoke with an accent of pity in which there was almost a hint of contempt.

"A rivederci, Signore," he added, pushing off the little boat.

"A rivederci, Gaspare."

Artois took the oars and paddled very gently out, keeping near to the cliffs of the opposite shore.

"Even San Francesco looks weary to-day," he said, glancing across the pool at the Saint on his pedestal. "I should not be surprised if, when we return, we find that he has laid down his cross and is reclining like the tired fishermen who come here in the night. Where shall we go?"

"To the Grotto of Virgil."

"I wonder if Virgil was ever in his grotto? I wonder if he ever came here on such a day of **sirocco as** this, and felt that the world was very old, and he was even older than the world?"

"Do you feel like that to-day?"

"I feel that this is a world suitable for the old, for those who have white hairs to accord with the white waters, and whose nights are the white nights of age."

"Was that why you were smiling **so strangely just** now when I came in?"

"Yes."

A SPIRIT IN PRISON

He rowed on softly. The boat slipped out of the Pool of the Saint, and then they saw the Capo Coroglio and the Island of Nisida with its fort. On their right, and close to them, rose the weary-looking cliffs, honey-combed with caverns, and seamed with fissures as an old and haggard face is seamed with the wrinkles that tell of many cares."

"Here is the grotto," said Hermione, almost directly. "Row in gently."

He obeyed her and turned the boat, sending it in under the mighty roof of rock.

A darkness fell upon them. They had a safe, en-closed sensation in escaping for a moment from the white day, almost as if they had escaped from a white enemy.

Artois let the oars lie still in the water, keeping his hands lightly upon them, and both Hermione and he were silent for a few minutes, listening to the tiny sounds made now and then by drops of moisture which fell from the cavern roof softly into the almost silent sea. At last Artois said:

"You are out of the whiteness now. This is a shad-owed place like a confessional, where murmuring lips tell to strangers the stories of their lives. I am not a stranger, but tell me, my friend, about yourself and Vere. Perhaps you scarcely know how deeply the mother and child problem interests me—that is, when mother and child are two real forces, as you and Vere are."

"Then you think Vere has force?"

"Do not you?"

"What kind of force?"

"You mean physical, intellectual, or moral? Suppose I say she has the force of charm!"

"Indeed she has that, as he had. That is one of the attributes she derives from Maurice,"

"Yes. He had a wonderful charm. And then, Vere has passion."

"You think so?"

"I am sure of it. Where does she get that from?"

"He was full of the passion of the South."

"I think Vere has a touch of Northern passion in her, too, combined perhaps with the other. And that, I think, she derives from you. Then I discern in Vere intellectual force, immature, embryonic if you like, but unmistakable."

"That does not come from me," Hermione said, suddenly, almost with bitterness.

"Why—why will you be unnecessarily humiliated?" Artois exclaimed.

His voice was confusedly echoed by the cavern, which broke into faint, but deep mutterings. Hermione looked up quickly to the mysterious vault which brooded above them, and listened till the chaotic noises died away. Then she said:

"Do you know what they remind me of?"

"Of what?"

"My efforts. Those efforts I made long ago to live again in work."

"When you wrote?"

"Yes, when I tried to throw my mind and my heart down upon paper. How strange it was! I had Vere— but she wasn't enough to still the ache. And I knew what work can be, what a consolation, because I knew you. And I stretched out my hands to it—I stretched out my soul. And it was no use; I wasn't made to be a successful writer. When I spoke from my heart to try and move men and save myself, my words were seized, as yours were just now by the rock—seized, and broken, and flung back in confusion. They struck my heart like stones. Emile, I'm one of those people who can only do one thing: I can only feel."

38

A SPIRIT IN PRISON

"It is true that you could never be an artist. Perhaps you were made to be an inspiration."

"But that's not enough. The rôle of starter to those who race—I haven't the temperament to reconcile myself to that. It's not that I have in me a conceit which demands to be fed. But I have in me a force that clamors to exercise itself. Only when I was living on Monte Amato with Maurice did I feel that that force was being used as God meant it to be used."

"In loving?"

"In loving passionately something that was utterly worthy to be loved."

Artois was silent. He knew Hermione's mistake. He knew what had never been told him: that Maurice had been false to her for the love of the peasant girl Maddalena. He knew that Maurice had been done to death by the betrayed girl's father, Salvatore. And Gaspare knew those things, too. But through all these years these two men had so respected silence, the nobility of it, the grand necessity of it in certain circumstances of life, that they had never spoken to each other of the black truth known to them both. Indeed, Artois believed that even now, after more than sixteen years, if he ventured one word against the dead man Gaspare would be ready to fly at his throat in defence of the loved Padrone. For this divined and persistent loyalty Artois had a sensat'on of absolute love. Between him and Gaspare there must always be the barrier of a great and mutual reserve. Yet that very reserve, because there was something truly delicate, and truly noble in it, was as a link of steel between them. They were watchdogs of Hermione. They had been watchdogs through all these years, guarding her from the knowledge of a truth. And so well had they done her service that now to-day she was able to say, with clasped hands and the light of passion in her eyes:

39

"Something that was utterly worthy to be loved."

When Artois spoke again he said:

"And that force cannot be fully used in loving Vere?"

"No, Emile. Is that very horrible, very unnatural?"

"Why should it be?"

"I have tried—I have tried for years, Emile, to make Vere enough. I have even been false with myself. I have said to myself that she was enough. I did that after I knew that I could never produce work of any value. When Vere was a baby I lived only for her. Again, when she was beginning to grow up, I tried to live, I did live only for her. And I remember I used to say, I kept on saying to myself, 'This is enough for me. I do not need any more than this. I have had my life. I am now a middle-aged woman. I must live in my child. This will be my satisfaction. This is my satisfaction. This is using rightly and naturally all that force I feel within me.' I kept on saying this. But there is something within one which rises up and defies a lie—however beautiful the lie is, however noble it is. And I think even a lie can sometimes be both. Don't you, Emile?"

It almost seemed to him for a moment that she knew his lie and Gaspare's.

"Yes," he said. "I do think so."

"Well, that lie of mine—it was defied. And it had no more courage."

"I want you to tell me something," he said, quietly. "I want you to tell me what has happened to-day?"

"To-day?"

"Yes. Something has happened either to-day or very recently—I am sure of it—that has stirred up within you this feeling of acute dissatisfaction. It was always there. But something has called it into the open. What has done that?"

Hermione hesitated.

"Perhaps you don't know," he said.

"I was wondering—yes, I do know. I must be truthful with myself—with you. I do know. But it seems so strange, so almost inexplicable, and even rather absurd."

"Truth often seems absurd."

"It was that boy, that diver for *frutti di mare*—Ruffo."

"The boy with the Arab eyes?"

"Yes. Of course I have seen many boys full of life and gayety and music. There are so many in Italy. But—well, I don't know—perhaps it was partly Vere."

"How do you mean?"

"Vere was so interested in him. It may have been that. Or perhaps it was something in his look and in his voice when he was singing. I don't really know what it was. But that boy made me feel—more horribly than I have ever felt before—that Vere is not enough. Emile, there is some hunger, so persistent, so peculiar, so intense, that one feels as if it must be satisfied eventually, as if it were impossible for it not to be satisfied. I think the human hunger for immortal life is like that, and I think my hunger for a son is like that. I know my hunger can never be satisfied. And yet it lives on in me just as if it knew more than I know, as if it knew that it could and must. After all these years I can't, no, I can't reconcile myself to the fact that Maurice was taken from me so utterly, that he died without stamping himself upon a son. It seems as if it couldn't be. And I feel to-day that I cannot bear that it is."

There were tears standing in her eyes. She had spoken with a force of feeling, with a depth of sincerity, that startled Artois, intimately as he knew her. Till this moment he had not quite realized the wonderful persistence of love in the hearts of certain women, and not only the persistence of love's existence, but of its existence undiminished, unabated by time.

"How am I to bear it?" she said, as he did not speak.

A SPIRIT IN PRISON

"I cannot tell. I am not worthy to know. And besides, I must say to you, Hermione, that one of the greatest mysteries in human life, at any rate to me, is this: how some human beings do bear the burdens laid upon them. Christ bore His cross. But there has only been, since the beginning of things, one Christ, and it is unthinkable that there can ever be another. But all these who are not Christ, how is it they bear what they do bear? It is easy to talk of bravery, the necessity for it in life. It is always very easy to talk. The thing that is impossible is to understand. How can you come to me to help you, my friend? And suppose I were to try. How could I try, except by saying that I think Vere is very worthy to be loved with all your love?"

"You love Vere, don't you, Emile?"

"Yes."

"And I do. You don't doubt that?"

"Never."

"After all I have said, the way I have spoken, you might."

"I do not doubt it for a moment."

"I wonder if there is any mother who would not, if I spoke to her as I have spoken to you to-day?"

"I think there is a great deal of untruth spoken of mother's love, a great deal of misconception about it, as there is about most very strange, and very wonderful and beautiful things. But are you so sure that if your husband had stamped himself upon a boy this force within you could have been satisfied?"

"I have believed so."

She was silent. Then she added, quietly "I do believe so."

He did not speak, but sat looking down at the sea, which was full of dim color in the cave.

"I think you are doubting that it would have been so?" she said, at last.

"Yes, that is true. I am doubting."

"I wonder why?"

"I cannot help feeling that there is passion in you, such passion as could not be satisfied in any strict, maternal relationship."

"But I am old, dear Emile," she said, very simply.

"When I was standing by that window, looking at the mountains of Ischia, I was saying to myself, 'This is an old, tired world, suitable for me—and for you. We are in our right environment to-day.' I was saying that, Hermione, but was I believing it, really? I don't think I was. And I am ten years older than you, and I have been given a nature that was, I think, always older than yours could ever be."

"I wonder if that is so."

She looked at him very directly, even searchingly, not with eager curiosity, but with deep inquiry.

"You know, Emile," she added, "I tell you very much, but you tell me very little. Not that I wish to ask anything—no. I respect all your reserve. And about your work: you tell me all that. It is a great thing in my life, your work. Perhaps you don't realize how sometimes I live in the book that you are doing, almost as if I were writing it myself. But your inner life—"

"But I have been frankness itself with you," said Artois. "To no one have I ever said so much as to you."

"Yes, I know, about many things. But about emotion, love,—not friendship, the other love—do you get on without that? When you say your nature has always been older than mine, do you mean that it has always been harder to move by love, that it has had less need of love?"

"I think so. For many years in my life I think that work has filled the place love occupies in many, perhaps in most men's lives. Everything comes second to work. I know that, because if any one attempts to interfere with my work, or to usurp any of the time that should be given to it, any regard I may have for that person turns at once to irritation, almost to hatred."

"I have never done that?"

"You—no. Of course, I have been like other men. When I was young—well, Hermione, after all I am a Frenchman, and though I am of Normandy, still I passed many years in Paris, as you know."

"All that I understand. But the real thing? Such as I have known?"

"I have never broken my heart for any one, though I have known agitations. But even those were long ago. And since I was thirty-five I have never felt really dominated by any one. Before that time I occasionally passed under the yoke, I believe, like other men. Why do you fix your eyes on me like that?"

"I was wondering if you could ever pass under the yoke again."

"Honestly, I do not think so. I am not sure. When can one be certain that one will never be, or do, this or that? Surely,"—he smiled,—"you are not afraid for me?"

"I do not say that. But I think you have forces in you not fully exercised even by your work."

"Possibly. But there the years do really step in and count for something, even for much. There is no doubt that as the years increase, the man who cares at all for intellectual pleasures is able to care for them more, is able to substitute them, without keen regret, without wailing and gnashing of teeth, for certain other pleasures, to which, perhaps, formerly he clung. That is why the man who is mentally and bodily—you know what I mean?"

"Yes."

44

A SPIRIT IN PRISON

"Has such an immense advantage in years of decline over the man who is merely a bodily man."

"I am sure that is true. But—"

"What is it?"

"The heart? What about that?"

"Perhaps there are some hearts that can fulfil themselves sufficiently in friendship."

As Artois said this his eyes rested upon Hermione with an expression in them that revealed much that he never spoke in words. She put out her hand, and took his, and pressed it, holding hers over it upon the oar.

"Emile," she said, "sometimes you make me feel unworthy and ungrateful because—because I still need, I dare to need more than I have been given. Without you I don't know how I should have faced it."

"Without me you would never have had to face it."

That was the cry that rose up perpetually in the heart of Artois, the cry that Hermione must never hear. He said to her now:

"Without you, Hermione, I should be dust in the dust of Africa!"

"Perhaps we each owe something to the other," she said. "It is blessed to have a debt to a friend."

"Would to God that I could pay all my debt to you!" Artois exclaimed.

Again the cavern took up his voice and threw it back to the sea in confused and hollow mutterings. They both looked up, as if some one were above them, warning them or rebuking them. At that instant they had the feeling that they were being watched. But there was only the empty gray sea about them, and over their heads the rugged, weary rock that had leaned over the sea for countless years.

"Hark!" said Artois, "it is telling me that my debt to you can never be paid: only in one way could it be partially discharged. If I could show you a path to

45

happiness, the happiness you long for, and need, the passionate happiness of the heart that is giving where it rejoices to give—for your happiness must always lie in generosity—I should have partially paid my debt to you. But that is impossible."

"I've made you sad to-day by my complaining," she said, with self-rebuke; "I'm sorry. You didn't realize?"

"How it was with you? No, not quite—I thought you were more at peace than you are."

"Till to-day I believe I was half deceived too."

"That singing boy, that—what is his name?"

"Ruffo."

"That Ruffo, I should like to run a knife into him under the left shoulder-blade. How dare he, a raga-muffin from some hovel of Naples, make you know that you are unhappy?"

"How strange it is what outside things, or people who have no connection with us or with our lives, can do to us unconsciously!" she said. "I have heard a hundred boys sing on the Bay, seen a hundred rowing their boats into the Pool—and just this one touches some chord, and all the strings of my soul quiver."

"Some people act upon us somewhat as nature does sometimes. And Vere paid the boy. There is another irony of unconsciousness. Vere, bone of your bone, flesh of your flesh, rewards your pain-giver. How we hide ourselves from those we love best and live with most intimately! You, her mother, are a stranger to Vere. Does not to-day prove it?"

"Ah, but Vere is not a stranger to me. That is where the mother has the advantage of the child."

Artois did not make any response to this remark. To cover his silence, perhaps, he grasped the oars more firmly and began to back the boat out of the cave. Both felt that it was no longer necessary to stay in this confessional of the rock.

46

A SPIRIT IN PRISON

As they came out under the grayness of the sky, Hermione, with a change of tone, said:

"And your friend? The Marchese—what is his name?"

"Isidoro Panacci."

"Tell me about him."

"He is a very perfect type of a complete Neapolitan of his class. He has scarcely travelled at all, except in Italy. Once he has been in Paris, where I met him, and once to Lucerne for a fortnight. Both his father and mother are Neapolitans. He is a charming fellow, utterly unintellectual, but quite clever; shrewd, sharp at reading character, marvellously able to take care of himself, and hold his own with anybody. A cat to fall on his feet! He is apparently born without any sense of fear, and with a profound belief in destiny. He can drive four-in-hand, swim for any number of hours without tiring, ride—well, as an Italian cavalry officer can ride, and that is not badly. His accomplishments? He can speak French—abominably, and pick out all imaginable tunes on the piano, putting instinctively quite tolerable basses. I don't think he ever reads anything, except the *Giorno* and the *Mattino*. He doesn't care for politics, and likes cards, but apparently not too much. They're no craze with him. He knows Naples inside out, and is as frank as a child that has never been punished."

"I should think he must be decidedly attractive?"

"Oh, he is. One great attraction he has—he appears to have no sense at all that difference of age can be a barrier between two men. He is twenty-four, and I am what I am. He is quite unaware that there is any gulf between us. In every way he treats me as if I were twenty-four."

"Is that refreshing or embarrassing?"

"I find it generally refreshing. His family accepts

47

the situation with perfect naïveté. I am welcomed as
Doro's chum with all the good-will in the world."

Hermione could not help laughing, and Artois echoed
her laugh.

"Merely talking about him has made you look years
younger," she declared. "The influence of the day has
lifted from you."

"It would not have fallen upon Isidoro, I think.
And yet he is full of sentiment. He is a curious instance
of a very common Neapolitan obsession."

"What is that?"

"He is entirely obsessed by woman. His life centres
round woman. You observe I use the singular. I do
that because it is so much more plural than the plural
in this case. His life is passed in love-affairs, in a sort
of chaos of amours."

"How strange that is!"

"You think so, my friend?"

"Yes. I never can understand how human beings
can pass from love to love, as many of them do. I never
could understand it, even before I—even before Sicily."

"You are not made to understand such a thing."

"But you do?"

"I? Well, perhaps. But the loves of men are not as
your love."

"Yet his was," she answered. "And he was a true
Southerner, despite his father."

"Yes, he was a true Southerner," Artois replied.

For once he was off his guard with her, and uttered
his real thought of Maurice, not without a touch of the
irony that was characteristic of him.

Immediately he had spoken he was aware of his indis-
cretion. But Hermione had not noticed it. He saw by
her eyes that she was far away in Sicily. And when the
boat slipped into the Saint's Pool, and Gaspare came to
the water's edge to hold the prow while they got out, she

rose from her seat slowly, and almost reluctantly, like one disturbed in a dream that she would fain continue.

"Have you seen the Signorina, Gaspare?" she asked him. "Has she been out?"

"No, Signora. She is still in the house."

"Still reading!" said Artois. "Vere must be quite a book-worm!"

"Will you stay to dinner, Emile?"

"Alas, I have promised the Marchesino Isidoro to dine with him. Give me a cup of tea *a la Russe*, and one of Ruffo's cigarettes, and then I must bid you adieu. I'll take the boat to the Antico Giuseppone, and then get another there as far as the gardens."

"One of Ruffo's cigarettes!" Hermione echoed, as they went up the steps. "That boy seems to have made himself one of the family already."

"Yet I wish, as I said in the cave, that I had put a knife into him under the left shoulder-blade—before this morning."

They spoke lightly. It seemed as if each desired for the moment to get away from their mood in the confessional of Virgil's Grotto, and from the sadness of the white and silent day.

As to Ruffo, about whom they jested, he was in sight of Naples, and not far from Mergellina, still rowing with tireless young arms, and singing to "Bella Napoli," with a strong resolve in his heart to return to the Saint's Pool on the first opportunity and dive for more cigarettes.

CHAPTER IV

AT the Antico Giuseppone, Artois left the boat from the islet and, taking another, was rowed towards the public gardens of Naples, whose trees were faintly visible far off across the Bay. Usually he talked familiarly to any Neapolitan with whom he found himself, but to-day he was taciturn, and sat in the stern of the broad-bottomed craft looking towards the city in silence while the boatman plied his oars. The memory of his conversation with Hermione in the Grotto of Virgil, of her manner, the look in her eyes, the sound of her voice there, gave him food for thought that was deep and serious.

Although Artois had an authoritative, and often an ironical manner that frightened timid people, he was a man capable of much emotion and of great loyalty. He did not easily trust or easily love, but in those whose worth he had thoroughly proved he had a confidence as complete as that of a child. And where he placed his complete confidence he placed also his affection. The one went with the other almost as inevitably as the wave goes with the wind.

In their discussion about the emotion of the heart Artois had spoken the truth to Hermione. As he had grown older he had felt the influence of women less. The pleasures of sentiment had been gradually superseded in his nature—or so at least he honestly believed —by the purely intellectual pleasures. More and more completely and contentedly had he lived in his work, and in the life of preparation for it. This life could never be narrow, for Artois was a traveller, and studied many lands.

In the years that had elapsed since the tragedy in Sicily, when the husband of Hermione had met his death suddenly in the sea, almost in sight of the home of the girl he had betrayed, the fame of Artois had grown steadily. And he was jealous of his fame almost as a good woman is jealous of her honor. This jealousy had led him to a certain selfishness of which he was quite aware—even to a certain hardness such as he had hinted to Hermione. Those who strove, or seemed likely to strive to interrupt him in his work, he pushed out of his life. Even if they were charming women he got rid of them. And the fact that he did so proved to him, and not improbably to them, that he was more wrapped up in the gratification of the mind than in the gratification of the heart, or of the body. It was not that the charm of charming women had ceased to please him, but it seemed to have ceased really to fascinate him.

Long ago, before Hermione married, he had felt for her a warm and intimate friendship. He had even been jealous of Maurice. Without being at all in love, he had cared enough for Hermione to be jealous. Before her marriage he had looked forward in imagination down a vista of long years, and had seen her with a husband, then with children, always more definitely separated from himself.

And he had seen himself exceptionally alone, even almost miserably alone.

Then fate had spun tragedy into her web. He had nearly died in Africa, and had been nursed back to life by this friend of whom he had been jealous. And they had gone together to Sicily, to the husband whose memory Hermione still adored. And then had followed swiftly the murder, the murderer's departure to America, saved by the silence of Gaspare, and the journey of the bereaved woman to Italy, where Artois had left her and returned to France.

Once more Artois had his friend, released from the love of another man. But he wished it were not so. Hermione's generosity met with a full response of generosity from him. All his egotism and selfishness dropped from him then, shaken down like dead leaves by the tempest of a genuine emotion. His knowledge of her grief, his understanding of its depth, brought to him a sorrow that was keen, and even exquisitely painful. For a long while he was preoccupied by an intense desire to assuage it. He strove to do so by acting almost in defiance of his nature, by fostering deception. From the Abetone Hermoine had written him letters, human documents—the tale of the suffering of a woman's heart. Many reserves she had from him and from every one. The most intimate agony was for her alone, and she kept it in her soul as the priest keeps the Sacred Host in its tabernacle. But some of her grief she showed in her letters, and some of her desire for comfort. And without any definite intention, she indicated to her subtle and devoted friend the only way in which he could console her.

For once, driven by his emotion, he took that way.

He allowed Hermione to believe that he agreed with her in the conception she had formed of her husband's character and of her husband's love for her. It was difficult for him to do this, for he had an almost cruel passion for truth, and generally a clear insight into human character. Far less than many others would have condemned did he, in his mind, condemn the man who was dead for the sin against love that he had committed. He had understood Maurice as Hermione had not understood him, and knowledge is full of pardon. But though he could pardon easily he could not easily pretend. By pretending he sinned against himself, and helped his friend some steps along the way to peace. He thought he had helped her to go much farther along that way than she had gone. And he thought that Vere had helped her, too.

Now the hollow mutterings of the rock in Virgil's Grotto seemed to be in his heart, as he realized how permanent was the storm in Hermione's nature. Something for her he had done. And something—much more, no doubt—Vere had done. But how little it all was!

Their helplessness gave to him a new understanding of woman.

Hermione had allowed him great privileges, had allowed him to protect her, had taken his advice. After Vere was born she had wished to go back again to Sicily. The house of the priest, where she had been so happy, and so sad, drew her. She longed for it. She desired to make it her home. He had fought against her in this matter, and had been aided by Gaspare.

There had been a subtle understanding, never expressed, between the boy and him.

Artois had played upon her intellect, had appealed, too, to her mother's heart.

He had not urged her to try to forget, but he had urged her not morbidly to remember, not to cherish and to foster the memory of the tragedy which had broken her life. To go back to that tiny home, solitary in its beautiful situation, in the changed circumstances which were hers, would be, he told her, to court and to summon sorrow. He was even cruel to be kind. When Hermione combated his view, assuring him that to her Monte Amato was like a sacred place, a place hallowed by memories of happiness, he recalled the despair in which that happiness had ended. With all the force at his command, and it was great, he drew the picture of the life that would be in comparison with the life that had been. And he told her finally that what she wished to do was morbid, was unworthy of her strength of character, was even wicked now that she was a mother. He brought before her mind those widows who make a cult of their dead. Would she be one of them? Would she steep a little child in such an atmosphere of memories, casting a young and tender mind backward into a cruel past instead of leading it forward into a joyous present? Maurice had been the very soul of happiness. Vere must be linked with the sunbeams. With his utmost subtlety Artois described and traced the effect upon a tiny and sensitive child of a mother's influence, whether for good or evil, until Hermione, who had a deep reverence for his knowledge of all phases of human nature, at last, almost in despite of the truth within her, of the interior voice which said to her, "With you and Vere it would not be so," caught alarm from his apparent alarm, drew distrust of herself from his apparent distrust of her.

Gaspare, too, played his part. When Hermione spoke to him of returning to the priest's house, almost wildly, and with the hot energy that bursts so readily up in Sicilians, he begged her not to go back to the *maledetta casa* in which his Padrone's dead body had lain. As he spoke a genuine fear of the cottage came upon him. All the latent superstition that dwells in the contadino was stirred as dust by a wind. In clouds it flew up about his mind. Fear looked out of his great eyes. Dread was eloquent in his gestures. And he, too, referred to the child, to the *povera piccola bambina*. It would cast ill-luck on the child to bring her up in a chamber of death. Her saint would forsake her. She too would die. The boy worked himself up into a fever. His face was white. Drops of sweat stood on his forehead.

He had set out to be deceptive—what he would have called *un poco birbante*, and he had even deceived himself. He knew that it would be dangerous for his Padrona to live again near Marechiaro. Any day a chance scrap of gossip might reach her ears. In time she would be certain almost to hear something of the dead Padrone's close acquaintance with the dwellers in the Casa delle Sirene. She would question him, perhaps. She would suspect something. She would inquire. She would search. She would find out the hideous truth. It was this fear which made him argue on the same side as Artois. But in doing so he caught another fear from his own words. He became really natural, really truthful in his fear. And—she scarcely knew why—Hermione was even more governed by him than by Artois. He had lived with them in the Casa del Prete, been an intimate part of their life there. And he was Sicilian of the soil. The boy had a real power to move, to dominate her, which he did not then suspect.

Again and again he repeated those words, "*La povera bambina—la povera piccola bambina.*" And at last Hermione was overcome.

"I won't go to Sicily," she said to Artois. "For if I went there I could only go to Monte Amato. I won't go until Vere is old enough to wish to go, to wish to see the house where her father and I were happy."

And she had never gone back. For Artois had not been satisfied with this early victory.

In returning from a tour in North Africa the following spring, when Vere was nearly two years old, he had paid a visit to Marechiaro, and, while there, had seen the contadino from whom Hermione had rented, and still rented, the house of the priest. The man was middle-aged, ignorant but shrewd, and very greedy. Artois made friends with him, and casually, over a glass of *moscato*, talked about his affairs and the land question in Sicily. The peasant became communicative and, of course, loud in his complaining. His land yielded nothing. The price of almonds had gone down. The lemon crop had been ruined by the storms. As to the vines—

they were all devoured by the phylloxera, and he had no money to buy and plant vines from America. Artois hinted that he received a good rent from the English lady for the cottage on Monte Amato. The contadino acknowledged that he received a fair price for the cottage and the land about it; but the house, he declared, would go to rack and ruin with no one ever in it, and the land was lying idle, for the English lady would have everything left exactly as it had been when she lived there with her husband. Artois seized upon this hint of what was in the peasant's mind, and bemoaned with him his situation. The house ought to be occupied, the land all about it, up to the very door, and behind upon the sunny mountain-side, planted with American vines. If it belonged to him that was what he would do—plant American vines, and when the years of yielding came, give a good percentage on all the wine made and sold to the man who had tended the vineyard. .

The peasant's love of money awoke. He only let the cottage to Hermione year by year, and had no contract with her extending beyond a twelve-months' lease. Before Artois left Marechiaro the tender treachery was arranged. When the year's lease was up, the contadino wrote to her declining to renew it. She answered, protesting, offering more money. But it was all in vain. The man replied that he had already let the cottage and the land around it to a grower of vines for a long term of years, and that he was getting double the annual price she offered.

Hermione was indignant and bitterly distressed. When this letter reached her she was at Fiesole with Vere in a villa which she had taken. She would probably have started at once for Sicily; but Vere was just then ill with some infantile complaint, and could not be left. Artois, who was in Rome, and had received from her the news of this carefully arranged disaster, offered to go to Sicily on her behalf—and actually went. He returned to tell her that the house of the priest was already occupied by contadini, and all the land up to the very door in process of being dug up and planted with vines. It was useless to make any further offer. The thing was done.

Hermione said nothing, but Artois saw in her eyes how keenly she was suffering, and turned his own eyes away. He was only trying to preserve her from greater unhappiness, the agony of ever finding out the truth; but he felt guilty at that moment, and as if he had been cruel to the woman who roused all his tenderness, all his protective instinct.

"I shall not go back to Marechiaro now," Hermione said. "I shall not go back even to see the grave. I could never feel that anything of his spirit lingered there. But I did feel, I should have felt again, as if something of him still loved that little house on the mountain, still stayed among the oak-trees. It seemed to me that when I took Vere to the Casa del Prete she would have learned to know something of her father there that she could never have learned to know in another place. But now — no, I shall not go back. If I did I should even lose my memories, perhaps, and I could not bear that."

And she had not returned. Gaspare went to Marechiaro sometimes, to see his family and his friends. He visited the grave and saw that it was properly kept. But Hermione remained in Italy. For some time she lived near Florence, first at Fiesole, later at Bellosguardo. When the summer heat came she took a villa at the Abetone. Or she spent some months with Vere beside the sea. As the girl grew older she developed a passion for the sea, and seemed to care little for the fascination of the pine forests. Hermione, noting this, gave up going to the Abetone and took a house by the sea for the whole summer. Two years they were at Santa Margherita, one year at Sorrento.

Then, sailing one evening on the sea towards Bagnoli, they saw the house on the islet beyond the Pool of San Francesco. Vere was enchanted by it.

"To live in it," she exclaimed, "would be almost like living in the sea!"

Hermione, too, was fascinated by its situation, the loneliness, the wildness, yet the radiant cheerfulness of it. She made inquiries, found that it was owned by a Neapolitan who scarcely ever went there, and eventually succeeded in getting it on a long lease. For two years now she and Vere had spent the summer there.

Artois had noticed that since Hermione had been in the Casa del Mare an old desire had begun to revive in her. She spoke more frequently of Sicily. Often she stood on the rock and looked across the sea, and he knew that she was thinking of those beloved coasts—of the Ionian waters, of the blossoming almond-trees among the olives and the rocks, of the scarlet geraniums glowing among the thorny cactus, of the giant watercourses leading up into the mountains. A hunger was awake in her, now that she had a home so near the enchanted island.

He realized it. But he was no longer much afraid. So many years had passed that even if Hermione revisited Marechiaro he believed there would be little or no danger now of her ever learning the truth. It had never been known in the village, and if it had been supsected, all the suspicions must have long ago died down. He had been successful in his protection. He was thankful for that. It was the one thing he had been able to do for the friend who had done so much for him.

The tragedy had occurred because of him. Because of him all knowledge of it had been kept from Hermione, and would now be kept from her forever—because of him and Gaspare.

This he had been able to do. But how powerless he was, and how powerless was Vere!

Now he looked vaguely at the villas of Posilipo, and he realized this thoroughly.

Something for her he had done, and something Vere had done. But how little it all was!

To-day a new light had been thrown upon Hermione, and he realized what she was as he had never realized it before. No, she was right. She could never live fully in a girl child—she was not made to do that. Why had he ever thought, hoped that perhaps it might be so, that perhaps Vere might some day completely and happily fill her life? Long ago he had encouraged her to work, to write. Misled by her keen intelligence, her enthusiasm, her sincerity and vitality, by the passion that was in her, the great heart, the power of feeling, the power of criticising and inspiring another which she had freely shown to him, Artois had believed—as he had once said to her in London—that she might be an artist, but that she preferred to be simply a woman. But he found it was not so. Hermione had not the peculiar gift of the writer. She could feel, but she could not arrange. She could discern, but she could not expose. A flood of words came to her, but not the inevitable word. She could not take that exquisite leap from the known into the unknown which genius can take with the certainty of alighting on firm ground. In short, she was not formed and endowed to be an artist. About such matters Artois knew only how to be sincere. He was sincere with his friend, and she thanked him for being so.

One possible life was taken from Hermione, the life of the artist who lives in the life of the work.

There remained the life in Vere.

To-day Artois knew from Hermione's own lips that

she could not live completely in her child, and he felt that he had been blind as men are often blind about women, are blind because they are secretly selfish. The man lives for himself, but he thinks it natural, even distinctively womanly, that women should live for others— for him, for some other man, for their children. What man finds his life in his child? But the woman—she surely ought to, and without difficulty. Hermione had been sincere to-day, and Artois knew his blindness, and knew his secret selfishness.

The gray was lifting a little over Naples, the distant shadowy form of Vesuvius was becoming clearer, more firm in outline. But the boatman rowed slowly, influenced by the scirocco.

How, then, was Hermione to live? How was she to find happiness or peace? It was a problem which he debated with an ardor that had in it something of passion. And he began to wonder how it would have been if he had acted differently, if he had allowed her to find out what he suspected to be the exact truth of the dead man. Long ago he had saved her from suffering. But by doing so had he not dedicated her, not to a greater, but to a longer suffering? He might have defiled a beautiful memory. He must have done so had he acted differently. But if he had defiled it, might not Hermione have been the subject of a great revulsion? Horror can kill, but it can also cure. It can surely root out love. But from such a heart as Hermione's?

Despite all his understanding of women, Artois felt at a loss to-day. He could not make up his mind what would have been the effect upon Hermione if she had learned that her husband had betrayed her.

Presently he left that subject and came to Vere.

When he did this he was conscious at once of a change within him. His tenderness and pity for Hermione were replaced by another tenderness and pity. And these were wholly for Vere. Hermione was suffering because of Maurice. But Vere was surely suffering, subconsciously, because of Hermione.

There were two links in the chain of suffering, that between Maurice and Hermione, and that between Hermione and Vere.

For a moment he felt as if Vere were bereaved, were motherless. The sensation passed directly he realized the exaggeration in his mind. But he still felt as if the girl were deprived of something which she ought to possess, which, till now, he had thought she did possess. It seemed to him that Vere stood quite outside of her mother's life, instead of in it, in its centre, its core; and he pitied the child, almost as he pitied other children from time to time, children to whom their parents were indifferent. And yet Hermione loved Vere, and Vere could not know what he had only known completely to-day—that the mother often felt lonely with the child.

Vere did not know that, but surely some day she would find it out.

Artois knew her character well, knew that she was very sensitive, very passionate, quick to feel and quick to understand. He discovered in her qualities inherited both from her father and her mother, attributes both English and Sicilian. In appearance she resembled her father. She had "thrown back" to the Sicilian ancestor, as he had. She had the Southern eyes, the Southern grace, the Southern vivacity and warmth that had made him so attractive. But Artois divined a certain stubbornness in Vere that had been lacking in the dead man, a stubbornness that took its rise not in stupidity but in a secret consciousness of force.

Vere, Artois thought, might be violent, but would not be fickle. She had a loyalty in her that was Sicilian in its fervor, a sense of gratitude such as the contadini have, although by many it is denied to them; a quick and lively temper, but a disposition that responded to joy, to brightness, to gayety, to sunlight, with a swiftness, almost a fierceness, that was entirely un-English.

Her father had been the dancing Faun. She had not, could never have his gift of thoughtlessness. For she had intellect, derived from Hermione, and an odd truthfulness that was certainly not Sicilian. Often there were what Artois called "Northern Lights" in her sincerity. The strains in her, united, made, he thought, a fascinating blend. But as yet she was undeveloped—an interesting, a charming child, but only a child. In many ways she was young for her age. Highly intelligent, she was anything rather than "knowing." Her innocence was like clear water in a spring. The graciousness of youth was hers to the full.

As Artois thought of it he was conscious, as of a new thing, of the wonderful beauty of such innocent youth.

It was horrible to connect it with suffering. And yet that link in the chain did exist. Vere had not something that surely she ought to have, and, without consciously missing it, she must sometimes subtly, perhaps vaguely, be aware that there was a lack in her life. Her mother gave her great love. But she was not to her mother what a son would have been. And the love that is mingled with regret has surely something shadowy in it.

Maurice Delarey had been as the embodiment of joy. It was strange that from the fount of joy sorrow was thrown up. But so it was. From him sorrow had come. From him sorrow might still come, even for Vere.

In the white and silent day Artois again felt the stirring of intuition, as he had felt it long ago. But now he roused himself, and resolutely, almost angrily, detached his mind from its excursions towards the future.

"Do you often think of to-morrow?" he suddenly said to the boatman, breaking from his silence.

A SPIRIT IN PRISON

"Signore?"

"Do you often wonder what is going to happen to-morrow, what you will do, whether you will be happy or sad?"

The man threw up his head.

"No, Signore. Whatever comes is destiny. If I have food to-day it is enough for me. Why should I bother about to-morrow's maccheroni?"

Artois smiled. The boat was close in now to the platform of stone that projected beneath the wall of the Marina.

As he stepped out he gave the boatman a generous *buonamano*.

"You are quite right, comrade," he said. "It is the greatest mistake in the world to bother about to-morrow's maccheroni."

CHAPTER V

THREE days after Artois' conversation with Hermione in the Grotto of Virgil the Marchesino Isidoro Panacci came smiling into his friend's apartments in the Hotel Royal des Etrangers. He was smartly dressed in the palest possible shade of gray, with a bright pink tie, pink socks, brown shoes of the rather boat-like shape affected by many young Neopolitans, and a round straw hat, with a small brim, that was set slightly on the side of his curly head. In his mouth was a cigarette, and in his buttonhole a pink carnation. He took Artois' hand with his left hand, squeezed it affectionately, murmured "Caro Emilio," and sat down in an easy attitude on the sofa, putting his hat and stick on a table near by.

It was quite evident that he had come for no special reason. He had just dropped in, as he did whenever he felt inclined, to gossip with "Caro Emilio," and it never occurred to him that possibly he might be interrupting an important piece of work. The Marechesino could not realize work. He knew his friend published books. He even saw him sometimes actually engaged in writing them, pen in hand. But he was sure anybody would far rather sit and chatter with him, or hear him play a valse on the piano, or a bit of the "Bohême," than bend over a table all by himself. And Artois always welcomed him. He liked him. But it was not only that which made him complaisant. Doro was a type, and a singularly perfect one.

A SPIRIT IN PRISON

Now Artois laid down his pen, and pulled forward an arm-chair opposite to the sofa.

"Mon Dieu, Doro! How fresh you look, like a fish just pulled out of the sea!"

The Marchesino showed his teeth in a smile which also shone in his round and boyish eyes.

"I have just come out of the sea. Papa and I have been bathing at the Eldorado. We swam round the Castello until we were opposite your windows, and sang 'Funiculì, funiculà!' in the water, to serenade you. Why didn't you hear us? Papa has a splendid voice, almost like Tamagno's in the gramophone, when he sings the 'Addio' from 'Otello.' Of course we kept a little out at sea. Papa is so easily recognized by his red mustaches. But still you might have heard us."

"I did."

"Then why didn't you come unto the balcony, amico mio?"

"Because I thought you were street singers."

"Davvero? Papa would be angry. And he is in a bad temper to-day anyhow."

"Why?"

"Well, I believe Gilda Mai is going to bring a *causa* against Viviano. Of course he won't marry her, and she never expected he could. Why, she used to be a milliner in the Toledo. I remember it perfectly, and now Sigismondo— But it's really Gilda that has made papa angry. You see, he has paid twice for me, once four thousand lire, and the other time three thousand five hundred. And then he has lost a lot at Lotto lately. He has no luck. And then he, too, was in a row yesterday evening."

"The Marchese?"

"Yes, in the Chiaia. He slapped Signora Merani's face twice before every one."

A SPIRIT IN PRISON

"Diavolo! What! a lady?"

"Well, if you like to call her so," returned Doro, negligently. "Her husband is an impiegato of the Post-office, or something of the kind."

"But why should the Marchese slap her face in the Chiaia?"

"Because she provoked him. They took a flat in the house my father owns in the Strada Chiatamone. After a time they got behind with the rent. He let them stay on for six months without paying, and then he turned them out. What should he do?" Doro began to gesticulate. He held his right hand up on a level with his face, with the fingers all drawn together and pressed against the thumb, and moved it violently backwards and forwards, bringing it close to the bridge of his nose, then throwing it out towards Artois. "What else, I say? Was he to give his beautiful rooms to them for nothing? And she with a face like — have you, I ask you, Emilio, have you seen her teeth?"

"I have never seen the Signora in my life!"

"You have never seen her teeth? Dio mio!" He opened his two hands, and, lifting his arms, shook them loosely above his head, shutting his eyes for an instant as if to ward off some dreadful vision. "They are like the keys of a piano from Bordicelli's! Basta!" He dropped his hands and opened his eyes. "Yesterday papa was walking in the Chiaia. He met Signori Merani, and she began to abuse him. She had a red parasol. She shook it at him! She called him vigliacco—papa, a Panacci, dei Duchi di Vedrano! The parasol—it was a bright red, it infuriated papa. He told the Signora to stop. She knows his temper. Every one in Naples knows our tempers, every one! I, Viviano, even Sigismondo, we are all the same, we are all exactly like papa. If we are insulted we cannot control ourselves. You know it, Emilio!"

66

"'YOU HAVE NEVER SEEN HER TEETH? DIO MIO!'"

A SPIRIT IN PRISON

"I am perfectly certain of it," said Artois. "I am positive you none of you can."

"It does not matter whether it is a man or a woman. We must do something with our hands. We have got to. Papa told the Signora he should strike her at once unless she put down the red parasol and was silent. What did she do, the imbecile? She stuck out her face like this,"—he thrust his face forward with the right cheek turned towards Artois—"and said, 'Strike me! strike me!' Papa obeyed her. Poom! poom! He gave her a smack on each cheek before every one. 'You want education!' he said to her. 'And I shall give it you.' And now she may bring a *processo* too. But did you really think we were street singers?" He threw himself back, took the cigarette from his mouth, and laughed. Then he caught hold of his blond mustache with both hands, gave it an upward twist, at the same time pouting his big lips, and added:

"We shall bring a *causa* against you for that!"

"No, Doro, you and I must never quarrel. By the way, though, I want to see you angry. Every one talks of the Panacci temper, but when I am with you I always see you smiling or laughing. As to the Marchese, he is as lively as a boy. Viviano—"

"Oh, Viviano is a buffone. Have you ever seen him imitate a monkey from whom another monkey has snatched a nut?"

"No."

"It is like this—"

With extraordinary suddenness he distorted his whole face into the likeness of an angry ape, hunching his shoulders and uttering fierce simian cries.

"No, I can't do it."

With equal suddenness and self-possession he became his smiling self again.

"Viviano has studied in the monkey-house. And the

67

monk looking the other way when he passes along the Marina where the women are bathing in the summer! He shall do that for you on Sunday afternoon when you come to Capodimonte. It makes even mamma die of laughing, and you know how religious she is. But then, of course, men—that does not matter. Religion is for women, and they understand that quite well."

The Marchesino never made any pretence of piety. One virtue he had in the fullest abundance. He was perfectly sincere with those whom he considered his friends. That there could be any need for hypocrisy never occurred to him.

"Mamma would hate it if we were saints," he continued.

"I am sure the Marchesa can be under no apprehension on that score," said Artois.

"No, I don't think so," returned the Marchesino, quite seriously.

He had a sense of humor, but it did not always serve him. Occasionally it was fitful, and when summoned by irony remained at a distance.

"It is true, Emilio, you have never seen me angry," he continued, reverting to the remark of Artois; "you ought to. Till you have seen a Panacci angry you do not really know him. With you, of course, I could never be angry—never, never. You are my friend, my comrade. To you I tell everything."

A sudden remembrance seemed to come to him. Evidently a new thought had started into his active mind, for his face suddenly changed, and became serious, even sentimental.

"What is it?" asked Artois.

"To-day, just now in the sea, I have seen a girl—Madonna! Emilio, she had a little nose that was perfect—perfect. How she was simpatica! What a beautiful girl!"

A SPIRIT IN PRISON

His whole face assumed a melting expression, and he pursed his lips in the form of a kiss.

"She was in the sea, too?" asked Artois.

"No. If she had been! But I was with papa. It was just after we had been serenading you. She had heard us, I am sure, for she was laughing. I dived under the boat in which she was. I did all my tricks for her. I did the mermaid and the seal. She was delighted. She never took her eyes from me. As to papa—she never glanced at him. Poor papa! He was angry. She had her mother with her, I think—a Signora, tall, flat, ugly, but she was simpatica, too. She had nice eyes, and when I did the seal she could not help laughing, though I think she was rather sad."

"What sort of boat were they in?" Artois asked, with sudden interest.

"A white boat with a green line."

"And they were coming from the direction of Posilipo?"

"Ma sì! Emilio, do you know them? Do you know the perfect little nose?"

The Marchesino laid one hand eagerly on the arm of his friend.

"I believe you do! I am sure of it! The mother—she is flat as a Carabiniere, and quite old, but with nice eyes, sympathetic, intelligent. And the girl is a little brown—from the sun—with eyes full of fun and fire, dark eyes. She may be Italian, and yet—there is something English, too. But she is not blonde, she is not cold. And when she laughs! Her teeth are not like the keys of a piano from Bordicelli's. And she is full of passion, of flame, of sentiment, as I am. And she is young, perhaps sixteen. Do you know her? Present me, Emilio! I have presented you to all my friends."

"Mio caro, you have made me your debtor for life."

"It isn't true!"

"Indeed it is true. But I do not know who these ladies are. They may be Italians. They may be tourists. Perhaps to-morrow they will have left Naples. Or they may come from Sorrento, Capri. How can I tell who they are?"

The Marchesino suddenly changed. His ardor vanished. His gesticulating hands fell to his sides. His expressive face grew melancholy.

"Of course. How can you tell? Directly I was out of the sea and dressed, I went to Santa Lucia. I examined every boat. but the white boat with the green line was not there, Basta!"

He lit a fresh cigarette and was silent for a moment. Then he said:

"Emilio caro, will you come out with me to-night?"

"With pleasure."

"In the boat. There will be a moon. We will dine at the Antico Giuseppone."

"So far off as that?" Artois said, rather abruptly.

"Why not? To-day I hate the town. I want tranquillity. At the Antico Giuseppone there will be scarcely any one. It is early in the season. And afterwards we will fish for sarde, or saraglie. Take me away from Naples, Emilio; take me away! For to-night, if I stay —well, I feel that I shall not be santo."

Artois burst into his big roaring laugh.

"And why do you want to be santo to-night?" he asked.

"The beautiful girl! I wish to keep her memory, if only for one night."

"Very well, then. We will fish, and you shall be a saint."

"Caro Emilio! Perhaps Viviano will come, too. But I think he will be with Lidia. She is singing to-night at the Teatro Nuovo. Be ready at half-past seven. I will call for you. And now I shall leave you."

A SPIRIT IN PRISON

He got up, went over to a mirror, carefully arranged his tie, and put on his straw hat at exactly the most impudent angle.

"I shall leave you to write your book while I meet papa at the villa. Do you know why papa is so careful to be always at the villa at four o'clock just now?"

"No!"

"Nor does mamma! If she did! Povera mamma! But she can always go to Mass. A rivederci, Emilio."

He moved his hat a little more to one side and went out, swinging his walking-stick gently to and fro in a manner that was pensive and almost sentimental.

CHAPTER VI

THE Marchesino Panacci was generally very sincere with his friends, and the boyish expression in his eyes was not altogether deceptive, for despite his wide knowledge of certain aspects of life, not wholly admirable, there was really something of the simplicity of a child—of a child that could be very naughty—in his disposition. But if he could be naïve he could also be mischievous and even subtle, and he was very swift in grasping a situation, very sharp in reading character, very cunning in the pursuit of his pleasure, very adroit in deception, if he thought that publicity of pursuit would be likely to lead to the frustration of his purpose.

He had seen at once that Artois either knew, or suspected, who were the occupants of the white boat with the green line; and he had also seen that, influenced perhaps by one of those second thoughts which lead men into caution, Artois desired to conceal his knowledge, or suspicion. Instantly the Marchesino had, therefore, dropped the subject, and as instantly he had devised a little plan to clear the matter up.

The Marchesino knew that when Artois had arrived in Naples he had had no friends in the town or neighborhood. But he also knew that recently an Englishwoman, an old friend of the novelist, had come upon the scene, that she was living somewhere not far off, and that Artois had been to visit her once or twice by sea. Artois had spoken of her very casually, and the Marchesino's interest in her had not been awakened. He was not an inquisitive man by nature, and was always very busy with his own pursuit of pleasure. But he remembered now that once he had seen his friend being rowed in the direction of Posilipo, and that in the evening of the same day Artois had mentioned having been to visit his English friend. This fact had suggested to the Marchesino that if his suspicion were correct, and the ladies in the white boat with the green line were this English friend and a daughter, they probably lived in some villa as easily reached by sea as by land. Such villas are more numerous towards the point of the Capo di Posilipo than nearer Naples, as the high road, after the Mergellina, mounts the hill and diverges farther and farther from the sea. The Antico Giuseppone is a small waterside ristorante at the point of the Capo di Posilipo, a little below the Villa Rosebery.

The Marchesino's suggestion of a dinner there that evening had been prompted by the desire to draw his friend into the neighborhood which he suspected to be the neighborhood of his charmer of the sea. Once there he might either find some pretext for making her acquaintance through Artois—if Artois did know her—or, if that were impossible, he might at least find out where she lived. By the manner of Artois when the Antico Giuseppone was mentioned, he knew at once that he was playing his cards well. The occupants of the white boat were known to the novelist. They did live somewhere near the Antico Giuseppone. And certainly Artois had no desire to bring about his—the Marchesino's—acquaintance with them.

That this was so, neither surprised nor seriously vexed the Marchesino. He knew a good deal of his friend's character, knew that Artois, despite his geniality and friendliness, was often reserved—even with him. During their short intimacy he had certainly told Artois a great deal more about his affairs with women than had been told to him in return. This fact was borne in upon him now. But he did not feel angry. A careless good-nature was an essential part of his character. He did not feel angry at his friend's secrecy, but he did feel mischievous. His lively desire to know the girl with "the perfect little nose" was backed up now by another desire—to teach "Caro Emilio" that it was better to meet complete frankness with complete frankness.

He had strolled out of his friend's room pensively, acting the melancholy youth who had lost all hope of succeeding in his desire; but directly the door was shut his manner changed. Disregarding the lift, he ran lightly down the stairs, made his way swiftly by the revolving door into the street, crossed it, and walked towards the harbor of Santa Lucia, where quantities of pleasure-boats lie waiting for hire, and the boatmen are gathered in knots smoking and gossiping, or are strolling singly up and down near the water's edge, keeping a sharp look-out for possible customers.

As the Marchesino turned on to the bridge that leads towards Castel dell' Ovo one of these boatmen met him and saluted him.

"Good-day, Giuseppe," said the Marchesino, address-ing him familiarly with a broad Neapolitan accent.

"Good-day, Signorino Marchesino," replied the man. "Do you want a boat? I will take you for—"

The Marchesino drew out his cigarette case.

"I don't want a boat. But perhaps you can tell me something."

"What is it, Signorino Marchesino?" said the man, looking eagerly at the cigarette case which was now open, and which displayed two tempting rows of fat Egyptian cigarettes reposing side by side.

"Do you know a boat—white with a green line—which sometimes comes into the harbor from the di-rection of Posilipo? It was here this afternoon, or it

74

passed here. I don't know whether it went on to the Arsenal."

"White with a green line?" said the man. "That might be—who was there in it, Signorino Marchesino?"

"Two ladies, one old and one very young. The young lady—"

"Those must be the ladies from the island," interrupted the man. "The English ladies who come in the summer to the Casa del Mare as they call it, on the island close to the Grotto of Virgilio by San Francesco's Pool. They were here this afternoon, but they're gone back. Their boat is white with a green line, Signorino Marchesino."

"Grazie, Giuseppe," said the Marchesino, with an immovable countenance. "Do you smoke cigarettes?"

"Signorino Marchesino, I do when I have any soldi to buy them with."

"Take these."

The Marchesino emptied one side of his cigarette case into the boatman's hand, called a hired carriage, and drove off towards the Villa—the horse going at a frantic trot, while the coachman, holding a rein in each hand, ejaculated, "A—ah!" every ten seconds, in a voice that was fiercely hortatory.

Artois, from his window, saw the carriage rattle past, and saw his friend leaning back in it, with alert eyes, to scan every woman passing by. He stood on the balcony for a moment till the noise of the wheels on the stone pavement died away. When he returned to his writing-table the mood for work was gone. He sat down in his chair. He took up his pen. But he found himself thinking of two people, the extraordinary difference between whom was the cause of his now linking them together in his mind. He found himself thinking of the Marchesino and of Vere.

Not for a moment did he doubt the identity of the

two women in the white boat. They were Hermione
and Vere. The Marchesino had read him rightly, but
Artois was not aware of it. His friend had deceived
him, as almost any sharp-witted Neapolitan can deceive
even a clever forestiere. Certainly he did not particularly wish to introduce his friend to Vere. . Yet now he
was thinking of the two in connection, and not without
amusement. What would they be like together? How
would Vere's divine innocence receive the amiable seduc-
tions of the Marchesino? Artois, in fancy, could see his
friend Doro for once completely disarmed by a child.
Vere's innocence did not spring from folly, but was
backed up by excellent brains. It was that fact which
made it so beautiful. The innocence and the brains together might well read Doro a pretty little lesson. And
Vere after the lesson—would she be changed? Would
she lose by giving, even if the gift were a lesson?

Artois had certainly felt that his instinct told him not
to do what Doro wanted. He had been moved, he supposed now, by a protective sentiment. Vere was delicious as she was. And Doro—he was delightful as he
was. The girl was enchanting in her ignorance. The
youth—to Artois the Marchesino seemed almost a boy,
indeed, often quite a boy—was admirable in his pre-
cocity. He embodied Naples, its gay *furberia*, and yet
that was hardly the word—perhaps rather one should
say its sunny naughtiness, its reckless devotion to life
purged of thought. And Vere—what did she embody?
Not Sicily, though she was in some ways so Sicilian.
Not England; certainly not that!

Suddenly Artois was conscious that he knew Doro
much better than he knew Vere. He remembered the
statement of an Austrian psychologist, that men are far
more mysterious than women, and shook his head over
it now. He felt strongly the mystery that lay hidden
deep down in the innocence of Vere, in the innocence of

every girl-child of Vere's age who had brains, temperament and perfect purity. What a marvellous combination they made! He imagined the clear flame of them burning in the night of the world of men. Vere must be happy.

When he said this to himself he knew that, perhaps for the first time, he was despairing of something that he ardently desired. He was transferring a wish, that was something like a prayer in the heart of one who had seldom prayed. He was giving up hope for Hermione and fastening hope on Vere. For a moment that seemed like treachery, like an abandoning of Hermione. Since their interview on the sea Artois had felt that, for Hermione, all possibility of real happiness was over. She could not detach her love. It had been fastened irrevocably on Maurice. It was now fastened irrevocably on Maurice's memory. Long ago, had she, while he was alive, found out what he had done, her passion for him might have died, and in the course of years she might have been able to love again. But now it was surely too late. She had lived with her memory too long. It was her blessing—to remember, to recall, how love had blessed her life for a time. And if that memory were desecrated now she would be as one wrecked in the storm of life. Yet with that memory how she suffered!

What could he do for her? His chivalry must exercise itself. He must remain in the lists, if only to fight for Hermione in Vere. And the Marchesino? Artois seemed to divine that he might be an enemy in certain circumstances.

A warmth of sentiment, not very common in Artois, generated within him by such thoughts as these, thoughts that detained him from work, still glowed in his heart when evening fell and the Marchesino came gayly in to take him out upon the sea.

"There's a little wind, Emilio," he said, as they got

into the boat in the harbor of Santa Lucia; "we can sail to the Antico Giuseppone. And after dinner we'll fish for sarde. Isn't it warm? One could sleep out on such a night."

They had two men with them. When they got beyond the breakwater the sail was set, the Marchesino took the helm, and the boat slipped through the smooth sea, rounded the rocks on which the old fort stands to stare at Capri, radiant now as a magic isle in the curiously ethereal light of evening, and headed for the distant point of land which hid Ischia from their eyes. The freedom of the Bay of Naples was granted them—the freedom of the sea. As they ran out into the open water, and Artois saw the round gray eyes of the Marchesino dancing to the merry music of a complete bodily pleasure, he felt like a man escaping. He looked back at the city almost as at a sad life over, and despite his deep and persistent interest in men he understood the joy of the hermit who casts them from him and escapes into the wilds. The radiance of the Bay, one of the most radiant of all the inlets of the sea, bold and glaring in the brilliant daytime, becomes exquisitely delicate towards night. Vesuvius, its fiery watcher, looks like a kindly guardian, until perhaps the darkness shows the flame upon its flanks, the flame bursting forth from the mouth it opens to the sky; and the coast-line by Sorrento, the lifted crest of Capri, even the hill of Posilipo, appear romantic and enticing, calling lands holding wonderful pleasures for men, joys in their rocks and trees, joys in their dim recesses, joys and soft realities fulfilling every dream upon their coasts washed by the whispering waves.

The eyes of the Marchesino were dancing with physical pleasure. Artois wondered how much he felt the beauty of the evening, and how. His friend evidently saw the question in his eyes, for he said:

A SPIRIT IN PRISON

"The man who knows not Naples knows not pleasure."

"Is that a Neapolitan saying?" asked Artois.

"Yes, and it is true. There is no town like Naples for pleasure. Even your Paris, Emilio, with all its theatres, its cocottes, its restaurants—no, it is not Naples. No wonder the forestieri come here. In Naples they are free. They can do what they will. They know we shall not mind. We are never shocked."

"And do you think we are easily shocked in Paris?"

"No, but it is not the same. You have not Vesuvius there. You have not the sea, you have not the sun."

Artois began laughingly to protest against the last statement, but the Marchesino would not have it.

"No, no, it shines—I know that,—but it is not the sun we have here."

He spoke to the seamen in the Neapolitan dialect. They were brown, muscular fellows. In their eyes were the extraordinary boldness and directness of the sea. Neither of them looked gay. Many of the Neapolitans who are much upon the sea have serious, even grave faces. These were intensely, almost overpoweringly male. They seemed to partake of the essence of the elements of nature, as if blood of the sea ran in their veins, as if they were hot with the grim and inner fires of the sun. When they spoke their faces showed a certain changefulness that denoted intelligence, but never lost the look of force, of an almost tense masculinity ready to battle, perpetually alive to hold its own.

The Marchesino was also very masculine, but in a different way and more consciously than they were. He was not cultured, but such civilization as he had endowed him with a power to catch the moods of others not possessed by these men, in whom persistence was more visible than adroitness, unless indeed any question of money was to the fore.

"We shall get to the Giuseppone by eight, Emilio,"

the Marchesino said, dropping his conversation with the men, which had been about the best hour and place for their fishing. "Are you hungry?"

"I shall be," said Artois. "This wind brings an appetite with it. How well you steer!"

The Marchesino nodded carelessly.

As the boat drew ever nearer to the point, running swiftly before the light breeze, its occupants were silent. Artois was watching the evening, with the eyes of a lover of nature, but also with the eyes of one who takes notes. The Marchesino seemed to be intent on his occupation of pilot. As to the two sailors, they sat in the accustomed calm and staring silence of seafaring men, with wide eyes looking out over the element that ministered to their wants. They saw it differently, perhaps, from Artois, to whom it gave now an intense æsthetic pleasure, differently from the Marchesino, to whom it was just a path to possible excitement, possible gratification of a new and dancing desire. They connected it with strange superstitions, with gifts, with deprivations, with death. Familiar and mysterious it was purely to them as to all seamen, like a woman possessed whose soul is far away.

Just as the clocks of Posilipo were striking eight the Marchesino steered the boat into the quay of the Antico Guiseppone.

Although it was early in the season a few deal tables were set out by the waterside, and a swarthy waiter, with huge mustaches and a napkin over his arm, came delicately over the stones to ask their wishes.

"Will you let me order dinner, Emilio?" said the Marchesino: "I know what they do best here."

Artois agreed, and while the waiter shuffled to carry out the Marchesino's directions the two friends strolled near the edge of the sea.

The breeze had been kindly. Having served them well it was now dying down to its repose, leaving the evening that was near to night profoundly calm. As Artois walked along the quay he felt the approach of calm like the approach of a potentate, serene in the vast consciousness of power. Peace was invading the sea, irresistible peace. The night was at hand. Already Naples uncoiled its chain of lamps along the Bay. In the gardens of Posilipo the lights of the houses gleamed. Opposite, but very far off across the sea, shone the tiny flames of the houses of Portici, of Torre del Greco, of Torre Annunziata, of Castellamare. Against the gathering darkness Vesuvius belched slowly soft clouds of rose-colored vapor, which went up like a menace into the dim vault of the sky. The sea was without waves. The boats by the wharf, where the road ascends past the villa Rosebery to the village of Posilipo, scarcely moved. Near them, in a group, lounging against the wall and talking rapidly, stood the two sailors from Naples with the boatmen of the Guiseppone. Oil lamps glimmered upon two or three of the deal tables, round one of which was gathered a party consisting of seven large women, three children, and two very thin middle-aged men with bright eyes, all of whom were eating oysters. Farther on, from a small arbor that gave access to a fisherman's house, which seemed to be constructed partially in a cave of the rock, and which was gained by a steep and crumbling stairway of stone, a mother called shrilly to some half-naked little boys who were fishing with tiny hand-nets in the sea. By the table which was destined to the Marchesino and Artois three ambulant musicians were hovering, holding in their broad and dirty hands two shabby mandolins and a guitar. In the distance a cook with a white cap on his head and bare arms was visible, as he moved to and fro in the lighted kitchen of the old ristorante, preparing a "zuppa di pesce" for the gentlemen from Naples.

"Che bella notte!" said the Marchesino, suddenly.

A SPIRIT IN PRISON

His voice sounded sentimental. He twisted his mustaches and added:

"Emilio, we ought to have brought two beautiful women with us to-night. What are the moon and the sea to men without beautiful women?"

"And the fishing?" said Artois.

"To the devil with the fishing," replied the young man. "Ecco! our dinner is ready, with thanks to the Madonna!"

They sat down, one on each side of the small table, with a smoking lamp between them.

"I have ordered vino bianco," said the Marchesino, who still looked sentimental. "Cameriere, take away the lamp. Put it on the next table. Va bene. We are going to have 'zuppa di pesce,' gamberi and veal cutlets. The wine is Capri. Now then," he added, with sudden violence and the coarsest imaginable Neapolitan accent, "if you fellows play 'Santa Lucia,' 'Napoli Bella,' or 'Sole mio' you'll have my knife in you. I am not an Inglese. I am a Neapolitan. Remember that!"

He proved it with a string of gutter words and oaths, at which the musicians smiled with pleasure. Then, turning again to Artois, he continued:

"If one doesn't tell them they think one is an imbecile. Emilio caro, do you not love to see the moon with a beautiful girl?"

His curious assumption that Artois and he were contemporaries because they were friends, and his apparently absolute blindness to the fact that a man of sixty and a man of twenty-four are hardly likely to regard the other sex with an exactly similar enthusiasm, always secretly entertained the novelist, who made it his business with this friend to be accommodating, and who seldom, if ever, showed himself authoritative, or revealed any part of his real inner self.

82

A SPIRIT IN PRISON

"Ma sì!" he replied; "the night and the moon are made for love."

"Everything is made for love," returned the Marchesino. "Take plenty of soaked bread, Emilio. They know how to make this zuppa here. Everything is made for love.—Look! There is a boat coming with women in it!"

At a short distance from the shore a rowing boat was visible; and from it now came shrill sounds of very common voices, followed by shouts of male laughter.

"Perhaps they are beautiful," said the Marchesino, at once on the alert.

The boat drew in to the quay, and from it there sprang, with much noise and many gesticulations, two over-dressed women—probably, indeed almost certainly, *canzonettiste*—and two large young men, whose brown fingers and whose chests gleamed with false diamonds. As they passed the table where the two friends were sitting, the Marchesino raked the women with his bold gray eyes. One of them was large and artificially blonde, with a spreading bust, immense hips, a small waist, and a quantity of pale dyed hair, on which was perched a bright blue hat. The other was fiercely dark, with masses of coarse black hair, big, blatant eyes that looked quite black in the dim lamplight, and a figure that suggested a self-conscious snake. Both were young. They returned the Marchesino's stare with vigorous impudence as they swung by.

"What sympathetic creatures!" he murmured. "They are two angels. I believe I have seen one of them at the Margherita. What was her name—Maria Leoni, I fancy."

He looked enviously at the young men. The arrival of the lobster distracted his attention for the moment; but it was obvious that the appearance of these women had increased the feeling of sentimentality already generated in him by the softness and stillness of the night.

The three musicians, rendered greedy rather than inspired by the presence of more clients, now began to pluck a lively street tune from their instruments; and the waiter, whose mustaches seemed if possible bigger now that night was fully come, poured the white wine into the glasses with the air of one making a libation.

As the Marchesino ate, he frequently looked towards the party at the neighboring table. He was evidently filled with envy of the two men whose jewels glittered as they gesticulated with their big brown hands. But presently their pleasure and success recalled to him something which he had momentarily forgotten, the reason why he had planned this expedition. He was in pursuit. The recollection cheered him up, restored to him the strength of his manhood, put him right with himself. The envy and the almost sickly sentimentality vanished from him, and he broke into the usual gay conversation which seldom failed him, either by day or night.

It was past nine before they had finished their coffee. The two boatmen had been regaled and had drunk a bottle of wine, and the moon was rising and making the oil lamps of the Giuseppone look pitiful. From the table where the canzonettiste were established came peals of laughter, which obviously upset the seven large and respectable women who had been eating oysters, and who now sat staring heavily at the gay revellers, while the two thin middle-aged men with bright eyes began to look furtively cheerful, and even rather younger than they were. The musicians passed round a small leaden tray for soldi, and the waiter brought the Marchesino the bill, and looked inquiringly at Artois, aware that he at least was not a Neapolitan. Artois gave him something and satisfied the musicians, while the Marchesino disputed the bill, not because he minded paying, but merely to prove that he was a Neapolitan and not an imbecile. The matter was settled at last, and they went towards the boat; the Marchesino casting many backward glances towards the two angels, who, with their lovers, were becoming riotous in their gayety as the moon came up.

"Are we going out into the Bay?" said Artois, as they stepped into the boat, and were pushed off.

"Where is the best fishing-ground?" asked the Marchesino of the elder of the two men.

"Towards the islet, Signorino Marchesino," he replied at once, looking his interlocutor full in the face with steady eyes, but remaining perfectly grave.

Artois glanced at the man sharply. For the first time it occurred to him that possibly his friend had arranged this expedition with a purpose other than that which he had put forward. It was not the fisherman's voice which had made Artois wonder, but the voice of the Marchesino.

"There are generally plenty of sarde round the islet," continued the fisherman, "but if the Signori would not be too tired it would be best to stay out the night. We shall get many more fish towards morning, and we can run the boat into the Pool of San Francesco, and have some sleep there, if the Signori like. We others generally take a nap there, and go to work further on in the night. But of course it is as the Signori prefer."

"They want to keep us out all night to get more pay," said the Marchesino to Artois, in bad French.

He had divined the suspicion that had suddenly risen up in his friend, and was resolved to lay it to rest, without, however, abandoning his purpose, which had become much more ardent with the coming of the night. The voices of the laughing women were ringing in his ears. He felt adventurous. The youth in him was rioting, and he was longing to be gay, as the men with those women were being gay.

"What do you think, Emilio caro?" he asked.

Then before Artois could reply, he said:

"After all, what do a few soldi matter? Who could sleep in a room on such a night? It might be August, when one bathes at midnight, and sings canzoni till dawn. Let us do as he says. Let us rest in the—what is the pool?" he asked of the fishermen, pretending not to know the name.

"The pool of San Francesco, Signorino Marchesino."

"Pool of San Francesco. I remember now. That is the place where all the fishermen along the coast towards Nisida go to sleep. I have slept there many times when I was a boy, and so has Viviano. To-night shall we do as the fishermen, Emilio?"

There was no pressure in his careless voice. His eyes for the moment looked so simple, though as eager, as a child's.

"Anything you like, mon ami," said Artois.

He did not want to go to San Francesco's Pool with the Marchesino, but he did not wish to seem reluctant to go. And he said to himself now that his interior hesitation was absurd. Night had fallen. By the time they reached the Pool the inmates of the Casa del Mare would probably be asleep. Even if they were not, what did it matter? The boat would lie among the vessels of the fishermen. The Marchesino and he would share the fishermen's repose. And even if Hermione and Vere should chance to be out of doors they would not see him, or, if they did, would not recognize him in the night.

His slight uneasiness, prompted by a vague idea that the Marchesino was secretly mischievous, had possibly some plan in his mind connected with the islet, was surely without foundation.

He told himself so as the fishermen laid hold of their

oars and set the boat's prow towards the point of land which conceals the small harbor of the Villa Rosebery.

The shrill voices of the two singers died away from their ears, but lingered in the memory of the Marchesino, as the silence of the sea took the boat to itself, the sea silence and the magic of the moon.

He turned his face towards the silver, beyond which, hidden as yet, was the islet where dwelt the child he meant to know.

CHAPTER VII

ALTHOUGH Hermione had told Artois that she could not find complete rest and happiness in her child, that she could not live again in Vere fully and intensely as she had lived once, as she still had it in her surely to live, she and Vere were in a singularly close relationship. They had never yet been separated for more than a few days. Vere had not been to school, and much of her education had been undertaken by her mother. In Florence she had been to classes and lectures. She had had lessons in languages, French, German, and Italian, in music and drawing. But Hermione had been her only permanent teacher, and until her sixteenth birthday she had never been enthusiastic about anything without carrying her enthusiasm to her mother, for sympathy, explanation, or encouragement.

Sorrow had not quenched the élan of Hermione's nature. What she had told Artois had been true—she was not a finished woman, nor would she ever be, so long as she was alive and conscious. Her hunger for love, her passionate remembrance of the past, her incapacity to sink herself in any one since her husband's death, her persistent, though concealed, worship of his memory, all these things proved her vitality. Artois was right when he said that she was a force. There was something in her that was red-hot, although she was now a middle-aged woman. She needed much more than most people, because she had much more than most people have to give.

A SPIRIT IN PRISON

Her failure to express herself in an art had been a tragedy. From this tragedy she turned, not with bitterness, but perhaps with an almost fiercer energy, to Vere. Her intellect, released from fruitless toil, was running loose demanding some employment. She sought that employment in developing the powers of her child. Vere was not specially studious. Such an out-of-door temperament as hers could never belong to a bookworm or a recluse. But she was naturally clever, as her father had not been, and she was enthusiastic not only in pleasure but in work. Long ago Hermione, trying with loving anxiety to educate her boyish husband, to make him understand certain subtleties of her own, had found herself frustrated. When she made such attempts with Vere she was met half way. The girl understood with swiftness even those things with which she was not specially in sympathy. Her father's mind had slipped away, ever so gracefully, from all which it did not love. Vere's could grasp even the unloved subject. There was mental grit in her—Artois knew it. In all her work until her sixteenth year Vere had consulted her mother. Nothing of her child till then was ever hidden from Hermione, except those things which the human being cannot reveal, and sometimes scarcely knows of. The child drew very much from her mother, responded to her enthusiasm, yet preserved instinctively, and quite without self-consciousness, her own individuality.

Artois had noticed this, and this had led him to say that Vere also was a force.

But when she was sixteen Vere woke up to something. Until now no one but herself knew to what. Sometimes she shut herself up alone in her room for long periods. When she came out she looked lazy, her mother thought, and she liked to go then to some nook of the rocks and sit alone, or to push a boat out into the centre of the Saint's Pool, and lie in it with her hands clasped behind her head looking up at the passing clouds or at the radiance of the blue.

Hermione knew how fond Vere was of reading, and supposed that this love was increasing as the child grew older. She sometimes felt a little lonely, but she was unselfish. Vere's freedom was quite innocent. She, the mother, would not seek to interfere with it. Soon after dinner on the evening of the Marchesino's expedition with Artois, Vere had got up from the sofa, on which she had been sitting with a book of Rossetti's poems in her hand, had gone over to one of the windows, and had stood for two or three minutes looking out over the sea. Then she had turned round, come up to her mother and kissed her tenderly—more tenderly, Hermione thought, even than usual.

"Good-night, Madre mia," she had said.

And then, without another word, she had gone swiftly out of the room.

After Vere had gone the room seemed very silent. In the evening, if they stayed in the house, they usually sat in Hermione's room up-stairs. They had been sitting there to-night. The shutters were not closed. The window that faced the sea towards Capri was open. A little moonlight began to mingle subtly with the light from the two lamps, to make it whiter, cleaner, suggestive of outdoor things and large spaces. Hermione had been reading when Vere was reading. She did not read now Vere was gone. Laying down her book she sat listening to the silence, realizing the world without. Almost at her feet was the sea, before her a wide-stretching expanse, behind her, confronted by the desolate rocks, the hollow and mysterious caverns. In the night, the Saint, unwearied, watched his Pool. Not very far off, yet delightfully remote, lay Naples with its furious activities, its gayeties, its intensities of sin, of misery, of pleasure. In the Galleria, tourists from the hotels and from the ships were wandering rather vaguely, watched and followed by newspaper sellers, by touts, by greedy, pale-faced boys, and old, worn-out men, all hungry for money and indifferent how it was gained. Along the Marina, with its huge serpent of lights, the street singers and players were making their nightly pilgrimage, pausing, wherever they saw a lighted window or a dark figure on a balcony, to play and sing the tunes of which they were weary long ago. On the wall, high above the sea, were dotted the dilettante fishermen with their long rods and lines. And below, before each stone staircase that descended to the water, was a waiting boat, and in the moonlight rose up the loud cry of "Barca! Barca!" to attract the attention of any casual passer-by.

And here, on this more truly sea-like sea, distant from the great crowd and from the thronging houses, the real fishermen who live by the sea were alert and at work, or were plunged in the quiet sleep that is a preparation for long hours of nocturnal wakefulness.

Hermione thought of it all, was aware of it, felt it, as she sat there opposite to the open window. Then she looked over to her writing-table, on which stood a large photograph of her dead husband, then to the sofa where Vere had been. She saw the volume of Rossetti lying beside the cushion that still showed a shallow dent where the child's head had been resting.

And then she shut her eyes, and asked her imagination to take her away for a moment, over the sea to Messina, and along the curving shore, and up by winding paths to a mountain, and into a little room in a tiny, whitewashed house, not the house of the sea, but of the priest. It still stood there, and the terrace was still before it. And the olive-trees rustled, perhaps, just now in the wind beneath the stars.

Yes, she was there. Lucrezia and Gaspare were in bed. But she and Maurice were sitting in the straw chairs on each side of the table, facing the open French window and the flight of shallow steps that led down to the terrace.

Faintly she heard the whisper of the sea about the islet, but she would not let it hinder her imagination: she translated it by means of her imagination into the whisper of the wind low down there, in the ravine among the trees. And that act made her think of the ravine, seemed presently to set her in the ravine. She was there in the night with Gaspare. They were hurrying down towards the sea. He was behind her, and she could hear his footsteps—longing to go faster. But she was breathless, her heart was beating, there was terror in her soul. What was that? A rattle of stones in the darkness, and then an old voice muttering "Benedicite!"

She opened her eyes and moved suddenly, like one intolerably stirred. What a foe the imagination can be—what a foe! She got up and went to the window. She must drive away that memory of the ravine, of all that followed after. Often she lingered with it, but to-night, somehow, she could not, she dared not. She was less brave than usual to-night.

She leaned out of the window.

"Am I a fool?"

That was what she was saying to herself. And she was comparing herself now with other people, other women. Did she know one who could not uproot an old memory, who could suffer, and desire, and internally weep, after more than sixteen years?

"I suppose it is preposterous."

She deliberately chose that ugly word to describe her own condition of soul. But instantly it seemed to her as if far down in that soul something rose up and answered:

"No, it is not. It is beautiful. It is divine. It is more—it is due. He gave you the greatest gift. He gave you what the whole world is always seeking; even in blindness, even in ignorance, even in terrible vice. He gave you love. How should you forget him?"

Far away on the sea that was faintly silvered by the moon there was a black speck. It was, or seemed from this distance to be, motionless. Hermione's eyes were attracted to it, and again her imagination carried her to Sicily. She stood on the shore by the inlet, she saw the boat coming in from the open sea. Then it stopped midway—like that boat.

She heard Gaspare furiously weeping.

But the boat moved, and the sound that was in her imagination died away, and she said to herself, "All that was long ago."

The boat out there was no doubt occupied by Neapolitan fishermen, and she was here on the islet in the Sea of Naples, and Sicily was far away across the moonlit waters. As to Gaspare—she was sure he was not weeping, faithful though he was to the memory of the dead Padrone.

And Vere? Hermione wondered what Vere was doing. She felt sure, though she did not know why, that Vere had not gone to bed. She realized to-night that her child was growing up rapidly, was passing from the stage of childhood to the stage of girlhood, was on the threshold of all the mysterious experiences that life holds for those who have ardent temperaments and eager interests, and passionate desires and fearless hearts.

To-night Hermione felt very strongly the difference between the father and the daughter. There was a gravity in Vere, a firmness, that Maurice had lacked. Full of life and warmth as she was, she was not the pure spirit of joy that he had been in those first days in Sicily. She was not irresponsible. She was more keenly aware of others, of just how they were feeling, of just how they were thinking, than Maurice had been.

A SPIRIT IN PRISON

Vere was very individual.

With that thought there came to Hermione a deeper sense of loneliness. She was conscious now in this moment, as she had never been conscious before, of the independence of her child's character. The knowledge of this independence seemed to come upon her suddenly —she could not tell why; and she saw Vere apart from her, detached, like a column in a lonely place.

And she herself—was not she also like a column in a lonely place? She turned back into the room, and saw again the cushion on the sofa with the shallow dent where the head of Vere had rested only a few minutes ago, and, moved by a sudden impulse, she went over to the sofa, sank down on it and pressed her head against the cushion just where her child's head had been. She shut her eyes and strove to think herself into Vere, and to call Vere's mind into hers. She was driven by the tragic desire of woman—specially tragic in her case because frustrated— to be one with another individuality, to merge herself, to be fused, to be no longer as a lonely column set in a desert place.

Vere must not escape from her. She must accompany her child step by step. She must not be left alone. She had told Emile that she could not live again in Vere. And that was true. Vere was not enough. But Vere was very much. Without Vere, what would her life be?

A wave of melancholy flowed over her to-night, a tide come from she knew not where. Making an effort to stem it, she recalled her happiness with Maurice after that day of the Tarantella. How groundless had really been her melancholy then! She had imagined him escaping from her, but he had remained with her, and loved her. He had been good to her until the end, tender and faithful. If she had ever had a rival, that rival had been Sicily. Always her imagination was her torturer.

Her failure in art had been a tragedy because of this.

94

A SPIRIT IN PRISON

If she could have set her imagination free in an art she would have been far safer than she was. Emile Artois was really lonelier than she, for he had not a child. But his art surely saved him securely from her sense of desolation. And then he was a man, and men must need far less than women do. Hermione felt that it was so. She thought of Emile in his most helpless moment, in that period when he was ill in Kairouan before she came. Even then she believed that he could not have felt quite so much alone as she did now; for men never long to be taken care of as women do. And yet she was well, in this tranquil house which was her own—with Vere, her child, and Gaspare, her devoted servant.

As mentally she recounted her benefits, the strength there was in her arose, protesting. She called herself harsh names: egoist, craven, *fainéant*. But it was no use to attack herself. In the deeps of her poor, eager, passionate, hungry woman's nature something wept, and needed, and could not be comforted, and could not be schooled. It complained as one feeble, but really it must be strong; for it was pitilessly persistent in its grieving. It had a strange endurance. Life, the passing of the years, could not change it, could not still it. Those eternal hungers of which Hermione had spoken to Artois —they must have their meaning. Somewhere, surely, there are the happy hunting-grounds, dreamed of by the red man—there are the Elysian Fields where the souls that have longed and suffered will find the ultimate peace.

There came a tap at the door.

Hermione started up from the cushion against which she had pressed her head, and opened her eyes, instinctively laying her hand on Vere's volume of Rossetti, and pretending to read it.

"Avanti!" she said.

The door opened and Gaspare appeared. Hermione felt an immediate sensation of comfort.

"Gaspare," she said, "what is it? I thought you were in bed."

"Ha bisogna Lei?" he said.

It was a most familiar phrase to Hermione. It had been often on Gaspare's lips when he was a boy in Sicily, and she had always loved it, feeling as if it sprang from a nature pleasantly ready to do anything in her service. But to-night it had an almost startling appropriateness, breaking in as if in direct response to her gnawing hunger of the heart. As she looked at Gaspare, standing by the door in his dark-blue clothes, with an earnest expression on his strong, handsome face, she felt as if he must have come just then because he was conscious that she had so much need of help and consolation. And she could not answer "no" to his simple question.

"Come in, Gaspare," she said, "and shut the door. I'm all alone. I should like to have a little talk with you."

He obeyed her, shut the door gently, and came up to her with the comfortable confidence of one safe in his welcome, desired not merely as a servant but as a friend by his Padrona.

"Did you want to say anything particular, Gaspare?" Hermione asked him. "Here—take a cigarette."

She gave him one. He took it gently, twitching his nose as he did so. This was a little trick he had when he was pleased.

"You can smoke it here, if you like."

"Grazie, Signora."

He lit it gravely and took a whiff. Then he said:

"The Signorina is outside."

"Is she?"

Hermione looked towards the window.

"It is a lovely night."

"Sì, Signora."

He took another whiff, and turned his great eyes here

and there, looking about the room. Hermione began to wonder what he had to say to her. She was certain that he had come to her for some reason other than just to ask if she had need of him.

"It does the Signorina good to get a breath of air before she goes to bed," Hermione added, after a moment of silence. "It makes her sleep."

"Sì, Signora."

He still stood calmly beside her, but now he looked at her with the odd directness which had been characteristic of him as a boy, and which he had not lost as a man.

"The Signorina is getting quite big, Signora," he said. "Have you noticed? Per Dio! In Sicily, if the Signorina was a Sicilian, the giovinotti would be asking to marry her."

"Ah, but, Gaspare, the Signorina is not a Sicilian," she said. "She is English, you know, and English girls do not generally think of such things till they are much older than Sicilians."

"But, Signora," said Gaspare, with the bluntness which in him was never rudeness, but merely the sincerity which he considered due to his Padrona — due also to himself, "my Padrone was like a real Sicilian, and the Signorina is his daughter. She must be like a Sicilian too, by force."

"Your Padrone, yes, he was a real Sicilian," Hermione said, softly. "But, well, the Signorina has much more English blood in her veins than Sicilian. She has only a little Sicilian blood."

"But the Signorina thinks she is almost a Sicilian. She wishes to be a Sicilian."

"How do you know that, Gaspare?" she asked, smiling a little at his firmness and persistence.

"The Signorina said so the other day to the giovinotto who had the cigarettes, Signora. I talked to him, and he told me. He said the Signorina had said to him that she was partly a Sicilian, and that he had said 'no,' that she was English. And when he said that—he said to me—the Signorina was quite angry. He could see that she was angry by her face."

"I suppose that is the Sicilian blood, Gaspare. There is some in the Signorina's veins, of course. And then, you know, both her father and I loved your country. I think the Signorina must often long to see Sicily."

"Does she say so?" asked Gaspare, looking rather less calm.

"She has not lately. I think she is very happy here. Don't you?"

"Sì, Signora. But the Signorina is growing up now, and she is a little Sicilian anyhow, Signora."

He paused, looking steadily at his Padrona.

"What is it, Gaspare? What do you want to say to me?"

"Signora, perhaps you will say it is not my business, but in my country we do not let girls go about by themselves after they are sixteen. We know it is better not. Ecco!"

Hermione had some difficulty in not smiling. But she knew that if she smiled he might be offended. So she kept her countenance and said:

"What do you mean, Gaspare? The Signorina is nearly always with me."

"No, Signora. The Signorina can go wherever she likes. She can speak to any one she pleases. She is free as a boy is free."

"Certainly she is free. I wish her to be free."

"Va bene, Signora, va bene."

A cloud came over his face, and he moved as if to go. But Hermione stopped him.

"Wait a minute, Gaspare. I want you to understand. I like your care for the Signorina. You know I trust

98

you and depend on you more than on almost any one. But you must remember that I am English, and in England, you know, things in some ways are very different from what they are in Sicily. Any English girl would be allowed the freedom of the Signorina."

"Why?"

"Why not? What harm does it do? The Signorina does not go to Naples alone."

"Per Dio!" he interrupted, in a tone almost of horror.

"Of course I should never allow that. But here on the island—why, what could happen to her here? Come, Gaspare, tell me what it is you are thinking of. You haven't told me yet. I knew directly you came in that you had something you wanted to say. What is it?"

"I know it is not my business," he said. "And I should never speak to the Signorina, but—"

"Well, Gaspare?"

"Signora, all sorts of people come here to the island— men from Naples. We do not know them. We cannot tell who they are. And they can all see the Signorina. And they can even talk to her."

"The fishermen, you mean?"

"Any one who comes in a boat."

"Well, but scarcely any one ever comes but the fishermen. You know that."

"Oh, it was all very well when the Signorina was a little girl, a child, Signora," he said, almost hotly. "But now it is different. It is quite different."

Suddenly Hermione understood. She remembered what Vere had said about Gaspare being jealous. He must certainly be thinking of the boy-diver, of Ruffo.

"You think the Signorina oughtn't to talk to the fishermen?" she said.

"What do we know of the fishermen of Naples, Signora? We are not Neapolitans. We are strangers here. We do not know their habits. We do not know what they think. They are different from us. If we were in Sicily! I am a Sicilian. I can tell. But when men come from Naples saying they are Sicilians, how can I tell whether they are ruffiani or not?'

Gaspare's inner thought stood revealed.

"I see, Gaspare," Hermione said, quietly. "You think I should not have let the Signorina talk to that boy the other day. But I saw him myself, and I gave the Signorina leave to take him some cigarettes. And he dived for her. She told me all about it. She always tells me everything."

"I do not doubt the Signorina," said Gaspare. "But I thought it was my duty to tell you what I thought, Signora. Why should people come here saying they are of my country, saying they are Sicilians, and talking as the Neapolitans talk?"

"Well, but at the time you didn't doubt that boy was what he said he was, did you?"

"Signora, I did not know. I could not know. But since then I have been thinking."

"Well, Gaspare, you are quite right to tell me. I prefer that. I have much faith in you, and always shall have. But we must not say anything like this to the Signorina. She would not understand what we meant."

"No, Signora. The Signorina is too good."

"She would not understand, and I think she would be hurt"—Hermione used the word "offesa,"—"as you would be if you fancied I thought something strange about you."

"Sì, Signora."

"Good-night, Gaspare."

"Good-night, Signora. Buon riposo."

He moved towards the door. When he reached it he stopped and added:

"I am going to bed, Signora."

"Go. Sleep well."

"Grazie, Signora. The Signorina is still outside, I am sure."

"She goes out for a minute nearly every evening, Gaspare. She likes the air and to look at the sea."

"Sì, Signora; in a minute I shall go to bed. Buon riposo."

And he went out.

When he had gone Hermione remained at first where she was. But Gaspare had effectually changed her mood, had driven away what she chose to call her egoism, had concentrated all her thoughts on Vere. He had never before spoken like this about the child. It was a sudden waking up on his part to the fact that Vere was growing up to womanhood.

When he chose, Gaspare could always, or nearly always, make his Padrona catch his mood; there was something so definite about him that he made an impression. And, though he was easily inclined to be suspicious of those whom he did not know well, Hermione knew him to be both intelligent and shrewd, especially about those for whom he had affection. She wondered now whether it were possible that Gaspare saw, understood, or even divined intuitively, more clearly than she did—she, a mother!

It was surely very unlikely.

She remembered that Gaspare had a jealous nature, like most of his countrymen.

Nevertheless he had suddenly made the islet seem different to her. She had thought of it as remote, as pleasantly far away from Naples, isolated in the quiet sea. But it was very easy to reach from Naples, and, as Gaspare had said, what did they know, or understand, of the Neapolitans, they who were strangers in the land?

She wondered whether Vere was still outside. To-night she certainly envisaged Vere newly. Never till to-night had she thought of her as anything but a child; as characteristic, as ardent, as determined sometimes, perhaps as forceful even, but always with a child's mind behind it all.

But to the people of the South Vere was already a woman—even to Gaspare, who had held her in his arms when she was in long clothes. At least Hermione supposed so now, after what Gaspare had said about the giovinotti, who, in Sicily, would have been wishing to marry Vere, had she been Sicilian. And perhaps even the mind of Vere was more grown-up than her mother had been ready to suppose.

The mother was conscious of a slight but distinct uneasiness. It was vague. Had she been asked to explain it she could not, perhaps, have done so.

Presently, after a minute or two of hesitation, she went to the window that faced north, opened it, and stood by it, listening. It was from the sea on this side that the fishermen who lived in the Mergellina, and in the town of Naples, came to the islet. It was from this direction that Ruffo had come three days ago.

Evidently Gaspare had been turning over the boy's acquaintance with Vere in his mind all that time, disapproving of it, secretly condemning Hermione for having allowed it. No, not that; Hermione felt that he was quite incapable of condemning her. But he was a watchdog who did not bark, but who was ready to bite all those who ventured to approach his two mistresses unless he was sure of their credentials. And of this boy's, Ruffo's, he was not sure.

Hermione recalled the boy; his brown healthiness, his laughing eyes and lips, his strong young body, his careless happy voice. And she found herself instinctively listening by the window to hear that voice again.

Now, as she looked out, the loveliness of the night appealed to her strongly, and she felt sure that Vere must be still outside, somewhere under the moon.

Just beneath the window was the narrow terrace, on to which she had stepped out, obedient to Vere's call, three days ago. Perhaps Vere was there, or in the garden beyond. She extinguished the lamp. She went to her bedroom to get a lace shawl, which she put over her head and drew round her shoulders like a mantilla. Then she looked into Vere's room, and found it empty.

A moment later she was on the terrace bathed in the radiance of the moon.

CHAPTER VIII

VERE was outside under the stars. When she had said good-night and had slipped away, it was with the desire to be alone, to see no one, to speak with no one till next morning. But the desires of the young change quickly, and Vere's presently changed.

She came out of the house, and passing over the bridge that connected together the two cliffs of which the islet was composed, reached the limit of the islet. At the edge of the precipice was a seat, and there she sat down. For some time she rested motionless, absorbing the beauty and the silence of the night. She was looking towards Ischia. She wished to look that way, to forget all about Naples, the great city which lay behind her.

Here were the ancient caves darkening with their mystery the silver wonder of the sea. Here the venerable shore stretched towards lands she did not know. They called to the leaping desires of her heart as the city did not call. They carried her away.

Often, from this seat, on dark and moonless nights, she had watched the fishermen's torches flaring below her in the blackness, and had thrilled at the mystery of their occupation, and had imagined them lifting from the sea strange and wonderful treasures, that must change the current of their lives: pearls such as had never before been given to the breasts of women, caskets that had lain for years beneath the waters, bottles in which were stoppered up magicians who, released, came forth in smoke, as in the Eastern story.

A SPIRIT IN PRISON

Once she had spoken of this last imagination to Gaspare, and had seen his face suddenly change and look excited, vivid, and then sad. She had asked him why he looked like that, and, after a moment of hesitation, he had told her how, long ago, before she was born, his Padrone had read to him such a tale as they lay together upon a mountain side in Sicily. Vere had eagerly questioned him, and he, speaking with vehemence in the heat of his recollection, had brought before her a picture of that scene in his simple life; had shown her how he lay, and how the Padrone lay, he listening, the Padrone, book in hand, reading about the "mago africano." He had even told Vere of their conversation afterwards, and how he had said that he would always be free, that he would never be "stoppered up," like the "mago africano." And when she had wondered at his memory, growing still more excited he had told her many other things of which his Padrone and he had talked together, and had made her feel the life of the past on Monte Amato as no cultured person, she believed, could ever have made her feel it. But when she had sought to question him about her father's death he had become silent, and she had seen that it would be impossible to make him obey her and tell her all the details that she longed to know.

To-night Vere could see no fishermen at work. The silver of the sea below her was unbroken by the black forms of gliding boats, the silence was unbroken by calling voices. And to-night she was glad that it was so; for she was in the mood to be quite alone. As she sat there very still she seemed to herself to be drawing nearer to the sea, and drawing the sea to her. Indeed, she was making some such imaginative attempt as her mother was making in the house—to become, in fancy at least, one with something outside of her, to be fused with the sea, as her mother desired to be fused with her. But Vere's endeavor was not tragic, like her mother's, but was almost tenderly happy. She thought she felt the sea responding to her as she responded to the sea. And she was very glad in that thought.

Presently she began to wonder about the fishermen.

How did they feel about the sea? To her the sea was romantic and personal. Was it romantic and personal to them? They were romantic to her because of their connection with the sea,which had imprinted upon them something of itself, showed forth in them, by means of them, something surely of its own character; but probably, almost certainly, she supposed, they were unconscious of this. They lived by the sea. Perhaps they thought of it as of a vast money-bag, into which they dipped their hands to get enough to live by. Or perhaps they thought of it as an enemy, against which they lived in perpetual war, from which they wrung, as it were at the sword's point, a poor and precarious booty.

As she sat thinking about this Vere began to change in her desire, to wish there were some fishermen out to-night about the islet, and that she could have speech of them. She would like to find out from one of them how they regarded the sea.

She smiled as she imagined a conversation between herself and some strong, brown, wild Neapolitan, she questioning and he replying. How he would misunderstand her! He would probably think her mad. And yet sometimes the men of the sea in their roughness are imaginative. They are superstitous. But a man—no, she could not question a man. Her mind went to the boy diver, Ruffo. She had often thought about Ruffo during the last three days. She had expected to see him again. He had said nothing about returning to the islet, but she had felt sure he would return, if only in the hope of being given some more cigarettes. Boys in his position, she knew well, do not get a present of Khali Targa cigarettes every day of the week. How happy he had looked

when he was smoking them! She remembered exactly
the expression of his brown face now, as she sat watching the empty, moonlit sea. It was not greedy. It was
voluptuous. She remembered seeing somewhere a picture of some Sultan of the East reclining on a divan
and smoking a chibouk. She thought Ruffo had looked
rather like the Sultan, serenely secure of all earthly enjoyment. At that moment the Pool of San Francesco
had stood to the boy for the Paradise of Mahomet.

But Ruffo had not come again.

Each morning Vere had listened for his voice, had
looked down upon the sea for his boat, but all in vain.
On the third day she had felt almost angry with him
unreasonably. But then she had remembered that he
was not his own master, not the owner of the boat. Of
course, he could not do what he liked. If he could—well,
then he would have come back. She was positive of that.

If he ever did come back, she said to herself now, she
would question him about the sea. She would get at his
thoughts about the sea, at his feelings. She wondered
if they could possibly be at all like hers. It was unlikely,
she supposed. They two were so very different. And
yet—!

She smiled to herself again, imagining question and
answer with Ruffo. He would not think her mad, even
if she puzzled him. They understood each other. Even
her mother had said that they seemed to be in sympathy.
And that was true. Difference of rank need not, indeed
cannot, destroy the magic chain if it exists, cannot prevent its links from being forged. She knew that her
mother was in sympathy with Gaspare, and Gaspare with
her mother. So there was no reason why she should not
be in sympathy with Ruffo.

If he were here to-night she would begin at once to
talk to him about the sea. But of course he would
never come at night to the islet.

A SPIRIT IN PRISON

Vere knew that the Neapolitan fishermen usually keep each to his own special branch of the common profession. By this time of night, no doubt, Ruffo was in his home at the Mergellina, sitting in the midst of his family, or was strolling with lively companions of his own age, or, perhaps, was fast asleep in bed.

Vere felt that it would be horrible to go to bed on such a night, to shut herself in from the moon and the sea. The fishermen who slept in the shelter of the Saint's Pool were enviable. They had the stars above them, the waters about them, the gentle winds to caress them as they lay in the very midst of romance.

She wondered whether there were any boats in the Saint's Pool to-night. She had not been to see. A few steps and she could look over. She got up and went back to the bridge, treading softly because she was thinking of repose. There she stopped and looked down. She saw two boats on the far side of the Pool almost at the feet of the Saint. The men in them must be lying down, for Vere could see only the boats, looking black, and filled with a confused blackness—of sails probably, and sleeping men. The rest of the pool was empty, part of it bright with the radiance of the moon, part of it shading away to the mysterious dimness of still water at night under the lee of cliffs.

For some time the girl stood, watching. Just at that moment her active brain almost ceased to work, stilled by the reverie that is born of certain night visions. Without those motionless boats the Pool of the Saint would have been calm. With them, its stillness seemed almost ineffably profound. The hint of life bound in the cords of sleep, prisoner to rest, deepened Nature's impression and sent Vere into reverie. There were no trees here. No birds sang, for although it was the month of the nightingales, none ever came to sing to San Francesco. No insects chirped or hummed. All was stark and almost fearfully still as in a world abandoned; and the light fell on the old faces of the rocks faintly, as if it feared to show the ravages made in them by the storms of the long ages they had confronted and defied.

Vere had a sensation of sinking very slowly down into a gulf, as she stood there, not falling, but sinking, down into some world of quiet things, farther and farther down, leaving all the sounds of life far up in light above her. And descent was exquisite, easy and natural, and, indeed, inevitable. Nothing called her from below. For where she was going there were no voices. Yet she felt that at last there would be something to receive her; mystical stillness, mystical peace.

A silky sound — far off — checked that imaginative descent that seemed so physical, first merely arrested it, then, always silky, but growing louder, took her swiftly and softly back to the summit she had left. Now she was conscious again of herself and of the night. She was listening. The sound that had broken her reverie was the gentle sweep of big-bladed oars through the calm sea. As she knew this she saw, away to the right, a black shadow stealing across the silver waste beyond the islet. It pushed its way to the water at her very feet, and chose that as its anchorage.

The figure of the rower stood up straight and black for a moment, looking lonely in the night.

Vere could not see his face, but she knew at once that he was Ruffo. Her inclination was to bend down with the soft cry of "Pescator!" which she had sent to him on the sunny morning of their meeting. She checked it, why she scarcely knew, in obedience to some imperious prompting of her nature. But she kept her eyes on him. And they were full of will. She was willing him not to lie down in the bottom of the boat and sleep. She knew that he and his companions must have come to the pool at that hour to rest. There were three other men in the boat. Two had been sitting on the gunwale of it, and now lay down. The third, who was in the bows, exchanged some words with the rower, who replied. Vere could hear the sound of their voices, but not what they said. The conversation continued for two or three minutes, while Ruffo was taking in the oars and laying them one on each side of the boat. When he had done this he stretched up his arms to their full length above his head, and a loud noise of a prolonged yawn came up to Vere, and nearly made her laugh. Long as it was, it seemed to her to end abruptly. The arms dropped down.

She felt sure he had seen her watching, and stayed quite still, wondering what he was going to do. Perhaps he would tell the other man. She found herself quickly hoping that he would not. That she was there ought to be their little secret.

All this that was passing through her mind was utterly foreign to any coquetry. Vere had no more feeling of sex in regard to Ruffo than she would have had if she had been a boy herself. The sympathy she felt with him was otherwise founded, deep down in mysteries beyond the mysteries of sex.

Again Ruffo and the man who had not lain down spoke together. But the man did not look up to Vere. He must have looked if his attention had been drawn to the fact that she was there—a little spy upon the men of the sea, considering them from her eminence.

Ruffo had not told. She was glad.

Presently the man moved from his place in the bows. She saw him lift a leg to get over into the stern, treading carefully in order not to trample on his sleeping companions. Then his black figure seemed to shut up like a telescope. He had become one with the dimness in the boat, was no longer detached from it. Only Ruffo was still detached. Was he going to sleep, too?

A certain tenseness came into Vere's body. She kept her eyes, which she had opened very wide, fixed upon the black figure. It remained standing. The head moved. He was certainly looking up. She realized that he was not sleepy, despite that yawn,—that he would like to speak to her—to let her know that he knew she was there.

Perhaps he did not dare to—or, not that, perhaps fishermen's etiquette, already enshrined in his nature, did not permit him to come ashore. The boat was so close to the land that he could step on to it easily.

She leaned down.

"Pescator!"

It was scarcely more than a whisper. But the night was so intensely still that he heard it. Or, if not that, he felt it. His shadow—so it seemed in the shadow of the cliff—flitted out of the boat and disappeared.

He was coming—to have that talk about the sea.

CHAPTER IX

"Buona sera, Signorina."

"Buona sera, Ruffo."

She did not feign surprise when he came up to her.

"So you fish at night?" she said. "I thought the divers for *frutti di mare* did not do that."

"Signorina, I have been taken into the boat of Mandano Giuseppe."

He spoke rather proudly, and evidently thought she would know of whom he was telling her. "I fish for sarde now."

"Is that better for you?"

"Sì, Signorina, of course."

"I am glad of that."

"Sì, Signorina."

He stood beside her quite at his ease. To-night he had on a cap, but it was pushed well off his brow, and showed plenty of his thick, dark hair.

"When did you see me?" she asked.

"Almost directly, Signorina."

"And what made you look up?"

"Signorina?"

"Why did you look up directly?"

"Non lo so, Signorina."

"I think it was because I made you feel that I was there," she said. "I think you obey me without knowing it. You did the same the other day."

"Perhaps, Signorina."

"Have you smoked all the cigarettes?"

She saw him smile, showing his teeth.

"Sì, Signorina, long ago. I smoked them the same day."

"You shouldn't. It is bad for a boy, and you are younger than I am, you know."

The smile grew wider.

"What are you laughing at?"

"I don't know, Signorina."

"Do you think it is funny to be younger than I am?"

"Sì, Signorina."

"I suppose you feel quite as if you were a man?"

"If I could not work as well as a man Giuseppe would not have taken me into his boat. But of course with a lady it is all different. A lady does not have to work. Poor women get old very soon, Signorina."

"Your mother, is she old?"

"My mamma! I don't know. Yes, I suppose she is rather old."

He seemed to be considering.

"Sì, Signorina, my mamma is rather old. But then she has had a lot of trouble, my poor mamma!"

"I am sorry. Is she like you?"

"I don't know, Signorina; I have never thought about it. What does it matter?"

"It may not matter, but such things are interesting sometimes."

"Are they, Signorina?"

Then, evidently with a polite desire to please her and carry on the conversation in the direction indicated by her, he added:

"And are you like your Signora Madre, Signorina?"

Vere felt inclined to smile, but she answered, quite seriously.

"I don't believe I am. My mother is very tall, much taller than I am, and not so dark. My eyes are much darker than hers and quite different."

"I think you have the eyes of a Sicilian, Signorina."

Again Vere was conscious of a simple effort on the part of the boy to be gallant. And he had a good memory too. He had not forgotten her three-days'-old claim to Sicilian blood. The night mitigated the blunders of his temperament, it seemed. Vere could not help being pleased. There was something in her that ever turned towards the Sicily she had never seen. And this boy had not seen Sicily either.

"Isn't it odd that you and I have never seen Sicily?" she said, "and that both our mothers have? And mine is all English, you know."

"My mamma would be very glad to kiss the hand of your Signora Mother," replied Ruffo. "I told her about the kind ladies who gave me cigarettes, and that the Signorina had never seen her father. When she heard that the Signorina was born after her father was dead, and that her father had died in Sicily, she said—my poor mamma!—'If ever I see the Signorina's mother, I shall kiss her hand. She was a widow before she was a mother; may the Madonna comfort her.' My mamma spoke just like that, Signorina. And then she cried for a long time. But when Patrigno came in she stopped crying at once."

"Did she? Why was that?"

"I don't know, Signorina."

Vere was silent for a moment. Then she said:

"Is your Patrigno kind to you, Ruffo?"

The boy looked at her, then swiftly looked away.

"Kind enough, Signorina," he answered.

Then they both kept silence. They were standing side by side thus, looking down rather vaguely at the Saint's Pool, when another boat floated gently into it, going over to the far side, where already lay the two boats at the feet of San Francesco. Vere saw it with indifference. She was accustomed to the advent of the fishermen at this hour. Ruffo stared at it for a moment with a critical, inquiring gaze. The boat drew up near the land and stopped. There was a faint murmur of voices, then silence again.

The Marchesino had told the two sailors that they could have an hour or two of sleep before beginning to fish.

The men lay down, shut their eyes, and seemed to sleep at once. But Artois and the Marchesino, lounging on a pile of rugs deftly arranged in the bottom of the stern of the boat, smoked their cigars in a silence laid upon them by the night silence of the Pool. Neither of them had as yet caught sight of the figures of Vere and Ruffo, which were becoming more clearly relieved as the moon rose and brought a larger world within the radiance of its light. Artois was satisfied that the members of the Casa del Mare were in bed. As they approached the house he had seen no light from its windows. The silence about the islet was profound, and gave him the impression of being in the very heart of the night. And this impression lasted, and so tricked his mind that he forgot that the hour was not really late. He lay back, lazily smoking his cigar, and drinking in the stark beauty round about him, a beauty delicately and mysteriously fashioned by the night, which, as by a miracle, had laid hold of bareness and barren ugliness, and turned them to its exquisite purposes, shrinking from no material in its certainty of its own power to transform.

The Marchesino, too, lay back, with his great, gray eyes staring about him. While the feelings of his friend had moved towards satisfaction, his had undergone a less pleasant change. His plan seemed to be going awry, and he began to think of himself as of a fool. What had he anticipated? What had he expected of this expedition? He had been, as usual, politely waiting on destiny. He had come to the islet in the hope that Destiny would meet him there and treat him with every kindness and hospitality, forestalling his desires. But lo! he was abandoned in a boat among a lot of taciturn men, while the object of all his thoughts and pains, his plots and hopes, was, doubtless, hermetically sealed in the home on the cliff above him.

Several Neapolitan words, familiar in street circles, ran through his mind, but did not issue from his lips, and his face remained perfectly calm—almost seraphic in expression.

Out of the corners of his eyes he stole a glance at "caro Emilio." He wished his friend would follow the example of the men and go to sleep. He wanted to feel himself alone in wakefulness and unobserved. For he was not resigned to an empty fate. The voices of the laughing women at the Antico Giuseppone still rang through his memory. He was adventurous by nature. What he would do if Emilio would only slumber he did not know. But it was certain he would do something. The islet, dark and distinct in outline beneath the moon, summoned him. Was he a Neapolitan and not beneath her window? It was absurd. And he was not at all accustomed to control himself or to fight his own impulses. For the moment "caro Emilio" became "maledetto Emilio" in his mind. Sleepless as Providence, Emilio reclined there. A slightly distracted look came into the Marchesino's eyes as he glanced away from his friend and stared once more at the islet, which he longed so ardently to invade.

This time he saw the figures of Vere and Ruffo above him in the moonlight, which now sharply relieved them. He gazed. And as he gazed they moved away from the bridge, going towards the seat where Vere had been before she had seen Ruffo.

Vere had on a white dress.

The heart of the Marchesino leaped. He was sure it was the girl of the white boat. Then the inhabitants of the house on the islet were not asleep, were not even in bed. They—she at least, and that was all he cared for—were out enjoying the moon and the sea. How favorable was the night! But who was with her?

The Marchesino had very keen eyes. And now he used them with almost fierce intensity. But Ruffo was on the far side of Vere. It was not possible to discern more than that he was male, and taller than the girl in the white dress.

Jealousy leaped up in the Marchesino, that quick and almost frivolous jealousy which, in the Southerner, can so easily deepen into the deadliness that leads to crime. Not for a moment did he doubt that the man with Vere was a lover. This was a blow which, somehow, he had not expected. The girl in the white boat had looked enchantingly young. When he had played the seal for her she had laughed like a child. He—even he, who believed in no one's simplicity, made sceptical by his own naughtiness so early developed towards a fine maturity! —had not expected anything like this. And these English, who pride themselves upon their propriety, their stiffness, their cold respectability! These English misses!

"Ouf!"

It was out of the Marchesino's mouth before he was aware of it, an exclamation of cynical disgust.

"What's the matter, amico mio?" said Artois, in a low voice.

"Niente!" said the Marchesino, recollecting himself. "Are not you going to sleep?"

"Yes," said Artois, throwing away his cigar end. "I am. And you?"

"I too!"

The Marchesino was surprised by his friend's reply. He did not understand the desire of Artois not to have his sense of the romance of their situation broken in upon by conversation just then. The romance of women was not with Artois, but the romance of Nature was. He wanted to keep it. And now he settled himself a little lower in the boat, under the shadow of its side, and seemed to be giving himself to sleep.

The Marchesino thanked the Madonna, and made his little pretence of slumber too, but he kept his head above the gunwale, leaning it on his arm with a supporting cushion beneath; and though he really did shut both his eyes for a short time, to deceive caro Emilio, he very soon opened them again, and gazed towards the islet. He could not see the two figures now. Rage seized him. First the two men at the Antico Giuseppone, and now this man on the islet! Every one was companioned. Every one was enjoying the night as it was meant to be enjoyed. He—he alone was the sport of "il maledetto destino." He longed to commit some act of violence. Then he glanced cautiously round without moving.

The two sailors were sleeping. He could hear their regular and rather loud breathing. Artois lay quite still. The Marchesino turned his body very carefully so that he might see the face of his friend. As he did so Artois, who had been looking straight up at the stars, shut his eyes, and simulated sleep. His suspicion of Doro, that this expedition had been undertaken with some hidden motive, was suddenly renewed by this sly and furtive movement, which certainly suggested purpose and the desire to conceal it.

So caro Emilio slept very peacefully, and breathed with the calm regularity of a sucking child. But in this sleep of a child he was presently aware that the boat was moving—in fact was being very adroitly moved. Though his eyes were shut he felt the moonlight leave his face presently, and knew they were taken by the shadow of the islet. Then the boat stopped.

A moment later Artois was aware that the boat contained three people instead of four.

A SPIRIT IN PRISON

The Marchesino had left it to take a little stroll on shore.

Artois lay still. He knew how light is the slumber of seamen in a boat with the wide airs about them, and felt sure that the sailors must have been waked by the tour of the boat across the Pool. Yet they had not moved, and they continued apparently to sleep. He guessed that a glance from their "Padrone" had advised them not to wake. And this was the truth.

At the first movement of the boat both the men had looked up and had received their message from the Marchesino's expressive eyes. They realized at once that he had some design which he wished to keep from the knowledge of his friend, the forestiere. Of course it must be connected with a woman. They were not particularly curious. They had always lived in Naples, and knew their aristocracy. So they merely returned the Marchesino's glance with one of comprehension and composed themselves once more to repose.

The Marchesino did not come back, and presently Artois lifted himself up a little, and looked out.

The boat was right under the lee of the islet, almost touching the shore, but the sea was so perfectly still that it scarcely moved, and was not in any danger of striking against the rock. The sailors had seen that, too, before they slept again.

Artois sat quite up. He wondered a good deal what his friend was doing. One thing was certain—he was trespassing. The islet belonged to Hermione, and no one had any right to be upon it without her invitation. Artois had that right, and was now considering whether or not he should use it, follow the Marchesino and tell him —what he had not told him—that the owner of the islet was the English friend of whom he had spoken.

For Artois the romance of the night in which he had been revelling was now thoroughly disturbed. He looked

again towards the two sailors, suspecting their sleep.
Then he got up quietly, and stepped out of the boat onto
the shore. His doing so gave a slight impetus to the
boat, which floated out a little way into the Pool. But
the men in it seemed to sleep on.

Artois stood still for a moment at the edge of the sea.
His great limbs were cramped, and he stretched them.
Then he went slowly towards the steps. He reached the
plateau before the Casa del Mare. The Marchesino
was not there. He looked up at the house. As he
did so the front door opened and Hermione came out,
wrapped in a white lace shawl.

"Emile?" she said, stopping with her hand on the
door. "Why—how extraordinary!"

She came to him.

"Have you come to pay us a nocturnal visit, or—
there's nothing the matter?"

"No," he said.

For perhaps the first time in his life he felt embarrassed
with Hermione. He took her hand.

"I don't believe you meant me to know you were here,"
she said, guided by the extraordinary intuition of woman.

"To tell the truth," he answered, "I did not expect to
see you. I thought you were all in bed."

"Oh no. I have been on the terrace and in the garden.
Vere is out somewhere. I was just going to look for her."

There was a distinct question in her prominent eyes as
she fixed them on him.

"No, I haven't seen Vere," he said, answering it.

"Are you alone?" she asked, abruptly.

"No. You remember my mentioning my friend, the
Marchesino Panacci? Well, he is with me. We were
going to fish. The fishermen suggested our sleeping in
the Saint's Pool for an hour of two first. I found Doro
gone, and came to look for him."

There was still a faint embarrassment in his manner.

"THEY TURNED ROUND AS IF MOVED BY A MUTUAL IMPULSE"

"I believe you have seen him," he added. "He was bathing the other day when you were passing in the boat, —I think it was you. Did you see a young man who did some tricks in the water?"

"Oh yes, an impudent young creature. He pretended to be a porpoise and a seal. He made us laugh. Vere was delighted with him. Is that your friend? Where can he be?"

"Where is Vere?" said Artois.

Their eyes met, and suddenly his embarrassment passed away.

"You don't mean that—?"

"My friend, you know what these Neapolitans are. Doro came back from his bathe raving about Vere. I did not tell him I knew her. I think—I am sure he has guessed it, and much more. Let us go and find him. It seems you are to know him. È il destino."

"You don't want me to know him?" she said, as they turned away from the house.

"I don't know that there is any real reason why you should not. But my instinct was against the acquaintance. Where can Vere be? Does she often come out alone at night?"

"Very often. Ah! There she is, beyond the bridge, and—is that the Marchesino Panacci with her? Why— no, it's—"

"It is Ruffo," Artois said.

Vere and the boy were standing near the edge of the cliff and talking earnestly together, but as Hermione and Artois came towards them they turned round as if moved by a mutual impulse. Ruffo took off his cap and Vere cried out:

"Monsieur Emile!"

She came up to him quickly. He noticed that her face looked extraordinarily alive, that her dark eyes were fiery with expression.

"Good-evening, Vere," he said.

He took her small hand.

"Buona sera, Ruffo," he added.

He looked from one to the other, and saw the perfect simplicity of both.

"Tell me, Vere," he said. "Have you seen any one on the islet to-night?"

"Yes, just now. Why? What made you think so?"

"Well?"

"A man—a gentleman came. I told him he was trespassing."

Artois smiled. Ruffo stood by, his cap in his hand, looking attentively at Vere, who had spoken in French. She glanced at him, and suddenly broke into Italian.

"He was that absurd boy we saw in the sea, Madre, the other day, who pretended to be a seal, and made me laugh. He reminded me of it, and asked me if I didn't recognize him."

"What did you say?"

"I said 'No' and 'Good-night.'"

"And did he go?" asked Artois.

"No, he would not go. I don't know what he wanted. He looked quite odd, as if he were feeling angry inside, and didn't wish to show it. And he began trying to talk. But as I didn't really know him—after all, laughing at a man because he pretends to be a seal is scarcely knowing him, is it, Monsieur Emile?"

"No," he said, smiling at her smile.

"I said 'good-night' again in such a way that he had to go."

"And so he went!" said Artois.

"Yes. Do you know him, Monsieur Emile?"

"Yes. He came with me to-night."

A little look of penitence came into the girl's face.

"Oh, I am sorry."

"Why should you be?"

"Well, he began saying something about knowing friends of mine, or—I didn't really listen very much, because Ruffo was telling me about the sea—and I thought it was all nonsense. He was absurdly complimentary first, you see! and so, when he began about friends, I only said 'good-night' again. And—and I'm really afraid I turned my back upon him. And now he's a friend of yours. Monsieur Emile! I am sorry!"

Already the Marchesino had had that lesson of which Artois had thought in Naples. Artois laughed aloud.

"It doesn't matter, Vere. My friend is not too sensitive."

"Buona sera, Signorina! Buona sera, Signora! Buon riposo!"

It was Ruffo preparing to go, feeling that he scarcely belonged to this company, although he looked in no way shy, and had been smiling broadly at Vere's narrative of the discomfiture of the Marchesino.

"Ruffo," said Hermione, "you must wait a moment."

"Sì, Signora?"

"I am going to give you a few more cigarettes."

Vere sent a silent but brilliant "Thank you" to her mother. They all walked towards the house.

Vere and her mother were in front, Artois and Ruffo behind. Artois looked very closely and even curiously at the boy.

"Have I ever seen you before?" he asked, as they came to the bridge.

"Signore?"

"Not the other morning. But have we ever met in Naples?"

"I have seen you pass by sometimes at the Mergellina, Signore."

"That must be it then!" Artois thought, "I have seen you there without consciously noticing you."

"You live there?" he said.

"Sì, Signore; I live with my mamma and my Patrigno."

"Your Patrigno," Artois said, merely to continue the conversation. "Then your father is dead?"

"Sì, Signore, my Babbo is dead."

They were on the plateau now, before the house.

"If you will wait a moment, Ruffo, I will fetch the cigarettes," said Hermione.

"Let me go, Madre," said Vere, eagerly.

"Very well, dear."

The girl ran into the house. As she disappeared they heard a quick step, and the Marchesino came hurrying up from the sea. He took off his hat when he saw Hermione, and stopped.

"I was looking for you, Emilio."

He kept his hat in his hand. Evidently he had recovered completely from his lesson. He looked gay and handsome. Artois realized how very completely the young rascal's desires were being fulfilled. But of course the introduction must be made. He made it quietly.

"Marchese Isidoro Panacci—Mrs. Delarey."

The Marchesino bent and kissed Hermione's hand. As he did so Vere came out of the house, her hands full of Khali Targa cigarettes, her face eager at the thought of giving pleasure to Ruffo.

"This is my daughter, Vere," Hermione said. "Vere, this is the Marchese Isidoro Panacci, a friend of Monsieur Emile's."

The Marchesino went to kiss Vere's hand, but she said:

"I'm very sorry—look!"

She showed him that they were full of cigarettes, and so escaped from the little ceremony. For those watching it was impossible to know whether she wished to avoid the formal salutation of the young man's lips or not.

"Here, Ruffo!" she said. She went up to the boy. "Put your hands together."

Ruffo gladly obeyed. He curved his brown hands

124

into a cup, and Vere filled this cup with the big cigarettes, while Hermione, Artois, and the Marchesino looked on; each one of them with a fixed attention which—surely—the action scarcely merited. But there was something about these two, Vere and the boy, which held the eyes and the mind.

"Good-night, Ruffo. You must carry them to the boat. They'll be crushed if you put them into your trousers-pocket."

"Sì, Signorina!"

He waited a moment. He wanted to salute them, but did not know how to. That was evident. His expressive eyes, his whole face told it to them.

Artois suddenly set his lips together in his beard. For an instant it seemed to him that the years had rolled back, that he was in London, in Caminiti's restaurant, that he saw Maurice Delarey, with the reverential expression on his face that had been so pleasing. Yes, the boy Ruffo looked like him in that moment, as he stood there, wishing to do his devoir, to be polite, but not knowing how to.

"Never mind, Ruffo." It was Vere's voice. "We understand! or—shall I?" A laughing look came into her face. She went up to the boy and, with a delicious, childish charm and delicacy, that quite removed the action from impertinence, she took his cap off. "There!" She put it gently back on his dark hair. "Now you've been polite to us. Buona notte!"

"Buona notte, Signorina."

The boy ran off, half laughing, and carrying carefully the cigarettes in his hands still held together like a cup.

Hermione and Artois were smiling. Artois felt something for Vere just then that he could hardly have explained, master though he was of the explanation of the feelings of man. It seemed to him that all the purity, and the beauty, and the whimsical unselfconsciousness, and the touchingness of youth that is divine, appeared in that little, almost comic action of the girl. He loved her for the action, because she was able to perform it just like that. And something in him suddenly adored youth in a way that seemed new to his heart.

"Well," said Hermione, when Ruffo had disappeared. "Will you come in? I'm afraid all the servants are in bed, but—"

"No, indeed it is too late," Artois said.

Without being aware of it he spoke with an authority that was almost stern.

"We must be off to our fishing," he added. "Good-night. Good-night, Vere."

"Good-night, Signora."

The Marchesino bowed, with his hat in his hand. He kissed Hermione's hand again, but he did not try to take Vere's.

"Good-night," Hermione said.

A glance at Artois had told her much that he was thinking.

"Good-night, Monsieur Emile," said Vere. "Good-night, Marchese. Buona pesca!"

She turned and followed her mother into the house.

"Che simpatica!"

It was the Marchesino's voice, breathing the words through a sigh: "Che simpatica Signorina!" Then an idea seemed to occur to him, and he looked at his friend reproachfully. "And you knew the girl with the perfect little nose, Emilio—all the time you knew her!"

"And all the time you knew I knew her!" retorted Artois.

They looked at each other in the eyes and burst out laughing.

"Emilio, you are the devil! I will never forgive you. You do not trust me."

"Caro amico, I do trust you—always to fall in love

A SPIRIT IN PRISON

with every girl you meet. But "—and his voice changed —"the Signorina is a child. Remember that, Doro."

They were going down the steps to the sea. Almost as Artois spoke they reached the bottom, and saw their boat floating in the moonlight nearly in the centre of the Pool. The Marchesino stood still.

"My dear Emilio," he said, staring at Artois with his great round eyes, "you make me wonder whether you know women."

Artois felt amused.

"Really?" he said.

"Really! and yet you write books."

"Writing books does not always prove that one knows much. But explain to me."

They began to stroll on the narrow space at the sea edge. Close by lay the boat to which Ruffo belonged. The boy was already in it, and they saw him strike a match and light one of the cigarettes. Then he lay back at his ease, smoking, and staring up at the moon.

"A girl of sixteen is not a child, and I am sure the Signorina is sixteen. But that is not all. Emilio, you do not know the Signorina."

Artois repressed a smile. The Marchesino was perfectly in earnest.

"And you—do you know the Signorina?" Artois asked.

"Certainly I know her," returned the Marchesino with gravity.

They reached Ruffo's boat. As they did so, the Marchesino glanced at it with a certain knowing impudence that was peculiarly Neapolitan.

"When I came to the top of the islet the Signorina was with that boy," the Marchesino continued.

"Well?" said Artois.

"Oh, you need not be angry, Emilio caro."

"I am not angry," said Artois.

127

Nor was he. It is useless to be angry with racial characteristics, racial points of view. He knew that well. The Marchesino stared at him.

"No, I see you are not."

"The Signorina was with that boy. She has talked to him before. He has dived for her. He has sung for her! She has given him cigarettes, taken from her mother's box, with her mother's consent. Everything the Signorina does her mother knows and approves of. You saw the Signora send the Signorina for more cigarettes to give the boy to-night. Ebbene?"

"Ebbene. They are English!"

And he laughed.

"Madre mia!"

He laughed again, seized his mustaches, twisted them, and went on.

"They are English, but for all that the Signorina is a woman. And as to that boy—"

"Perhaps he is a man."

"Certainly he is. Dio mio, the boy at least is a Neapolitan."

"No, he isn't."

"He is not?"

"He's a Sicilian."

"How do you know?"

"I was here the other day when he was diving for *frutti di mare.*"

"I have seen him at the Mergellina ever since he was a child."

"He says he is a Sicilian."

"Boys like that say anything if they can get something by it. Perhaps he thought you liked the Sicilians better than the Neapolitans. But anyhow—Sicilian or Neapolitan, it is all one! He is a Southerner, and at fifteen a Southerner is already a man. I was."

"I know it. But you were proving to me that the

A SPIRIT IN PRISON

Signorina is a woman. The fact that she, an English girl, is good friends with that fisher boy does not prove it."

"Ah, well!"

The Marchesino hesitated.

"I had seen the Signorina before I came to meet you at the house."

"Had you?"

"Didn't you know it?"

"Yes, I did."

"I knew she told you."

"What?"

"She told you! she told you! She is birbante. She is a woman, for she pretended as only a woman can pretend."

"What did she pretend?"

"That she was not pleased at my coming, at my finding out where she lived, and seeking her. Why, Emilio, even when I was in the sea, when I was doing the seal, I could read the Signorina's character. She showed me from the boat that she wanted me to come, that she wished to know me. Ah, che simpatica! Che simpatica ragazza!"

The Marchesino looked once more at Ruffo.

"Come here a minute!" he said, in a low voice, not wishing to wake the still sleeping fishermen.

The boy jumped lightly out and came to them. When he stood still the Marchesino said, in his broadest Neapolitan:

"Now then, you tell me the truth! I'm a Neapolitan, not a forestiere. You've seen me for years at the Mergellina."

"Sì, Signore."

"You're a Napolitano."

"No, Signore. I am a Sicilian."

There was a sound of pride in the boy's voice.

"I am quite sure he speaks the truth," Artois said, in French.

"Why do you come here?" asked the Marchesino.

"Signore, I come to fish."

"For cigarettes?"

"No, Signore, for sarde. Buona notte, Signore."

He turned away from them with decision, and went back to his boat.

"He is a Sicilian," said Artois. "I would swear to it."

"Why? Hark at his accent."

"He is a Sicilian!"

"But why are you so sure?"

Artois only said:

"Are you going to fish?"

"Emilio, I cannot fish to-night. My soul is above such work as fishing. It is indeed. Let us go back to Naples."

"Va bene."

Artois was secretly glad. He, too, had no mind—or was it no heart?—for fishing that night, after the episode of the islet. They hailed the sailors, who were really asleep this time, and were soon far out on the path of the moonlight setting their course towards Naples.

CHAPTER X

On the following morning Hermione and Vere went for an excursion to Capri. They were absent from the island for three nights. When they returned they found a card lying upon the table in the little hall—"Marchese Isidoro Panacci di Torno"—and Gaspare told them that it had been left by a Signore, who had called on the day of their departure, and had seemed very disappointed to hear that they were gone.

"I do not know this Signore," Gaspare added, rather grimly.

Vere laughed, and suddenly made her eyes look very round, and staring, and impudent.

"He's like that, Gaspare," she said.

"Vere!" said her mother.

Then she added to Gaspare:

"The Marchese is a friend of Don Emilio's. Ah! and here is a letter from Don Emilio."

It was lying beside the Marchese's card with some other letters. Hermione opened it first, and read that Artois had been unexpectedly called away to Paris on business, but intended to return to Naples as soon as possible, and to spend the whole summer on the Bay.

"I feel specially that this summer I should like to be near you," he wrote. "I hope you wish it."

At the end of the letter there was an allusion to the Marchesino, "that gay and admirably characteristic Neapolitan product, the Toledo incarnate."

There was not a word of Vere.

Hermione read the letter aloud to Vere, who was standing beside her, evidently hoping to hear it. When she had finished, Vere said:

"I am glad Monsieur Emile will be here all the summer."

"Yes."

"But why specially this summer, Madre?"

"I am not sure what he means by that," Hermione answered.

But she remembered the conversation in the Grotto of Virgil, and wondered if her friend thought she needed the comfort of his presence.

"Well, Madre?"

Vere's bright eyes were fixed upon her mother.

"Well, Vere? What is it?"

"Is there no message for me from Monsieur Emile?"

"No, Vere."

"How forgetful of him! But never mind!" She went up-stairs, looking disappointed.

Hermione re-read the letter. She wondered, perhaps more than Vere, why there was no message for the child. The child—she was still calling Vere that in her mind, even after the night conversation with Gaspare. Two or three times she re-read that sentence, "I feel specially that this summer I should like to be near you," and considered it; but she finally put the letter away with a strong feeling that most of its meaning lay between the lines, and that she had not, perhaps, the power to interpret it.

Vere had said that Emile was forgetful. He might be many things, but forgetful he was not. One of his most characteristic qualities was his exceptionally sharp consciousness of himself and of others. Hermione knew that he was incapable of writing to her and forgetting Vere while he was doing so.

She did not exactly know why, but the result upon her

of this letter was a certain sense of depression, a slight and vague foreboding. And yet she was glad, she was even thankful, to know that her friend was going to spend the summer on the Bay. She blamed herself for her melancholy, telling herself that there was nothing in the words of Artois to make her sad. Yet she continued to feel sad, to feel as if some grievous change were at hand, as if she had returned to the island to confront some untoward fate. It was very absurd of her. She told herself that.

The excursion to Capri had been a cheerful one. She had enjoyed it. But all the time she had been watching Vere, studying her, as she had not watched and studied her before. Something had suddenly made her feel unaccustomed to Vere. It might be the words of Gaspare, the expression in the round eyes of the Marchesino, or something new, or newly apparent, in Vere. She did not know. But she did know that now the omission of Artois to mention Vere in his letter seemed to add to the novelty of the child for her.

That seemed strange, yet it was a fact. How absolutely mysterious are many of the currents in our being, Hermione thought. They flow far off in subterranean channels, unseen by us, and scarcely ever realized, but governing, carrying our lives along upon their deeps towards the appointed end.

Gaspare saw that his Padrona was not quite as usual, and looked at her with large-eyed inquiry, but did not at first say anything. After tea, however, when Hermione was sitting alone in the little garden with a book, he said to her bluntly:

"Che ha Lei?"

Hermione put the book down in her lap.

"That is just what I don't know, Gaspare."

"Perhaps you are not well."

"But I believe I am, perfectly well. You know I am

always well. I never even have fever. And you have
that sometimes."

He continued to look at her searchingly.

"You have something."

He said it firmly, almost as if he were supplying her
with information which she needed and had lacked.

Hermione made a sound that was like a little laugh,
behind which there was no mirth.

"I don't know what it is."

Then, after a pause, she added that phrase which is so
often upon Sicilian lips:

"Ma forse è il destino."

Gaspare moved his head once as if in acquiescence.

"When we are young, Signora," he said, "we do what
we want, but we have to want it. And we think we are
very free. And when we are old we don't feel to want
anything, but we have to do things just the same.
Signora, we are not free. It is all destiny."

And again he moved his head solemnly, making his
liquid brown eyes look more enormous than usual.

"It is all destiny," Hermione repeated, almost
dreamily.

Just then she felt that it was so—that each human
being, and she most of all, was in the grasp of an inflexible, of an almost fierce guide, who chose the paths,
and turned the feet of each traveller, reluctant or not,
into the path the will of the guide had selected. And
now, still dreamily, she wondered whether she would
ever try to rebel if the path selected for her were one
that she hated or feared, one that led into any horror of
darkness, or any horror of too great light. For light,
too, can be terrible, a sudden great light that shines pitilessly upon one's own soul. She was of those who
possess force and impulse, and she knew it. She knew,
too, that these are often rebellious. But to-day it
seemed to her that she might believe so much in destiny,

be so entirely certain of the inflexible purpose and power of the guide, that her intellect might forbid her to rebel, because of rebellion's fore-ordained inutility. Nevertheless, she supposed that if it was her instinct to rebel, she would do so at the psychological moment, even against the dictates of her intellect.

Gaspare remained beside her quietly. He often stood near her after they had been talking together, and calmly shared the silence with her. She liked that. It gave her an impression of his perfect confidence in her, his perfect ease in her company.

"Don't you ever think that you can put a knife into Destiny, Gaspare," she asked him presently, using an image he would be likely to understand, "as you might put a knife into a man who tried to force you to do something you didn't wish to do?"

"Signora, what would be the use? The knife is no good against Destiny, nor the revolver either. And I have the permesso to carry one," he added, with a smile, as if he realized that he was being whimsical.

"Well, then, we must just hope that Destiny will be very kind to us, be a friend to us, a true comrade. I shall hope that and so must you."

"Sì, Signora."

He realized that the conversation was finished, and went quietly away.

Hermione kept the letter of Artois. When he came back to the Bay she wanted to show it to him, to ask him to read for her the meaning between its lines. She put it away in her writing-table drawer, and then resolved to forget the peculiar and disagreeable effect it had made upon her.

A fortnight passed away before Artois' return. June came in upon the Bay, bringing with it a more vivid life in the environs of Naples. As the heat of the sun increased the vitality of the human motes that danced in its beams seemed to increase also, to become more blatant, more persistent. The wild oleander was in flower. The thorny cactus put forth upon the rim of its grotesque leaves pale yellow blossoms to rival the red geraniums that throng about it insolently in Italy. In the streets of the city ragged boys ran by crying, "Fragole!" and holding aloft the shallow baskets in which the rosy fruit made splashes of happy color. The carters wore bright carnations above their dusty ears. The children exposed their bare limbs to the sun, and were proud when they were given morsels of ice wrapped up in vine leaves to suck in the intervals of their endless dances and their play. On the hill of Posilipo the Venetian blinds of the houses, in the gardens clouded by the rounded dusk of the great stone pines, were thrust back, the windows were thrown open, the glad sun-rays fell upon the cool paved floors, over which few feet had trodden since the last summer died. Loud was the call of "Aqua!" along the roads where there were buildings, and all the lemons of Italy seemed to be set forth in bowers to please the eyes with their sharp, yet soothing color, and tempt the lips with their poignant juice. Already in the Galleria, an "avviso" was prominently displayed, stating that Ferdinando Bucci, the famous maker of Sicilian ice-creams, had arrived from Palermo for the season. In the Piazza del Plebiscito, hundreds of chairs were ranged before the bandstand, and before the kiosk where the women sing on the nights of summer near the Caffè Turco. The "Margherita" was shutting up. The "Eldorado" was opening. And all along the sea, from the vegetable gardens protected by brushwood hedges on the outskirts of the city towards Portici, to the balconies of the "Mascotte," under the hill of Posilipo, the wooden bathing establishments were creeping out into the shallow waters, and displaying proudly to the passers-by above their names: "Stabilimento Elena,"

A SPIRIT IN PRISON

"Stabilimento Donn' Anna," "Stabilimento delle Sirene," "Il piccolo Paradiso."

And all along the sea by night there was music.

From the Piazza before the Palace the band of the Caffè Gambrinus sent forth its lusty valses. The posturing women of the wooden kiosk caught up the chain of sound, and flung it on with their shrill voices down the hill towards Santa Lucia, where, by the waterside and the crowding white yachts, the itinerant musicians took it into the keeping of their guitars, their mandolins, their squeaky fiddles, and their hot and tremulous voices. The "Valse Bleu," "Santa Lucia," "Addio, mia bella Napoli," "La Frangese," "Sole Mio," "Marechiaro," "Carolina," "La Ciociara"; with the chain of lights the chain of songs was woven round the bay; from the Eldorado, past the Hotel de Vesuve, the Hotel Royal, the Victoria, to the tree-shaded alleys of the Villa Nazionale, to the Mergellina, where the naked urchins of the fisherfolk took their evening bath among the resting boats, to the "Scoglio di Frisio," and upwards to the Ristorante della Stella, and downwards again to the Ristorante del Mare, and so away to the point, to the Antico Giuseppone.

Long and brilliant was the chain of lamps, and long and ardent was the chain of melodies melting one into the other, and stretching to the wide darkness of the night and to the great stillness of the sea. The night was alive with music, with the voices that beat like hearts overcharged with sentimental longings.

But at the point where stood the Antico Giuseppone the lights and the songs died out. And beyond there was the mystery, the stillness of the sea.

And there, beyond the chain of lights, the chain of melodies, the islet lay in its delicate isolation; nevertheless, it, too, was surely not unaware of the coming of summer. For even here, Nature ran up her flag to

137

honor her new festival. High up above the rock on the mainland opposite there was a golden glory of ginestra, the broom plant, an expanse of gold so brilliant, so daring in these bare surroundings, that Vere said, when she saw it:

"There is something cruel even in beauty, Madre. Do you like successful audacity?"

"I think I used to when I was your age," said Hermione. "Anything audacious was attractive to me then. But now I sometimes see through it too easily, and want something quieter and a little more mysterious."

"The difference between the Marchesino and Monsieur Emile?" said the girl, with a little laugh.

Hermione laughed, too.

"Do you think Monsieur Emile mysterious?" she asked.

"Yes—certainly. Don't you?"

"I have known him so intimately for so many years."

"Well, but that does not change him. Does it?"

"No. But it may make him appear very differently to me from the way in which he shows himself to others."

"I think if I knew Monsieur Emile for centuries I should always wonder about him."

"What is it in Emile that makes you wonder?" asked her mother, with a real curiosity.

"The same thing that makes me wonder when I look at a sleepy lion."

"You call Emile sleepy!" said Hermione.

"Oh, not his intellect, Madre! Of course that is horribly, horribly wide awake."

And Vere ran off to her room, or the garden, or the Saint's Pool—who knew where?—leaving her mother to say to herself, as she had already said to herself in these last days of the growing summer, "When I said that to

138

Emile, what a fool I was!" She was thinking of her statement that there was nothing in her child that was hidden from her. As if in answer to that statement, Vere was unconsciously showing to her day by day the folly of it. Emile had said nothing. Hermione remembered that, and realized that his silence had been caused by his disagreement. But why had he not told her she was mistaken? Perhaps because she had just been laying bare to him the pain that was in her heart. Her call had been for sympathy, not merely for truth. She wondered whether she was a coward. Since they had returned from Capri the season and Vere had surely changed. Then, and always afterwards, Hermione thought of those three days in Capri as a definite barrier, a dividing line between two periods. Already, while in Capri, she had begun to watch her child in a new way. But that was, perhaps, because of an uneasiness, partly nervous, within herself. In Capri she might have been imagining. Now she was not imagining, she was realizing.

Over the sea came to the islet the intensity of summer. Their world was changing. And in this changing world Vere was beginning to show forth more clearly than before her movement onward—whither?

As yet the girl herself was unconscious of her mother's new watchfulness. She was happy in the coming of summer, and in her happiness was quite at ease, like a kitten that stretches itself luxuriously in the sun. To Vere the world never seemed quite awake till the summer came. Only in the hot sunshine did there glow the truthfulness and the fulness of life. She shared it with the ginestra. She saw and felt a certain cruelty in the gold, but she did not fear or condemn it, or wish it away. For she was very young, and though she spoke of cruelty she did not really understand it. In it there was force, and force already appealed to the girl as few things did.

A SPIRIT IN PRISON

As, long ago, her father had gloried in the coming of summer to the South, she gloried in it now. She looked across the Pool of the Saint to the flood of yellow that was like sunlight given a body upon the cliff opposite, and her soul revelled within her, and her heart rose up and danced, alone, and yet as if in a glad company of dancers, all of whom were friends. Her brain, too, sprang to the alert. The sun increased the feeling of intelligence within her.

And then she thought of her room, of the hours she passed shut in there, and she was torn by opposing impulses.

But she told no one of them. Vere could keep her secrets, although she was a girl.

How the sea welcomed the summer! To many this home on the island would have seemed an arid, inhospitable place, desolate and lost amid a cruel world of cliffs and waters. It was not so to Vere. For she entered into the life of the sea. She knew all its phases, as one may know all the moods of a person loved. She knew when she would find it intensely calm, at early morning and when the evening approached. At a certain hour, with a curious regularity, the breeze came, generally from Ischia, and turned it to vivacity. A temper that was almost frivolous then possessed it, and it broke into gayeties like a child's. The waves were small, but they were impertinently lively. They made a turmoil such as urchins make at play. Heedless of reverence, but not consciously impious, they flung themselves at the feet of San Francesco, casting up a tiny tribute of spray into the sun.

Then Vere thought that the Saint looked down with pleasure at them, as a good old man looks at a crowd of laughing children who have run against him in the street, remembering his own youth. For even the Saints were young! And, after that, surely the waves were a little less boisterous. She thought she noted a greater calm. But perhaps it was only that the breeze was dying down as the afternoon wore on.

She often sat and wondered which she loved best—the calm that lay upon the sea at dawn, or the calm that was the prelude to the night. Silvery were these dawns of the summer days. Here and there the waters gleamed like the scales of some lovely fish. Mysterious lights, like those in the breast of the opal, shone in the breast of the sea, stirred, surely travelled as if endowed with life, then sank away to the far-off kingdoms that man may never look on. Those dawns drew away the girl's soul as if she were led by angels, or, like Peter, walked upon the deep at some divine command. She felt that though her body was on the islet the vital part of her, the real "I," was free to roam across the great expanse that lay flat and still and delicately mysterious to the limits of eternity.

She had strange encounters there, the soul of her, as she went towards the East.

The evening calm was different. There was, Vere thought, less of heaven about it, but perhaps more of the wonder of this world. And this made her feel as if she had been nearer to heaven at her birth than she would be at her death. She knew nothing of the defilements of life. Her purity of mind was very perfect; but, taking a parable from Nature, she applied it imaginatively to Man, and she saw him covered with dust because of his journey through the world. Poor man!

And then she pitied herself too. But that passed. For if the sea at evening held most of the wonder of this world, it was worth the holding. Barely would she substitute the heavenly mysteries for it. The fishermen's boats were dreams upon a dream. Each sail was akin to a miracle. A voice that called across the water from a distance brought tears to Vere's eyes when the magic was at its fullest. For it seemed to mean all things that were tender, all things that were wistful, all things that trembled with hope—that trembled with love.

With summer Vere could give herself up to the sea, and not only imaginatively but by a bodily act.

Every day, and sometimes twice a day, she put on her bathing-dress in the Casa del Mare, threw a thin cloak over her, and ran down to the edge of the sea, where Gaspare was waiting with the boat. Hermione did not bathe. It did not suit her now. And Gaspare was Vere's invariable companion. He had superintended her bathing when she was little. He had taught her to swim. And with no one else would he ever trust his Padroncina when she gave herself to the sea. Sometimes he would row her out to a reef of rocks in the open water not many yards from the island, and she would dive from them. Sometimes, if it was very hot, he would take her to the Grotto of Virgil. Sometimes they went far out to sea, and then, like her father in the Ionian Sea before the Casa delle Sirene, Vere would swim away and imagine that this was her mode of travel, that she was journeying alone to some distant land, or that she had been taken by the sea forever.

But very soon she would be sure to hear the soft splash of oars following her, and, looking back, would see the large, attentive eyes of the faithful Gaspare cautiously watching her dark head. Then she would lift up one hand, and call to him to go, and say she did not want him, that she wished to be alone, smiling and yet imperious. He only followed quietly and inflexibly. She would dive. She would swim under water. She would swim her fastest, as if really anxious to escape him. It was a game between them now. But always he was there, intent upon her safety.

Vere did not know the memories within Gaspare that

made him such a guardian to the child of the Padrone he
had loved; but she loved him secretly for his watchfulness, even though now and then she longed to be quite
alone with the sea. And this she never was when
bathing, for Hermione had exacted a promise from her
not to go to bathe without Gaspare. In former days
Vere had once or twice begun to protest against this
prohibition, but something in her mother's eyes had
stopped her. And she had remembered:

"Father was drowned in the sea."

Then, understanding something of what was in her
mother's heart, she threw eager arms about her, and
anxiously promised to be good.

One afternoon of the summer, towards the middle of
June, she prolonged her bathe in the Grotto of Virgil
until Gaspare used his authority, and insisted on her
coming out of the water.

"One minute more, Gaspare! Only another minute!"

"Ma Signorina!"

She dived. She came up.

"Ma veramente Signorina!"

She dived again.

Gaspare waited. He was standing up in the boat with
the oars in his hands, ready to make a dash at his
Padroncina directly she reappeared, but she was wily,
and came up behind the boat with a shrill cry that
startled him. He looked round reproachfully over his
shoulder.

"Signorina," he said, turning the boat round, "you
are like a wicked baby to-day."

"What is it, Gaspare?" she asked, this time letting
him come towards her.

"I say that you are like a wicked baby. And only
the other day I was saying to the Signora—"

"What were you saying?"

She swam to the boat and got in.

"What?" she repeated, sitting down on the gunwale, while he began to row towards the islet.

"I was saying that you are nearly a woman now."

Vere seemed extraordinarily thin and young as she sat there in her dripping bathing-dress, with her small, bare feet distilling drops into the bottom of the boat, and her two hands, looking drowned, holding lightly to the wood on each side of her. Even Gaspare, as he spoke, was struck by this, and by the intensely youthful expression in the eyes that now regarded him curiously.

"Really, Gaspare?"

Vere asked the question quite seriously.

"Sì, Signorina."

"A woman!"

She looked down, as if considering herself. Her wet face had become thoughtful, and for a moment she said nothing.

"And what did mother say?" she asked, looking up again. "But I know. I am sure she laughed at you."

Gaspare looked rather offended. His expressive face, which always showed what he was feeling, became almost stern, and he began to row faster than before.

"Why should the Signora laugh? Am I an imbecile, Signorina?"

"You?"

She hastened to correct the impression she had made.

"Why, Gaspare, you are our Providence!"

"Va bene, but—"

"I only meant that I am sure Madre wouldn't agree with you. She thinks me quite a child. I know that."

She spoke with conviction, nodding her head.

"Perhaps the Signora does not see."

Vere smiled.

"Gaspare, I believe you are horribly sharp," she said. "I often think you notice everything. You are birbante. I am half afraid of you."

Gaspare smiled, too. He had quite recovered his good humor. It pleased him mightily to fancy he had seen what the Padrona had not seen.

"I am a man, Signorina," he observed, quietly. "And I do not speak till I know. Why should I? And I was at your baptism. When we came back to the house I put five lire on the bed to bring you luck, although you were not a Catholic. But it is just the same. Your Saint will take care of you."

"Well, but if I am almost a woman—what then, Gaspare?"

"Signorina?"

"Mustn't I play about any more? Mustn't I do just what I feel inclined to, as I did in the Grotto just now?"

"There is no harm in that, Signorina. I was only joking then. But—"

He hesitated, looking at her firmly with his unfaltering gaze.

"But what? I believe you want to scold me about something. I am sure you do."

"No, Signorina, never! But women cannot talk to everybody, as children can. Nobody thinks anything of what children say. People only laugh and say 'Ecco, it's a baby talking.' But when we are older it is all different. People pay attention to us. We are of more importance then."

He did not mention Ruffo. He was too delicate to do that, for instinctively he understood how childish his Padroncina still was. And, at that moment, Vere did not think of Ruffo. She wondered a little what Gaspare was thinking. That there was some special thought behind his words, prompting them, she knew. But she did not ask him what it was, for already they were at the islet, and she must run in, and put on her clothes. Gaspare put her cloak carefully over her shoulders, and she hurried lightly up the steps and into her room. Her mother was not in the house. She had gone to Naples that day to see some poor people in whom she was interested. So Vere was quite alone. She took off her bathing-dress, and began to put on her things rather slowly. Her whole body was deliciously lulled by its long contact with the sea. She felt gloriously calm and gloriously healthy just then, but her mind was working vigorously though quietly.

A woman! The word sounded a little solemn and heavy, and, somehow, dreadfully respectable. And she thought of her recent behavior in the Grotto, and laughed aloud. She was so very slim, too. The word woman suggested to her some one more bulky than she was. But all that was absurd, of course. She was thinking very frivolously to-day.

She put on her dress and fastened it. At the age of sixteen she had put up her hair, but now it was still wet, and she had left it streaming over her shoulders. In a moment she was going out onto the cliff to let the sun dry it thoroughly. The sun was so much better than any towel. With her hair down she really looked like a child, whatever Gaspare thought. She said that to herself, standing for a moment before the glass. Vere was almost as divinely free from self-consciousness as her father had been. But the conversation in the boat had made her think of herself very seriously, and now she considered herself, not without keen interest.

"I am certainly not a wicked baby," she said to herself. "But I don't think I look at all like a woman."

Her dark eyes met the eyes in the glass and smiled.

"And yet I shall be seventeen quite soon. What can have made Gaspare talk like that to Madre? I wonder what he said exactly. And then that about 'women cannot talk to everybody as children can.' Now what—?"

Ruffo came into her mind.

"Ah!" she said, aloud.

The figure in the glass made a little gesture. It **threw** up its hand.

"That's it! That's it! Gaspare thinks—"

"Signorina! Signorina!" •

Gaspare's voice was speaking outside the door. And now there came a firm knock. Vere turned round, rather startled. She had been very much absorbed by her colloquy.

"What is it, Gaspare?"

"Signorina, there's a boat coming in from Naples with Don Emilio in it."

"Don Emilio! He's come back! Oh!" There was a pause. Then she cried out, "Capital! Capital!"

She ran to the door and opened it.

"Just think of Don Emilio's being back already, Gaspare. But Madre! She will be sorry."

"Signorina?"

"Why? What's the matter?"

"Are you coming like that?"

"What?—Oh, you mean my hair?"

"Sì, Signorina."

"Gaspare, you ought to have been a lady's maid! Go and bring in Don Emilio to Madre's room. And— wait—you're not to tell him Madre is away. Now mind!"

"Va bene, Signorina."

He went away.

"Shall I put up my hair?"

Vere went again to the glass, and stood considering herself.

"For Monsieur Emile! No, it's too absurd! Gaspare really is . . . I sha'n't!"

And she ran out just as she was to meet Artois.

CHAPTER XI

WHEN she reached her mother's sitting-room Artois
was already there speaking to Gaspare by a window.
He turned rather quickly as Vere came in, and exclaimed:

"Vere! Why—"

"Oh!" she cried, "Gaspare hasn't gone!"

A look almost of dread, half pretence but with some
reality in it, too, came into her face.

"Gaspare, forgive me! I was in such a hurry. And
it is only Don Emilio!"

Her voice was coaxing. Gaspare looked at his
Padroncina with an attempt at reprobation; but his nose
twitched, and though he tried to compress his lips they
began to stretch themselves in a smile.

"Signorina! Signorina!" he exclaimed. "Madonna!"

On that exclamation he went out, trying to make
his back look condemnatory.

"Only Don Emilio!" Artois repeated.

Vere went to him, and took and held his hand for a
moment.

"Yes—only! That's my little compliment. Madre
would say of you, 'He's such an old shoe!' Such compliments come from the heart, you know."

She still held his hand.

"I should have to put my hair up for anybody else.
And Gaspare wanted me to for you."

Artois was looking rather grave and tired. She noticed
that now, and dropped his hand and moved towards a
bell.

148

A SPIRIT IN PRISON

"Tea!" she said, "all alone with me—for a treat!"

"Isn't your mother in?"

"No. She's gone to Naples. I'm very, very sorry. Make the best of it, Monsieur Emile, for the sake of my *amour propre.* I said I was sorry—but that was only for you, and Madre."

Artois smiled.

"Is an old shoe a worthy object of gross flattery?" he said.

"No."

"Then—"

"Don't be cantankerous, and don't be subtle, because I've been bathing."

"I notice that."

"And I feel so calm and delicious. Tea, please, Giulia."

The plump, dark woman who had opened the door smiled and retreated.

"So calm and so delicious, Monsieur Emile, and as if I were made of friendliness from top to toe."

"The all-the-world feeling. I know."

He sat down, rather heavily.

"You are tired. When did you come?"

"I arrived this morning. It was hot travelling, and I shared my compartment in the wagon-lit with a German gentleman very far advanced in several unæsthetic ailments. Basta! Thank Heaven for this. Calm and delicious!"

His large, piercing eyes were fixed upon Vere.

"And about twelve," he added, "or twelve-and-a-half."

"I?"

"Yes, you. I am not speaking of myself, though I believe I am calm also."

"I am a woman—practically."

"Practically?"

149

"Yes; isn't that the word people always put in when they mean 'that's a lie'?"

"You mean you aren't a woman! This afternoon I must agree with you."

"It's the sea! But just now, when you were coming, I was looking at myself in the glass and saying, 'You're a woman'—solemnly, you know, as if it was a dreadful truth."

Artois had sat down on a sofa. He leaned back now with his hands behind his head. He still looked at Vere, and, as he did so, he heard the faint whisper of the sea.

"Child of nature," he said—"call yourself that. It covers any age, and it's blessedly true."

Giulia came in at this moment with tea. She smiled again broadly on Artois, and received and returned his greeting with the comfortable and unembarrassed friendliness of the Italian race. As she went out she was still smiling.

"Addio to the German gentleman with the unæsthetic ailments!" said Artois.

An almost boyish sensation of sheer happiness invaded him. It made him feel splendidly untalkative. And he felt for a moment, too, as if his intellect lay down to sleep.

"Cara Giula!" he added, after a rapturous silence.

"What?"

"Carissima Giulia!"

"Yes, Giulia is—"

"They all are, and the island, and the house upon it, and this clear yellow tea, and this brown toast, and this butter from Lombardy. They all are."

"I believe you are feeling good all over, Monsieur Emile."

"San Gennaro knows I am."

He drank some tea, and ate some toast, spreading the butter upon it with voluptuous deliberation.

"Then I'm sure he's pleased."

"Paris, hateful Paris!"

"Oh, but that's abusive. A person who feels good all over should not say that."

"You are right, Vere. But when are you not right? You ought always to wear your hair down, mon enfant, and always to have just been bathing."

"And you ought always to have just been travelling."

"It is true that a dreadful past can be a blessing as well as a curse. It is profoundly true. Why have I never realized that before?"

"If I am twelve and a half, I think you are about— about—"

"For the love of the sea make it under twenty, Vere."

"Nineteen, then."

"Were you going to make it under twenty?"

"Yes, I was."

"I don't believe you. Yes, I do, I do! You are an artist. You realize that truth is a question of feeling, not a question of fact. You penetrate beneath the gray hairs as the prosaic never do. This butter is delicious! And to think that there have been moments when I have feared butter, when I have kept an eye upon a corpulent future. Give me some more, plenty more."

Vere stretched out her hand to the tea-table, but it shook. She drew it back, and burst into a peal of laughter.

"What are you laughing at?" said Artois, with burlesque majesty.

"At you. What's the matter with you, Monsieur Emile? How can you be so foolish?"

She lay back in her chair, with her hair streaming about her, and her thin body quivered, as if the sense of fun within her were striving to break through its prison walls.

A SPIRIT IN PRISON

"This," said Artois, "this is sheer impertinence. I venture to inquire for butter, and—"

"To inquire! One, two, three, four—five pats of butter right in front of you! And you inquire—!"

Artois suddenly sent out a loud roar to join her childish treble.

The tea had swept away his previous sensation of fatigue, even the happy stolidity that had succeeded it for an instant. He felt full of life and gayety, and a challenging mental activity. A similar challenging activity, he thought, shone in the eyes of the girl opposite to him.

"Thank God I can still be foolish!" he exclaimed. "And thank God that there are people in the world devoid of humor. My German friend was without humor. Only that fact enabled me to endure his prodigious collection of ailments. But for the heat I might even have revelled in them. He was asthmatic, without humor; dyspeptic, without humor. He had a bad cold in the head, without humor, and got up into the top berth with two rheumatic legs and a crick in the back, without humor. Had he seen the fun of himself, the fun would have meant much less to me."

"You cruel person!"

"There is often cruelty in humor—perhaps not in yours, though, yet."

"Why do you say—yet, like that?"

"The hair is such a kindly veil that I doubt the existence of cruelty behind it."

He spoke with a sort of almost tender and paternal gentleness.

"I don't believe you could ever be really cruel, Monsieur Emile."

"Why not?"

"I think you are too intelligent."

"Why should that prevent me?"

A SPIRIT IN PRISON

"Isn't cruelty stupid, unimaginative?"

"Often. But it can be brilliant, artful, intellectual, full of imagination. It can be religious. It can be passionate. It can be splendid. It can be almost everything."

"Splendid!"

"Like Napoleon's cruelty to France. But why should I educate you in abominable knowledge?"

"Oh," said the girl, thrusting forward her firm little chin, "I have no faith in mere ignorance."

"Yet it does a great deal for those who are not ignorant."

"How?"

"It shows them how pretty, how beautiful even, sometimes, was the place from which they started for their journey through the world."

Vere was silent for a moment. The sparkle of fun had died out of her eyes, which had become dark with the steadier fires of imagination. The strands of her thick hair, falling down on each side of her oval face, gave to it a whimsically mediæval look, suggestive of legend. Her long-fingered, delicate, but strong little hands were clasped in her lap, and did not move. It was evident that she was thinking deeply.

"I believe I know," she said, at last. "Yes, that was my thought, or almost."

"When?"

She hesitated, looking at him, not altogether doubtfully, but with a shadow of reserve, which might easily, he fancied, grow deeper, or fade entirely away. He saw the resolve to speak come quietly into her mind.

"You know, Monsieur Emile, I love watching the sea," she said, rather slowly and carefully. "Especially at dawn, and in the evening before it is dark. And it always seems to me as if at dawn it is more heavenly than it is after the day has happened, though it is so very lovely then. And sometimes that has made me feel that our dawn is our most beautiful time—as if we were nearest the truth then. And, of course, that is when we are most ignorant, isn't it? So I suppose I have been thinking a little bit like you. Haven't I?"

She asked it, earnestly. Artois had never heard her speak quite like this before, with a curious deliberation that was nevertheless without self-consciousness. Before he could answer she added, abruptly, as if correcting, or even almost condemning herself:

"I can put it much better than that. I have."

Artois leaned forward. Something, he did not quite know what, made him feel suddenly a deep interest in what Vere said—a strong curiosity even.

"You have put it much better?" he said.

Vere suddenly looked conscious. A faint wave of red went over her face and down to her small neck. Her hands moved and parted. She seemed half ashamed of something for a minute.

"Madre doesn't know," she murmured, as if she were giving him a reason for something. "It isn't interesting," she added. "Except, of course, to me."

Artois was watching her.

"I think you really want to tell me," he said now.

"Oh yes, in a way I do. I have been half wanting to for a long time—but only half."

"And now?"

She looked at him, but almost instantly looked down again, with a sort of shyness he had never seen in her before. And her eyes had been full of a strange and beautiful sensitiveness.

"Never mind, Vere," he said, quickly, obedient to those eyes, and responding to their delicate subtlety. "We all have our righteous secrets, and should all respect the righteous secrets of others."

"Yes, I think we should. And I know you would be

the very last, at least Madre and you, to—I think I'm
being rather absurd, really." The last words were said
with a sudden change of tone to determination, as if
Vere were taking herself to task. "I'm making a lot of
almost nothing. You see, if I am a woman, as Gaspare
is making out, I'm at any rate a very young one, am I
not?"

"The youngest that exists."

As he said that Artois thought, "Mon Dieu! If the
Marchesino could only see her now!"

"If humor is cruel, Monsieur Emile," Vere continued,
"you will laugh at me. For I am sure, if I tell you—
and I know now I'm going to—you will think this fuss is
as ridiculous as the German's cold in the head, and poor
legs, and all. I wrote that about the sea."

She said the last sentence with a sort of childish defiance.

"Wait," said Artois. "Now I begin to understand."

"What?"

"All those hours spent in your room. Your mother
thought you were reading."

"No," she said, still rather defiantly; "I've been writing that, and other things—about the sea."

"How? In prose?"

"No. That's the worst of it, I suppose."

And again the faint wave of color went over her face
to her neck.

"Do you really feel so criminal? Then what ought I
to feel?"

"You? Now that is really cruel!" she cried, getting up
quickly, almost as if she meant to hurry away.

But she only stood there in front of him, near the
window.

"Never mind!" she said. "Only you remember that
Madre tried. She has never said much about it to me.
But now and then from just a word I know that she feels

bad, that she wishes very much she could do something. Only the other day she said to me, 'We have the instinct, men the vocabulary.' She was meaning that you had. She even told me to ask you something that I had asked her, and she said, 'I feel all the things that he can explain.' And there was something in her voice that hurt me—for her. And Madre is so clever. Isn't she clever?"

"Yes."

"And if Madre can't do things, you can imagine that I feel rather absurd now that I'm telling you."

"Yes, being just as you are, Vere, I can quite imagine that you do. But we can have sweet feelings of absurdity that only arise from something moral within us, a moral delicacy. However, would you like me to look at what you have been writing about the sea?"

"Yes, if you can do it quite seriously."

"I could not do it in any other way."

"Then—thank you."

She went out of the room, not without a sort of simple dignity that was utterly removed from conceit or pretentiousness.

What a strange end, this, to their laughter!

Vere was away several minutes, during which at first Artois sat quite still, leaning back, with his great frame stretched out, and his hands once more behind his head. His intellect was certainly very much awake now, and he was setting a guard upon it, to watch it carefully, lest it should be ruthless, even with Vere. And was he not setting also another guard to watch the softness of his nature, lest it should betray him into foolish kindness?

Yet, after a minute, he said to himself that he was wasting his time in both these proceedings. For Vere's eyes were surely a touchstone to discover honesty. There is something merciless in the purity of untarnished youth. What can it not divine at moments?

A SPIRIT IN PRISON

Artois poured out another cup of tea and drank it, considering the little funny situation. Vere and he with a secret from Hermione shared between them! Vere submitting verses to his judgment! He remembered Hermione's half-concealed tragedy, which, of course, had been patent to him in its uttermost nakedness. Even Vere had guessed something of it. Do we ever really hide anything from every one? And yet each one breaths mystery too. The assertive man is the last of fools. Of that at least Artois just then felt certain.

If Vere should really have talent! He did not expect it, although he had said that there was intellectual force in the girl. There was intellectual force in Hermione, but she could not create. And Vere! He smiled as he thought of her rush into the room with her hair streaming down, of her shrieks of laughter over his absurdity. But she was full of changes.

The door opened, and Vere came in holding some manuscript in her hand. She had done up her hair while she had been away. When Artois saw that he heaved himself up from the sofa.

"I must smoke," he said.

"Oh yes. I'll get the Khali Targas."

"No. I must have a pipe. And you prefer that, I know."

"Generally, but—you do look dreadfully as if you meant business when you are smoking a pipe."

"I do mean business now."

He took his pipe from his pocket, filled it and lit it.

"Now then, Vere!" he said.

She came to sit down on the sofa.

He sat down beside her.

CHAPTER XII

MORE than an hour had passed. To Vere it had seemed like five minutes. Her cheeks were hotly flushed. Her eyes shone. With hands that were slightly trembling she gathered together her manuscripts, and carefully arranged them in a neat packet and put a piece of ribbon round them, tying it in a little bow. Meanwhile Artois, standing up, was knocking the shreds of tobacco out of his pipe against the chimney-piece into his hand. He carried them over to the window, dropped them out, then stood for a minute looking at the sea.

"The evening calm is coming, Vere," he said, "bringing with it the wonder of this world."

"Yes."

He heard a soft sigh behind him, and turned round.

"Why was that? Has dejection set in, then?"

"No, no."

"You know the Latin saying: 'Festina lente'? If you want to understand how slowly you must hasten, look at me."

He had been going to add, "Look at these gray hairs," but he did not. Just then he felt suddenly an invincible reluctance to call Vere's attention to the signs of age apparent in him.

"I spoke to you about the admirable incentive of ambition," he continued, after a moment. "But you must understand that I meant the ambition for perfection, not at all the ambition for celebrity. The satisfaction of the former may be a deep and exquisite joy—the partial

158

satisfaction, for I suppose it can never be anything more than that. But the satisfaction of the other will certainly be Dead-sea fruit—fruit of the sea unlike that brought up by Ruffo, without lasting savor, without any real value. One should never live for that."

The last words he spoke as if to himself, almost like a warning addressed to himself.

"I don't believe I ever should," Vere said, quickly. "I never thought of such a thing."

"The thought will come, though, inevitably."

"How dreadful it must be to know so much about human nature as you do!"

"And yet how little I really know!"

There came up a distant cry from the sea. Vere started.

"There is Madre! Of course, Monsieur Emile, I don't want—but you understand!"

She hurried out of the room, carrying the packet with her.

Artois felt that the girl was strongly excited. She was revealing more of herself to him, this little Vere whom he had known, and not known, ever since she had been a baby. The gradual revelation interested him intensely—so intensely that in him, too, there was excitement now. So many truths go to make up the whole round truth of every human soul. Hermione saw some of these truths of Vere, Gaspare others, perhaps; he again others. And even Ruffo and the Marchesino—he put the Marchesino most definitely last—even they saw still other truths of Vere, he supposed.

To whom did she reveal the most? The mother ought to know most, and during the years of childhood had doubtless known most. But those years were nearly over. Certainly Vere was approaching, or was on, the threshold of the second period of her life.

And she and he had a secret from Hermione. This

secret was a very innocent one. Still, of course, it had the two attributes that belong to every secret: of drawing together those who share it, of setting apart from them those who know it not. And there was another secret, too, connected with it, and known only to Artois: the fact that the child, Vere, possessed the very small but quite definite beginnings, the seed, as it were, of something that had been denied to the mother, Hermione.

"Emile, you have come back! I am glad!"

Hermione came into the room with her eager manner and rather slow gait, holding out both her hands, her hot face and prominent eyes showing forth with ardor the sincerity of her surprise and pleasure.

"Gaspare told me. I nearly gave him a hug. You know his sly look when he has something delightful up his sleeve for one! Bless you!"

She shook both his hands.

"And I had come back in such bad spirits! But now—"

She took off her hat and put it on a table.

"Why were you in bad spirits, my friend?"

"I had been with Madame Alliani, seeing something of the intense misery and wickedness of Naples. I have seen a girl—such a tragedy! What devils men can be in these Southern places! What hideous things they will do under the pretence of being driven by love! But— no, don't let us spoil your arrival. Where is Vere? I thought she was entertaining you."

"We have been having tea together. She has this moment gone out of the room."

"Oh!"

She seemed to expect some further explanation. As he gave none she sat down.

"Wasn't she very surprised to see you?"

"I think she was. She had just been bathing, and came running in with her hair all about her, looking like an Undine with a dash of Sicilian blood in her. Here she is!"

"Are you pleased, Madre? You poor, hot Madre!"

Vere sat down by her mother and put one arm round her. Subtly she was trying to make up to her mother for the little secret she was keeping from her for a time.

"Are you very, very pleased?"

"Yes, I think I am."

"Think! You mischievous Madre!"

Hermione laughed.

"But I feel almost jealous of you two sitting here in the cool, and having a quiet tea and a lovely talk while— Never mind. Here is my tea. And there's another thing. Oh, Emile, I do wish I had known you would arrive to-day!"

"Why specially?"

"I've committed an unusual crime. I've made—actually—an engagement for this evening."

Artois and Vere held up their hands in exaggerated surprise.

"Are you mad, my dear Hermione?" asked Artois.

"I believe I am. It's dangerous to go to Naples. I met a young man."

"The Marchesino!" cried Vere. "The Marchesino! I see him in your eye, Madre."

"C'est cela!" said Artois, "and you mean to say—!"

"That I accepted an invitation to dine with him to-night, at nine, at the Scoglio di Frisio. There! Why did I? I have no idea. I was hot from a horrible vicolo. He was cool from the sea. What chance had I against him? And then he is through and through Neapolitan, and gives no quarter to a woman, even when she is 'una vecchia.'"

As she finished Hermione broke into a laugh, evidently at some recollection.

"Doro made his eyes very round. I can see that," said Artois.

"Like this!" cried Vere.

And suddenly there appeared in her face a reminiscence of the face of the Marchesino.

"Vere, you must not! Some day you will do it by accident when he is here."

"Is he coming here?"

"In a launch to fetch me—us."

"Am I invited?" said Vere. "What fun!"

"I could not get out of it," Hermione said to Artois. "But now I insist on your staying here till the Marchesino comes. Then he will ask you, and we shall be a quartet."

"I will stay," said Artois, with a sudden return of his authoritative manner.

"It seems that I am wofully ignorant of the Bay," continued Hermione. "I have never dined at Frisio's. Everybody goes there at least once. Everybody has been there. Emperors, kings, queens, writers, singers, politicians, generals—they all eat fish at Frisio's."

"It's true."

"You have done it?"

"Yes. The Padrone is worth knowing. He—but to-night you will know him. Yes, Frisio's is characteristic. Vere will be amused."

With a light tone he hid a faint chagrin.

"What fun!" repeated Vere. "If I had diamonds I should put them on."

She too was hiding something, one sentiment with another very different. But her youth came to her aid, and very soon the second excitement really took the place of the first, and she was joyously alive to the prospect of a novel gayety.

"I must not eat anything more," said Hermione. "I believe the Marchesino is ordering something marvellous for us, all the treasures of the sea. We must be up to the mark. He really is a good fellow."

"Yes," said Artois. "He is. I have a genuine liking for him."

He said it with obvious sincerity.

"I am going," said Vere. "I must think about clothes. And I must undo my hair again and get Maria to dry it thoroughly, or I shall look frightening."

She went out quickly, her eyes sparkling.

"Vere is delighted," said Hermione.

"Yes, indeed she is."

"And you are not. Would you rather avoid the Marchesino to-night, Emile, and not come with us? Perhaps I am selfish. I would so very much rather have you with us."

"If Doro asks me I shall certainly come. It's true that I wish you were not engaged to-night—I should have enjoyed a quiet evening here. But we shall have many quiet, happy evenings together this summer, I hope."

"I wonder if we shall?" said Hermione, slowly.

"You—why?"

"I don't know. Oh, I am absurd, probably. One has such strange ideas, houses based on sand, or on air, or perhaps on nothing at all."

She got up, went to her writing-table, opened a drawer, and took out of it a letter.

"Emile," she said, coming back to him with it in her hand, "would you like to explain this to me?"

"What is it?"

"The letter I found from you when I came back from Capri."

"But does it need explanation?"

"It seemed to me as if it did. Read it and see."

He took it from her, opened it and read it.

"Well?" he said.

163

"Isn't the real meaning between the lines?"

"If it is, cannot you decipher it?"

"I don't know. I don't think so. Somehow it depressed me. Perhaps it was my mood just then. Was it?"

"Perhaps it was merely mine."

"But why—'I feel specially this summer I should like to be near you'? What does that mean exactly?"

"I did feel that."

"Why?"

"I don't think I can tell you now. I am not sure that I could even have told you at the time I wrote that letter."

She took it from him and put it away again in the drawer.

"Perhaps we shall both know later on," she said, quietly. "I believe we shall."

He did not say anything.

"I saw that boy, Ruffo, this afternoon," she said, after a moment of silence.

"Did you?" said Artois, with a change of tone, a greater animation. "I forgot to ask Vere about him. I suppose he has been to the island again while I have been away?"

"Not once. Poor boy, I find he has been ill. He has had fever. He was out to-day for the first time after it. We met him close to Mergellina. He was in a boat, but he looked very thin and pulled down. He seemed so delighted to see me. I was quite touched."

"Hasn't Vere been wondering very much why he did not come again?"

"She has never once mentioned him. Vere is a strange child sometimes."

"But you—haven't you spoken of him to her?"

"No, I don't think so."

"Vere's silence made you silent?"

"I suppose so. I must tell her. She likes the boy very much."

"What is it that attracts her to this boy, do you think?"

The question was ordinary enough, but there was a peculiar intonation in Artois' voice as he asked it, an intonation that awakened surprise in Hermione.

"I don't know. He is an attractive boy."

"You think so too?"

"Why, yes. What do you mean, Emile?"

"I was only wondering. The sea breeds a great many boys like Ruffo, you know. But they don't all get Khali Targa cigarettes given to them, for all that."

"That's true. I have never seen Vere pay any particular attention to the fishermen who come to the island. In a way she loves them all because they belong to the sea, she loves them as a décor. But Ruffo is different. I felt it myself."

"Did you?"

He looked at her, then looked out of the window and pulled his beard slowly.

"Yes. In my case, perhaps, the interest was roused partly by what Vere told me. The boy is a Sicilian, you see, and just Vere's age.

"Vere's interest perhaps comes from the same reason."

"Very likely it does."

Hermione spoke the last words without conviction. Perhaps they both felt that they were not talking very frankly — were not expressing their thoughts to each other with their accustomed sincerity. At any rate, Artois suddenly introduced another topic of conversation, the reason of his hurried visit to Paris, and for the next hour they discussed literary affairs with a gradually increasing vivacity and open-heartedness. The little difficulty between them—of which both had been sensitive and fully conscious—passed away, and when at length Hermione got up to go to her bedroom and change her dress for the evening, there was no cloud about them.

When Hermione had gone Artois took up a book, but he sat till the evening was falling and Giulia came smiling to light the lamp, without reading a word of it. Her entry roused him from his reverie, and he took out his watch. It was already past eight. The Marchesino would soon be coming. And then—the dinner at Frisio's!

He got up and moved about the room, picking up a book here and there, glancing at some pages, then putting it down. He felt restless and uneasy.

"I am tired from the journey," he thought. "Or— I wonder what the weather is this evening. The heat seems to have become suffocating since Hermione went away."

He went to one of the windows and looked out. Twilight was stealing over the sea, which was so calm that it resembled a huge sheet of steel. The sky over the island was clear. He turned and went to the opposite window. Above Ischia there was a great blackness like a pall. He stood looking at it for some minutes. His erring thoughts, which wandered like things fatigued that cannot rest, went to a mountain village in Sicily, through which he had once ridden at night during a terrific thunder-storm. In a sudden, fierce glare of lightning he had seen upon the great door of a gaunt Palazzo, which looked abandoned, a strip of black cloth. Above it were the words, "Lutto in famiglia."

That was years ago. Yet now he saw again the palace door, the strip of cloth soaked by the pouring rain, the dreary, almost sinister words which he had read by lightning:

"Lutto in famiglia."

He repeated them as he gazed at the blackness above Ischia.

A SPIRIT IN PRISON

"Monsieur Emile!"

"Vere!"

The girl came towards him, a white contrast to what he had been watching.

"I'm all ready. It seems so strange to be going out to a sort of party. I've had such a bother with my hair."

"You have conquered," he said. "Undine has disappeared."

"What?"

"Come quite close to the lamp."

She came obediently.

"Vere transformed!" he said. "I have seen three Veres to-day already. How many more will greet me to-night?"

She laughed gently, standing quite still. Her dress and her gloves were white, but she had on a small black hat, very French, and at the back of her hair there was a broad black ribbon tied in a big bow. This ribbon marked her exact age clearly, he thought.

"This is a new frock, and my very smartest," she said; "and you dared to abuse Paris!"

"Being a man. I must retract now. You are right, we cannot do without it. But—have you an umbrella?"

"An umbrella?"

She moved and laughed again, much more gayly.

"I am serious. Come here and look at Ischia."

She went with him quickly to the window.

"That blackness does look wicked. But it's a long way off."

"I think it is coming this way."

"Oh, but"—and she went to the opposite window—"the sky is perfectly clear towards Naples. And look how still the sea is."

"Too still. It is like steel."

A SPIRIT IN PRISON

"Hush! Listen!"

She held up her hand. They both heard a far-off sound of busy panting on the sea.

"That must be the launch!" she said.

Her eyes were gay and expectant. It was evident that she was in high spirits, that she was looking forward to this unusual gayety.

"Yes."

"Doesn't it sound in a hurry, as if the Marchesino was terribly afraid of being late?"

"Get your umbrella, Vere, and a waterproof. You will want them both."

At that moment Hermione came in.

"Madre, the launch is coming in a frightful hurry, and Monsieur Emile says we must take umbrellas."

"Surely it isn't going to rain?"

"There is a thunder-storm coming up from Ischia, I believe," said Artois.

"Then we will take our cloaks in case. It is fearfully hot. I thought so when I was dressing. No doubt the launch will have a cabin."

A siren hooted.

"That is the Marchesino saluting us!" cried Vere. "Come along, Madre! Maria! Maria!"

She ran out, calling for the cloaks.

"Do you like Vere's frock, Emile?" said Hermione, as they followed.

"Yes. She looks delicious—but quite like a little woman of the world."

"Ah, you like her best as the Island child. So do I. Oh, Emile!"

"What is it?"

"I can't help it. I hate Vere's growing up."

"Few things can remain unchanged for long. This sea will be unrecognizable before we return."

Gaspare met them on the landing with solemn eyes.

"There is going to be a great storm, Signora," he said. "It is coming from Ischia."

"So Don Emilio thinks. But we will take wraps, and we are going in a launch. It will be all right, Gaspare."

"Shall I come with you, Signora?"

"Well, Gaspare, you see it is the Marchese's launch—"

"If you would like me to come, I will ask the Signor Marchese."

"We'll see how much room there is."

"Sì, Signora."

He went down to receive the launch.

"Emile," Hermione said, as he disappeared, "can you understand what a comfort to me Gaspare is? Ah, if people knew how women love those who are ready to protect them! It's quite absurd, but just because Gaspare said that, I'd fifty times rather have him with us than go without him."

"I understand. I love your watch-dog, too."

She touched his arm.

"No one could ever understand the merits of a watch-dog better than you. That's right, Maria; we shall be safer with these."

The Marchesino stood at the foot of the cliff, bare-headed, to receive them. He was in evening dress, what he called "smoking," with a flower in his button-hole, and a straw hat, and held a pair of white kid gloves in his hand. He looked in rapturous spirits, but ceremonial. When he caught sight of Artois on the steps behind Hermione and Vere, however, he could not repress an exclamation of "Emilio!"

He took Hermione's and Vere's hands, bowed over them and kissed them. Then he turned to his friend.

"Caro Emilio! You are back! You must come with us! You must dine at Frisio's."

"May I?" said Artois.

"You must. This is delightful. See, Madame,"

he added to Hermione, suddenly breaking into awful French, "we have the English flag! Your Jack! Voilá, the great, the only Jack! I salute him! Let me help you!"

As Hermione stepped into the launch she said:

"I see there is plenty of room. I wonder if you would mind my taking my servant, Gaspare, to look after the cloaks and umbrellas. It seems absurd, but he says a storm is coming, and—"

"A storm!" cried the Marchesino. "Of course your Gaspare must come. Which is he?"

"There."

The Marchesino spoke to Gaspare in Italian, telling him to join the two sailors in the stern of the launch. A minute afterwards he went to him and gave him some cigarettes. Then he brought from the cabin two bouquets of flowers, and offered them to Hermione and Vere, who, with Artois, were settling themselves in the bows. The siren sounded. They were off, cutting swiftly through the oily sea.

"A storm, Signora! Cloaks and umbrellas!" said the Marchesino, shooting a glance of trumph at "Caro Emilio," whose presence to witness his success completed his enjoyment of it. "But it is a perfect night. Look at the sea. Signorina, let me put the cushion a little higher behind you. It is not right. You are not perfectly comfortable. And everything must be perfect for you to-night—everything." He arranged the cushion tenderly. "The weather, too! Why, where is the storm?"

"Over Ischia," said Artois.

"It will stay there. Ischia! It is a volcano. Anything terrible may happen there."

"And Vesuvius?" said Hermione, laughing.

The Marchesino threw up his chin.

"We are not going to Vesuvius I know Naples,

Signora, and I promise you fine weather. We shall take our coffee after dinner outside upon the terrace at the one and only Frisio's."

He chattered on gayly. His eyes were always on Vere, but he talked chiefly to Hermione, with the obvious intention of fascinating the mother in order that she might be favorably disposed towards him, and later on smile indulgently upon his flirtation with the daughter. His proceedings were carried on with a frankness that should have been disarming, and that evidently did disarm Hermione and Vere, who seemed to regard the Marchesino as a very lively boy. But Artois was almost immediately conscious of a secret irritation that threatened to spoil his evening.

The Marchesino was triumphant. Emilio had wished to prevent him from knowing these ladies. Why? Evidently because Emilio considered him dangerous. Now he knew the ladies. He was actually their host. And he meant to prove to Emilio how dangerous he could be. His eyes shot a lively defiance at his friend, then melted as they turned to Hermione, melted still more as they gazed with unwinking sentimentality into the eyes of Vere. He had no inward shyness to contend against, and was perfectly at his ease; and Artois perceived that his gayety and sheer animal spirits were communicating themselves to his companions. Vere said little, but she frequently laughed, and her face lit up with eager animation. And she, too, was quite at her ease. The direct, and desirous, glances of the Marchesino did not upset her innocent self-possession at all, although they began to upset the self-possession of Artois. As he sat, generally in silence, listening to the frivolous and cheerful chatter that never stopped, while the launch cut its way through the solemn, steel-like sea towards the lights of Posilipo, he felt that he was apart because he was clever, as if his cleverness caused loneliness.

They travelled fast. Soon the prow of the launch was directed to a darkness that lay below, and to the right of a line of brilliant lights that shone close to the sea; and a boy dressed in white, holding a swinging lantern, and standing, like a statue, in a small niche of rock almost flush with the water, hailed them, caught the gunwale of the launch with one hand, and brought it close in to the wall that towered above them.

"Do we get out here? But where do we go?" said Hermione.

"There is a staircase. Let me—"

The Marchesino was out in a moment and helped them all to land. He called to the sailors that he would send down food and wine to them and Gaspare. Then, piloted by the boy with the lantern, they walked up carefully through dark passages and over crumbling stairs, turned to the left, and came out upon a small terrace above the sea and facing the curving lamps of Naples. Just beyond was a long restaurant, lined with great windows on one side and with mirrors on the other, and blazing with light.

"Ecco!" cried the Marchesino. "Ecco lo Scoglio di Frisio! And here is the Padrone!" he added, as a small, bright-eyed man, with a military figure and fierce mustaches, came briskly forward to receive them.

CHAPTER XIII

THE dinner, which was served at a table strewn with red carnations close to an open window, was a gay one, despite Artois. It could hardly have been otherwise with a host so complacent, so attentive, so self-possessed, so hilarious as the Marchesino. And the Padrone of the restaurant warmly seconded the efforts of the giver of the feast. He hovered perpetually, but always discreetly, near, watchfully directing the middle - aged waiters in their duties, smiling to show his teeth, stained with tobacco juice, or drawing delicately close to relate anecdotes connected with the menu.

The soup, a "zuppa di pesce alla marinara" remarkable for its beautiful red color, had been originally invented by the chef of Frisio's for the ex-Queen Natalie of Servia, who had deigned to come, heavily veiled, to lunch at the Scoglio, and had finally thrown off her veil and her incognito, and written her name in the visitors' book for all to see. The Macaroni à l'Impératrice had been the favorite *plat* of the dead Empress Elizabeth of Austria, who used to visit Frisio's day after day, and who always demanded two things—an eruption of Vesuvius and "Funiculì, funiculà!" William Ewart Gladstone had deigned to praise the "œufs à la Gladstone," called henceforth by his name, when he walked over from the Villa Rendel to breakfast; and the delicious punch served before the dolce, and immediately after the "Pollo panato alla Frisio," had been lauded by the late Czar of all the Russias, who was drinking a glass of it—according

173

to the solemn asservation of the Padrone—when the telegram announcing the assassination of his father was put into his hand.

Names of very varied popular and great ones of the earth floated about the table. Here, it appeared, Mario Costa and Paolo Tosti had composed their most celebrated songs between one course and another. Here Zola and Tolstoy had written. Here Sarah Bernhardt had ordered a dozen bottles of famous old wine to be sent to the Avenue Pereire from the cellars of Frisio, and had fallen in love with a cat from Greece. Here Matilde Serao had penned a lasting testimony to the marital fidelity of her husband.

Everything—everything had happened here, just here, at Frisio's.

Seeing the amused interest of his guests, the Marchesino encouraged the Padrone to talk, called for his most noted wines, and demanded at dessert a jug of Asti Spumante, with snow in it, and strawberries floating on the top.

"You approve of Frisio's, Signorina?" he said, bending towards Vere. "You do not find your evening dull?"

The girl shook her head. A certain excitement was noticeable in her gayety—had been noticed by her mother all through the evening. It was really due to the afternoon's incident with Artois, succeeded by this unexpected festival, in which the lively homage of the Marchesino was mingled with the long procession of celebrated names introduced by the Padrone. Vere was secretly strung up, had been strung up even before she stepped into the launch. She felt very happy, but in her happiness there was something feverish, which was not customary to any mood of hers. She never drank wine, and had taken none to-night, yet as the evening wore on she was conscious of an effervescence, as if her brain were full of winking bubbles such as rise to the surface of champagne.

Her imagination was almost furiously alive; and as the Padrone talked, waving his hands and striking postures like those of a military dictator, she saw the dead Empress, with her fan before her face, nodding her head to the jig of "Funiculì, funiculà," while she watched the red cloud from Vesuvius rising into the starry sky; she saw Sarah Bernhardt taking the Greek cat upon her knee; the newly made Czar reading the telegram with his glass of punch beside him; Tosti tracing lines of music; Gladstone watching the sea; and finally the gaunt figure and the long beard of Tolstoy bending over the book in which he wrote clearly so many years ago, "Vedi Napoli e poi mori."

"Monsieur Emile, you must write in the wonderful book of Frisio's," she exclaimed.

"We will all write, Signorina!" cried the Marchesino. "Bring the book, Signor Masella!"

The Padrone hastened away to fetch it, but Vere shook her head.

"No, no, we must not write! We are nobodies. Monsieur Emile is a great man. Only he is worthy of such a book. Isn't it so, Madre?"

Artois felt the color rising to his face at this unexpected remark of the girl. He had been distrait during the dinner, certainly neither brilliant nor amusing, despite his efforts to seem talkative and cheerful. A depression had weighed upon him, as it had weighed upon him in the launch during the voyage from the island. He had felt as if he were apart, even almost as if he were *de trop*. Had Vere noticed it? Was that the reason of this sudden and charming demonstration in his favor.

He looked across at her, longing to know. But she was arguing gayly with the Marchesino, who continued to insist that they must all write their names as a souvenir of the occasion.

"We are nobodies," she repeated.

"You dare to say that you are a nobody!" exclaimed the young man, looking at her with ardent eyes. "Ah, Signorina, you do wrong to drink no wine. In wine there is truth, they say. But you—you drink water, and then you say these dreadful things that are not—are not true. Emilio"—he suddenly appealed to Artois—"would not the Signorina honor any book by writing her name in it? I ask you if—"

"Marchese, don't be ridiculous!" said Vere, with sudden petulance. "Don't ask Monsieur Emile absurd questions!"

"But he thinks as I do. Emilio, is it not so? Is it not an honor for any book to have the Signorina's name?"

He spoke emphatically and looked really in earnest. Artois felt as if he were listening to a silly boy who understood nothing.

"Let us all write our names," he said. "Here comes the book."

The Padrone bore it proudly down between the mirrors and the windows.

But Vere suddenly got up.

"I won't write my name," she said, sticking out her chin with the little determined air that was sometimes characteristic of her. "I am going to see what Gaspare and the sailors are doing."

And she walked quickly away towards the terrace.

The Marchesino sprang up in despair.

"Shall we all go, Madame?" he said. "I have ordered coffee. It will be brought in a moment to the terrace."

Hermione glanced at Artois.

"I will stay here for a little. I want to look at the book," she said. "We will come in a moment. I don't take coffee."

"Then—we will be upon the terrace. A rivederci per un momento—pour un moment, Madame,"

He bowed over Hermione's hand, and hurried away after Vere.

The Padrone put his book very carefully down between Hermione and Artois, and left them with a murmured apology that he had to look after another party of guests which had just come into the restaurant.

"I thought you would be glad to get rid of those young things for a minute," said Hermione, in explanation of what she had done.

Artois did not reply, but turned over the leaves of the book mechanically.

"Oh, here is Tolstoy's signature," he said, stopping.

Hermione drew her chair nearer.

"What a clear handwriting!" she said.

"Yes, isn't it? 'Vedi Napoli e poi mori.'"

"Where are you going to write?"

He was looking towards the outer room of the restaurant which led onto the terrace.

He turned the leaves.

"I?—oh—here is a space."

He took up a pen the Padrone had brought, dipped it into the ink.

"What's the good?" he said, making a movement as if to push the book away.

"No; do write."

"Why should I?"

"I agree with Vere. Your name will add something worth having to the book."

"Oh, well—"

A rather bitter expression had come into his face.

"Dead-sea fruit!" he muttered.

But he bent, wrote something quickly, signed his name, blotted and shut the book. Hermione had not been able to see the sentence he had written. She did not ask what it was.

There was a noise of rather shuffling footsteps on the

paved floor of the room. Three musicians had come in. They were shabbily dressed. One was very short, stout, and quite blind, with a gaping mouth that had an odd resemblance to an elephant's mouth when it lifts its trunk and shows its rolling tongue. He smiled perpetually. The other two were thin and dreary, middle-aged, and hopeless-looking. They stood not far from the table and began to play on guitars, putting wrong harmonies to a well-known Neapolitan tune, whose name Artois could not recall.

"What a pity it is they never put the right bass!" said Hermione.

"Yes. One would suppose they would hit it sometimes by mistake. But they seldom do."

Except for the thin and uncertain music the restaurant was almost silent. The people who had just come in were sitting down far away at the end of the long room. Hermione and Artois were the only other visitors, now that Vere and the Marchesino were outside on the terrace.

"Famous though it is, Frisio's does not draw the crowd," said Hermione.

To-night she found it oddly difficult to talk to her friend, although she had refused the Marchesino's invitation on purpose to do so.

"Perhaps people were afraid of the storm."

"Well, but it doesn't come."

"It is close," he said. "Don't you feel it? I do."

His voice was heavy with melancholy, and made her feel sad, even apprehensive.

"Where are the stars?" he added.

She followed his example and leaned out of the great window. Not a star was visible in all the sky.

"You are right. It is coming. I feel it now. The sea is like lead, and the sky, too. There is no sense of freedom to-night, no out-of-doors feeling. And the water is horribly calm."

178

A SPIRIT IN PRISON

As they both leaned out they heard, away to the left at some distance, the voices of Vere and the Marchesino.

"I stayed because I thought—I fancied all the chatter was getting a little on your nerves, Emile," Hermione said now. "They are so absurdly young, both of them. Wasn't it so?"

"Am I so old that youth should get upon my nerves?" he returned, with a creeping irritation, which, however, he tried to keep out of his voice.

"No. But of course we can hardly enjoy nonsense that might amuse them immensely. Vere is such a baby, and your friend is a regular boy, in spite of his self-assurance."

"Women often fancy men to be young in ways in which they are not young," said Artois. "Panacci is very much of a man, I can assure you."

"Panacci! I never heard you call him that before."

Her eager brown eyes went to his face curiously for a moment. Artois saw that, and said, rather hastily:

"It's true that nearly every one calls him Doro."

Once more they heard the chattering voices, and then a sound of laughter in the darkness. It made Hermione smile, but Artois moved uneasily. Just then there came to them from the sea, like a blow, a sudden puff of wind. It hit their faces.

"Do you want to avoid the storm?" Artois said.

"Yes. Do you think—"

"I am sure you can only avoid it by going at once. Look!"

He pointed towards the sea. The blackness before them was cut at some distance off by a long, level line of white.

"What's that?" asked Hermione, peering out.

"Foam."

"Foam! But surely it can't be!"

A SPIRIT IN PRISON

The wind struck them again. It was like a hot, almost like a sweating hand, coarse and violent, and repugnant.

Hermione drew in.

"There is something disgusting in nature to-night," she said—"something that seems almost unnatural."

The blind man began to sing behind them. His voice was soft and throaty. The phrasing was sickly. Some notes trembled. As he sang he threw back his head, stared with his sightless eyes at the ceiling, and showed his tongue. The whole of his fat body swayed. His face became scarlet. The two hopeless, middle-aged men on either side of him stared into vacancy as, with dirty hands on which the veins stood out, they played wrong basses to the melody on their guitars.

Suddenly Hermione was seized with a sensation of fear.

"Let us go. We had better go. Ah!"

She cried out. The wind, returning, had caught the white table-cloth. It flew up towards her, then sank down.

"What a fool I am!" she said. "I thought—I didn't know——"

She felt that really it was something in Artois which had upset her nerves, but she did not say so. In that moment, when she was startled, she had instinctively put out her hand towards him. But, as instinctively, she drew it back without touching him.

"Oh, here is Gaspare!" she said.

An immense, a really ridiculous sense of relief came to her as she saw Gaspare's sturdy legs marching decisively towards them, his great eyes examining the row of mirrors, the tables, the musicians, then settling comfortably upon his Padrona. Over his arms he carried the cloaks, and his hands grasped the two umbrellas. At that moment, if she had translated her impulse into an action, Hermione would have given Gaspare a good hug—just for being himself; for being always the same: honest, watchful, perfectly fearless, perfectly natural, and perfectly determined to take care of his Padrona and his Padroncina.

Afterwards she remembered that she had found in his presence relief from something that had distressed her in her friend.

"Signora, the storm is coming. Look at the sea!" said Gaspare. He pointed to the white line which was advancing in the blackness.

"I told the Signorina, and that Signore—"

A fierce flash of lightning zigzagged across the window-space, and suddenly the sound of the wind was loud upon the sea, and mingled with the growing murmur of waves.

"Ecco!" said Gaspare. "Signora, you ought to start at once. But the Signor Marchese—"

The thunder followed. Hermione had been waiting for it, and felt almost relieved when it came crashing above the Scoglio di Frisio.

"The Signor Marchese, Gaspare?" she asked, putting on the cloak he was holding for her.

"He only laughs, Signora," said Gaspare, rather contemptuously. "The Signor Marchese thinks only of his pleasure."

"Well, he must think of yours now," said Artois, decisively, to Hermione. "You will have a rough voyage to the island, even as it is."

They were walking towards the entrance. Hermione had noticed the pronoun, and said, quietly:

"You will take a carriage to the hotel, or a tram?"

"The tram, I think. It passes the door here."

He glanced at her and added:

"I noticed that the cabin of the launch is very small, and as Gaspare is with you—"

"Oh, of course!" she said, quickly. "It would be ridiculous for you to come all the way back with us. Besides, there is not room in the cabin."

She did not know why, but she felt guilty for a moment. Yet she had done nothing.

"There is the rain," said Artois.

They were just entering the outer room from which the terrace opened.

"Vere!" called Hermione.

As she called the lightning flashed again, and showed her Vere and the Marchesino running in from the darkness. Vere was laughing, and looked more joyous than before.

"Such a storm, Madre! The sea is a mass of foam. It's glorious! Hark at the fishermen!"

From the blackness below rose hoarse shouts and prolonged calls—some near, some far. Faintly with them mingled the quavering and throaty voice of the blind man, now raised in "Santa Lucia."

"What are we going to do, Monsieur Emile?"

"We must get home at once before it gets worse," said Hermione. "Marchese, I am so sorry, but I am afraid we must ask for the launch."

"But, madame, it is only a squall. By midnight it will be all over. I promise you. I am a Neapolitan."

"Ah, but you promised that there would be no storm at all."

"Sa-a-nta-a Lu-u-ci-i-a! Santa Lu-cia!"

The blind man sounded like one in agony. The thunder crashed again just above him, as if it desired to beat down his sickly voice.

Artois felt a sharp stab of neuralgia over his eyes.

Behind, in the restaurant, the waiters were running over the pavement to shut the great windows. The rush of the rain made a noise like quantities of silk rustling.

The Marchesino laughed, quite unabashed. His cheeks were slightly flushed and his eyes shone.

A SPIRIT IN PRISON

"Could I tell the truth, Signora? You might have refused to come. But now I speak the solemn truth. By midnight—"

"I'm afraid we really can't stay so late as that."

"But there is a piano. I will play valses. I will sing."

He looked ardently at Vere, who was eagerly watching the sea from the window.

"And we will dance, the Signorina and I."

Artois made a brusque movement towards the terrace, muttering something about the launch. A glare of lightning lit up the shore immediately below the terrace, showing him the launch buffeted by the waves that were now breaking over the sandy beach. There came a summoning call from the sailors.

"If you do stay," Artois said to the Marchesino, turning back to them, "you must send the launch round to Mergellina. I don't believe it can stop here."

"Well, but there are rocks, Caro Emilio. It is protected!"

"Not enough."

"Signora," said Gaspare, "we had better go. It will only get worse. The sea is not too bad yet."

"Come along!" Hermione cried, with decision. "Come, Vere! I'm very sorry, Marchese, but we must really get back at once. Good-night, Emile! Gaspare, give me your arm."

And she set off at once, clinging to Gaspare, who held an open umbrella over her.

"Good-night, Vere!" said Artois.

The girl was looking at him with surprised eyes.

"You are going—"

"I shall take the tram."

"Oh—of course. That is your quickest way."

"Signorina—the umbrella!"

The Marchesino was offering his arm to conduct Vere

to the launch. He cast a challenging look of triumph at Artois.

"I would come in the launch," Artois, said hastily. "But— Good-night!"

He turned away.

"À rivederci, Emilio!" called the Marchesino.

"—derci!"

The last syllables only came back to them through the wind and the rain.

"Take my arm, Signorina."

"Grazie, it is all right like this."

"Ma—"

"I am quite covered, really, thank you."

She hurried on, smiling, but not taking his arm. She knew how to be obstinate.

"Ma Signorina—mais Mademoiselle—"

"Gaspare! Is Madre all safe in the launch?"

Vere glided from under the Marchesino's umbrella and sought the shade of Gaspare's. Behind, the Marchesino was murmuring to himself Neapolitan street expressions.

"Sì, Signorina."

Gaspare's face had suddenly lighted up. His Padroncina's little hand was holding tightly to his strong arm.

"Take care, Signorina. That is water!"

"Oh, I was nearly in. I thought—"

He almost lifted her into the launch, which was rising and falling on the waves.

"Madre! What a night!"

Vere sank down on the narrow seat of the little cabin. The Marchesino jumped aboard. The machine in the stern throbbed. They rushed forward into the blackness of the impenetrable night, the white of the leaping foam, the hissing of the rain, the roaring of the wind. In a blurred and hasty vision the lights of Frisio's ran before them, fell back into the storm like things defeated. Hermione fancied she discerned for a second the blind man's scarlet face and open mouth, the Padrone at a window waving a frantic adieu, having only just become aware of their departure. But if it were so they were gone before she knew—gone into mystery, with Emile and the world.

The Marchesino inserted himself reproachfully into the cabin. He had turned up the collar of his "smoking," and drawn the silk lapels forward over his soft shirt-front. His white gloves were saturated. He came to sit down by Vere.

"Madame!" he said, reproachfully, "we should have waited. The sea is too rough. Really, it is dangerous. And the Signorina and I—we could have danced together."

Hermione could not help laughing, though she did not feel gay.

"I should not have danced," said Vere. "I could not. I should have had to watch the storm."

She was peering out of the cabin window at the wild foam that leaped up round the little craft and disappeared in the darkness. There was no sensation of fear in her heart, only a passion of interest and an odd feeling of triumph.

To dance with the Marchesino at the Scoglio di Frisio would have been banal in comparison with this glorious progress through the night in the teeth of opposing elements. She envied Gaspare, who was outside with the sailors, and whose form she could dimly see, a blur against the blackness. She longed to take off her smart little hat and her French frock, and be outside too, in the wind and the rain.

"It is ridiculous to be dressed like this!" she said, quickly, taking off the glove she had put on her left hand. "You poor Marchese!"

She looked at his damp "smoking," his soaking gloves and deplorable expression, and could not repress a little rush of laughter.

A SPIRIT IN PRISON

"Do forgive me! Madre, I know I'm behaving shamefully, but we are all so hopelessly inappropriate. Your diamond brooch, Madre! And your hat is all on one side. Gaspare must have knocked it with the umbrella. I am sure we all look like hens in a shower!"

She leaned back against the swaying side of the cabin and laughed till the tears were in her eyes. The sudden coming of the storm had increased the excitement that had been already within her, created by the incidents of the day.

"Vere!" said her mother, but smiling through the protest.

The Marchesino showed his big white teeth. Everything that Vere did seemed to develop his admiration for her. He was delighted with this mood, and forgot his disappointment. But there was a glint of wonder in his eyes, and now he said:

"But the Signorina is not afraid! She does not cry out! She does not call upon the Madonna and the Saints! My mother, my sisters, if they were here—"

The prow of the launch struck a wave which burst over the bows, scattering spray to the roof of the cabin.

"But I like it, I love it!" said Vere. "Don't you?—don't you, Madre?"

Before Hermione could reply the Marchesino exclaimed:

"Signorina, in the breast of an angel you have the heart of a lion! The sea will never harm you. How could it? It will treat you as it treats the Saint of your pool, San Francesco. You know what the sailors and the fishermen say? In the wildest storms, when the sea crashes upon the rocks, never, never does it touch San Francesco. Never does it put out the lamp that burns at San Francesco's feet."

"Yes, I have heard them say that," Vere said.

Suddenly her face had become serious. The romance

186

in the belief of the seamen had got hold of her, had touched her. The compliment to herself she ignored. Indeed, she had already forgotten it.

"Only the other night—" she began.

But she stopped suddenly.

"You know," she said, changing to something else, "that when the fishermen pass under San Francesco's pedestal they bend down, and lift a little water from the sea, and sprinkle it into the boat, and make the sign of the cross. They call it 'acqua benedetta.' I love to see them do that."

Another big wave struck the launch and made it shiver. The Marchesino crossed himself, but quite mechanically. He was intent on Vere.

"I wonder," the girl said, "whether to-night San Francesco will not be beaten by the waves, whether his light will be burning when we reach the island."

She paused, then she added, in a lower voice:

"I do hope it will—don't you, Madre?"

"Yes, Vere," said her mother.

Something in her mother's voice made the girl look up at her swiftly, then put a hand into hers, a hand that was all sympathy. She felt that just then her mother's imagination was almost, or quite, one with hers. The lights of Naples were gone, swallowed by the blackness of the storm. And the tiny light at the feet of the Saint, of San Francesco, who protected the men of the sea, and the boys—Ruffo, too!—would it greet them, star of the sea to their pool, star of the sea to their island, their Casa del Mare, when they had battled through the storm to San Francesco's feet?

"I do hope it will."

Why did Hermione's heart echo Vere's words with such a strenuous and sudden passion, such a deep desire? She scarcely knew then. But she knew that she wanted a light to be shining for her when she neared home—

longed for it, needed it specially that night. If San Francesco's lamp were burning quietly amid the fury of the sea in such a blackness as this about them—well, it would seem like an omen. She would take it as an omen of happiness.

And if it were not burning?

She, too, longed to be outside with Gaspare and the sailors, staring into the darkness with eyes keen as those of a seaman, looking for the light. Since Vere's last words and her reply they had sat in silence. Even the Marchesino's vivacity was suddenly abated, either by the increasing violence of the storm or by the change in Vere. It would have been difficult to say by which. The lightning flashed. The thunder at moments seemed to split the sky asunder as a charge of gunpowder splits asunder a rock. The head wind rushed by, yet had never passed them, but was forever coming furiously to meet them. On the roof of the little cabin the rain made a noise that was no longer like the rustle of silk, but was like the crackle of musketry.

There was something oppressive, something even almost terrible, in being closely confined, shut in by low roof and narrow walls from such sweeping turbulence, such a clamor of wind and water and the sky.

Hermione looked at her diamond brooch, then at her cloak.

Slowly she lifted her hand and began to button it.

Vere moved and began to button up hers. Hermione glanced at her, and saw a watchful, shining, half-humorous, half-passionate look in her eyes that could not be mistaken.

She dropped her hands.

"No, Vere!"

"Yes, Madre! Yes, yes, yes!"

The Marchesino stared.

"No, I did not—"

"You did! You did, Madre! It's no use! I understood directly."

She began quickly to take off her hat.

"Marchese, we are going out."

"Vere, this is absurd."

"We are going outside, Marchese. Madre wants air."

The Marchesino, accustomed only to the habits and customs of Neapolitan women, looked frankly as if he thought Hermione mad.

"Poor Madre must have a breath of air."

"I will open the window, Signora!"

"And the rain all over her, and the thunder close above her, and the sea in her face, the sea—the sea!"

She clapped her hands.

"Gaspare! Gaspare!"

She put her face to the glass. Gaspare, who was standing up in the stern, with his hands holding fast to the rail that edged the cabin roof, bent down till his brown face was on a level with hers, and his big eyes were staring inquiringly into her eyes.

"We are coming out."

On the other side of the glass Gaspare made violently negative gestures. One word only came to those inside the cabin through the uproar of the elements.

"Impossible!"

"Signorina," said the Marchesino, "you cannot mean it. But you will be washed off. And the water—you will be drowned. It cannot be."

"Marchese, look at Madre! If she stays inside another minute she will be ill. She is stifling! Quickly! Quickly!"

The Marchesino, whose sense of humor was not of a kind to comprehend this freak of Vere's, was for once really taken aback. There were two sliding doors to the cabin, one opening into the bows of the launch, the other into the stern. He got up, looking very grave and rather confused, and opened the former. The wind rushed in, carrying with it spray from the sea. At the same moment there was a loud tapping on the glass behind them. Vere looked round. Gaspare was crouching down with his face against the pane. She put her ear to the glass by his mouth.

"Signorina, you must not go into the bows," he called. "If you will come out, come here, and I will take care of you."

He knew Vere's love of the sea and understood her desire.

"Go, Vere," said Hermione.

The Marchesino shut the door and stood by it, bending and looking doubtful.

"I will stay here with the Marchese. I am really too old to face such a tempest, and the Marchese has no coat. He simply can't go."

"But, Signora, it does not matter! I am ready."

"Impossible. Your clothes would be ruined. Go along, Vere! Turn up your collar."

She spoke almost as if to a boy, and like a gay boy Vere obeyed her and slipped out to Gaspare.

"You really won't come, Madre?"

"No. But—tell me if you see the light."

The girl nodded, and the door moved into its place, shutting out the wind.

Then the Marchesino sat down and looked at his damp patent-leather boots.

He really could not comprehend these English ladies. That Vere was greatly attracted by him he thoroughly believed. How could it be otherwise? Her liveliness he considered direct encouragement. And then she had gone out to the terrace after dinner, leaving her mother. That was to make him follow her, of course. She wanted to be alone with him. In a Neapolitan girl such conduct would have been a declaration. A Neapolitan mother would not have allowed them to sit together on the terrace without a chaperon. But the English mother had deliberately remained within and had kept Caro Emilio with her. What could such conduct mean, if not that the Signorina was in love with him, the Marchesino, and that the Signorina's mamma was perfectly willing for him to make love to her child?

And yet—and yet?

There was something in Vere that puzzled him, that had kept him strangely discreet upon the terrace, that made him silent and thoughtful now. Had she been a typical English girl he might have discerned something of the truth of her. But Vere was lively, daring, passionate, and not without some traces of half-humorous and wholly innocent coquetry. She was not at all what the Neapolitan calls "a lump of snow to cool the wine." In her innocence there was fire. That was what confused the Marchesino.

He stared at the cabin door by which Vere had gone out, and his round eyes became almost pathetic for a moment. Then it occurred to him that perhaps this exit was a second ruse, like Vere's departure to the terrace, and he made a movement as if to go out and brave the storm. But Hermione stopped him decisively.

"No, Marchese," she said, "really I cannot let you expose yourself to the rain and the sea in that airy costume. I might be your mother."

"Signora, but you—"

"No, compliments apart, I really might be, and you must let me use a mother's authority. Till we reach the island stay here and make the best of me."

Hermione had touched the right note. Metaphorically, the Marchesino cast himself at her feet. With a gallant assumption of undivided adoration he burst into conversation, and, though his eyes often wandered to the blurred glass, against which pressed and swayed a blackness that told of those outside, his sense of his duty as a host gradually prevailed, and he and Hermione were soon talking quite cheerfully together.

Vere had forgotten him as utterly as she had forgotten Naples, swallowed up by the night. Just then only the sea, the night, Gaspare, and the two sailors who were managing the launch were real to her—besides herself. For a moment even her mother had ceased to exist in her consciousness. As the sea swept the deck of the little craft it swept her mind clear to make more room for itself.

She stood by Gaspare, touching him, and clinging on, as he did, to the rail. Impenetrably black was the night. Only here and there, at distances she could not begin to judge of, shone vaguely lights that seemed to dance and fade and reappear like marsh lights in a world of mist. Were they on sea or land? She could not tell and did not ask. The sailors doubtless knew, but she respected them and their duty too much to speak to them, though she had given them a smile as she came out to join them, and had received two admiring salutes in reply. Gaspare, too, had smiled at her with a pleasure which swiftly conquered the faint reproach in his eloquent eyes. He liked his Padroncina's courage, liked the sailors of the Signor Marchese to see it. He was soaked to the skin, but he, too, was enjoying the adventure, a rare one on this summer sea, which had slept through so many shining days and starry nights like a "bambino in dolce letargo."

To-night it was awake, and woke up others, Vere's nature and his.

"Where is the island, Gaspare?" cried Vere through the wind to him.

"Chi lo sa, Signorina."

He waved one hand to the blackness before them.

"It must be there."

A SPIRIT IN PRISON

She strained her eyes, then looked away towards where the land must be. At a long distance across the leaping foam she saw one light. As the boat rose and sank on the crests and into the hollows of the waves the light shone and faded, shone and faded. She guessed it to be a light at the Antico Giuseppone. Despite the head wind and the waves that met them the launch travelled bravely, and soon the light was gone. She told herself that it must have been at the Giuseppone, and that now they had got beyond the point, and were opposite to the harbor of the Villa Rosebery. But no lights greeted them from the White Palazzo in the wood, or from the smaller white house low down beside the sea. And again she looked straight forward.

Now she was intent on San Francesco. She was thinking of him, of the Pool, of the island. And she thrilled with joy at the thought of the wonderful wildness of her home. As they drew on towards it the waves were bigger, the wind was stronger. Even on calm nights there was always a breeze when one had passed the Giuseppone going towards Ischia, and beyond the island there was sometimes quite a lively sea. What would it be to-night? Her heart cried out for a crescendo. Within her, at that moment, was a desire like the motorist's for speed. More! more! More wind! more sea! more uproar from the elements!

And San Francesco all alone in this terrific blackness! Had he not been dashed from his pedestal by the waves? Was the light at his feet still burning?

"Il Santo!" she said to Gaspare.

He bent his head till it was close to her lips.

"Il Santo! What has become of him, Gaspare?"

"He will be there, Signorina."

So Gaspare, too, held to the belief of the seamen of the Bay. He had confidence in the obedience of the sea, this sea that roared around them like a tyrant. Sud-

193

denly she had no doubt. It would be so. The saint would be untouched. The light would still be burning. She looked for it. And now she remembered her mother. She must tell her mother directly she saw it. But all was blackness still.

And the launch seemed weary, like a live thing whose strength is ebbing, who strains and pants and struggles gallantly, not losing heart but losing physical force. Surely it was going slower. She laid one hand upon the cabin roof as if in encouragement. Her heart was with the launch, as the seaman's is with his boat when it resists, surely for his sake consciously, the assault of the great sea.

"Coraggio!"

She was murmuring the word. Gaspare looked at her. And the word was in his eyes as it should be in all eyes that look at youth. And the launch strove on.

"Coraggio! Coraggio!"

The spray was in her face. Her hair was wet with the rain. Her French frock—that was probably ruined! But she knew that she had never felt more happy. And now—it was like a miracle! Suddenly out of the darkness a second darkness shaped itself, a darkness that she knew—the island. And almost simultaneously there shone out a little, steady light.

"Ecco il Santo!"

"Ecco! Ecco!"

Vere called out: "Madre! Madre!"

She bent down.

"Madre! The light is burning."

The sailors, too, bent down, right down to the water. They caught at it with their hands, Gaspare, too. Vere understood, and, kneeling on the gunwale, firmly in Gaspare's grasp, she joined in their action.

She sprinkled the boat with the acqua benedetta and made the sign of the cross.

CHAPTER XIV

WHEN, the next day, Artois sat down at his table to work he found it impossible to concentrate his mind. The irritation of the previous evening had passed away. He attributed it to the physical effect made upon him by the disturbed atmosphere. Now the sun shone, the sky was clear, the sea calm. He had just come out of an ice-cold bath, had taken his coffee, and smoked one · cigarette. A quiet morning lay before him. Quiet?

He got up and went to the window.

On the wooden roof of the bath establishment opposite rows of towels, hung out to dry, were moving listlessly to and fro in the soft breeze. Capri was almost hidden by haze in the distance. In the sea, just below him, several heads of swimmers moved. One boy was "making death." He floated on his back with his eyes closed and his arms extended. His body, giving itself without resistance to every movement of the water, looked corpselike and ghostly.

A companion shouted to him. He threw up his arms suddenly and shouted a reply in the broadest Neapolitan, then began to swim vigorously towards the slimy rocks at the base of Castel dell' Ovo. Upon the wooden terrace of the baths among green plants in pots stood three women, probably friends of the proprietor. For though it was already hot, the regular bathing season of Naples had not yet begun and the baths were not completed. Only in July, after the festa of the Madonna del Carmine, do the Neapolitans give themselves heart and soul to the

195

sea. Artois knew this, and wondered idly what the women were doing on the terrace. One had a dog. It sat in the sun and began to cough. A long wagon on two wheels went by, drawn by two mules and a thin horse harnessed abreast. It was full of white stone. The driver had bought some green stuff and flung it down upon the white. He wore a handkerchief on his head. His chest was bare. As he passed beneath the window he sang a loud song that sounded Eastern, such a song as the Spanish wagoners sing in Algeria, as they set out by night on their long journeys towards the desert. Upon a tiny platform of wood, fastened to slanting stakes which met together beneath it in a tripod, a stout man in shirt and trousers, with black whiskers, was sitting on a chair fishing with a rod and line. A boy sat beside him dangling his legs over the water. At a little distance a large fishing-smack, with sails set to catch the breeze farther out in the Bay, was being laboriously rowed towards the open sea by half-naked men, who shouted as they toiled at the immense oars.

Artois wondered where they were going. Their skins were a rich orange color. From a distance in the sunlight they looked like men of gold. Their cries and their fierce movements suggested some fantastic quest to lands of mysterious tumult.

Artois wished that Vere could see them.

What were the inhabitants of the island doing?

To-day his mind was beyond his governance, and roamed like a vagrant on a long, white road. Everything that he saw below him in the calm radiance of the morning pushed it from thought to thought. Yet none of these thoughts were valuable. None seemed fully formed. They resembled henids, things seen so far away that one cannot tell what they are, but is only aware that they exist and can attract attention.

He came out upon his balcony. As he did so he looked

down into the road, and saw a hired carriage drive up, with Hermione in it.

She glanced up and saw him.

"May I come in for a minute?"

He nodded, smiling, and went out to meet her, glad of this interruption.

They met at the door of the lift. As Hermione stepped out she cast a rather anxious glance at her friend, a glance that seemed to say that she was not quite certain of her welcome. Artois' eyes reassured her.

"I feel guilty," she said.

"Why?"

"Coming at such an hour. Are you working?"

"No. I don't know why, but I am incapable of work. I feel both lazy and restless, an unfruitful combination. Perhaps something in me secretly knew that you were coming."

"Then it is my fault."

They came into his sitting-room. It had four windows, two facing the sea, two looking on the road, and the terraces and garden of the Hotel Hassler. The room scarcely suggested its present occupant. It contained a light-yellow carpet with pink flowers strewn over it, red-and-gold chairs, mirrors, a white marble mantelpiece, a gray-and-pink sofa with a pink cushion. Only the large writing-table, covered with manuscripts, letters, and photographs in frames, said something individual to the visitor. Hermione and Vere were among the photographs.

Hermione sat down on the sofa.

"I have come to consult you about something, Emile."

"What is it?"

"I really meant to ask you last night, but somehow I couldn't."

"Why?"

A SPIRIT IN PRISON

"I don't know. We—I—there seemed to be a sort of barrier between us—didn't there?"

"I was in a bad humor. I was tired after the journey, and perhaps the weather upset me."

"It's all right—one can't be always— Well, this is what I wanted to say. I alluded to it yesterday when I told you about my visit to Naples with Madame Alliani. Do you remember?"

"You hinted you had seen, or heard of, some tragedy."

"Yes. I believe it is a quite ordinary one in Naples. We went to visit a consumptive woman in one of those narrow streets going uphill to the left of the Via Roma, and while there by chance I heard of it. In the same house as the sick woman there is a girl. Not many days ago she was beautiful!"

"Yes? What has happened to her?"

"I'll tell you. Her name is Peppina. She is only nineteen, but she has been one of those who are not given a chance. She was left an orphan very young and went to live with an aunt. This aunt is a horrible old woman. I believe—they say she goes to the Galleria—"

Hermione paused.

"I understand," said Artois.

"She is greedy, wicked, merciless. We had the story from the woman we were visiting, a neighbor. This aunt forced Peppina into sin. Her beauty, which must have been extraordinary, naturally attracted attention and turned people's heads. It seems to have driven one man nearly mad. He is a fisherman, not young, and a married man. It seems that he is notoriously violent and jealous, and thoroughly unscrupulous. He is a member of the Camorra, too. He pestered Peppina with his attentions, coming day after day from Mergellina, where he lives with his wife. One night he entered the house and made a scene. Peppina refused finally to

198

receive his advances, and told him she hated him before all the neighbors. He took out a razor and—"

Hermione stopped.

"I understand," said Artois. "He disfigured her."

"Dreadfully."

"It is often done here. Sometimes a youth does it simply to show that a girl is his property. But what is it you wish to do for Peppina? I see you have a plan in your head."

"I want to have her on the island."

"In what capacity?"

"As a servant. She can work. She is not a bad girl. She has only—well, Emile, the aunt only succeeded in forcing one lover on her. That is the truth. He was rich and bribed the aunt. But of course the neighbors all know, and—the population here has its virtues, but it is not exactly a delicate population."

"Per Bacco!"

"And now that the poor girl is disfigured the aunt is going to turn her out-of-doors. She says Peppina must go and earn money for herself. Of course nobody will take her. I want to. I have seen her, talked to her. She would be so thankful. She is in despair. Think of it! Nineteen, and all her beauty gone! Isn't it devilish?"

"And the man?"

"Oh, they say he'll get scarcely anything, if anything. Two or three months, perhaps. He is 'protected.' It makes my blood boil."

Artois was silent, waiting for her to say more, to ask questions.

"The only thing is—Vere, Emile," she said.

"Vere?"

"Yes. You know how friendly she is with the servants. I like her to be. But of course till now they have been all right—so far as I know."

"You do well to add that proviso."

"Peppina would not wait on us. She would be in the kitchen. Am I justified in taking her? Of course I could help her with money. If I had not seen her, talked to her, that is what I should have done, no doubt. But she wants—she wants everything, peace, a decent home, pure air. I feel she wants the island?"

"And the other servants?"

"They need only know she was attacked. They need not know her past history. But all that does not matter. It is only the question of Vere that troubles me."

"You mean that you are not decided whether you ought to bring into the house with Vere a girl who is not as Vere is?"

"Yes."

"And you want me to advise you?"

"Yes."

"I can't do that, Hermione."

She looked at him almost as if she were startled.

"Why not? I always rely—"

"No, no. This is not a man's business, my business."

He spoke with an odd brusqueness, and there were traces of agitation in his face. Hermione did not at all understand what feeling was prompting him, but again, as on the previous evening, she felt as if there were a barrier between them — very slight, perhaps, very shadowy, but definite nevertheless. There was no longer complete frankness in their relations. At moments her friend seemed to be subtly dominated by some secret irritation, or anxiety, which she did not comprehend. She had been aware of it yesterday. She was aware of it now. After his last exclamation she said nothing.

"You are going to this girl now?" he asked.

"I meant to. Yes, I shall go."

She sat still for a minute, looking down at the pink-and-yellow carpet.

"And what will you do?"

She looked up at him.

"I think I shall take her to the island. I am almost sure I shall. Emile, I don't believe in cowardice, and I sometimes think I am inclined to be a coward about Vere. She is growing up. She will be seventeen this year, very soon. There are girls who marry at sixteen, even English girls."

"That is true."

She could gather nothing from his tone; and now his face was perfectly calm.

"My instinct is to keep Vere just as she is, to preserve the loveliness of childhood in her as long as possible, to keep away from her all knowledge of sin, sorrow, the things that distract and torture the world. But I mustn't be selfish about Vere. I mustn't keep her wrapped in cotton wool. That is unwholesome. And, after all, Vere must have her life apart from me. Last night I realized that strongly."

"Last night?"

"Yes, from the way in which she treated the Marchese, and later from something else. Last night Vere showed two sides of a woman's nature—the capacity to hold her own, what is vulgarly called 'to keep her distance,' and the capacity to be motherly."

"Was Vere motherly to the Marchesino, then?" asked Artois, not without irony.

"No—to Ruffo."

"That boy? But where was he last night?"

"When we got back to the island, and the launch had gone off, Vere and I stood for a minute at the foot of the steps to listen to the roaring of the sea. Vere loves the sea."

"I know that."

As he spoke he thought of something that Hermione did not know.

"The pool was protected, and under the lee of the island it was comparatively calm. But the rain was falling in torrents. There was one fishing-boat in the pool, close to where we were, and as we were standing and listening Vere said, suddenly, 'Madre, that's Ruffo's boat!' I asked her how she knew — because he has changed into another boat lately—she had told me that. 'I saw his head,' she answered. 'He's there and he's not asleep. Poor boy, in all this rain!' Ruffo has been ill with fever, as I told you, and when Vere said that I remembered it at once."

"Had you told Vere yet?" interposed Artois.

"No. But I did then. Emile, she showed an agitation that—well, it was almost strange, I think. She begged me to make him come into the house and spend the night there, safe from the wind and the rain."

"And you did, of course?"

"Yes. He was looking very pale and shaky. The men let him come. They were nice and sympathetic. I think they are fond of the boy."

"Ruffo seems to know how to attract people to him."

"Yes."

"And so Vere played the mother to Ruffo?"

"Yes. I never saw that side of her before. She was a woman then. Eventually Ruffo slept with Gaspare."

"And how did Gaspare accept the situation?"

"Better than I should have expected. I think he likes Ruffo personally, though he is inclined to be suspicious and jealous of any strangers who come into our lives. But I haven't had time to talk to him this morning."

"Is Ruffo still in the house?"

"Oh no. He went off in the boat. They came for him about eight."

"Ah!"

Artois went to the window and looked out. But now

he saw nothing, although the three women were still talking and gesticulating on the terrace of the bath-house, more fishing-boats were being towed or rowed out into the Bay, carts were passing by, and people were strolling in the sun.

"You say that Vere showed agitation last night?" he said, turning round after a moment.

"About Ruffo's illness? It really almost amounted to that. But Vere was certainly excited. Didn't you notice it?"

"I think she was."

"Emile," Hermione said, after an instant of hesitation, "you remember my saying to you the other day that Vere was not a stranger to me?"

"Yes, quite well."

"You said nothing—I don't think you agreed. Well, since that day—only since then—I have sometimes felt that there is much in Vere that I do not understand, much that is hidden from me. Has she changed lately?"

"She is at an age when development seems sudden, and is often striking, even startling."

"I don't know why, but—but I dread something," Hermione said. "I feel as if—no, I don't know what I feel. But if Vere should ever drift away from me I don't know how I could bear it. A boy—one expects him to go out into the world. But a girl! I want to keep Vere. I must keep Vere. If anything else were to be taken from me I don't think I could bear it."

"Vere loves you. Be sure of that."

"Yes."

Hermione got up.

"Well, you won't give me your advice?"

"No, Hermione."

He looked at her steadily.

"You must treat Vere as you think best, order her life as you think right. In some things you do wisely to consult me. But in this you must rely on yourself. Let your heart teach you. Do not ask questions of my head."

"Your head!" she exclaimed.

There was a trace of disappointment, even of surprise, in her voice. She looked at him as if she were going to say more, but again she was disconcerted by something in his look, his attitude.

"Well, good-bye, Emile."

"I will come with you to the lift."

He went with her and touched the electric bell. As they waited for a moment he added:

"I should like to have an evening quietly on the island."

"Come to-night, or whenever you like. Don't fix a time. Come when the inclination whispers—'I want to be with friends.'"

He pressed her hand.

"Shall I see Peppina?"

"Chi lo sa?"

"And Ruffo?"

She laughed.

"The Marchesino, too, perhaps."

"No," said Artois, emphatically. "Disfigured girls and fisher-boys—as many as you like, but not the alta aristocrazia Napoletana."

"But I thought—"

"I like Doro, but—I like him in his place."

"And his place?"

"Is not the island—when I wish to be quiet there."

The lift descended. Artois went out once more onto the balcony, and watched her get into the carriage and drive away towards Naples. She did not look up again.

"She has gone to fetch that girl Peppina," Artois said to himself, "and I might have prevented it."

He knew very well the reason why he had not interfered. He had not interfered because he had wished too much to interfere. The desire had been strong enough to startle him, to warn him.

An islet! That suggests isolation. Like Hermione, he wished to isolate Vere, to preserve her as she was in character. He did not know when the wish had first been consciously in his mind, but he knew that since he had been consulted by Vere, since she had broken through her reserve and submitted to him her poems, unveiling for him alone what was really to her a holy of holies, the wish had enormously increased. He told himself that Vere was unique, and that he longed to keep her unique, so that the talent he discerned in her might remain unaffected. How great her talent was he did not know. He would not know, perhaps, for a very long time. But it was definite, it was intimate. It was Vere's talent, no one else's.

He had made up his mind very soon about Hermione's incapacity to produce work of value. Although Vere was such a child, so inexperienced, so innocent, so cloistered, he knew at once that he dared not dash her hopes. It was possible that she might eventually become what her mother certainly could never be.

But she must not be interfered with. Her connection with the sea must not be severed. And people were coming into her life—Ruffo, the Marchesino, and now this wounded girl Peppina.

Artois felt uneasy. He wished Hermione were less generous-hearted, less impulsive. She looked on him as a guide, a check. He knew that. But this time he would not exercise his prerogative. Ruffo he did not mind—at least he thought he did not. The boy was a sea creature. He might even be an inspiring force to Vere. Something Artois had read had taught him that. And Ruffo interested him, attracted him too.

A SPIRIT IN PRISON

But he hated Vere's acquaintance with the Mar
chesino. He knew that the Marchesino would make
love to her. And the knowledge was odious to him.
Let Vere be loved by the sea, but by no man as
yet.

And this girl, Peppina?

He thought of the horrors of Naples, of the things that
happen "behind the shutter," of the lives led by some
men and women, some boys and girls of the great city
beneath the watching volcano. He thought of evenings
he had spent in the Galleria. He saw before him an old
woman about whom he had often wondered. Always
at night, and often in the afternoon, she walked in the
Galleria. She was invariably alone. The first time he
had seen her he had noticed her because she had a slightly humped back. Her hair was snow white, and was
drawn away from her long, pale face and carefully arranged under a modest bonnet. She carried a small
umbrella and a tiny bag. Glancing at her casually, he
had supposed her to be a respectable widow of the bor-
ghese class. But then he had seen her again and again,
and by degrees he had come to believe that she was
something very different. And then one night in late
spring he had seen her in a new light dress with white
thread gloves. And she had noticed him watching her,
and had cast upon him a look that was unmistakable,
a look from the world "behind the shutter"; and he
had understood. Then she had followed him persistently. When he sat before the "Gran caffè" sipping
his coffee and listening to the orchestra of women that
plays on the platform outside the caffè, she had passed
and repassed, always casting upon him that glance of
sinister understanding, of invitation, of dreary wickedness that sought for, and believed that it had found,
an answering wickedness in him.

Terrible old woman! Peppina's aunt might well be

like that. And Peppina would sleep, perhaps to-night, in the Casa del Mare, under the same roof as Vere.

He resolved to go that evening to the island, to see Peppina, to see Vere. He wished, too, to have a little talk with Gaspare about Ruffo.

The watch-dog instinct, which dwelt also in Gaspare, was alive in him.

But to-day it was alive to do service for Vere, not for Hermione. He knew that, and said to himself that it was natural. For Hermione was a woman, with experience of life; but Vere was only upon the threshold of the world. She needed protection more than Hermione.

Some time ago, when he was returning to Naples from the island on an evening of scirocco, Artois had in thought transferred certain hopes of his from Hermione to Vere. He had said to himself that he must henceforth hope for Hermione in Vere.

Now was he not transferring something else from the mother to the child?

CHAPTER XV

ARTOIS had intended to go that evening to the island.
But he did not fulfil his intention. When the sun began
to sink he threw a light coat over his arm and walked
down to the harbor of Santa Lucia. A boatman whom
he knew met him and said:

"Shall I take you to the island, Signore?"

Artois was there to take a boat. He meant to say
yes. Yet when the man spoke he answered no. The
fellow turned away and found another customer. Two
or three minutes later Artois saw his boat drawing out
to sea in the direction of Posilipo. It was a still evening, and very clear after the storm of the preceding
night. Artois longed to be in that travelling boat,
longed to see the night come from the summit of the
island with Hermione and Vere. But he resisted the
sea, its wide peace, its subtle summons, called a carriage and drove to the Galleria. Arrived there, he took
his seat at a little table outside the "Gran Caffè," ordered a small dinner, and, while he was eating it, watched the people strolling up and down, seeking among them
for a figure that he knew.

As the hour drew near for the music to begin, and the
girls dressed in white came out one by one to the platform that, surrounded by a white railing edged with red
velvet, is built out beyond the caffè to face the crowd,
the number of promenaders increased, and many stood
still waiting for the first note, and debating the looks
of the players. Others thronged around Artois, taking
possession of the many little tables, and calling for ices,

lemon - water, syrups, and liqueurs. Priests, soldiers, sailors, students, actors—who assemble in the Galleria to seek engagements—newsboys, and youths whose faces suggested that they were "ruffiani," mingled with foreigners who had come from the hotels and from the ships in the harbor, and whose demeanor was partly curious and partly suspicious, as of one who longs to probe the psychology of a thief while safely guarding his pockets. The buzz of voices, the tramp of feet, gained a peculiar and vivid sonorousness from the high and vaulted roof; and in the warm air, under the large and winking electric lights, the perpetually moving figures looked strangely capricious, hungry, determined, furtive, ardent, and intent. On their little stands the electric fans whirred as they slowly revolved, casting an artificial breeze upon pallid faces, and around the central dome the angels with gilded wings lifted their right arms as if pointing the unconscious multitude the difficult way to heaven.

A priest sat down with two companions at the table next to Artois. He had a red cord round his shaggy black hat. His face was like a parroquet's, with small, beady eyes full of an unintellectual sharpness. His plump body suggested this world, and his whole demeanor, the movements of his dimpled, dirty hands, and of his protruding lips, the attitude of his extended legs, the pose of his coarse shoulders, seemed hostile to things mystical. He munched an ice, and swallowed hasty draughts of iced water, talking the while with a sort of gluttonous vivacity. Artois looked at him and heard, with his imagination, the sound of the bell at the Elevation, and saw the bowed heads of the crouching worshippers. The irony of life, that is the deepest mystery of life, came upon him like the wave of some Polar sea. He looked up at the gilded angels, then dropped his eyes and saw what he had come to see.

A SPIRIT IN PRISON

Slowly threading her way through the increasing throng, came the old woman whom he had watched so often and by whom he had been watched. To-night she had on her summer dress, a respectable, rather shiny gown of grayish mauve, a bonnet edged with white ribbon, a pair of white thread gloves. She carried her little bag and a small Japanese fan. Walking in a strange, flat-footed way that was peculiar to her, and glancing narrowly about her, yet keeping her head almost still, she advanced towards the band-stand. As she came opposite to Artois the orchestra of women struck up the "Valse Noir," and the old woman stood still, impeded by the now dense crowd of listeners. While the demurely sinister music ran its course, she remained absolutely immobile. Artois watched her with a keen interest.

It had come into his mind that she was the aunt of Peppina, the disfigured girl, who perhaps to-night was sleeping in the Casa del Mare with Vere.

Presently, attracted, no doubt, by his gaze, the old woman looked across at Artois and met his eyes. Instantly a sour and malignant expression came into her long, pale face, and she drew up a corner of her upper lip, as a dog sometimes does, showing a tooth that was like a menace.

She was secretly cursing Artois.

He knew why. Encouraged by his former observation of her, she had scented a client in him and had been deceived, and this deception had bred within her an acrid hatred of him. To-night he would chase away that hatred. For he meant to speak to her. The old woman looked away from him, holding her head down as if in cold disdain. Artois read easily what was passing in her mind. She believed him wicked, but nervous in his wickedness, desirous of her services but afraid to invite them. And she held him in the uttermost contempt. Well, to-night he would undeceive her on one point at least. He kept his eyes upon her so firmly that she looked at him again. This time he made a sign of recognition, of understanding. She stared as if in suspicious amazement. He glanced towards the dome, then at her once more. At this moment the waiter came up. Artois paid his bill slowly and ostentatiously. As he counted out the money upon the little tray he looked up once, and saw the eyes in the long, pale face of the venerable temptress glitter while they watched. The music ceased, the crowd before the platform broke up, and began quickly to melt away. Only the woman waited, holding her little bag and her cheap Japanese fan.

Artois drew out a cigar, lit it slowly, then got up, and began to move out among the tables.

The priest looked after him, spoke rapidly to his companions, and burst into a throaty laugh which was loudly echoed.

"Maria Fortunata is in luck to-night!" said some one.

Then the band began again, the waiter came with more ices, and the tall, long-bearded forestiere was forgotten.

Without glancing at the woman, Artois strolled slowly on. Many people looked at him, but none spoke to him, for he was known now, as each stranger who stays long in Naples is known, summed up, labelled, and either ignored or pestered. The touts and the ruffiani were aware that it was no use to pester the Frenchman, and even the decrepit and indescribably seedy old men who hover before the huge plate-glass windows of the photograph shops, or linger near the entrance to the cinematograph, never peeped at him out of the corners of their bloodshot eyes or whispered a word of the white slaves in his ear.

When he was beneath the dome, and could see the

light gleaming upon the wings of the pointing angels,
Artois seemed to be aware of an individual step among
the many feet behind him, a step soft, furtive, and obstinate, that followed him like a fate's. He glanced up
at the angels. A melancholy and half-bitter smile came
to his lips. Then he turned to the right and made his
way still slowly towards the Via Roma, always crowded
from the early afternoon until late into the night. As
he went, as he pushed through the mob of standing men
at the entrance of the Galleria, and crossed the street to
the far side, from which innumerable narrow and evil-
looking alleys stretch away into the darkness up the
hill, the influence of the following old woman increased
upon him, casting upon him like a mist her hateful
eagerness. He desired to be rid of it, and, quickening
his walk, he turned into the first alley he came to, walked
a little way up it, until he was in comparative solitude
and obscurity, then stopped and abruptly turned.

The shiny, grayish mauve gown and the white-
trimmed bonnet were close to him. Between them he
faintly perceived a widely smiling face, and from this
face broke at once a sickly torrent of speech, half Neapolitan dialect, half bastard French.

"Silenzio!" Artois said, sternly.

The old harridan stopped in surprise, showing her
tooth.

"What has become of Peppina?"

"Maria Santissima!" she ejaculated, moving back a
step in the darkness.

She paused. Then she said:

"You know Peppina!"

She came forward again, quite up to him, and peered
into his face, seeking there for an ugly truth which till
now had been hidden from her.

"What had you to do with Peppina?"

"Nothing. Tell me about her, and—"

A SPIRIT IN PRISON

He put his hand to the inside pocket of his coat, and showed her the edge of a little case containing paper notes. The woman misunderstood him. He knew that by her face, which for the moment was as a battle-field on which lust fought with a desperate anger of disappointment. Then cunning came to stop the battle.

"You have heard of Peppina, Signore? You have never seen her?"

Artois played with her for a moment.

"Never."

Her smile widened. She put up her thin hands to her hair, her bonnet, coquettishly.

"There is not a girl in Naples as beautiful as Peppina. Mother of—"

But the game was too loathsome with such a player.

"Beautiful! Macchè!"

He laughed, made a gesture of pulling out a knife and smashing his face with it.

"Beautiful! Per Dio!"

The coquetry, the cunning, dropped out of the long, pale face.

"The Signore knows?"

"Ma sì! All Naples knows."

The old woman's face became terrible. Her two hands shot up, dropped, shot up again, imprecating, cursing the world, the sky, the whole scheme of the universe, it seemed. She chattered like an ape. Artois soothed her with a ten-lire note.

That night, when he went back to the hotel, he had heard the aunt's version of Peppina, and knew—that which really he had known before—that Hermione had taken her to live on the island.

Hermione! What was she? An original, clever and blind, great-hearted and unwise. An enthusiast, one created to be carried away.

Never would she grow really old, never surely would

the primal fires within her die down into the gray ashes that litter so many of the hearths by which age sits, a bleak, uncomely shadow.

And Peppina was on the island, a girl from the stews of Naples; not wicked, perhaps, rather wronged, injured by life—nevertheless, the niece of that horror of the Galleria.

He thought of Vere and shuddered.

Next day towards four o'clock the Marchesino strolled into Artois' room, with a peculiarly impudent look of knowledge upon his face.

"Buon giorno, Caro Emilio," he said. "Are you busy?"

"Not specially."

"Will you come with me for a stroll in the Villa? Will you come to see the gathering together of the geese?"

"Che Diavolo! What's that?"

"This summer the Marchesa Pontini has organized a sort of club, which meets in the Villa every day except Sundays. Three days the meeting is in the morning, three days in the afternoon. The silliest people of the aristocracy belong to this club, and the Marchesa is the mother goose. Ecco! Will you come, or—or have you some appointment?" He smiled in his friend's face.

Artois wondered, but could not divine, what was at the back of his mind.

"No, I had thought of going on the sea."

"Or to the Toledo, perhaps?"

The Marchesino laughed happily.

"The Toledo? Why should I go there?"

"Non lo so. Put on your chapeau and come. Il fait très beau cet après-midi."

Doro was very proud of his French, which made Artois secretly shiver, and generally spoke it when he was in specially good spirits, or was feeling unusually mischievous. As they walked along the sea-front a moment later, he continued in Italian:

"You were not at the island yesterday, Emilio?"

"No. Were you?"

"I naturally called to know how the ladies were after that terrible storm. What else could I do?"

"And how were they?"

"The Signora was in Naples, and of course the Signorina could not have received me alone. But the saints were with me, Emilio. I met her on the sea, quite by herself, on the sea of the Saint's Pool. She was lying back in a little boat, with no hat on, her hands behind her head—so, and her eyes—her beautiful eyes, Emilio, were full of dreams, of dreams of the sea."

"How do you know that?" said Artois, rather sharply.

"Cosa?"

"How do you know the Signorina was dreaming of the sea? Did she—did she tell you?"

"No, but I am sure. We walked together from the boats. I told her she was an enchantress of the sea, the spirit of the wave—I told her!"

He spread out his hands, rejoicing in the remembrance of his graceful compliments.

"The Signorina was delighted, but she could not stay long. She had a slight headache and was a little tired after the storm. But she would have liked to ask me to the house. She was longing to. I could see that."

He seized his mustache.

"She turned her head away, trying to conceal from me her desire, but—"

He laughed.

"Le donne! Le donne!" he happily exclaimed.

Artois found himself wondering why, until Doro had made the acquaintance of the dwellers on the island, he had never wished to smack his smooth, complacent cheeks.

A SPIRIT IN PRISON

They turned from the sea into the broad walk of the
Villa, and walked towards the kiosk. Near it, on the
small, green chairs, were some ladies swathed in gigantic
floating-veils, talking to two or three very smart young
men in white suits and straw hats, who leaned forward eying them steadily with a determined yet rather
vacuous boldness that did not disconcert them. One
of the ladies, dressed in black-and-white check, was immensely stout. She seemed to lead the conversation,
which was carried on with extreme vivacity in very
loud and not melodious voices.

"Ecco the gathering of the geese!" said the Marchesino, touching Artois on the arm. "And that"—he
pointed to the stout lady, who at this moment tossed
her head till her veil swung loose like a sail suddenly
deserted by the wind—"is the goose-mother. Buona
sera, Marchesa! Buona sera — molto piacere. Carlo,
buona sera—a rivederci, Contessa! A questa sera."

He showed his splendid teeth in a fixed but winning
smile, and, hat in hand, went by, walking from his hips.
Then, replacing his hat on his head, he added to his
friend:

"The Marchesa is always hoping that the Duchessa
d'Aosta will come one day, if only for a moment, to
smile upon the geese. But—well, the Duchessa prefers
to climb to the fourth story to see the poor. She has
a heart. Let us sit here, Emilio."

They sat down under the trees, and the Marchesino
looked at his pointed boots for a moment in silence,
pushing forward his under lip until his blond mustache
touched the jaunty tip of his nose. Then he began to
laugh, still looking before him.

"Emilio! Emilio!"

He shook his head repeatedly.

"Emilio mio! And that you should be asking me to
show you Naples! It is too good! C'est parfait!"

A SPIRIT IN PRISON

The Marchesino turned towards Artois.

"And Maria Fortunata! Santa Maria of the Toledo, the white-haired protectress of the strangers! Emilio— you might have come to me! But you do not trust me. Ecco! You do not—"

Artois understood.

"You saw me last night?"

"Ma sì! All Naples saw you. Do you not know that the Galleria is full—but full—of eyes?"

"Va bene! But you don't understand."

"Emilio!"

He shrugged his shoulders, lifted his hands, his eyebrows. His whole being seemed as if it were about to mount ironically towards heaven.

"You don't understand. I repeat it."

Artois spoke quietly, but there was a sound in his voice which caused his frivolous companion to stare at him with an inquiry that was, for a moment, almost sulky.

"You forget, Doro, how old I am."

"What has that to do with it?"

"You forget—"

Artois was about to allude to his real self, to point out the improbability of a man so mental, so known, so travelled as he was, falling like a school-boy publicly into a sordid adventure. But he stopped, realizing the uselessness of such an explanation. And he could not tell the Marchesino the truth of his shadowy colloquy in a by-street with the old creature from behind the shutter.

"You have made a mistake about me," he said. "But it is of no consequence. Look! There is another goose coming."

He pointed with his cane in the direction of the chatterers near the kiosk.

"It is papa! It is papa!"

A SPIRIT IN PRISON

"Pardon! I did not recognize—"

The Marchesino got up.

"Let us go there. The Marchesa with papa—it is better than the Compagnia Scarpetta! I will present you."

But Artois was in no mood for a cataract of nothingness.

"Not now," he said. "I have—"

The Marchesino shot a cruel glance of impudent comprehension at him, and touched his left hand in token of farewell.

"I know! I know! The quickest horse to the Toledo. A-ah! A-ah! May the writer's saint go with you! Addio, mio caro!"

There was a hint of real malice in his voice. He cocked his hat and strutted away towards the veils and the piercing voices. Artois stared after him for a moment, then walked across the garden to the sea, and leaned against the low wall looking towards Capri. He was vexed at this little episode—unreasonably vexed. In his friend Doro he now discerned a possible enemy. An Italian who has trusted does not easily forgive if he is not trusted in return. Artois was conscious of a dawning hostility in the Marchesino. No doubt he could check it. Doro was essentially good-tempered and light-hearted. He could check it by an exhibition of frankness. But this frankness was impossible to him, and as it was impossible he must allow Doro to suspect him of sordid infamies. He knew, of course, the Neapolitan's habitual disbelief in masculine virtue, and did not mind it. Then why should he mind Doro's laughing thought of himself as one of the elderly crew who cling to forbidden pleasures? Why should he feel sore, angry, almost insulted?

Vere rose before him, as one who came softly to bring him the answer to his questionings. And he knew that

218

his vexation arose from the secret apprehension of a future in which he would desire to stand between her and the Marchesino with clean hands, and tell Doro certain truths which are universal, not national. Such truths would come ill from one whom the lectured held unclean.

As he walked home to the hotel his vexation grew.

When he was once more in his room he remembered his remark to Hermione, "We shall have many quiet, happy evenings together this summer, I hope," and her strange and doubtful reply. And because he felt himself invaded by her doubts he resolved to set out for the island. If he took a boat at once he could be there between six and seven o'clock.

And perhaps he would see the new occupant of the Casa del Mare. Perhaps he would see Peppina.

15

CHAPTER XVI

"I HAVE come, you see," said Artois that evening, as he entered Hermione's room, "to have the first of our quiet, happy evenings, about which you were so doubtful."

"Was I?"

She smiled at him from her seat between the big windows.

Outside the door he had, almost with a sudden passion, dismissed the vague doubts and apprehensions that beset him. He came with a definite brightness, a strong intimacy, holding out his hands, intent really on forcing Fate to weave her web in accordance with his will.

"We women are full of little fears, even the bravest of us. Chase mine away, Emile."

He sat down.

"What are they?"

She shook her head.

"Formless—or almost. But perhaps that adds to the uneasiness they inspire. To put them into words would be impossible."

"Away with them!"

"Willingly."

Her eyes seemed to be asking him questions, to be not quite satisfied, not quite sure of something.

"What is it?" he asked.

"I wonder if you have it in you to be angry with me."

"Make your confession."

A SPIRIT IN PRISON

"I have Peppina here."

"Of course."

"You knew—?"

"I have known you as an impulsive for—how many years? Why should you change?"

He looked at her in silence for a moment. Then he continued:

"Sometimes you remind me—in spots, as it were—of George Sand."

She laughed, not quite without bitterness.

"In spots, indeed!"

"She described herself once in a book as having 'a great facility' for illusions, a blind benevolence of judgment, a tenderness of heart that was inexhaustible—"

"Oh!"

"Wait! From these qualities, she said, came hurry, mistakes innumerable, heroic devotion to objects that were worthless, much weakness, tremendous disappointments."

Hermione said nothing, but sat still looking grave.

"Well? don't you recognize something of yourself in the catalogue, my friend?"

"Have I a great facility for illusions? Am I capable of heroic devotion to worthless objects?"

Suddenly Artois remembered all he knew and she did not know.

"At least you act hastily often," he said, evasively. "And I think you are often so concentrated upon the person who stands, perhaps suffering, immediately before you, that you forget who is on the right, who is on the left."

"Emile, I asked your advice yesterday, and you would not give it me."

"A fair hit!" he said. "And so Peppina is here. How did the servants receive her?"

"I think they were rather surprised. Of course they don't know the truth."

"They will within—shall we say twenty-four hours, or less?"

"How can they? Peppina won't tell them."

"You are sure? And when Gaspare goes into Naples to 'fare la spesa'?"

"I told Gaspare last night."

"That was wisdom. You understand your watch-dog's character."

"You grant that Gaspare is not an instance of a worthless object made the recipient of my heroic devotion?"

"Give him all you like," said Artois, with warmth. "You will never repent of that. Was he angry when you told him?"

"I think he was."

"Why?"

"I heard him saying 'Testa della Madonna!' as he was leaving me."

Artois could not help smiling.

"And Vere?" he said, looking directly at her.

"I have not told Vere anything about Peppina's past," Hermione said, rather hastily. "I do not intend to. I explained that Peppina had had a sad life and had been attacked by a man who had fallen in love with her, and for whom she didn't care."

"And Vere was all sympathy and pity?" said Artois, gently.

"She didn't seem much interested, I thought. She scarcely seemed to be listening. I don't believe she has seen Peppina yet. When we arrived she was shut up in her room."

As she spoke she was looking at him, and she saw a slight change come over his face.

"Do you think—?" she began, and paused. "I wonder if she was reading," she added, slowly, after a moment.

"Even the children have their secrets," he answered. As he spoke he turned his head and looked out of the window towards Ischia. "How clear it is to-night! There will be no storm."

"No. We can dine outside. I have told them." Her voice sounded slightly constrained. "I will go and call Vere," she added.

"She is in the house?"

"I think so."

She went out, shutting the door behind her.

So Vere was working. Artois felt sure that her conversation with him had given to her mind, perhaps to her heart, too, an impulse that had caused an outburst of young energy. Ah! the blessed ardors of youth! How beautiful they are, and, even in their occasional absurdity, how sacred. What Hermione had said had made him realize acutely the influence which his celebrity and its cause—the self that had made it—must have upon a girl who was striving as Vere was. He felt a thrill of pleasure, even of triumph, that startled him, so seldom now, jealous and careful as he was of his literary reputation, did he draw any definite joy from it. Would Vere ever do something really good? He found himself longing that she might, as the proud godparent longs for his godchild to gain prizes. He remembered the line at the close of Maeterlinck's "Pelleas and Melisande," a line that had gone like a silver shaft into his soul when he first heard it—"Maintenant c'est au tour de la pauvre petite" (Now its the child's turn.)

"Now it's the child's turn," he said it to himself, forming the words with his lips. At that moment he was freed entirely from the selfishness of age, and warm with a generous and noble sympathy with youth, its aspirations, its strivings, its winged hopes. He got up from his chair. He had a longing to go to Vere and tell her all he was feeling, a longing to pour into her—as just then he could have poured it—inspiration molten in a long-tried furnace. He had no heed of any one but Vere.

The door opened and Hermione came back.

"Vere is coming, Emile," she said.

"You told her I was here?"

She looked at him swiftly, as if the ringing sound in his voice had startled her.

"Yes. She is glad, I know. Dear little Vere!"

Her voice was dull, and she spoke—or he fancied so —rather mechanically. He remembered all she did not know and was conscious of her false position. In their intercourse she had so often, so generally, been the enthusiastic sympathizer. More than she knew she had inspired him.

"Dear Hermione! How good it is to be here with you!" he said, turning towards her the current of his sympathy. "As one grows old one clings to the known, the proved. That passion at least increases while so many others fade away, the passion for all that is faithful in a shifting world, for all that is leal, that does not suffer corruption, disintegration! How adorable is Time where Time is powerless!"

"Is Time ever powerless?" she said. "Ah, here is Vere!"

They dined outside upon the terrace facing Vesuvius. Artois sat between mother and child. Vere was very quiet. Her excitement, her almost feverish gayety of the evening of the storm had vanished. To-night dreams hung in her eyes. And the sea was quiet as she was, repentant surely of its former furies. There seemed something humble, something pleading in its murmur, as if it asked forgiveness and promised amendment.

The talk was chiefly between Hermione and Artois. It was not very animated. Perhaps the wide peace of the evening influenced their minds. When coffee was carried out Artois lit his pipe, and fell into complete silence, watching the sea. Giulia brought to Hermione a bit of embroidery on which she was working, cleared away the dessert and quietly disappeared. From the house now and then came a sound of voices, of laughter. It died away, and the calm of the coming night, the calm of the silent trio that faced it, seemed to deepen as if in delicate protest against the interference. The stillness of Nature to-night was very natural. But was the human stillness natural? Presently Artois, suddenly roused, he knew not why, to self-consciousness, found himself wondering. Vere lay back in her wicker chair like one at ease. Hermione was leaning forward over her work with her eyes bent steadily upon it. Far off across the sea the smoke from the summit of Vesuvius was dyed at regular intervals by the red fire that issued from the entrails of the mountain. Silently it rose from its hidden world, glowed angrily, menacingly, faded, then glowed again. And the life that is in fire, and that seems to some the most intense of all the forces of life, stirred Artois from his peace. The pulse of the mountain, whose regular beating was surely indicated by the regularly recurring glow of the rising flame, seemed for a moment to be sounding in his ears, and, with it, all the pulses that were beating through the world. And he thought of the calm of their bodies, of Hermione's, of Vere's, of his own, as he had thought of the calm of the steely sky, the steely sea, that had preceded the bursting of the storm that came from Ischia. He thought of it as something unnatural, something almost menacing, a sort of combined lie that strove to conceal, to deny, the leaping fires of the soul.

Suddenly Vere got up and went quietly away. While she had been with them silence had been easy. Directly she was gone Artois felt that it was difficult, in another moment that it was no longer possible.

A SPIRIT IN PRISON

"Am I to see Peppina to-night?" he asked.

"Do you wish to?"

Hermione's hands moved a little faster about their work when he spoke.

"I feel a certain interest in her, as I should in any new inhabitant of the island. A very confined space seems always to heighten the influence of human personality, I think. On your rock everybody must mean a good deal, perhaps more than you realize, Hermione."

"I am beginning to realize that," she answered, quietly. "Perhaps they mean too much. I wonder if it is wise to live as we do?"

"In such comparative isolation, you mean?"

"Yes."

She laid her work down in her lap.

"I'm afraid that by nature I am a monopolist," she said. "And as I could never descend into the arena of life to struggle to keep what I have, if others desired to take it from me, I am inclined jealously to guard it."

She took up her work again.

"I've been thinking that I am rather like the dog that buries his bone," she added, bending once more over the embroidery.

"Are you thinking of—of your husband?"

"Yes, and of Vere. I isolated myself with Maurice. Now I am isolating myself with Vere. Perhaps it is unwise, weak, this instinct to keep out the world."

"Are you thinking of changing your mode of life, then?" he asked.

In his voice there was a sound of anxiety which she noticed.

"Perhaps. I don't know."

She glanced at him and away, and he thought that there was something strange in her eyes. After a pause, she said:

"What would you advise?"

"Surely you are happy here. And—and Vere is happy."

"Vere is happy—yes."

He realized the thoughtlessness of his first sentence.

"But I must think of Vere's development. Lately, in these last days, I have been realizing that Vere is moving, is beginning to move very fast. Perhaps it is time to bring her into contact with more people. Perhaps—"

"You once asked my advice," he interrupted. "I give it now. Leave Vere alone. What she needs she will obtain. Have no fear of that."

"You are sure?"

"Quite sure. Sometimes, often, the children know instinctively more than their elders know by experience."

Hermione's lips trembled.

"Sometimes," she said, in a low voice, "I think Vere knows far more than I do. But—but I often feel that I am very blind, very stupid. You called me an impulsive—I suppose I am one. But if I don't follow my impulses, what am I to follow? One must have a guide."

"Yes, and reason is often such a dull one, like a verger showing one over a cathedral and destroying its mystery and its beauty with every word he speaks. When one is young one does not feel that one needs a guide at all."

"Sometimes—often—I feel very helpless now," she said.

He was acutely conscious of the passionate longing for sympathy that was alive within her, and more faintly aware of a peculiar depression that companioned her to-night. Yet, for some reason unknown to him, he could not issue from a certain reserve that checked him, could not speak to her as he had spoken not long ago in the cave. Indeed, as she came in her last words a little towards him, as one with hands tremblingly and a little doubtfully held out, he felt that he drew back.

"I think we all feel helpless often when we have passed our first youth," he answered.

He got up and stretched himself, towering above her.

"Shall we stroll about a little?" he added. "I feel quite cramped with sitting."

"You go. I'll finish this flower."

"I'll take a turn and come back."

As he went she dropped her embroidery and sat staring straight before her at the sea.

Artois heard voices in the house, and listened for a new one, the voice of Peppina. But he could not distinguish it. He went down into the tiny garden. No one was there, and he returned, and passing through the house came out on its farther side. Here he met Gaspare coming up from the sea.

"Good-evening, Gaspare," he said.

"Good-evening, Signore."

"I hear there's a new-comer in the house."

"Signore?"

"A new servant."

Gaspare lifted his large eyes towards heaven.

"Testa della Madonna?" said Artois.

"Signore?"

"Have a cigar, Gaspare?"

"Grazie, Signore."

"Is she a good sort of girl, do you think?"

"Who, Signore?"

"This Peppina."

"She is in the kitchen, Signore. I have nothing to do with her."

"I see."

Evidently Gaspare did not mean to talk. Artois decided to change the subject.

"I hear you had that boy, Ruffo, sleeping in the house the other night," he said.

"Sì, Signore; the Signorina wished it."

Gaspare's voice sounded rather more promising.

"He seems popular on the island."

"He had been ill, Signore, and it was raining hard. Poveretto! He had had the fever. It was bad for him to be out in the boat."

"So Ruffo's getting hold of you too!" thought Artois.

He pulled at his cigar once or twice. Then he said:

"Do you think he looks like a Sicilian?"

Gaspare's eyes met his steadily.

"A Sicilian, Signore?"

"Yes."

"Signore, he is a Sicilian. How should he not look like one?"

Gaspare's voice sounded rebellious.

"Va bene, Gaspare, va bene. Have you seen the Signorina?"

"I think she is at the wooden seat, Signore. The Signorina likes to look at the sea from there."

"I will go and see if I can find her."

"Va bene, Signore. And I will go to speak with the Signora."

He took off his hat and went into the house. Artois stood for a moment looking after him and pulling at his beard. There was something very forcible in Gaspare's personality. Artois felt it the more because of his knowledge of Gaspare's power of prolonged, perhaps of eternal silence. The Sicilian was both blunt and subtle, therefore not always easily read. To-night he puzzled Artois because he impressed him strongly, yet vaguely. He seemed to be quietly concealing something that was not small. What it was Artois could not divine. Only he felt positive that there was something. In Gaspare's eyes that evening he had seen an expression such as had been in them long ago in Sicily, when Artois rode up after Maurice's death to see Hermione, and Gaspare turned from him and looked over the wall of the ravine: an expression of dogged and impenetrable reserve, that was like a door closing upon unseen, just not seen, vistas.

"Che Diavolo!" muttered Artois.

Then he went up to look for Vere.

A little wind met him on the crest of the cliff, the definite caress of the night, which had now fallen ever so softly. The troop of the stars was posted in the immeasurable deeps of the firmament. There was, there would be, no moon, yet it was not black darkness, but rather a dimly purple twilight which lifted into its breast the wayward songs of the sea. And the songs and the stars seemed twin children of the wedded wave and night. Divinely soft was the wind, divinely dreamy the hour, and bearing something of youth as a galley from the East bears odors. Over the spirit of Artois a magical essence seemed scattered. And the youngness that lives forever, however deeply buried, in the man who is an artist, stirred, lifted itself up, stood erect to salute the night. As he came towards Vere he forgot. The poppy draught was at his lips. The extreme consciousness, which was both his strength and his curse, sank down for a moment and profoundly slept.

"Vere!" he said. "Vere, do I disturb you?"

The girl turned softly on the bench and looked at him.

"No. I often come here. I like to be here at nightfall. Madre knows that. Did she tell you?"

"No."

"You guessed?"

"I met Gaspare."

He stood near her.

"Where is Madre?"

"On the terrace. She preferred to stay quietly there. And so you have been working very hard?"

He spoke gently, half smilingly, but not at all derisively.

"Yes. But how did you know?"

"I gathered it from something your mother said. Do you know, Vere, I think soon she will begin to wonder what you do when you are shut up for so long in your room."

The girl's face looked troubled for a moment.

"She doesn't—she has no idea."

"Oh no."

Vere was silent for a while.

"I wonder if I ought to tell her, Monsieur Emile," she said, at length.

"Tell her!" Artois said, hastily. "But I thought—"

He checked himself, suddenly surprised at the keenness of his own desire to keep their little secret.

"I know. You mean what I said the other day. But—if Madre should be hurt. I don't think I have ever had a secret from her before, a real secret. But—it's like this. If Madre knows I shall feel horribly self-conscious, because of what I told you—her having tried and given it up. I shall feel guilty. Is it absurd?"

"No."

"And—and—I don't believe I shall be able to go on. Of course some day, if it turns out that I ever can do anything, I must tell. But that would be different. If it's certain that you can do a thing well it seems to me that you have a right to do it. But—till then—I'm a little coward, really."

She ended with a laugh that was almost deprecating.

"Don't tell your mother yet, Vere," said Artois, decisively. "It is as you say: if you told her before you have thoroughly tried your wings you might be paralyzed. When, if ever, you can show her something really good she will be the first to encourage you. But —till then—I think with you that her influence in that direction would probably be discouraging. Indeed, I feel sure of it."

"But if she should really begin to wonder! Perhaps she will ask. It's absurd, but I can't help feeling as if we, you and I, were conspirators, Monsieur Emile."

He laughed happily.

"What a blessed place this is!" he said. "One is made free of the ocean here. What is that far-away light?"

He pointed.

"Low down? Oh, that must be the light of a fisherman, one of those who seek in the rocks for shell-fish."

"How mysterious it looks, moving to and fro! One feels life there, the doings of unknown men in the darkness."

"I wonder if—would you hate to go out a little way in the boat? The men look so strange when one is near them, almost like fire-people."

"Hate! Let us go."

"And we'll get Madre to come too."

"Oh yes."

Vere got up and they went into the house. As they came out upon the terrace Hermione took up her embroidery, and Gaspare, who was standing beside her, picked up the tray with the coffee-cups and went off with it towards the kitchen.

"Well, Vere?"

"Madre, we are going out a little way in the boat, and we want you to come with us."

"Where are you going?"

"To see the fishermen, just beyond the Grotto of Virgilio. You will come?"

"Do come, my friend," added Artois.

But Hermione sat still.

"I'm a little tired to-night," she answered. "I think I would rather stay quietly here. You won't be long, will you?"

"Oh no, Madre. Only a few minutes. But, really, won't you?" Vere laid her hand on her mother's. "It's so lovely on the sea to-night."

"I know. But honestly, I'm lazy to-night."

Vere looked disappointed. She took away her hand gently.

"Then we'll stay with you, won't we, Monsieur Emile?"

"No, Vere," said her mother quickly, before he could answer. "You two go. I sha'n't be dull. You won't be very long?"

"No, of course. But—"

"Go, dearest, go. Are you going to row, Emile?"

"I could. Or shall we take Gaspare?"

"It's Gaspare's supper-time," said Vere.

"Hush, then!" said Artois, putting his finger to his lips. "Let us creep down softly, or he will think it his duty to come with us, starving, and that would spoil everything. Au revoir, Hermione," he whispered.

"Good-bye, Madre," whispered Vere.

They glided away, the big man and the light-footed child, going on tiptoe with elaborate precaution.

As Hermione looked after them, she said to herself: "How young Emile is to-night!"

At that moment she felt as if she were much older than he was.

They slipped down to the sea without attracting the attention of Gaspare, got into the little boat, and rowed gently out towards Nisida.

"I feel like a contrabandista," said Artois, as they stole under the lee of the island towards the open sea— "as if Gaspare would fire upon us if he heard the sound of oars."

"Quick! Quick! Let us get away. Pull harder, Monsieur Emile! How slow you are!"

Laughingly Artois bent to the oars.

"Vere, you are a baby!" he said.

"And what are you, then, I should like to know?" she answered, with dignity.

"I! I am an old fellow playing the fool."

Suddenly his gayety had evaporated, and he was conscious of his years. He let the boat drift for a moment.

"Check me another time, Vere, if you see me inclined to be buffo," he said.

"Indeed I won't. Why should I? I like you best when you are quite natural."

"Do you?"

"Yes. Look! There are the lights! Oh, how strange they are. Go a little nearer, but not too near."

"Tell me, then. Remember, I can't see."

"Yes. One, two, three—"

She counted. Each time she said a number he pulled. And she, like a little coxswain, bent towards him with each word, giving him a bodily signal for the stroke. Presently she stretched out her hand.

"Stop!"

He stopped at once. For a minute the boat glided on. Then the impetus he had given died away from it, and it floated quietly without perceptible movement upon the bosom of the sea.

"Now, Monsieur Emile, you must come and sit by me."

Treading softly he obeyed her, and sat down near her, facing the shadowy coast.

"Now watch!"

They sat in silence, while the boat drifted on the smooth and oily water almost in the shadow of the cliffs. At some distance beyond them the cliffs sank, and the shore curved sharply in the direction of the island with its fort. There was the enigmatic dimness, though not dense darkness, of the night. Nearer at hand the walls of rock made the night seem more mysterious, more profound, and at their base flickered the flames which had attracted Artois' attention. Fitfully now these flames, rising from some invisible brazier, or from some torch fed by it, fell upon half-naked forms of creatures mysteriously busy about some hidden task. Men they were, yet hardly men they seemed, but rather unknown denizens of rock, or wave, or underworld; now red-bodied against the gleam, now ethereally black as are shadows, and whimsical and shifty, yet always full of meaning that could not be divined. They bent, they crouched. They seemed to die down like a wave that is, then is not. Then rising they towered, lifting brawny arms towards the stars. Silence seemed to flow from them, to exude from their labors. And in the swiftness of their movements there was something that was sad. Or was it, perhaps, only pathetic, wistful with the wistfulness of the sea and of all nocturnal things? Artois did not ask, but his attention, the attention of mind and soul, was held by these distant, voiceless beings as by a magic. And Vere was still as he was, tense as he was. All the poetry that lay beneath his realism, all the credulity that slept below his scepticism, all the ignorance that his knowledge strove to dominate, had its wild moment of liberty under the smiling stars. The lights moved and swayed. Now the seamed rock, with its cold veins and slimy crevices, was gilded, its nudity clothed with fire. Now on the water a trail of glory fell, and travelled and died. Now the red men were utterly revealed, one watching with an ardor that was surely not of this world, some secret in the blackness, another turning as if to strike in defence of his companion. Then both fell back and were taken by the night. And out of the night came a strong voice across the water.

"Madre di Dio, che splendore!"

Artois got up, turned the boat, and began to row gently away, keeping near the base of the cliffs. He meant to take Vere back at once to the island, leaving the impression made upon her by the men of fire vivid, and undisturbed by speech. But when they came to the huge mouth of the Grotto of Virgil, Vere said:

"Go in for a moment, please, Monsieur Emile."

He obeyed, thinking that the mother's love for this dark place was echoed by the child. Since his conversation with Hermione on the day of scirocco he had not been here, and as the boat glided under the hollow blackness of the vault, and there lay still, he remembered their conversation, the unloosing of her passion, the strength and tenacity of the nature she had shown to him, gripping the past with hands almost as unyielding as the tragic hands of death. ·

And he waited in silence, and with a deep expectation, for the revelation of the child. It seemed to him that Vere had her purpose in coming here, as Hermione had had hers. And once more the words of the old man in "Pelleas and Melisande" haunted him. Once more he heard them in his heart.

"Now it's the child's turn."

Vere dropped her right hand over the gunwale till it touched the sea, making a tiny splash.

"Monsieur Emile!" she said.

"Yes, Vere."

"Do you believe in the evil eye?"

Artois did not know what he had expected Vere to say, but her question seemed to strike his mind like a soft blow, it was so unforeseen.

"No," he answered.

She was silent. It was too dark for him to see her

face at all clearly. He had only a vague general impression of her, of her slightness, vitality, youth, and half-dreamy excitement.

"Why do you ask me?"

"Giulia said to me this evening that she was sure the new servant had the evil eye."

"Peppina?"

"Yes, that is the name."

"Have you seen her?"

"No, not yet. It's odd, but I feel as if I would rather not."

"Have you any reason for such a feeling?"

"I don't think so. Poor thing! I know she has a dreadful scar. But I don't believe it's that. It's just a feeling I have."

"I dare say it will have gone by the time we get back to the island."

"Perhaps. It's nice and dark here."

"Do you like darkness, Vere?"

"Sometimes. I do now."

"Why?"

"Because I can talk better and be less afraid of you."

"Vere! what nonsense! You are incapable of fear."

She laughed, but the laugh sounded serious, he thought.

"Real fear—perhaps. But you don't know"—she paused—"you don't know how I respect you."

There was a slight pressure on the last words.

"For all you've done, what you are. I never felt it as I have just lately, since—since—you know."

Artois was conscious of a movement of his blood.

"I should be a liar if I said I am not pleased. Tell me about the work, Vere—now we are in the dark."

And then he heard the revelation of the child, there under the weary rock, as he had heard the revelation of the mother. How different it was! Yet in it, too, there was the beating of the pulse of life. But there was no regret, no looking back into the past, no sombre exhibition of force seeking—as a thing groping desperately in a gulf—an object on which to exercise itself. Instead there was aspiration, there was expectation, there was the wonder of bright eyes lifted to the sun. And there was a reverence that for a moment recalled to Artois the reverence of the dead man from whose loins this child had sprung. But Vere's was the reverence of understanding, not of a dim amazement—more beautiful than Maurice's. When he had been with Hermione under the brooding rock Artois had been impregnated with the passionate despair of humanity, and had seen for a moment the world with out-stretched hands, seeking, surely, for the nonexistent, striving to hold fast the mirage. Now he was impregnated with humanity's passionate hope. He saw life light-footed in a sweet chase for things ideal. And all the blackness of the rock and of the silent sea was irradiated with the light that streamed from a growing soul.

> "Sento n' addore 'e rose e de viole
> Sempe che passo pe sott 'o barcone
> Addo assettata staie. Na canzone
> Se sperde sola sola . . . e 'a cante tu!

> " Ah—tu nun saie
> Quanto stu core
> Spantica e more
> Luntano a 'te.—
> Nocchie lucente
> Vocca addurosa
> Occhiu de na rosa
> Beila tu si."

A voice—an inquiring, searching voice, surely, rose quivering from some distance on the sea, startling Vere and Artois. It was untrained but unshy, and the singer forced it with a resolute hardihood that was indifferent to the future. Artois had never heard the Marchesino sing before, but he knew at once that it was he. Some one at the island must surely have told the determined youth that Vere was voyaging, and he was now in quest of her, sending her an amorous summons couched in the dialect of Naples.

Vere moved impatiently.

"Really!" she began.

But she did not continue. The quivering voice began another verse. Artois had said nothing, but, as he sat listening to this fervid protestation, a message illuminated as it were by the vibrato, he began to hate the terrible frankness of the Italian nature which, till now, he had thought he loved. The beauty of reticence appealed to him in a new way. There was savagery in a bellowed passion. The voice was travelling. They heard it moving onward towards Nisida. Artois wondered if Vere knew who was the singer. She did not leave him long in doubt.

"Now's our chance, Monsieur Emile!" she said, suddenly, leaning towards him. "Row to the island for your life, or the Marchesino will catch us!"

Without a word he bent to the oars.

> "Occhiu de na rosa
> Bella tu si . . . bella tu si. . . ."

Towards the men of fire it went. It died away upon the sea.

"How absurd the Marchesino is!"

Vere spoke aloud, released from fear.

"Absurd? He is Neapolitan."

"Very well, then! The Neapolitans are absurd!" said Vere, with decision. "And what a voice! Ruffo doesn't sing like that. That shaking sounds—sounds so artificial."

"And yet I dare say he is very much in earnest."

239

A SPIRIT IN PRISON

Artois was almost pleading a cause against his will.
"Oh!"

The girl gave almost a little puff that suggested a rather childish indignation.

"I like the people best," she added. "They say what they feel simply, and it means ever so much more. Am I a democrat?"

He could not help laughing.

"Chi lo sa? An anarchist perhaps."

She laughed too.

"Bella tu si—Bella tu si! It's too absurd! One would think—"

"What, Vere?"

"Never mind. Don't be inquisitive, Monsieur Emile."

He rowed on meekly.

"There is San Francesco's light," she said, in a moment. "I wonder if it is late. Have we been away long? I have no idea."

"No more have I."

Nor had he.

When they reached land he made the boat fast and turned to walk up to the house with her. He found her standing very still just behind him at the edge of the sea, with a startled look on her face.

"What is it, Vere?" he asked.

"Hush!"

She held up her hand and bent her head a little to one side, as one listening intently.

"I thought I heard—I did hear—something—"

"Something?"

"Yes—so strange—I can't hear it now."

"What was it like?"

She looked fixedly at him.

"Like some one crying—horribly."

"Where? Near us?"

"Not far. Listen again."

"AS VERE SAW IT, SHOWING REDLY THROUGH THE DARK-
NESS, SHE RECOILED"

He obeyed, holding his breath. But he heard nothing except the very faint lapping of the sea at their feet.

"Perhaps I imagined it," she said, at length.

"Let us go up to the house," he said. "Come, Vere."

He had a sudden wish to take her into the house. But she remained where she was.

"Could it have been fancy, Monsieur Emile?"

"No doubt."

Her eyes were intensely grave, almost frightened.

"But—just look, will you? Perhaps there really is somebody."

"Where? It's so dark."

Artois hesitated; but Vere's face was full of resolution, and he turned reluctantly to obey her. As he did so there came to them both through the dark the sound of a woman crying and sobbing convulsively.

"What is it? Oh, who can it be?" Vere cried out.

She went swiftly towards the sound.

Artois followed, and found her bending down over the figure of a girl who was crouching against the cliff, and touching her shoulder.

"What is it? What is the matter? Tell me."

The girl looked up, startled, and showed a passionate face that was horribly disfigured. Upon the right cheek, extending from the temple almost to the line of the jaw, a razor had cut a sign, a brutal sign of the cross. As Vere saw it, showing redly through the darkness, she recoiled. The girl read the meaning of her movement, and shrank backward, putting up her hand to cover the wound. But Vere recovered instantly, and bent down once more, intent only on trying to comfort this sorrow, whose violence seemed to open to her a door into a new and frightful world.

"Vere!" said Artois. "Vere, you had better—"

The girl turned round to him.

"It must be Peppina!" she said.

"Yes. But—"

"Please go up to the house, Monsieur Emile. I will come in a moment."

"But I can't leave you—"

"Please go. Just tell Madre I'm soon coming."

There was something inexorable in her voice. She turned away from him and began to speak softly to Peppina.

Artois obeyed and left her.

He knew that just then she would not acknowledge his authority. As he went slowly up the steps he wondered—he feared. Peppina had cried with the fury of despair, and the Neapolitan who is desperate knows no reticence.

Was the red sign of passion to be scored already upon Vere's white life? Was she to pass even now, in this night, from her beautiful ignorance to knowledge?

CHAPTER XVII

THAT night the Marchesino failed in his search for
Vere, and he returned to Naples not merely disappointed
but incensed. He had learned from a fisherman in the
Saint's Pool that she was out upon the sea "with a Signore," and he had little difficulty in guessing who this
Signore was. Of course it was "Caro Emilio," the
patron of Maria Fortunata. He began to consider his
friend unfavorably. He remembered how frankly he
had always told Emilio of his little escapades, with what
enthusiasm, in what copious detail. Always he had
trusted Emilio. And now Emilio was trying to play
him false—worse, was making apparently a complete
success of the attempt. For Emilio and Vere must
have heard his beautiful singing, must have guessed
from whom that vibrant voice proceeded, must have
deliberately concealed themselves from its possessor.
Where had they lain in hiding? His shrewd suspicion
fell upon the very place. Virgilio's Grotto had surely
been their refuge.

"Ladro! Vigiliacco!" Words of no uncertain meaning flowed from his overcharged heart. His whole hot
nature was aroused. His spirit was up in arms. And
now, almost for the first time, he drew a comparison
between his age and Emilio's. Emilio was an old man.
He realized it. Why had he never realized it before?
Was he, full of youth, beauty, chivalrous energy and
devotion, to be interfered with, set aside, for a man
with gray hairs thick upon his head, for a man who

spent half his hours bent over a writing-table? Emilio
had never wished him to know the ladies of the island.
He knew the reason now, and glowed with a fiery lust
of battle. Vere had attracted him from the first. But
this opposition drove on attraction into something
stronger, more determined. He said to himself that he
was madly in love. Never yet had he been worsted
in an amour by any man. The blood surged to his head
at the mere thought of being conquered in the only
battle of life worth fighting—the battle for a woman,
and by a man of more than twice his age, a man who
ought long ago to have been married and have had
children as old as the Signorina Vere.

Well, he had been a good friend to Emilio. Now
Emilio should see that the good friend could be the
good enemy. Late that night, as he sat alone in front
of the Caffè Turco smoking innumerable cigarettes, he
resolved to show these foreigners the stuff a Neapolitan
was made of. They did not know. Poor, ignorant
beings from cold England, drowned forever in perpetual
yellow fogs, and from France, country of volatility but
not of passion, they did not know what the men of the
South, of a volcanic soil, were capable of, once they were
roused, once their blood spoke and their whole nature responded! It was time they learned. And he would under-
take to teach them. As he drove towards dawn up the
dusty hill to Capodimonte he was in a fever of excitement.

There was excitement, too, in the house on the island,
but it did not centre round the Marchesino.

That night, for the first time in her young life, Vere
did not sleep. She heard the fishermen call, but the
enchantment of sea doings did not stir her. She was
aware for the first time of the teeming horrors of life.
There, in the darkness beneath the cliff, Peppina had
sobbed out her story, and Vere, while she listened, had
stepped from girlhood into womanhood.

A SPIRIT IN PRISON

She had come into the house quietly, and found Artois waiting for her alone. Hermione had gone to bed, leaving word that she had a headache. And Vere was glad that night not to see her mother. She wished to see no one, and she bade Artois good-bye at once, telling him nothing, and not meeting his eyes when he touched her hand in adieu. And he had asked nothing. Why should he, when he read the truth in the grave, almost stern face of the child?

Vere knew.

The veils that hang before the happy eyes of childhood had been torn away, and those eyes had looked for the first time into the deeps of an unhappy human heart.

And he had thought it possible to preserve, perhaps for a long while, Vere's beautiful ignorance untouched. He had thought of the island as a safe retreat in which her delicate, and as yet childish talent, might gradually mature under his influence and the influence of the sea. She had been like some charming and unusual plant of the sea, shot with sea colors, wet with sea winds, fresh with the freshness of the smooth-backed waves. And now in a moment she was dropped into the filthy dust of city horrors. What would be the result upon her and upon her dawning gift?

The double question was in his mind, and quite honestly. For his interest of the literary man in Vere was very vivid. Never yet had he had a pupil or dreamed of having one. There are writers who found a school, whose fame is carried forward like a banner by young and eager hands. Artois had always stood alone, ardently admired, ardently condemned, but not imitated. And he had been proud of his solitude. But—lately—had not underthoughts come into his mind, thoughts of leaving an impress on a vivid young intellect, a soul that was full of life, and the beginnings of energy? Had not he dreamed, however vaguely, of forming, like some sculptor of genius, an exquisite statuette—poetry, in the slim form of a girl-child singing to the world?

And now Peppina had rushed into Vere's life, with sobs and a tumult of cries to the Madonna and the saints, and, no doubt, with imprecations upon the wickedness of men. And where were the dreams of the sea? And his dreams, where were they?

That night the irony that was in him woke up and smiled bitterly, and he asked himself how he, with his burden of years and of knowledge of life, could have been such a fool as to think it possible to guard any one against the assaults of the facts of life. Hermione, perhaps, had been wiser than he, and yet he could not help feeling something that was almost like anger against her for what he called her quixotism. The woman of passionate impulses—how dangerous she is, even when her impulses are generous, are noble! Action without thought, though the prompting heart behind it be a heart of gold—how fatal may it be!

And then he remembered a passionate impulse that had driven a happy woman across a sea to Africa, and he was ashamed.

Yet again the feeling that was almost like hostility returned. He said to himself that Hermione should have learned caution in the passing of so many years, that she ought to have grown older than she had. But there was something unconquerably young, unconquerably naïve, in her—something that, it seemed, would never die. Her cleverness went hand in hand with a short-sightedness that was like a rather beautiful, yet sometimes irritating stupidity. And this latter quality might innocently make victims, might even make a victim of her own child.

And then a strange desire rose up in Artois, a desire to protect Vere against her own mother.

A SPIRIT IN PRISON

But how could that be done?

Vere, guarded by the beautiful unconsciousness of youth, was unaware of the subtleties that were brought' into activity by her. That the Marchesino was, or thought himself, in love with her she realized. But she could not connect any root-sincerity with his feeling. She was accustomed vaguely to think of all young Southern Italians as perpetually sighing for some one's dark eyes. The air of the South was full of love songs that rose and fell without much more meaning than a twitter of birds, that could not be stilled because it was so natural. And the Marchesino was a young aristocrat who did absolutely nothing of any importance to the world. The Northern blood in Vere demanded other things of a man than imitations of a seal, the clever driving of a four-in-hand, light-footed dancing, and songs to the guitar. In Gaspare she saw more reality than she saw as yet in the Marchesino. The dawning intellect of her began to grasp already the nobility of work. Gaspare had his work to do, and did it with loyal efficiency. Ruffo, too, had his profession of the sea. He drew out of the deep his livelihood. Even with the fever almost upon him he had been out by night in the storm. That which she liked and respected in Gaspare, his perfect and natural acceptance of work as a condition of his life, she liked and respected in Ruffo.

On the morning after the incident with Peppina, Vere came down looking strangely grave and tired. Her mother, too, was rather heavy-eyed, and the breakfast passed almost severely. When it was over Hermione, who still conducted Vere's education, but with a much relaxed vigor in the summer months, suggested that they should read French together.

"Let us read one of Monsieur Emile's books, Madre," said Vere, with an awakening of animation. "You know I have never read one, only two or three baby stories, and articles that don't count."

"Yes, but Emile's books are not quite suitable for you yet, Vere."

"Why, Madre?"

"They are very fine, but they dive deep into life, and life contains many sad and many cruel things."

"Oughtn't we to prepare ourselves for them, then?"

"Not too soon, I think. I am nearly sure that if you were to read Emile's books just yet you would regret it."

Vere said nothing.

"Don't you think you can trust me to judge for you in this matter, figlia mia? I—I am almost certain that Emile himself would think as I do."

It was not without an effort, a strong effort, that Hermione was able to speak the last sentence. Vere came nearer to her mother, and stood before her, as if she were going to say something that was decisive or important. But she hesitated.

"What is it, Vere?" Hermione asked, gently.

"I might learn from life itself what Monsieur Emile's books might teach me."

"Some day. And when that time comes neither I nor he would wish to keep them out of your hands."

"I see. Well, Madre dear, let us read whatever you like."

Vere had been on the verge of telling her mother about the previous night and Peppina. But, somehow, at the last moment she could not.

And thus, for the moment at least, Artois and she shared another secret of which Hermione was unaware.

But very soon Hermione noticed that Vere was specially kind always to Peppina. They did not meet, perhaps, very often, but when by chance they did Vere spoke to the disfigured girl with a gentleness, almost a tenderness, that were striking.

A SPIRIT IN PRISON

"You like Peppina, Vere?" asked her mother one day.

"Yes, because I pity her so much."

There was a sound that was almost like passion in the girl's voice; and, looking up, Hermione saw that her eyes were full of light, as if the spirit had set two lamps in them.

"It is strange," Vere continued, in a quieter tone; "but sometimes I feel as if on the night of the storm I had had a sort of consciousness of her coming—as if, when I saw the Saint's light shining, and bent down to the water and made the sign of the Cross, I already knew something of Peppina's wound, as if I made the sign to protect our Casa del Mare, to ward off something evil."

"That was coming to us with Peppina, do you mean?"

"I don't know, Madre."

"Are you thinking of Giulia's foolish words about the evil eye?"

"No. It's all vague, Madre. But Peppina's cross sometimes seems to me to be a sign, a warning come into the house. When I see it it seems to say there is a cross to be borne by some one here, by one of us."

"How imaginative you are, Vere!"

"So are you, Madre! But you try to hide it from me."

Hermione was startled. She took Vere's hand, and held it for a moment in silence, pressing it with a force that was nervous. And her luminous, expressive eyes, immensely sensitive, beautiful in their sensitiveness, showed that she was moved. At last she said:

"Perhaps that is true. Yes, I suppose it is."

"Why do you try to hide it?"

"I suppose—I think because—because it has brought to me a great deal of pain. And what we hide from others we sometimes seem almost to be destroying by that very act, though of course we are not."

"No. But I think I should like to encourage my imagination."

"Do you encourage it?" the mother asked, looking at her closely.

Again, as Vere had been on the edge of telling her mother all she knew about Peppina, she was on the edge of telling her about the poems of the sea. And again, moved by some sudden, obstinate reluctance, come she knew not why, she withheld the words that were almost on her lips.

And each time the mother was aware of something avoided, of an impulse stifled, and therefore of a secret deliberately kept. The first time Hermione had not allowed her knowledge to appear. But on this second occasion for a moment she lost control of herself, and when, after a perceptible pause, Vere said, "I know I love it," and was silent, she exclaimed:

"Keep your secrets, Vere. Every one has a right to their freedom."

"But, Madre—" Vere began, startled by her mother's abrupt vehemence.

"No, Vere, no! My child, my dearest one, never tell me anything but of your own accord, out of your own heart and desire. Such a confidence is beautiful. But anything else—anything else, I could not bear from you."

And she got up and left the room, walking with a strange slowness, as if she put upon herself an embargo not to hasten.

The words and—specially that—the way in which they were spoken made Vere suddenly and completely aware of something that perhaps she had already latently known—that the relation between her mother and herself had, of late, not been quite what once it was. At moments she had felt almost shy of her mother, only at moments. Formerly she had always told her mother everything, and had spoken—as her mother had just said—out of her own heart and desire, with eagerness, inevitably. Now—well, now she could not always do that. Was it because she was growing older? Children are immensely frank. She had been a child. But now —she thought of the Marchesino, of Peppina, of her conversation with Monsieur Emile in the Grotto of Virgilio, and she realized the blooming of her girlhood, was aware that she was changing. And she felt half frightened, then eager, ardently eager. An impulse filled her, the impulse towards a fulness of life that, till now, she had not known. And for a moment she loved those little, innocent secrets that she kept.

But then she thought again of her mother, the most beloved of all her world. There had been in her mother's voice a sound of tragedy.

Vere stood for a long while by the window thinking.

The day was very hot. She longed to bathe, to wash away certain perplexities that troubled her in the sea. But Gaspare was not on the island. He had gone she knew not where. She looked at the sea with longing. When would Gaspare be back? Well, at least she could go out in the small boat. Then she would be near to the water. She ran down the steps and embarked. At first she only rowed a little way out into the Saint's Pool, and then leaned back against the white cushions, and looked up at the blue sky, and let her hand trail in the water. But she was restless today. The Pool did not suffice her, and she began to paddle out along the coast towards Naples. She passed a ruined, windowless house named by the fisherfolk "The Palace of the Spirits," and then a tiny hamlet climbing up from a minute harbor to an antique church. Children called to her. A fisherman shouted: "Buon viaggio, Signorina!" She waved her hand to them apathetically and rowed slowly on. Now she had a bourne. A little farther on there was a small inlet of the sea containing two caves, not gloomy and imposing like the Grotto of Virgilio, but cosey, shady, and serene. Into the first of them she ran the boat until its prow touched the sandy bottom. Then she lay down at full length, with her hands behind her head on the cushions, and thought—and thought.

Figures passed through her mind, a caravan of figures travelling as all are travelling: her mother, Gaspare, Giulia, with her plump and swarthy face; Monsieur Emile, to whom she had drawn so pleasantly, interestingly near in these last days; the Marchesino (strutting from the hips and making his bold eyes round), Peppina, Ruffo. They went by and returned, gathered about her, separated, melted away as people do in our musings. Her eyes were fixed on the low roof of the cave. The lilt of the water seemed to rock her soul in a cradle. "Madre —Ruffo! Madre—Ruffo!" The words were in her mind like a refrain. And then the oddity, the promiscuity of life struck her. How many differences there were in this small group of people by whom she was surrounded! What would their fates be, and hers? Would her life be happy? She did not feel afraid. Youth ran in her veins. But—would it be? She saw the red cross on Peppina's cheek. Why was one singled out for misery, another for joy? Which would be her fate? Ruffo seemed to be standing near her. She had seen him several times in these last days, but only at evening, fugitively, when he came in the boat with the fishermen. He was stronger now. He had saluted her eagerly. She had spoken to him from the shore. But he had not landed again on the island. She felt as if she saw his bright and beaming eyes. And Ruffo—would he be happy? She hoped so. She wanted him to be happy. He was such a dear, active, bold boy—such a real boy. What must it be like to have a brother? Gaspare approved of Ruffo now, she thought; and Gaspare did not like everybody, and was fearfully blunt in expressing his opinion. She loved his bluntness. How delightfully his nose twitched when he was pleased! Dear old Gaspare! She could never feel afraid of anything or anybody when he was near. Monsieur Emile —the poems—the Marchesino singing. She closed her eyes to think the better.

"Signorina! Signorina!"

Vere woke and sat up.

"Signorina!"

Gaspare was looking at her from his boat.

"Gaspare!"

She began to realize things.

"I was—I was thinking."

"Sì, Signorina. I always think like that when I am in bed."

She laughed. She was wide awake now.

"How did you find me?"

"I met one of the fishermen. He had seen you row into the cave."

"Oh!"

She looked at him more steadily. His brown face was hot. Perspiration stood on his forehead just under the thick and waving hair.

"Where have you been, Gaspare? Not to Naples in all this heat?"

"I have been to Mergellina, Signorina."

"Mergellina! Did you see Ruffo?"

"Sì, Signorina."

There was something very odd about Gaspare to-day, Vere thought. Or was she still not thoroughly awake? His eyes looked excited, surely, as if something unusual had been happening. And they were fixed upon her face with a scrutiny that was strange, almost as if he saw her now for the first time.

"What is it, Gaspare? Why do you look at me like that?"

Gaspare turned his eyes away.

"Like what, Signorina? Why should I not look at you?"

"What have you been doing at Mergellina?"

She spoke rather imperiously.

"Nothing particular, Signorina."

"Oh!"

She paused, but he did not speak.

"Where did you see Ruffo?"

"At the harbor, Signorina."

"Tell me, Gaspare, do you like him?"

"Ruffo?"

"Yes."

"I do not dislike him, Signorina. He has never done me any harm."

"Of course not. Why should he?"

"I say—he has not."

"I like Ruffo."

"Lo so."

Again he looked at her with that curious expression in his eyes. Then he said:

"Come, Signorina! It is getting late. We must go to the island."

And they pulled out round the point to the open sea.

During the hot weather the dwellers in the Casa del Mare made the siesta after the mid-day meal. The awnings and blinds were drawn. Silence reigned, and the house was still as the Palace of the Sleeping Beauty. At the foot of the cliffs the sea slept in the sunshine, and it was almost an empty sea, for few boats passed by in those hot, still hours.

To-day the servants were quiet in their quarters. Only Gaspare was outside. And he, in shirt and trousers, with a white linen hat covering his brown face, was stretched under the dwarf trees of the little garden, in the shadow of the wall, resting profoundly after the labors of the morning. In their respective rooms Hermione and Vere were secluded behind shut doors. Hermione was lying down, but not sleeping. Vere was not lying down. Generally she slept at this time for an hour. But to-day, perhaps because of her nap in the cave, she had no desire for sleep.

She was thinking about her mother. And Hermione was thinking of her. Each mind was working in the midst of its desert space, its solitude eternal.

What was growing up between them, and why was it growing?

Hermione was beset by a strange sensation of impotence. She felt as if her child were drifting from her. Was it her fault, or was it no one's, and inevitable? Had Vere been able to divine certain feelings in her, the mother, obscure pains of the soul that had travelled to mind and heart? She did not think it possible. Nor had it been possible for her to kill those pains, although she had made her effort—to conceal them. Long ago, before she was married to Maurice, Emile had spoken to them of jealousy. At the time she had not understood it. She remembered thinking, even saying, that she could not be jealous.

But then she had not had a child.

Lately she had realized that there were forces in her of which she had not been aware. She had realized her passion for her child. Was it strange that she had not always known how deep and strong it was? Her mutilated life was more vehemently centred upon Vere than she had understood. Of Vere she could be jealous. If Vere put any one before her, trusted any one more than her, confided anything to another rather than to her, she could be frightfully jealous.

Recently she had suspected—she had imagined—

Restlessly she moved on her bed. A mosquito-curtain protected it. She was glad of that, as if it kept out prying eyes. For sometimes she was ashamed of the vehemence within her.

She thought of her friend Emile, whom she had dragged back from death.

He, too, had he not drifted a little from her in these last days? It seemed to her that it was so. She knew that it was so. Women are so sure of certain things, more almost than men are ever sure of anything. And why should Vere have drifted, Emile have drifted, if there were not some link between them—some link between the child and the middle-aged man which they would not have her know of?

Vere had told to Emile something that she had kept, that she still kept from her mother. When Vere had been shut up in her room she had not been reading. Emile knew what it was that she did during those long hours when she was alone. Emile knew that, and perhaps other things of Vere that she, Hermione, did not know, was not allowed to know.

Hermione, in their long intimacy, had learned to read Artois more clearly, more certainly than he realized. Although often impulsive, and seemingly unconscious of the thoughts of others, she could be both sharply observant and subtle, especially with those she loved. She had noticed the difference between his manner when first they spoke of Vere's hidden occupation and his manner when last they spoke of it. In the interval he had found out what it was, and that it was not reading. Of that she was positive. She was positive also that he did not wish her to suspect this. Vere must have told him what it was.

It was characteristic of Hermione that at this moment she was free from any common curiosity as to what it was that Vere did during those many hours when she was shut up in her room. The thing that hurt her, that seemed to humiliate her, was that Emile should know what it was and not she, that Vere should have told Emile and not told her.

As she lay there she cowered under the blow a mutual silence can give, and something woke up in her, something fiery, something surely that could act with violence. It startled her, almost as a stranger rushing into her room would have startled her.

For a moment she thought of her child and her loved friend with a bitterness that was cruel.

How long had they shared their secret? She wondered, and began to consider the recent days, searching their hours for those tiny incidents, those small reticences, avoidances, that to women are revelations. When had she first noticed a slight change in Emile's manner to her? When had Vere and he first seemed a little more intimate, a little more confidential than before? When had she, Hermione, first felt a little "out of it," not perfectly at ease with these two dear denizens of her life?

Her mind fastened at once upon the day of the storm. On the night of the storm, when she and Emile had been left alone in the restaurant, she had felt almost afraid of him. But before then, in the afternoon on the island, there had been something. They had not been always at ease. She had been conscious of trying to tide over moments that were almost awkward—once or twice, only once or twice. But that was the day. Her woman's instinct told her so. That was the day on which Vere had told Emile the secret she had kept from her mother. How excited Vere had been, almost feverishly excited! And Emile had been very strange. When the Marchesino and Vere went out upon the terrace, how restless, how irritable he—

Suddenly Hermione sat up in her bed. The heat, the stillness, the white cage of the mosquito-net, the silence had become intolerable to her. She pulled aside the net. Yes, that was better. She felt more free. She would lie down outside the net. But the pillow was hot. She turned it, but its pressure against her cheek almost maddened her, and she got up, went across the room to the wash-hand stand and bathed her face with cold water. Then she put some *eau de Cologne* on her forehead, opened a drawer and drew out a fan, went over to an arm-chair near the window and sat down in it.

What had Emile written in the visitors' book at the Scoglio di Frisio? With a strange abruptness, with a flight that was instinctive as that of a homing pigeon, Hermione's mind went to that book as to a book of revelation. Just before he wrote he had been feeling acutely—something. She had been aware of that at the time. He had not wanted to write. And then suddenly, almost violently, he had written and had closed the book.

She longed to open that book now, at once, to read what he had written. She felt as if it would tell her very much. There was no reason why she should not read it. The book was one that all might see, was kept to be looked over by any chance visitor. She would go one day, one evening, to the restaurant and see what Emile had written. He would not mind. If she had asked him that night of course he would have shown her the words. But she had not asked him. She had been almost afraid of things that night. She remembered how the wind had blown up the white table-cloth, her cold, momentary shiver of fear, her relief when she had seen Gaspare walking sturdily into the room.

And now, at once, this thought of Gaspare brought to her a sense of relief again, of relief so great, so sharp—piercing down into the very deep of her nature—that by it she was able to measure something, her inward

258

desolation at this moment. Yes, she clung to Gaspare, because he was loyal, because he loved her, because he had loved Maurice—but also because she was terribly alone.

Because he had loved Maurice! Had there been a time, really a time, when she had possessed one who belonged utterly to her, who lived only in and for her? Was that possible? To-day, with a fierceness of one starving, she fastened upon this memory, her memory, hers only, shared by no one, never shared by living or dead. That at least she had, and that could never be taken from her. Even if Vere, her child, slipped from her, if Emile, her friend, whose life she had saved, slipped from her, the memory of her Sicilian was forever hers, the memory of his love, his joy in their mutual life, his last kiss. Long ago she had taken that kiss as a gift made to two—to her and to Vere unborn. To-day, almost savagely, she took it to herself, alone, herself—alone. Hers it was, hers only, no part of it Vere's.

That she had — her memory, and Gaspare's loyal, open-hearted devotion. He knew what she had suffered. He loved her as he had loved his dead Padrone. He would always protect her, put her first without hesitation, conceal nothing from her that it was her right—for surely even the humblest, the least selfish, the least grasping, surely all who love have their rights—that it was her right to know.

Her cheeks were burning. She felt like one who had been making some physical exertion.

Deeply silent was the house. Her room was full of shadows, yet full of the hidden presence of the sun. There was a glory outside, against which she was protected. But inside, and against assaults that were inglorious, what protection had she? Her own personality must protect her, her own will, the determination, the strength, the courage that belong to all who are worth

anything in the world. And she called upon herself.
And it seemed to her that there was no voice that answered.

There was a hideous moment of drama.

She sat there quietly in her chair in the pretty room.
And she called again, and she listened—and again there
was silence.

Then she was afraid. She had a strange and horrible
feeling that she was deserted by herself, by that which,
at least, had been herself and on which she had been
accustomed to rely. And what was left was surely utterly incapable, full of the flabby wickedness that seems
to dwell in weakness. It seemed to her that if any one
who knew her well, if Vere, Emile, or even Gaspare, had
come into the room just then, the intruder would have
paused on the threshold amazed to see a stranger there.
She felt afraid to be seen and yet afraid to remain alone.
Should she do something definite, something defiant, to
prove to herself that she had will and could exercise it?

She got up, resolved to go to Vere. When she was
there, with her child, she did not know what she was
going to do. She had said to Vere, "Keep your secrets."
What if she went now and humbled herself, explained to
the child quite simply and frankly a mother's jealousy,
a widow's loneliness, made her realize what she was in
a life from which the greatest thing had been ruthlessly
withdrawn? Vere would understand surely, and all
would be well. This shadow between them would pass
away. Hermione had her hand on the door. But she
did not open it. An imperious reserve, autocrat, tyrant,
rose up suddenly within her. She could never make
such a confession to Vere. She could never plead for
her child's confidence—a confidence already given to
Emile, to a man. And now for the first time the common curiosity to which she had not yet fallen a victim
came upon her, flooded her. What was Vere's secret?

A SPIRIT IN PRISON

That it was innocent, probably even childish, Hermione did not question even for a moment. But what was it?

She heard a light step outside and drew back from the door. The step passed on and died away down the paved staircase. Vere had gone out to the terrace, the garden, or the sea.

Hermione again moved forward, then stopped abruptly. Her face was suddenly flooded with red as she realized what she had been going to do, she who had exclaimed that every one has a right to their freedom.

For an instant she had meant to go to Vere's room, to try to find out surreptitiously what Emile knew.

A moment later Vere, coming back swiftly for a pencil she had forgotten, heard the sharp grating of a key in the lock of her mother's door.

She ran on lightly, wondering why her mother was locking herself in, and against whom.

CHAPTER XVIII

DURING the last days Artois had not been to the island,
nor had he seen the Marchesino. A sudden passion for
work had seized him. Since the night of Vere's meeting
with Peppina his brain had been in flood with thoughts.
Life often acts subtly upon the creative artist, repres-
sing or encouraging his instinct to bring forth, depres-
sing or exciting him when, perhaps, he expects it least.
The passing incidents of life frequently have their hidden, their unsuspected part in determining his activities.
So it was now with Artois. He had given an impetus
to Vere. That was natural, to be expected, considering
his knowledge and his fame, his great experience and
his understanding of men. But now Vere had given an
impetus to him—and that was surely stranger. Since
the conversation among the shadows of the cave, after
the vision of the moving men of darkness and of fire,
since the sound of Peppina sobbing in the night, and the
sight of her passionate face lifted to show its gashed
cross to Vere, Artois' brain and heart had been alive with
a fury of energy that forcibly summoned him to work,
that held him working. He even felt within him something that was like a renewal of some part of his vanished
youth, and remembered old days of student life, nights
in the Quartier Latin, his début as a writer for the papers, the sensation of joy with which he saw his first
article in the *Figaro*, his dreams of fame, his hopes of
love, his baptism of sentiment. How he had worked in
those days and nights! How he had hunted experience

in the streets and the by-ways of the great city! How passionate and yet how ruthless he had been, as artists often are, governed not only by their quick emotions, but also by the something watchful and dogged underneath, that will not be swept away, that is like a detective hidden by a house door to spy out all the comers in the night. Something, some breath from the former days, swept over him again. In his ears there sounded surely the cries of Paris, urging him to the assault of the barricades of Fame. And he sat down, and he worked with the vehement energy, with the pulsating eagerness of one of "les jeunes." Hour after hour he worked. He took coffee, and wrote through the night. He slept when the dawn came, got up, and toiled again.

He shut out the real world and he forgot it—until the fit was past. And then he pushed away his paper, he laid down his pen, he stretched himself, and he knew that his great effort had tired him tremendously—tremendously.

He looked at his right hand. It was cramped. As he held it up he saw that it was shaking. He had drunk a great deal of black coffee during those days, had drunk it recklessly as in the days of youth, when he cared nothing about health because he felt made of iron.

"Pf-f-f!"

And so there was Naples outside, the waters of the Bay dancing in the sunshine of the bright summer afternoon; people bathing and shouting to one another from the diving platforms and the cabins; people galloping by in the little carriages to eat oysters at Posilipo. Lazy, heedless, pleasure-loving wretches! He thought of Doro as he looked at them.

He had given strict orders that he was not to be disturbed while he was at work, unless Hermione came. And he had not once been disturbed. Now he rang the bell. An Italian waiter, with crooked eyes and a fair beard, stepped softly in.

A SPIRIT IN PRISON

"Has any one been to see me? Has any one asked for me lately?" he said. "Just go down, will you, and inquire of the concierge."

The waiter departed, and returned to say that no one had been for the Signore.

"Not the Marchese Isidoro Panacci?"

"The concierge says that no one has been, Signore."

"Va bene."

The man went out.

So Doro had not come even once! Perhaps he was seriously offended. At their last parting in the Villa he had shown a certain irony that had in it a hint of bitterness. Artois did not know of the fisherman's information, that Doro had guessed who was Vere's companion that night upon the sea. He supposed that his friend was angry because he believed himself distrusted. Well, that could soon be put right. He thought of the Marchesino now with lightness, as the worker who has just made a great and prolonged effort is inclined to think of the habitual idler. Doro was like a feather on the warm wind of the South. He, Artois, was not in the mood just then to bother about a feather. Still less was he inclined for companionship. He wanted some hours of complete rest out in the air, with gay and frivolous scenes before his eyes.

He wanted to look on, but not to join in, the merry life that was about him, and that for so long a time he had almost violently ignored.

He resolved to take a carriage, drive slowly to Posilipo, and eat his dinner there in some eyrie above the sea; watching the pageant that unfolds itself on the evenings of summer about the ristoranti and the osterie, round the stalls of the vendors of Frutti di Mare, and the piano-organs, to the accompaniment of which impudent men sing love songs to the saucy, dark-eyed beauties posed upon balconies, or gathered in knots upon the little terraces that dominate the bathing establishments, and the distant traffic of the Bay. His brain longed for rest, but it longed also for the hum and the stir of men. His heart lusted for the sight of pleasure, and must be appeased.

Catching up his hat, almost with the hasty eagerness of a boy, he went down-stairs. On the opposite side of the road was a smart little carriage in which the coachman was asleep, with his legs cocked up on the driver's seat, displaying a pair of startling orange-and-black socks. By the socks Artois knew his man.

"Pasqualino! Pasqualino!" he cried.

The coachman sprang up, showing a round, rosy face, and a pair of shrewd, rather small dark eyes.

"Take me to Posilipo."

"Sì, Signore."

Pasqualino cracked his whip vigorously.

"Ah—ah! Ah—ah!" he cried to his gayly bedizened little horse, who wore a long feather on his head, flanked by bunches of artificial roses.

"Not too fast, Pasqualino. I am in no hurry. Keep along by the sea."

The coachman let the reins go loose, and instantly the little horse went slowly, as if all his spirit and agility had suddenly been withdrawn from him.

"I have not seen you for several days, Signore. Have you been ill?"

Pasqualino had turned quite round on his box, and was facing his client.

"No, I've been working."

"Sì?"

Pasqualino made a grimace, as he nearly always did when he heard a rich Signore speak of working.

"And you? You have been spending money as usual. All your clothes are new."

Pasqualino smiled, showing rows of splendid teeth under his little twisted-up mustache.

"Sì, Signore, all! And I have also new underclothing."

"Per Bacco!"

"Ecco, Signore!"

He pulled his trousers up to his knees, showing a pair of pale-blue drawers.

"The suspenders—they are new, Signore!" He drew attention to the scarlet elastics that kept the orange-and-black socks in place. "My boots!" He put his feet up on the box that Artois might see his lemon-colored boots, then unbuttoned and threw open his waistcoat. "My shirt is new! My cravat is new! Look at the pin!" He flourished his plump, brown, and carefully washed hands. "I have a new ring." He bent his head. "My hat is new."

Artois broke into a roar of laughter that seemed to do him good after his days of work.

"You young dandy! And where do you get the money?"

Pasqualino looked doleful and hung his head.

"Signore, I am in debt. But I say to myself, 'Thank the Madonna, I have a rich and generous Padrone who wishes his coachman to be chic. When he sees my clothes he will be contented, and—who knows what he will do?'"

"Per Bacco! And who is this rich and generous Signore?"

"Ma!" Pasqualino passionately flung out the ringed hand that was not holding the reins—"Ma!—you, Signore."

"You young rascal! Turn round and attend to your driving!"

But Artois laughed again. The impudent boyishness of Pasqualino, and his childish passion for finery, were

refreshing, and seemed to belong to a young and thoughtless world. The sea-breeze was soft as silk, the afternoon sunshine was delicately brilliant. The Bay looked
as it often does in summer—like radiant liberty held in
happy arms, alluring, full of promises. And a physical
well-being invaded Artois such as he had not known
since the day when he had tea with Vere upon the island.

He had been shut in. Now the gates were thrown
open, and to what a brilliant world! He issued forth
into it with almost joyous expectation.

They went slowly, and presently drew near to the
Rotonda. Artois leaned a little forward and saw that
the fishermen were at work. They stood in lines upon
the pavement pulling at the immense nets which were
still a long way out at sea. When the carriage reached
them Artois told Pasqualino to draw up, and sat watching the work and the fierce energy of the workers. Half
naked, with arms and legs and chests that gleamed in
the sun like copper, they toiled, slanting backward,
one towards another, laughing, shouting, swearing with
a sort of almost angry joy. In their eyes there was a
carelessness that was wild, in their gestures a lack of
self-consciousness that was savage. But they looked
like creatures who must live forever. And to Artois,
sedentary for so long, the sight of them brought a feeling almost of triumph, but also a sensation of envy.
Their vigor made him pine for movement.

"Drive on slowly, Pasqualino," he said. "I will follow you on foot, and join you at the hill."

"Sì Signore."

He got out, stood for a moment, then strolled on towards the Mergellina. As he approached this part of the
town, with its harbor and its population of fisherfolk,
the thought of Ruffo came into his mind. He remembered that Ruffo lived here. Perhaps he might see the
boy this afternoon.

A SPIRIT IN PRISON

On the mole that serves as a slight barrier between the open sea and the snug little harbor several boys were fishing. Others were bathing, leaping into the water with shouts from the rocks. Beyond, upon the slope of dingy sand among the drawn-up boats, children were playing, the girls generally separated from the boys. Fishermen, in woollen shirts and white linen trousers, sat smoking in the shadow of their craft, or leaned muscular arms upon them, standing at ease, staring into vacancy or calling to each other. On the still water there was a perpetual movement of boats; and from the distance came a dull but continuous uproar, the yells and the laughter of hundreds of bathers at the Stabilimento di Bagni beyond the opposite limit of the harbor.

Artois enjoyed the open-air gayety, the freedom of the scene; and once again, as often before, found himself thinking that the out-door life, the life loosed from formal restrictions, was the only one really and fully worth living. There was a carelessness, a camaraderie among these people that was of the essence of humanity. Despite their frequent quarrels, their intrigues, their betrayals, their vendettas, they hung together. There was a true and vital companionship among them.

He passed on with deliberation, observing closely, yet half-lazily—for his brain was slack and needed rest— the different types about him, musing on the possibilities of their lives, smiling at the gambols of the intent girls, and the impudent frolics of the little boys who seemed the very spawn of sand and sea and sun, till he had nearly passed the harbor, and was opposite to the pathway that leads down to the jetty, to the left of which lie the steam-yachts.

At the entrance to this pathway there is always a knot of people gathered about the shanty where the seamen eat maccaroni and strange messes, and the

268

stands where shell-fish are exposed for sale. On the far side of the tramway, beneath the tall houses which are let out in rooms and apartments for families, there is an open space, and here in summer are set out quantities of strong tables, at which from noon till late into the evening the people of Mergellina, and visitors of the humbler classes from Naples, sit in merry throngs, eating, smoking, drinking coffee, syrups, and red and white wine.

Artois stood still for a minute to watch them, to partake from a distance, and unknown to them, in their boisterous gayety. He had lit a big cigar, and puffed at it as his eyes roved from group to group, resting now on a family party, now on a quartet of lovers, now on two stout men obviously trying to drive a bargain with vigorous rhetoric and emphatic gestures, now on an elderly woman in a shawl spending an hour with her soldier son in placid silence, now on some sailors from a ship in the distant port by the arsenal bent over a game of cards, or a party of workmen talking wages or politics in their shirt-sleeves with flowers above their ears.

What a row they made, these people! Their animation was almost like the animation of a nightmare. Some were ugly, some looked wicked; others mischievous, sympathetic, coarse, artful, seductive, boldly defiant or boisterously excited. But however much they differed, in one quality they were nearly all alike. They nearly all looked vivid. If they lacked anything, at least it was not life. Even their sorrows should be energetic.

As this thought came into his mind Artois' eyes chanced to rest on two people sitting a little apart at a table on which stood a coffee-cup, a thick glass half full of red wine, and a couple of tumblers of water. One was a woman, the other—yes, the other was Ruffo.

A SPIRIT IN PRISON

When Artois realized this he kept his eyes upon them.
He forgot his interest in the crowd.

At first he could only see Ruffo's side-face. But the
woman was exactly opposite to him.

She was neatly dressed in some dark stuff, and wore
a thin shawl, purple in color, over her shoulders. She
looked middle-aged. Had she been an Englishwoman
Artois would have guessed her to be near fifty. But
as she was evidently a Southerner it was possible that
she was very much younger. Her figure was broad and
matronly. Her face, once probably quite pretty, was
lined, and had the battered and almost corrugated look
that the faces of Italian women of the lower classes
often reveal when the years begin to increase upon them.
The cheek-bones showed harshly in it, by the long and
dark eyes, which were surrounded by little puckers of
yellow flesh. But Artois' attention was held not by
this woman's quite ordinary appearance, but by her
manner. Like the people about her she was vivacious,
but her vivacity was tragic—she had not come here to
be gay. Evidently she was in the excitement of some
great grief or passion. She was speaking vehemently
to Ruffo, gesticulating with her dark hands, on which
there were two or three cheap rings, catching at her
shawl, swaying her body, nodding her head, on which
the still black hair was piled in heavy masses. And
her face was distorted by an emotion that seemed of
sorrow and anger mingled. In her ears, pretty and almost delicate in contrast to the ruggedness of her face,
were large gold rings, such as Sicilian women often wear.
They swayed in response to her perpetual movements.
Artois watched her lips as they opened and shut, were
compressed or thrust forward, watched her white teeth
gleaming. She lifted her two hands, doubled into fists,
till they were on a level with her shoulders, shook them
vehemently, then dashed them down on the table. The

coffee-cup was overturned. She took no notice of it. She was heedless of everything but the subject which evidently obsessed her.

The boy, Ruffo, sat quite still listening to her. His attitude was calm. Now and then he sipped his wine, and presently he took from his pocket a cigarette, lighted it carefully, and began to smoke. There was something very boyish and happy-go-lucky in his attitude and manner. Evidently, Artois thought, he was very much at home with this middle-aged woman. Probably her vehemence was to him an every-day affair. She laid one hand on his arm and bent forward. He slightly shrugged his shoulders and shook his head. She kept her hand on his arm, went on talking passionately, and suddenly began to weep. Tears rushed out of her eyes. Then the boy took her hand gently, stroked it, and began to speak to her, always keeping her hand in his. The woman, with a despairing movement, laid her face down on the table, with her forehead touching the wood. Then she lifted it up. The paroxysm seemed to have passed. She took out a handkerchief from inside the bodice of her dress and dried her eyes. Ruffo struck the table with his glass. An attendant came. He paid the bill, and the woman and he got up to go. As they did so Ruffo presented for a moment his full face to Artois, and Artois swiftly compared it with the face of the woman, and felt sure that they were mother and son.

Artois moved on towards the hill of Posilipo, but after taking a few steps turned to look back. The woman and Ruffo had come into the road by the tram-line. They stood there for a moment, talking. Then Ruffo crossed over to the path, and the woman went away slowly towards the Rotonda. Seeing Ruffo alone Artois turned to go back, thinking to have a word with the boy. But before he could reach him he saw a man

step out from behind the wooden shanty of the fishermen and join him.

This man was Gaspare.

Ruffo and Gaspare strolled slowly away towards the
jetty where the yachts lie, and presently disappeared.

Artois found Pasqualino waiting for him rather impatiently not far from the entrance to the Scoglio di
Frisio.

"I thought you were dead, Signore," he remarked, as
Artois came up.

"I was watching the people."

He got into the carriage.

"They are canaglia," said Pasqualino, with the profound contempt of the Neapolitan coachman for those
who get their living by the sea. He lived at Fuorigrotta, and thought Mergellina a place of outer darkness.

"I like them," returned Artois.

"You don't know them, Signore. I say—they are
canaglia. Where shall I drive you?"

Artois hesitated, passing in mental review the various
ristoranti on the hill.

"Take me to the Ristorante della Stella," he said, at
length.

Pasqualino cracked his whip, and drove once more
merrily onward.

When Artois came to the ristorante, which is perched
high up on the side of the road farthest from the sea,
he had almost all the tables to choose from, as it was
still early in the evening, and in summer the Neapolitans
who frequent the more expensive restaurants usually
dine late. He sat down at a table in the open air close
to the railing, from which he could see a grand view of
the Bay, as well as all that was passing on the road
beneath, and ordered a dinner to be ready in half an
hour. He was in no hurry, and wanted to finish his cigar.

There was a constant traffic below. The tram - bell

sounded its reiterated signal to the crowds of dusty
pedestrians to clear the way. Donkeys toiled upward,
drawing carts loaded with vegetables and fruit. Animated young men, wearing tiny straw hats cocked impertinently to one side, drove frantically by in light gigs
that looked like the skeletons of carriages, holding a
rein in each hand, pulling violently at their horses'
mouths, and shouting "Ah—ah!" as if possessed of the
devil. Smart women made the evening "Passeggiata"
in landaus and low victorias, wearing flamboyant hats,
and gazing into the eyes of the watching men ranged
along the low wall on the sea-side with a cool steadiness
that was almost Oriental. Some of them were talking.
But by far the greater number leaned back almost immobile against their cushions; and their pale faces
showed nothing but the languid consciousness of being observed and, perhaps, desired. Stout Neapolitan
fathers, with bulging eyes, immense brown cheeks, and
peppery mustaches, were promenading with their children and little dogs, looking lavishly contented with
themselves. Young girls went primly past, holding
their narrow, well-dressed heads with a certain virginal
stiffness that was yet not devoid of grace, and casting
down eyes that were supposed not yet to be enlightened.
Their governesses and duennas accompanied them.
Barefooted brown children darted in and out, dodging
pedestrians and horses. Priests and black-robed students chattered vivaciously. School-boys with peaked
caps hastened homeward. The orphans from Queen
Margherita's Home, higher up the hill, marched sturdily
through the dust to the sound of a boyish but desperately
martial music. It was a wonderfully vivid world, but the
eyes of Artois wandered away from it, over the terraces,
the houses, and the tree-tops. Their gaze dropped down
to the sea. Far off, Capri rose out of the light mist produced by the heat. And beyond was Sicily.

A SPIRIT IN PRISON

Why had that woman, Ruffo's mother, wept just now?
What was her tragedy? he wondered. Accurately he
recalled her face, broad now, and seamed with the wrinkles
brought by trouble and the years.

He recalled, too, Ruffo's attitude as the boy listened
to her vehement, her almost violent harangue. How
boyish, how careless it had been—yet not unkind or
even disrespectful; only wonderfully natural and wonderfully young.

"He was the deathless boy."

Suddenly those words started into Artois' mind. Had
he read them somewhere? For a moment he wondered. Or had he heard them? They seemed to suggest speech, a voice whose intonations he knew. His
mind was still fatigued by work, and would not be commanded by his will. Keeping his eyes fixed on the
ethereal outline of Capri, he strove to remember, to find
the book which had contained those words and given
them to his eyes, or the voice that had spoken them
and given them to his ears.

"He was the deathless boy."

A piano-organ struck up below him, a little way up
the hill to the right, and above its hard accompaniment
there rose a powerful tenor voice singing:

> "Quanno fa notte 'nterra Mergellina,
>   Se sceta 'o mare e canta chiano chiano
> Se fa chiu doce st 'aria d 'a marina,
>   Pure 'e serene cantano 'a luntano.
>
> "Quanno fa notte 'nterra Mergellina—"

The song must have struck forcibly upon some part of
his brain that was sleeping, must have summoned it to
activity. For instantly, ere the voice had sung the first
verse, he saw imaginatively a mountain top in Sicily,
evening light—such as was then shining over and trans-

figuring Capri—and a woman, Hermione. And he heard
her voice, very soft, with a strange depth and stillness in it, saying those words: "He was the deathless
boy."

Of course! How could he have forgotten? They
had been said of Maurice Delarey. And now idly,
strangely, he had recalled them as he thought of Ruffo's
young and careless attitude by the table of the ristorante
that afternoon.

The waiter, coming presently to bring the French
Signore the plate of oysters from Fusaro, which he had
ordered as the prelude to his dinner, was surprised by
the deep gravity of his face, and said:

"Don't you like 'A Mergellina,' Signore? We are all
mad about it. And it won the first prize at last year's
festa of Piedigrotta."

"Comment donc?" exclaimed Artois, as if startled.
"What?—no—yes. I like it. It's a capital song.
Lemon? That's right—and red pepper. Va bene!"

And he bent over his plate rather hurriedly and began to eat.

The piano-organ and the singing voice died away
down the hill, going towards Mergellina:

> "E custa luna dint' 'essere e state
>   Lo vularria durmi, ma nun e cosa;
> Me scentene d' 'o suonno 'e sti sarate,
>   O' Mare 'e Mergellina e l' uocchie 'e Rosa."

But the effect, curious and surely unreasonable, of
the song remained. Often, while he ate, Artois turned
his eyes towards the mountain of Capri, and each time
that he did so he saw, beyond it and its circling sea,
Sicily, Monte Amato, the dying lights on Etna, the evening star above its plume of smoke, the figure of a woman
set in the shadow of her sorrow, yet almost terribly
serene; and then another woman, sitting at a table,

vehemently talking, then bowing down her head passionately as if in angry grief.

When he had finished his dinner the sun had set, and night had dropped down softly over the Bay. Capri had disappeared. The long serpent of lights had uncoiled itself along the sea. Down below, very far down, there was the twang and the thin, acute whine of guitars and mandolines, the throbbing cry of Southern voices. The stars were out in a deep sky of bloomy purple. There was no chill in the air, but a voluptuous, brooding warmth, that shed over the city and the waters a luxurious benediction, giving absolution, surely, to all the sins, to all the riotous follies of the South.

Artois rested his arms on the balustrade.

The ristorante was nearly full now, gay with lights and with a tempest of talk. The waiter came to ask if the Signore would take coffee.

Artois hesitated a moment, then shook his head. He realized that his nerves had been tried enough in these last days and nights. He must let them rest for a while.

The waiter went away, and he turned once more towards the sea. To-night he felt the wonder of Italy, of this part of the land and of its people, as he had not felt it before, in a new and, as it seemed to him, a mysterious way. A very modern man and, in his art, a realist, to-night there was surely something very young alert within him, something of vague sentimentality that was like an echo from Byronic days. He felt overshadowed, but not unpleasantly, by a dim and exquisite melancholy, in which he thought of nature and of human nature pathetically, linking them together; those singing voices with the stars, the women who leaned on balconies to listen with the sea that was murmuring below them, the fishermen upon that sea with the deep and marvellous sky that watched their labors.

A SPIRIT IN PRISON

In a beautiful and almost magical sadness he too was one with the night, this night in Italy. It held him softly in its arms. A golden sadness streamed from the stars. The voices below expressed it. The fishermen's torches in the Bay, those travelling lights that are as the eyes of the South searching for charmed things in secret places, lifted the sorrows of earth towards the stars, and they were golden too. There was a joy even in the tears wept on such a night as this.

He loved detail. It was, perhaps, his fault to love it too much. But now he realized that the magician, Night, knew better than he what were the qualities of perfection. She had changed Naples into a diaper of jewels sparkling softly in the void. He knew that behind that lacework of jewels there were hotels, gaunt and discolored houses full of poverty, shame, and wickedness, galleries in which men hunted the things that gratify their lusts, alleys infected with disease and filth indescribable. He knew it, but he no longer felt it. The glamour of the magician was upon him. Perhaps behind the stars there were terrors, too. But who, looking upon them, could believe it? Detail might create a picture; its withdrawal let in upon the soul the spirit light of the true magic.

It was a mistake to search too much, to draw too near, to seek always to see clearly.

The Night taught that in Italy, and many things not to be clothed with words.

Reluctantly at last he lifted his arms from the balcony rail and got up to leave the restaurant. He dreaded the bustle of the street. As he came out into it he heard the sharp "Ting! ting!" of a tram-bell higher up the hill, and stepped aside to let the tram go by. Idly he looked at it as it approached. He was still in the vague, the almost sentimental mood that had come upon him with the night. The tram came up level with him and slipped slowly by. There was a number of people in it, but on the last seat one woman sat alone. He saw her clearly as she passed, and recognized Hermione.

She did not see him. She was looking straight before her.

"Ah-ah! Ah-ah!"

A shower of objurgations in the Neapolitan dialect fell upon Artois from the box of a carriage coming up the hill. He jumped back and gained the path. There again he stood still. The sweet and half-melancholy vagueness had quite left him now. The sight of his friend had swept it away. Why was she going to Mergellina at that hour? And why did she look like that?

And he thought of the expression he had seen on her face as the tram slipped by, an expression surely of excitement, but also a furtive expression.

Artois had seen Hermione in all her moods, and hers was a very changeful face. But never before had he seen her look furtive. Nor could he have conceived it possible that she could look so.

Perhaps the lights had deceived him. And he had only seen her for an instant.

But why was she going to Mergellina?

Then suddenly it occurred to him that she might be going to Naples, not to Mergellina at all. He knew no reason why her destination should be Mergellina. He began to walk down the hill rather quickly. Some hundreds of yards below the Ristorante della Stella there is a narrow flight of steps between high walls and houses, which leads eventually down to the sea at a point where there are usually two or three boats waiting for hire. Artois, when he started, had no intention of going to sea that night, but when he reached the steps he paused, and finally turned from the path and began to descend them.

He had realized that he was really in pursuit, and

abruptly relinquished his purpose. Why should he wish to interfere with an intention of Hermione's that night?

He would return to Naples by sea.

As he came in sight of the water there rose up to him in a light tenor voice a melodious cry:

"Barca! Barca!"

He answered the call.

"Barca!"

The sailor who was below came gayly to meet him.

"It is a lovely night for the Signore. I could take the Signore to Sorrento or to Capri to-night."

He held Artois by the right arm, gently assisting him into the broad-bottomed boat.

"I only want to go to Naples."

"To which landing, Signore?"

"The Vittoria. But go quietly and keep near the shore. Go round as near as you can to the Mergellina."

"Va bene, Signore."

They slipped out, with a delicious, liquid sound, upon the moving silence of the sea.

CHAPTER XIX

HERMIONE was not going to Mergellina, but to the Scoglio di Frisio. She had only come out of her room late in the afternoon. During her seclusion there she had once been disturbed by Gaspare, who had come to ask her if she wanted him for anything, and, if not, whether he might go over to Mergellina for the rest of the afternoon to see some friends he had made there. She told him he was free till night, and he went away quickly, after one searching, wide-eyed glance at the face of his Padrona.

When he had gone Hermione told herself that she was glad he was away. If he had been on the island she might have been tempted to take one of the boats, to ask him to row her to the Scoglio that evening. But now, of course, she would not go. It was true that she could easily get a boatman from the village on the mainland near by, but without Gaspare's companionship she would not care to go. So that was settled. She would think no more about it. She had tea with Vere, and strove with all her might to be natural, to show no traces in face or manner of the storm that had swept over her that day. She hoped, she believed that she was successful. But what a hateful, what an unnatural effort that was!

A woman who is not at her ease in her own home with her own girl—where can she be at ease?

It was really the reaction from that effort that sent Hermione from the island that evening. She felt as if

she could not face another meal with Vere just then.
She felt transparent, as if Vere's eyes would be able to
see all that she must hide if they were together in the
evening. And she resolved to go away. She made
some excuse—that she wished for a little change, that
she was fidgety and felt the confinement of the island.

"I think I'll go over to the village," she said, "and
walk up to the road and take the tram."

"Will you, Madre?"

Hermione saw in Vere's eyes that the girl was waiting
for something.

"I'll go by myself, Vere," she said. "I should be bad
company to-day. The black dog is at my heels."

She laughed, and added:

"If I am late in coming back, have dinner without
me."

"Very well, Madre."

Vere waited a moment; then, as if desiring to break
forcibly through the restraint that bound them, put out
her hand to her mother's and said:

"Why don't you go in to Naples and have dinner with
Monsieur Emile? He would cheer you up, and it is
ages since we have seen him."

"Only two or three days. No. I won't disturb
Emile. He may be working."

Vere felt that somehow her eager suggestion had
deepened the constraint. She said no more, and Hermione presently crossed over to the mainland and began
her walk to the road that leads from Naples to Bagnoli.

Where was she going? What was she really about
to do?

Certainly she would not adopt the suggestion of Vere.
Emile was the last person whom she wished to see—by
whom she wished to be seen—just then.

The narrow path turned away from the sea into the
shadow of high banks. She walked very slowly, like

one out for a desultory stroll; a lizard slipped across
the warm earth in front of her, almost touching her foot,
climbed the bank swiftly, and vanished among the dry
leaves with a faint rustle.

She felt quite alone to-day in Italy, and far off, as if
she had no duties, no ties, as if she were one of those
solitary, drifting, middle-aged women who vaguely
haunt the beaten tracks of foreign lands. It was sultry
in this path away from the sea. She was sharply conscious of the change of climate, the inland sensation, the
falling away of the freedom from her, the freedom that
seems to exhale from wave and wind of the wave.

She walked on, meeting no one and still undecided
what to do. The thought of the Scoglio di Frisio returned to her mind, was dismissed, returned again. She
might go and dine there quietly alone. Was she deceiving herself, and had she really made up her mind to
go to the Scoglio before she left the island? No, she had
come away mainly because she felt the need of solitude,
the difficulty of being with Vere just for this one night.
To-morrow it would be different. It should be different
to-morrow.

She saw a row of houses in the distance, houses of poor
people, and knew that she was nearing the road. Clothes
were hanging to dry. Children were playing at the edge
of a vineyard. Women were washing linen, men sitting
on the doorsteps mending *nasse*. As she went by she
nodded to them, and bade them "Buona sera." They
answered courteously, some with smiling faces, others
with grave and searching looks—or so she thought.

The tunnel that runs beneath the road at the point
where this path joins it came in sight. And still Hermione did not know what she was going to do. As she
entered the tunnel she heard above her head the rumble
of a tram going towards Naples. This decided her. She
hurried on, turned to the right, and came out on the

highway before the little lonely ristorante that is set here to command the view of vineyards and of sea.

The tram was already gliding away at some distance down the road.

A solitary waiter came forward in his unsuitable black into the dust to sympathize with the Signora, and to suggest that she should take a seat and drink some lemon water, or gazzosa, while waiting for the next tram. Or would not the Signora dine in the upper room and watch the *tramontare del sole*. It would be splendid this evening. And he could promise her an excellent risotto, sardines with pomidoro, and a bifteck such as certainly she could not get in the restaurants of Naples.

"Very well," Hermione answered, quickly, "I will dine here, but not directly—in half an hour or three-quarters."

What Artois was doing at the Ristorante della Stella she was doing at the Trattoria del Giardinetto.

She would dine quietly here, and then walk back to the sea in the cool of the evening.

That was her decision. Yet when the evening fell, and her bill was paid, she took the tram that was going down to Naples, and passed presently before the eyes of Artois. The coming of darkness had revived within her much of the mood of the afternoon. She felt that she could not go home without doing something definite, and she resolved to go to the Scoglio di Frisio, have a cup of coffee there, look through the visitors' book, and then take a boat and return by night to the island. The sea wind would cool her, would do her good.

Nothing told her when the eyes of her friend were for an instant fixed upon her, when the mind of her friend for a moment wondered at the strange, new look in her face. She left the tram presently at the doorway above which is Frisio's name, descended to the little terrace from which Vere had run in laughing with the Marchesino, and stood there for a moment hesitating.

A SPIRIT IN PRISON

The long restaurant was lit up, and from it came the sound of music—guitars, and a voice singing. She recognized the throaty tenor of the blind man raised in a spurious and sickly rapture:

"Sa-anta-a Lu-u-ci-ia! Santa Luci—a!"

It recalled her sharply to the night of the storm. For a moment she felt again the strange, the unreasonable sense of fear, indefinable but harsh, which had come upon her then, as fear comes suddenly sometimes upon a child.

Then she stepped into the restaurant.

As on the other night, there were but few people dining there, and they were away at the far end of the big room. Near them stood the musicians under a light— seedy, depressed; except the blind man, who lifted his big head, rolled his tongue, and swelled and grew scarlet in an effort to be impressive.

Hermione sat down at the first table.

For a moment no one saw her. She heard men s voices talking loudly and gayly, the clatter of plates, the clink of knives and forks. She looked round for the visitors' book. If it were lying near she thought she would open it, search for what Emile had written, and then slip away at once unobserved.

There was a furtive spirit within her to-night.

But she could not see the book; so she sat still, listening to the blind man and gazing at the calm sea just below her. A boat was waiting there. She could see the cushions, which were white and looked ghastly in the darkness, the dim form of the rower standing up to search for clients.

"Barca! Barca!"

He had seen her.

She drew back a little. As she did so her chair made a grating noise, and instantly the sharp ears of the

A SPIRIT IN PRISON

Padrone caught a sound betokening the presence of a new-comer in his restaurant. It might be a queen, an empress! Who could tell?

With his stiff yet alert military gait, he at once came marching down towards her, staring hard with his big, bright eyes. When he saw who it was he threw up his brown hands.

"The Signora of the storm!" he exclaimed. He moved as if about to turn around. "I must tell—"

But Hermione stopped him with a quick, decisive gesture.

"One moment, Signore."

The Padrone approached aristocratically.

"The Marchese Isidoro Panacci is here dining with friends, the Duca di—"

"Yes, yes. But I am only here for a moment, so it is not worth while to tell the Marchese."

"You are not going to dine, Signora! The food of Frisio does not please you!"

He cast up his eyes in deep distress.

"Indeed it does. But I have dined. What I want is a cup of coffee, and—and a liqueur—une fine. And may I look over your wonderful visitors' book? To tell the truth, that is what I have come for, to see the marvellous book. I hadn't enough time the other night. May I?"

The Padrone was appeased. He smiled graciously and turned upon his. heels.

"At once, Signora."

"And—not a word to the Marchese! He is with friends. I would rather not disturb him."

The Padrone threw up his chin and clicked his tongue against his teeth. A shrewd, though not at all impudent, expression had come into his face. A Signora alone, at night, in a restaurant! He was a man of the great world. He understood. What a mercy it was to be "educato"!

A SPIRIT IN PRISON

He came back again almost directly, bearing the book as a sacristan might bear a black-letter Bible.

"Ecco, Signora."

With a superb gesture he placed it before her.

"The coffee, the fine. Attendez, Signora, pour un petit momento."

He stood to see the effect of his French upon her. She forced into her face a look of pious admiration, and he at once departed. Hermione opened the book rather furtively. She had the unpleasant sensation of doing a surreptitious action, and she was an almost abnormally straightforward woman by nature. The book was large, and contained an immense number of inscriptions and signatures in handwritings that varied as strangely as do the characters of men. She turned the leaves hastily. Where had Emile written? Not at the end of the book. She remembered that his signature had been followed by others, although she had not seen, or tried to see, what he had written. Perhaps his name was near Tolstoy's. They had read together Tolstoy's *Vedi Napoli e poi Mori*.

But where was Tolstoy's name?

A waiter came with the coffee and the brandy. She thanked him quickly, sipped the coffee without tasting it, and continued the search.

The voice of the blind man died away. The guitars ceased.

She started. She was afraid the musicians would come down and gather round her. Why had she not told the Padrone she wished to be quite alone? She heard the shuffle of feet. They were coming. Feverishly she turned the pages. Ah! here it was! She bent down over the page.

"La conscience, c'est la quantité de science innée que nous avons en nous. EMILE ARTOIS.

"Nuit d'orage. Juin."

A SPIRIT IN PRISON

The guitars began a prelude. The blind man shifted from one fat leg to another, cast up his sightless eyes, protruded and drew in his tongue, coughed, spat—

"Cameriere!"

Hermione struck upon the table sharply. She had forgotten all about the Marchesino. She was full of the desire to escape, to get away and be out on the sea.

"Cameriere!"

She called more loudly.

A middle-aged waiter came shuffling over the floor.

"The bill, please."

As she spoke she drank the brandy.

"Sì, Signora."

He stood beside her.

"One coffee?"

"Sì."

"One cognac?"

"Sì, sì."

The blind man burst into song.

"One fifty, Signora."

Hermione gave him a two-lire piece and got up to go.

"Signora—buona sera! What a pleasure!"

The Marchesino stood before her, smiling, bowing. He took her hand, bent over it, and kissed it.

"What a pleasure!" he repeated, glancing round. "And you are alone? The Signorina is not here?"

He stared suspiciously towards the terrace.

"And our dear friend Emilio?"

"No, no. I am quite alone."

The blind man bawled, as if he wished to drown the sound of speech.

"Please—could you stop him, Marchese?" said Hermione. "I—really—give him this for me."

She gave the Marchese a lira.

"Signora, it isn't necessary. Silenzio! Silenzio! P-sh-sh-sh!"

287

He hissed sharply, almost furiously. The musicians abruptly stopped, and the blind man made a gurgling sound, as if he were swallowing the unfinished portion of his song.

"No; please pay them."

"It's too much."

"Never mind."

The Marchese gave the lire to the blind man, and the musicians went drearily out.

Then Hermione held out her hand at once.

"I must go now. It is late."

"You are going by sea, Signora?"

"Yes."

"I will accompany you."

"No, indeed. I couldn't think of it. You have friends."

"They will understand. Have you your own boat?"

"No."

"Then of course I shall come with you."

But Hermione was firm. She knew that to-night the company of this young man would be absolutely unbearable.

"Marchese, indeed I cannot—I cannot allow it. We Englishwomen are very independent, you know. But you may call me a boat and take me down to it, as you are so kind."

"With pleasure, Signora."

He went to the open window. At once the boatman's cry rose up.

"Barca! barca!"

"That is Andrea's voice," said the Marchesino. "I know him. Barca—sì!"

The boat began to glide in towards the land.

As they went out the Marchesino said:

"And how is the Signorina?"

"Very well."

"I have had a touch of fever, Signora, or I should have come over to the island again. I stayed too long in the sea the other day, or—" He shrugged his shoulders.

"I'm sorry," said Hermione. "You are very pale to-night."

For the first time she looked at him closely, and saw that his face was white, and that his big and boyish eyes held a tired and yet excited expression.

"It is nothing. It has passed. And our friend— Emilio? How is he?"

A hardness had come into his voice. Hermione noticed it.

"We have not seen him lately. I suppose he has been busy."

"Probably. Emilio has much to do in Naples," said the Marchesino, with an unmistakable sneer. "Do allow me to escort you to the island, Signora."

They had reached the boat. Hermione shook her head and stepped in at once.

"Then when may I come?"

"Whenever you like."

"To-morrow?"

"Certainly."

"At what time?"

Hermione suddenly remembered his hospitality and felt that she ought to return it.

"Come to lunch—half-past twelve. We shall be quite alone."

"Signora, for loneliness with you and the Signorina I would give up every friend I have ever had. I would give up—"

"Half-past twelve, then, Marchese. Addio!"

"A rivederci, Signora! A demain! Andrea, take care of the Signora. Treat her as you would treat the Madonna. Do you hear?"

The boatman grinned and took off his cap, and the

boat glided away across the path of yellow light that was shed from the window of Frisio's.

Hermione leaned back against the white cushions. She was thankful to escape. She felt tired and confused. That dreadful music had distracted her, that—and something else, her tricked expectation. She knew now that she had been very foolish, perhaps even very fantastic. She had felt so sure that Emile had written in that book —what?

As the boat went softly on she asked herself exactly what she had expected to find written there, and she realized that her imagination had, as so often before, been galloping like a frightened horse with the reins upon its neck. And then she began to consider what he had written.

"La conscience, c'est la quantité de science innée que nous avons en nous."

She did not know the words. Were they his own or another's? And had he written them simply because they had chanced to come into his mind at the moment, or because they expressed some underthought or feeling that had surged up in him just then? She wished she knew.

It was a fine saying, she thought, but for the moment she was less interested in it than in Emile's mood, his mind, when he had written it. She realized now, on this calm of the sea, how absurd had been the thought that a man so subtle as Emile would flagrantly reveal a passing phase of his nature, a secret irritability, a jealousy, perhaps, or a sudden hatred in a sentence written for any eyes that chose to see. But he might covertly reveal himself to one who understood him well.

She sat still, trying to match her subtlety against his.

From the shore came sounds of changing music, low down or falling to them from the illuminated heights where people were making merry in the night. Now and then a boat passed them. In one, young men were singing, and interrupting their song to shout with laughter. Here and there a fisherman's torch glided like a great fire-fly above the oily darkness of the sea. The distant trees of the gardens climbing up the hill made an ebony blackness beneath the stars, a blackness that suggested impenetrable beauty that lay deep down with hidden face. And the lights dispersed among them, gaining significance by their solitude, seemed to summon adventurous or romantic spirits to come to them by secret paths and learn their revelation. Over the sea lay a delicate warmth, not tropical, not enervating, but softly inspiring. And beyond the circling lamps of Naples Vesuvius lit up the firmament with a torrent of rose-colored fire that glowed and died, and glowed again, constantly as beats a heart.

And to Hermione came a melancholy devoid of all violence, soft almost as the warmth upon this sea, quiet as the resignation of the fatalistic East. She felt herself for a moment such a tiny, dark thing caught in the meshes of the great net of the Universe, this Universe that she could never understand. What could she do? She must just sink down upon the breast of mystery, let it take her, hold her, do with her what it would.

Her subtlety against Emile's! She smiled to herself in the dark. What a combat of midgets! She seemed to see two marionettes battling in the desert.

And yet — and yet! She remembered a saying of Flaubert's, that man is like a nomad journeying on a camel through the desert; and he is the nomad, and the camel—and the desert.

How true that was, for even now, as she felt herself to be nothing, she felt herself to be tremendous.

She heard the sound of oars from the darkness before them, and saw the dim outline of a boat, then the eyes of Emile looking straight into hers.

"Emile!"

"Hermione!"

His face was gone. But yielding to her impulse she made Andrea stop, and, turning round, saw that the other boat had also stopped a little way from hers. It began to back, and in a moment was level with them.

"Emile! How strange to meet you! Have — you haven't been to the island?"

"No. I was tired. I have been working very hard. I dined quietly at Posilipo."

He did not ask her where she had been.

"Yes. I think you look tired," she said. He did not speak, and she added: "I felt restless, so I took the tram from the Trattoria del Giardinetto as far as the Scoglio di Frisio, and am going back, as you see, by boat."

"It is exquisite on the sea to-night," he said.

"Yes, exquisite; it makes one sad."

She remembered all she had been through that day, as she looked at his powerful face.

"Yes," he answered. "It makes one sad."

For a moment she felt that they were again in perfect sympathy, as they used to be. Their sadness, born of the dreaming hour, united them.

"Come soon to the island, dear Emile," she said, suddenly and with the impulsiveness that was part of her, forgetting all her jealousy and all her shadowy fears. "I have missed you."

He noticed that she ruled out Vere in that sentence; but the warmth of her voice stirred warmth in him, and he answered:

"Let me come to-morrow."

"Do—do!"

"In the morning, to lunch, and to spend a long day."

Suddenly she remembered the Marchesino and the sound of his voice when he had spoken of his friend.

"Lunch?" she said.

Instantly he caught her hesitation, her dubiety.

"It isn't convenient, perhaps?"

"Perfectly, only—only the Marchesino is coming."

"To-morrow?—To lunch?"

The hardness of the Marchesino's voice was echoed now in the voice of Artois. There was antagonism between these men. Hermione realized it.

"Yes. I invited him this evening."

There was a slight pause. Then Artois said:

"I'll come some other day, Hermione. Well, my friend, au revoir, and bon voyage to the island."

His voice had suddenly become cold, and he signed to his boatman.

"Avanti!"

The boat slipped away and was lost in the darkness.

Hermione had said nothing. Once again—why, she did not know—her friend had made her feel guilty.

Andrea, the boatman, still paused. Now she saw him staring into her face, and she felt like a woman publicly deserted, almost humiliated.

"Avanti, Andrea!" she said.

Her voice trembled as she spoke.

He bent to his oars and rowed on.

And man is the nomad, and the camel—and the desert.

Yes, she carried the desert within her, and she was wandering in it alone. She saw herself, a poor, starved, shrinking figure, travelling through a vast, a burning, a waterless expanse, with an iron sky above her, a brazen land beneath. She was in rags, barefoot, like the poorest nomad of them all.

But even the poorest nomad carries something.

Against her breast, to her heart, she clasped—a memory—the sacred memory of him who had loved her, who had taken her to be his, who had given her himself.

CHAPTER XX

THAT night when Hermione drew near to the island she saw the Saint's light shining, and remembered how, in the storm, she had longed for it—how, when she had seen it above the roaring sea, she had felt that it was a good omen. To-night it meant nothing to her. It was just a lamp lit, as a lamp might be lit in a street, to give illumination in darkness to any one who passed. She wondered why she had thought of it so strangely.

Gaspare met her at the landing. She noticed at once a suppressed excitement in his manner. He looked at Andrea keenly and suspiciously.

"How late you are, Signora!"

He put out his strong arm to help her to the land.

"Am I, Gaspare? Yes, I suppose I am—you ought all to be in bed."

"I should not go to bed while you were out, Signora."

Again she linked Gaspare with her memory, saw the nomad not quite alone on the journey.

"I know."

"Have you been to Naples, Signora?"

"No—only to—"

"To Mergellina?"

He interrupted her almost sharply.

"No, to the Scoglio di Frisio. Pay the boatman this, Gaspare. Good-night, Andrea."

"Good-night, Signora."

Gaspare handed the man his money, and at once the boat set out on its return to Posilipo.

A SPIRIT IN PRISON

Hermione stood at the water's edge watching its departure. It passed below the Saint, and the gleam of his light fell upon it for a moment. In the gleam the black figure of Andrea was visible stooping to the water. He was making the fishermen's sign of the Cross. The cross on Peppina's face—was it an enemy of the Cross that carried with it San Francesco's blessing? Vere's imagination! She turned to go up to the house.

"Is the Signorina in bed yet, Gaspare?"

"No, Signora."

"Where is she? Still out?"

"Sì, Signora."

"Did she think I was lost?"

"Signora, the Signorina is on the cliff with Ruffo."

"With Ruffo?"

They were going up the steps.

"Sì, Signora. We have all been together."

Hermione guessed that Gaspare had been playing chaperon, and loved him for it.

"And you heard the boat coming from the cliff?"

"I saw it pass under the Saint's light, Signora. I did not hear it."

"Well, but it might have been a fisherman's boat."

"Sì, Signora. And it might have been your boat."

The logic of this faithful watcher was unanswerable. They came up to the house.

"I think I'll go and see Ruffo," said Hermione.

She was close to the door of the house, Gaspare stood immediately before her. He did not move now, but he said:

"I can go and tell the Signorina you are here, Signora. She will come at once."

Again Hermione noticed a curious, almost dogged, excitement in his manner. It recalled to her a night of years ago when he had stood on a terrace beside her in the darkness and had said: "I will go down to the sea. Signora, let me go down to the sea!"

"There's nothing the matter, is there, Gaspare?" she said, quickly. "Nothing wrong?"

"Signora, of course not! What should there be?"

"I don't know."

"I will fetch the Signorina."

On that night, years ago, she had battled with Gaspare. He had been forced to yield to her. Now she yielded to him.

"Very well," she answered. "Go and tell the Signorina I am here."

She turned and went into the house and up to the sitting-room. Vere did not come immediately. To her mother it seemed as if she was a very long time coming; but at last her light step fell on the stairs, and she entered quickly.

"Madre! How late you are! Where have you been?"

"Am I late? I dined at the little restaurant at the top of the hill where the tram passes."

"There? But you haven't been there all this time?"

"No. Afterwards I took the tram to Posilipo and came home by boat. And what have you been doing?"

"Oh, all sorts of things—what I always do. Just now I've been with Ruffo."

"Gaspare told me he was here."

"Yes. We've been having a talk."

Hermione waited for Vere to say something more, but she was silent. She stood near the window looking out, and the expression on her face had become rather vague, as if her mind had gone on a journey.

"Well," said the mother at last, "and what does Ruffo say for himself, Vere?"

"Ruffo? Oh, I don't know."

She paused, then added:

"I think he has rather a hard time, do you know, Madre?"

Hermione had taken off her hat. She laid it on a table and sat down. She was feeling tired.

"But generally he looks so gay, so strong. Don't you remember that first day you saw him?"

"Ah—then!"

"Of course, when he had fever—"

"No, it isn't that. Any one might be ill. I think he has things at home to make him unhappy sometimes."

"Has he been telling you so?"

"Oh, he doesn't complain," Vere said, quickly, and almost with a touch of heat. "A boy like that couldn't whine, you know, Madre. But one can understand things without hearing them said. There is some trouble. I don't know what it is exactly. But I think his step-father—his Patrigno, as he calls him—must have got into some bother, or done something horrible. Ruffo seemed to want to tell me, and yet not to want to tell me. And, of course, I couldn't ask. I think he'll tell me to-morrow, perhaps."

"Is he coming here to-morrow?"

"Oh, in summer I think he comes nearly every night."

"But you haven't said anything about him just lately."

"No. Because he hasn't landed till to-night since the night of the storm."

"I wonder why?" said Hermione.

She was interested; but she still felt tired, and the fatigue crept into her voice.

"So do I," Vere said. "He had a reason, I'm sure. You're tired, Madre, so I'll go to bed. Good-night."

She came to her mother and kissed her. Moved by a sudden overwhelming impulse of tenderness, and need of tenderness, Hermione put her arms round the child's slim body. But even as she did so she remembered Vere's secret, shared with Emile and not with her. She could not abruptly loose her arms without surprising her child. But they seemed to her to stiffen, against her will, and her embrace was surely mechanical. She wondered if Vere noticed this, but she did not look into her eyes to see.

"Good-night, Vere."

"Good-night."

Vere was at the door when Hermione remembered her two meetings of that evening.

"By-the-way," she said, "I met the Marchesino to-night. He was at the Scoglio di Frisio."

"Was he?"

"And afterwards on the sea I met Emile."

"Monsieur Emile! Then he isn't quite dead!"

"There was a sound almost of irritation in Vere's voice.

"He has been working very hard."

"Oh, I see."

Her voice had softened.

"The Marchesino is coming here to lunch to-morrow."

"Oh, Madre!"

"Does he bore you? I had to ask him to something after accepting his dinner, Vere."

"Yes, yes, of course. The Marchese is all right."

She stood by the door with her bright, expressive eyes fixed on her mother. Her dark hair had been a little roughened by the breeze from Ischia, and stuck up just above the forehead, giving to her face an odd, almost a boyish look.

"What is it, Vere?"

"And when is Monsieur Emile coming? Didn't he say?"

"No. He suggested to-morrow, but when I told him the Marchese was coming he said he wouldn't."

As Hermione said this she looked very steadily at her child. Vere's eyes did not fall, but met hers simply, fearlessly, yet not quite childishly.

"I don't wonder," she said. "To tell the truth, Madre, I can't see how a man like the Marchesino could interest a man like Monsieur Emile — at any rate, for long. Well—" She gave a little sigh, throwing up her pretty chin. "A letto si va!"

And she vanished.

When she had gone Hermione thought she too would go to bed. She was very tired. She ought to go. Yet now she suddenly felt reluctant to go, and as if the doings of the day for her were not yet over. And, besides, she was not going to sleep well. That was certain. The dry, the almost sandy sensation of insomnia was upon her. What was the matter with Gaspare to-night? Perhaps he had had a quarrel with some one at Mergellina. He had a strong temper as well as a loyal heart.

Hermione went to a window. The breeze from Ischia touched her. She opened her lips, shut her eyes, drank it in. It would be delicious to spend the whole night upon the sea, like Ruffo. Had he gone yet? or was he in the boat asleep, perhaps in the Saint's Pool? How interested Vere was in all the doings of that boy—how innocently, charmingly interested!

Hermione stood by the window for two or three minutes, then went out of the room, down the stairs, to the front door of the house. It was already locked. Yet Gaspare had not come up to say good-night to her. And he always did that before he went to bed. She unlocked the door, went out, shut it behind her, and stood still.

How strangely beautiful and touching the faint noise of the sea round the island was at night, and how full of meaning not quite to be divined! It came upon her heart like the whisper of a world trying to tell its secret to the darkness. What depths, what subtleties, what unfailing revelations of beauty, and surely, too, of love, there were in Nature! And yet in Nature what terrible indifference there was: a powerful, an almost terrific inattention, like that of the sphinx that gazes at what men cannot see. Hermione moved away from the house.

A SPIRIT IN PRISON

She walked to the brow of the island and sat down on the seat that Vere was fond of. Presently she would go to the bridge and look over into the Pool and listen for the voices of fishermen. She sat there for some time gaining a certain peace, losing something of her feeling of weary excitement and desolation under the stars. At last she thought that sleep might come if she went to bed. But before doing so she made her way to the bridge and leaned on the rail, looking down into the Pool.

It was very dark, but she saw the shadowy shape of a fishing - boat lying close to the rock. She stood and watched it, and presently she lost herself in a thicket of night thoughts, and forgot where she was and why she had come there. She was recalled by hearing a very faint voice singing, scarcely more than humming, beneath her.

> "Oh, dolce luna bianca de l' Estate
>   Mi fugge il sonno accanto a la marina:
>   Mi destan le dolcissime serate
>   Gil occhi di Rosa e il mar di Mergellina."

It was the same song that Artois had heard that day as he leaned on the balcony of the Ristorante della Stella. But this singer of it sang the Italian words, and not the dialetto. The song that wins the prize at the Piedigrotta Festival is on the lips of every one in Naples. In houses, in streets, in the harbor, in every piazza, and upon the sea it is heard incessantly.

And now Ruffo was singing it softly and rather proudly in the Italian, to attract the attention of the dark figure he saw above him. He was not certain who it was, but he thought it was the mother of the Signorina, and —he did not exactly know why—he wished her to find out that he was there, squatting on the dry rock with his back against the cliff wall. The ladies of the Casa del Mare had been very kind to him, and to-night he was not very happy, and vaguely he longed for sympathy.

Hermione listened to the pretty, tripping words, the happy, youthful words. And Ruffo sang them again, still very softly.

"Oh, dolce luna bianca de l' Estate—"

And the poor nomad wandering in the desert? But she had known the rapture of youth, the sweet white moons of summer in the South. She had known them long ago for a little while, and therefore she knew them while she lived. A woman's heart is tenacious, and wide as the world, when it contains that world which is the memory of something perfect that gave it satisfaction.

"Mi destan le dolcissime serate
Gli occhi di Rosa e il mar di Mergellina."

Dear, happy, lovable youth that can sing to itself like that in the deep night! Like that once Maurice, her sacred possession of youth, sang. She felt a rush of tenderness for Ruffo, just because he was so young, and sang—and brought back to her the piercing truth of the everlasting renewal that goes hand in hand with the everlasting passing away.

"Ruffo!—Ruffo!"

Almost as Vere had once called "Pescator!" she called. And as Ruffo had once come running up to Vere he came now to Vere's mother.

"Good-evening, Ruffo."

"Good-evening, Signora."

She was looking at the boy as at a mystery which yet she could understand. And he looked at her simply, with a sort of fearless gentleness, and readiness to receive the kindness which he knew dwelt in her for him to take.

"Are you better?"

"Sì, Signora, much better. The fever has gone. I am strong, you know."

"You are so young."

She could not help saying it, and her eyes were tender just then.

"Sì, Signora, I am very young."

His simple voice almost made her laugh, stirred in her that sweet humor which has its dwelling at the core of the heart.

"Young and happy," she said.

And as she said it she remembered Vere's words that evening: "I think he has rather a hard time."

"At least, I hope you are happy, Ruffo," she added.

"Sì, Signora."

He looked at her. She was not sure which he meant, whether his assent was to her hope or to the fact of his happiness. She wondered which it was.

"Young people ought to be happy," she said.

"Ought they, Signora?"

"You like your life, don't you? You like the sea?"

"Sì, Signora. I could not live away from the sea. If I could not see the sea every day I don't know what I should do."

"I love it, too."

"The Signorina loves the sea."

He had ignored her love for it and seized on Vere's. She thought that was very characteristic of his youth.

"Yes. She loves being here. You talked to her to-night, didn't you?"

"Sì, Signora."

"And to Gaspare?"

"Sì, Signora. And this afternoon, too. Gaspare was at Mergellina this afternoon."

"And you met there, did you?"

"Sì, Signora. I had been with my mamma, and when I left my mamma—poveretta—I met Gaspare."

"I hope your mother is well."

"Signora, she is not very well just now. She is a little sad just now."

Hermione felt that the boy had some trouble which, perhaps, he would like to tell her. Perhaps some instinct made him know that she felt tender towards him, very tender that night.

"I am sorry for that," she said—"very sorry."

"Sì, Signora. There is trouble in our house."

"What is it, Ruffo?"

The boy hesitated to answer. He moved his bare feet on the bridge and looked down towards the boat. Hermione did not press him, said nothing.

"Signora," Ruffo said, at last, coming to a decision, "my Patrigno is not a good man. He makes my mamma jealous. He goes after others."

It was the old story of the South, then! Hermione knew something of the persistent infidelities of Neapolitan men. Poor women who had to suffer them!

"I am sorry for your mother," she said, gently. "That must be very hard."

"Sì, Signora, it is hard. My mamma was very unhappy to-day. She put her head on the table, and she cried. But that was because my Patrigno is put in prison."

"In prison! What has he done?"

Ruffo looked at her, and she saw that the simple expression had gone out of his eyes.

"Signora, I thought perhaps you knew."

"I? But I have never seen your step-father."

"No, Signora. But—but you have that girl here in your house."

"What girl?"

Suddenly, almost while she was speaking, Hermione understood.

"Peppina!" she said. "It was your Patrigno who wounded Peppina?"

A SPIRIT IN PRISON

"Sì, Signora."

There was a silence between them. Then Hermione said, gently:

"I am very sorry for your poor mother, Ruffo—very sorry. Tell me, can she manage? About money, I mean?"

"It was not so much the money she was crying about, Signora. But, of course, while Patrigno is in prison he cannot earn money for her. I shall give her my money. But my mamma does not like all the neighbors knowing about that girl. It is a shame for her."

"Yes, of course it is. It is very hard."

She thought a moment. Then she said:

"It must be horrible—horrible!"

She spoke with all the vehemence of her nature. Again, as long ago, when she knelt before a mountain shrine in the night, she had put herself imaginatively in the place of a woman, this time in the place of Ruffo's mother. She had realized how she would have felt if her husband, her "man," had ever been faithless to her.

Ruffo looked at her almost in surprise.

"I wish I could see your poor mother, Ruffo," she said. "I would go to see her, only—well, you see, I have Peppina here, and—"

She broke off. Perhaps the boy would not understand what she considered the awkwardness of the situation. She did not quite know how these people regarded certain things.

"Wait here a moment, Ruffo," she said. "I am going to give you something for your mother. I won't be a moment."

"Grazie, Signora."

Hermione went away to the house. The perfect naturalness and simplicity of the boy appealed to her. She was pleased, too, that he had not told all this to Vere. It showed a true feeling of delicacy. And she was sure he was a good son. She went up to her room, got two ten-lira notes, and went quickly back to Ruffo, who was standing upon the bridge.

"There, Ruffo," she said, giving them to him. "These are for your mother."

The boy's brown face flushed, and into his eyes there came an expression of almost melting gentleness.

"Oh, Signora!" he said.

And there was a note of protest in his voice.

"Take them to her, Ruffo. And—and I want you to promise me something. Will you?"

"Sì, Signora. I will do anything—anything for you."

Hermione put her hand on his shoulder.

"Be very, very kind to your poor mother, Ruffo."

"Signora, I always am good for my poor mamma."

He spoke with warm eagerness.

"I am sure you are. But just now, when she is sad, be very good to her."

"Sì, Signora."

She took her hand from the boy's shoulder. He bent to kiss her hand, and again, as he was lifting up his head, she saw that melting look in his eyes. This time it was unmingled with amazement, and it startled her.

"Oh, Ruffo!" she said, and stopped, staring at him in the darkness.

"Signora! What is it? What have you?"

"Nothing. Good-night, Ruffo."

"Good-night, Signora."

He took off his cap and ran down to the boat. Hermione leaned over the railing, bending down to see the boy reappear below. When he came he looked like a shadow. From this shadow there rose a voice singing very softly.

"Oh, dolce luna bianca de l' Estate—"

The shadow went over to the boat, and the voice died away.

"Gli occhi di Rosa e il mar di Mergellina."

Hermione still was bending down. And she formed the last words with lips that trembled a little.

"Gli occhi di Rosa e il mar di Mergellina."

Then she said: "Maurice—Maurice!"

And then she stood trembling.

Yes, it was Maurice whom she had seen again for an instant in the melting look of Ruffo's face. She felt frightened in the dark. Maurice—when he kissed her for the last time, had looked at her like that. It could not be fancy. It was not.

Was this the very first time she had noticed in Ruffo a likeness to her dead husband? She asked herself if it was. Yes. She had never—or had there been something? Not in the face, perhaps. But—the voice? Ruffo's singing? His attitude as he stood up in the boat? Had there not been something? She remembered her conversation with Artois in the cave. She had said to him that—she did not know why—the boy, Ruffo, had made her feel, had stirred up within her slumbering desires, slumbering yearnings.

"I have heard a hundred boys sing on the Bay—and just this one touches some chord, and all the strings of my soul quiver."

She had said that.

Then there was something in the boy, something not merely fleeting like that look of gentleness—something permanent, subtle, that resembled Maurice.

Now she no longer felt frightened, but she had a passionate wish to go down to the boat, to see Ruffo again, to be with him again, now that she was awake to this strange, and perhaps only faint, imitation by another of the one whom she had lost. No—not imitation; this fragmentary reproduction of some characteristic, some—

She lifted herself up from the railing. And now she knew that her eyes were wet. She wiped them with her handkerchief, drew a deep breath, and went back to the house. She felt for the handle of the door, and, when she found it, opened the door, went in, and shut it rather heavily, then locked it. As she bent down to push home the bolt at the bottom a voice called out:

"Who's there?"

She was startled and turned quickly.

"Gaspare!"

He stood before her half dressed, with his hair over his eyes, and a revolver in his hand.

"Signora! It is you!"

"Sì. What did you think? That it was a robber?"

Gaspare looked at her almost sternly, went to the door, bent down and bolted it, then he said:

"Signora, I heard a noise in the house a few minutes ago. I listened, but I heard nothing more. Still, I thought it best to get up. I had just put on my clothes when again I heard a noise at the door. I myself had locked it for the night. What should I think?"

"I was outside. I came back for something. That was what you heard. Then I went out again."

"Sì."

He stood there staring at her in a way that seemed, she fancied, to rebuke her. She knew that he wished to know why she had gone out so late, returned to the house, then gone out once more.

"Come up-stairs for a minute, Gaspare," she said. "I want to speak to you."

He looked less stern, but still unlike himself.

"Sì, Signora. Shall I put on my jacket?"

"No, no, never mind. Come like that."

She went up-stairs, treading softly, lest she might disturb Vere. He followed. When they were in her sitting-room she said:

"Gaspare, why did you go to bed without coming to say good-night to me?"

He looked rather confused.

"Did I forget, Signora? I was tired. Forgive me."

"I don't know whether you forgot. But you never came."

As Hermione spoke, suddenly she felt as if Gaspare, too, were going, perhaps, to drift from her. She looked at him with an almost sharp intensity which hardened her whole face. Was he, too, being insincere with her, he whom she trusted so implicitly?

"Did you forget, Gaspare?" she said.

"Signora," he repeated, with a certain, almost ugly doggedness, "I was tired. Forgive me."

She felt sure that he had chosen deliberately not to come to her for the evening salutation. It was a trifle, yet to-night it hurt her. For a moment she was silent, and he was silent, looking down at the floor. Then she opened her lips to dismiss him. She intended to say a curt "Good-night"; but—no—she could not let Gaspare retreat from her behind impenetrable walls of obstinate reserve. And she did know his nature through and through. If he was odd to-night, unlike himself, there was some reason for it; and it could not be a reason that, known to her, would make her think badly of him. She was certain of that.

"Never mind, Gaspare," she said, gently. "But I like you to come and say good-night to me. I am accustomed to that, and I miss it if you don't come."

"Sì, Signora," he said, in a very low voice.

He turned a little away from her, and made a small noise with his nose as if he had a cold.

"Gaspare," she said, with an impulse to be frank, "I saw Ruffo to-night."

He turned round quickly. She saw moisture in his eyes, but they were shining almost fiercely.

"He told me something about his Patrigno. Did you know it?"

"His Patrigno and Peppina?"

Hermione nodded.

"Sì Signora; Ruffo told me."

"I gave the boy something for his mother."

"His mother—why?"

There was quick suspicion in Gaspare's voice.

"Poor woman! Because of all this trouble. Her husband is in prison."

"Lo so. But he will soon be out again. He is 'protected.'"

"Who protects him?"

But Gaspare evaded the answer, and substituted something that was almost a rebuke.

"Signora," he said, bluntly, "if I were you I would not have anything to do with these people. Ruffo's Patrigno is a bad man. Better leave them alone."

"But, Ruffo?"

"Signora?"

"You like him, don't you?"

"Sì, Signora. There is no harm in him."

"And the poor mother?"

"I am not friends with his mother, Signora. I do not want to be."

Hermione was surprised by his harshness.

"But why not?"

"There are people at Mergellina who are bad people," he said. "We are not Neapolitan. We had better keep to ourselves. You have too much heart, Signora, a great deal too much heart, and you do not always know what people are."

"Do you think I ought not to have given Ruffo that money for his mother?" Hermione asked, almost meekly.

"Sì, Signora. It is not for you to give his mother money. It is not for you."

"Well, Gaspare, it's done now."

"Sì, it's done now."

"You don't think Ruffo bad, do you?"

After a pause, Gaspare answered:

"No, Signora. Ruffo is not bad."

Hermione hesitated. She wanted to ask Gaspare something, but she was not sure that the opportunity was a good one. He was odd to-night. His temper had surely been upset. Perhaps it would be better to wait. She decided not to speak of what was in her mind.

"Well, Gaspare, good-night," she said.

"Good-night, Signora."

She smiled at him.

"You see, after all, you have had to say good-night to me!"

"Signora," he answered, earnestly, "even if I do not come to say good-night to you always, I shall stay with you till death."

Again he made the little noise with his nose, as he turned away and went out of the room.

That night, ere she got into bed, Hermione called down on that faithful watch-dog's dark head a blessing, the best that heaven contained for him. Then she put out the light, and lay awake so long that when a boat came round the cliff from the Saint's Pool to the open sea, in the hour before the dawn, she heard the soft splash of the oars in the water and the sound of a boy's voice singing.

> "Oh, dolce luna bianca de l' Estate
>   Mi fugge il sonno accanto a la marina:
> Mi destan le dolcissime serate
>   Gli occhi di Rosa e il mar di Mergellina."

A SPIRIT IN PRISON

She lifted herself up on her pillow and listened—listened until across the sea, going towards the dawn, the song was lost.

"Gli occhi di Rosa e il mar di Mergellina."

When the voice was near, had not Maurice seemed near to her? And when it died away, did not he fade with it—fade until the Ionian waters took him?

She sat up in the darkness until long after the song was hushed. But she heard it still in the whisper of the sea.

CHAPTER XXI

THE Marchesino had really been unwell, as he had told Hermione. The Panacci disposition, of which he had once spoken to Artois, was certainly not a calm one, and Isidoro was, perhaps, the most excitable member of an abundantly excitable family. Although changeable, he was vehement. He knew not the meaning of the word patience, and had always been accustomed to get what he wanted exactly when he wanted it. Delay in the gratification of his desires, opposition to his demands, rendered him as indignant as if he were a spoiled child unable to understand the fixed position and function of the moon. And since the night of his vain singing along the shore to Nisida he had been ill with fever, brought on by jealousy and disappointment, brought on partly also by the busy workings of a heated imagination which painted his friend Emilio in colors of inky black.

The Marchesino had not the faintest doubt that Artois was in love with Vere. He believed this not from any evidence of his eyes, for, even now, in not very lucid moments, he could not recall any occasion on which he had seen Emilio paying court to the pretty English girl. But, then, he had only seen them together twice—on the night of his first visit to the island and on the night of the storm. It was the general conduct of his friend that convinced him, conduct in connection not with Vere, but with himself—apart from that one occasion when Emilio must have lain hidden with Vere among the shadows of the Grotto of Virgil. He had been deceived by

Emilio. He had thought of him as an intellectual, who was also a bon vivant and interested in Neapolitan life. But he had not thought of him as a libertine. Yet that was what he certainly was. The interview with Maria Fortunata in the alley beyond the Via Roma had quite convinced the Marchesino. He had no objection whatever to loose conduct, but he had a contempt for hypocrisy which was strong and genuine. He had trusted Emilio. Now he distrusted him, and was ready to see subtlety, deceit, and guile in all his undertakings.

Emilio had been trying to play with him. Emilio looked upon him as a boy who knew nothing of the world. The difference in their respective ages, so long ignored by him, now glared perpetually upon the Marchesino, even roused within him a certain condemnatory something that was almost akin to moral sense, a rare enough bird in Naples. He said to himself that Emilio was a wicked old man, "un vecchio briccone." The delights of sin were the prerogative of youth. Abruptly this illuminating fact swam, like a new comet, within the ken of the Marchesino. He towered towards heights of virtuous indignation. As he lay upon his fevered pillow, drinking a tisane prepared by his anxious mamma, he understood the inner beauty of settling down—for the old; and white-haired age, still intent upon having its fling, appeared to him so truly pitiable and disgusting that he could almost have wept for Emilio had he not feared to make himself more feverish by such an act of enlightened friendship.

And this sense and appreciation of the true morality, ravishing in its utter novelty for the young barbarian, was cherished by the Marchesino until he began almost to swell with virtue, and to start on stilts to heaven, big with the message that wickedness was for the young and must not be meddled with by any one over thirty—the age at which, till now, he had always proposed to himself to marry some rich girl and settle down to the rigid asceticism of Neapolitan wedded life.

And as the Marchesino had lain in bed tingling with morality, so did he get up and issue forth to the world, and even set sail upon the following day for the island. Morality was thick upon him, as upon that "briccone," Emilio, something else was thick. About mediæval chivalry he knew precisely nothing. Yet, as the white wings of his pretty yacht caught the light breeze of morning, he felt like a most virtuous knight *sans peur et sans reproche.* He even felt like a steady-going person with a mission.

But he wished he thoroughly understood the English nation. Towards the English he felt friendly, as do most Italians; but he knew little of them, except that they were very rich, lived in a perpetual fog, and were "un poco pazzi." But the question was how mad—in other words, how different from Neapolitans—they were! He wished he knew. It would make things easier for him in his campaign against Emilio.

Till he met the ladies of the island he had never said a hundred words to any English person. The Neapolitan aristocracy is a very conservative body, and by no means disposed to cosmopolitanism. To the Panacci Villa at Capodimonte came only Italians, except Emilio. The Marchesino had inquired of Emilio if his mother should call upon the Signora Delarey, but Artois, knowing Hermione's hatred of social formalities, had hastened to say that it was not necessary, that it would even be a surprising departure from the English fashion of life, which ordained some knowledge of each other by the ladies of two families, or at least some formal introduction by a mutual woman friend, before an acquaintance could be properly cemented. Hitherto the Marchesino had felt quite at ease with his new friends. But hitherto he had been, as it were, merely at play with them. The interlude of fever had changed his views and enlarged his consciousness. And Emilio was no longer at hand to be explanatory if desired.

The Marchesino wished very much that he thoroughly understood the inner workings of the minds of English ladies.

How mad were the English? How mad exactly, for instance, was the Signora Delarey? And how mad exactly was the Signorina? It would be very valuable to know. He realized that his accurate knowledge of Neapolitan women, hitherto considered by him as amply sufficient to conduct him without a false step through all the intricacies of the world feminine, might not serve him perfectly with the ladies of the island. His fever had, it seemed, struck a little blow on his self-confidence, and rendered him so feeble as to be almost thoughtful.

And then, what exactly did he want? To discomfit Emilio utterly? That, of course, did not need saying, even to himself. And afterwards? There were two perpendicular lines above his eyebrows as the boat drew near to the island.

But when he came into the little drawing-room, where Hermione was waiting to receive him, he looked young and debonair, though still pale from his recent touch of illness.

Vere was secretly irritated by his coming. Her interview with Peppina had opened her eyes to many things, among others to a good deal that was latent in the Marchesino. She could never again meet him, or any man of his type, with the complete and masterful simplicity of ignorant childhood that can innocently coquet by instinct, that can manage by heredity from Eve, but that does not understand thoroughly, either, what it is doing or why it is doing it.

Vere was not in the mood for the Marchesino.

She had been working, and she had been dreaming, and she wanted to have another talk with Monsieur Emile. Pretty, delicate, yet strong-fibred ambitions were stirring within her, and the curious passion to use life as a material, but not all of life that presented itself to her. With the desire to use that might be greedy arose the fastidious prerogative of rejection.

And that very morning, mentally, Vere had rejected the Marchesino as something not interesting in life, something that was only lively, like the very shallow stream. What a bore it would be having to entertain him, to listen to his compliments, to avoid his glances, to pretend to be at ease with him.

For Vere felt now that she would no longer be quite at ease in his company.

Through her Venetian blinds she saw his boat come into the Pool's tranquillity, and in a leisurely manner prepared herself to go down and greet him.

"But Madre can have him for a little first," she said to herself, as she looked into the glass to see that her hair was presentable. "Madre asked him to come. I didn't. I shall have nothing to say to him."

She had quite forgotten her eagerness on the night of the storm, when she heard the cry of the siren that betokened his approach. Again she looked in the glass and gave a pat to her hair. And just as she was doing it she thought of that day after the bathe, when Gaspare had come to tell her that Monsieur Emile was waiting for her. She had run down, then, just as she was, and now—

"Mamma mia! Am I getting vain!" she said to herself.

And she turned from the glass, and reluctantly went to meet their guest.

She had said to herself that it was a bore having the Marchesino to lunch, that he was uninteresting, frivolous, empty-headed. But directly she set eyes upon him, as he stood in the drawing-room by her mother, she felt a change in him. What had happened to him? She could not tell. But she was conscious that he seemed much more definite, much more of a personage, than he had seemed to her before. Even his face looked different, though paler, stronger. She was aware of surprise.

The Marchesino, too, though much less instinctively observant than Vere, noted a change in her. She looked more developed, more grown up. And he said to himself:

"When I told Emile she was a woman I was right."

Their meeting was rather grave and formal, even a little stiff. The Marchesino paid Vere two or three compliments, and she inquired perfunctorily after his health, and expressed regret for his slight illness.

"It was only a chill, Signorina. It was nothing."

"Perhaps you caught it that night," Vere said.

"What night, Signorina?"

Vere had been thinking of the night when he sang for her in vain. Suddenly remembering how she and Monsieur Emile had lain in hiding and slipped surreptitiously home under cover of the darkness, she flushed and said:

"The night of the storm—you got wet, didn't you?"

"But that was long ago, Signorina," he answered, looking steadily at her, with an expression that was searching and almost hard.

Had he guessed her inadvertence? She feared so, and felt rather guilty, and glad when Giulia came in to announce that lunch was ready.

Hermione, when they sat down, feeling a certain constraint, but not knowing what it sprang from, came to the rescue with an effort. She was really disinclined for talk, and was perpetually remembering that the presence of the Marchesino had prevented Emile from coming to spend a long day. But she remembered also her guest's

317

hospitality at Frisio's, and her social instinct defied her natural reluctance to be lively. She said to herself that she was rapidly developing into a fogey, and must rigorously combat the grievous tendency. By a sheer exertion of will-power she drove herself into a different, and conversational, mood. The Marchesino politely responded. He was perfectly self-possessed, but he was not light-hearted. The unusual effort of being thoughtful had, perhaps, distressed or even outraged his brain. And the worst of it was that he was still thinking—for him quite profoundly.

However, they talked about risotto, they talked about Vesuvius, they spoke of the delights of summer in the South and of the advantages of living on an island.

"Does it not bore you, Signora, having the sea all round?" asked the Marchesino. "Do you not feel in a prison and that you cannot escape?"

"We don't want to escape, do we, Madre?" said Vere, quickly, before Hermione could answer.

"I am very fond of the island, certainly," said Hermione. "Still, of course, we are rather isolated here."

She was thinking of what she had said to Artois—that perhaps her instinct to shut out the world was morbid, was bad for Vere. The girl at once caught the sound of hesitation in her mother's voice.

"Madre!" she exclaimed. "You don't mean to say that you are tired of our island life?"

"I do not say that. And you, Vere?"

"I love being here. I dread the thought of the autumn."

"In what month do you go away, Signora?" asked the Marchesino.

"By the end of October we shall have made our flitting, I suppose."

"You will come in to Naples for the winter?"

Hermione hesitated. Then she said:

"I almost think I shall take my daughter to Rome. What do you say, Vere?"

The girl's face had become grave, even almost troubled.

"I can't look forward in this weather," she said. "I think it's almost wicked to. Oh, let us live in the moment, Madre, and pretend it will be always summer, and that we shall always be living in our Casa del Mare!"

There was a sound of eager youth in her voice as she spoke, and her eyes suddenly shone. The Marchesino looked at her with an admiration he did not try to conceal.

"You love the sea, Signorina?" he asked.

But Vere's enthusiasm abruptly vanished, as if she feared that he might destroy its completeness by trying to share it.

"Oh yes," she said. "We all do here; Madre, Gaspare, Monsieur Emile—everybody."

It was the first time the name of Artois had been mentioned among them that day. The Marchesino's full red lips tightened over his large white teeth.

"I have not seen Signor Emilio for some days," he said.

"Nor have we," said Vere, with a touch of childish discontent.

He looked at her closely.

Emilio—he knew all about Emilio. But the Signorina? What were her feelings towards the "vecchio briccone"? He did not understand the situation, because he did not understand precisely the nature of the madness of the English. Had the ladies been Neapolitans, Emilio an Italian, he would have felt on sure ground. But in England, so he had heard, there is a fantastic, cold, sexless something called friendship that can exist between unrelated man and woman.

"Don Emilio writes much," he said, with less than his usual alacrity. "When one goes to see him he has always a pen in his hand."

He tried to speak of Emilio with complete detachment, but could not resist adding:

"When one is an old man one likes to sit, one cannot be forever running to and fro. One gets tired, I suppose."

There was marked satire in the accent with which he said the last words. And the shrug of his shoulders was an almost audible "What can I know of that?"

"Monsieur Emile writes because he has a great brain, not because he has a tired body," said Vere, with sudden warmth.

Her mother was looking at her earnestly.

"Oh, Signorina, I do not mean— But for a man to be always shut up," began the Marchesino, "it is not life."

"You don't understand, Marchese. One can live in a little room with the door shut as one can never live—"

Abruptly she stopped. A flush ran over her face and down to her neck. Hermione turned away her eyes. But they had read Vere's secret. She knew what her child was doing in those hours of seclusion. And she remembered her own passionate attempts to stave off despair by work. She remembered her own failure.

"Poor little Vere!" That was her first thought. "But what is Emile doing?" That was the second. He had discouraged her. He had told her the truth. What was he telling Vere? A flood of bitter curiosity seemed to rise in her, drowning many things.

"What I like is life, Signorina," said the Marchesino. "Driving, riding, swimming, sport, fencing, being with beautiful ladies—that is life."

"Yes, of course, that is life," she said.

What was the good of trying to explain to him the inner life? He had no imagination.

Her youth made her very drastic, very sweeping, in her secret mental assertions.

She labelled the Marchesino "Philistine," and popped him into his drawer.

A SPIRIT IN PRISON

Lunch was over, and they got up.

"Are you afraid of the heat out-of-doors, Marchese?" Hermione asked, "or shall we have coffee in the garden? There is a trellis, and we shall be out of the sun."

"Signora, I am delighted to go out."

He got his straw hat, and they went into the tiny garden and sat down on basket-work chairs under a trellis, set in the shadow of some fig-trees. Giulia brought them coffee, and the Marchesino lighted a cigarette.

He said to himself that he had never been in love before.

Vere wore a white dress. She had no hat on, but held rather carelessly over her small, dark head a red parasol. It was evident that she was not afraid even of the midday sun. That new look in her face, soft womanhood at the windows gazing at a world more fully, if more sadly, understood, fascinated him, sent the blood up to his head. There was a great change in her. To-day she knew what before she had not known.

As he stared at Vere with adoring eyes suddenly there came into his mind the question: "Who has taught her?"

And then he thought of the night when all in vain he had sung upon the sea, while the Signorina and "un Signore" were hidden somewhere near him.

The blood sang in his head, and something seemed to expand in his brain, to press violently against his temples, as if striving to force its way out. He put down his coffee-cup, and the two perpendicular lines appeared above his eyebrows, giving him an odd look, cruel and rather catlike.

"If Emilio—"

At that moment he longed to put a knife into his friend.

But he was not sure. He only suspected.

Hermione's rôle in this summer existence puzzled him exceedingly. The natural supposition in a Neapolitan

321

would, of course, have been that Artois was her lover.
But when the Marchesino looked at Hermione's eyes he
could not tell.

What did it all mean? He felt furious at being puzzled, as if he were deliberately duped.

"Your cigarette has gone out, Marchese," said Hermione. "Have another."

The young man started.

"It's nothing."

"Vere, run in and get the Marchese a Khali Targa."

The girl got up quickly.

"No, no! I cannot permit—I have another here."

He opened his case. It was empty.

Vere laughed.

"You see!"

She went off before he could say another word, and
the Marchesino was alone for a moment with Hermione.

"You are fortunate, Signora, in having such a daughter," he said, with a sigh that was boyish.

"Yes," Hermione said.

That bitter curiosity was still with her, and her voice
sounded listless, almost cold. The Marchesino looked
up. Ah! Was there something here that he could
understand? Something really feminine? A creeping
jealousy? He was on the *qui vive* at once.

"And such a good friend as Don Emilio," he added.
"You have known Emilio for a long time, Signora?"

"Oh yes, for a very long time."

"He is a strange man," said the Marchesino, with
rather elaborate carelessness.

"Do you think so? In what way?"

"He likes to know, but he does not like to be known."

There was a great deal of truth in the remark. Its
acuteness surprised Hermione, who thought the Marchesino quick witted but very superficial.

"As he is a writer, I suppose he has to study people a good deal," she said, quietly.

"I do not think I can understand these great people. I think they are too grand for me."

"Oh, but Emile likes you very much. He told me so."

"It is very good of him," said the Marchesino, pulling at his mustaches.

He was longing to warn Hermione against Emilio—to hint that Emilio was not to be trusted. He believed that Hermione must be very blind, very unfitted to look after a lovely daughter. But when he glanced at her face he did not quite know how to hint what was in his mind. And just then Vere came back and the opportunity was gone. She held out a box to the Marchesino. As he thanked her and took a cigarette he tried to look into her eyes. But she would not let him. And when he struck his match she returned once more to the house, carrying the box with her. Her movement was so swift and unexpected that Hermione had not time to speak before she was gone.

"But—"

"I should not smoke another, Signora," said the Marchesino, quickly.

"You are sure?"

"Quite."

"Still, Vere might have left the box. She is inhospitable to-day."

Hermione spoke lightly.

"Oh, it is bad for cigarettes to lie in the sun. It ruins them."

"But you should have filled your case. You must do it before you go."

"Thank you."

His head was buzzing again. The touch of fever had really weakened him. He knew it now. Never gifted with much self-control, he felt to-day that, with a very slight incentive, he might lose his head. The new atmosphere which Vere diffused around her excited him strangely. He was certain that she was able to understand something of what he was feeling, that on the night of the storm she would not have been able to understand. Again he thought of Emilio, and moved restlessly in his chair, looking sideways at Hermione, then dropping his eyes. Vere did not come back.

Hermione exerted herself to talk, but the task became really a difficult one, for the Marchesino looked perpetually towards the house, and so far forgot himself as to show scarcely even a wavering interest in anything his hostess said. As the minutes ran by a hot sensation of anger began to overcome him. A spot of red appeared on each cheek.

Suddenly he got up.

"Signora, you will want to make the siesta. I must not keep you longer."

"No, really; I love sitting out in the garden, and you will find the glare of the sun intolerable if you go so early."

"On the sea there is always a breeze. Indeed, I must not detain you. All our ladies sleep after the colazione until the bathing hour. Do not you?"

"Yes, we lie down. But to-day—"

"You must not break the habit. It is a necessity. My boat will be ready, and I must thank you for a delightful entertainment."

His round eyes were fierce, but he commanded his voice.

"A rive—"

"I will come with you to the house if you really will not stay a little longer."

"Perhaps I may come again?" he said, quickly, with a sudden hardness, a fighting sound in his voice. "One evening in the cool. Or do I bore you?"

"No; do come."

Hermione felt rather guilty, as if they had been inhospitable, she and Vere; though, indeed, only Vere was in fault.

"Come and dine one night, and I shall ask Don Emilio." As she spoke she looked steadily at her guest.

"He was good enough to introduce us to each other, wasn't he?" she added. "We must all have an evening together, as we did at Frisio's."

The Marchesino bowed.

"With pleasure, Signora."

They came into the house.

As they did so Peppina came down the stairs. When she saw them she murmured a respectful salutation and passed quickly by, averting her wounded cheek. Almost immediately behind her was Vere. The Marchesino looked openly amazed for a moment, then even confused. He stared first at Hermione, then at Vere.

"I am sorry, Madre; I was kept for a moment," the girl said. "Are you coming up-stairs?"

"The Marchese says he must go, Vere. He is determined not to deprive us of our siesta."

"One needs to sleep at his hour in the hot weather," said the Marchesino.

The expression of wonder and confusion was still upon his face, and he spoke slowly.

"Good-bye, Marchese,'" Vere said, holding out her hand.

He took it and bowed over it and let it go. The girl turned and ran lightly up-stairs.

Directly she was gone the Marchesino said to Hermione:

"Pardon me, Signora, I—I—"

He hesitated. His self-possession seemed to have deserted him for the moment. He looked at Hermione swiftly, searchingly, then dropped his eyes,

"What is it, Marchese?" she asked, wondering what was the matter with him.

He still hesitated. Evidently he was much disturbed. At last he said again:

"Pardon me, Signora. I—as you know, I am Neapolitan. I have always lived in Naples."

"Yes, I know."

"I know Naples like my pocket—"

He broke off.

Hermione waited for him to go on. She had no idea what was coming.

"Yes?" she said, at length to help him.

"Excuse me, Signora! But that girl—that girl who passed by just now—"

"My servant, Peppina."

He stared at her.

"Your servant, Signora?"

"Yes."

"Do you know what she is, where she comes from? But no, it is impossible."

"I know all about Peppina, Marchese," Hermione replied, quietly.

"Truly? Ah!"

His large round eyes were still fixedly staring at her.

"Good-bye, Signora!" he said. "Thank you for a very charming colazione. And I shall look forward with all my heart to the evening you have kindly suggested."

"I shall write directly I have arranged with Don Emilio."

"Thank you! Thank you! A rivederci, Signora."

He cast upon her one more gravely staring look, and was gone.

When he was outside and alone, he threw up his hands and talked to himself for a moment, uttering many exclamations. In truth, he was utterly amazed. Maria Fortunata had spread abroad diligently the fame of her niece's beauty, and the Marchesino, like the rest of the gay young men of Naples, had known of and had misjudged her. He had read in the papers of the violence done to her, and had at once dismissed her from his mind with a murmured "Povera Ragazza!"

She was no longer beautiful.

And now he discovered her living as a servant with the ladies of the island. Who could have put her there? He thought of Emilio's colloquy with Maria Fortunata. But the Signora? A mother? What did it all mean? Even the madness of the English could scarcely be so pronounced as to make such a proceeding as this quite a commonplace manifestation of the national life and eccentricity. He could not believe that.

He stepped into his boat. As the sailors rowed it out from the Pool—the wind had gone down and the sails were useless—he looked earnestly up to the windows of the Casa del Mare, longing to pierce its secrets.

What was Emilio in that house? A lover, a friend, a bad genius? And the Signora? What was she?

The Marchesino was no believer in the virtue of women. But the lack of beauty in Hermione, and her age, rendered him very doubtful as to her rôle in the life on the island. Vere's gay simplicity had jumped to the eyes. But now she, too, was become something of a mystery.

He traced it all to Emilio, and was hot with a curiosity that was linked closely with his passion.

Should he go to see Emilio? He considered the question and resolved not to do so. He would try to be patient until the night of the dinner on the island. He would be birbante, would play the fox, as Emilio surely had done. The Panacci temper should find out that one member of the family could control it, when such control served his purpose.

He was on fire with a lust for action as he made his resolutions. Vere's coolness to him, even avoidance of him, had struck hammer-like blows upon his *amour propre.* He saw her now—yes, he saw her—coming down the stairs behind Peppina. Had they been together? Did they talk together, the cold, the prudish Signorina Inglese—so he called Vere now in his anger—and the former decoy of Maria Fortunata?

And then a horrible conception of Emilio's rôle in all this darted into his mind, and for a moment he thought of Hermione as a blind innocent, like his subservient mother, of Vere as a preordained victim. Then the blood coursed through his veins like fire, and he felt as if he could no longer sit still in the boat.

"Avanti! avanti!" he cried to the sailors. "Dio mio! There is enough breeze to sail. Run up the sail! Madonna Santissima! We shall not be to Naples till it is night. Avanti! avanti!"

Then he lay back, crossed his arms behind his head, and, with an effort, closed his eyes.

He was determined to be calm, not to let himself go. He put his fingers on his pulse.

"That cursed fever! I believe it is coming back," he said to himself.

He wondered how soon the Signora would arrange that dinner on the island. He did not feel as if he could wait long without seeing Vere again. But would it ever be possible to see her alone? Emilio saw her alone. His white hairs brought him privileges. He might take her out upon the sea.

The Marchesino still had his fingers on his pulse. Surely it was fluttering very strangely. Like many young Italians, he was a mixture of fearlessness and weakness, of boldness and childishness.

"I must go to mamma! I must have medicine—the doctor," he thought, anxiously. "There is something wrong with me. Perhaps I have been looked on by the evil eye."

And down he went to the bottom of a gulf of depression.

CHAPTER XXII

HERMIONE was very thankful that the Marchesino had gone. She felt that the lunch had been a failure, and was sorry. But she had done her best. Vere and the young man himself had frustrated her, she thought. It was a bore having to entertain any one in the hot weather. As she went up-stairs she said to herself that her guest's addio had been the final fiasco of an unfortunate morning. Evidently he knew something of Peppina, and had been shocked to find the girl in the house. Emile had told her—Hermione—that she was an impulsive. Had she acted foolishly in taking Peppina? She had been governed in the matter by her heart, in which dwelt pity and a passion for justice. Surely the sense of compassion, the love of fair dealing could not lead one far astray. And yet, since Peppina had been on the island the peace of the life there had been lessened. Emile had become a little different, Vere too. And even Gaspare—was there not some change in him?

She thought of Giulia's assertion that the disfigured girl had the evil eye.

She had laughed at the idea, and had spoken very seriously to Giulia, telling her that she was not to communicate her foolish suspicion to the other servants. But certainly the joy of their life in this House of the Sea was not what it had been. And even Vere had had forebodings with which Peppina had been connected. Perhaps the air of Italy, this clear, this radiant atmosphere which seemed created to be the environment of happiness, contained some subtle poison that was working in them all, turning them from cool reason.

She thought of Emile, calling up before her his big frame, his powerful face with the steady eyes. And a wave of depression went over her, as she understood how very much she had relied on him since the death of Maurice. Without him she would indeed have been a derelict.

Again that bitter flood of curiosity welled up in her. She wondered where Vere was, but she did not go to the girl's room. Instead, she went to her own sitting-room. Yesterday she had been restless. She had felt driven. To-day she felt even worse. But to-day she knew what yesterday she had not known—Vere's solitary occupation. Why had not Vere told her, confided in her? It was a very simple matter. The only reason why it now assumed an importance to her was because it had been so carefully concealed. Why had not Vere told her all about it, as she told her other little matters of their island life, freely, without even a thought of hesitation?

She sought the reason of this departure which was paining her. But at first she did not find it.

Perhaps Vere wanted to give her a surprise. For a moment her heart grew lighter. Vere might be preparing something to please or astonish her mother, and Emile might be in the secret, might be assisting in some way. But no! Vere's mysterious occupation had been followed too long. And then Emile had not always known what it was. He had only known lately.

Those long reveries of Vere upon the sea, when she lay in the little boat in the shadow cast by the cliffs over the Saint's Pool—they were the prelude to work; imaginative, creative perhaps.

And Vere was not seventeen.

Hermione smiled to herself rather bitterly, thinking of the ignorance, of the inevitable folly of youth. The child, no doubt, had dreams of fame. What clever, what imaginative and energetic child has not such dreams at some period or other? How absurd we all are, thinking to climb to the stars almost as soon as we can see them!

And then the smile died away from Hermione's lips as the great tenderness of the mother within her was moved by the thought of the disappointments that come with greater knowledge of life. Vere would suffer when she learned the truth, when she knew the meaning of failure.

Quite simply and naturally Hermione was including her child inevitably within the circle of her own disaster.

If Emile knew, why did he not tell Vere what he had told her mother?

But Emile had surely shown much greater interest in Vere just lately than ever before?

Was Emile helping Vere in what she was doing? But if he was, then he must believe in Vere's capacity to do something that was worth doing.

Hermione knew the almost terrible sincerity of Artois in the things of the intellect, his clear, unwavering judgment, his ruthless truthfulness. Nothing would ever turn him from that. Nothing, unless he—

Her face became suddenly scarlet, then pale. A monstrous idea had spung up in her mind, an idea so monstrous that she strove to thrust it away violently, without even contemplating it. Why had Vere not told her? There must be some good and sufficient reason. Vehemently—to escape from that monstrous idea—she sought it. Why had everything else in her child been revealed to her, only this one thing been hidden from her?

She searched the past, Vere and herself in that past. And now, despite her emotion, her full intelligence was roused up and at work. And presently she remembered that Emile and Vere shared the knowledge of her own

desire to create, and her utter failure to succeed in creation. Emile knew the whole naked truth of that. Vere
did not. But Vere knew something. Could that mutual
knowledge be the reason of this mutual secrecy? As
women often do, Hermione had leaped into the very core
of the heart of the truth, had leaped out of the void,
guided by some strange instinct never alive in man. But,
as women very seldom do, she shrank away from the
place she had gained. Instead of triumphing, she was
afraid. She remembered how often her imagination had
betrayed her, how it had created phantoms, had ruined
for her the lagging hours. Again and again she had said
to herself, "I will beware of it." Now she accused it of
playing her false once more, of running wild. Sharply
she pulled herself up. She was assuming things. That
was her great fault, to assume that things were that
which perhaps they were not.

How often Emile had told her not to trust her imagination! She would heed him now. She knew nothing.
She did not even know for certain that Vere's flush,
Vere's abrupt hesitation at lunch, were a betrayal of
the child's secret.

But that she would find out.

Again the fierce curiosity besieged and took possession
of her. After all, she was a mother. A mother had
rights. Surely she had a right to know what another
knew of her child.

"I will ask Vere," she said to herself.

Once before she had said to herself that she would do
that, and she had not done it. She had felt that to do
it would be a humiliation. But now she was resolved
to do it, for she knew more of her own condition and was
more afraid of herself. She began to feel like one who
has undergone a prolonged strain of work, who believes
that it has not been too great and has been capably supported, and who suddenly is aware of a yielding, of a

downward and outward movement, like a wide and spreading disintegration, in which brain, nerves, the whole body are involved.

Yet what had been the strain that she had been supporting, that now suddenly she began to feel too much? The strain of a loss. Time should have eased it. But had Time eased it, or only lengthened the period during which she had been forced to carry her load? People ought to get accustomed to things. She knew that it is supposed by many that the human body, the human mind, the human heart can get accustomed—by which is apparently meant can cease passionately and instinctively to strive to repel—can get accustomed to anything. Well, she could not. Never could she get accustomed to the loss of love, of man's love. The whole world might proclaim its proverbs. For her they had no truth. For her—and for how many other silent women!

And now suddenly she felt that for years she had been struggling, and that the struggle had told upon her far more than she had ever suspected. Nothing must be added to her burden or she would sink down. The dust would cover her. She would be as nothing—or she would be as something terrible, nameless.

She must ask Vere, do what she had said to herself that she would not do. Unless she had the complete confidence of her child she could not continue to do without the cherishing love she had lost. She saw herself a cripple, something maimed. Hitherto she had been supported by blessed human crutches: by Vere, Emile, Gaspare. How heavily she had leaned upon them! She knew that now. How heavily she must still lean if she were to continue on her way. And a fierce, an almost savage something, desperate and therefore arbitrary, said within her:

"I will keep the little that I have: I will—I will."

A SPIRIT IN PRISON

"The little!" Had she said that? It was wicked of
her to say that. But she had had the wonderful thing.
She had held for a brief time the magic of the world
within the hollow of her hands, within the shadow of
her heart. And the others? Children slip from their
parents' lives into the arms of another whose call means
more to them than the voices of those who made them
love. Friends drift away, scarcely knowing why, divided from each other by the innumerable channels that
branch from the main stream of existence. Even a
faithful servant cannot be more than a friend.

There is one thing that is great, whose greatness makes
the smallness of all the other things. And so Hermione
said, "the little that I have," and there was truth in it.
And there was as vital a truth in the fact of her whole
nature recognizing that little's enormous value to her.
Not for a moment did she underrate her possession. Indeed, she had to fight against the tendency to exaggeration. Her intellect said to her that, in being so
deeply moved by such a thing as the concealment from
her by Vere of something innocent of which Emile
knew, she was making a water drop into an ocean. Her
intellect said that. But her heart said no.

And the voice of her intellect sank away like the frailest
echo that ever raised its spectral imitation of a reality.
And the voice of her heart rang out till it filled her world.

And so the argument was over.

She thought she heard a step below, and looked out
of the window into the sunshine.

Gaspare was there. It was his hour of repose, and
he was smoking a cigarette. He was dressed in white
linen, without a coat, and had a white linen hat on his
head. He stood near the house, apparently looking
out to sea. And his pose was meditative. Hermione
watched him. The sight of him reminded her of another
question she wished to ask.

A SPIRIT IN PRISON

Gaspare had one hand in the pocket of his white trousers. With the other he held the cigarette. Hermione saw the wreaths of pale smoke curling up and evaporating in the shining, twinkling air, which seemed full of joyous, dancing atoms. But presently his hand forgot to do its work. The cigarette, only half smoked, went out, and he stood there as if plunged in profound thought. Hermione wondered what he was thinking about.

"Gaspare!"

She said it softly. Evidently he did not hear.

"Gaspare! Gaspare!"

Each time she spoke a little louder, but still he took no notice.

She leaned farther out and called:

"Gaspare!"

This time he heard and started violently, dropped the cigarette, then, without looking up, bent down slowly, recovered it, and turned round.

"Signora?"

The sun shone full on his upturned face, showing to Hermione the dogged look which sometimes came to it when anything startled him.

"I made you jump."

"No, Signora."

"But I did. What were you thinking about?"

"Nothing, Signora. Why are you not asleep?"

He spoke almost as if she injured him by being awake.

"I couldn't sleep to-day. What are you going to do this afternoon?"

"I don't know, Signora. Do you wish me to do anything for you?"

"Well—"

She had a wish to clear things up, to force her life, the lives of those few she cared for, out of mystery into a clear light. She had a desire to chastise thought by strong, bracing action.

335

"I rather want to send a note to Don Emilio."

"Sì, Signora."

His voice did not sound pleased.

"It is too hot to row all the way to Naples. Couldn't you go to the village and take the tram to the hotel—if I write the note?"

"If you like, Signora."

"Or would it be less bother to row as far as Mergellina, and take a tram or carriage from there?"

"I can do that, Signora."

He sounded a little more cheerful.

"I think I'll write the note, Gaspare, then. And you might take it some time—whenever you like. You might come and fetch it in five minutes."

"Very well, Signora."

He moved away, and she went to her writing-table. She sat down, and slowly, with a good deal of hesitation and thought, she wrote part of a letter asking Emile to come to dine whenever he liked at the island. And now came the difficulty. She knew Emile did not want to meet the Marchesino there. Yet she was going to ask them to meet each other. She had told the Marchesino so. Should she tell Emile? Perhaps, if she did, he would refuse to come. But she could never lay even the smallest trap for a friend. So she wrote on, asking Emile to let her know the night he would come, as she had promised to invite the Marchesino to meet him.

"Be a good friend and do this for me," she ended, "even if it bores you. The Marchese lunched here alone with us to-day, and it was a fiasco. I think we were very inhospitable, and I want to wipe away the recollection of our dulness from his mind. Gaspare will bring me your answer."

At the bottom she wrote "Hermione." But just as she was going to seal the letter in its envelope she took it out, and added, "Delarey" to her Christian name.

"Hermione Delarey." She looked at the words for a long time before she rang the bell for Gaspare.

When she gave him the letter, "Are you going by Mergellina?" she asked him.

"Sì, Signora."

He stood beside her for a moment; then, as she said nothing more, turned to go out.

"Gaspare, wait one minute," she said, quickly.

"Sì, Signora."

"I meant to ask you last night, but—well, we spoke of other things, and it was so late. Have you ever noticed anything about that boy, Ruffo, anything at all, that surprised you?"

"Surprised me, Signora?"

"Surprised you, or reminded you of anything?"

"I don't know what you mean, Signora."

Gaspare's voice was hard and cold. He looked steadily at Hermione, as a man of strong character sometimes looks when he wishes to turn his eyes away from the glance of another, but will not, because of his manhood.

Hermione hesitated to go on, but something drove her to be more explicit.

"Have you never noticed in Ruffo a likeness to—to your Padrone?" she said, slowly.

"My Padrone!"

Gaspare's great eyes dropped before hers, and he stood looking on the floor. She saw a deep flush cover his brown skin.

"I am sure you have noticed it, Gaspare," she said. "I can see you have. Why did you not tell me?"

At that moment she felt angry with herself and almost angry with him. Had he noticed this strange, this subtle resemblance between the fisher-boy and the dead man at once, long before she had? Had he been swifter to see such a thing than she?

"What do you mean, Signora? What are you talking about?"

He looked ugly.

"How can a fisher-boy, a nothing from Mergellina, look like my Padrone?"

Now he lifted his eyes, and they were fierce—or so she thought.

"Signora, how can you say such a thing?"

"Gaspare?" she exclaimed, astonished at his sudden vehemence.

"Signora—scusi! But—but there will never be another like my Padrone."

He opened the door and went quickly out of the room, and when the door shut it was as if an iron door shut upon a furnace.

Hermione stood looking at this door. She drew a long breath.

"But he has seen it!" she said, aloud. "He has seen it."

And Emile?

Had she been a blind woman, she who had so loved the beauty that was dust? She thought of Vere and Ruffo standing together, so youthful, so happy in their simple, casual intercourse.

It was as if Vere had been mysteriously drawn to this boy because of his resemblance to the father she had never seen.

Vere! Little Vere!

Again the mother's tenderness welled up in Hermione's heart, this time sweeping away the reluctance to be humble.

"I will go to Vere now."

She went to the door, as she had gone to it the previous day. But this time she did not hesitate to open it. A strong impulse swept her along, and she came to her child's room eagerly.

338

A SPIRIT IN PRISON

"Vere!"

She knocked at the door.

"Vere! May I come in?"

She knocked again. There was no answer.

Then she opened the door and went in. Possibly Vere was sleeping. The mosquito-net was drawn round the bed, but Hermione saw that her child was not behind it. Vere had gone out somewhere.

The mother went to the big window which looked out upon the sea. The green Venetian blind was drawn. She pushed up one of its flaps and bent to look through. Below, a little way out on the calm water, she saw Vere's boat rocking softly in obedience to the small movement that is never absent from the sea. The white awning was stretched above the stern-seats, and under it lay Vere in her white linen dress, her small head, not protected by a hat, supported by a cushion. She lay quite still, one arm on the gunwale of the boat, the other against her side. Hermione could not see whether her eyes were shut or open.

The mother watched her for a long time through the blind.

How much of power was enclosed in that young figure that lay so still, so perfectly at ease, cradled on the great sea, warmed and cherished by the tempered fires of the sun! How much of power to lift up and to cast down, to be secret, to create sorrow, to be merciful! Wonderful, terrible human power!

The watching mother felt just then that she was in the hands of the child.

"Now it's the child's turn."

Surely Vere must be asleep. Such absolute stillness must mean temporary withdrawal of consciousness.

Just as Hermione was thinking this, Vere's left hand moved. The girl lifted it up to her face, and gently and repeatedly rubbed her eyebrow.

339

A SPIRIT IN PRISON

Hermione dropped the flap of the blind. The little, oddly natural movement had suddenly made her feel that it was not right to be watching Vere when the child must suppose herself to be unobserved and quite alone with the sea.

As she came away from the window she glanced quickly round the room, and upon a small writing-table at the foot of the bed she saw a number of sheets of paper lying loose, with a piece of ribbon beside them. They had evidently been taken out of the writing-table drawer, which was partially open, and which, as Hermione could see, contained other sheets of a similar kind. Hermione looked, and then at once looked away. She passed the table and reached the door. When she was there she glanced again at the sheets of paper. They were covered with writing. They drew, they fascinated her eyes, and she stood still, with her hand resting on the door-handle. As a rule it would have seemed perfectly natural to her to read anything that Vere had left lying about, either in her own room or anywhere else. Until just lately her child had never had, or dreamed of having, any secret from her. Never had Vere received a letter that her mother had not seen. Secrets simply did not exist between them—secrets, that is, of the child from the mother.

But it was not so now. And that was why those sheets of paper drew and held the mother's eyes.

She had, of course, a perfect right to read them. Or had she—she who had said to Vere, "Keep your secrets"? In those words had she not deliberately relinquished such a right? She stood there thinking, recalling those words, debating within herself this question—and surely with much less than her usual great honesty.

Emile, she was sure, had read the writing upon those sheets of paper.

She did not know exactly why she was certain of this

—but she was certain, absolutely certain. She remembered the long-ago days, when she had submitted to him similar sheets. What Emile had read surely she might read. Again that intense and bitter curiosity mingled with something else, a strange, new jealousy in which it was rooted. She felt as if Vere, this child whom she had loved and cared for, had done her a cruel wrong, had barred her out from the life in which she had always been till now the best loved, the most absolutely trusted dweller. Why should she not take that which she ought to have been given?

Again she was conscious of that painful, that piteous sensation of one who is yielding under a strain that has been too prolonged. Something surely collapsed within her, something of the part of her being that was moral. She was no longer a free woman in that moment. She was governed. Or so she felt, perhaps deceiving herself.

She went swiftly and softly over to the table and bent over the sheets.

At first she stood. Then she sat down. She took up the paper, handled it, held it close to her eyes.

Verses! Vere was writing verses. Of course! Every one begins by being a poet. Hermione smiled, almost laughed aloud. Poor little Vere with her poor little secret! There was still that bitterness in the mother, that sense of wrong. But she read on and on. And her face was very grave, even earnest. And presently she started and her hand shook.

She had come to a poem that was corrected in Vere's handwriting, and on the margin was written, "Monsieur Emile's idea."

So there had been a conference, and Emile was advising Vere.

Hermione's hand shook so violently that she could not go on reading for a moment, and she laid the paper down. She felt like one who has suddenly unmasked a conspiracy against herself. It was useless for her intellect to deny this conspiracy, for her heart proclaimed it.

Long ago Emile had told her frankly that it was in vain for her to waste her time in creative work, that she had not the necessary gift for it. And now he was secretly assisting her own child—a child of sixteen—to do what he had told her, the mother, not to do. Why was he doing this?

Again the monstrous idea that she had forcibly dismissed from her mind that day returned to Hermione. There is one thing that sometimes blinds the most clearsighted men, so that they cannot perceive truth.

But—Hermione again bent over the sheets of paper, this time seeking for a weapon against the idea which assailed her. On several pages she found emendations, excisions, on one a whole verse completely changed. And on the margins were pencilled "Monsieur Emile's suggestion"; "Monsieur E.'s advice"; and once "These two lines invented by Monsieur Emile."

When had Vere and Emile had the opportunity for this long and secret discussion? On the day of the storm they had been together alone. They had had tea together alone. And on the night Emile dined on the island they had been out in the boat together for a long time. All this must have been talked over then.

Yes.

She read on. Had Vere talent? Did her child possess what she had longed for, and had been denied? She strove to read critically, but she was too excited, too moved to do so. All necessary calm was gone. She was painfully upset. The words moved before her eyes, running upward in irregular lines that resembled creeping things, and she saw rings of light, yellow in the middle and edged with pale blue.

She pushed away the sheets of paper, got up and went

again to the window. She must look at Vere once more, look at her with this new knowledge, look at her critically, with a piercing scrutiny. And she bent down as before, and moved a section of the blind, pushing it up.

There was no boat beneath her on the sea.

She dropped the blind sharply, and all the blood in her body seemed to make a simultaneous movement away from the region of the heart.

Vere was perhaps already in the house, running lightly up to the room. She would come in and find her mother there. She would guess what her mother had been doing.

Hermione did not hesitate. She crossed the room swiftly, opened the door, and went out. She reached her own room without meeting Vere. But she had not been in it for more than a minute and a half when she heard Vere come up-stairs, the sound of her door open and shut.

Hermione cleared her throat. She felt the need of doing something physical. Then she pulled up her blinds and let the hot sun stream in upon her.

She felt dark just then—black.

In a moment she found that she was perspiring. The sun was fierce—that, of course, must be the reason. But she would not shut the sun out. She must have light around her, although there was none within her.

She was thankful she had escaped in time. If she had not, if Vere had run into the room and found her there, she was sure she would have frightened her child by some strange outburst. She would have said or done something—she did not at all know what—that would perhaps have altered their relations irrevocably. For, in that moment, the sense of self-control, of being herself—so she put it—had been withdrawn from her.

She would regain it, no doubt. She was even now regaining it. Already she was able to say to herself that she was not seeing things in their true proportions, that some sudden crisis of the nerves, due perhaps to some purely physical cause, had plunged her into a folly of feeling from which she would soon escape entirely. She was by nature emotional and unguarded: therefore specially likely to be the victim in mind of any bodily ill.

And then she was not accustomed to be unwell. Her strength of body was remarkable. Very seldom had she felt weak.

She remembered one night, long ago in Sicily, when an awful bodily weakness had overtaken her. But that had been caused by dread. The mind had reacted upon the body. Now, she was sure of it, body had reacted on mind.

Yet she had not been ill.

She felt unequal to the battle of pros and cons that was raging within her.

"I'll be quiet," she thought. "I'll read."

And she took up a book.

She read steadily for an hour, understanding thoroughly all she read, and wondering how she had ever fancied she cared about reading. Then she laid the book down and looked at the clock. It was nearly four. Tea would perhaps refresh her. And after tea? She had loved the island, but to-day she felt almost as if it were a prison. What was there to be done? She found herself wondering for the first time how she had managed to "get through" week after week there. And in a moment her wonder made her realize the inward change in her, the distance that now divided her from Vere, the gulf that lay between them.

A day with a stranger may seem long, but a month with a friend how short! To live with Vere had been like living with a part of herself. But now what would it be like? And when Emile came, and they three were together?

When Hermione contemplated that reunion, she felt

that it would be to her intolerable. And yet she desired it. For she wanted to know something, and she was certain that if she, Vere, and Emile could be together, without any fourth person, she would know it.

A little while ago, when she had longed for bracing action, she had resolved to ask Emile to meet the Marchesino. She had felt as if that meeting would clear the air, would drive out the faint mystery which seemed to be encompassing them about. The two men, formerly friends, were evidently in antagonism now. She wanted to restore things to their former footing, or to make the enmity come out into the open, to understand it thoroughly, and to know if she and Vere had any part in it. Her desire had been to throw open windows and let in light.

But now things were changed. She understood, she knew more. And she wanted to be alone with Emile and with Vere. Then, perhaps, she would understand everything.

She said this to herself quite calmly. Her mood was changed. The fire had died down in her, and she felt almost sluggish, although still restless. The monstrous idea had come to her again. She did not vehemently repel it. By nature she was no doubt an impulsive. But now she meant to be a watcher. Before she took up her book and began to read she had been, perhaps, almost hysterical, had been plunged in a welter of emotion in which reason was drowned, had not been herself.

But now she felt that she was herself.

There was something that she wished to know, something that the knowledge she had gained in her child's room that day suggested as a possibility.

She regretted her note to Emile. Why had not she asked him to come alone, to-morrow, or even to-night— yes, to-night?

If she could only be with him and Vere for a few minutes to-night!

CHAPTER XXIII

WHEN Artois received Hermione's letter he asked who had brought it, and obtained from the waiter a fairly accurate description of Gaspare.

"Please ask him to come up," he said. "I want to speak to him."

Two or three minutes later there was a knock at the door and Gaspare walked in, with a large-eyed inquiring look.

"Good-day, Gaspare. You've never seen my quarters before, I think," said Artois, cordially.

"No, Signore. What a beautiful room!"

"You're not in a great hurry, are you?"

"No, Signore."

"Then smoke a cigar, and I'll write an answer to this letter."

"Thank you, Signore."

Artois gave him a cigar, and sat down to answer the letter, while Gaspare went out on to the balcony and stood looking at the bathers who were diving from the high wooden platform of the bath establishment over the way. When Artois had finished writing he joined Gaspare. He had a great wish that day to break down a reserve he had respected for many years, but he knew Gaspare's determined character, his power of obstinate, of dogged silence. Gaspare's will had been strong when he was a boy. The passing of the years had certainly not weakened it. Nevertheless, Artois was moved to make the attempt which he foresaw would probably end in failure.

He gave Gaspare the letter, and said:

"Don't go for a moment. I want to have a little talk with you."

"Sì, Signore."

Gaspare put the letter into the inner pocket of his jacket, and stood looking at Artois, holding the cigar in his left hand. In all these years Artois had never found out whether Gaspare liked him or not. He wished now that he knew.

"Gaspare," he said, "I think you know that I have a great regard for your Padrona."

"Sì, Signore. I know it."

The words sounded rather cold.

"She has had a great deal of sorrow to bear."

"Sì, Signore."

"One does not wish that she should be disturbed in any way—that any fresh trouble should come into her life."

Gaspare's eyes were always fixed steadily upon Artois, who, as he spoke the last words, fancied he saw come into them an expression that was almost severely ironical. It vanished at once as Gaspare said:

"No, Signore."

Artois felt the iron of this faithful servant's impenetrable reserve, but he continued very quietly and composedly:

"You have always stood between the Padrona and trouble whenever you could. You always will—I am sure of that."

"Sì, Signore."

"Do you think there is any danger to the Signora's happiness here?"

"Here, Signore?"

Gaspare's emphasis seemed to imply where they were just then standing. Artois was surprised, then for a moment almost relieved. Apparently Gaspare had no

23   347

thought in common with the strange, the perhaps fantastic thought that had been in his own mind.

"Here—no!" he said, with a smile. "Only you and I are here, and we shall not make the Signora unhappy."

"Chi lo sa?" returned Gaspare.

And again that ironical expression was in his eyes.

"By here I meant here in Naples, where we all are—or on the island, for instance."

"Signore, in this life there is trouble for all."

"But some troubles, some disasters can be avoided."

"It's possible."

"Gaspare"—Artois looked at him steadily, searchingly even, and spoke very gravely—"I respect you for your discretion of many years. But if you know of any trouble, any danger that is near to the Signora, and against which I could help you to protect her, I hope you will trust me and tell me. I think you ought to do that."

"I don't know what you mean, Signore."

"Are you quite sure, Gaspare? Are you quite sure that no one comes to the island who might make the Signora very unhappy?"

Gaspare had dropped his eyes. Now he lifted them, and looked Artois straight in the face.

"No, Signore, I am not sure of that," he said.

There was nothing rude in his voice, but there was something stern. Artois felt as if a strong, determined man stood in his path and blocked the way. But why? Surely they were at cross purposes. The working of Gaspare's mind was not clear to him.

After a moment of silence, he said:

"What I mean is this. Do you think it would be a good thing if the Signora left the island?"

"Left the island, Signore?"

"Yes, and went away from Naples altogether."

"The Signorina would never let the Padrona go. The

Signorina loves the island and my Padrona loves the Signorina."

"But the Signorina would not be selfish. If it was best for her mother to go—"

"The Signorina would not think it was best; she would never think it was best to leave the island."

"But what I want to know, Gaspare, is whether you think it would be best for them to leave the island. That's what I want to know—and you haven't told me."

"I am a servant, Signore. I cannot tell such things."

"You are a servant—yes. But you are also a friend. And I think nobody could tell better than you."

"I am sure the Signora will not leave the island till October, Signore. She says we are all to stay until the end of October."

"And now it's July."

"Sì, Signore. Now it's July."

In saying the last words Gaspare's voice sounded fatalistic, and Artois believed that he caught an echo of a deep-down thought of his own. With all his virtues Gaspare had an admixture of the spirit of the East that dwells also in Sicily, a spirit that sometimes, brooding over a nature however fine, prevents action, a spirit that says to a man, "This is ordained. This is destiny. This is to be."

"Gaspare," Artois said, strong in this conviction, "I have heard you say, 'è il destino.' But you know we can often get away from things if we are quick-witted."

"Some things, Signore."

"Most things, perhaps. Don't you trust me?"

"Signore!"

"Don't you think, after all these years, you can trust me?"

"Signore, I respect you as I respect my father."

"Well, Gaspare, remember this. The Signora has had trouble enough in her life. We must keep out any more."

"Signore, I shall always do what I can to spare my Padrona. Thank you for the cigar, Signore. I ought to go now. I have to go to Mergellina for the boat."

"To Mergellina?"

Again Artois looked at him searchingly.

"Sì, Signore; I left the boat at Mergellina. It is very hot to row all the way here."

"Yes. A rivederci, Gaspare. Perhaps I shall sail round to the island to-night after dinner. But I'm not sure. So you need not say I am coming."

"A rivederci, Signore."

When Gaspare had gone, Artois said to himself, "He does not trust me."

Artois was surprised to realize how hurt he felt at Gaspare's attitude towards him that day. Till now their mutual reserve had surely linked them together. Their silence had been a bond. But there was a change, and the bond seemed suddenly loosened.

"Damn the difference between the nations!" Artois thought. "How can we grasp the different points of view? How can even the cleverest of us read clearly in others of a different race from our own?"

He felt frustrated, as he had sometimes felt frustrated by Orientals. And he knew an anger of the brain as well as an anger of the heart. But this anger roused him, and he resolved to do something from which till now he had instinctively shrunk, strong-willed man though he was. If Gaspare would not help him he would act for himself. Possibly the suspicion, the fear that beset him was groundless. He had put it away from him more than once, had said that it was absurd, that his profession of an imaginative writer rendered him, perhaps, more liable to strange fancies than were other men, that it encouraged him to seek instinctively for drama, and that what a man instinctively and perpetually seeks he will often imagine that he has found. Now he would try to prove what was the truth.

He had written to Hermione saying that he would be glad to dine with her on any evening that suited the Marchesino, that he had no engagements. Why she wished him to meet the Marchesino he did not know. No doubt she had some woman's reason. The one she gave was hardly enough, and he divined another beneath it. Certainly he did not love Doro on the island, but perhaps it was as well that they should meet there once, and get over their little antagonism, an antagonism that Artois thought of as almost childish. Life was not long enough for quarrels with boys like Doro. Artois had refused Hermione's invitation on the sea abruptly. He had felt irritated for the moment, because he had for the moment been unusually expansive, and her announcement that Doro was to be there had fallen upon him like a cold douche. And then he had been nervous, highly strung from overwork. Now he was calm, and could look at things as they were. And if he noticed anything leading him to suppose that the Marchesino was likely to try to abuse Hermione's hospitality he meant to have it out with him. He would speak plainly and explain the English point of view. Doro would no doubt attack him on the ground of his interview with Maria Fortunata. He did not care. Somehow his present preoccupation with Hermione's fate, increased by the visit of Gaspare, rendered his irritation against the Marchesino less keen than it had been. But he thought he would probably visit the island to-night—after another visit which he intended to pay. He could not start at once. He must give Gaspare time to take the boat and row off. For his first visit was to Mergellina.

After waiting an hour he started on foot, keeping along by the sea, as he did not wish to meet acquaintances, and was likely to meet them in the Villa. As he drew near

to Mergellina he felt a great and growing reluctance to
do what he had come to do, to make inquiries into a certain matter; and he believed that this reluctance, awake
within him although perhaps he had scarcely been aware
of it, had kept him inactive during many days. Yet he
was not sure of this. He was not sure when a faint suspicion had first been born in his mind. Even now he
said to himself that what he meant to do, if explained
to the ordinary man, would probably seem to him ridiculous, that the ordinary man would say, "What a wild
idea! Your imagination runs riot." But he thought
of certain subtle things which had seemed like indica-
tions, like shadowy pointing fingers; of a look in Gaspare's eyes when they had met his—a hard, defiant look
that seemed shutting him out from something; of a look
in another face one night under the moon; of some words
spoken in a cave with a passion that had reached his
heart; of two children strangely at ease in each other's
society. And again the thought pricked him, "Is not
everything possible—even that?" All through his life
he had sought truth with persistence, sometimes almost
with cruelty, yet now he was conscious of timidity, almost of cowardice—as if he feared to seek it.

Long ago he had known a cowardice akin to this, in
Sicily. Then he had been afraid, not for himself but
for another. To-day again the protective instinct was
alive in him. It was that instinct which made him
afraid, but it was also that instinct which kept him to
his first intention, which pushed him on to Mergellina.
No safety can be in ignorance for a strong man. He
must know. Then he can act.

When Artois reached Mergellina he looked about for
Ruffo, but he could not see the boy. He had never inquired Ruffo's second name. He might make a guess at it.
Should he? He looked at a group of fishermen who were
talking loudly on the sand just beyond the low wall.

A SPIRIT IN PRISON

One of them had a handsome face bronzed by the sun, frank hazel eyes, a mouth oddly sensitive for one of his class. His woollen shirt, wide open, showed a medal resting on his broad chest, one of those amulets that are said to protect the fishermen from the dangers of the sea. Artois resolved to ask this man the question he wished, yet feared to put to some one. Afterwards he wondered why he had picked out this man. Perhaps it was because he looked happy.

Artois caught the man's eye.

"You want a boat, Signore?"

With a quick movement the fellow was beside him on the other side of the wall.

"I'll take your boat—perhaps this evening."

"At what hour, Signore?"

"We'll see. But first perhaps you can tell me something."

"What is it?"

"You live here at Mergellina?"

"Sì, Signore."

"Do you know any one called—called Buonavista?"

The eyes of Artois were fixed on the man's face.

"Buonavista—sì, Signore."

"You do?"

"Ma sì, Signore," said the man, looking at Artois with a sudden flash of surprise. "The family Buonavista, I have known it all my life."

"The family? Oh, then there are many of them?"

The man laughed.

"Enrico Buonavista has made many children, and is proud of it, I can tell you. He has ten—his father before him—"

"Then they are Neapolitans?"

"Neapolitans! No, Signore. They are from Mergellina."

Artois smiled. The tension which had surprised the sailor had left his face.

353

"I understand. But there is no Sicilian here called Buonavista?"

"A Sicilian, Signore? I never heard of one. Are there Buonavistas in Sicily?"

"I have met with the name there once. But perhaps you can tell me of a boy, one of the fishermen, called Ruffo?"

"Ruffo Scarla? You mean Ruffo Scarla, who fishes with Giuseppe—Mandano Giuseppe, Signore?"

"It may be. A young fellow, a Sicilian by birth, I believe."

"Il Siciliano! Sì, Signore. We call him that, but he has never been in Sicily, and was born in America."

"That's the boy."

"Do you want him, Signore? But he is not here to-day. He is at sea to-day."

"I did want to speak to him."

"But he is not a boatman, Signore. He does not go with the travellers. He is a fisherman."

"Yes. Do you know his mother?"

"Sì, Signore."

"What is her name?"

"Bernari, Signore. She is married to Antonio Bernari, who is in prison."

"In prison? What's he been doing?"

"He is always after the girls, Signore. And now he has put a knife into one."

The man shrugged his shoulders.

"Diavolo! He is jealous. He has not been tried yet, perhaps he never will be. His wife has gone into Naples to-day to see him."

"Oh, she's away?"

"Sì, Signore."

"And her name, her Christian name? It's Maria, isn't it?"

"No, Signore, Maddalena—Maddalena Bernari."

A SPIRIT IN PRISON

Artois said nothing for a minute. Then he added:

"I suppose there are plenty of Maddalenas here in Mergellina?"

The man laughed.

"Sì, Signore. Marias and Maddalenas—you find them everywhere. Why, my own mamma is Maddalena, and my wife is Maria, and so is my sister."

"Exactly. And your name? I want it, so that when next I take a boat here I can ask for yours."

"Fabiano, Signore, Lari Fabiano, and my boat is the *Stella del Mare*."

"Thank you, Fabiano."

Artois put a lira into his hand.

"I shall take the *Star of the Sea* very soon."

"This evening, Signore; it will be fine for sailing this evening."

"If not this evening, another day. A rivederci, Fabiano."

"A rivederci, Signore. Buon passeggio."

The man went back to his companions, and, as Artois walked on began talking eagerly to them, and pointing after the stranger.

Artois did not know what he would do later on in the evening, but he had decided on the immediate future. He would walk up the hill to the village of Posilipo, then turn down to the left, past the entrance to the Villa Rosebery, and go to the Antico Giuseppone, where he would dine by the waterside. It was quiet there, he knew; and he could have a cutlet and a zampaglione, a cup of coffee and a cigar, and sit and watch the night fall. And when it had fallen? Well, he would not be far from the island, nor very far from Naples, and he could decide then what to do.

He followed out this plan, and arrived at the Giuseppone at evening. As he came down the road between the big buildings near the waterside he saw in the distance a small group of boys and men lounging by the

355

three or four boats that lie at the quay, and feared to find, perhaps, a bustle and noise of people round the corner at the ristorante. But when he turned the corner and came to the little tables that were set out in the open air, he was glad to see only two men who were bending over their plates of fish soup. He glanced at them, almost without noticing them, so preoccupied was he with his thoughts, sat down at an adjoining table and ordered his simple meal. While it was being got ready he looked out over the sea.

The two men near him conversed occasionally in low voices. He paid no heed to them. Only when he had dined slowly and was sipping his black coffee did they attract his attention. He heard one of them say to the other in French:

"What am I to do? It would be terrible for me! How am I to prevent it from happening?"

His companion replied:

"I thought you had been wandering all the winter in the desert."

"I have. What has that to do with it?"

"Have you not learned its lesson?"

"What lesson?"

"The lesson of resignation, of obedience to the thing that must be."

Artois looked towards the last speaker and saw that he was an Oriental, and that he was very old. His companion was a young Frenchman.

"What do those do who have not learned?" continued the Oriental. "They seek, do they not? They rebel, they fight, they try to avoid things, they try to bring things about. They lift up their hands to disperse the grains of the sand-storm. They lift up their voices to be heard by the wind from the South. They stretch forth their hands to gather the mirage into their bosom. They follow the drum that is beaten among the dunes.

They are afraid of life because they know it has two kinds of gifts; and one they snatch at, and one they would refuse. And they are afraid still more of the door that all must enter, Sultan and Nomad—he who has washed himself and made the threefold pilgrimage, and he who is a leper and is eaten by flies. So it is. And nevertheless all that is to come must come, and all that is to go must go at the time appointed; just as the cloud falls and lifts at the time appointed, and the wind blows and fails, and Ramadan is here and is over."

As he ceased from speaking he got up from his chair, and, followed by the young Frenchman, he passed in front of Artois, went down to the waterside, stepped into a boat, and was rowed away into the gathering shadows of night.

Artois sat very still for a time. Then he, too, got into a boat and was rowed away across the calm water to the island.

He found Hermione sitting alone, without a lamp, on the terrace, meditating, perhaps, beneath the stars. When she saw him she got up quickly, and a strained look of excitement came into her face.

"You have come!"

"Yes. You—are you surprised? Did you wish to be alone?"

"No. Will you have some coffee?"

He shook his head.

"I dined at the Giuseppone. I had it there."

He glanced round.

"Are you looking for Vere? She is out on the cliff, I suppose. Shall we go to her?"

He was struck by her nervous uneasiness. And he thought of the words of the old Oriental, which had made upon him a profound impression, perhaps because they had seemed spoken, not to the young Frenchman, but in answer to unuttered thoughts of his own.

"Let us sit here for a minute," he said.

Hermione sat down again in silence. They talked for a little while about trifling things. And then Artois was moved to tell her of the conversation he had that evening overheard, to repeat to her, almost word for word, what the old Oriental had said. When he had finished Hermione was silent for a minute. Then she moved her chair and said, in an unsteady voice:

"I don't think I should ever learn the lesson of the desert. Perhaps only those who belong to it can learn from it."

"If it is so it is sad—for the others."

"Let us go and find Vere," she said.

"Are you sure she is on the cliff?" he asked, as they passed out by the front door.

"I think so. I am almost certain she is."

They went forward, and almost immediately heard a murmur of voices.

"Vere is with some one," said Artois.

"It must be Ruffo. It is Ruffo."

She stood still. Artois stood still beside her. The night was windless. Voices travelled through the dreaming silence.

"Don't be afraid. Sing it to me."

Vere's voice was speaking. Then a boy's voice rang out in the song of Mergellina. The obedient voice was soft and very young, though manly. And it sounded as if it sang only for one person, who was very near. Yet it was impersonal. It asked nothing from, it told nothing to, that person. Simply, and very naturally, it just gave to the night a very simple and a very natural song.

> "Oh, dolce luna bianca de l' Estate
>   Mi fugge il sonno accanto a la marina:
> Mi destan le dolcissime serate
>   Gli occhi di Rosa e il mar di Mergellina."

A SPIRIT IN PRISON

As Artois listened he felt as if he learned what he had not been able to learn that day at Mergellina. Strange as this thing was—if indeed it was—he felt that it must be, that it was ordained to be, it and all that might follow from it. He even felt almost that Hermione must already know it, have divined it, as if, therefore, any effort to hide it from her must be fruitless, or even contemptible, as if indeed all effort to conceal truth of whatever kind was contemptible.

The words of the Oriental had sunk deep into his soul.

When the song was over he turned resolutely away. He felt that those children should not be disturbed. Hermione hesitated for a moment. Then she fell in with his caprice. At the house door he bade her good-bye. She scarcely answered. And he left her standing there alone in the still night.

CHAPTER XXIV

HER unrest was greater than ever, and the desire that consumed her remained ungratified, although Emile had come to the island as if in obedience to her fierce mental summons. But she had not seen him even for a moment with Vere. Why had she let him go? When would he come again? She might ask him to come for a long day, or she might get Vere to ask him.

Vere must surely be longing to have a talk with her secret mentor, with her admirer and inspirer. And then Hermione remembered how often she had encouraged Emile, how they had discussed his work together, how he had claimed her sympathy in difficult moments, how by her enthusiasm she had even inspired him—so at least he had told her. And now he was fulfilling in her child's life an office akin to hers in his life.

The knowledge made her feel desolate, driven out. Yes, she felt as if this secret shared by child and friend had expelled her from their lives. Was that unreasonable? She wished to be reasonable, to be calm.

Calm! She thought of the old Oriental, and of his theory of resignation. Surely it was not for her, that theory. She was of different blood. She did not issue from the loins of the immutable East. And yet how much better it was to be resigned, to sit enthroned above the chances of life, to have conquered fate by absolute submission to its decrees!

Why was her heart so youthful in her middle-aged body? Why did it still instinctively clamor for sym-

pathy, like a child's? Why could she be so easily and
so cruelly wounded? It was weak. It was contemptible. She hated herself. But she could only be the
thing she at that moment hated.

Her surreptitious act of the afternoon seemed to have
altered her irrevocably, to have twisted her out of shape
—yet she could not wish it undone, the knowledge gained
by it withheld. She had needed to know what Emile
knew, and chance had led her to learn it, as she had
learned it, with her eyes instead of from the lips of her
child.

She wondered what Vere would have said if she had
been asked to reveal the secret. She would never know
that now. But there were other things that she felt she
must know: why Vere had never told her—and something else.

Her act of that day had twisted her out of shape.
She was awry, and she felt that she must continue to
be as she was, that her fearless honesty was no longer
needed by her, could no longer rightly serve her in the
new circumstances that others had created for her.
They had been secret. She could not be open. She
was constrained to watch, to conceal—to be awry, in
fact.

Yet she felt guilty even while she said this to herself,
guilty and ashamed, and then doubtful. She doubted
her new capacity to be furtive. She could watch, but
she did not know whether she could watch without showing what she was doing. And Emile was terribly observant.

This thought, of his subtlety and her desire to conceal,
made her suddenly realize their altered relations with
a vividness that frightened her. Where was the beautiful friendship that had been the comfort, the prop of
her bereaved life? It seemed already to have sunk
away into the past. She wondered what was in store for

her, if there were new sorrows being forged for her in the cruel smithy of the great Ruler, sorrows that would hang like chains about her till she could go no farther. The Egyptian had said: "What is to come will come, and what is to go will go, at the time appointed." And Vere had said she felt as if perhaps there was a cross that must be borne by some one on the island, by "one of us." Was she, Hermione, picked out to bear that cross? Surely God mistook the measure of her strength. If He had He would soon know how feeble she was. When Maurice had died, somehow she had endured it. She had staggered under the weight laid upon her, but she had upheld it. But now she was much older, and she felt as if suffering, instead of strengthening, had weakened her character, as if she had not much "fight" left in her.

"I don't believe I could endure another great sorrow," she said to herself. "I'm sure I couldn't."

Just then Vere came in to bid her good-night.

"Good-night, Vere," Hermione said.

She kissed the girl gently on the forehead, and the touch of the cool skin suddenly made her long to sob, and to say many things. She took her lips away.

"Emile has been here," she said.

"Monsieur Emile!"

Vere looked round.

"But—"

"He has gone."

"Gone! But I haven't seen him!"

Her voice sounded thoroughly surprised.

"He only stayed five minutes or so."

"Oh, Madre, I wish I had known!"

There was a touch of reproach in Vere's tone, and there was something so transparently natural, so transparently innocent and girlish in her disappointment, that it told her mother something she was glad to know.

Not that she had doubted it — but she was glad to know.

"We came to look for you."

"Well, but I was only on the cliff, where I always go. I was there having a little talk with Ruffo."

"I know."

"And you never called me, Madre!" Vere looked openly hurt. "Why didn't you?"

In truth, Hermione hardly knew. Surely it had been Emile who had led them away from the singing voice of Ruffo.

"Ruffo was singing."

"A song about Mergellina. Did you hear it? I do like it and the way he sings it."

The annoyance had gone from her face at the thought of the song.

"And when he sings he looks so careless and gay. Did you listen?"

"Yes, for a moment, and then we went away. I think it was Emile who made us go. He didn't want to disturb you, I think."

"I understand."

Vere's face softened. Again Hermione felt a creeping jealousy at her heart. Vere had surely been annoyed with her, but now she knew that it was Emile who had not wished to disturb the *tête-à-tête* on the cliff she did not mind. She even looked as if she were almost touched. Could the mother be wrong where the mere friend was right? She felt, when Vere spoke and her expression changed, the secret understanding from which she was excluded.

"What is the matter, Madre?"

"The matter! Nothing. Why?"

"You looked so odd for a minute. I thought—"

But she did not express what she had thought, for Hermione interrupted her by saying:

"We must get Emile to come for a long day. I wish you would write him a note to-morrow morning, Vere. Write for me and ask him to come on Thursday. I have a lot to do in the morning. Will you save me the trouble?" She tried to speak, carelessly. "I've a long letter to send to Evelyn Townley," she added.

"Of course, Madre. And I'll tell Monsieur Emile all I think of him for neglecting us as he has. Ah! But I remember; he's been working."

"Yes, he's been working; and one must forgive everything to the worker, mustn't one?"

"To such a worker as Monsieur Emile is, yes. I do wish you'd let me read his books, Madre."

For a moment Hermione hesitated, looking at her child.

"Why are you so anxious to read them all of a sudden?" she asked.

"Well, I'm growing up and—and I understand things I used not to understand."

Her eyes fell for a moment before her mother's, and there was a silence, in which the mother felt some truth withheld. Vere looked up again.

"And I want to appreciate Monsieur Emile properly—as you do, Madre. It seems almost ridiculous to know him so well, and not to know him really at all."

"But you do know him really."

"I'm sure he puts most of his real self into his work."

Hermione remembered her conception of Emile Artois long ago, when she only knew him through two books; that she had believed him to be cruel, that she had thought her nature must be in opposition to his. Vere did not know that side of "Monsieur Emile."

"Vere, it is true you are growing up," she said, speaking rather slowly, as if to give herself time for something. "Perhaps I was wrong the other day in what I said. You may read Emile's books if you like."

A SPIRIT IN PRISON

"Madre!"

Vere's face flushed with eager pleasure.

"Thank you, Madre!"

She went up to bed radiant.

When she had gone Hermione stood where she was. She had just done a thing that was mean, or at least she had done a thing from a mean, a despicable motive. She knew it as the door shut behind her child, and she was frightened of herself. Never before had she been governed by so contemptible a feeling as that which had just prompted her. If Emile ever knew, or even suspected what it was, she felt that she could never look into his face again with clear, unfaltering eyes. What madness was upon her? What change was working within her? Revulsion came, and with it the desire to combat at once, strongly, the new, the hateful self which had frightened her.

She hastened after Vere, and in a moment was knocking at the child's door.

"Who's there? Who is it?"

"Vere!" called the mother.

As she called she tried the door, and found it locked.

"Madre! It's you!"

"Yes. May I come in?"

"One tiny moment."

The voice within sounded surely a little startled and uneven, certainly not welcoming. There was a pause. Hermione heard the rustling of paper, then a drawer shut sharply.

Vere was hiding away her poems!

When Hermione understood that, she felt the strong, good impulse suddenly shrivel within her, and a bitter jealousy take its place. Vere came to the door and opened it.

"Oh, come in, Madre! What is it?" she asked.

In her bright eyes there was the look of one unexpectedly disturbed. Hermione glanced quickly at the writing-table.

"You—you weren't writing my note to Monsieur Emile?" she said.

She stepped into the room. She wished she could force Vere to tell her about the poems, but without asking. She felt as if she could not continue in her present condition, excluded from Vere's confidence. Yet she knew now that she could never plead for it.

"No, Madre. I can do it to-morrow."

Vere looked and sounded surprised, and the mother felt more than ever like an intruder. Yet something dogged kept her there.

"Are you tired, Vere?" she asked.

"Not a bit."

"Then let us have a little talk."

"Of course."

Vere shut the door. Hermione knew by the way she shut it that she wanted to be alone, to go on with her secret occupation. She came back slowly to her mother, who was sitting on a chair by the bedside. Hermione took her hand, and Vere pushed up the edge of the mosquito-curtain and sat down on the bed.

"About those books of Emile's—" Hermione began.

"Oh, Madre, you're not going to— But you've promised!"

"Yes."

"Then I may?"

"Why should you wish to read such books? They will probably make you sad, and—and they may even make you afraid of Emile."

"Afraid! Why?"

"I remember long ago, before I knew him, I had a very wrong conception of him, gained from his books."

"Oh, but I know him beforehand. That makes all the difference."

"A man like Emile has many sides."

"I think we all have, Madre. Don't you?"

Vere looked straight at her mother. Hermione felt that a moment had come in which, perhaps, she could force the telling of that truth which already she knew.

"I suppose so, Vere; but we need not surely keep any side hidden from those we love, those who are nearest to us."

Vere looked a little doubtful—even, for a moment, slightly confused.

"N—o?" she said.

She seemed to consider something. Then she added:

"But I think it depends. If something in us might give pain to any one we love, I think we ought to try to hide that. I am sure we ought."

Hermione felt that each of them was thinking of the same thing, even speaking of it without mentioning it. But whereas she knew that Vere was doing so, Vere could not know that she was. So Vere was at a disadvantage. Vere's last words had opened the mother's eyes. What she had guessed was true. This secret of the poems was kept from her because of her own attempt to create and its failure. Abruptly she wondered if Vere and Emile had ever talked that failure over. At the mere thought of such a conversation her whole body tingled. She got up from her chair.

"Well, good-night, Vere," she said.

And she left the room, leaving her child amazed.

Vere did not understand why her mother had come, nor why, having come, she abruptly went away. There was something the matter with her mother. She had felt that for some time. She was more conscious than ever of it now. Around her mother there was an atmosphere of uneasiness in which she felt herself involved. And she was vaguely conscious of the new distance between them, a distance daily growing wider. Now and then, lately, she had felt almost uncomfortable with her mother, in the sitting-room when she was saying good-night, and just now when she sat on the bed. Youth is terribly quick to feel hostility, however subtle. The thought that her mother could be hostile to her had never entered Vere's head. Nevertheless, the mother's faint and creeping hostility—for at times Hermione's feeling was really that, though she would doubtless have denied it even to herself—disagreeably affected the child.

"What can be the matter with Madre?" she thought.

She went over to the writing-table, where she had hastily shut up her poems on hearing the knock at the door, but she did not take them out again. Instead, she sat down and wrote the note to Monsieur Emile. As she wrote the sense of mystery, of uneasiness, departed from her, chased away, perhaps, by the memory of Monsieur Emile's kindness to her and warm encouragement, by the thought of having a long talk with him again, of showing him certain corrections and developments carried out by her since she had seen him. The sympathy of the big man meant a great deal to her, more even than he was aware of. It lifted up her eager young heart. It sent the blood coursing through her veins with a new and ardent strength. Hermione's enthusiasm had been inherited by Vere, and with it something else that gave it a peculiar vitality, a power of lasting—the secret consciousness of talent.

Now, as she wrote her letter, she forgot all her uneasiness, and her pen flew.

At last she signed her name—"Vere."

She was just going to put the letter into its envelope when something struck her, and she paused. Then she added:

"P.S.—Just now Madre gave me leave to read your books."

CHAPTER XXV

THE words of the old Oriental lingered in the mind of Artois. He was by nature more fatalistic than Hermione, and moreover he knew what she did not. Long ago he had striven against a fate. With the help of Gaspare he had conquered it—or so he had believed till now. But now he asked himself whether he had not only delayed its coming. If his suspicion were well founded,—and since his last visit to the island he felt as if it must be,—then surely all he had done with Gaspare would be in vain at the last.

If his suspicion were well founded, then certain things are ordained. They have to happen for some reason, known only to the hidden Intelligence that fashions each man's character, that develops it in joy or grief, that makes it glad with feasting, or forces it to feed upon the bread of tears.

Did Gaspare know? If the truth were what Artois suspected, and Gaspare did know it, what would Gaspare do?

That was a problem which interested Artois intensely.

The Sicilian often said of a thing "È il Destino." Yet Artois believed that for his beloved Padrona he would fight to the death. He, Artois, would leave this fight against destiny to the Sicilian. For him the Oriental's philosophy; for him resignation to the inevitable, whatever it might be.

He said to himself that to do more than he had

369

already done to ward off the assaults of truth would be impious. Perhaps he ought never to have done anything. Perhaps it would have been far better to have let the wave sweep over Hermione long ago. Perhaps even in that fight of his there had been secret selfishness, the desire that she should not know how by his cry from Africa her happy life had been destroyed. And perhaps he was to be punished some day for that.

He did not know. But he felt, after all these years, that if to that hermitage of the sea Fate had really found the way he must let things take their course. And it seemed to him as if the old Oriental had been mysteriously appointed to come near him just at that moment, to make him feel that this was so. The Oriental had been like a messenger sent to him out of that East which he loved, which he had studied, but from which, perhaps, he had not learned enough.

Vere's letter came. He read it with eagerness and pleasure till he came to the postcript. But that startled him. He knew Vere had never read his books. He thought her far too young to read them. Till lately he had almost a contempt for those who write with one eye on "la jeune fille." Now he could conceive writing with a new pleasure something that Vere might read. But those books of his! Why had Hermione suddenly given that permission? He remembered Peppina. Vere must have told her mother of the scene with Peppina, and how her eyes had been opened to certain truths of life, how she had passed from girlhood to womanhood through that gate of knowledge. And Hermione must have thought that it was useless to strive to keep Vere back.

But did he wish Vere to read all that he had written?

On Thursday he went over to the island with mingled eagerness and reluctance. That little home in the sea, washed by blue waters, roofed by blue skies, sun-kissed and star-kissed by day and night, drew and repelled him. There was the graciousness of youth there, of youth and promise; but there was tragedy there, too, in the heart of Hermione, and in Peppina, typified by the cross upon her cheek. And does not like draw like?

For a moment he saw the little island with a great cloud above it. But when he landed and met Vere he felt the summer, and knew that the sky was clear.

Hermione was not on the island, Vere told him. She had left many apologies, and would be home for lunch. She had had to go in to Naples to see the dentist. A tooth had troubled her in the night. She had gone by tram. As Vere explained Artois had a moment of surprise, a moment of suspicion—even of vexation. But it passed when Vere said:

"I'm afraid poor Madre suffered a great deal. She looked dreadful this morning, as if she hadn't slept all night."

"Poveretta!" said Artois.

He looked earnestly at Vere. This was the first time they had met since the revelation of Peppina. What the Marchesino had seen Artois saw more plainly, felt more strongly than the young Neapolitan had felt. But he looked at Vere, too, in search of something else, thinking of Ruffo, trying to probe into the depth of human mysteries, to find the secret spring that carried child to child.

"What do you want, Monsieur Emile?"

"I want to know how the work goes," he answered, smiling.

She flushed a little.

"And I want to tell you something," he added. "My talk with you roused me up. Vere, you set me working as I have not worked for a long while."

A lively pleasure showed in her face.

"Is that really true? But then I must be careful, or

you will never come to see us any more. You will always be shut up in the hotel writing."

They mounted the cliff together and, without question or reply, as by a mutual instinct, turned towards the seat that faced Ischia, clear to-day, yet romantic with the mystery of heat. When they had sat down Vere added:

"And besides, of course I know that it is Madre who encourages you when you are depressed about your work. I have heard you say so often."

"Your mother has done a great deal for me," said Artois, seriously—"far more than she will ever know."

There was a sound of deep, surely of eternal feeling in his voice, which suddenly touched the girl to the quick.

"I like to hear you say that—like that," she said, softly. "I think Madre does a great deal for us all."

If Hermione could have heard them her torn heart might perhaps have ceased to bleed. It had been difficult for her to do what she had done—to leave the island that morning. She had done it to discipline her nature, as Passionists scourge themselves by night before the altar. She had left Emile alone with Vere simply because she hated to do it.

The rising up of jealousy in her heart had frightened her. All night she had lain awake feeling this new and terrible emanation from her soul, conscious of this monster that lifted up its head and thrust it forth out of the darkness.

But one merit she had. She was frank with herself. She named the monster before she strove to fight it, to beat it back into the darkness from which is was emerging.

She was jealous, doubly jealous. The monopolizing instinct of strong-natured and deeply affectionate women was fiercely alive in her. Always, no doubt, she had had it. Long ago, when first she was in Sicily alone,

372

she had dreamed of a love in the South—far away from the world. When she married she had carried her Mercury to the exquisite isolation of Monte Amato. And when that love was taken from her, and her child came and was at the age of blossom, she had brought her child to this isle, this hermitage of the sea. Emile, too, her one great friend, she had never wished to share him. She had never cared much to meet him in society. Her instinct was to have him to herself, to be with him alone in unfrequented places. She was greedy or she was timid. Which was it? Perhaps she lacked self-confidence, belief in her own attractive power. Life in the world is a fight. Women fight for their lovers, fight for their friends, with other women: those many women who are born thieves, who are never happy unless they are taking from their sisters the possessions those sisters care for most. Hermione could never have fought with other women for the love or the friendship of a man. Her instinct, perhaps, was to carry her treasure out of all danger into the wilderness.

Two treasures she had—Vere her child, Emile her friend. And now she was jealous of each with the other. And the enormous difference in their ages made her jealousy seem the more degrading. Nevertheless, she could not feel that it was unnatural. By a mutual act they had excluded her from their lives, had withdrawn from her their confidence while giving it to each other. And their reason for doing this—she was sure of it now—was her own failure to do something in the world of art.

She was jealous of Vere because of that confidence given to Emile, and of Emile because of his secret advice and help to Vere—advice and help which he had not given to the mother, because he had plainly seen that to do so would be useless.

And when she remembered this Hermione was jealous,

too, of the talent Vere must have, a talent she had longed
for, but which had been denied to her. For even if
Emile . . . and then again came the most hateful suspicion of all—but Emile could not lie about the things of
art.

Had they spoken together of her failure? Again and
again she asked herself the question. They must have
spoken. They had spoken. She could almost hear
their words—words of regret or of pity. "We must not
hurt her. We must keep it from her. We must temper
the wind to the shorn lamb." The elderly man and the
child had read together the secret of her suffering, had
understood together the tragedy of her failure. To the
extremes of life, youth and age, she had appeared an
object of pity.

And then she thought of her dead husband's reverence of her intellect, boyish admiration to her mental
gifts; and an agony of longing for his love swept over
her again, and she felt that he was the only person who
had been able to love her really, and that now he was
gone there was no one.

At that moment she forgot Gaspare. Her sense of
being abandoned, and of being humiliated, swept out
many things from her memory. Only Maurice had
loved her really. Only he had set her on high, where
even the humblest woman longs to be set by some one.
Only he had thought her better, braver, more worship-
ful, more lovable, than any other woman. Such love,
without bringing conceit to the creature loved, gives
power, creates much of what it believes in. The lack
of any such love seems to withdraw the little power
that there is.

Hermione, feeling in this humiliation of the imagination that she was less than nothing, clung desperately
to the memory of him who had thought her much. The
dividing years were gone. With a strange, a beautiful

and terrible freshness, the days of her love came back. She saw Maurice's eyes looking at her with that simple, almost reverent admiration which she had smiled at and adored.

And she gripped her memory. She clung to it feverishly as she had never clung to it before. She told herself that she would live in it as in a house of shelter. For there was the desolate wind outside.

And she thought much of Ruffo, and with a strange desire—to be with him, to search for the look she loved in him. For a moment with him she had seemed to see her Mercury in the flesh. She must watch for his return.

When the morning came she began her fight. She made her excuse, and left the morning free for Emile to be with Vere.

Two dreary hours she spent in Naples. The buzzing city affected her like a nightmare. Coming back through Mergellina, she eagerly looked for Ruffo. But she did not see him. Nor had she seen him in the early morning, when she passed by the harbor where the yachts were lying in the sun.

Gaspare came with the boat to take her over from the nearest village to the island.

"Don Emilio has come?" she asked him, as she stepped into the boat.

"Sì, Signora. He has been on the island a long time."

Gaspare sat down facing his Padrona and took the oars. As he rowed the boat out past the ruined "Palace of the Spirits" he looked at Hermione, and it seemed to her that his eyes pitied her.

Could Gaspare see what she was feeling, her humiliation, her secret jealousy? She felt as if she were made of glass. But she returned his gaze almost sternly, and said:

"What's the matter, Gaspare? Why do you look at me like that?"

"Signora!"

He seemed startled, and slightly reddened, then looked hurt and almost sulky.

"May I not look at you, Signora?" he asked, rather defiantly. "Have I the evil eye?"

"No—no, Gaspare! Only—only you looked at me as if something were the matter. Do I look ill?"

She asked the question with a forced lightness, with a smile. He answered, bluntly:

"Sì, Signora. You look very ill."

She put up her hand to her face instinctively, as if to feel whether his words were true.

"But I'm perfectly well," she said.

"You look very ill, Signora," he returned.

"I'm a little bit tired, perhaps."

He said no more, and rowed steadily on for a while. But presently she found him looking gravely at her again.

"Signora," he began, "the Signorina loves the island."

"Yes, Gaspare."

"Do you love it?"

The question startled her. Had he read her thoughts in the last days?

"Don't you think I love it?" she asked.

"You go away from it very often, Signora."

"But I must occasionally go in to Naples!" she protested.

"Sì, Signora."

"Well, but mustn't I?"

"Non lo so, Signora. Perhaps we have been here long enough. Perhaps we had better go away from here."

He spoke slowly, and with something less than his usual firmness, as if in his mind there was uncertainty, some indecision or some conflict of desires.

376

A SPIRIT IN PRISON

"Do you want to go away?" she said.

"It is not for me to want, Signora."

"I don't think the Signorina would like to go, Gaspare. She hates the idea of leaving the island."

"The Signorina is not every one," he returned.

Habitually blunt as Gaspare was, Hermione had never before heard him speak of Vere like this, not with the least impertinence, but with a certain roughness. To-day it did not hurt her. Nor, indeed, could it ever have hurt her, coming from one so proven as Gaspare. But to-day it even warmed her, for it made her feel that some one was thinking exclusively of her—was putting her first. She longed for some expression of affection from some one. She felt that she was starving for it. And this feeling made her say:

"How do you mean, Gaspare?"

"Signora, it is for you to say whether we shall go away or stay here."

"You—you put me first, Gaspare?"

She was ashamed of herself for saying it. But she had to say it.

"First, Signora? Of course you are first."

He looked genuinely surprised.

"Are you not the Padrona?" he added. "It is for you to command."

"Yes. But I don't quite mean that."

She stopped. But she had to go on:

"I mean, would you rather do what I wanted than what any one else wanted?"

"Sì, Signora—much rather."

There was more in his voice than in his words.

"Thank you, Gaspare," she said.

"Signora," he said, "if you think we had better leave the island, let us leave it. Let us go away."

"Well, but I have never said I wished to go. I am—" she paused. "I have been very contented to be here."

377

A SPIRIT IN PRISON

"Va bene, Signora."

When they reached the island Hermione felt nervous—almost as if she were to meet strangers who were critical, who would appraise her and be ready to despise her. She told herself that she was mad to feel like that; but when she thought of Emile and Vere talking of her failure—of their secret combined action to keep from her the knowledge of the effort of the child—that seemed just then to her a successful rivalry concealed—she could not dismiss the feeling.

She dreaded to meet Emile and Vere.

"I wonder where they are," she said, as she got out. "Perhaps they are on the cliff, or out in the little boat. I'll go into the house."

"Signora, I will go to the seat and see if they are there."

"Oh, don't bother—" she began.

But he ran off, springing up the steps with a strong agility, like that of a boy.

She hurried after him and went into the house. After what he had said in the boat she wished to look at herself in the glass, to see if there was anything strange or painful, anything that might rouse surprise, in her appearance. She gained her bedroom, and went at once to the mirror.

Hermione was not by nature at all a self-conscious woman. She knew that she was plain, and had sometimes, very simply, regretted it. But she did not generally think about her appearance, and very seldom now wondered what others were thinking of it. When Maurice had been with her she had often indeed secretly compared her ugliness with his beauty. But a great love breeds many regrets as well as many joys. And that was long ago. It was years since she had looked at herself in the glass with any keen feminine anxiety, any tremor of fear, or any cruel self-criticism. But now she stood for a long time before the glass, quite still, looking at her reflection with wide, almost with staring, eyes.

It was true what Gaspare said. She saw that she was looking ill, very different from her usual strong self. There was not a thread of white in her thick hair, and this fact, combined with the eagerness of her expression, the strong vivacity and intelligence that normally shone in her eyes, deceived many people as to her age. But to-day her face was strained, haggard, and feverish. Under the brown tint that the sunrays had given to her complexion there seemed to lurk a sickly white, which was most markedly suggested at the corners of the mouth. The cheek-bones seemed unusually prominent. And the eyes held surely a depth of uneasiness, of—

Hermione approached her face to the mirror till it almost touched the glass. The reflected eyes drew hers. She gazed into them with a scrutiny into which she seemed to be pouring her whole force, both of soul and body. She was trying to look at her nature, to see its shape, its color, its expression, so that she might judge of what it was capable—whether for good or evil. The eyes into which she looked both helped her and frustrated her. They told her much—too much. And yet they baffled her. When she would know all, they seemed to substitute themselves for that which she saw through them, and she found herself noticing their size, their prominence, the exact shade of their brown hue. And the quick human creature behind them was hidden from her.

But Gaspare was right. She did look ill. Emile would notice it directly.

She washed her face with cold water, then dried it almost cruelly with a rough towel. Having done this, she did not look again into the glass, but went at once down-stairs. As she came into the drawing-room she heard voices in the garden. She stood still and listened.

They were the voices of Vere and Emile talking tirelessly. She could not hear what they said. Had she been able to hear it she would not have listened. She could only hear the sound made by their voices, that noise by which human beings strive to explain, or to conceal, what they really are. They were talking seriously. She heard no sounds of laughter. Vere was saying most. It seemed to Hermione that Vere never talked so much and so eagerly to her, with such a ceaseless vivacity. And there was surely an intimate sound in her voice, a sound of being warmly at ease, as if she spoke in an atmosphere of ardent sympathy.

Again the jealousy came in Hermione, acute, fierce, and travelling—like a needle being moved steadily, point downwards, through a network of quivering nerves.

"Vere!" she called out. "Vere! Emile!"

Was her voice odd, startling?

They did not hear her. Emile was speaking now. She heard the deep, booming sound of his powerful voice, that seemed expressive of strength and will.

"Vere! Emile!"

As she called again she went towards the window. She felt passionately excited. The excitement had come suddenly to her when they had not heard her first call.

"Emile! Emile!" she repeated. "Emile!"

"Madre!"

"Hermione!"

Both voices sounded startled.

"What's the matter?"

Vere appeared at the window, looking frightened.

"Hermione, what is it?"

Emile was there beside her. And he, too, looked anxious, almost alarmed.

"I only wanted to let you know I had come back," said Hermione, crushing down her excitement and forcing herself to smile.

"But why did you call like that?"

Vere spoke.

"Like what? What do you mean, figlia mia?"

"It sounded—"

She stopped and looked at Artois.

"It frightened me. And you, Monsieur Emile?"

"I, too, was afraid for a moment that something unpleasant had happened."

"You nervous people! Isn't it lunch-time?"

As they looked at her she felt they had been talking about her, about her failure. And she felt, too, as if they must be able to see in her eyes that she knew the secret Vere had wished to keep from her and thought she did not know. Emile had given her a glance of intense scrutiny, and the eyes of her child still questioned her with a sort of bright and searching eagerness.

"You make me feel as if I were with detectives," she said, laughing, but uneasily. "There's really nothing the matter."

"And your tooth, Madre? Is it better?"

"Yes, quite well. I am perfectly well. Let us go in."

Hermione had said to herself that if she could see Emile and Vere together, without any third person, she would know something that she felt she must know. When she was with them she meant to be a watcher. And now her whole being was strung to attention. But it seemed to her that for some reason they, too, were on the alert, and so were not quite natural. And she could not be sure of certain things unless the atmosphere was normal. So she said to herself now, though before she had had the inimitable confidence of woman in certain detective instincts claimed by the whole sex. At one moment the thing she feared—and her whole being recoiled from the thought of it with a shaking disgust— the thing she feared seemed to her fact. Then something occurred to make her distrust herself. And she felt that betraying imagination of hers at work, obscuring all issues, tricking her, punishing her.

And when the meal was over she did not know at all. And she felt as if she had perhaps been deliberately baffled—not, of course, by Vere, of whose attitude she was not, and never had been, doubtful, but by Emile.

When they got up from the table Vere said:

"I'm going to take the siesta."

"You look remarkably wide awake, Vere," Artois said, smiling.

"But I'm going to, because I've had you all to myself the whole morning. Now it's Madre's turn. Isn't it, Madre?"

The girl's remark showed her sense of their complete triple intimacy, but it emphasized to Hermione her own cruel sense of being in the wilderness. And she even felt vexed that it should be supposed she wanted Emile's company. Nevertheless, she restrained herself from making any disclaimer. Vere went up-stairs, and she and Artois went out and sat down under the trellis. But with the removal of Vere a protection and safety-valve seemed to be removed, and neither Hermione nor Emile could for a moment continue the conversation. Again a sense of humiliation, of being mindless, nothing, in the eyes of Artois came to Hermione, diminishing all her powers. She was never a conceited, but she had often been a self-reliant woman. Now she felt a humbleness such as she knew no one should ever feel—a humbleness that was contemptible, that felt itself incapable, unworthy of notice. She tried to resist it, but when she thought of this man, her friend, talking over her failure with her child, in whom he must surely believe, she could not. She felt "Vere can talk to Emile better than I can. She interests him more than I." And then her years seemed to gather round her and whip her. She shrank beneath the thongs of age, which had not even brought to her those gifts of the mind with which it often partially replaces the bodily gifts and graces it is so eager to remove.

"Hermione!"

"Yes, Emile."

She turned slowly in her chair, forcing herself to face him.

"Are you sure you are not feeling ill?"

"Quite sure. Did you have a pleasant morning with Vere?"

"Yes. Oh"—he sat forward in his chair—"she told me something that rather surprised me—that you had told her she might read my books."

"Well?"

Hermione's voice was rather hard.

"Well, I never meant them for 'la jeune fille.'"

"You consider Vere—"

"Is she not?"

She felt he was condemning her secretly for her permission to Vere. What would he think if he knew her under-reason for giving it?

"You don't wish Vere to read your books, then?"

"No. And I ventured to tell her so."

Hermione felt hot.

"What did she say?"

"She said she would not read them."

"Oh."

She looked up and met his eyes, and was sure she read condemnation in them.

"After I had told Vere—" she began.

She was about to defend herself, to tell him how she had gone to Vere's room intending to withdraw the permission given; but suddenly she realized clearly that she, a mother, was being secretly taken to task by a man for her conduct to her child.

That was intolerable.

And Vere had yielded to Emile's prohibition, though she had eagerly resisted her mother's attempt to retreat from the promise made. That was more intolerable.

She sat still without saying anything. Her knees were trembling under her thin summer gown. Artois felt something of her agitation, perhaps, for he said, with a kind of hesitating diffidence, very rare in him:

"Of course, my friend, I would not interfere between you and Vere, only, as I was concerned, as they were my own writings that were in question—" He broke off. "You won't misunderstand my motives?" he concluded.

"Oh no."

He was more conscious that she was feeling something acutely.

"I feel that I perfectly understand why you gave the permission at this particular moment," he continued, anxious to excuse her to herself and to himself.

"Why?" Hermione said, sharply.

"Wasn't it because of Peppina?"

"Peppina?"

"Yes; didn't you—"

He looked into her face and saw at once that he had made a false step, that Vere had not told her mother of Peppina's outburst.

"Didn't I—what?"

He still looked at her.

"What?" she repeated. "What has Peppina to do with it?"

"Nothing. Only—don't you remember what you said to me about not keeping Vere in cotton-wool?"

She knew that he was deceiving her. A hopeless, desperate feeling of being in the dark rushed over her. What was friendship without complete sincerity? Nothing—less than nothing. She felt as if her whole body stiffened with a proud reserve to meet the reserve with which he treated her. And she felt as if her friend of years, the friend whose life she had perhaps saved in Africa, had turned in that moment into a stranger, or —or even into an enemy. For this furtive withdrawal from their beautiful and open intimacy was like an act of hostility. She was almost dazed for an instant. Then her brain worked with feverish activity. What had Emile meant? Her permission to Vere was connected in his mind with Peppina. He must know something about Vere and Peppina that she did not know. She looked at him, and her face, usually so sensitive, so receptive, so warmly benign when it was turned to his, was hard and cold.

"Emile," she said, "what was it you meant about Peppina? I think I have a right to know. I brought her into the house. Why should Peppina have anything to do with my giving Vere permission to read your books?"

Artois' instinct was not to tell what Vere had not told, and therefore had not wished to be known. Yet he hated to shuffle with Hermione. He chose a middle course.

"My friend," he said, quietly, but with determination, "I made a mistake. I was following foolishly a wrong track. Let us say no more about it. But do not be angry with me about the books. I think my motive in speaking as I did to Vere was probably partly a selfish one. It is not only that I wish Vere to be as she is for as long a time as possible, but that I—well, don't think me a great coward if I say that I almost dread her discovery of all the cruel knowledge that is mine, and that I have, perhaps wrongly, brought to the attention of the world."

Hermione was amazed.

"You regret having written your books!" she said.

"I don't know—I don't know. But I think the happy confidence, the sweet respect of youth, makes one regret a thousand things. Don't you, Hermione? Don't you think youth is often the most terrible tutor age can have?"

She thought of Ruffo singing, "Oh, dolce luna bianca de l' Estate"—and suddenly she felt that she could not stay any longer with Artois just then. She got up.

"I don't feel very well," she said.

Artois sprang up and came towards her with a face full of concern. But she drew back.

"I didn't sleep last night—and then going into Naples— I'll go to my room and lie down. I'll keep quiet. Vere will look after you. I'll be down at tea."

She went away before he could say or do anything. For some time he was alone. Then Vere came. Hermione had not told her of this episode, and she had only come because she thought the pretended siesta had lasted long enough. When Artois told her about her mother, she wanted to run away at once, and see what was the matter—see if she could do something. But Artois stopped her.

"I should leave her to rest," he said. "I—I feel sure she wishes to be alone."

Vere was looking at him while he spoke, and her face caught the gravity of his, reflected it for a moment, then showed an uneasiness that deepened into fear. She laid her hand on his arm.

"Monsieur Emile, what is the matter with Madre?"

"Only a headache, I fancy. She did not sleep last night, and—"

"No, no: the real matter, Monsieur Emile."

"What do you mean, Vere?"

The girl looked excited. Her own words had revealed

to her a feeling of which till then she had only been vaguely aware.

"Madre has seemed different lately," she said—"been different. I am sure she has. What is it?"

As the girl spoke, and looked keenly at him with her bright, searching eyes, a thought came, like a flash, upon Artois — a thought that almost frightened him. He could not tell it to Vere, and almost immediately he thrust it away from his mind. But Vere had seen that something had come to him.

"You know what it is!" she said.

"I don't know."

"Monsieur Emile!"

Her voice was full of reproach.

"Vere, I am telling you the truth," he said, earnestly. "If there is anything serious troubling your mother I do not know what it is. She has sorrows, of course. You know that."

"This is something fresh," the girl said. She thrust forward her little chin decisively. "This is something new."

"It cannot be that," Artois said to himself. "It cannot be that."

To Vere he said: "Sleeplessness is terribly distressing."

"Well—but only one night."

"Perhaps there have been others."

In reply Vere said:

"Monsieur Emile, you remember this morning, when we were in the garden, and mother called?"

"Yes."

"D'you know, the way she called made me feel frightened?"

"We were so busy talking that the sudden sound startled us."

"No, it wasn't that."

"But when we came your mother was smiling—she was perfectly well. You let your imagination—"

"No, Monsieur Emile, indeed I don't."

He did not try any more to remove her impression. He saw that to do so would be quite useless.

"I should like to speak to Gaspare," Vere said, after a moment's thought.

"Gaspare! Why?"

"Perhaps you will laugh at me! But I often think Gaspare understands Madre better than any of us, Monsieur Emile."

"Gaspare has been with your mother a very long time."

"Yes, and in his way he is very clever. Haven't you noticed it?"

Artois did not answer this. But he said:

"Follow your instincts, Vere. I don't think they will often lead you wrong."

At tea-time Hermione came from her bedroom looking calm and smiling. There was something deliberate about her serenity, and her eyes were tired, but she said the little rest had done her good. Vere instinctively felt that her mother did not wish to be observed, or to have any fuss made about her condition, and Artois took Vere's cue. When tea was over, Artois said:

"Well, I suppose I ought to be going."

"Oh no," Hermione said. "We asked you for a long day. That means dinner."

The cordiality in her voice sounded determined, and therefore formal. Artois felt chilled. For a moment he looked at her doubtfully.

"Well, but, Hermione, you aren't feeling very well."

"I am much better now. Do stay. I shall rest, and Vere will take care of you."

It struck him for the first time that she was becoming very ready to substitute Vere for herself as his companion. He wondered if he had really offended or hurt her in any way. He even wondered for a moment whether she was not pleased at his spending the summer

388

in Naples—whether, for some reason, she had wished, and still wished, to be alone with Vere.

"Perhaps Vere will get sick of looking after an—an old man," he said.

"You are not an old man, Monsieur Emile. Don't tout!"

"Tout?"

"Yes, for compliments about your youth. You meant me, you meant us both, to say how young you are."

She spoke gayly, laughingly, but he felt she was cleverly and secretly trying to smooth things out, to cover up the difficulty that had intruded itself into their generally natural and simple relations.

"And your mother says nothing," said Artois, trying to fall in with her desire, and to restore their wonted liveliness. "Don't you look upon me as almost a boy, Hermione?"

"I think sometimes you seem wonderfully young," she said.

Her voice suggested that she wished to please him, but also that she meant what she said. Yet Artois had never felt his age more acutely than when she finished speaking.

"I am a poor companion for Vere," he said, almost bitterly. "She ought to be with friends of her own age."

"You mean that I am a poor companion for you, Monsieur Emile. I often feel how good you are to put up with me in the way you do."

The gayety had gone from her now, and she spoke with an earnestness that seemed to him wonderfully gracious. He looked at her, and his eyes thanked her gently.

"Take Emile out in the boat, Vere," Hermione said, "while I read a book till dinner-time."

At that moment she longed for them to be gone. Vere looked at her mother, then said:

"Come along, Monsieur Emile. I'm sorry for you, but Madre wants rest."

She led the way out of the room.

Hermione was on the sofa. Before he followed Vere, Artois went up to her and said:

"You are sure you won't come out with us, my friend? Perhaps the air on the sea would do you good."

"No, thank you, Emile; I really think I had better stay quietly here."

"Very well."

He hesitated for a moment, then he went out and left her. But she had seen a question in his eyes.

When he had gone, Hermione took up a book, and read for a little while, always listening for the sound of oars. She was not sure Vere and Emile would go out in the boat, but she thought they would. If they came out to the open sea beyond the island it was possible that she might hear them. Presently, as she did not hear them, she got up. She wanted to satisfy herself that they were at sea. Going to the window she looked out. But she saw no boat, only the great plain of the radiant waters. They made her feel alone—why, she did not know then. But it was really something of the same feeling which had come to her long ago during her first visit to Sicily. In the contemplation of beauty she knew the need of love, knew it with an intimacy that was cruel.

She came away from the window and went to the terrace. From there she could not see the boat. Finally she went to the small pavilion that overlooked the Saint's Pool. Leaning over the parapet, she perceived the little white boat just starting around the cliff towards the Grotto of Virgil. Vere was rowing. Hermione saw her thin figure, so impregnated with the narrow charm of youth, bending backward and forward to the oars, Emile's big form leaning against the cushions as if at ease. From the dripping oars came twinkling lines of light, that rayed out and spread like the opened sticks of a fan upon the sea. Hugging the shore, the boat slipped out of sight.

"Suppose they had gone forever—gone out of my life!"

Hermione said that to herself. She fancied she still could see the faint commotion in the water that told where the boat had passed. Now it was turning into the Grotto of Virgil. She felt sure of that. It was entering the shadows where she had shown to Emile not long ago the very depths of her heart.

How could she have done that? She grew hot as she thought of it. In her new and bitter reserve she hated to think of his possession that could never be taken from him, the knowledge of her hidden despair, her hidden need of love. And by that sensation of hatred of his knowledge she measured the gulf between them. When had come the very first narrow fissure she scarcely knew. But she knew how to-day the gulf had widened.

That permission of hers to Vere to read Emile's books! And Emile's authority governing her child, substituted surely for hers! The gulf had been made wider by her learning that episode; and the fact that secretly she felt her permission ought never to have been given caused her the more bitterness. Vere had yielded to Emile because he had been in the right. Instinctively her child had known which of the two with whom she had to deal was swayed by an evil mood, and which was thinking rightly, only for her.

Could Vere see into her mother's heart?

Hermione had a moment of panic. Then she laughed at her folly.

And she thought of Peppina, of that other secret which certainly existed, but which she had never suspected till that day.

The boat was gone, and she knew where. She went back into the house and rang the bell. Giulia came.

"Oh, Giulia," Hermione said, "will you please ask Peppina to come to my sitting-room. I want to speak to her for a moment."

"Sì, Signora."

Giulia looked at her Padrona, then added:

"Signora, I am sure I was right. I am sure that girl has the evil eye."

"Giulia, what nonsense! I have told you often that such ideas are silly. Peppina has no power to do us harm. Poor girl, we ought to pity her."

Giulia's fat face was very grave and quite unconvinced.

"Signora, since she is here the island is not the same. The Signorina is not the same, you are not the same, the French Signore is not the same. Even Gaspare is different. One cannot speak with him now. Trouble is with us all, Signora."

Hermione shook her head impatiently. But when Giulia was gone she thought of her words about Gaspare. Words, even the simplest, spoken just before some great moment of a life, some high triumph, or deep catastrophe, stick with resolution in the memory. Lucrezia had once said of Gaspare on the terrace before the Casa del Prete: "One cannot speak with him to-day." And she had added: "He is terrible to-day." That was on the evening of the night on which Maurice's dead body was found. Often since then Hermione had thought that Gaspare had seemed to have a prevision of the disaster that was approaching.

And now Giulia said of him: "One cannot speak with him now."

The same words. Was Gaspare as a stormy petrel?

There came a knock at the door of the sitting-room, to which Hermione had gone to wait for the coming of Peppina.

A SPIRIT IN PRISON

"Come in."

The door opened and the disfigured girl entered, looking anxious.

"Come in, Peppina. It's all right. I only want to speak to you for a moment."

Hermione spoke kindly, but Peppina still looked nervous.

"Sì, Signora," she murmured.

And she remained standing near the door, looking down.

"Peppina," Hermione said, "I'm going to ask you something, and I want you to tell me the truth without being afraid."

"Sì, Signora."

"You remember, when I took you, I told you not to say anything to my daughter, the Sinorina, about your past life, your aunt, and—and all you had gone through. Have you said anything?"

Peppina looked more frightened.

"Signora," she began. "Madonna! It was not my fault, it was not my fault!"

She raised her voice, and began to gesticulate.

"Hush, Peppina! Now don't be afraid of me."

"You are my preserver, Signora! My saint has forgotten me, but you—"

"I will not leave you to the streets. You must trust me. And now tell me—quietly—what have you told the Signorina?"

And presently Peppina was induced to be truthful, and Hermione knew of the outburst in the night, and that "the foreign Signore" had known of it from the moment of its happening.

"The Signorina was so kind, Signora, that I forgot. I told her all!—I told her all—I told her—"

Once Peppina had begun to be truthful she could not stop. She recalled—or seemed to—the very words she had spoken to Vere, all the details of her narration.

393

"And the foreign Signore? Was he there, too?" Hermione asked, at the end.

"No, Signora. He went away. The Signorina told him to go away and leave us."

Hermione dismissed Peppina quietly.

"Please don't say anything about this conversation, Peppina," she said, as the agitated girl prepared to go. "Try to obey me this time, will you?"

She spoke very kindly but very firmly.

"May the Madonna take out my tongue if I speak, Signora!" Peppina raised her hand.

As she was going out Hermione stared at the cross upon her cheek.

CHAPTER XXVI

ARTOIS stayed to dine. The falling of night deepened Hermione's impression of the gulf which was now between them, and which she was sure he knew of. When darkness comes to intimacy it seems to make that intimacy more perfect. Now surely it caused reserve, restraint, to be more complete. The two secrets which Hermione now knew, but which were still cherished as secrets by Vere and Artois, stood up between the mother and her child and friend, inexorably dividing them.

Hermione was strung up to a sort of nervous strength that was full of determination. She had herself in hand, like a woman of the world who faces society with the resolution to deceive it. While Vere and Artois had been out in the boat she had schooled herself. She felt more competent to be the watcher of events. She even felt calmer, for knowledge increased almost always brings an undercurrent of increased tranquillity, because of the sense of greater power that it produces in the mind. She looked better. She talked more easily.

When dinner was over they went as usual to the garden, and when they were there Hermione referred to the projected meeting with the Marchesino.

"I made a promise," she said. "I must keep it."

"Of course," said Artois. "But it seems to me that I am always being entertained, and that I am inhospitable —I do nothing in return. I have a proposal to make. Monday will be the sixteenth of July, the festa of the Madonna del Carmine—Santa Maria del Carmine. It is one of the prettiest of the year, they tell me. Why should not you and Vere come to dine at the Hotel, or in the Galleria, with me? I will ask Panacci to join us, and we will all go on afterwards to see the illuminations, and the fireworks, and the sending up of the fire-balloons. What do you say?"

"Would you like it, Vere?"

"Immensely, Madre."

She spoke quietly, but she looked pleased at the idea.

"Won't the crowd be very bad, though?" asked Hermione.

"I'll get tickets for the enclosure in the Piazza. We shall have seats there. And you can bring Gaspare, if you like. Then you will have three cavaliers."

"Yes, I should like Gaspare to come," said Hermione.

There was a sound of warmth in her hitherto rather cold voice when she said that.

"How you rely on Gaspare!" Artois said, almost as if with a momentary touch of vexation.

"Indeed I do," Hermione answered.

Their eyes met, surely almost with hostility.

"Madre knows how Gaspare adores her," said Vere, gently. "If there were any danger he'd never hesitate. He'd save Madre if he left every other human being in the world to perish miserably—including me."

"Vere!"

"You know quite well he would, Madre."

They talked a little more. Presently Vere seemed to be feeling restless. Artois noticed it, and watched her. Once or twice she got up, without apparent reason. She pulled at the branches of the fig-trees. She gathered a flower. She moved away, and leaned upon the wall. Finally, when her mother and Artois had fallen into conversation about some new book, she slipped very quietly away.

Hermione and Artois continued their conversation, though without much animation. At length, however, some remark of Hermione led Artois to speak of the book he was writing. Very often and very openly in the days gone by she had discussed with him his work. Now, feeling the barrier between them, he fancied that perhaps it might be removed most easily by such another discussion. And this notion of his was not any proof of want of subtlety on his part. Without knowing why, Hermione felt a lack of self-confidence, a distressing, an almost unnatural humbleness to-day. He partially divined the feeling. Possibly it sprang from their difference of opinion on the propriety of Vere's reading his books. He thought it might be so. And he wanted to oust Hermione gently from her low stool and to show her himself seated there. Filled with this idea, he began to ask her advice about the task upon which she was engaged. He explained the progress he had made during the days when he was absent from the island and shut perpetually in his room. She listened in perfect silence.

They were sitting near each other, but not close together, for Vere had been between them. It was dark under the fig-trees. They could see each other's faces, but not quite clearly. There was a small breeze which made the trees move, and the leaves rustled faintly now and then, making a tiny noise which joined the furtive noise of the sea, not far below them.

Artois talked on. As his thoughts became more concentrated upon his book he grew warmer. Having always had Hermione's eager, even enthusiastic sympathy and encouragement in his work, he believed himself to have them now. And in his manner, in his tone, even sometimes in his choice of words, he plainly showed that he assumed them. But presently, glancing across at Hermione, he was surprised by the expression on her face. It seemed to him as if a face of stone had suddenly looked bitterly satirical. He was so astonished that the words stopped upon his lips.

A SPIRIT IN PRISON

"Go on, Emile," she said, "I am listening."

The expression which had startled him was gone. Had it ever been? Perhaps he had been deceived by the darkness. Perhaps the moving leaves had thrown their little shadows across her features. He said to himself that it must be so—that his friend, Hermione, could never have looked like that. Yet he was chilled. And he remembered her passing by in the tram at Posilipo, and how he had stood for a moment and watched her, and seen upon her face a furtive look that he had never seen there before, and that had seemed to contradict her whole nature as he knew it.

Did he know it?

Never before had he asked himself this question. He asked it now. Was there living in Hermione some one whom he did not know, with whom he had had no dealings, had exchanged no thoughts, had spoken no words?

"Go on, Emile," she said again.

But he could not. For once his brain was clouded, and he felt confused. He had completely lost the thread of his thoughts.

"I can't," he said, abruptly.

"Why not?"

"I've forgotten. I've not thoroughly worked the thing out. Another time. Besides—besides, I'm sure I bore you with my eternal talk about my work. You've been such a kind, such a sympathetic friend and encourager that—"

He broke off, thinking of that face. Was is possible that through all these years Hermione had been playing a part with him, had been pretending to admire his talent, to care for what he was doing, when really she had been bored by it? Had the whole thing been a weariness to her, endured perhaps because she liked him as a man? The thought cut him to the very quick, seared his self-respect, struck a blow at his pride which

398

made it quiver, and struck surely also a blow at something else.

His life during all these years—what would it have been without Hermione's friendship? Was he to learn that now?

He looked at her. Now her face was almost as usual, only less animated than he had seen it.

"Your work could never bore me. You know it," she said.

The real Hermione sounded in her voice when she said that, for the eternal woman deep down in her had heard the sound almost of helplessness in his voice, had felt the leaning of his nature, strong though it was, on her, and had responded instantly, inevitably, almost passionately. But then came the thought of his secret intercourse with Vere. She saw in the dark words: "Monsieur Emile's idea." "Monsieur Emile's suggestion." She remembered how Artois had told her that she could never be an artist. And again the intensely bitter feeling of satire, that had set in her face the expression which had startled him, returned, twisting, warping her whole nature.

"I am to encourage you—you who have told me that I can do nothing!"

That was what she had been feeling. And, as by a search-light, she had seen surely for a moment the whole great and undying selfishness of man, exactly as it was. And she had seen surely, also, the ministering world of women gathered round about it, feeding it, lest it should fail and be no more. And she had seen herself among them!

"Where can Vere have gone to?" he said.

There had been a pause. Neither knew how long it had lasted.

"I should not wonder if she is on the cliff," said Hermione. "She often goes there at his hour. She goes to meet Ruffo."

The name switched the mind of Artois on to a new and profoundly interesting train of thought.

"Ruffo," he began, slowly. "And you think it wise—?"

He stopped. To-night he no longer dared frankly to speak all his mind to Hermione.

"I was at Mergellina the other day," he said. "And I saw Ruffo with his mother."

"Did you? What is she like?"

"Oh, like many middle-aged women of the South, rather broad and battered-looking, and probably much older in appearance than in years."

"Poor woman! She has been through a great deal."

Her voice was quite genuine now. And Artois said to himself that the faint suspicion he had had was ill-founded.

"Do you know anything about her?"

"Oh yes. I had a talk with Ruffo the other night. And he told me several things."

Each time Hermione mentioned Ruffo's name it seemed to Artois that her voice softened, almost that she gave the word a caress. He longed to ask her something, but he was afraid to.

He would try not to interfere with Fate. But he would not hasten its coming—if it were coming. And he knew nothing. Perhaps the anxious suspicion which had taken up its abode in his mind, and which, without definite reason, seemed gradually changing into a conviction, was erroneous. Perhaps some day he would laugh at himself, and say to himself, "I was mad to dream of such a thing."

"Those women often have a bad time," he said.

"Few women do not, I sometimes think."

He said nothing, and she went on rather hastily, as if wishing to cover her last words.

"Ruffo told me something that I did not know about

Peppina. His step-father was the man who cut that cross on Peppina's face."

"Perdio!" said Artois.

He used the Italian exclamation at that moment quite naturally. Suddenly he wished more than ever before that Hermione had not taken Peppina to live on the island.

"Hermione," he said, "I wish you had not Peppina here."

"Still because of Vere?" she said.

And now she was looking at him steadily.

"I feel that she comes from another world, that she had better keep away from yours. I feel as if misfortune attended her."

"It is odd. Even the servants say she has the evil eye. But, if she has, it is too late now. Peppina has looked upon us all."

"Perhaps that old Eastern was right." Artois could not help saying it. "Perhaps all that is to be is ordained long beforehand. Do you think that, Hermione?"

"I have sometimes thought it, when I have been depressed. I have sometimes said to myself, 'É il destino!'"

She remembered at that moment her feeling on the day when she returned from the expedition with Vere to Capri—that perhaps she had returned to the island to confront some grievous fate. Had Artois such a thought, such a prevision? Suddenly she felt frightened, like a child when, at night, it passes the open door of a room that is dark.

She moved and got up from her chair. Like the child, when it rushes on and away, she felt in her panic the necessity of physical activity.

Artois followed her example. He was glad to move.

"Shall we go and see what Vere is doing?" he said.

"If you like. I feel sure she is with Ruffo."

They went towards the house. Artois felt a deep curiosity, which filled his whole being, to know what Hermione's exact feeling towards Ruffo was.

"Don't you think," he said, "that perhaps it is a little dangerous to allow Vere to be so much with a boy from Mergellina?"

"Oh no."

In her tone there was the calm of absolute certainty.

"Well, but we don't know so very much about him."

"Do you think two instincts could be at fault?"

"Two instincts?"

"Vere's and mine?"

"Perhaps not. Then your instinct—"

He waited. He was passionately interested.

"Ruffo is all right," Hermione answered.

It seemed to him as if she had deliberately used that bluff expression to punish his almost mystical curiosity. Was she warding him off consciously?

They passed through the house and came out on its farther side, but they did not go immediately to the cliff top. Both of them felt certain the two children must be there, and both of them, perhaps, were held back for a moment by a mutual desire not to disturb their innocent confidences. They stood upon the bridge, therefore, looking down into the dimness of the Pool. From the water silence seemed to float up to them, almost visibly, like a lovely, delicate mist—silence, and the tenderness of night, embracing their distresses.

The satire died out of Hermione's poor, tormented heart. And Artois for a moment forgot the terrible face half seen in the darkness of the trees.

"There is the boat. He is here."

Hermione spoke in a low voice, pointing to the shadowy form of a boat upon the Pool.

"Yes."

Artois gazed at the boat. Was it indeed a Fate that

came by night to the island softly across the sea, ferried by the ignorant hands of men? He longed to know. And Hermione longed to know something, too: whether Artois had ever seen the strange likeness she had seen, whether Maurice had ever seemed to gaze for a moment at him out of the eyes of Ruffo. But to-night she could not ask him that. They were too far away from each other. And because of the gulf between them her memory had suddenly become far more sacred, far more necessary to her even, than it had been before.

It had been a solace, a beautiful solace. But now it was much more than that—now it was surely her salvation.

As she felt that, a deep longing filled her heart to look again on Ruffo's face, to search again for the expression that sent back the years. But she wished to do that without witnesses, to be alone with the boy, as she had been alone with him that night upon the bridge. And suddenly she was impatient of Vere's intercourse with him. Vere could not know what that tender look meant, if it came. For she had never seen her father's face.

"Let us go to the cliff," Hermione said, moved by this new feeling of impatience.

She meant to interrupt the children, to get rid of Vere and Emile, and have Ruffo to herself for a moment. Just then she felt as if he were nearer, far nearer, to her than they were: they who kept things from her, who spoke of her secretly, pitying her.

And again that evening she came into acute antagonism with her friend. For the instinct was still alive in him not to interrupt the children. The strange suspicion that had been born and that lived within him gathered strength, caused him to feel almost as if they might be upon holy ground, those two so full of youth, who talked together in the night; as if they knew mysteriously things that were hidden from their elders, from those wiser, yet far less full of the wisdom that is eternal, the wisdom of instinct, than themselves. There is always something sacred about children. And he had never lost the sense of it amid the dust of his worldly knowledge. But about these children, about them or within them, there floated, perhaps, something that was mystic, something that was awful and must not be disturbed. Hermione did not feel it. How could she? He himself had withheld from her for many years the only knowledge that could have made her share his present feeling. He could tell her nothing. Yet he could not conceal his intense reluctance to go to that seat upon the cliff.

"But it's delicious here. I love the Pool at night, don't you? Look at the Saint's light, how quietly it shines!"

She took her hands from the rail. His attempt at detention irritated her whole being. She looked at the light. On the night of the storm she had felt as if it shone exclusively for her. That feeling was dead. San Francesco watched, perhaps, over the fishermen. He did not watch over her.

And yet that night she, too, had made the sign of the cross when she knew that the light was shining.

She did not answer Artois' remark, and he continued, always for the children's sake, and for the sake of what he seemed to divine secretly at work in them:

"This Pool is a place apart, I think. The Saint has given his benediction to it."

He was speaking at random to keep Hermione there. And yet his words seemed chosen by some one for him to say.

"Surely good must come to the island over that waterway."

"You think so!"

404

Her stress upon thé pronoun made him reply:

"Hermione, you do not think me the typical Frenchman of this century, who furiously denies over a glass of absinthe the existence of the Creator of the world?"

"No. But I scarcely thought you believed in the efficacy of a plaster Saint."

"Not of the plaster—no. But don't you think it possible that truth, emanating from certain regions and affecting the souls of men, might move them unconsciously to embody it in symbol? What if this Pool were blessed, and men, feeling that it was blessed, put San Francesco here with his visible benediction?"

He said to himself that he was playing with his imagination, as sometimes he played with words, half-sensuously and half-æsthetically; yet he felt to-night as if within him there was something that might believe far more than he had ever suspected it would be possible for him to believe.

And that, too, seemed to have come to him from the hidden children who were so near.

"I don't feel at all as if the Pool were blessed," said Hermione. She sighed.

"Let us go to the cliff," she said, again, this time with a strong impatience.

He could not, of course, resist her desire, so they moved away, and mounted to the summit of the island.

The children were there. They could just see them in the darkness, Vere seated upon the wooden bench, Ruffo standing beside her. Their forms looked like shadows, but from the shadows voices came.

When he saw them, Artois stood still. Hermione was going on. He put his hand upon her arm to stop her. She sent an almost sharp inquiry to him with her eyes.

"Don't you think," he said—"don't you think it is a pity to disturb them?"

"Why?"

"They seem so happy together."

He glanced at her for sympathy, but she gave him none.

"Am I to have nothing?" she thought. And a passion of secret anger woke up in her. "Am I to have nothing at all? May I not even speak to this boy, in whom I have seen Maurice for a moment—because if I do I may disturb some childish gossip?"

Her eyes gave to Artois a fierce rebuke.

"I beg your pardon, Hermione," he said, hastily. "Of course if you really want to talk to Ruffo—"

"I don't think Vere will mind," she said.

Her lips were actually trembling, but her voice was calm.

They walked forward.

When they were close to the children they both saw there was a third figure on the cliff. Gaspare was at a little distance. Hermione could see the red point of his cigarette gleaming.

"Gaspare's there, too," she said.

"Yes."

"Why is he there?" Artois thought.

And again there woke up in him an intense curiosity about Gaspare.

Ruffo had seen them, and now he took off his cap. And Vere turned her head and got up from the seat.

Neither the girl nor the boy gave any explanation of their being together. Evidently they did not think it necessary to do so. Hermione was the first to speak.

"Good-evening, Ruffo," she said.

Artois noticed a peculiar kindness and gentleness in her voice when she spoke to the boy, a sound apart, that surely did not come into her voice even when it spoke to Vere.

"Good-evening, Signora." He stood with his cap in his hand. "I have been telling the Signorina what you have done for my poor mamma, Signora. I did not tell her before because I thought she knew. But she did not know."

Vere was looking at her mother with a shining of affection in her eyes.

At this moment Gaspare came up slowly, with a careless walk.

Artois watched him.

"About the little money, you mean?" said Hermione, rather hastily.

"Sì, Signora. When I gave it to my poor mamma she cried again. But that was because you were so kind. And she said to me, 'Ruffo, why should a strange lady be so kind to me? Why should a strange lady think about me?' she said. 'Ruffino,' she said, 'it must be Santa Maddalena who has sent her here to be good to me.' My poor mamma!"

"The Signora does not want to be bothered with all this!" It was Gaspare who had spoken, roughly, and who now pushed in between Ruffo and those who were listening to his simple narrative.

Ruffo looked surprised, but submissive. Evidently he respected Gaspare, and the two understood each other. And though Gaspare's words were harsh, his eyes, as they looked at Ruffo, seemed to contradict them. Nevertheless, there was excitement, a strung-up look in his face.

"Gaspare!" said Vere.

Her eyes shot fire.

"Signorina?"

"Madre does like to hear what Ruffo has to say. Don't you, Madre?"

Gaspare looked unmoved. His whole face was full of a dogged obstinacy. Yet he did not forget himself. There was nothing rude in his manner as he said, before Hermione could reply:

"Signorina, the Signora does not know Ruffo's mother, so such things cannot interest her. Is it not so, Signora?"

Hermione was still governed by the desire to be alone for a little while with Ruffo, and the sensation of intense reserve—a reserve that seemed even partially physical— that she felt towards Artois made her dislike Ruffo's public exhibition of a gratitude that, expressed in private, would have been sweet to her. Instead, therefore, of agreeing with Vere, she said, in rather an off-hand way:

"It's all right, Ruffo. Thank you very much. But we must not keep Don Emilio listening to my supposed good deeds forever. So that's enough."

Vere reddened. Evidently she felt snubbed. She said nothing, but she shot a glance of eager sympathy at Ruffo, who stood very simply looking at Hermione with a sort of manly deference, as if all that she said, or wished, must certainly be right. Then she moved quietly away, pressing her lips rather firmly together, and went slowly towards the house. After a moment's hesitation, Artois followed her. Hermione remained by Ruffo, and Gaspare stayed doggedly with his Padrona.

Hermione wished he would go. She could not understand his exact feeling about the fisher-boy's odd little intimacy with them. Her instinct told her that secretly he was fond of Ruffo. Yet sometimes he seemed to be hostile to him, to be suspicious of him, as of some one who might bring them harm. Or, perhaps, he felt it his duty to be on guard against all strangers who approached them. She knew well his fixed belief that she and Vere depended entirely on him, felt always perfectly safe when he was near. And she liked to have him near— but not just at this moment. Yet she did not feel that she could ask him to go.

"Thank you very much for your gratitude, Ruffo," she said. "You mustn't think—"

She glanced at Gaspare.

"I didn't want to stop you," she continued, trying to steer an even course. "But it's a very little thing. I hope your mother is getting on pretty well. She must have courage."

As she said the last sentence she thought it came that night oddly from her lips.

Gaspare moved as if he felt impatient, and suddenly Hermione knew an anger akin to Vere's, an anger she had scarcely ever felt against Gaspare.

She did not show it at first, but went on with a sort of forced calmness and deliberation, a touch even perhaps of obstinacy that was meant for Gaspare.

"I am interested in your mother, you know, although I have not seen her. Tell me how she is."

Gaspare opened his lips to speak, but something held him silent; and as he listened to Ruffo's carefully detailed reply, delivered with the perfect naturalness of one sure of the genuine interest taken in his concerns by his auditors, his large eyes travelled from the face of the boy to the face of his Padrona with a deep and restless curiosity. He seemed to inquire something of Ruffo, something of Hermione, and then, at the last, surely something of himself. But when Ruffo had finished, he said, brusquely:

"Signora, it is getting very late. Will not Don Emilio be going? He will want to say good-night, and I must help him with the boat."

"Run and see if Don Emilio is in a hurry, Gaspare. If he is I'll come."

Gaspare looked at her, hesitating.

"What's the matter?" she exclaimed, her secret irritation suddenly getting the upper hand in her nature. "Are you afraid that Ruffo will hurt me?"

"No, Signora."

As Vere had reddened, he reddened, and he looked with

deep reproach at his Padrona. That look went to Hermione's heart; she thought, "Am I going to quarrel with the one true and absolutely loyal friend I have?" She remembered Vere's words in the garden about Gaspare's devotion to her, a devotion which she felt like a warmth round about her life.

"I'll come with you, Gaspare," she said, with a revulsion of feeling. "Good-night, Ruffo."

"Good-night, Signora."

"Perhaps we shall see you to-morrow."

She was just going to turn away when Ruffo bent down to kiss her hand. Since she had given charity to his mother it was evident that his feeling for her had changed. The Sicilian in him rose up to honor her like a Padrona.

"Signora," he said, letting go her hand. "Benedicite e buon riposo."

He was being a little whimsical, was showing to her and to Gaspare that he knew how to be a Sicilian. And now he looked from one to the other to see how they took his salutation: looked gently, confidentially, with a smile dawning in his eyes under the deference and the boyish affection and gratitude.

And again it seemed to Hermione for a moment that Maurice stood there before her in the night. Her impulse was to catch Gaspare's arm, to say to him, "Look! Don't you see your Padrone?"

She did not do this, but she did turn impulsively to Gaspare. And as she turned she saw tears start into his eyes. The blood rushed to his temples, his forehead. He put up his hand to his face.

"Signora," he said, "are you not coming?"

He cleared his throat violently. "I have taken a cold," he muttered.

He caught hold of his throat with his left hand, and again cleared his throat.

SHE WAS JUST GOING TO TURN AWAY WHEN RUFFO BENT
DOWN TO KISS HER HAND"

A SPIRIT IN PRISON

"Madre di Dio!"

He spoke very roughly.

But his roughness did not hurt Hermione; for suddenly she felt far less lonely and deserted. Gaspare had seen what she had seen—she knew it.

As they went back to the house it seemed to her that she and Gaspare talked together.

And yet they spoke no words.

CHAPTER XXVII

NEITHER Artois nor the Marchesino visited the island during the days that elapsed before the Festa of the Madonna del Carmine. But Artois wrote to tell Hermione that the Marchesino had accepted his invitation, and that he hoped she and Vere would be at the Hôtel des Étrangers punctually by eight o'clock on the night of the sixteenth. He wrote cordially, but a little formally, and did not add any gossip or any remarks about his work to the few sentences connected with the projected expedition. And Hermione replied as briefly to his note. Usually, when she wrote to Artois, her pen flew, and eager thoughts, born of the thought of him, floated into her mind. But this time it was not so. The energies of her mind in connection with his mind were surely failing. As she put the note into its envelope she had the feeling of one who had been trying to "make" conversation with an acquaintance, and who had not been successful, and she found herself almost dreading to talk with Emile.

Yet for years her talks with him had been her greatest pleasure, outside of her intercourse with Vere and her relations with Gaspare.

The change that had come over their friendship, like a mist over the sea, was subtle, yet startling in its completeness. She wondered if she saw and felt this mist as definitely as she did, if he regretted the fair prospect it had blotted out, if he marvelled at its coming.

He was so acute that he must be aware of the drooping of their intimacy. To what could he attribute it? And would he care to fight against the change?

She remembered the days when she had nursed him in Kairouan. She felt again the hot dry atmosphere. She heard the ceaseless buzzing of the flies. How pale his face had been, how weak his body! He had returned to the weakness of a child. He had depended upon her. That fact, that he had for a time utterly depended upon her, had forged a new link in their friendship, the strongest link of all. At least she had felt it to be so. For she was very much of a woman, and full of a secret motherliness.

But perhaps he had forgotten all that.

In these days she often felt as if she did not understand men at all, as if their natures were hidden from her, and perhaps, of necessity, from all women.

"We can't understand each other."

She often said that to herself, and partly to comfort herself a little. She did not want to be only one of a class of women from whom men's natures were hidden.

And yet it was not true.

For Maurice, at least, she had understood. She had not feared his gayeties, his boyish love of pleasure, his passion for the sun, his joy in the peasant life, his almost fierce happiness in the life of the body. She had feared nothing in him, because she had felt that she understood him thoroughly. She had read the gay innocence of his temperament rightly, and so she had never tried to hold him back from his pleasures, to keep him always with her, as many women would have done.

And she clung to the memory of her understanding of Maurice as she faced the mist that had swept up softly and silently over that sea and sky which had been clear. He had been simple. There was nothing to dread in cleverness, in complexity. One got lost in a nature that was full of winding paths. Just then, and for the time, she forgot her love of, even her passion for, mental things. The beauty of the straight white road appealed to her. She saw it leading one onward to the glory of the sun.

Vere and she did not see very much of each other during those days. They met, of course, at meals, and often for a few minutes at other times. But it seemed as if each tacitly, and almost instinctively, sought to avoid any prolonged intercourse with the other. Hermione was a great deal in her sitting-room, reading, or pretending to read. And Vere made several long expeditions upon the sea in the sailing-boat with Gaspare and a boy from the nearest village, who was hired as an extra hand.

Hermione had a strange feeling of desertion sometimes, when the white sail of the boat faded on the blue and she saw the empty sea. She would watch the boat go out, standing at a window and looking through the blinds. The sailor-boy pulled at the oars. Vere was at the helm, Gaspare busy with the ropes. They passed quite close beneath her. She saw Vere's bright and eager face looking the way they were going, anticipating the voyage; Gaspare's brown hands moving swiftly and deftly. She saw the sail run up, the boat bend over. The oars were laid in their places now. The boat went faster through the water. The forms in it dwindled. Was that Vere's head, or Gaspare's? Who was that standing up? The fisher-boy? What were they now, they and the boat that held them? Only a white sail on the blue, going towards the sun.

And how deep was the silence that fell about the house, how deep and hollow! She saw her life then like a cavern that was empty. No waters flowed into it. No lights played in its recesses. No sounds echoed through it.

She looked up into the blue, and remembered her

thought, that Maurice had been taken by the blue. Hark! Was there not in the air the thin sound of a reed flute playing a tarantella? She shut her eyes, and saw the gray rocks of Sicily. But the blue was too vast. Maurice was lost in it, lost to her forever. And she gazed up into it again, with the effort to travel through it, to go on and on and on. And it seemed as if her soul ached from that journey.

The sail had dipped down below the horizon. She let fall the blind. She sat down in the silence.

Vere was greatly perplexed about her mother. One day in the boat she followed her instinct and spoke to Gaspare about her. Hermione and she between them had taught Gaspare some English. He understood it fairly well, and could speak it, though not correctly, and he was very proud of his knowledge. Because of the fisher-boy, Vere said what she had to say slowly in English. Gaspare listened with the grave look of learning that betokened his secret sensation of being glorified by his capacities. But when he grasped the exact meaning of his Padroncina's words, his expression changed. He shook his head vigorously.

"Not true!" he said. "Not true! No matter—there is not no matter with my Padrona."

"But Gaspare—"

Vere protested, explained, strong in her conviction of the change in her mother.

But Gaspare would not have it. With energetic gestures he affirmed that his Padrona was just as usual. But Vere surprised a look in his eyes which told her he was watching her to see if he deceived her. Then she realized that for some reason of his own Gaspare did not wish her to know that he had seen the change, wished also to detach her observation from her mother.

She wondered why this was.

Her busy mind could not arrive at any conclusion in

the matter, but she knew her mother was secretly sad. And she knew that she and her mother were no longer at ease with each other. This pained her, and the pain was beginning to increase. Sometimes she felt as if her mother disliked something in her, and did not choose to say so, and was irritated by the silence that she kept. But what could it be? She searched among her doings carefully. Had she failed in any way in her conduct towards her mother? Had she been lacking in anything? Certainly she had not been lacking in love. And her knowledge of that seemed simply to exclude any possibility of serious shortcomings. And her mother?

Vere remembered how her mother had once longed to have a son, how she had felt certain she was going to have a son. Could it be that? Could her mother be dogged by that disappointment? She felt chilled to the heart at that idea. Her warm nature protested against it. The love she gave to her mother was so complete that it had always assumed the completeness of that which it was given in return. But it might be so, Vere supposed. It was possible. She pondered over this deeply, and when she was with her mother watched for signs that might confirm or dispel her fears. And thus she opposed to the mother's new watchfulness the watchfulness of the child. And Hermione noticed it, and wondered whether Vere had any suspicion of the surreptitious reading of her poems.

But that was scarcely possible.

Hermione had not said a word to Vere of her discovery that Peppina had done what she had been told not to do—related the story of her fate. Almost all delicate-minded mothers and daughters find certain subjects difficult, if not impossible of discussion, even when an apparent necessity of their discussion arrives in the course of life. The present reserve between Hermione and Vere rendered even the idea of any plain speaking about the revelation of Peppina quite insupportable to the mother. She could only pretend to ignore that it had ever been made. And this she did. But now that she knew of it she felt very acutely the difference it had made in Vere. That difference was owing to her own impulsive action. And Emile knew the whole truth. She understood now what he had been going to say about Peppina and Vere when they had talked about the books.

He did condemn her in his heart. He thought she was not a neglectful, but a mistaken mother. He thought her so impulsive as to be dangerous, perhaps, even to those she loved best. Almost she divined that curious desire of his to protect Vere against her. And yet without her impulsive nature he himself might long ago have died.

She could not help at this time dwelling secretly on one or two actions of hers, could not help saying to herself now and then: "I have been some good in the world. I am capable of unselfishness sometimes. I did leave my happiness for Emile's sake, because I had a great ideal of friendship and was determined to live up to it. My impulses are not always crazy and ridiculous."

She did this, she was obliged to do it, to prevent the feeling of impotence from overwhelming her. She had to do it to give herself strength to get up out of the dust. The human creature dares not say to itself, "You are nothing." And now Hermione, feeling the withdrawal from her of her friend, believing in the withdrawal from her of her child, spoke to herself, pleading her own cause to her own soul against invisible detractors.

One visitor the island had at this time. Each evening, when the darkness fell, the boat of Ruffo's employer glided into the Pool of San Francesco. And the boy always came ashore while his companions slept. Since Hermione had been charitable to his mother, and since he had explained to her about his Patrigno and Peppina, he evidently had something of the ready feeling that springs up in Sicilians in whom real interest has been shown—the feeling of partly belonging to his benefactor. There is something dog-like in this feeling. And it is touching and attractive because of the animalism of its frankness and simplicity. And as the dog who has been kindly, tenderly treated has no hesitation in claiming attention with a paw, or in laying its muzzle upon the knee of its benefactor, so Ruffo had no hesitation in relating to Hermione all the little intimate incidents of his daily life, in crediting her with an active interest in his concerns. There was no conceit in this, only a very complete boyish simplicity.

Hermione found in this new attitude of Ruffo's a curious solace for the sudden loneliness of soul that had come upon her. Originally Ruffo's chief friendship had obviously been for Vere, but now Vere, seeing her mother's new and deep interest in the boy, gave way a little to it, yet without doing anything ostentatious, or showing any pique. Simply she would stay in the garden, or on the terrace, later than usual, till after Ruffo was sure to be at the island, and let her mother stroll to the cliff top. Or, if she were there with him first, she would soon make an excuse to go away, and casually tell her mother that he was there alone or with Gaspare. And all this was done so naturally that Hermione did not know it was deliberate, but merely fancied that perhaps Vere's first enthusiasm for the fisherboy was wearing off, that it had been a child's sudden fancy, and that it was lightly passing away.

Vere rather wondered at her mother's liking for Ruffo, although she herself had found him so attractive, and had drawn her mother's attention to his handsome face and bold, yet simple bearing. She wondered, because she felt in it something peculiar, a sort of heat and anxiety, a restlessness, a watchfulness; attributes which sprang from the observation of that resemblance to the dead man which drew her mother to Ruffo, but of which her mother had never spoken to her.

Nor did Hermione speak of it again to Gaspare. He had almost angrily denied it, but since the night of Artois' visit she knew that he had seen it, been startled, moved by it, almost as she had been.

She knew that quite well. Yet Gaspare puzzled her. He had become moody, nervous, and full of changes. She seemed to discern sometimes a latent excitement in him. His temper was uneven. Giulia had said that one could not speak with him. Since that day she had grumbled about him again, but discreetly, with a certain vagueness. For all the servants thoroughly appreciated his special position in the household as the "cameriere di confidenza" of the Padrona. One thing which drew Hermione's special attention was his extraordinary watchfulness of her. When they were together she frequently surprised him looking at her with a sort of penetrating and almost severe scrutiny which startled her. Once or twice, indeed, she showed that she was startled.

"What's the matter, Gaspare?" she said, one day "Do I look ill again?"

For she had remembered his looking at her in the boat.

"No, Signora," he answered, this time, quickly. "You are not looking ill to-day."

And he moved off, as if anxious to avoid further questioning.

Another time she thought that there was something wrong with her dress, or her hair, and said so.

"Is there anything wrong with me?" she exclaimed. "What is it?" And she instinctively glanced down at her gown, and put up her hands to her head.

And this time he had turned it off with a laugh, and had said:

"Signora, you are like the Signorina! Once she told me I was—I was"—he shook his head—"I forget the word. But I am sure it was something that a man could never be. Per dio!"

And then he had gone off into a rambling conversation that had led Hermione's attention far away from the starting-point of their talk.

Vere, too, noticed the variations of his demeanor.

"Gaspare was very 'jumpy' to-day in the boat," she said, one evening, after returning from a sail; "I wonder what's the matter with him. Do you think he can be in love, Madre?"

"I don't know. But he is *fidanzato*, Vere, with a girl in Marechiaro, you remember?"

"Yes, but that lasts forever. When I speak of it he always says: 'There is plenty of time, Signorina. If one marries in a hurry, one makes two faces ugly!' I should think the girl must be sick of waiting."

Hermione was sure that there was some very definite reason for Gaspare's curious behavior, but she could not imagine what it was. That it was not anything to do with his health she had speedily ascertained. Any small discipline of Providence in the guise of a cold in the head, or a pain in the stomach, despatched him promptly to the depths. But he had told her that he was perfectly well and "made of iron," when she had questioned him on the subject.

She supposed time would elucidate the mystery, and meanwhile she knew it was no use troubling about it. Years had taught her that when Gaspare chose to be silent not heaven nor earth could make him speak.

Although Vere could not know why Ruffo attracted her mother, Hermione knew that Gaspare must understand, at any rate partially, why she cared so much to be with him. During the days between the last visit of Artois and the Festa of the Madonna del Carmine her acquaintance with the boy had progressed so rapidly that sometimes she found herself wondering what the days had been like before she knew him, the evenings before his boat slipped into the Saint's Pool, and his light feet ran up from the water's edge to the cliff top. Possibly, had Ruffo come into her life when she was comparatively happy and at ease, she would never have drawn so closely to him, despite the resemblance that stirred her to the heart. But he came when she was feeling specially lonely and sad; and when he, too, was in trouble. Both wanted sympathy. Hermione gave Ruffo hers in full measure. She could not ask for his. But giving had always been her pleasure. It was her pleasure now. And she drew happiness from the obvious and growing affection of the boy. Perfectly natural at all times, he kept back little from the kind lady of the island. He told her the smallest details of his daily life, his simple hopes and fears, his friendships and quarrels, his relations with the other fishermen of Mergellina, his intentions in the present, his ambitions for the future. Some day he hoped to be the Padrone of a boat of his own. That seemed to be the ultimate aim of his life. Hermione smiled as she heard it, and saw his eyes shining with the excitement of anticipation. When he spoke the word "Padrone," his little form seemed to expand with authority and conscious pride. He squared his shoulders. He looked almost a man. The pleasures of command dressed all his person, as flags dress a ship on a festival day. He stood before Hermione a boy exuberant.

And she thought of Maurice bounding down the mountain-side to the fishing, and rousing the night with his "Ciao, Ciao, Ciao, Morettina bella—Ciao!"

But Ruffo was sometimes reserved. Hermione could

not make him speak of his father. All she knew of him was that he was dead. Sometimes she gave Ruffo good advice. She divined the dangers of Naples for a lad with the blood bounding in his veins, and she dwelt upon the pride of man's strength, and how he should be careful to preserve it, and not dissipate it before it came to maturity. She did not speak very plainly, but Ruffo understood, and answered her with the unconscious frankness that is characteristic of the people of the South. And at the end of his remarks he added:

"Don Gaspare has talked to me about that. Don Gaspare knows much, Signora."

He spoke with deep respect. Hermione was surprised by this little revelation. Was Gaspare secretly watching over this boy? Did he concern himself seriously with Ruffo's fate? She longed to question Gaspare. But she knew that to do so would be useless. Even with her Gaspare would only speak freely of things when he chose. At other times he was calmly mute. He wrapped himself in a cloud. She wondered whether he had ever given Ruffo any hints or instructions as to suitable conduct when with her.

Although Ruffo was so frank and garrulous about most things, she noticed that if she began to speak of his mother or his Patrigno, his manner changed, and he became uncommunicative. Was this owing to Gaspare's rather rough rebuke upon the cliff before Artois and Vere? Or had Gaspare emphasized that by further directions when alone with Ruffo? She tried deftly to find out, but the boy baffled her. But perhaps he was delicate about money, unlike Neapolitans, and feared that if he talked too much of his mother the lady of the island would think he was "making misery," was hoping for another twenty francs. As to his Patrigno, the fact that Peppina was living on the island made that subject rather a difficult one. Nevertheless, Hermione could not help suspecting that Gaspare had told the boy not to bother her with any family troubles.

She had not offered him money again. The giving of the twenty francs had been a sudden impulse to help a suffering woman, less because she was probably in poverty than because she was undoubtedly made unhappy by her husband. Since she had suffered at the hands of death, Hermione felt very pitiful for women. She would gladly have gone to see Ruffo's mother, have striven to help her more, both materially and morally. But as to a visit—Peppina seemed to bar the way. And as to more money help—she remembered Gaspare's warning. Perhaps he knew something of the mother that she did not know. Perhaps the mother was an objectionable, or even a wicked woman.

But when she looked at Ruffo she could not believe that. And then several times he had spoken with great affection of his mother.

She left things as they were, taking her cue from the boy in despite of her desire. And here, as in some other directions, she was secretly governed by Gaspare.

Only sometimes did she see in Ruffo's face the look that had drawn her to him. The resemblance to Maurice was startling, but it was nearly always fleeting. She could not tell when it was coming, nor retain it when it came. But she noticed that it was generally when Ruffo was moved by affection, by a sudden sympathy, by a warm and deferent impulse that the look came in him. And again she thought of the beautiful obedience that · springs directly from love, of Mercury poised for flight to the gods, his mission happily accomplished.

She wondered if Artois had ever thought of it when he was with Ruffo. But she felt now that she could never ask him.

And, indeed, she cherished her knowledge, her recognition, as something almost sacred, silently shared with Gaspare.

To no one could that look mean what it meant to her. To no other heart could it make the same appeal.

And so in those few days between Hermione and the fisher-boy a firm friendship was established.

And to Hermione this friendship came like a small ray of brightly golden light, falling gently in a place that was very dark.

CHAPTER XXVIII

When the Marchesino received the invitation of Artois
to dine with him and the ladies from the island on the
night of the Festa of the Madonna del Carmine he was
again ill in bed with fever.   But nevertheless he returned
an immediate acceptance.   Then he called in the family
doctor, and violently demanded to be made well, "perfectly well," by the evening of the sixteenth.   The
doctor, who guessed at once that some amorous adventure was on foot, promised to do his best, and so
ingeniously plied his patient with drugs and potions that
on the sixteenth Doro was out of bed, and busily doing
gymnastics to test his strength for the coming campaign.

Artois' invitation had surprised him.   He had lost
all faith in his friend, and at first almost suspected an
ambush.   Emilio had not invited him out of love—that
was certain.   But perhaps the ladies of the island had
desired his presence, his escort.   He was a Neapolitan.
He knew the ways of the city.   That was probably the
truth.   They wanted him, and Emilio had been obliged
to ask him.

He saw his opportunity.   His fever, coming at such a
time, had almost maddened him, and during the days of
forced inaction the Panacci temper had been vigorously
displayed in the home circle.   As he lay in bed his imagination ran riot.   The day and the night were filled
with thoughts and dreams of Vere.   And always Emilio
was near her, presiding over her doings with a false
imitation of the paternal manner.

A SPIRIT IN PRISON

But now at the last the Marchesino saw his opportunity to strike a blow at Emilio. Every year of his
life since he was a child he had been to the festa in honor
of the Madonna del Carmine. He knew the crowds that
assembled under the prison walls and beneath Nuvolo's
tall belfry, the crowds that overflowed into the gaunt
Square of the Mercato and streamed down the avenues
of fire into the narrow side streets. In those crowds it
would be easy to get lost. Emilio, when he heard his
friend's voice singing, had hidden with the Signorina
in the darkness of a cave. He might be alone with the
Signorina when he would. The English ladies trusted
his white hairs. Or the English ladies did not care for
the *convenances*. Since he had found Peppina in the
Casa del Mare, the Marchesino did not know what to
think of its Padrona. And now he was too reckless to
care. He only knew that he was in love, and that circumstances so far had fought against him. He only
knew that he had been tricked, and that he meant to
trick Emilio in return. His anxiety to revenge himself
on Emilio was quite as keen as his desire to be alone with
Vere. The natural devilry of his temperament, a boy's
devilry, not really wicked, but compounded of sen-
suality, vanity, the passion for conquest, and the determination to hold his own against other males and to
shine in his world's esteem, was augmented by abstinence
from his usual life. The few days in the house seemed
to him a lifetime already wasted. He meant to make up
for it, and he did not care at whose expense, so long as
some of the debt was paid by Emilio.

On the sixteenth he issued forth into life again in a
mood that was dangerous. The fever that had abandoned his body was raging in his mind. He was in the
temper which had governed his papa on the day of the
slapping of Signora Merani's face in the Chiaia.

The Marchesino always thought a great deal about

his personal appearance, but his toilet on the night of the sixteenth was unusually prolonged. On several matters connected with it he was undecided. Should he wear a waistcoat of white piqué or one of black silk? Should he put on a white tie, or a black? And what about rings?

He loved jewelry, as do most Neapolitans, both male and female, and had quantities of gaudy rings, studs, sleeve-links, and waistcoat buttons. In his present mood he was inclined to adorn himself with as many of them as possible. But he was not sure whether the English liked diamonds and rubies on a man. He hesitated long, made many changes, and looked many times in the glass. At last he decided on a black tie, a white waistcoat with pearl buttons, a pearl shirt-stud surrounded with diamonds, pearl and diamond sleeve-links, and only three rings—a gold snake, a seal ring, and a ring set with turquoises. This was a modest toilet, suited, surely, to the taste of the English, which he remembered to have heard of as sober.

He stood long before the mirror when he was ready, and had poured over his handkerchief a libation of "Rose d'amour."

Certainly he was a fine-looking fellow—his natural sincerity obliged him to acknowledge it. Possibly his nose stuck out too much to balance perfectly the low forehead and the rather square chin. Possibly his cheek-bones were too prominent. But what of that? Women always looked at a man's figure, his eyes, his teeth, his mustaches. And he had a splendid figure, enormous gray eyes, large and perfectly even white teeth between lips that were very full and very red, and blond mustaches whose turned-up points were like a cry of victory.

He drew himself up from the hips, enlarged his eyes by opening them exaggeratedly, stretched his lips till his teeth were well exposed, and vehemently twisted the ends of his mustaches.

A SPIRIT IN PRISON

Yes, he was a very handsome fellow, and boyish-looking, too—but not too boyish.

It really was absurd of Emilio to think of cutting him out with a girl—Emilio, an old man, all beard and brains! As if any living woman really cared for brains! Impertinence, gayety, agility, muscle—that was what women loved in men. And he had all they wanted.

He filled his case with cigarettes, slipped on a very smart fawn-colored coat, cocked a small-brimmed black bowler hat over his left ear, picked up a pair of white gloves and a cane surmounted by a bunch of golden grapes, and hurried down-stairs, humming "Lili Kangy," the "canzonetta birichina" that was then the rage in Naples.

The dinner was to be at the Hôtel des Étrangers. On consideration, Artois had decided against the Galleria. He had thought of those who wander there, of Peppina's aunt, of certain others. And then he had thought of Vere. And his decision was quickly taken. When the Marchesino arrived, Artois was alone in his sitting-room. The two men looked into each other's eyes as they met, and Artois saw at once that Doro was in a state of suppressed excitement and not in a gentle mood. Although Doro generally seemed full of good-humor, and readiness to please and to be pleased, he could look very cruel. And when, in rare moments, he did so, his face seemed almost to change its shape: the cheek-bones to become more salient, the nose sharper, the eyes catlike, the large but well-shaped mouth venomous instead of passionate. He looked older and also commoner directly his insouciance departed from him, and one could divine a great deal of primitive savagery beneath his lively grace and boyish charm.

But to-night, directly he spoke to Artois, his natural humor seemed to return. He explained his illness, which accounted for his not having come as usual to see his friend, and drew a humorous picture of a Panacci in a bed surrounded by terror-stricken nurses.

"And you, Emilio, what have you been doing?" he concluded.

"Working," said Artois.

He pointed to his writing-table, on which lay a pile of manuscript.

The Marchesino glanced at it carelessly, but the two vertical lines suddenly appeared in his forehead just above the inside corners of his eyes.

".Work! work!" he said. "You make me feel quite guilty, amico mio. I live for happiness, for love. But you—you live for duty."

He put his arm through his friend's with a laugh, and drew him towards the balcony.

"Nevertheless," he added, "even you have your moments of pleasure, haven't you?"

He pressed Artois' arm gently, but in the touch of his fingers there was something that seemed to hint a longing to close them violently and cause a shudder of pain.

"Even you have moments when the brain goes to sleep and—and the body wakes up. Eh, Emilio? Isn't it true?"

"My dear Doro, when have I claimed to be unlike other men?"

"No, no! But you workers inspire reverence, you know. We, who do not work, we see your pale faces, your earnest eyes, and we think—mon Dieu, Emilio!—-we think you are saints. And then, if, by chance, one evening we go to the Galleria, and find it is not so, that you are like ourselves, we are glad."

He began to laugh.

"We are glad; we feel no longer at a disadvantage."

Again he pressed Artois' arm gently.

"But, amico mio, you are deceptive, you workers," he said. "You take us all in. We are children beside you, we who say all we feel, who show when we hate and when we love. We are babies. If I ever want to become really birbante, I shall become a worker."

He spoke always lightly, laughingly; but Artois understood the malice at his heart, and hesitated for a moment whether to challenge it quietly and firmly, or whether laughingly to accept the sly imputations of secrecy, of hypocrisy, in a "not-worth-while" temper. If things developed—and Artois felt that they must with such a protagonist as the Marchesino—a situation might arise in which Doro's enmity must come out into the open and be dealt with drastically. Till then was it not best to ignore it, to fall in with his apparent frivolity? Before Artois could decide—for his natural temper and an under-sense of prudence and contempt pulled different ways—the Marchesino suddenly released his arm, leaned over the balcony rail, and looked eagerly down the road. A carriage had just rattled up from the harbor of Santa Lucia only a few yards away.

"Ecco!" he exclaimed. "Ecco! But—but who is with them?"

"Only Gaspare," replied Artois.

"Gaspare! That servant who came to the Guiseppone? Oh, no doubt he has rowed the ladies over and will return to the boat?"

"No, I think not. I think the Signora will bring him to the Carmine."

"Why?" said the Marchesino, sharply.

"Why not? He is a strong fellow, and might be useful in a crowd."

"Are not we strong? Are not we useful?"

"My dear Doro, what's the matter?"

"Niente—niente!"

He tugged at his mustaches.

"Only I think the Signora might trust to us."

"Tell her so, if you like. Here she is."

A SPIRIT IN PRISON

At this moment the door opened and Hermione came in, followed by Vere.

As Artois went to welcome them he was aware of a strange mixture of sensations, which made these two dear and close friends, these intimates of his life, seem almost new. He was acutely conscious of the mist of which Hermione had thought. He wondered about her, as she about him. He saw again that face in the night under the trellis. He heard the voice that had called to him and Vere in the garden. And he knew that enmity, mysterious yet definite, might arise even between Hermione and him; that even they two—inexorably under the law that has made all human beings separate entities, and incapable of perfect fusion—might be victims of misunderstanding, of ignorance of the absolute truth of personality. Even now he was companioned by the sudden and horrible doubt which had attacked him in the garden: that perhaps she had been always playing a part when she had seemed to be deeply interested in his work, that perhaps there was within her some one whom he did not know, had never even caught a glimpse of until lately, once when she was in the tram going to the Scoglio di Frisio, and once the last time they had met. And yet this was the woman who had nursed him in Africa—and this was the woman against whose impulsive actions he had had the instinct to protect Vere—the Hermione Delarey whom he had known for so many years.

Never before had he looked at Hermione quite as he looked at her to-night. His sense of her strangeness woke up in him something that was ill at ease, doubtful, almost even suspicious, but also something that was quivering with interest.

For years this woman had been to him "dear Hermione," "ma pauvre amie," comrade, sympathizer, nurse, mother of Vere.

431

Now—what else was she? A human creature with a heart and brain capable of mystery; a soul with room in it for secret things; a temple whose outside he had seen, but whose god, perhaps, he had never seen.

And Vere was involved in her mother's strangeness, and had her own strangeness too. Of that he had been conscious before to-night. For Vere was being formed. The plastic fingers were at work about her, moulding her into what she must be as a woman.

But Hermione! She had been a woman so long.

Perhaps, too, she was standing on the brink of a precipice. That suspicion, that fear, not to be banished by action, added to the curiosity, as about an unknown land, that she aroused.

And the new and vital sense of Hermione's strangeness which was alive in Artois was met by a feeling in her that was akin to it, only of the feminine sex.

Their eyes encountered like eyes that say, "What are you?"

After swift greeting they went down-stairs to dine in the public room. As there were but few people in the house, the large dining-room was not in use, and their table was laid in the small restaurant that looks out on the Marina, and was placed close to the window.

"At last we are repeating our *partie carrée* of the Giuseppone," said Artois, as they sat down.

He felt that as host he must release himself from subtleties and under-feelings, must stamp down his consciousness of secret inquiries and of desires or hatreds half-concealed. He spoke cheerfully, even conventionally.

"Yes, but without the storm," said Hermione, in the same tone. "There is no feeling of electricity in the air to-night."

Even while she spoke she felt as if she were telling a lie which was obvious to them all. And she could not help glancing hastily round. She met the large round

432

eyes of the Marchesino, eyes without subtlety though often expressive.

"No, Signora," he said, smiling at her, rather obviously to captivate her by the sudden vision of his superb teeth—"La Bruna is safe to-night."

"La Bruna?"

"The Madonna del Carmine."

They talked of the coming festa.

Vere was rather quiet, much less vehement in appearance and lively in manner than she had been at the Marchesino's dinner. Artois thought she looked definitely older than she had then, though even then she had played quite well the part of a little woman of the world. There was something subdued in her eyes to-night which touched him, because it made him imagine Vere sad. He wondered if she were still troubled about her mother, if she had fulfilled her intention and asked Gaspare what he thought. And he longed to ask her, to know what Gaspare had said. The remembrance of Gaspare made him say to Hermione:

"I gave orders that Gaspare was to have a meal here. Did they tell you?"

"Yes. He has gone to the servants' room."

The Marchesino's face changed.

"Your Gaspare seems indispensable, Signora," he said to Hermione in his lightest, most boyish manner—a manner that the determination in his eyes contradicted rather crudely. "Do you take him everywhere, like a little dog?"

"I often take him—but not like a little dog, Marchese," Hermione said, quietly.

"Signora, I did not mean— Here, in Naples, we use that expression for anything, or any one, we like to have always with us."

"I see. Well, call Gaspare a watch-dog if you like," she answered, with a smile; "he watches over me carefully."

"A watch-dog, Signora! But do you like to be watched? Is it not unpleasant?"

He was speaking now to get rid of the impression his first remark had evidently made upon her.

"I think it depends how," she replied. "If Gaspare watches me it is only to protect me—I am sure of that."

"But, Signora, do you not trust Don Emilio, do you not trust me, to be your watch-dogs to-night at the festa?"

There was a little pressure in his voice, but he still preserved his light and boyish manner. And now he turned to Vere.

"Speak for us, Signorina! Tell the Signora that we will take care of her to-night, that there is no need of the faithful Gaspare."

Vere looked at him gravely. She had wondered a little why her mother had brought Gaspare, why, at least, she had not left him free till they returned to the boat at Santa Lucia. But her mother wanted him to come with them, and that was enough for her. She opened her lips, and Artois thought she was going to snub her companion. But perhaps she suddenly changed her mind, for she only said:

"Who would trust you, Marchese?"

She met his eyes with a sort of child's impertinence. She had abruptly become the Vere of the Scoglio di Frisio.

"Who would take you for a watch-dog?"

"Ma—Signorina!"

"As a seal—yes, you are all very well! But—"

The young man was immediately in the seventh Heaven. The Signorina remembered his feats in the water. All his self-confidence returned, all his former certainty that the Signorina was secretly devoted to him. His days of doubt and fury were forgotten. His jealousy of Emilio vanished in a cloud of happy contempt for the disabilities of age, and he began to talk to Vere with a vivacity that was truly Neapolitan. When the Marchesino was joyous he had charm, the charm that emanates from the bounding life that flows in the veins of youth. Even the Puritan feels, and fears, the grace that is Pagan. The Marchesino had a Pagan grace. And now it returned to him and fell about him like a garment, clothing body and soul. And Vere seemed to respond to it. She began to chatter, too. She talked half-serious nonsense. She bantered her gay companion lightly, flicking him with little whips of sarcasm that did not hurt, but only urged him on. The humor of a festa night began to flow from these two.

And again, instead of infecting Artois, it seemed to set him apart, to rebuke silently his gifts, his fame—to tell him that they were useless, that they could do nothing for him.

The Marchesino was not troubled with an intellect. Yet with what ease he found words to play with the words of Vere! His Latin vivacity seemed a perfect substitute for thought, for imagination, for every subtlety. He bubbled like champagne. And when champagne winks and foams at the edge of the shining glass, do the young think of, or care for, the sober gravity, the lingering bouquet of claret, even if it be Château Margaux?

As Artois half listened to the young people, while he talked quietly with Hermione, playing the host with discretion, he felt the peculiar cruelty which ordains that the weapons of youth, even if taken up and used by age with vigor and competence, shall be only reeds in those hands whose lines tell of the life behind.

Yet how Vere and he had laughed together on the day of his return from Paris! One gust of such mutual laughter is worth how many days of earnest talk!

Vere was gleaming with fun to-night.

The waiters, as they went softly about the table, looked at her with kind eyes. Secretly they were enjoying her gayety because it was so pretty. Her merriment was as airy as the flight of a bird.

The Marchesino was entranced. Did she care for that?

Artois wondered secretly, and was not sure. He had a theory that all women like to feel their power over men. Few men have not this theory. But there was in Vere something immensely independent, that seemed without sex, and that hinted at a reserve not vestal, but very pure—too pure, perhaps, to desire an empire which is founded certainly upon desire.

And the Marchesino was essentially and completely the young animal; not the heavy, sleek, and self-contented young animal that the northern countries breed, but the frolicsome, playful, fiery young animal that has been many times warmed by the sun.

Hermione felt that Artois' mood to-night echoed his mood at Frisio's, and suddenly she thought once more of the visitors' book and of what he had written there, surely in a moment of almost heated impulse. And as she thought of it she was moved to speak of her thought. She had so many secret reserves from Emile now that this one she could dispense with.

"You remember that night when I met you on the sea?" she said to him.

He looked away from Vere and answered:

"Yes. What about it?"

"When I was at the Scoglio di Frisio I looked again over that wonderful visitors' book."

"Did you?"

"Yes. And I saw what you had written."

Their eyes met. She wondered if by the expression in hers he divined why she had made that expedition, moved by what expectation, by what curiosity. She could tell nothing by his face, which was calm and inscrutable.

After an instant's pause he said:

"Do you know from whom those words come?"

"No. Are they your own?"

"Victor Hugo's. Do you like them?"

But her eyes were asking him a question, and he saw it.

"What is it?" he said.

"Why did you write them?" she said.

"I had to write something. You made me."

"Vere suggested it first."

He looked again at Vere, but only for a moment. She was laughing at something the Marchesino was saying.

"Did she?—Oh! Take some of that salade à la Russe. I gave the chef the recipe for it.—Did she?"

"Don't you remember?"

"Those words were in my head. I put them down."

"Are you fond of them?"

Her restless curiosity was still quite unsatisfied.

"I don't know. But one has puzzled about conscience. Hasn't one?"

He glanced at the Marchesino, who was bending forward to Vere, and illustrating something he was telling her by curious undulating gestures with both hands that suggested a flight.

"At least some of us have," he continued. "And some never have, and never will."

Hermione understood the comment on their fellow-guest.

"Do you think that saying explains it satisfactorily?" she said.

"I believe sometimes we know a great deal more than we know we know," he answered. "That sounds like some nonsense game with words, but it's the best way to put it. Conscience seems to speak out of the silence. But there may be some one in the prompter's box— our secret knowledge."

"But is it knowledge of ourselves, or of others?"

"Which do you think?"

"Of ourselves, I suppose. I think we generally know far less of others than we believe ourselves to know."

She expressed his thought of her earlier in the evening.

"Probably. And nevertheless we may know things of them that we are not aware we know—till after we have instinctively acted on our knowledge."

Their eyes met again. Hermione felt in that moment as if he knew why she had given Vere the permission to read his books.

But still she did not know whether he had written that sentence in the book at Frisio's carelessly, or prompted by some violent impulse to express a secret thought or feeling of the moment.

"Things good or evil?" she said, slowly.

"Perhaps both."

The Marchesino burst into a laugh. He leaned back in his chair, shaking his head, and holding the table with his two hands. His white teeth gleamed.

"What is the joke?" asked Artois.

Vere turned her head.

"Oh, nothing. It's too silly. I can't imagine why the Marchesino is so much amused by it."

Artois felt shut out. But when Vere and he had laughed over the tea-table in a blessed community of happy foolishness, who could have understood their mirth? He remembered how he had pitied the imagined outsider.

He turned again to Hermione, but such conversation as theirs, and indeed all serious conversation, now seemed to him heavy, portentous, almost ludicrous. The young alone knew how to deal with life, chasing it as a child chases a colored air-ball, and when it would sink, and fail and be inert, sending it with a gay blow soaring once more towards the blue.

Perhaps Hermione had a similar thought, or perhaps she knew of it in him. At any rate, for a moment she had nothing to say. Nor had he. And so, tacitly excluded, as it seemed, from the merriment of the young ones, the two elders remained looking towards each other in silence, sunk in a joint exile.

Presently Artois began to fidget with his bread. He pulled out some of the crumb from his roll, and pressed it softly between his large fingers, and scattered the tiny fragments mechanically over the table-cloth near his plate. Hermione watched his moving hand. The Marchesino was talking now. He was telling Vere about a paper-chase at Capodimonte, which had started from the Royal Palace. His vivacity, his excitement made a paper-chase seem one of the most brilliant and remarkable events in a brilliant and remarkable world. He had been the hare. And such a hare! Since hares were first created and placed in the Garden of Eden there had been none like unto him. He told of his cunning exploits.

The fingers of Artois moved faster. Hermione glanced at his face. Its massiveness looked heavy. The large eyes were fixed upon the table-cloth. His hand just then was more expressive. And as she glanced at it again something very pitiful awoke in her, something pitiful for him and for herself. She felt that very often lately she had misunderstood him—she had been confused about him. But now, in this moment, she understood him perfectly.

He pulled some more crumb out of his roll.

She was fascinated by his hand. Much as it had written, it had never written more clearly on paper than it was writing now.

But suddenly she felt as if she could not look at it any

more, as if it was intolerable to look at it. And she turned towards the open window.

"What is it?" Artois asked her. "Is there too much air for you?"

"Oh no. It isn't that. I was only thinking what a quantity of people pass by, and wondering where they were all going, and what they were all thinking and hoping. I don't know why they should have come into my head just then. I suppose it will soon be time for us to start for the festa."

"Yes. We'll have coffee in my sitting-room—when they are ready." He looked again at Vere and the Marchesino.

"Have we all finished? I thought we would go and have coffee up-stairs. What do you say, Vere?"

He spoke cheerfully.

"Yes; do let us."

They all got up. As Hermione and Vere moved towards the door Artois leaned out of the window for a moment.

"You needn't be afraid. There will be no storm to-night, Emilio!" said the Marchesino, gayly—almost satirically.

"No—it's quite fine."

Artois drew in. "We ought to have a perfect evening," he added, quietly.

CHAPTER XXIX

"How are we going to drive to the Carmine?" said Artois to Hermione, when she had taken her cloak and was ready to go down.

"We must have two carriages."

"Yes."

"Vere and I will go in one, with Gaspare on the box, and you and the Marchese can follow in the other."

"Signora," said the Marchesino, drawing on his white gloves, "you still do not trust us? You are still determined to take the watch-dog? It is cruel of you. It shows a great want of faith in Emilio and in me."

"Gaspare must come."

The Marchesino said no more, only shrugged his shoulders with an air of humorous resignation which hid a real chagrin. He knew how watchful a Sicilian can be, how unyielding in attention to his mistresses, if he thinks they need protection.

But perhaps this Gaspare was to be bribed.

Instinctively the Marchesino put his hand into his waistcoat-pocket, and began to feel the money there.

Yes, there was a gold piece.

"Come, Panacci!"

Emilio's hand touched his shoulder, and he followed the ladies out of the room.

Emilio had called him "Panacci." That sounded almost like a declaration of war. Well, he was ready. At dinner his had been the triumph, and Emilio knew it. He meant his triumph to be a greater one before the evening was over. The reappearance of the gay child in Vere, grafted upon the comprehending woman whom he had seen looking out of her eyes on the day of his last visit to the island, had put the finishing touch to the amorous madness of the Marchesino. He deemed Vere an accomplished coquette. He believed that her cruelty on the night of his serenade, that her coldness and avoidance of him on the day of the lunch, were means devised to increase his ardor. She had been using Emilio merely as an instrument. He had been a weapon in her girlish hands. That was the suitable fate of the old—usefulness.

The Marchesino was in a fever of anticipation. Possibly Vere would play into his hands when they got to the festa. If not, he must manage things for himself. The Signora, of course, would make Emilio her escort. Vere would naturally fall to him, the Marchesino.

But there was the fifth—this Gaspare.

When they came out to the pavement the Marchesino cast a searching glance at the Sicilian, who was taking the cloaks, while the two carriages which had been summoned by the hotel porter were rattling up from the opposite side of the way. Gaspare had saluted him, but did not look at him again. When Hermione and Vere were in the first carriage, Gaspare sprang on to the box as a matter of course. The Marchesino went to tell the coachman which way to drive to the Carmine. When he had finished he looked at Gaspare and said:

"There will be a big crowd. Take care the Signora does not get hurt in it."

He laid a slight emphasis on the word "Signora," and put his hand significantly into his waistcoat-pocket.

Gaspare regarded him calmly.

"Va bene, Signor Marchese," he replied. "I will take care of the Signora and the Signorina."

The Marchesino turned away and jumped into the

second carriage with Emilio, realizing angrily that his gold piece would avail him nothing.

As they drove off Artois drew out some small square bits of paper.

"Here's your ticket for the enclosure," he said, giving one to the Marchesino.

"Grazie. But we must walk about. We must show the ladies the fun in the Mercato. It is very dull to stay all the evening in the enclosure."

"We will do whatever they like, of course."

"Keep close to the other carriage! Do you hear?" roared the Marchesino to the coachman.

The man jerked his head, cracked his whip, pulled at his horse's mouth. They shot forward at a tremendous pace, keeping close by the sea at first, then turning to the left up the hill towards the Piazza del Plebiscito. The Marchesino crossed his legs, folded his arms, and instinctively assumed the devil-may-care look characteristic of the young Neapolitan when driving through his city.

"Emilio," he said, after a moment, looking at Artois out of the corners of his eyes without moving his head, "when I was at the island the other day, do you know whom I saw in the house?"

"No."

"A girl of the town. A bad girl. You understand?"

"Do you mean a girl with a wounded cheek?"

"Yes. How can the Signora have her there?"

"The Signora knows all about her," said Artois, dryly.

"She thinks so!"

"What do you mean?"

"If the Signora really knew, could she take such a girl to live with the Signorina?"

The conversation was rapidly becoming insupportable to Artois.

"This is not our affair," he said.

"I do not say it is. But still, as I am a Neapolitan, I think it a pity that some one does not explain to the Signora how impossible—"

"Caro mio!" Artois exclaimed, unable to endure his companion's obvious inclination to pose as a protector of Vere's innocence, "English ladies do not care to be governed. They are not like your charming women. They are independent and do as they choose. You had much better not bother your head about what happens on the island. Very soon the Signora may be leaving it and going away from Naples."

"Davvero?"

The Marchesino turned right round in the little carriage, forgetting his pose.

"Davvero? No. I don't believe it. You play with me. You wish to frighten me."

"To frighten you! I don't understand what you mean. What can it matter to you? You scarcely know these ladies."

The Marchesino pursed his lips together. But he only said, "Sì, sì." He did not mean to quarrel with Emilio yet. To do so might complicate matters with the ladies.

As they entered the Via del Popolo, and drew near to the Piazza di Masaniello, his excitement increased, stirred by the sight of the crowds of people, who were all streaming in the same direction past the iron rails of the port, beyond which, above the long and ghostly sheds that skirt the sea, rose the tapering masts of vessels lying at anchor. Plans buzzed in his head. He called upon all his shrewdness, all his trickiness of the South. He had little doubt of his capacity to out-manœuvre Emilio and the Signora. And if the Signorina were favorable to him, he believed that he might even get the better of Gaspare, in whom he divined a watchful hostility. But would the Signorina help him? He could not tell. How can one ever tell what a girl will do at a given moment?

With a jerk the carriage drew up beneath the walls of the prison that frowns upon the Piazza di Masaniello, and the Marchesino roused himself to the battle and sprang out. The hum of the great crowd already assembled, the brilliance of the illuminations that lit up the houses, Nuvolo's tower, the façade of the Church of the Carmine, and the adjoining monastery, the loud music of the band that was stationed in the Kosk before the enclosure, stirred his young blood. As he went quickly to help Hermione and Vere, he shot a glance almost of contempt at the gray hairs of Emilio, who was getting out of the carriage slowly. Artois saw the glance and understood it. For a moment he stood still. Then he paid the coachman and moved on, encompassed by the masses of people who were struggling gayly towards the centre of the Square, intent upon seeing the big doll that was enthroned there dressed as Masaniello.

"We had better go into the enclosure. Don't you think so?" he said to Hermione.

"If you like. I am ready for anything."

"We can walk about afterwards. Perhaps the crush will be less when the fire-balloon has gone up."

The Marchesino said nothing, and they gained the enclosure, where rows of little chairs stood on the short grass that edges the side of the prison that looks upon the Piazza. Gaspare, who on such occasions was full of energy and singularly adroit, found them good places in a moment.

"Ecco, Signora! Ecco, Signorina!"

"Madre, may I stand on my chair?"

"Of course, Signorina. Look! Others are standing!"

Gaspare helped his Padroncina up, then took his place beside her, and stood like a sentinel. Artois had never liked him better than at that moment. Hermione, who

looked rather tired, sat down on her chair. The loud
music of the band, the lines of fire that brought the discolored houses into sharp relief, and that showed her
with a distinctness that was fanciful and lurid the
moving faces of hundreds of strangers, the dull roar of
voices, and the heat that flowed from the human bodies,
seemed to mingle, to become concrete, to lie upon her
spirit like a weight. Artois stood by her, leaning on his
stick and watching the crowd with his steady eyes. The
Marchesino was looking up at Vere, standing in a position
that seemed to indicate a longing that she should rest
her hand upon his shoulder.

"You will fall, Signorina!" he said. "Be careful.
Let me—"

"I am quite safe."

But she dropped one hand to the shoulder of Gaspare.

The Marchesino moved, almost as if he were about to
go away. Then he lit a cigarette and spoke to Hermione.

"You look tired, Signora. You feel the heat. It is
much fresher outside, when one is walking. Here, under
the prison walls, it is always like a furnace in summer.
It is unwholesome. It puts one into a fever."

Hermione looked at him, and saw a red spot burning
on each side of his face near his cheek-bones.

"Perhaps it would be better to walk," she said,
doubtfully.

Her inclination was for movement, for her fatigue was
combined with a sensation of great restlessness.

"What do you say, Vere?" she added.

"Oh, I should love to go among the people and see
everything," she answered, eagerly.

The Marchesino's brow cleared.

"Let us go, Emilio! You hear what the Signorina
says."

"Very well," said Artois.

His voice was reluctant, even cold. Vere glanced at him quickly.

"Would you rather stay here, Monsieur Emile?" she said.

"No, Vere, no. Let us go and see the fun."

He smiled at her.

"We must keep close together," he added, looking at the Marchesino. "The crowd is tremendous."

"But they are all in good humor," he answered, carelessly. "We Neapolitans, we are very gay, that is true, but we do not forget our manners when we have a festa. There is nothing to fear. This is the best way out. We must cross the Mercato. The illuminations of the streets beyond are always magnificent. The Signorina shall walk down paths of fire, but she shall not be burned."

He led the way with Vere, going in front to disarm the suspicion which he saw plainly lurking in Emilio's eyes. Artois followed with Hermione, and Gaspare came last. The exit from the enclosure was difficult, as many people were pouring in through the narrow opening, and others, massed together outside the wooden barrier, were gazing at the seated women within; but at length they reached the end of the Piazza, and caught a glimpse of the Masaniello doll, which faced a portrait of the Madonna del Carmine framed in fire. Beyond, to the right, above the heads of the excited multitude, rose the pale-pink globe of the fire-balloon, and as for a moment they stood still to look at it the band struck up a sonorous march, the balloon moved sideways, swayed, heeled over slightly like a sailing-yacht catching the breeze beyond the harbor bar, recovered itself, and lifted its blazing car above the gesticulating arms of the people. A long murmur followed it as it glided gently away, skirting the prodigious belfry with the apparent precaution of a living thing that longed for, and sought, the dim freedom of the sky. The children instinctively stretched out their arms to it. All faces were lifted towards the stars, as if a common aspiration at that moment infected the throng, a universal, though passing desire to be free of the earth, to mount, to travel, to be lost in the great spaces that encircle terrestrial things. At the doors of the trattorie the people, who had forsaken their snails, stood to gaze, many of them holding glasses of white wine in their hands. The spighe arrosto, the watermelons, were for a moment forgotten on the stalls of their vendors, who ceased from shouting to the passers-by. There was a silence in which was almost audible the human wish for wings. Presently the balloon, caught by some vagrant current of air, began to travel abruptly, and more swiftly, sideways, passing over the city towards its centre. At once the crowd moved in the same direction. Aspiration was gone. A violence of children took its place, and the instinct to follow where the blazing toy led. The silence was broken. People called and gesticulated, laughed and chattered. Then the balloon caught fire from the brazier beneath it. A mass of flames shot up. A roar broke from the crowd and it pressed more fiercely onward, each unit of it longing to see where the wreck would fall. Already the flames were sinking towards the city.

"Where are Vere and the Marchesino?"

Hermione had spoken. Artois, whose imagination had been fascinated by the instincts of the crowd, and whose intellect had been chained to watchfulness during its strange excitement, looked sharply round.

"Vere—isn't she here?"

He saw at once that she was gone. But he saw, too, that Gaspare was no longer with them. The watchdog had been more faithful than he.

"They must be close by," he added. "The sudden movement separated us, no doubt."

"Yes. Gaspare has vanished too!"

"With them," Artois said.

He spoke with an emphasis that was almost violent.

"But—you didn't see—" began Hermione.

"Don't you know Gaspare yet?" he asked.

Their eyes met. She was startled by the expression in his.

"You don't think—" she began.

She broke off.

"I think Gaspare knows his Southerner," Artois replied. "We must look for them. They are certain to have gone with the crowd."

They followed the people into the Mercato. The burning balloon dropped down and disappeared.

"It had fallen into the Rettifilo!" cried a young man close to them.

"Macchè!" exclaimed his companion.

"I will bet you five lire—"

He gesticulated furiously.

"We shall never find them," Hermione said.

"We will try to find them."

His voice startled her now, as his eyes had startled her. A man in the crowd pressed against her roughly. Instinctively she caught hold of Artois' arm.

"Yes, you had better take it," he said.

"Oh, it was only—"

"No, take it."

And he drew her hand under his arm.

The number of people in the Mercato was immense, but it was possible to walk on steadily, though slowly. Now that the balloon had vanished the crowd had forgotten it, and was devoting itself eagerly to the pleasures of the fair. In the tall and barrack-like houses candles gleamed in honor of Masaniello. The streets that led away towards the city's heart were decorated with arches of little lamps, with columns and chains of lights, and the pedestrians passing through them looked strangely black in this great frame of fire. From the Piazza before the Carmine the first rocket rose, and, exploding, showered its golden rain upon the picture of the Virgin.

"Perhaps they have gone back into the Piazza."

Hermione spoke after a long silence, during which they had searched in vain. Artois stood still and looked down at her. His face was very stern.

"We sha'n't find them," he said.

"In this crowd, of course, it is difficult, but—"

"We sha'n't find them."

"At any rate, Gaspare is with them."

"How do we know that?"

The expression in his face frightened her.

"But you said you were sure—"

"Panacci was too clever for us; he may have been too clever for Gaspare."

Hermione was silent for a moment. Then she said:

"You surely don't think the Marchese is wicked?"

"He is young, he is Neapolitan, and to-night he is mad. Vere has made him mad."

"But Vere was only gay at dinner as any child—"

"Don't think I am blaming Vere. If she has fascination, she cannot help it."

"What shall we do?"

"Will you let me put you into a cab? Will you wait in my room at the hotel until I come back with Vere? I can search for her better alone. I will find her—if she is here."

Their eyes met steadily as he finished speaking, and he saw, or thought he saw, in hers a creeping menace, as if she had the intention to attack or to defy him.

"I am Vere's mother," she said.

"Let me take you to a cab, Hermione."

He spoke coldly, inexorably. This moment of enforced inactivity was a very difficult one for him. And the violence that was blazing within him made him fear that if Hermione did not yield to his wish he might lose his self-control.

"You can do nothing," he added.

Her eyes left his, her lips quivered. Then she said: "Take me, then."

She did not look at him again until she was in a cab and Artois had told the driver to go to the Hôtel Royal. Then she glanced at him with a strange expression of acute self-consciousness which he had never before seen on her face.

"You don't believe that—that there is any danger to Vere?" she said, in a low voice. "You cannot believe that."

"I don't know."

She leaned forward, and her face changed.

"Go and bring her back to me."

The cabman drove off, and Artois was lost in the crowd.

He never knew how long his search lasted, how long he heard the swish and the bang of rockets, the vehement music of the band, the cries and laughter of the people, the sound of footsteps as if a world were starting on some pilgrimage; how long he saw the dazzling avenues of fire stretching away into the city's heart; how long he looked at the faces of strangers, seeking Vere's face. He was excessively conscious of almost everything except of time. It might have been two hours later, or much less, when he felt a hand upon his arm, turned round, and saw Gaspare beside him.

"Where is the Signora?"

"Gone to the hotel. And the Signorina?"

Gaspare looked at Artois with a sort of heavy gloom, then looked down to the ground.

"You have lost her?"

"Sì."

There was a dulness of fatalism in his voice.

Artois did not reproach him.

"Did you lose them when the balloon went up?" he asked.

"Macchè! It was not the balloon!" Gaspare said, fiercely.

"What was it?"

Artois felt suddenly that Gaspare had some perfect excuse for his inattention.

"Some one spoke to me. When I—when I had finished the Signorina and that Signore were gone."

"Some one spoke to you. Who was it?"

"It was Ruffo."

Artois stared at Gaspare.

"Ruffo! Was he alone?"

"No, Signore."

"Who was with him?"

"His mother was with him."

"His mother. Did you speak to her?"

"Sì, Signore."

There was a silence between them. It was broken by a sound of bells.

"Signore, it is midnight."

Artois drew out his watch quickly. The hands pointed to twelve o'clock. The crowd was growing thinner, was surely melting away.

"We had better go to the hotel," Artois said. "Perhaps they are there. If they are not there—"

He did not finish the sentence. They found a cab and drove swiftly towards the Marina. All the time the little carriage rattled over the stony streets Artois expected Gaspare to speak to him, to tell him more, to tell him something tremendous. He felt as if the Sicilian were beset by an imperious need to break a long reserve. But, if it were so, this reserve was too strong for its enemy. Gaspare's lips were closed. He did not say a word till the cabman drew up before the hotel.

As Artois got out he knew that he was terribly excited. The hall was almost dark, and the night concierge came from his little room on the right of the door to turn on the light and accompany Artois to the lift.

"There is a lady waiting in your room, Signore," he said.

Artois, who was walking quickly towards the lift, stopped. He looked at Gaspare.

"A lady!" he said.

"Shall I go back to the Piazza, Signore?"

He half turned towards the swing door.

"Wait a minute. Come up-stairs first and see the Signora."

The lift ascended. As Artois opened the door of his sitting-room he heard a woman's dress rustle, and Hermione stood before them.

"Vere?" she said.

She laid her hand on his arm.

"Gaspare!"

There was a sound of reproach in her voice. She took her hand away from Artois.

"Gaspare?" she repeated, interrogatively.

"Signora!" he answered, doggedly.

He did not lift his eyes to hers.

"You have lost the Signorina?"

"Sì, Signora."

He attempted no excuse, he expressed no regret.

"Gaspare!" Hermione said.

Suddenly Artois put his hand on Gaspare's shoulder. He said nothing, but his touch told the Sicilian much— told him how he was understood, how he was respected, by this man who had shared his silence.

"We thought they might be here," Artois said.

453

"They are not here."

Her voice was almost hard, almost rebuking. She was still standing in the door-space.

"I will go back and look again, Signora."

"Sì," she said.

She turned back into the room. Artois held out his hand to Gaspare:

"Signore?"

Gaspare looked surprised, hesitating, then moved. He took the out-stretched hand, grasped it violently, and went away.

Artois shut the sitting-room door and went towards Hermione.

"You are staying?" she said.

By her intonation he could not tell whether she was glad or almost angrily astonished.

"They may come here immediately," he said. "I wish to see Panacci—when he comes."

She looked at him quickly.

"It must be an accident," she said. "I can't—I won't believe that—no one could hurt Vere."

He said nothing.

"No one could hurt Vere," she repeated.

He went out on to the balcony and stood there for two or three minutes, looking down at the sea and at the empty road. She did not follow him, but sat down upon the sofa near the writing-table. Presently he turned round.

"Gaspare has gone."

"It would have been better if he had never come!"

"Hermione," he said, "has it come to this, that I must defend Gaspare to you?"

"I think Gaspare might have kept with Vere, ought to have kept with Vere."

Artois felt a burning desire to make Hermione understand the Sicilian, but he only said, gently:

"Some day, perhaps, you will know Gaspare's character better, you will understand all this."

"I can't understand it now. But—oh, if Vere— No, that's impossible, impossible!"

She spoke with intense vehemence.

"Some things cannot happen," she exclaimed, with a force that seemed to be commanding destiny.

Artois said nothing. And his apparent calm seemed to punish her, almost as if he struck her with a whip.

"Why don't you speak?" she said.

She felt almost confused by his silence.

He went out again to the balcony, leaned on the railing and looked over. She felt that he was listening with his whole nature for the sound of wheels. She felt that she heard him listening, that she heard him demanding the sound. And as she looked at his dark figure, beyond which she saw the vagueness of night and some stars, she was conscious of the life in him as she had never been conscious of it before, she was conscious of all his manhood terribly awake.

That was for Vere.

A quarter of an hour went by. Artois remained always on the balcony, and scarcely moved. Hermione watched him, and tried to learn a lesson; tried to realize without bitterness and horror that in the heart of man everything has been planted, and that therefore nothing which grows there should cause too great amazement, too great condemnation, or the absolute withdrawal of pity; tried to face someth'ng which must completely change her life, sweeping away more than mere illusions, sweeping away a long reverence which had been well founded, and which she had kept very secret in her heart, replacing its vital substance with a pale shadow of compassion.

She watched him, and she listened for the sound of wheels, until at last she could bear it no longer.

"Emile, what are we to do? What can we do?" she said, desperately.

"Hush!" he said.

He held up his hand. They both listened and heard far off the noise of a carriage rapidly approaching. He looked over into the road. The carriage rattled up. She heard it stop, and saw him bend down. Then suddenly he drew himself up, turned, and came into the room.

"They have come," he said.

He went to the door and opened it, and stood by it.

And his face was terrible.

CHAPTER XXX

Two minutes later there was the sound of steps coming quickly down the uncarpeted corridor, and Vere entered, followed, but not closely, by the Marchesino. Vere went up at once to her mother, without even glancing at Artois.

"I am so sorry, Madre," she said, quietly. "But—but it was not my fault."

The Marchesino had paused near the door, as if doubtful of Vere's intentions. Now he approached Hermione, pulling off his white gloves.

"Signora," he said, in a hard and steady voice, but smiling boyishly, "I fear I am the guilty one. When the balloon went up we were separated from you by the crowd, and could not find you again immediately. The Signorina wished to go back to the enclosure. Unfortunately I had lost the tickets, so that we should not have been readmitted. Under these circumstances I thought the best thing was to show the Signorina the illuminations, and then to come straight back to the hotel. I hope you have not been distressed. The Signorina was of course perfectly safe with me."

"Thank you, Marchese," said Hermione, coldly. "Emile, what are we to do about Gaspare?"

"Gaspare?" asked Vere.

"He has gone back to the Piazza to search for you again."

"Oh!"

She flushed, turned away, and went up to the window.

There she hesitated, and finally stepped out on to the balcony.

"You had better spend the night in the hotel," said Artois.

"But we have nothing!"

"The housemaid can find you what is necessary in the morning."

"As to our clothes—that doesn't matter. Perhaps it will be the best plan."

Artois rang the bell. They waited in silence till the night porter came.

"Can you give these two ladies rooms for the night?" said Artois. "It is too late for them to go home by boat, and their servant has not come back yet."

"Yes, sir. The ladies can have two very good rooms."

"Good-night, Emile," said Hermione. "Good-night, Marchese. Vere!"

Vere came in from the balcony.

"We are going to sleep here, Vere. Come!"

She went out.

"Good-night, Monsieur Emile," Vere said to Artois, without looking at him.

She followed her mother without saying another word.

Artois looked after them as they went down the corridor, watched Vere's thin and girlish figure until she turned the corner near the staircase, walking slowly and, he thought, as if she were tired and depressed. During this moment he was trying to get hold of his own violence, to make sure of his self-control. When the sound of the footsteps had died completely away he drew back into the room and shut the door.

The Marchesino was standing near the window. When he saw the face of Artois he sat down in an arm-chair and put his hat on the floor.

"You don't mind if I stay for a few minutes, Emilio?"

he said. "Have you anything to drink? I am thirsty after all this walking in the crowd."

Artois brought him some Nocera and lemons.

"Do you want brandy, whiskey?"

"No, no. Grazie."

He poured out the Nocera gently, and began carefully to squeeze some lemon-juice into it, holding the fruit lightly in his strong fingers, and watching the drops fall with a quiet attention.

"Where have you been to-night?"

The Marchesino looked up.

"In the Piazza di Masaniello."

"Where have you been?"

"I tell you—the Piazza, the Mercato, down one or two streets to see the illuminations. What's the matter, caro mio? Are you angry because we lost you in the crowd?"

"You intended to lose us in the crowd before we left the hotel to-night."

"Not at all, amico mio. Not at all."

His voice hardened again, the furrows appeared on his forehead.

"Now you are lying," said Artois.

The Marchesino got up and stood in front of Artois. The ugly, cat-like look had come into his face, changing it from its usual boyish impudence to a hardness that suggested age. At that moment he looked much older than he was.

"Be careful, Emilio!" he said. "I am Neapolitan, and I do not allow myself to be insulted."

His gray eyes contracted.

"You did not mean to get lost with the Signorina?" said Artois.

"One leaves such things to destiny."

"Destiny! Well, to-night it is your destiny to go out of the Signorina's life forever."

"How dare you command me? How dare you speak for these ladies?"

Suddenly Artois went quite white, and laid his hand on the Marchesino's arm.

"Where have you been? What have you been doing all this time?" he said.

Questions blazed in his eyes. His hand closed more firmly on the Marchesino.

"Where did you take that child? What did you say to her? What did you dare to say?"

"I! And you?" said the Marchesino, sharply.

He threw out his hand towards the face of Artois. "And you—you!" he repeated.

"I?"

"Yes—you! What have you said to her? Where have you taken her? I at least am young. My blood speaks to me. I am natural, I am passionate. I know what I am, what I want; I show it; I say it; I am sincere. I—I am ready to go naked into the sun before the whole world, and say, 'There! There! This is Isidoro Panacci; and he is this—and this—and this! Like it or hate it—that does not matter! It is not his fault. He is like that. He is made like that. He is meant to be like that, and he is that—he is that!' Do you hear? That is what I am ready to do. But you— you—! Ah, Madonna! Ah, Madre benedetta!"

He threw up both his hands suddenly, looked at the ceiling and shook his head sharply from side to side. Then he slapped his hands gently and repeatedly against his knees, and a prim and almost venerable look came into his mobile face.

"The great worker! The man of intellect! The man who is above the follies of that little Isidoro Panacci, who loves a beautiful girl, and who is proud of loving her, and who shows that he loves her, that he wants her, that he wishes to take her! Stand still!"—he suddenly hissed

out the words. "The man with the white hairs who
might have had many children of his own, but who prefers to play papa—caro papa, Babbo bello!—to the child
of another on a certain little island. Ah, buon Dio!
The wonderful writer, respected and admired by all;
by whose side the little Isidoro seems only a small boy
from college, about whom nobody need bother! How
he is loved, and how he is trusted on the island! Nobody must come there but he and those whom he wishes.
He is to order, to arrange all. The little Isidoro—he
must not come there. He must not know the ladies.
He is nothing; but he is wicked. He loves pleasure.
He loves beautiful girls! Wicked, wicked Isidoro!
Keep him out! Keep him away! But the great writer
—with the white hairs—everything is allowed to him
because he is Caro Papa. He may teach the Signorina.
He may be alone with her. He may take her out at
night in the boat."—His cheeks were stained with red
and his eyes glittered.—"And when the voice of that
wicked little Isidoro is heard— Quick! quick! To the
cave! Let us escape! Let us hide where it is dark, and
he will never find us! Let us make him think we are at
Nisida! Hush! the boat is passing. He is deceived!
He will search all night till he is tired! Ah—ah—ah!
That is good! And now back to the island—quick!—
before he finds out!"—He thrust out his arm towards
Artois.—"And that is my friend!" he exclaimed. "He
who calls himself the friend of the little wicked Isidoro.
P—f!"—He turned his head and spat on to the balcony.
—"Gran Dio! And this white-haired Babbo! He steals
into the Galleria at night to meet Maria Fortunata! He
puts a girl of the town to live with the Signorina upon
the island, to teach her—"

"Stop!" said Artois.

"I will not stop!" said the Marchesino, furiously.
"To teach the Signorina all the—"

Artois lifted his hand.

"Do you want me to strike you on the mouth?" he said.

"Strike me!"

Artois looked at him with a steadiness that seemed to pierce.

"Then—take care, Panacci. You are losing your head."

"And you have lost yours!" cried the Marchesino. "You, with your white hairs, you are mad. You are mad about the 'child.' You play papa, and all the time you are mad, and you think nobody sees it. But every one sees it, every one knows it. Every one knows that you are madly in love with the Signorina."

Artois had stepped back.

"I—in love!" he said.

His voice was contemptuous, but his face had become flushed, and his hands suddenly clinched themselves.

"What! you play the hypocrite even with yourself! Ah, we Neapolitans, we may be shocking; but at least we are sincere! You do not know?—then I will tell you. You love the Signorina madly, and you hate me because you are jealous of me—because I am young and you are old. I know it; the Signora knows it; that Sicilian—Gaspare—he knows it! And now you—you know it!"

He suddenly flung himself down on the sofa that was behind him. Perspiration was running down his face, and even his hands were wet with it.

Artois said nothing, but stood where he was, looking at the Marchesino, as if he were waiting for something more which must inevitably come. The Marchesino took out his handkerchief, passed it several times quickly over his lips, then rolled it up into a ball and shut it up in his left hand.

"I am young and you are old," he said. "And that is all the matter. You hate me, not because you think

A SPIRIT IN PRISON

I am wicked and might do the Signorina harm, but because I am young. You try to keep the Signorina from me because I am young. You do not dare to let her know what youth is, really, really to know, really, really to feel. Because, if once she did know, if once she did feel, if she touched the fire"—he struck his hand down on his breast—"she would be carried away, she would be gone from you forever. You think, 'Now she looks up to me! She reverences me! She admires me! She worships me as a great man!' And if once, only once she touched the fire—ah!"—he flung out both his arms with a wide gesture, opened his mouth, then shut it, showing his teeth like an animal.—"Away would go everything—everything. She would forget your talent, she would forget your fame, she would forget your thoughts, your books, she would forget you, do you hear?—all, all of you. She would remember only that you are old and she is young, and that, because of that, she is not for you. And then"—his voice dropped, became cold and serious and deadly, like the voice of one proclaiming a stark truth—"and then, if she understood you, what you feel, and what you wish, and how you think of her—she would hate you! How she would hate you!"

He stopped abruptly, staring at Artois, who said nothing.

"Is it not true?" he said.

He got up, taking his hat and stick from the floor.

"You do not know! Well—think! And you will know that it is true. A rivederci, Emilio!"

His manner had suddenly become almost calm. He turned away and went towards the door. When he reached it he added:

"To-morrow I shall ask the Signora to allow me to marry the Signorina."

Then he went out.

A SPIRIT IN PRISON

The gilt clock on the marble table beneath the mirror struck the half-hour after one. Artois looked at it and at his watch, comparing them. The action was mechanical, and unaccompanied by any thought connected with it. When he put his watch back into his pocket he did not know whether its hands pointed to half-past one or not. He carried a light chair on to the balcony, and sat down there, crossing his legs, and leaning one arm on the rail.

"If she touched the fire." Those words of the Marchesino remained in the mind of Artois—why, he did not know. He saw before him a vision of a girl and of a flame. The flame aspired towards the girl, but the girl hesitated, drew back—then waited.

What had happened during the hours of the Festa? Artois did not know. The Marchesino had told him nothing, except that he—Artois—was madly in love with Vere. Monstrous absurdity! What trivial nonsense men talked in moments of anger, when they desired to wound!

And to-morrow the Marchesino would ask Vere to marry him. Of course Vere would refuse. She had no feeling for him. She would tell him so. He would be obliged to understand that for once he could not have his own way. He would go out of Vere's life, abruptly, as he had come into it.

He would go. That was certain. But others would come into Vere's life. Fire would spring up round about her, the fire of the love of men for a girl who has fire within her, the fire of the love of youth for youth.

Youth! Artois was not by nature a sentimentalist —and he was not a fool. He knew how to accept the inevitable things life cruelly brings to men, without futile struggling, without contemptible pretence. Quite calmly, quite serenely, he had accepted the snows of middle age. He had not secretly groaned or cursed,

464

railed against destiny, striven to defy it by travesty, as do many men. He had thought himself to be "above" all that—until lately. But now, as he thought of the fire, he was conscious of an immense sadness that had in it something of passion, or a regret that was, for a moment, desperate, bitter, that seared, that tortured, that was scarcely to be endured. It is terrible to realize that one is at a permanent disadvantage, which time can only increase. And just then Artois felt that there was nothing, that there could never be anything, to compensate any human being for the loss of youth.

He began to wonder about the people of the island. The Marchesino had spoken with a strange assurance. He had dared to say:

"You love the Signorina. I know it; the Signora knows it; Gaspare—he knows it. And now you—you know it."

Was it possible that his deep interest in Vere, his paternal delight in her talent, in her growing charm, in her grace and sweetness, could have been mistaken for something else, for the desire of man for woman? Vere had certainly never for a moment misunderstood him. That he knew as surely as he knew that he was alive. But Gaspare and—Hermione? He fell into deep thought, and presently he was shaken by an emotion that was partly disgust and partly anxiety. He got up from his chair and looked out into the night. The weather was exquisitely still, the sky absolutely clear. The sea was like the calm that dwells surely in the breast of God. Naples was sleeping in the silence. But he was terribly awake, and it began to seem to him as if he had, perhaps, slept lately, slept too long. He was a lover of truth, and believed himself to be a discerner of it. The Marchesino was but a thoughtless, passionate boy, headstrong, Pagan, careless of intellect, and immensely physical. Yet it was possible that he had been enabled to see a truth which Artois had neither seen nor suspected. Artois began to believe it possible, as he remembered many details of the conduct of Hermione and of Gaspare in these last summer days. There had been something of condemnation sometimes in the Sicilian's eyes as they looked into his. He had wondered what it meant. Had it meant—that? And that night in the garden with Hermione—

With all his force and fixity of purpose he fastened his mind upon Hermione, letting Gaspare go.

If what the Marchesino had asserted were true— not that—but if Hermione had believed it to be true, much in her conduct that had puzzled Artois was made plain. Could she have thought that? Had she thought it? And if she had—? Always he was looking out to the stars, and to the ineffable calm of the sea. But now their piercing brightness, and its large repose, only threw into a sort of blatant relief in his mind its consciousness of the tumult of humanity. He saw Hermione involved in that tumult, and he saw himself. And Vere?

Was it possible that in certain circumstances Vere might hate him? It was strange that to-night Artois found himself for the first time considering the Marchesino seriously, not as a boy, but as a man who perhaps knew something of the world and of character better than he did. The Marchesino had said:

"If she understood you—how she would hate you."

But surely Vere and he understood each other very well.

He looked out over the sea steadily, as he wished, as he meant, to look now at himself, into his own heart and nature, into his own life. Upon the sea, to the right and far off, a light was moving near the blackness of the breakwater. It was the torch of a fisherman—one of those eyes of the South of which Artois had thought. His eyes became fascinated by it, and he watched it with intensity. Sometimes it was still. Then it travelled gently onward, coming towards him. Then it

466

stopped again. Fire—the fire of youth. He thought
of the torch as that; as youth with its hot strength, its
beautiful eagerness, its intense desires, its spark-like
hopes, moving without fear amid the dark mysteries of
the world and of life; seeking treasure in the blackness,
the treasure of an answering soul, of a completing nature,
of the desired and desirous heart, seeking its complement
of love—the other fire.

He looked far over the sea. But there was no other
fire upon it.

And still the light came on.

And now he thought of it as Vere.

She was almost a child, but already her fire was being
sought, longed for. And she knew it, and must be
searching, too, perhaps without definite consciousness
of what she was doing, instinctively. She was searching there in the blackness, and in her quest she was
approaching him. But where he stood it was all dark.
There was no flame lifting itself up that could draw her
flame to it. The fire that was approaching would pass
before him, would go on, exploring the night, would
vanish away from his eyes. Elsewhere it would seek
the fire it needed, the fire it would surely find at last.

And so it was. The torch came on, passed softly by,
slipped from his sight beneath the bridge of Castel dell'
Uovo.

When it had gone Artois felt strangely deserted and
alone, strangely unreconciled with life. And he remembered his conversation with Hermione in Virgil's Grotto;
how he had spoken like one who scarcely needed love,
having ambition and having work to do, and being no
longer young.

To-night he felt that every one needs love first—that
all the other human needs come after that great necessity.
He had thought himself a man full of self-knowledge,
full of knowledge of others. But he had not known

himself. Perhaps even now the real man was hiding somewhere, far down, shrinking away for fear of being known, for fear of being dragged up into the light.

He sought for this man, almost with violence.

A weariness lay beneath his violence to-night, a physical fatigue such as he sometimes felt after work. It had been produced, no doubt, by the secret anger he had so long controlled, the secret but intense curiosity which was not yet satisfied, and which still haunted him and tortured him. This curiosity he now strove to expel from his mind, telling himself that he had no right to it. He had wished to preserve Vere just as she was, to keep her from all outside influences. And now he asked the real man why he had wished it? Had it been merely the desire of the literary godfather to cherish a pretty and promising talent? Or had something of the jealous spirit so brutally proclaimed to him that night by the Marchesino really entered into the desire? This torturing curiosity to know what had happened at the Festa surely betrayed the existence of some such spirit.

He must get rid of it.

He began to walk slowly up and down the little balcony, turning every instant like a beast in its cage. It seemed to him that the real man had indeed lain in hiding, but that he was coming forth reluctantly into the light.

Possibly he had been drifting without knowing it towards some nameless folly. He was not sure. To-night he felt uncertain of himself and of everything, almost like an ignorant child facing the world. And he felt almost afraid of himself. Was it possible that he, holding within him so much of knowledge, so much of pride, could ever draw near to a crazy absurdity, a thing that the whole world would laugh at and despise? Had he drawn near to it? Was he near it now?

He thought of all his recent intercourse with Vere,

going back mentally to the day in spring when he arrived in Naples. He followed the record day by day until he reached that afternoon when he had returned from Paris, when he came to the island to find Vere alone, when she read to him her poems. Very pitilessly, despite the excitement still raging within him, he examined that day, that night, recalling every incident, recalling every feeling the incidents of those hours had elicited from his heart. He remembered how vexed he had been when Hermione told him of the engagement for the evening. He remembered the moments after the dinner, his sensation of loneliness when he listened to the gay conversation of Vere and the Marchesino, his almost irritable anxiety when she had left the restaurant and gone out to the terrace in the darkness. He had felt angry with Panacci then. Had he not always felt angry with Panacci for intruding into the island life?

He followed the record of his intercourse with Vere until he reached the Festa of that night, until he reached the moment in which he was pacing the tiny balcony while the night wore on towards dawn.

That was the record of himself with Vere.

He began to think of Hermione. How had all this that he had just been telling over in his mind affected her? What had she been thinking of it—feeling about it? And Gaspare?

Even now Artois did not understand himself, did not know whither his steps might have tended had not the brutality of the Marchesino roused him abruptly to this self-examination, this self-consideration. He did not fully understand himself, and he wondered very much how Hermione and the Sicilian had understood him—judged him.

Artois had a firm belief in the right instincts of sensitive but untutored natures, especially when linked with strong hearts capable of deep love and long fidelity.

He did not think that Gaspare would easily misread the character or the desires of one whom he knew well. Hermione might. She was tremendously emotional and impulsive, and might be carried away into error. But there was a steadiness in Gaspare which was impressive, which could not be ignored.

Artois wondered very much what Gaspare had thought.

There was a tap at the door, and Gaspare came in, holding his soft hat in his hand, and looking tragic and very hot and tired.

"Oh, Gaspare!" said Artois, coming in from the balcony, "they have come back."

"Lo so, Signore."

"And they are sleeping here for the night."

"Sì, Signore."

Gaspare looked at him as if inquiring something of him.

"Sit down a minute," said Artois, "and have something to drink. You must spend the night here, too. The porter will give you a bed."

"Grazie, Signore."

Gaspare sat down by the table, and Artois gave him some Nocera and lemon-juice. He would not have brandy or whiskey, though he would not have refused wine had it been offered to him.

"Where have you been?" Artois asked him.

"Signore, I have been all over the Piazza di Masaniello and the Mercato. I have been through all the streets near by. I have been down by the harbor. And the Signorina?"

He stared at Artois searchingly above his glass. His face was covered with perspiration.

"I only saw her for a moment. She went to bed almost immediately."

"And that Signore?"

"He has gone home."

Gaspare was silent for a minute. Then he said:

"If I had met that Signore—" He lifted his right hand, which was lying on the table, and moved it towards his belt.

He sighed, and again looked hard at Artois.

"It is better that I did not meet him," he said, with naïve conviction. "It is much better. The Signorina is not for him."

Artois was sitting opposite to him, with the table between them.

"The Signorina is not for him," repeated Gaspare, with a dogged emphasis.

His large eyes were full of a sort of cloudy rebuke and watchfulness. And as he met them Artois felt that he knew what Gaspare had thought. He longed to say, "You are wrong. It is not so. It was never so." But he only said:

"The Signor Marchese will know that to-morrow."

And as he spoke the words he was conscious of an immense sensation of relief which startled him. He was too glad when he thought of the final dismissal of the Marchesino.

Gaspare nodded his head and put his glass to his lips. When he set it down again it was empty. He moved to get up, but Artois detained him.

"And so you met Ruffo to-night?" he said.

Gaspare's expression completely changed. Instead of the almost cruel watcher, he became the one who felt that he was watched.

"Sì, Signore."

"Just when the balloon went up?"

"Sì, Signore. They were beside me in the crowd."

"Was he alone with his mother?"

"Sì, Signore. Quite alone."

"Gaspare, I have seen Ruffo's mother."

Gaspare looked startled.

A SPIRIT IN PRISON

"Truly, Signore?"

"Yes. I saw her with him one day at the Mergellina. She was crying."

"Perhaps she is unhappy. Her husband is in prison."

"Because of Peppina."

"Sì."

"And to-night you spoke to her for the first time?"

Artois laid a strong emphasis on the final words.

"Signore, I had never met her with Ruffo before."

The two men looked steadily at each other. A question that could not be evaded, a question that would break like a hammer upon a mutual silence of years, was almost upon Artois' lips. Perhaps Gaspare saw it, for he got up with determination.

"I am going to bed now, Signore. I am tired. Buona notte, Signore."

He took up his hat and went out.

Artois had not asked his question. But he felt that it was answered.

Gaspare knew. And he knew.

And Hermione — did Fate intend that she should know?

CHAPTER XXXI

It was nearly dawn when Artois fell asleep. He did not wake till past ten o'clock. The servant who brought his breakfast handed him a note, and told him that the ladies of the island had just left the hotel with Gaspare. As Artois took the note he was conscious of a mingled feeling of relief and disappointment. This swift, almost hurried departure left him lonely, yet he could not have met Hermione and Vere happily in the light of morning. To-day he felt a self-consciousness that was unusual in him, and that the keen eyes of women could not surely fail to observe. He wanted a little time. He wanted to think quietly, calmly, to reach a decision that he had not reached at night.

Hermione and Vere had a very silent voyage. Gaspare's tragic humor cast a cloud about his mistresses. He had met them in the morning with a look of heavy, almost sullen scrutiny in his great eyes, which seemed to develop into a definite demand for information. But he asked nothing. He made no allusion to the night before. To Vere his manner was almost cold. When they were getting into the boat at Santa Lucia she said, with none of her usual simplicity and self-possession, but like one making an effort which was repugnant:

"I'm very sorry about last night, Gaspare."

"It doesn't matter, Signorina."

"Did you get back very late?"

"I don't know, Signorina. I did not look at the hour."

She looked away from him and out to sea.

473

"I am very sorry," she repeated.

And he again said:

"It doesn't matter, Signorina."

It was nearly noon when they drew near to the island. The weather was heavily hot, languidly hot even upon the water. There was a haze hanging over the world in which distant objects appeared like unsubstantial clouds, or dream things impregnated with a mystery that was mournful. The voice of a fisherman singing not far off came to them like the voice of Fate, issuing from the ocean to tell them of the sadness that was the doom of men. Behind them Naples sank away into the vaporous distance. Vesuvius was almost blotted out, Capri an ethereal silhouette. And their little island, even when they approached it, did not look like the solid land on which they had made a home, but like the vague shell of some substance that had been destroyed, leaving its former abiding-place untenanted.

As they passed San Francesco Vere glanced at him, and Hermione saw a faint flush of red go over her face. Directly the boat touched the rock she stepped ashore, and without waiting for her mother ran up the steps and disappeared towards the house. Gaspare looked after her, then stared at his Padrona.

"Is the Signorina ill?" he asked.

"No, Gaspare. But I think she is tired to-day and a little upset. We had better take no notice of it."

"Va bene, Signora."

He busied himself in making fast the boat, while Hermione followed Vere.

In the afternoon about five, when Hermione was sitting alone in her room writing some letters, Gaspare appeared with an angry and suspicious face.

"Signora," he said, "that Signore is here."

"What Signore? The Marchese!"

"Sì, Signora."

Gaspare was watching his Padrona's face, and suddenly his own face changed, lightened, as he saw the look that had come into her eyes.

"I did not know whether you wished to see him—"

"Yes, Gaspare, I will see him. You can let him in. Wait a moment. Where is the Signorina?"

"Up in her room, Signora."

"You can tell her who is here, and ask her whether she wishes to have tea in her room or not."

"Sì, Signora."

Gaspare went out almost cheerfully. He felt that now he understood what his Padrona was feeling and what she meant to do. She meant to do in her way what he wanted to do in his. He ran down the steps to the water with vivacity, and his eyes were shining as he came to the Marchesino, who was standing at the edge of the sea looking almost feverishly excited, but determined.

"The Signora will see you, Signor Marchese."

The words hit the Marchesino like a blow. He stared at Gaspare for a moment almost stupidly, and hesitated. He felt as if this servant had told him something else.

"The Signora will see you," repeated Gaspare.

"Va bene," said the Marchesino.

He followed Gaspare slowly up the steps and into the drawing-room. It was empty. Gaspare placed a chair for the Marchesino. And again the latter felt as if he had received a blow. He glanced round him and sat down, while Gaspare went away. For about five minutes he waited.

When he had arrived at the island he had been greatly excited. He had felt full of an energy that was feverish. Now, in this silence, in this pause during which patience was forced upon him, his excitement grew, became fierce, dominant. He knew from Gaspare's way of speaking, from his action, from his whole manner, that his fate had been secretly determined in that house, and that it was being rejoiced over. At first he sat looking at the floor. Then he got up, went to the window, came back, stood in the middle of the room and glanced about it. How pretty it was, with a prettiness that he was quite unaccustomed to. In his father's villa at Capodimonte there was little real comfort. And he knew nothing of the cosiness of English houses. As he looked at this room he felt, or thought he felt, Vere in it. He even made an effort scarcely natural to him, and tried to imagine a home with Vere as its mistress.

Then he began to listen. Perhaps Emilio was in the house. Perhaps Emilio was talking now to the Signora, was telling her what to do.

But he heard no sound of voices speaking.

No doubt Emilio had seen the Signora that morning in the hotel. No doubt there had been a consultation. And probably at this consultation his—the Marchesino's —fate had been decided.

By Emilio?

At that moment the Marchesino actively, even furiously, hated his former friend.

There was a little noise at the door; the Marchesino turned swiftly, and saw Hermione coming in. He looked eagerly behind her. But the door shut. She was alone. She did not give her hand to him. He bowed, trying to look calm.

"Good-afternoon, Signora."

Hermione sat down. He followed her example.

"I don't know why you wish to see me, after yesterday, Marchese," she said, quietly, looking at him with steady eyes.

"Signora, pardon me, but I should have thought that you would know."

"What is it?"

"Signora, I am here to ask the great honor of your

daughter the Signorina's hand in marriage. My father, to whom—"

But Hermione interrupted him.

"You will never marry my daughter, Marchese," she said.

A sudden red burned in her cheeks, and she leaned forward slightly, but very quickly, almost as if an impulse had come to her to push the Marchesino away from her.

"But, Signora, I assure you that my family—"

"It is quite useless to talk about it."

"But why, Signora?"

"My child is not for a man like you," Hermione said, emphasizing the first word.

A dogged expression came into the Marchesino's face, a fighting look that was ugly and brutal, but that showed a certain force.

"I do not understand, Signora. I am like other men. What is the matter with me?"

He turned a little in his chair so that he faced her more fully.

"What is the matter with me, Signora?" he repeated, slightly raising his voice.

"I don't think you would be able to understand if I tried to tell you."

"Why not? You think me stupid, then?"

An angry fire shone in his eyes.

"Oh no, you are not stupid."

"Then I shall understand."

Hermione hesitated. There was within her a hot impulse towards speech, towards the telling to this self-satisfied young Pagan her exact opinion of him. Yet was it worth while? He was going out of their lives. They would see no more of him.

"I don't think it is necessary for me to tell you," she said.

"Perhaps there is nothing to tell because there is nothing the matter with me."

His tone stung her.

"I beg your pardon, Marchese. I think there is a good deal to tell."

"All I say is, Signora, that I am like other men."

He thrust forward his strong under jaw, showing his big, white teeth.

"There I don't agree with you. I am thankful to say I know many men who would not behave as you behaved last night."

"But I have come to ask for the Signorina's hand!" he exclaimed.

"And you think—you dare to think that excuses your conduct!"

She spoke with a sudden and intense heat.

"Understand this, please, Marchese. If I gave my consent to your request, and sent for my daughter—"

"Sì! Sì!" he said, eagerly leaning forward in his chair.

"Do you suppose she would come near you?"

"Certainly."

"You think she would come near a man she will not even speak of?"

"What!"

"She won't speak of you. She has told me nothing about last night. That is why I know so much."

"She has not—the Signorina has—not—?"

He stopped. A smile went over his face. It was sufficiently obvious that he understood Vere's silence as merely a form of deceit, a coquettish girl's cold secret from her mother.

"Signora, give me permission to speak to your daughter, and you will see whether it is you—or I—who understands her best."

"Very well, Marchese."

Hermione rang the bell. It was answered by Gaspare.

A SPIRIT IN PRISON

"Gaspare," said Hermione, "please go to the Signorina, tell her the Signor Marchese is here, and wishes very much to see her before he goes."

Gaspare's face grew dark, and he hesitated by the door.

"Go, Gaspare, please."

He looked into his Padrona's face, and went out as if reassured. Hermione and the Marchese sat in silence waiting for him to return. In a moment the door was reopened.

"Signora, I have told the Signorina."

"What did she say?"

Gaspare looked at the Marchese as he answered.

"Signora, the Signorina said to me, 'Please tell Madre that I cannot come to see the Signor Marchese.'"

"You can go, Gaspare."

He looked at the angry flush on the Marchesino's cheeks, and went out.

"Good-bye, Marchese."

Hermione got up. The Marchesino followed her example. But he did not go. He stood still for a moment in silence. Then he lifted his head up with a jerk.

"Signora," he said, in a hard, uneven voice that betrayed the intensity of his excitement, "I see how it is. I understand perfectly what is happening here. You think me bad. Well, I am like other men, and I am not ashamed of it—not a bit. I am natural. I live according to my nature, and I do not come from your north, but from Naples—from Naples." He threw out his arm, pointing at a window that looked towards the city. "If it is bad to have the blood hot in one's veins and the fire hot in one's head and in one's heart—very well! I am bad. And I do not care. I do not care a bit! But you think me stupid. Sì, Signora, you think me a stupid boy. And I am not that. And I will show you." He drew his fingers together, and bent towards

479

her, slightly lowering his voice. "From the first, from the very first moment, I have seen, I have understood all that is happening here. From the first I have understood all that was against me—"

"Marchese—!"

"Signora, pardon me! You have spoken, the Signorina has spoken, and now it is for me to speak. It is my right. I come here with an honorable proposal, and therefore I say I have a right—"

He put his fingers inside his shirt collar and pulled it fiercely out from his throat.

"E il vecchio!" he exclaimed, with sudden passion. "E il maledetto vecchio!"

Hermione's face changed. There had been in it a firm look, a calmness of strength. But now, at his last words, the strength seemed to shrink. It dwindled, it faded out of her, leaving her not collapsed, but cowering, like a woman who crouches down in a corner to avoid a blow.

"It is he! It is he! He will not allow it, and he is master here."

"Marchese—"

"I say he is master—he is master—he has always been master here!"

He came a step towards Hermione, moving as a man sometimes moves instinctively when he is determined to make something absolutely clear to one who does not wish to understand.

"And you know it, and every one knows it—every one. When I was in the sea, when I saw the Signorina for the first time, I did not know who she was, where she lived; I did not know anything about her. I went to tell my friend about her—my friend, you understand, whom I trusted, to whom I told everything!—I went to him. I described the Signora, the Signorina, the boat to him. He knew who the ladies were; he knew directly. I saw it in his face, in his manner. But what did he say? That he did not know, that he knew nothing. I was not to come to the island. No one was to come to the island but he. So he meant. But I—I was sharper than he, I who am so stupid! I took him to fish by night. I brought him to the island. I made him introduce me to you, to the Signorina. That night I made him. You remember? Well, then—ever since that night all is changed between us. Ever since that night he is my enemy. Ever since that night he suspects me, he watches me, he hides from me, he hates me. Oh, he tries to conceal it. He is a hypocrite. But I, stupid as I am, I see it all. I see what he is, what he wants, I see all—all that is in his mind and heart. For this noble old man, so respected, with the white hairs and the great brain, what is he, what does he do? He goes at night to the Galleria. He consults with Maria Fortunata, she who is known to all Naples, she who is the aunt of that girl—that girl of the town and of the bad life, whom you have taken to be your servant here. You have taken her because he—he has told you to take her. He has put her here—"

"Marchese!"

"I say he has put her here that the Signorina—"

"Marchese, I forbid you to say that! It is not true."

"It is true! It is true! Perhaps you are blind, perhaps you see nothing. I do not know. But I know that I am not blind. I love, and I see. I see, I have always seen that he—Emilio—loves the Signorina, that he loves her madly, that he wishes, that he means to keep her for himself. Did he not hide with her in the cave, in the Grotto of Virgil, that night when I came to serenade her on the sea? Yes, he took her, and he hid her, because he loves her. He loves her, he an old man! And he thinks—and he means—"

"Marchese—"

"He loves her; I say he loves her!"

"Marchese, I must ask you to go!"

"I say—"

"Marchese, I insist upon your going."

She opened the door. She was very pale, but she looked calm. The crouching woman had vanished. She was mistress of herself.

"Gaspare!" she called, in a loud, sharp voice that betrayed the inner excitement her appearance did not show.

"Signora," vociferated the Marchesino, "I say and I repeat—"

"Gaspare! Come here!"

"Signora!" cried a voice from below.

Gaspare came running.

"The Signor Marchese is going, Gaspare. Go down with him to the boat, please."

The Marchesino grew scarlet. The hot blood rushed over his face, up to his forehead, to his hair. Even his hands became red in that moment.

"Good-bye, Marchese."

She went out, and left him standing with Gaspare.

"Signor Marchese, shall I take you to the boat?"

Gaspare's voice was quite respectful. The Marchesino made no answer, but stepped out into the passage and looked up to the staircase that led to the top floor of the house. He listened. He heard nothing.

"Is the French Signore here?" he said to Gaspare. "Do you hear me? Is he in this house?"

"No, Signore!"

The Marchesino again looked towards the staircase and hesitated. Then he turned and saw Gaspare standing in a watchful attitude, almost like one about to spring.

"Stay there!" he said, loudly, making a violent, threatening gesture with his arm.

Gaspare stood where he was with a smile upon his face.

A moment later he heard the splash of oars in the sea, and knew that the Marchesino's boat was leaving the island.

He drew his lips together like one about to whistle. The sound of the oars died away.

Then he began to whistle softly "La Ciocciara."

CHAPTER XXXII

THE ghostly day sank into a ghostly night that laid
pale hands upon the island, holding it closely, softly, in
a hypnotic grasp, bidding it surely rest, it and those
who dwelled there with all the dreaming hours. A mist
hung over the sea, and the heat did not go with day,
but stayed to greet the darkness and the strange, enormous silence that lay upon the waters. In the Casa del
Mare the atmosphere was almost suffocating, although
every window was wide open. The servants went about
their duties leaden-footed, drooping, their Latin vivacity
quenched as by a spell. Vere was mute. It seemed,
since the episode of the Carmine, as if her normal spirit
had been withdrawn, as if a dumb, evasive personality
replaced it. The impression made upon Hermione was
that the real Vere had sunk far down in her child, out
of sight and hearing, out of reach, beyond pursuit, to a
depth where none could follow, where the soul enjoyed
the safety of utter isolation.

Hermione did not wish to pursue this anchorite. She
did not wish to draw near to Vere that evening. To
do so would have been impossible to her, even had Vere
been willing to come to her. Since the brutal outburst
of the Marchesino, she, too, had felt the desire, the necessity, of a desert place, where she could sit alone and
realize the bareness of her world.

In that outburst of passion the Marchesino had gathered together and hurled at her beliefs that had surely
been her own, but that she had striven to avoid, that

she had beaten back as spectres and unreal, that she had even denied, tricking, or trying to trick, her terrible sense of truth. His brutality had made the delicacy in her crouch and sicken. It had been almost intolerable to her to see her friend, Emile, thus driven out into the open, like one naked, to be laughed at, condemned, held up, that the wild folly, the almost insane absurdity of his secret self might be seen and understood even by the blind, the determined in stupidity.

She had always had a great reverence for her friend, which had been mingled with he· love for him, giving it its character. Was that reverence to be torn utterly away? Had it already been cast to the winds?

Poor Emile!

In the first moments after the departure of the Marchesino she pitied Emile intensely with all her heart of woman. If this thing were true, how he must have suffered, how he must still be suffering—not only in his heart, but in his mind! His sense of pride, his self-respect, his passion for complete independence, his meticulous consciousness of the fitness of things, of what could be and of what was impossible—all must be lying in the dust. She could almost have wept for him then.

But another feeling succeeded this sense of pity, a sensation of outrage that grew within her and became almost ungovernable. She had her independence too, her pride, her self-respect. And now she saw them in dust that Emile had surely heaped about them. A storm of almost hard anger shook her. She tasted an acrid bitterness that seemed to impregnate her, to turn the mainspring of her life to gall. She heard the violent voice of the young Neapolitan saying: "He is master, he is master, he has always been master here!" And she tried to look back over her life, and to see how things had been. And, shaken still by this storm of anger, she felt as if it were true, as if she had allowed Artois to take her life in his hands and to shape it according to his will, as if he had been governing her although she had not known it. He had been the dominant personality in their mutual friendship. His had been the calling voice, hers the obedient voice that answered. Only once had she risen to a strong act, an act that brought great change with it, and that he had been hostile to. That was when she had married Maurice.

And she had left Maurice for Artois. From Africa had come the calling, dominant voice. And even in her Garden of Paradise she had heard it. And even from her Garden of Paradise she had obeyed it. For the first time she saw that act of renunciation as the average man or woman would probably see it; as an extraordinary, quixotic act, to be wondered at blankly, or, perhaps, to be almost angrily condemned. She stood away from her own impulsive, enthusiastic nature, and stared at it critically—as even her friends had often stared—and realized that it was unusual, perhaps extravagant, perhaps sometimes preposterous. This readiness to sacrifice —was it not rather slavish than regally loyal? This forgetfulness of personal joy, this burnt-offering of personality—was it not contemptible? Could such actions bring into being the respect of others, the respect of any man? Had Emile respected her for rushing to Africa? Or had he, perhaps, then and through all these years, simply wondered how she could have done such a thing?

And Maurice—Maurice? Oh, what had he thought? How had he looked upon that action?

Often and often in lonely hours she had longed to go down into the grave, or to go up into the blue, to drag the body, the soul, the heart she loved back to her. She had been rent by a desire that had made her limbs shudder, or that had flushed her whole body with red, and set her temples beating. The longing of heart and flesh had been so vehement that it had seemed to her as if they must compel, or cease to be. Now, again, she desired to compel Maurice to come to her from his far, distant place, but in order that she might make him understand what he had perhaps died misunderstanding; why she had left him to go to Artois, exactly how she had felt, how desperately sad to abandon the Garden of Paradise, how torn by fear lest the perfect days were forever at an end, how intensely desirous to take him with her. Perhaps he had felt cruelly jealous! Perhaps that was why he had not offered to go with her at once. Yes, she believed that now. She saw her action, she saw her preceding decision as others had seen it, as no doubt Maurice had seen it, as perhaps even Artois had seen it. Why had she not more fully explained herself? Why had she instinctively felt that because her nature was as it was, and because she was bravely following it, every one must understand her? Oh, to be completely understood! If she could call Maurice back for one moment, and just make him see her as she had been then: loyal to her friend, and through and through passionately loyal to him! If she could! If she could!

She had left Maurice, the one being who had utterly belonged to her, to go to Artois. She had lost the few remaining days in which she could have been supremely happy. She had come back to have a few short hours devoid of calm, chilled sometimes by the strangeness that had intruded itself between her and Maurice, to have one kiss in which surely at last misunderstanding was lost and perfect love was found. And then—that "something" in the water! And then—the gulf.

In that gulf she had not been quite alone. The friend whom she had carried away from Africa and death had been with her. He had been closely in her life ever since. And now—

She heard the Marchesino's voice: "I see what he is, what he wants, I see all—all that is in his mind and heart.

I see, I have always seen, that he loves the Signorina, that he loves her madly."

Vere!

Hermione sickened. Emile and Vere in that relation!

The storm of anger was not spent yet. Would it ever be spent? Something within her, the something, perhaps, that felt rejected, strove to reject in its turn, did surely reject. Pride burned in her like a fire that cruelly illumines night, shining upon the destruction it is compassing.

The terrible sense of outrage that gripped her soul and body—her body because Vere was bone of her bone, flesh of her flesh—seemed to be forcibly changing her nature, as cruel hands, prompted by murder in a heart, change form, change beauty in the effort to destroy.

That evening Hermione felt herself being literally defaced by this sensation of outrage within her, a sensation which she was powerless to expel.

She found herself praying to God that Artois might not come to the island that night. And yet, while she prayed, she felt that he was coming.

She dined with Vere, in almost complete silence—trying to love this dear child as she had always loved her, even in certain evil moments of an irresistible jealousy. But she felt immensely far from Vere, distant from her as one who does not love from one who loves; yet hideously near, too, like one caught in the tangle of an enforced intimacy rooted in a past which the present denies and rejects. Directly dinner was over they parted, driven by the mutual desire to be alone.

And then Hermione waited for that against which she had prayed.

Artois would come to the island that night. Useless to pray! He was coming. She felt that he was on the sea, environed by this strange mist that hung to-night over the waters. She felt that he was coming to Vere.

A SPIRIT IN PRISON

She had gone to Africa to save him—in order that he might fall in love with her then unborn child.

Monstrosities, the monstrosities that are in life, deny them, beat them back, close our eyes to them as we will, rose up around her in the hot stillness. She felt haunted, terrified. She was forcibly changed, and now all the world was changing about her.

She must have relief. She could not sit there among spectres waiting for the sound of oars that would tell her Vere's lover had come to the island. How could she detach herself for a moment from this horror?

She thought of Ruffo.

As the thought came to her she got up and went out of the house.

Only when she was out-of-doors did she fully realize the strangeness of the night. The heat of it was flaccid. The island seemed to swim in a fatigued and breathless atmosphere. The mist that hung about it was like the mist in a vapor-bath.

Below the vague sea lay a thing exhausted, motionless, perhaps fainting in the dark. And in this heat and stillness there was no presage, no thrill, however subtle, of a coming change, of storm. Rather there was the deadness of eternity, as if this swoon would last forever, neither developing into life, nor deepening into death.

Hermione had left the house feverishly, yearning to escape from her company of spectres, yearning to escape from the sensation of ruthless hands defacing her. As she passed the door-sill it was only with difficulty that she suppressed a cry of "Ruffo!" a cry for help. But when the night took her she no longer had any wish to disturb it by a sound. She was penetrated at once by an atmosphere of fatality. Her pace changed. She moved on slowly, almost furtively. She felt inclined to creep.

Would Ruffo be at the island to-night? Would Artois

really come? It seemed unlikely, almost impossible. But if Ruffo were there, if Artois came, it would be fatality. That she was there was fatality.

She walked always slowly, always furtively, to the crest of the cliff.

She stood there. She listened.

Silence.

She felt as if she were quite alone on the island. She could scarcely believe that Vere, that Gaspare, that the servants were there—among them Peppina with her cross.

They said Peppina had the evil eye. Had she perhaps cast a spell to-night?

Hermione did not smile at such an imagination as she dismissed it.

She waited and listened, but not actively, for she did not feel as if Ruffo could ever stand with her in the embrace of such a night, he, a boy, with bright hopes and eager longings, he the happy singer of the song of Mergellina.

And yet, when in a moment she found him standing by her side, she accepted his presence as a thing inevitable.

It had been meant, perhaps for centuries, that they two should stand together that night, speak together as now they were about to speak.

"Signora, buona sera."

"Buona sera, Ruffo."

"The Signorina is not here to-night?"

"I think she is in the house. I think she is tired to-night."

"The Signorina is tired after the Festa, Signora."

"You knew we were at the Festa, Ruffo?"

"Ma sì, Signora."

"Did we tell you we were going? I had forgotten."

"It was not that, Signora. But I saw the Signorina at the Festa. Did not Don Gaspare tell you?"

"Gaspare said nothing. Did he see you?"

She spoke languidly. Quickness had died out of her under the influence of the night. But already she felt a slight yet decided sense of relief, almost of peace. She drew that from Ruffo. And, standing very close to him, she watched his eager face, hoping to see presently in it the expression that she loved.

"Did he see you, Ruffo?"

"Ma sì, Signora. I was with my poor mamma."

"Your mother! I wish I had met her!"

"Sì, Signora. I was with my mamma in the Piazza of Masaniello. We had been eating snails, Signora, and afterwards watermelon, and we had each had a glass of white wine. And I was feeling very happy, because my poor mamma had heard good news."

"What was that?"

"To-morrow my Patrigno is to be let out of prison."

"So soon! But I thought he had not been tried."

"No, Signora. But he is to be let out now. Perhaps he will be put back again. But now he is let out because "—he hesitated—"because—well, Signora, he has rich friends, he has friends who are powerful for him. And so he is let out just now."

"I understand."

"Well, Signora, and after the white wine we were feeling happy, and we were going to see everything: the Madonna, and Masaniello, and the fireworks, and the fire-balloon. Did you see the fire-balloon, Signora?"

"Yes, Ruffo. It was very pretty."

His simple talk soothed her. He was so young, so happy, so free from the hideous complexities of life; no child of tragedy, but the son surely of a love that had been gay and utterly contented.

"Sì, Signora! Per dio, Signora, it was wonderful! It was just before the fire-balloon went up, Signora, that I saw the Signorina with the Neapolitan Signorino.

And close behind them was Don Gaspare. I said to
my mamma, 'Mamma, ecco the beautiful Signorina of
the island!' My mamma was excited, Signora. She
held on to my arm, and she said: 'Ruffino,' she said,
'show her to me. Where is she?' my mamma said, Signora. 'And is the Signora Madre with her?' Just then,
Signora, the people moved, and all of a sudden there we
were, my mamma and I, right in front of Don Gaspare."

Ruffo stopped, and Hermione saw a change, a gravity,
come into his bright face.

"Well, Ruffo?" she said, wondering what was coming.

"I said to my mamma, Signora, 'Mamma, this is Don
Gaspare of the island.' Signora, my mamma looked at
Don Gaspare for a minute. Her face was quite funny.
She looked white, Signora, my mamma looked white,
almost like the man at the circus who comes in with the
dog to make us laugh. And Don Gaspare, too, he
looked"—Ruffo paused, then used a word beloved of
Sicilians who wish to be impressive—"he looked mysterious, Signora. Don Gaspare looked mysterious."

"Mysterious? Gaspare?"

"Sì, Signora, he did. And he looked almost white,
too, but not like my mamma. And then my mamma
said, 'Gaspare!' just like that, Signora, and put out her
hand—so. And Don Gaspare's face got red and hot.
And then for a minute they spoke together, Signora,
and I could not hear what they said. For Don Gaspare
stood with his back so that I should not hear. And then
the balloon went sideways and the people ran, and I
did not see Don Gaspare any more. And after that,
Signora, my mamma was crying all the time. And she
would not tell me anything. I only heard her say: 'To
think of its being Gaspare! To think of its being Gaspare on the island!' And when we got home she said
to me, 'Ruffo,' she said, 'has Gaspare ever said you were
like somebody?' What is it, Signora?"

"Nothing, Ruffo. Go on."

"But—"

"Go on, Ruffo."

"'Has Gaspare ever said you were like somebody?' my mamma said."

"And you—what did you say?"

"I said, 'No,' Signora. And that is true. Don Gaspare has never said I was like somebody."

The boy had evidently finished what he had to say. He stood quietly by Hermione, waiting for her to speak in her turn. For a moment she said nothing. Then she put her hand on Ruffo's arm.

"Whom do you think your mother meant when she said 'somebody,' Ruffo?"

"Signora, I do not know."

"But surely—didn't you ask whom she meant?"

"No, Signora. I told my mamma Don Gaspare had never said that. She was crying. And so I did not say anything more."

Hermione still held his arm for a moment. Then her hand dropped down.

Ruffo was looking at her steadily with his bright and searching eyes.

"Signora, do you know what she meant?"

"I! How can I tell, Ruffo? I have never seen your mother. How can I know what she meant?"

"No, Signora."

Again there was a silence. Then Hermione said:

"I should like to see your mother, Ruffo."

"Sì, Signora."

"I must see her."

Hermione said the last words in a low and withdrawn voice, like one speaking to herself. As she spoke she was gazing at the boy beside her, and in her eyes there was a mystery—a mystery almost like that of the night.

493

"Ruffo," she added, in a moment, "I want you to promise me something."

"Sì, Signora."

"Don't speak to any one about the little talk we have had to-night. Don't say anything, even to Gaspare."

"No, Signora."

For a short time they remained together talking of other things. Hermione spoke only enough to encourage Ruffo. And always she was watching him. But to-night she did not see the look she longed for, the look that made Maurice stand before her. Only she discerned, or believed she discerned, a definite physical resemblance in the boy to the dead man, a certain resemblance of outline, a likeness surely in the poise of the head upon the strong, brave-looking neck, and in a trait that suggested ardor about the full yet delicate lips. Why had she never noticed these things before? Had she been quite blind? Or was she now imaginative? Was she deceiving herself?

"Good-night, Ruffo," she said, at last.

He took off his cap and stood bareheaded.

"Good-night, Signora."

He put back the cap on his dark hair with a free and graceful gesture.

Was not that, too, Maurice?

"A rivederci, Signora."

He was gone.

Hermione stood alone in the fatal night. She had forgotten Vere. She had forgotten Artois. The words of Ruffo had led her on another step in the journey it was ordained that she should make. She felt the underthings. It seemed to her that she heard in the night the dull murmuring of the undercurrents, that carry through wayward, or terrible, channels the wind-driven bark of life. What could it mean, this encounter just

494

described to her: this pain, this emotion of a woman, her strange question to her son? And Gaspare's agitation, his pallor, his "mysterious" face, the colloquy that Ruffo was not allowed to hear!

What did it mean? That woman's question—that question!

"What is it? What am I near?" Ruffo's mother knew Gaspare, must have known him intimately in the past. When? Surely long ago in Sicily; for Ruffo was sixteen, and Hermione felt sure—knew, in fact—that till they came to the island Gaspare had never seen Ruffo.

That woman's question!

Hermione went slowly to the bench and sat down by the edge of the cliff.

What could it possibly mean?

Could it mean that this woman, Ruffo's mother, had once known Maurice, known him well enough to see in her son the resemblance to him?

But then—

Hermione, as sometimes happened, having reached truth instinctively and with a sure swiftness, turned to retreat from it. She had lost confidence in herself. She feared her own impulses. Now, abruptly, she told herself that this idea was wholly extravagant. Ruffo probably resembled some one else whom his mother and Gaspare knew. That was far more likely. That must be the truth.

But again she seemed to hear in the night the dull murmurings of those undercurrents. And many, many times she recurred mentally to that weeping woman's question to her son—that question about Gaspare.

Gaspare—he had been strange, disturbed lately. Hermione had noticed it; so had the servants. There had been in the Casa del Mare an oppressive atmosphere created by the mentality of some of its inhabitants.

Even she, on that day when she had returned from
Capri, had felt a sensation of returning to meet some
grievous tale.

She remembered Artois now, recalling his letter which
she had found that day.

Gaspare and Artois—did they both suspect, or both
know, something which they had been concealing from
her?

Suddenly she began to feel frightened. Yet she did
not form in her mind any definite conception of what
such a mutual secret might be. She simply began to
feel frightened, almost like a child.

She said to herself that this brooding night, with its
dumbness, its heat, its vaporous mystery, was affecting
her spirit. And she got up from the bench, and began
to walk very slowly towards the house.

When she did this she suddenly felt sure that while
she had been on the crest of the cliff Artois had arrived
at the island, that he was now with Vere in the house.
She knew that it was so.

And again there rushed upon her that sensation of
outrage, of being defaced, and of approaching a dwelling
in which things monstrous had taken up their abode.

She came to the bridge and paused by the rail. She
felt a sort of horror of the Casa del Mare in which Artois
was surely sitting—alone or with Vere? With Vere.
For otherwise he would have come up to the cliff.

She leaned over the rail. She looked into the Pool.
One boat was there just below her, the boat to which
Ruffo belonged. Was there another? She glanced to
the right. Yes; there lay by the rock a pleasure-boat
from Naples.

Artois had come in that.

She looked again at the other boat, searching its
shadowy blackness for the form of Ruffo. She longed
that he might be awake. She longed that he might

sing, in his happy voice, of the happy summer nights, of the sweet white moons that light the Southern summer nights, of the bright eyes of Rosa, of the sea of Mergellina. But from the boat there rose no voice, and the mist hung heavily over the silent Pool.

Then Hermione lifted her eyes and looked across the Pool, seeking the little light of San Francesco. Only the darkness and the mist confronted her. She saw no light—and she trembled like one to whom the omens are hostile.

She trembled and hid her face for a moment. Then she turned and went up into the house.

CHAPTER XXXIII

WHEN Hermione reached the door of the Casa del Mare she did not go in immediately, but waited on the step. The door was open. There was a dim lamp burning in the little hall, which was scarcely more than a passage. She looked up and saw a light shining from the window of her sitting-room. She listened; there was no sound of voices.

They were not in there.

She was trying to crush down her sense of outrage, to feel calm before she entered the house.

Perhaps they had gone into the garden. The night was terribly hot. They would prefer to be out-of-doors. Vere loved the garden. Or they might be on the terrace.

She stepped into the hall and went to the servants' staircase. Now she heard voices, a laugh.

"Giulia!" she called.

The voices stopped talking, but it was Gaspare who came in answer to her call. She looked down to him.

"Don't come up, Gaspare. Where is the Signorina?"

"The Signorina is on the terrace, Signora—with Don Emilio."

He looked up at her very seriously in the gloom. She thought of that meeting at the Festa, and longed to wring from Gaspare his secret.

"Don Emilio is here?"

"Sì, Signora."

"How long ago did he come?"

A SPIRIT IN PRISON

"About half an hour, I think, Signora."

"Why didn't you tell me?"

"Don Emilio told me not to bother you, Signora—
that he would just sit and wait."

"I see. And the Signorina?"

"I did not tell her, either. She was in the garden
alone, but I have heard her talking on the terrace with
the Signore. Are you ill, Signora?"

"No. All right, Gaspare!"

She moved away. His large, staring eyes followed
her till she disappeared in the passage. The passage
was not long, but it seemed to Hermione as if a multitude of impressions, of thoughts, of fears, of determina-
tions rushed through her heart and brain while she
walked down it and into the room that opened to the
terrace. This room was dark.

As she entered it she expected to hear the voices from
outside. But she heard nothing.

They were not on the terrace, then!

She again stood still. Her heart was beating violently,
and she felt violent all over, thrilling with violence like
one on the edge of some outburst.

She looked towards the French window. Through its
high space she saw the wan night outside, a sort of thin
paleness resting against the blackness in which she was
hidden. And as her eyes became accustomed to their
environment she perceived that the pallor without was
impinged upon by two shadowy darknesses. Very faint
they were, scarcely relieved against the night, very still
and dumb—two shadowy darknesses, Emile and Vere
sitting together in silence.

When Hermione understood this she remained where
she was, trying to subdue even her breathing. Why
were they not talking? What did this mutual silence,
this mutual immobility mean? She was only a few feet
from them. Yet she could not hear a human sound,

even the slightest. There was something unnatural, but also tremendously impressive to her in their silence. She felt as if it signified something unusual, something of high vitality. She felt as if it had succeeded some speech that was exceptional, and that had laid its spell, of joy or sorrow, upon both their spirits.

And she felt much more afraid, and also much more alone, than she would have felt had she found them talking.

Presently, as the silence continued, she moved softly back into the passage. She went down it a little way, then returned, walking briskly and loudly. In this action her secret violence was at play. When she came to the room she grasped the door-handle with a force that hurt her hand. She went in, shut the door sharply behind her, and without any pause came out upon the terrace.

"Emile!"

"Yes," he said, getting up from his garden-chair quickly.

"Gaspare told me you were here."

"I have been here about half an hour."

She had not given him her hand. She did not give it.

"I didn't hear you talking to Vere, so I wondered— I almost thought—"

"That I had gone without seeing you? Oh no. It isn't very late. You don't want to get rid of me at once?"

"Of course not."

His manner—or so it seemed to her—was strangely uneasy and formal, and she thought his face looked drawn, almost tortured. But the light was very dim. She could not be sure of that.

Vere had said nothing, had not moved from her seat.

There was a third chair. As Hermione took it and drew it slightly forward, she looked towards Vere, and

thought that she was sitting in a very strange position.
In the darkness it seemed to the mother as if her child's
body were almost crouching in its chair, as if the head
were drooping, as if—

"Vere! Is anything the matter with you?"

Suddenly, as if struck sharply, Vere sprang up and
passed into the darkness of the house, leaving a sound
that was like a mingled exclamation and a sob behind
her.

"Emile!"

.   .   .   .   .

"Emile!"

"Hermione?"

"What is the matter with Vere? What have you
been doing to Vere?"

"I!"

"Yes, you! No one else is here."

Hermione's violent, almost furious agitation was audible in her voice.

"I should never wish to hurt Vere—you know that."

His voice sounded as if he were deeply moved.

"I must— Vere! Vere!"

She moved towards the house. But Artois stepped
forward swiftly, laid a hand on her arm, and stopped
her.

"No, leave Vere alone to-night!" he said.

"Why?"

"She wishes to be alone to-night."

"But I find her here with you."

There was a harsh bitterness of suspicion, of doubt,
in her tone that he ought surely to have resented. But
he did not resent it.

"I was sitting on the terrace," he said, gently. "Vere
came in from the garden. Naturally she stayed to entertain me till you were here."

"And directly I come she rushes away into the house!"

"Perhaps there was—something may have occurred to upset her."

"What was it?"

Her voice was imperious.

"You must tell me what it was!" she said, as he was silent.

"Hermione, my friend, let us sit down. Let us at any rate be with each other as we always have been—till now."

He was almost pleading with her, but she did not feel her hardness melting. Nevertheless she sat down.

"Now tell me what it was."

"I don't think I can do that, Hermione."

"I am her mother. I have a right to know. I have a right to know everything about my child's life."

In those words, and in the way they were spoken, Hermione's bitter jealousy about the two secrets kept from her, but shared by Artois, rushed out into the light.

"I am sure there is nothing in Vere's life that might not be told to the whole world without shame; and yet there may be many things that an innocent girl would not care to tell to any one."

"But if things are told they should be told to the mother. The mother comes first."

He said nothing.

"The mother comes first!" she repeated, almost fiercely. "And you ought to know it. You do know it!"

"You do come first with Vere."

"If I did, Vere would confide in me rather than in any one else."

As Hermione said this, all the long-contained bitterness caused by Vere's exclusion of her from the knowledge that had been freely given to Artois brimmed up suddenly in her heart, overflowed boundaries, seemed to inundate her whole being.

A SPIRIT IN PRISON

"I do not come first," she said.

Her voice trembled, almost broke.

"You know that I do not come first. You have just told me a lie."

"Hermione!"

His voice was startled.

"You know it perfectly well. You have known it for a long time."

Hot tears were in her eyes, were about to fall. With a crude gesture, almost like that of a man, she put up her hands to brush them away.

"You have known it, you have known it, but you try to keep me in the dark."

Suddenly she was horribly conscious of the darkness of the night in which they were together, of the darkness of the world.

"You love to keep me in the dark, in prison. It is cruel, it is wicked of you."

"But Hermione—"

"Take care, Emile, take care—or I shall hate you for keeping me in the dark."

Her passionate words applied only to the later events in which Vere was concerned. But his mind rushed back to Sicily, and suddenly there came to his memory some words he had once read, he did not know when, or where:

"The spirit that resteth upon a lie is a spirit in prison."

As he remembered them he felt guilty, guilty before Hermione. He saw her as a spirit confined for years in a prison to which his action had condemned her. Yes, she was in the dark. She was in an airless place. She was deprived of the true liberty, that great freedom which is the accurate knowledge of the essential truths of our own individual lives. From his mind in that moment the cause of Hermione's outburst, Vere and her childish secrets, were driven out by a greater thing that came upon it like a strong and mighty wind—the memory of that lie, in which he had enclosed his friend's life for years, that lie on which her spirit had rested, on which it was resting still. And his sense of truth did not permit him to try to refute her accusation. Indeed, he was filled with a desire that nearly conquered him—there and then, brutally, clearly, nakedly, to pour forth to his friend all the truth, to say to her:

"You have a strong, a fiery spirit, a spirit that hates the dark, that hates imprisonment, a spirit that can surely endure, like the eagle, to gaze steadfastly into the terrible glory of the sun. Then come out of the darkness, come out of your prison. I put you there—let me bring you forth. This is the truth—listen! hear it!—it is this—it is this—and—this!"

This desire nearly conquered him. Perhaps it would have conquered him but for an occurrence that, simple though it was, changed the atmosphere in which their souls were immersed, brought in upon them another world with the feeling of other lives than their own.

The boat to which Ruffo belonged, going out of the Pool to the fishing, passed at this moment slowly upon the sea beneath the terrace, and from the misty darkness his happy voice came up to them in the song of Mergellina which he loved:

> "Oh, dolce luna bianca de l' Estate
>   Mi fugge il sonno accanto a la marina:
>   Mi destan le dolcissime serate
>   Gli occhi di Rosa e il mar di Mergellina."

Dark was the night, moonless, shrouded in the mist. But his boy's heart defied it, laughed at the sorrowful truths of life, set the sweet white moon in the sky, covered the sea with her silver. Artois turned towards the song and stood still. But Hermione, as if physically compelled towards it, moved away down the terrace, following in the direction in which the boat was going.

As she passed Artois he saw tears running down her cheeks. And he said to himself:

"No, I cannot tell her; I can never tell her. If she is to be told, let Ruffo tell her. Let Ruffo make her understand. Let Ruffo lift her up from the lie on which I have made her rest, and lead her out of prison."

As this thought came to him a deep tenderness towards Hermione flooded his heart. He stood where he was. Far off he still heard Ruffo's voice drifting away in the mist out to the great sea. And he saw the vague form of Hermione leaning down over the terrace wall, towards the sea, the song, and Ruffo.

How intensely strange, how mysterious, how subtle was the influence housed within the body of that singing boy, that fisher-boy, which, like an issuing fluid, or escaping vapor, or perfume, had stirred and attracted the childish heart of Vere, had summoned and now held fast the deep heart of Hermione.

Just then Artois felt as if in the night he was walking with the Eternities, as if that song, now fading away across the sea, came even from them. We do not die. For in that song to which Hermione bent down—the dead man lived when that boy's voice sang it. In that boat, now vanishing upon the sea, the dead man held an oar. In that warm young heart of Ruffo the dead man moved, and spoke—spoke to his child, Vere, whom he had never seen, spoke to his wife, Hermione, whom he had deceived, yet whom he had loved.

Then let him—let the dead man himself—speak out of that temple which he had created in a moment of lawless passion, out of that son whom he had made to live by the action which had brought upon him death.

Ruffo—all was in the hands of Ruffo, to whom Hermione, weeping, bent for consolation.

A SPIRIT IN PRISON

The song died away. Yet Hermione did not move, but still leaned over the sea. She scarcely knew where she was. The soul of her, the suffering soul, was voyaging through the mist with Ruffo, was voyaging through the mist and through the night with—her Sicilian and all the perfect past. It seemed to her at that moment that she had lost Vere in the dark, that she had lost Emile in the dark, that even Gaspare was drifting from her in a mist of secrecy which he did not intend that she should penetrate.

There was only Ruffo left.

He had no secrets. He threw no darkness round him and those who loved him. In his happy, innocent song was his happy, innocent soul.

She listened, she leaned down, almost she stretched out her arms towards the sea. And in that moment she knew in her mind and she felt in her heart that Ruffo was very near to her, that he meant very much to her, even that she loved him.

CHAPTER XXXIV

Artois left the island that night without speaking to Hermione. He waited a long time. But she did not move to come to him. And he did not dare to go to her. He did not dare! In all their long friendship never before had his spirit bent before, or retreated as if in fear from Hermione's. To-night he was conscious that in her fierce anger, and afterwards in her tears, she had emancipated herself from him. He was conscious of her force as he had never been conscious of it before. Something within him almost abdicated to her intensity. And at last he turned and went softly away from the terrace. He descended to the sea. He left the island.

Were they any longer friends?

As the boat gave itself to the mist he wondered. It had come to this, then—that he did not know whether Hermione and he were any longer friends. Almost imperceptibly, with movement so minute that it had seemed like immobility, they had been drifting apart through these days and nights of the summer. And now abruptly the gulf appeared between them.

He felt just then that they could never more be friends, that their old happy camaraderie could never be re-established.

That they could ever be enemies was unthinkable. Even in Hermione's bitterness and anger Artois felt her deep affection. In her cry, "Take care, Emile, or I shall hate you for keeping me in the dark!" he heard only the hatred that is the other side of love.

But could they ever be comrades again? And if they could not, what could they be?

As the boat slipped on, under the Saint's light, which was burning although the mist had hidden it from Hermione's searching eyes, and out to the open sea, Artois heard again her fierce exclamation. It blended with Vere's sob. He looked up and saw the faint lights of the Casa del Mare fading from him in the night. And an immense sadness, mingled with an immense, but chaotic, longing invaded him. He felt horribly lonely, and he felt a strange, new desire for the nearness to him of life. He yearned to feel life close to him, pulsing with a rhythm to which the rhythm of his being answered. He yearned for that strange and exquisite satisfaction, compounded of mystery and wonder, and thrilling with something akin to pain, that is called forth in the human being who feels another human being centring all its highest faculties, its strongest powers, its deepest hopes in him. He desired intensely, as he had never desired before, true communion with another, that mingling of bodies, hearts, and spirits, that is the greatest proof of God to man.

The lights of the Casa del Mare were lost to his eyes in the night. He looked for them still. He strained his eyes to see them. But the powerful night would not yield up its prey.

And now, in the darkness and with Hermione's last words ringing in his ears, he felt almost overwhelmed by the solitariness of his life in the world of lives.

That day, before he came to the island, he had met himself face to face like a man meeting his double. He had stripped himself bare. He had sear hed himself for the truth. Remembering all the Marchesino had said, he had demanded of his heart the truth, uncertain whether it would save or slay him. It had not slain him. When the colloquy was over he was still upright.

508

But he had realized as never before the delicate poise of human nature, set, without wings, on a peak with gulfs about it. Had he not looked in time, and with clear, steadfast eyes, might he not have fallen?

His affection for Vere was perfectly pure, was the love of a man without desire for a gracious and charming child. It still was that. He knew it for that by the wave of disgust that went over him when his imagination, prompted by the Marchesino's brutality, set pictures before him of himself in other relations with Vere. The real man in him recoiled so swiftly, so uncontrollably, that he was reassured as to his own condition. And yet he found much to condemn, something to be contemptuous of, something almost to weep over—that desire to establish a monopoly—that almost sickly regret for his vanished youth, that bitterness against the community to which all young things instinctively belong, whatever their differences of intellect, temperament, and feeling.

Could he have fallen?

Even now he did not absolutely know whether such a decadence might have been possible to him or not. But that now it would not be possible he felt that he did know.

Age could never complete youth, and Vere must be complete. He had desired to make her gift for song complete. He could never desire to mutilate her life. Had he not said to himself one day, as his boat glided past the sloping gardens of Posilipo, "Vere must be happy."

Yet that evening he had made her unhappy.

He had come to the island from his self-examination strong in the determination to be really himself, no longer half self-deceived and so deceiving. He had gone out upon the terrace, and waited there. But when Vere had come to join him, he had not been able to be natural. In his desire to rehabilitate himself thoroughly and swiftly in his own opinion he must have been almost harsh to the child. She had approached him a little doubtfully. She had needed specially just then to be met with even more than the usual friendship. Artois had seen in her face, in her expressive eyes, a plea not for forgiveness— there was no need of that, but for compassion, an appeal to him to ignore and yet to sympathize, that was exquisitely young and winning. But, because of his self-examination, and because he was feeling acutely, he had been abrupt, cold, changed in his manner. They had sat down together in the dark, and after some uneasy conversation, Vere, perhaps eager to make things easier between herself and "Monsieur Emile," had brought up the subject of her poems with a sort of anxious simplicity, and a touch of timidity that yet was confidential. And Artois, still recoiling secretly from that which might possibly have become a folly but could never have been anything more, had told Vere plainly and almost sternly that she must go on her literary path unaided, unadvised by him.

"I was glad to advise you at the beginning, Vere," he had said, finally; " but now I must leave you to yourself to work out your own salvation. You have talent. Trust it. Trust yourself. Do not lean on any one, least of all on me."

"No, Monsieur Emile," she had answered.

Those were the last words exchanged between them before Hermione came and questioned Vere. And only when Vere slipped into the house, leaving that sound of pain behind her, did Artois realize how cruel he must have seemed in his desire quickly to set things right.

He realized that; but, subtle though he was, he did not understand the inmost and root-cause of Vere's loss of self-control.

Vere was feeling bitterly ashamed, had been bending under this sense of undeserved shame, ever since the

Marchesino's stratagem on the preceding night. Although she was gay and fearless, she was exquisitely sensitive. Peppina's confession had roused her maidenhood to a theoretical knowledge of certain things in life, of certain cruel phases of man's selfishness and lust which, till then, she had never envisaged. The Marchesino's madness had carried her one step further. She had not actually looked into the abyss. But she had felt herself near to something that she hated even more than she feared it. And she had returned to the hotel full of a shrinking delicacy, not to be explained, intense as snow, which had made the meeting with her mother and Artois a torture to her, which had sealed her lips to silence that night, which had made her half apology to Gaspare in the morning a secret agony, which had even set a flush on her face when she looked at San Francesco. The abrupt change in Monsieur Emile's demeanor towards her made her feel as if she were despised by him because she had been the victim of the Marchesino's trick. Or perhaps Monsieur Emile completely misunderstood her; perhaps he thought—perhaps he dared to think, that she had helped the Marchesino in his manœuvre.

Vere felt almost crucified, but was too proud to speak of the pain and bitterness within her. Only when her mother came out upon the terrace did she suddenly feel that she could bear no more.

That night, directly she was in her room, she locked her door. She was afraid that her mother might follow her, to ask what was the matter.

But Hermione did not come. She, too, wished to be alone that night. She, too, felt that she could not be looked at by searching eyes that night.

She did not know when Artois left the terrace. Long after Ruffo's song had died away she still leaned over the sea, following his boat with her desirous heart.

Artois, too, was on the sea. She did not know it. She was, almost desperately, seeking a refuge in the past. The present failed her. That was her feeling. Then she would cling to the past. And in that song, prompted now by her always eager imagination, she seemed to hear it. For she was almost fiercely, feverishly, beginning to find resemblances in Ruffo to Maurice. At first she had noticed none, although she had been strangely attracted by the boy. Then she had seen that look, flceting but vivid, that seemed for a moment to bring Maurice before her. Then, on the cliff, she had discerned a likeness of line, a definite similarity of features.

And now—was not that voice like Maurice's? Had it not his wonderful thrill of youth in it, that sound of the love of life, which wakes all the pulses of the body and stirs all the depths of the heart?

"Oh, dolce luna bianca de l' estate——"

The voice upon the sea was singing always the song of Mergellina. But to Hermione it began to seem that the song was changing to another song, and that the voice that was dying away across the shrouded water was sinking into the shadows of a ravine upon a mountainside.

"Ciao, Ciao, Ciao,
Morettina bella, ciao——"

Maurice was going to the fishing under the sweet white moon of Sicily. And she—she was no longer leaning down from the terrace of the Casa del Mare, but from the terrace of the House of the Priest.

"Prima di partire
Un bacio ti voglio da!"

That kiss, which he had given her before he had gone away from her forever! She seemed to feel it on her

512

lips again, and she shut her eyes, giving herself up to a passion of the imagination.

When she opened them again she felt exhausted and terribly alone. Maurice had gone down into the ravine. He was never coming back. Ruffo was taken by the mists and by the night. She lifted herself up from the balustrade and looked round, remembering suddenly that she had left Artois upon the terrace. He had disappeared silently, without a word of good-bye.

And now, seeing the deserted terrace, she recollected her fierce attack upon Artois, she remembered how she had stood in the black room watching the two darknesses outside, listening to their silence. And she remembered her conversation with Ruffo.

Actualities rushed back upon her memory. She felt as if she heard them coming like an army to the assault. Her brain was crowded with jostling thoughts, her heart with jostling feelings and with fears. She was like one trying to find a safe path through a black troop of threatening secrets. What had happened that night between Vere and Emile? Why had Vere fled? Why had she wept? And the previous night with the Marchesino— Vere had not spoken of it to her mother. Hermione had found it impossible to ask her child for any details. There was a secret too. And there were the two secrets, which now she knew, but which Vere and Artois thought were unknown to her still. And then—that mystery of which Ruffo had innocently spoken that night.

As Hermione, moving in imagination through the black and threatening troop, came to that last secret, she was again assailed by a curious, and horrible, sensation of apprehension. She again felt very little and very helpless, like a child.

She moved away from the balustrade and turned towards the house. Above, in her sitting-room, the light still shone. The other windows on this side of the Casa del Mare were dark. She felt that she must go to that light quickly, and she hastened in, went cautiously—though now almost panic-stricken—through the black room with the French windows, and came into the dimly lighted passage that led to the front door.

Gaspare was there locking up. She came to him.

"Good-night, Gaspare," she said, stopping.

"Good-night, Signora," he answered, slightly turning his head, but not looking into her face.

Hermione turned to go up-stairs. She went up two or three steps. She heard a bolt shot into its place below her, and she stopped again. To-night she felt for the first time almost afraid of Gaspare. She trusted him as she had always trusted him—completely. Yet that trust was mingled with this new and dreadful sensation of fear bred of her conviction that he held some secret from her in his breast. Indeed, it was her trust in Gaspare which made her fear so keen. As she stood on the staircase she knew that. If Gaspare kept things, kept anything from her that at all concerned her life, it must be because he was faithfully trying to save her from some pain or misery.

But perhaps she was led away by her depression of to-night. Perhaps this mystery was her own creation, and he would be quite willing to explain, to clear it away with a word.

"Gaspare," she said, "have you finished locking up?"

"Not quite, Signora. I have the front of the house to do."

"Of course. Well, when you have finished come up to my room for a minute, will you?"

"Va bene, Signora."

Was there reluctance in his voice? She thought there was. She went up-stairs and waited in her sitting-room. It seemed to her that Gaspare was a very long time locking up. She leaned out of the window that overlooked

514

the terrace to hear if he was shutting the French windows. When she did so she saw him faintly below, standing by the balustrade. She watched him, wondering what he was doing, till at last she could not be patient any longer.

"Gaspare!" she called out.

He started violently.

"I am coming, Signora."

"I am waiting for you."

"A moment, Signora!"

Yes, his voice was reluctant; but he went at once towards the house and disappeared. Directly afterwards she heard the windows being shut and barred, then a step coming rather slowly up the staircase.

"Che vuole, Signora?"

How many times she had heard that phrase from Gaspare's lips! How many times in reply she had expressed some simple desire! To-night she found a difficulty in answering that blunt question. There was so much that she wished, wanted—wide and terrible want filled her heart.

"Che vuole?" he repeated.

As she heard it a second time, suddenly Hermione knew that for the moment she was entirely dominated by Ruffo and that which concerned, which was connected with him. The fisher-boy had assumed an abrupt and vast importance in her life.

"Gaspare," she said, "you know me pretty well by this time, don't you?"

"Know you, Signora! Of course I know you!" He gazed at her, then added, "Who should know you, Signora, if I do not?"

"That is just what I mean, Gaspare. I wonder—I wonder—" She broke off. "Do you understand, Gaspare, how important you are to me, how necessary you are to me?"

515

An expressive look that was full of gentleness dawned in his big eyes.

"Sì, Signora, I understand."

"And I think you ought to understand my character by this time." She looked at him earnestly. "But I sometimes wonder—I mean lately—I sometimes wonder whether you do quite understand me."

"Why, Signora?"

"Do you know what I like best from the people who are near me, who live with me?"

"Sì, Signora."

"What?"

"Affection, Signora. You like to be cared for, Signora."

She felt tears rising again in her eyes.

"Yes, I love affection. But—there's something else, too. I love to be trusted. I'm not curious. I hate to pry into people's affairs. But I love to feel that I am trusted, that those I trust and care for would never keep me in the dark—"

She thought again of Emile and of the night and her outburst.

"The dark, Signora?"

"Don't you understand what I mean? When you are in the dark you can't see anything. You can't see the things you ought to see."

"You are not in the dark, Signora."

He spoke rather stupidly, and looked towards the lamp, as if he misunderstood her explanation. But she knew his quickness of mind too well to be deceived.

"Gaspare," she said, "I don't know whether you are going to be frank with me, but I am going to be frank with you. Sit down for a minute, and—please shut the door first."

He looked at her, looked down, hesitated, then went slowly to the door and shut it softly. Hermione was sitting on the sofa when he turned. He came back and stood beside her.

"Sì, Signora?"

"I'd rather you sat too, Gaspare."

He took his seat on a hard chair. His face had changed. Generally it was what is called "an open face." Now it looked the opposite to that. When she glanced at him, almost furtively, Hermione was once more assailed by fear. She began to speak quickly, with determination, to combat her fear.

"Gaspare, I may be wrong, but for some time I have felt now and then as if you and I were not quite as we used to be together, as if—well, now and then it seems to me as if there was a wall, and I was on one side of the wall and you were on the other. I don't like that feeling, after having you with me so long. I don't like it, and I want to get rid of it."

She paused.

"Sì, Signora," he said, in a low voice.

He was now looking at the floor. His arms were resting on his knees, and his hands hung down touching each other.

"It seems to me that—I never noticed this thing between us until—until Ruffo came to the island."

"Ruffo?"

"Yes, Gaspare, Ruffo."

She spoke with increasing energy and determination, still combating her still formless fear. And because of this interior combat her manner and voice were not quite natural, though she strove to keep them so, knowing well how swiftly a Sicilian will catch the infection of a strange mood, will be puzzled by it, be made obstinate, even dogged by it.

"I am sure that all this—I mean that this has something to do with Ruffo."

Gaspare said nothing.

517

"I know you like Ruffo, Gaspare. I believe you like
him very much. Don't you?"

"Signora, Ruffo has never done me any harm."

"Ruffo is very fond of you."

She saw Gaspare redden.

"He respects and admires you more than other people. I have noticed that."

Gaspare cleared his throat but did not look up or
make any remark.

"Both the Signorina and I like Ruffo, too. We feel—
at least I feel—I feel as if he had become one of the
family."

Gaspare looked up quickly and his eyes were surely
fierce.

"One of the family!" he exclaimed.

Hermione wondered if he were jealous.

"I don't mean that I put him with you, Gaspare.
No—but he seems to me quite a friend. Tell me—do
you know anything against Ruffo?"

"Non, Signora."

It came very slowly from his lips.

"Absolutely nothing?"

"Signora, I don't know anything bad of Ruffo."

"I felt sure not. Don't you like his coming to the
island?"

Gaspare's face was still flushed.

"Signora, it is nothing to do with me."

A sort of dull anger seemed to be creeping into his
voice, an accent of defiance that he was trying to control. Hermione noticed it, and it brought her to a resolve that, till now, she had avoided. Her secret fear
had prompted her to delay, to a gradual method of
arriving at the truth. Now she sat forward, clasping
her hands together hard, and speaking quickly:

"Gaspare, I feel sure that you noticed long ago something very strange in Ruffo. Perhaps you noticed it

almost at once. I believe you did. It is this. Ruffo
has an extraordinary look in his face sometimes, a look
of—of your dead Padrone. I didn't see it for some time,
but I think you saw it directly. Did you? Did you,
Gaspare?"

There was no answer. Gaspare only cleared his
throat again more violently. Hermione waited for a
minute. Then, understanding that he was not going to
answer, she went on:

"You have seen it—we have both noticed it. Now I
want to tell you something—something that happened
to-night."

Gaspare started, looked up quickly, darted at his Padrona a searching glance of inquiry.

"What is it?" she said.

"Niente!"

He kept his eyes on her, staring with a tremendous
directness that was essentially southern. And she returned his gaze.

"I was with Ruffo this evening. We talked, and he
told me that he met you at the Festa last night. He
told me, too, that he was with his mother."

She waited, to give him a chance of speaking, of forestalling any question. But he only stared at her with
dilated eyes.

"He told me that you knew his mother, and that his
mother knew you."

"Why not?"

"Of course, there is no reason. What surprised me
rather"—she was speaking more slowly now, and more
unevenly—"was this—"

"Sì?"

Gaspare's voice was loud. He lifted up his hands and
laid them heavily on his knees.

"Sì?" he repeated.

"After you had spoken with her, she cried, Ruffo's

mother cried, Gaspare. And she said, 'To think of its being Gaspare on the island!'"

"Is that all?"

"No."

A look that was surely a look of fear came into his face, rendering it new to Hermione. Never before had she seen such an expression — or had she once — long ago — one night in Sicily?

"That isn't all. Ruffo took his mother home, and when they got home she said to him this, 'Has Gaspare ever said you were like somebody?'"

Gaspare said nothing.

"Did you hear, Gaspare?"

"Sì, Signora."

"Gaspare, it seems to me"—Hermione was speaking now very slowly, like one shaping a thought in her mind while she spoke—"it seems to me strange that you and Ruffo's mother should have known each other so well long before Ruffo was born, and that she should cry because she met you at the Festa, and that—afterwards— she should ask Ruffo that."

"Strange?"

The fear that had been formless was increasing now in Hermione, and surely it was beginning at last to take a form, but as yet only a form that was vague and shadowy.

"Yes. I think it very strange. Did you"—an intense curiosity was alive in her now—"did you know Ruffo's mother in Sicily?"

"Signora, it does not matter where I knew her."

"Why should she say that?"

"What?"

"'Has Gaspare ever said you were like somebody?'"

"I have never said Ruffo was like anybody!" Gaspare exclaimed, with sudden and intense violence. "May the Madonna let me die—may I die"—he held up his

520

arms—"may I die to-morrow if I have ever said Ruffo was like anybody!"

He got up from his chair. His face was red in patches, like the face of a man stricken with fever.

"Gaspare, I know that; but what could this woman have meant?"

"Madonna! How should I know? Signora, how can I tell what a woman like that means? Such women have no sense, they talk, they gossip—ah, ah, ah, ah!"—he imitated the voice of a woman of the people—"they are always on the door-step, their tongues are always going. Dio mio! Who is to say what they mean, or what nonsense goes through their heads?"

Hermione got up and laid her hand heavily on his arm.

"I believe you know of whom Ruffo's mother spoke, Gaspare. Tell me this—did Ruffo's mother ever know your Padrone?"

She looked straight into his eyes. It seemed to her as if, for the first time, there came from them to her a look that had something in it of dislike. This look struck her to a terrible melancholy, yet she met it firmly, almost fiercely, with a glance that fought it, that strove to beat it back. And with a steady voice she repeated the question he had not answered.

"Did Ruffo's mother ever know your Padrone?"

Gaspare moved his lips, passing his tongue over them. His eyes fell. He moved his arm, trying to shift it from his Padrona's hand. Her fingers closed on it more tenaciously.

"Gaspare, I order you to tell me."

"Signora," he said, "such things are not in my service. I am here to work, not to answer questions."

He spoke quietly now, heavily, and moved his feet on the carpet.

"You disobey me?"

"Signora, I shall always obey all your orders as a servant."

"And as a friend, Gaspare, as a friend! You are my friend, aren't you?"

Her voice had suddenly changed, and in answer to it his face changed. He looked into her face, and his eyes were full of a lustrous softness that was like a gentle and warm caress.

"Signora, you know what I am for you. Then leave me alone, Signora." He spoke solemnly. "You ought to trust me, Signora, you ought to trust me."

"I do trust you. But you—do you trust me?"

"Sì, Signora."

"In everything?"

"Signora, I trust you; I have always trusted you."

"And my courage—do you trust that?"

He did not answer.

"I don't think you do, Gaspare."

Suddenly she felt that he was right not to trust it. Again she felt beset by fear, and as if she had nothing within her that was strong enough to stand up in further combat against the assaults of the world and of destiny. The desire to know all, to probe this mystery, abruptly left her, was replaced by an almost frantic wish to be always ignorant, if only that ignorance saved her from any fresh sorrow or terror.

"Never mind," she said. "You needn't answer. I don't want— What does it all matter? It's—it's all so long ago."

Having got hold of that phrase, she clung to it as if for comfort.

"It's all so long ago," she repeated. "Years and years ago. We've forgotten it. We've forgotten Sicily, Gaspare. Why should we think of it or trouble about it any more? Good-night, Gaspare."

She smiled at him, but her face was drawn and looked old.

"Buona notte, Signora."

He did not smile, but gazed at her with earnest gentleness, and still with that lustrous look in his eyes, full of tenderness and protection.

"Buon riposo, Signora."

He went away, surely relieved to go.   At the door he said again:

"Buon riposo."

The door was shut.

"Buon riposo!"

Hermione repeated the words to herself.

"Riposo!"

The very thought of repose was like the most bitter irony.   She walked up and down the room.   To-night there was no stability in her.   She was shaken, lacerated mentally, by sharply changing moods that rushed through her, one chasing another.   Scarcely had Gaspare gone before she longed to call him back, to force him to speak, to explain everything to her.   The fear that cringed was suddenly replaced by the fear that rushes forward blindly, intent only on getting rid of uncertainty even at the cost of death.   Soldiers know that fear.   It has given men to bayonet points.

Now it increased rapidly within Hermione.   She was devoured by a terror that was acutely nervous, that gnawed her body as well as her soul.

Gaspare had known Ruffo's mother in Sicily.   And Maurice—he had known Ruffo's mother.   He must have known her.   But when?   How had he got to know her?

Hermione stood still.

"It must have been when I was in Africa!"

A hundred details of her husband's conduct, from the moment of his return from the fair till the last kiss he had given her before he went away down the side of Monte Amato, flashed through her mind.   And each one seemed to burn her mind as a spark, touching flesh, burns the flesh.

"It was when I was in Africa!"

She went to the window and leaned out into the night over the misty sea. Her lips moved. She was repeating to herself again and again:

"To-morrow I'll go to Mergellina! To-morrow I'll go to Mergellina!"

CHAPTER XXXV

HERMIONE did not sleep at all that night. When the
dawn came she got up and looked out over the sea. The
mist had vanished with the darkness. The vaporous
heat was replaced by a delicate freshness that embraced
the South as dew embraces a rose. On the as yet pale
waters, full of varying shades of gray, slate color, ethereal
mauve, very faint pink and white, were dotted many
fishing-boats. Hermione looked at them with her tired
eyes. Ruffo's boat was no doubt among them. There
was one only a few hundred yards beyond the rocks from
which Vere sometimes bathed. Perhaps that was his.

Ruffo's boat! Ruffo!

She put her elbows on the sill of the window and rested
her face in her hands.

Her eyes felt very dry, like sand she thought, and her
mind felt dry too, as if insomnia was withering it up.
She opened her lips to breathe in the salt freshness of
the morning.

Upon Anacapri a woolly white cloud lay lightly. The
distant coast, where dreams Sorrento, was becoming
clearer every moment.

Often and often in the summer-time had Hermione
been invaded by the radiant cheerfulness of the Bay of
Naples. She knew no sea that had its special gift of
magical gayety and stirring hopefulness, its laughing
Pagan appeal to all the light things of the soul. It
woke even the weary heart to holiday when, in the summer, it glittered and danced in the sun, whispering or

calling with a tender or bold vivacity along its lovely coast.

Out of this morning beauty, refined and exquisitely gentle, would rise presently that livelier Pagan spirit. It was not hers. She was no Pagan. But she had loved it, and she had, or thought she had, been able to understand it.

All that was long ago.

Now, as she leaned out, her soul felt old and haggard, and the contact with the youth and freshness of the morning emphasized its inability to be influenced any more by youthful wonders, by the graciousness and inspiration that are the gifts of dawn.

Was that Ruffo's boat?

Her mind was dwelling on Ruffo, but mechanically, heavily, like a thing with feet of lead, unable to lift itself once it had dropped down upon a surface.

All the night her brain had been busy. Now it did not slumber, but it brooded, like the mist that had so lately left the sea. It brooded upon the thought of Ruffo.

The light grew. Over the mountains the sky spread scarlet banners. The sea took, with a quiet readiness that was happily submissive, its burnished gift of gold. The gray was lost in gold.

And Hermione watched, and drank in the delicate air, but caught nothing of the delicate spirit of the dawn.

Presently the boat that lay not far beyond the rocks moved. A little black figure stood up in it, swayed to and fro, plying tiny oars. The boat diminished. It was leaving the fishing-ground. It was going towards Mergellina.

"To-day I am going to Mergellina."

Hermione said that to herself as she watched the boat till it disappeared in the shining gold that was making a rapture of the sea. She said it, but the words seemed to have little meaning, the fact which they conveyed to be unimportant to her.

And she leaned out of the window, with a weary and inexpressive face, while the gold spread ever more widely over the sea, and the Pagan spirit surely stirred from its brief repose to greet the brilliant day.

Presently she became aware of a boat approaching the island from the direction of Mergellina. She saw it first when it was a long distance off, and watched it idly as it drew near. It looked black against the gold, till it was off the Villa Pantano. But then, or soon after, she saw that it was white. It was making straight for the island, propelled by vigorous arms.

Now she thought it looked like one of the island boats. Could Vere have got up and gone out so early with Gaspare?

She drew back, lifted her face from her hands, and stood straight up against the curtain of the window. In a moment she heard the sound of oars in the water, and saw that the boat was from the island, and that Gaspare was in it alone. He looked up, saw her, and raised his cap, but with a rather reluctant gesture that scarcely indicated satisfaction or a happy readiness to greet her. She hesitated, then called out to him.

"Good-morning, Gaspare."

"Good-morning, Signora."

"How early you are up!"

"And you, too, Signora."

"Couldn't you sleep?"

"Signora, I never want much sleep."

"Where have you been?"

"I have been for a row, Signora."

He lifted his cap again and began to row in. The boat disappeared into the Saint's Pool.

"He has been to Mergellina."

A SPIRIT IN PRISON

The mind of Hermione was awake again. The sight of Gaspare had lifted those feet of lead. Once more she was in flight.

Arabs can often read the thoughts of those whom they know. In many Sicilians there is some Arab blood, and sometimes Hermione had felt that Gaspare knew well intentions of hers which she had never hinted to him. Now she was sure that in the night he had divined her determination to go to Mergellina, to see the mother of Ruffo, to ask her for the truth which Gaspare had refused to tell. He had divined this, and he had gone to Mergellina before her. Why?

She was fully roused now. She felt like one in a conflict. Was there, then, to be a battle between herself and Gaspare, a battle over this hidden truth?

Now she felt that it was vital to her to know this truth. Yet when her mind, or her tormented heart, was surely on the verge of its statement, was—or seemed to be—about to say to her, "Perhaps it is—that!" or "It is—that!" something within her, housed deep down in her, refused to listen, refused to hear, revolted from—what it did not acknowledge the existence of.

Paradox alone could hint the condition of her mind just then. She was in the thrall of fear, but, had she been questioned, would not have allowed that she was afraid.

Afterwards she never rightly knew what was the truth of her during this period of her life.

There was to be a conflict between her and Gaspare.

She came from the window, took a bath, and dressed. When she had finished she looked in the glass. Her face was calm, but set and grim. She had not known she could look like that. She hated her face, her expression, and she came away from the glass feeling almost afraid of herself.

At breakfast she and Vere always met. The table was

528

laid out-of-doors in the little garden or on the terrace if the weather was fine, in the dining-room if it was bad. This morning Hermione saw the glimmer of the white cloth near the fig-tree. She wondered if Vere was there, and longed to plead a headache and to have her coffee in her bedroom. Nevertheless, she went down resolved to govern herself.

In the garden she found Giulia smiling and putting down the silver coffee-pot in quite a bower of roses. Vere was not visible.

Hermione exchanged a good-morning with Giulia and sat down. The servant's smiling face brought her a mingled feeling of relief and wonder. The pungent smell of the coffee, conquering the soft scent of the many roses, pinned her mind abruptly down to the simple realities and animal pleasures and necessities of life. She made a strong effort to be quite normal, to think of the moment, to live for it. The morning was fresh and lovely; the warmth of the sun, the tonic vivacity of the air from the sea, caressed and quickened her blood.

The minute garden was secluded. A world that seemed at peace, a world of rocks and waters far from the roar of traffic, the uneasy hum of men, lay around her.

Surely the moment was sweet, was peaceful. She would live in it.

Vere came slowly from the house, and at once Hermione's newly made and not yet carried out resolution crumbled into dust. She forgot the sun, the sea, the peaceful situation and all material things. She was confronted by the painful drama of the island life! Vere with her secrets, Emile with his, Gaspare fighting to keep her, his Padrona, still in mystery. And she was confronted by her own passions, those hosts of armed men that have their dwelling in every powerful nature.

Vere came up listlessly.

"Good-morning, Madre," she said.

She kissed her mother's cheek with cold lips.

"What lovely roses!"

She smelled them and sat down in her place facing the sea-wall.

"Yes, aren't they?"

"And such a heavenly morning after the mist! What are we going to do to-day?"

Hermione gave her her coffee, and the little dry tap of a spoon on an egg-shell was heard in the stillness of the garden.

" Well, I—I am going across to take the tram."

"Are you?"

"Yes."

"Naples again? I'm tired of Naples."

There was in her voice a sound that suggested rather hatred than lassitude.

"I don't know that I shall go as far as Naples. I am going to Mergellina."

"Oh!"

Vere did not ask her what she was going to do there. She showed no special interest, no curiosity.

"What will you do, Vere?"

"I don't know."

She glanced round. Hermione saw that her usually bright eyes were dull and lack-lustre.

"I don't know what I shall do."

She sighed and began to eat her egg slowly, as if she had no appetite.

"Did you sleep well, Vere?"

"Not very well, Madre."

"Are you tired of the island?"

Vere looked up as if startled.

"Oh no! at least"—she paused—"No, I don't believe I could ever be really that. I love the island."

"What is it, then?"

"Sometimes—some days one doesn't know exactly what to do."

"Well, but you always seem occupied." Hermione spoke with slow meaning, not unkindly, but with a significance she hardly meant to put into her voice, yet could not keep out of it. "You always manage to find something to do."

Suddenly Vere's eyes filled with tears. She bent down her head and went on eating. Again she heard Monsieur Emile's harsh words. They seemed to have changed her world. She felt despised. At that moment she hated the Marchesino with a fiery hatred.

Hermione was not able to put her arm round her child quickly, to ask her what was the matter, to kiss her tears away, or to bid them flow quietly, openly, while Vere rested against her, secure that the sorrow was understood, was shared. She could only pretend not to see, while she thought of the two shadows in the garden last night.

What could have happened between Emile and Vere? What had been said, done, to cause that cry of pain, those tears? Was it possible that Emile had let Vere see plainly his—his—? But here Hermione stopped. Not even in her own mind, for herself alone, could she summon up certain spectres.

She went on eating her breakfast, and pretending not to notice that Vere was troubled. Presently Vere spoke again.

"Would you like me to come with you to Mergellina, Madre?" she said.

Her voice was rather uneven, almost trembling.

"Oh no, Vere!"

Hermione spoke hastily, abruptly, strongly conscious of the impossibility of taking Vere with her. Directly she had said the words she realized that they must have fallen on Vere like a blow. She realized this still more when she looked quickly up and saw that Vere's face was scarlet.

"I don't mean that I shouldn't like to have you with me, Vere," she added, hurriedly. "But—"

"It's all right, Madre. Well, I've finished. I think I shall go out a little in my boat."

She went away, half humming, half singing the tune of the Mergellina song.

Hermione put down her cup. She had not finished her coffee, but she knew she could not finish it. Life seemed at that moment utterly intolerable to her. She felt desperate, as a nature does that is forced back upon itself by circumstances, that is forced to be, or to appear to be, traitor to itself. And in her desperation action presented itself to her as imperatively necessary —necessary as air is to one suffocating.

She got up. She would start at once for Mergellina. As she went up-stairs she remembered that she did not know where Ruffo's mother lived, what she was like, even what her name was. The boy had always spoken of her as "Mia Mamma." They dwelt at Mergellina. That was all she knew.

She did not choose to ask Gaspare anything. She would go alone, and find out somehow for herself where Ruffo lived. She would ask the fishermen. Or perhaps she would come across Ruffo. Probably he had gone home by this time from the fishing.

Quickly, energetically she got ready.

Just before she left her room she saw Vere pass slowly by upon the sea, rowing a little way out alone, as she often did in the calm summer weather. Vere had a book, and almost directly she laid the oars in their places side by side, went into the stern, sat down under the awning, and began—apparently—to read. Hermione watched her for two or three minutes. She looked very lonely; and moved by an impulse to try to erase the impression made on her by the abrupt exclamation at the breakfast-table, the mother leaned out and hailed the child.

"Good-bye, Vere! I am just starting!" she cried out, trying to make her voice cheerful and ordinary.

Vere looked up for a second.

"Good-bye!"

She bent her head and returned to her book.

Hermione felt chilled.

She went down and met Giulia in the passage.

"Giulia, is Gaspare anywhere about? I want to cross to the mainland. I am going to take the tram."

"Signora, are you going to Naples? Maria says—"

"I can't do any commissions, because I shall probably not go beyond Mergellina. Find Gaspare, will you?"

Giulia went away and Hermione descended to the Saint's Pool. She waited there two or three minutes. Then Gaspare appeared above.

"You want the boat, Signora?"

"Yes, Gaspare."

He leaped down the steps and stood beside her.

"Where do you want to go?"

She hesitated. Then she looked him straight in the face and said:

"To Mergellina."

He met her eyes without flinching. His face was quite calm.

"Shall I row you there, Signora?"

"I meant to go to the village, and walk up and take the tram."

"As you like, Signora. But I can easily row you there."

"Aren't you tired after being out so early this morning?"

"No, Signora."

"Did you go far?"

"Not so very far, Signora."

Hermione hesitated. She knew Gaspare had been to Mergellina. She knew he had been to see Ruffo's mother. If that were so her journey would probably be in vain. In their conflict Gaspare had struck the first blow. Could anything be gained by her going?

Gaspare saw, and perhaps read accurately, her hesitation.

"It will get very hot to-day, Signora," he said, carelessly.

His words decided Hermione. If obstacles were to be put in her way she would overleap them. At all costs she would emerge from the darkness in which she was walking. A heat of anger rushed over her. She felt as if Gaspare, and perhaps Artois, were treating her like a child.

"I must go to Mergellina, Gaspare," she said. "And I shall go by tram. Please row me to the village."

"Va bene, Signora," he answered.

He went to pull in the boat.

CHAPTER XXXVI

WHEN Hermione got out of the boat in the little harbor of the village on the mainland Gaspare said again:

"I could easily row you to Mergellina, Signora. I am not a bit tired."

She looked at him as he stood with his hand on the prow of the boat. His shirt-sleeves were rolled up, showing his strong arms. There was something brave, something "safe"—so she called it to herself—in his whole appearance which had always appealed to her nature. How she longed at that moment to be quite at ease with him! Why would he not trust her completely? Perhaps in her glance just then she showed her thought, her desire. Gaspare's eyes fell before hers.

"I think I'll take the tram," she said, "unless—"

She was still looking at him, longing for him to speak. But he said nothing. At that moment a fisherman ran down the steps from the village and came over the sand to greet them.

"Good-bye, Gaspare," she said. "Don't wait, of course. Giovanni can row me back."

The fisherman smiled, but Gaspare said:

"I can come for you, Signora. You will not be very long, will you? You will be back for colazione?"

"Oh yes, I suppose so."

"I will come for you, Signora."

Again she looked at him, and felt his deep loyalty to her, his strong and almost doglike affection. And, feeling them, she was seized once more by fear. The thing Gaspare hid from her must be something terrible.

"Thank you, Gaspare."

"A rivederci, Signora."

Was there not a sound of pleading in his voice, a longing to retain her? She would not heed it. But she gave him a very gentle look as she turned to walk up the hill.

At the top, by the Trattoria del Giardinetto, she had to wait for several minutes before the tram came. She remembered her solitary dinner there on the evening when she had gone to the Scoglio di Frisio to look at the visitor's book. She had felt lonely then in the soft light of the fading day. She felt far more lonely now in the brilliant sunshine of morning. And for an instant she saw herself travelling steadily along a straight road, from which she could not diverge. She passed milestone after milestone. And now, not far off, she saw in the distance a great darkness in which the road ended. And the darkness was the ultimate loneliness which can encompass on earth the human spirit.

The tram-bell sounded. She lifted her head mechanically. A moment later she was rushing down towards Naples. Before the tram reached the harbor of Mergellina, on the hill opposite the Donn' Anna, Hermione got out. Something within her desired delay; there was plenty of time. She would walk a little way among the lively people who were streaming to the Stabilimenti to have their morning dip.

In the tram she had scarcely thought at all. She had given herself to the air, to speed, to vision. Now, at once, with physical action came an anxiety, a restlessness, that seemed to her very physical too. Her body felt ill, she thought, though she knew there was nothing the matter with her. All through her life her health had been robust. Never yet had she completely "broken down." She told herself that her body was perfectly well.

But she was afraid. That was the truth. And to feel fear was specially hateful to her, because she abhorred cowardice, and was inclined to despise all timidity as springing from weakness of character.

She dreaded reaching Mergellina. She dreaded seeing this woman, Ruffo's mother. And Ruffo? Did she dread seeing him?

She fought against her fear. Whatever might befall her she would remain herself, essentially separate from all other beings and from events, secure of the tremendous solitude that is the property of every human being on earth.

"Pain, misery, horror, come from within, not from without." She said that to herself steadily. "I am free so long as I choose, so long as I have the courage to choose, to be free."

And saying that, and never once allowing her mind to state frankly any fear, she came down to the harbor of Mergellina.

The harbor and its environs looked immensely gay in the brilliant sunshine. Life was at play here, even at its busiest. The very workers sang as if their work were play. Boats went in and out on the water. Children paddled in the shallow sea, pushing hand-nets along the sand. From the rocks boys were bathing. Their shouts travelled to the road where the fishermen were talking with intensity, as they leaned against the wall hot with the splendid sun.

Hermione looked for Ruffo's face among all these sun-browned faces, for his bright eyes among all the sparkling eyes of these children of the sea.

But she could not see him. She walked along the wall slowly.

"Ruffo—Ruffo—Ruffo!"

A SPIRIT IN PRISON

She was summoning him with her mind.

Perhaps he was among those bathing boys. She looked across the harbor to the rocks, and saw the brown body of one shoot through the shining air and disappear with a splash into the sea.

Perhaps that boy was he—how far away from her loneliness, her sadness, and her dread!

She began to despair of finding him.

"Barca! Barca!"

She had reached the steps now near the Savoy Hotel. A happy-looking boatman, with hazel eyes and a sensitive mouth, hailed her from the water. It was Fabiano Lari, to whom Artois had once spoken, waiting for custom in his boat the *Stella del Mare*.

Hermione was attracted to the man, as Artois had been, and she resolved to find out from him, if possible, where Ruffo's mother lived. She went down the steps. The man immediately brought his boat right in.

"No," she said, "I don't want the boat."

Fabiano looked a little disappointed.

"I am looking for some one who lives here, a Sicilian boy called Ruffo."

"Ruffo Scarla, Signora? The Sicilian?"

"That must be he. Do you know him?"

"Sì, Signora, I know Ruffo very well. He was here this morning. But I don't know where he is now." He looked round. "He may have gone home, Signora."

"Do you know where he lives?"

"Sì, Signora. It is near where I live. It's near the Grotto."

"Could you possibly leave your boat and take me there?"

"Sì, Signora! A moment, Signora."

Quickly he signed to a boy who was standing close by watching them. The boy ran down to the boat. Fabiano spoke to him in dialect. He got into the boat, while Fabiano jumped ashore.

538

"Signora, I am ready. We go this way."

They walked along together.

Fabiano was as frank and simple as a child, and began at once to talk. Hermione was glad of that, still more glad that he talked of himself, his family, the life and affairs of a boatman. She listened sympathetically, occasionally putting in a word, till suddenly Fabiano said:

"Antonio Bernari will be out to-day. I suppose you know that, Signora?"

"Antonio Bernari! Who is he? I never heard of him."

Fabiano looked surprised.

"But he is Ruffo's Patrigno. He is the husband of Maddalena."

Hermione stood still on the pavement. She did not know why for a moment. Her mind seemed to need a motionless body in which to work. It was surely groping after something, eagerly, feverishly, yet blindly.

Fabiano paused beside her.

"Signora," he said, staring at her in surprise, "are you tired? Are you not well?"

"I'm quite well. But wait a minute. Yes, I do want to rest for a minute."

She dared not move lest she should interfere with that mental search. Fabiano's words had sent her mind sharply to Sicily.

Maddalena!

She was sure she had known, or heard of, some girl in Sicily called Maddalena, some girl or some woman. She thought of the servant in the Casa del Prete, Lucrezia. Had she any sister, any relation called Maddalena? Or had Gaspare—?

Suddenly Hermione seemed to be on the little terrace above the ravine with Maurice and Artois. She seemed to feel the heat of noon in summer. Gaspare was there, too. She saw his sullen face. She saw him looking ugly. She heard him say:

"Salvatore and Maddalena, Signora."

Why had he said that? In answer to what question?

And then, in a flash, she remembered everything. It was she who had spoken first. She had asked him who lived in the House of the Sirens.

"Salvatore and Maddalena."

And afterwards—Maurice had said something. Her mind went in search, seized its prey.

"They're quite friends of ours. We saw them at the fair only yesterday."

Maurice had said that. She could hear his voice saying it.

"I'm rested now."

She was speaking to Fabiano. They were walking on again among the chattering people. They had come to the wooden station where the tram-lines converge.

"Is it this way?"

"Sì, Signora, quite near the Grotto. Take care, Signora."

"It's all right. Thank you."

They had crossed now and were walking up the street that leads directly to the tunnel, whose mouth confronted them in the distance. Hermione felt as if they were going to enter it, were going to walk down it to that great darkness which seemed to wait for her, to beckon her. But presently Fabiano turned to the right, and they came into a street leading up the hill, and stopped almost immediately before a tall house.

"Antonio and Maddalena live here, Signora."

"And Ruffo," she said, as if correcting him.

"Ruffo! Sì, Signora, of course."

Hermione looked at the house. It was evidently let out in rooms to people who were comparatively poor; not very poor, not in any destitution, but who made

540

a modest livelihood, and could pay their fourteen or fifteen lire a month for a lodging. She divined by its aspect that every room was occupied. For the building teemed with life, and echoed with the sound of calling, or screaming, voices. The inhabitants were surely all of them in a flurry of furious activity. Children were playing before and upon the door-step, which was flanked by an open shop, whose interior revealed with a blatant sincerity a rummage of mysterious edibles—fruit, vegetables, strings of strange objects that looked poisonous, fungi, and other delights. Above, from several windows, women leaned out, talking violently to one another. Two were holding babies, who testified their new-born sense of life by screaming shrilly. Across other window-spaces heads passed to and fro, denoting the continuous movement of those within. People in the street called to people in the house, and the latter shouted in answer, with that absolute lack of self-consciousness and disregard of the opinions of others which is the hall-mark of the true Neapolitan. From the corner came the rumble and the bell notes of the trams going to and coming from the tunnel that leads to Fuorigrotta. And from every direction rose the vehement street calls of ambulant venders of the necessaries of Neapolitan life.

"Ruffo lives here!" said Hermione.

She could hardly believe it. So unsuitable seemed such a dwelling to that bright-eyed child of the sea, whom she had always seen surrounded by the wide airs and the waters.

"Sì, Signora. They are on the third floor. Shall I take you up?"

Hermione hesitated. Should she go up alone?

"Please show me the way," she said, deciding.

Fabiano preceded her up a dirty stone staircase, dark and full of noises, till they came to the third floor.

"It is here, Signora!"

He knocked loudly on a door. It was opened very quickly, as if by some one who was on the watch, expectant of an arrival.

"Chi è?" cried a female voice.

And, almost simultaneously, a woman appeared with eyes that stared in inquiry.

By these eyes, their shape, and the long, level brows above them, Hermione knew that this woman must be Ruffo's mother.

"Good-morning, Donna Maddalena," said Fabiano, heartily.

"Good-morning," said the woman, directing her eyes with a strange and pertinacious scrutiny to Hermione, who stood behind him. "I thought perhaps it was—"

She stopped. Behind, in the doorway, appeared the head of a young woman, covered with blue-black hair, then the questioning face of an old woman with a skin like yellow parchment.

"Don Antonio?"

She nodded, keeping her long, Arab eyes on Hermione.

"No. Are you expecting him so early?"

"He may come at any time. Chi lo sa?"

She shrugged her broad, graceless shoulders.

"It isn't he! It isn't Antonio!" bleated a pale and disappointed voice, with a peculiarly irritating timbre.

It was the voice of the old woman, who now darted over Maddalena Bernari's shoulder a hostile glance at Hermione.

"Madonna Santissima!" baaed the woman with the blue-black hair. "Perhaps he will not be let out to-day!"

The old woman began to cry feebly, yet angrily.

"Courage, Madre Teresa!" said Fabiano. "Antonio will be here to-day for a certainty. Every one knows it. His friends"—he raised a big brown hand significantly—"his friends have managed well for him."

"Sì! sì! It is true!" said the black-haired woman, nodding her large head, and gesticulating towards Madre Teresa. "He will be here to-day. Antonio will be here."

They all stared at Hermione, suddenly forgetting their personal and private affairs.

"Donna Maddalena," said Fabiano, "here is a signora who knows Ruffo. I met her at the Mergellina, and she asked me to show her the way here."

"Ruffo is out," said Maddalena, always keeping her eyes on Hermione.

"May I come in and speak to you?" said Hermione.

Maddalena looked doubtful, yet curious.

"My son is in the sea, Signora. He is bathing at the Marina."

Hermione thought of the brown body she had seen falling through the shining air, of the gay splash as it entered the water.

"I know your son so well that I should like to know his mother," she said.

Fabiano by this time had moved aside, and the two women were confronting each other in the doorway. Behind Maddalena the two other women stared and listened with all their might, giving their whole attention to this unexpected scene.

"Are you the Signora of the island?" asked Maddalena.

"Yes, I am."

"Let the Signora in, Donna Maddalena," said Fabiano. "She is tired and wants to rest."

Without saying anything Maddalena moved her broad body from the doorway, leaving enough space for Hermione to enter.

"Thank you," said Hermione to Fabiano, giving him a couple of lire.

"Grazie, Signora. I will wait down-stairs to take you back."

He went off before she had time to tell him that was
not necessary.

Hermione walked into Ruffo's home.

There were two rooms, one opening into the other.
The latter was a kitchen, the former the sleeping-room.
Hermione looked quickly round it, and her eyes fell at
once upon a large green parrot, which was sitting at the
end of the board on which, supported by trestles of iron,
the huge bed of Maddalena and her husband was laid.
At present this bed was rolled up, and in consequence
towered to a considerable height. The parrot looked
at Hermione coldly, with round, observant eyes whose
pupils kept contracting and expanding with a monoto-
nous regularity. She felt as if it had a soul that was
frigidly ironic. Its pertinacious glance chilled and repelled her, and she fancied it was reflected in the faces
of the women round her.

"Can I speak to you alone for a few minutes?" she
asked Maddalena.

Maddalena turned to the two women and spoke to
them loudly in dialect. They replied. The old woman
spoke at great length. She seemed always angry and
always upon the verge of tears. Over her shoulders she
wore a black shawl, and as she talked she kept fidgeting
with it, pulling it first to one side, then to the other, or
dragging at it with her thin and crooked yellow fingers.
The parrot watched her steadily. Her hideous voice
played upon Hermione's nerves till they felt raw. At
length, looking back, as she walked, with bloodshot eyes,
she went into the kitchen, followed by the young woman.
They began talking together in sibilant whispers, like
people conspiring.

After a moment of apparent hesitation Maddalena
gave her visitor a chair.

"Thank you," Hermione said, taking it.

She looked round the room again. It was clean and

well kept, but humbly furnished. Ruffo's bed was rolled up in a corner. On the walls were some shields of post-cards and photographs, such as the poor Italians love, deftly enough arranged and fastened together by some mysterious not apparent means. Many of the post-cards were American. Near two small flags, American and Italian, fastened crosswise above the head of the big bed, was a portrait of Maria Addolorata, under which burned a tiny light. A palm, blessed, and fashioned like a dagger with a cross for the hilt, was nailed above it, with a coral charm to protect the household against the evil eye. And a little to the right of it was a small object which Hermione saw and wondered at without understanding why it should be there, or what was its use—a *Fattura della morte* (death-charm), in the form of a green lemon pierced with many nails. This hung by a bit of string to a nail projecting from the wall.

From the death-charm Hermione turned her eyes to Maddalena.

She saw a woman who was surely not very much younger than herself, with a broad and spreading figure, wide hips, plump though small-boned arms, heavy shoulders. The face—that, perhaps—yes, that, certainly—must have been once pretty. Very pretty? Hermione looked searchingly at it until she saw Maddalena's eyes drop before hers suddenly, as if embarrassed. She must say something. But now that she was here she felt a difficulty in opening a conversation, an intense reluctance to speak to this woman into whose house she had almost forced her way. With the son she was strangely intimate. From the mother she felt separated by a gulf.

And that fear of hers?

She looked again round the room. Had that fear increased or diminished? Her eyes fell on Maria Addolorata, then on the *Fattura della morte*. She did not know why, but she was moved to speak about it.

545

"You have nice rooms here," she said.

"Sì, Signora."

Maddalena had rather a harsh voice. She spoke politely, but inexpressively.

"What a curious thing that is on the wall!"

"Signora?"

"It's a lemon, isn't it? With nails stuck through it?"

Maddalena's broad face grew a dusky red.

"That is nothing, Signora!" she said, hastily.

She looked greatly disturbed, suddenly went over to the bed, unhooked the string from the nail, and put the death-charm into her pocket. As she came back she looked at Hermione with defiance in her eyes.

The gulf between them had widened.

From the kitchen came the persistent sound of whispering voices. The green parrot turned sideways on the board beyond the pile of rolled-up mattresses, and looked, with one round eye, steadfastly at Hermione.

An almost intolerable sensation of desertion swept over her. She felt as if every one hated her.

"Would you mind shutting that door?" she said to Maddalena, pointing towards the kitchen.

The sound of whispers ceased. The women within were listening.

"Signora, we always keep it open."

"But I have something to say to you that I wish to say in private."

"Sì!"

The exclamation was suspicious. The voice sounded harsher than before. In the kitchen the silence seemed to increase, to thrill with anxious curiosity.

"Please shut that door."

It was like an order. Maddalena obeyed it, despite a cataract of words from the old woman that voiced indignant protest.

"And do sit down, won't you? I don't like to sit while you are standing."

"Signora, I—"

"Please do sit down."

Hermione's voice began to show her acute nervous agitation. Maddalena stared, then took another chair from its place against the wall, and sat down at some distance from Hermione. She folded her plump hands in her lap. Seated, she looked bigger, more graceless, than before. But Hermione saw that she was not really middle-aged. Hard life and trouble doubtless had combined to destroy her youth and beauty early, to coarsen the outlines, to plant the many wrinkles that spread from the corners of her eyes and lips to her temples and her heavy, dusky cheeks. She was now a typical woman of the people. Hermione tried to see her as a girl, long ago — years and years ago.

"I know your son Ruffo very well," she said.

Maddalena's face softened.

"Sì, Signora. He has told me of you."

Suddenly she seemed to recollect something.

"I have never— Signora, thank you for the money," she said.

The harshness was withdrawn from her voice as she spoke now, and in her abrupt gentleness she looked much younger than before. Hermione divined in that moment her vanished beauty. It seemed suddenly to be unveiled by her tenderness.

"I heard you were in trouble."

"Sì, Signora—great trouble."

Her eyes filled with tears and her mouth worked. As if moved by an uncontrollable impulse, she thrust one hand into her dress, drew out the death-charm, and contemplated it, at the same time muttering some words that Hermione did not understand. Her face became full of hatred. Holding up the charm, and lifting her head, she exclaimed:

"Those who bring trouble shall have trouble!"

While she spoke she looked straight before her, and her voice became harsh again, seemed to proclaim to the world unalterable destiny.

"Yes," said Hermione, in a low voice.

Maddalena hid the death-charm once more with a movement that was surreptitious.

"Yes," Hermione said again, gazing into Maddalena's still beautiful eyes. "And you have trouble!"

Maddalena looked afraid, like an ignorant person whose tragic superstition is proved true by an assailing fact.

"Signora!"

"You have trouble in your house. Have you ever brought trouble to any one? Have you?"

Maddalena stared at her with dilated eyes, but made no answer.

"Tell me something." Hermione leaned forward. "You know my servant, Gaspare?"

Maddalena was silent.

"You know Gaspare. Did you know him in Sicily?"

"Sicily?" Her face and her voice had become stupid. "Sicily?" she repeated.

The parrot shifted on the board, lifted its left claw, and craned its head forward in the direction of the two women. The tram-bell sounded its reiterated appeal.

"Yes, in Sicily. You are a Sicilian?"

"Who says so?"

"Your son is a Sicilian. At the port they call him 'Il Siciliano.'"

"Do they?"

Her intellect seemed to be collapsing. She looked almost bovine.

Hermione's excitement began to be complicated by a feeling of hot anger.

A SPIRIT IN PRISON

"But don't you know it? You must know it!"

The parrot shuffled slowly along the board, coming nearer to them, and bowing its head obsequiously. Hermione could not help watching its movements with a strained attention. Its presence distracted her. She had a longing to take it up and wring its neck. Yet she loved birds.

"You must know it!" she repeated, no longer looking at Maddalena.

"Sì?"

All ignorance and all stupidity were surely enshrined in that word thus said.

"Where did you know Gaspare?"

"Who says I know Gaspare?"

The way in which she pronounced his name revealed to Hermione a former intimacy between them.

"Ruffo says so."

The parrot was quite at the edge of the board now, listening apparently with cold intensity to every word that was being said. And Hermione felt that behind the kitchen door the two women were straining their ears to catch the conversation. Was the whole world listening? Was the whole world coldly, cruelly intent upon her painful effort to come out of darkness into— perhaps a greater darkness?

"Ruffo says so. Ruffo told me so."

"Boys say anything."

"Do you mean it is not true?"

Maddalena's face was now almost devoid of expression. She had set her knees wide apart and planted her hands on them.

"Do you mean that?" repeated Hermione.

"Boys—"

"I know it is true. You knew Gaspare in Sicily. You come from Marechiaro."

At the mention of the last word light broke into Maddalena's face.

"You are from Marechiaro. Have you ever seen me before? Do you remember me?"

Maddalena shook her head.

"And I—I don't remember you. But you are from Marechiaro. You must be."

Maddalena shook her head again.

"You are not?"

Hermione looked into the long Arab eyes, searching for a lie. She met a gaze that was steady but dull, almost like that of a sulky child, and for a moment she felt as if this woman was only a great child, heavy, ignorant, but solemnly determined, a child that had learned its lesson and was bent on repeating it word for word.

"Did Gaspare come here early this morning to see you?" she asked, with sudden vehemence.

Maddalena was obviously startled. Her face flushed.

"Why should he come?" she said, almost angrily.

"That is what I want you to tell me."

Maddalena was silent. She shifted uneasily in her chair, which creaked under her weight, and twisted her full lips sideways. Her whole body looked half-sleepily apprehensive. The parrot watched her with supreme attention. Suddenly Hermione felt that she could no longer bear this struggle, that she could no longer continue in darkness, that she must have full light. The contemplation of this stolid ignorance—that yet knew how much?—confronting her like a featureless wall almost maddened her.

"Who are you?" she said. "What have you had to do with my life?"

Maddalena looked at her and looked away, bending her head sideways till her plump neck was like a thing deformed.

"What have you had to do with my life? What have you to do with it now? I want to know!" She stood up.

"I must know. You must tell me! Do you hear?"
She bent down. She was standing almost over Maddalena. "You must tell me!"

There was again a silence through which presently the tram-bell sounded. Maddalena's face had become heavily expressionless, almost like a face of stone. And Hermione, looking down at this face, felt a moment of impotent despair that was succeeded by a fierce, energetic impulse.

"Then," she said—"then—I'll tell you!"

Maddalena looked up.

"Yes, I'll tell you."

Hermione paused. She had begun to tremble. She put one hand down to the back of the chair, grasping it tightly as if to steady herself.

"I'll tell you."

What? What was she going to tell?

That first evening in Sicily—just before they went in to bed—Maurice had looked down over the terrace wall to the sea. He had seen a light—far down by the sea.

It was the light in the House of the Sirens.

"You once lived in Sicily. You once lived in the Casa delle Sirene, beyond the old wall, beyond the inlet. You were there when we were in Sicily, when Gaspare was with us as our servant."

Maddalena's lips parted. Her mouth began to gape. It was obvious that she was afraid.

"You—you knew Gaspare. You knew—you knew my husband, the Signore of the Casa del Prete on Monte Amato. You knew him. Do you remember?"

Maddalena only stared up at her with a sort of heavy apprehension, sitting widely in her chair, with her feet apart and her hands always resting on her knees.

"It was in the summer-time—" She was again in Sicily. She was tracing out a story. It was almost as if she saw words and read them from a book. "There were no forestieri in Sicily. They had all gone. Only we were there—" An expression so faint that it was like a fleeting shadow passed over Maddalena's face, the fleeting shadow of something that denied. "Ah, yes! Till I went away, you mean! I went to Africa. Did you know it then? But before I went—before—" She was thinking, she was burrowing deep down into the past, stirring the heap of memories that lay like drifted leaves. "They used to go—at least they went once— down to the sea. One night they went to the fishing. And they slept out all night. They slept in the caves. Ah, you know that? You remember that night!"

The trembling that shook her body was reflected in her voice, which became tremulous. She heard the tram-bell ringing. She saw the green parrot listening on its board. And yet she was in Sicily, and saw the line of the coast between Messina and Cattaro, the Isle of the Sirens, the lakelike sea of the inlet between it and the shore.

"I see that you remember it. You saw them there. They—they didn't tell me!"

As she said the last words she felt that she was entering the great darkness. Maurice and Gaspare—she had trusted them with all her nature. And they—had they failed her? Was that possible?

"They didn't tell me," she repeated, piteously, speaking now only for herself and to her own soul. "They didn't tell me!"

Maddalena shook her head like one in sympathy or agreement. But Hermione did not see the movement. She no longer saw Maddalena. She saw only herself, and those two, whom she had trusted so completely, and —who had not told her.

What had they not told her?

And then she was in Africa, beside the bed of Artois,

ministering to him in the torrid heat, driving away the flies from his white face.

What had been done in the Garden of Paradise while she had been in exile?

She turned suddenly sick. Her body felt ashamed, defiled. A shutter seemed to be sharply drawn across her eyes, blotting out life. Her head was full of sea-like noises.

Presently, from among these noises, one detached itself, pushed itself, as it were, forward to attract forcibly her attention—the sound of a boy's voice.

"Signora! Signora!"

"Signora!"

A hand touched her, gripped her.

"Signora!"

The shutter was sharply drawn back from her eyes, and she saw Ruffo. He stood before her, gazing at her. His hair, wet from the sea, was plastered down upon his brown forehead—as *his* hair had been when, in the night, they drew him from the sea.

She saw Ruffo in that moment as if for the first time. And she knew. Ruffo had told her.

CHAPTER XXXVII

HERMIONE was outside in the street, hearing the cries of the ambulant sellers, the calls of women and children, the tinkling bells and the rumble of the trams, and the voice of Fabiano Lari speaking—was it to her?

"Signora, did you see him?"

"Yes."

"He is glad to be out of prison. He is gay, but he looks wicked."

She did not understand what he meant. She walked on and came into the road that leads to the tunnel. She turned mechanically towards the tunnel, drawn by its darkness.

"But, Signora, this is not the way! This is the way to Fuorigrotta!"

"Oh!"

She went towards the sea. She was thinking of the green parrot expanding and contracting the pupils of its round, ironic eyes.

"Was Maddalena pleased to see him? Was Donna Teresa pleased?"

Hermione stood still.

"What are you talking about?"

"Signora! About Antonio Bernari, who has just come home from prison! Didn't you see him? But you were there—in the house!"

"Oh—yes, I saw him. A rivederci!"

"Ma—"

"A rivederci!"

554

She felt in her purse, found a coin, and gave it to him. Then she walked on. She did not see him any more. She did not know what became of him.

Of course she had seen the return of Antonio Bernari. She remembered now. As Ruffo stood before her with the wet hair on his forehead there had come a shrill cry from the old woman in the kitchen: a cry that was hideous and yet almost beautiful, so full it was of joy. Then from the kitchen the two women had rushed in, gesticulating, ejaculating, their faces convulsed with excitement. They had seized Maddalena, Ruffo. One of them—the old woman, she thought—had even clutched at Hermione's arm. The room had been full of cries.

"Ecco! Antonio!"

"Antonio is coming!"

"I have seen Antonio!"

"He is pale! He is white like death!"

"Mamma mia! But he is thin!"

"Ecco! Ecco! He comes! Here he is! Here is Antonio!"

And then the door had been opened, and on the sill a big, broad-shouldered man had appeared, followed by several other evil-looking though smiling men. And all the women had hurried to them. There had been shrill cries, a babel of voices, a noise of kisses.

And Ruffo! Where had he been? What had he done?

Hermione only knew that she had heard a rough voice saying:

"Sangue del Diavolo! Let me alone! Give me a glass of wine! Basta! basta!"

And then she went out in the street, thinking of the green parrot and hearing the cries of the sellers, the tram-bells, and Fabiano's questioning voice.

Now she continued her walk towards the harbor of Mergellina alone. The thought of the green parrot obsessed her mind.

A SPIRIT IN PRISON

She saw it before her on its board, with the rolled-up bed towering behind it. Now it was motionless—only the pupils of its eyes moved. Now it lifted its claw, bowed its head, shuffled along the board to hear their conversation better.

She saw it with extreme distinctness, and now she saw also on the wall of the room near it the "Fattura della Morte"—the green lemon with the nails stuck through it, like nails driven into a cross.

Vaguely the word "crucifixion" went through her mind. Many people, many women, had surely been crucified since the greatest tragedy the world had ever known. What had they felt, they who were only human, they who could not see the face of the Father, who could—some of them, perhaps—only hope that there was a Father? What had they felt? Perhaps scarcely anything. Perhaps merely a sensation of numbness, as if their whole bodies, and their minds, too, were under the influence of a great injection of cocaine. Her thoughts again returned to the parrot. She wondered where it had been bought, whether it had come with Antonio from America.

Presently she reached the tramway station and stood still. She had to go back to the "Trattoria del Giardinetto." She must take a tram here, one of those on which was written in big letters, "Capo di Posilipo." No, not that! That did not go far enough. The other one—what was written upon it? Something—" Sette Settembre." She looked for the words "Sette Settembre."

Tram after tram came up, paused, passed on. But she did not see those words on any of them. She began to think of the sea, of the brown body of the bathing boy which she had seen shoot through the air and disappear into the shining water before she had gone to that house where the green parrot was. She would go down to the sea, to the harbor.

A SPIRIT IN PRISON

She threaded her way across the broad space, going in
and out among the trams and the waiting people. Then
she went down a road not far from the Grand Hotel and
came to the Marina.

There were boys bathing still from the breakwater of
the rocks. And still they were shouting. She stood by
the wall and watched them, resting her hands on the
stone.

How hot the stone was! Gaspare had been right. It
was going to be a glorious day, one of the tremendous
days of summer.

The nails driven through the green lemon like nails
driven through a cross—Peppina—the cross cut on Peppina's cheek.

That broad-shouldered man who had come in at the
door had cut that cross on Peppina's cheek.

Was it true that Peppina had the evil eye? Had it
been a fatal day for the Casa del Mare when she had
been allowed to cross its threshold? Vere had said
something—what was it?—about Peppina and her cross.
Oh yes! That Peppina's cross seemed like a sign, a
warning come into the house on the island, that it seemed
to say, "There is a cross to be borne by some one here,
by one of us!"

And the fishermen's sign of the cross under the light of
San Francesco?

Surely there had been many warnings in her life.
They had been given to her, but she had not heeded
them.

She saw a brown body shoot through the air from the
rocks and disappear into the shining sea. Was it Ruffo?
With an effort she remembered that she had left Ruffo
in the tall house, in the room where the green parrot was.

She walked on slowly till she came to the place where
Artois had seen Ruffo with his mother. A number of
tables were set out, but there were few people sitting at

557

them. She felt tired. She crossed the road, went to a table, and sat down. A waiter came up and asked her what she would have.

"Acqua fresca," she said.

He looked surprised.

"Oh—then wine, vermouth—anything!"

He looked more surprised.

"Will you have vermouth, Signora?"

"Yes, yes—vermouth."

He brought her vermouth and iced water. She mixed them together and drank. But she was not conscious of tasting anything. For a considerable time she sat there. People passed her. The trams rushed by. On several of them were printed the words she had looked for in vain at the station. But she did not notice them.

During this time she did not feel unhappy. Seldom had she felt calmer, more at rest, more able to be still. She had no desire to do anything. It seemed to her that she would be quite satisfied to sit where she was in the sun forever.

While she sat there she was always thinking, but vaguely, slowly, lethargically. And her thoughts reiterated themselves, were like recurring fragments of dreams, and were curiously linked together. The green parrot she always connected with the death-charm, because the latter had once been green. Whenever the one presented itself to her mind it was immediately followed by the other. The shawl at which the old woman's yellow fingers had perpetually pulled led her mind to the thought of the tunnel, because she imagined that the latter must eventually end in blackness, and the shawl was black. She knew, of course, really that the tunnel was lit from end to end by electricity. But her mind arbitrarily put aside this knowledge. It did not belong to her strange mood, the mood of one drawing near to the verge either of some abominable collapse or

of some terrible activity. Occasionally, she thought of
Ruffo; but always as one of the brown boys bathing
from the rocks beyond the harbor, shouting, laughing,
triumphant in his glorious youth. And when the link
was, as it were, just beginning to form itself from the
thought-shape of youth to another thought-shape, her
mind stopped short in that progress, recoiled, like a
creature recoiling from a precipice it has not seen but
has divined in the dark. She sipped the vermouth and
the iced water, and stared at the drops chasing each
other down the clouded glass. And for a time she was
not conscious where she was, and heard none of the
noises round about her.

> "Quanno fa notte 'nterra Mergellina,
> Se sceta 'o mare e canta chiano, chiano,
> Si fa chiu doce st' aria d 'a Marina,
> Pure 'e serene cantano 'a luntano.
> Quanno fa notte 'nterra Mergellina,
> E custa luna dint' 'essere e state
> Lo vularria durmi, ma nun e cosa;
> Me scetene d' 'o suonno 'e sti sarate,
> O' Mare, 'e Mergellina, e l' uocchie 'e Rosa!"

It was the song of Mergellina, sung at some distance
off in dialect, by a tenor voice to the accompaniment of
a piano-organ. Hermione ceased from gazing at the
drops on the glass, looked up, listened.

The song came nearer. The tenor voice was hard,
strident, sang lustily but inexpressively in the glaring
sunshine. And the dialect made the song seem different,
almost new. Its charm seemed to have evaporated.
Yet she remembered vaguely that it had charmed her.
She sought for the charm, striving feebly to recapture it.

> "E custa luna dint' 'essere e state—"

The piano-organ hurt her, the hard voice hurt her.
It sounded cruel and greedy. But the song—once it had

appealed to her.   Once she had leaned down to hear it, she had leaned down over the misty sea, her soul had followed it out over the sea.

> "Oh, dolce luna bianca de l' estate
>   Mi fugge il sonno accanto a la Marina:
> Mi destan le dolcissime serate
>   Gli occhi di Rosa e il mar di Mergellina."

Those were the real words.   And what voice had sung them?

And then, suddenly, her brain worked once more with its natural swiftness and vivacity, her imagination and her heart awaked.   She was again alive.   She saw the people.   She heard the sounds about her.   She felt the scorching heat of the sun.   But in it she was conscious also of the opposite of day, of the opposite of heat.   At that moment she had a double consciousness.   For she felt the salt coolness of the night around the lonely island.   And she heard not only the street singer, but Ruffo in his boat.

Ruffo—in his boat.

Suddenly she could not see anything.   Her sight was drowned by tears.   She got up at once.   She felt for her purse, found it, opened it, felt for money, found some coins, laid them down on the table, and began to walk. She was driven by fear, the fear of falling down in the sun in the sight of all men, and crying, sobbing, with her face against the ground.   She heard a shout.   Some one gave her a violent push, thrusting her forward.   She stumbled, recovered herself.   A passer-by had saved her from a tram.   She did not know it.   She did not look at him or thank him.   He went away, swearing at the English.   Where was she going?

She must go home.   She must go to the island.   She must go to Vere, to Gaspare, to Emile—to her life.

Her body and soul revolted from the thought, her out-

560

raged body and her outraged soul, which were just beginning to feel their outrage, as flesh and nerves begin
to feel pain after an operation when the effect of the
anæsthetic gradually fades away.

She was walking up the hill and still crying.

She met a boy of the people, swarthy, with impudent
black eyes, tangled hair, and a big, pouting mouth, above
which a premature mustache showed like a smudge. He
looked into her face and began to laugh. She saw his
white teeth, and her tears rushed back to their sources.
At once her eyes were dry. And, almost at once, she
thought, her heart became hard as stone, and she felt
self-control like iron within her.

That boy of the people should be the last human being
to laugh at her.

She saw a tram stop. It went to the "Trattoria del
Giardinetto." She got in, and sat down next to two
thin English ladies, who held guide-books in their hands,
and whose pointed features looked piteously inquiring.

"Excuse me, but do you know this neighborhood?"

She was being addressed.

"Yes."

"That is fortunate—we do not. Perhaps you will
kindly tell us something about it. Is it far to Bagnoli?"

"Not very far."

"And when you get there?"

"I beg your pardon!"

"When you get there, is there much to see?"

"Not so very much."

"Can one lunch there?"

"No doubt."

"Yes. But I mean, what sort of lunch? Can one get
anything clean and wholesome, such as you get in England?"

"It would be Italian food."

"Oh, dear! Fanny, this lady says we can only get Italian food at Bagnoli!"

"Tcha! Tcha!"

"But perhaps—excuse me, but do you think we could get a good cup of tea there? We might manage with that—tea and some boiled eggs. Don't you think so, Fanny? Could we get a cup of—"

The tram stopped. Hermione had pulled the cord that made the bell sound. She paid and got down. The tram carried away the English ladies, their pointed features red with surprise and indignation.

Hermione again began to walk, but almost directly she saw a wandering carriage and hailed the driver.

"Carrozza!"

She got in.

"Put me down at the 'Trattoria del Giardinetto.'"

"Sì, Signora—but how much are you going to give me? I can't take you for less than—"

"Anything—five lire—drive on at once."

The man drove on, grinning.

Presently Hermione was walking through the short tunnel that leads to the path descending between vineyards to the sea. She must take a boat to the island. She must go back to the island. Where else could she go? If Vere had not been there she might—but Vere was there. It was inevitable. She must return to the island.

She stood still in the path, between the high banks.

Her body was demanding not to be forced by the will to go to the island.

"I must go back to the island."

She walked on very slowly till she could see the shining water over the sloping, vine-covered land. The sight of the water reminded her that Gaspare would be waiting for her on the sand below the village. When she remembered that she stopped again. Then she turned round, and began to walk back towards the highroad.

A SPIRIT IN PRISON

Gaspare was waiting. If she went down to the sand she would have to meet his great intent eyes, those watchful eyes full of questions. He would read her. He would see in a moment that—she knew. And he would see more than that! He would see that she was hating him. The hatred was only dawning, struggling up in her tangled heart. But it existed—it was there. And he would see that it was there.

She walked back till she reached the tunnel under the highroad. But she did not pass through it. She could not face the highroad with its traffic. Perhaps the English ladies would be coming back. Perhaps— She turned again and presently sat down on a bank, and looked at the dry and wrinkled ground. Nobody went by. The lizards ran about near her feet. She sat there over an hour, scarcely moving, with the sun beating upon her head.

Then she got up and walked fast, and with a firm step, towards the village and the sea.

The village is only a tiny hamlet, ending in a small trattoria with a rough terrace above the sea, overlooking a strip of sand where a few boats lie. As Hermione came to the steps that lead down to the terrace she stood still and looked over the wall on her left. The boat from the island was at anchor there, floating motionless on the still water. Gaspare was not in it, but was lying stretched on his back on the sand, with his white linen hat over his face.

He lay like one dead.

She stood and watched him, as she might have watched a corpse of some one she had cared for but who was gone from her forever.

Perhaps he was not asleep, for almost directly he became aware of her observation, sat up, and uncovered his face, turning towards her and looking up. Already, and from this distance, she could see a fierce inquiry in his eyes.

She made a determined effort and waved her hand.

Gaspare sprang to his feet, took out his watch, looked at it, then went and fetched the boat.

His action—the taking out of the watch—reminded Hermione of time. She looked at her watch. It was half-past two. On the island they lunched at half-past twelve. Gaspare must have been waiting for hours. What did it matter?

She made another determined effort and went down the remaining steps to the beach.

Gaspare should not know that she knew. She was resolved upon that, concentrated upon that. Continually she saw in front of her the pouting mouth, the white teeth of the boy who had laughed at her in the street. There should be no more crying, no more visible despair. No one should see any difference in her. All the time that she had been sitting still in the sun upon the bank she had been fiercely schooling herself in an act new to her—the act of deception. She had not faced the truth that to-day she knew. She had not faced the ruin that its knowledge had made of all that had been sacred and lovely in her life. She had fastened her whole force fanatically upon that one idea, that one decision and the effort that was the corollary of it.

"There shall be no difference in me. No one is to know that anything has happened."

At that moment she was a fanatic. And she looked like one as she came down upon the sand.

"I'm afraid I'm rather late—Gaspare."

It was difficult to her to say his name. But she said it firmly.

"Signora, it is nearly three o'clock."

"Half-past two. No, I can get in all right."

He had put out his arm to help her into the boat. But she could not touch him. She knew that. She felt that she would rather die at the moment than touch or be touched by him.

"You might take away your arm."

He dropped his arm at once.

Had she already betrayed herself?

She got into the boat and he pushed off.

Usually he sat, when he was rowing, so that he might keep his face towards her. But to-day he stood up to row, turning his back to her. And this change of conduct made her say to herself again:

"Have I betrayed myself already?"

Fiercely she resolved to be and to do the impossible. It was the only chance. For Gaspare was difficult to deceive.

"Gaspare!" she said.

"Sì, Signora," he replied, without turning his head.

"Can't you row sitting down?"

"If you like, Signora."

"We can talk better then."

"Va bene, Signora."

He turned round and sat down.

The boat was at this moment just off the "Palace of the Spirits." Hermione saw its shattered walls cruelly lit up by the blazing sun, its gaping window-spaces like eye-sockets, sightless, staring, horribly suggestive of ruin and despair.

She was like that. Gaspare was looking at her. Gaspare must know that she was like that.

But she was a fanatic just then, and she smiled at him with a resolution that had in it something almost brutal, something the opposite of what she was, of the sum of her.

"I forgot the time. It is so lovely to-day. It was so gay at Mergellina."

"Sì?"

"I sat for a long time watching the boats, and the

boys bathing, and listening to the music. They sang 'A Mergellina.'"

"Sì?"

She smiled again.

"And I went to visit Ruffo's mother."

Gaspare made no response. He looked down now as he plied his oars.

"She seems a nice woman. I—I dare say she was quite pretty once."

The voice that was speaking now was the voice of a fanatic.

"I am sure she must have been pretty."

"Chi lo sa?"

"If one looks carefully one can see the traces. But, of course, now—"

She stopped abruptly. It was impossible for her to go on. She was passionately trying to imagine what that spreading, graceless woman, with her fat hands resting on her knees set wide apart, was like once—was like nearly seventeen years ago. Was she ever pretty, beautiful? Never could she have been intelligent— never, never. Then she must have been beautiful. For, otherwise— Hermione's drawn face was flooded with scarlet.

"If—if it's easier to you to row standing up, Gaspare," she almost stammered, "never mind about sitting down."

"I think it is easier, Signora."

He got up, and once more turned his back upon her.

They did not speak again until they reached the island.

Hermione watched his strong body swinging to and fro with every stroke, and wondered if he felt the terrible change in her feeling for him—a change that a few hours ago she would have thought utterly impossible.

She wondered if Gaspare knew that she was hating him.

He was alive and, therefore, to be hated. For surely we cannot hate the dust!

"HE TURNED AND GAZED AFTER HER AS SHE WENT UP
THE STEPS"

CHAPTER XXXVIII

GASPARE did not offer to help Hermione out of the boat when they reached the island. He glanced at her face, met her eyes, looked away again immediately, and stood holding the boat while she got out. Even when she stumbled slightly he made no movement; but he turned and gazed after her as she went up the steps towards the house, and as he gazed his face worked, his lips muttered words, and his eyes, become almost ferocious in their tragic gloom, were clouded with moisture. Angrily he fastened the boat, angrily he laid by the oars. In everything he did there was violence. He put up his hands to his eyes to rub the moisture that clouded them away. But it came again. And he swore under his breath. He looked once more towards the Casa del Mare. The figure of his Padrona had disappeared, but he remembered just how it had gone up the steps— leaning forward, moving very slowly. It had made him think of an early morning long ago, when he and his Padrona had followed a coffin down the narrow street of Marechiaro, and over the mountain-path to the Campo Santo above the Ionian Sea. He shook his head, murmuring to himself. He was not swearing now. He shook his head again and again. Then he went away, and sat down under the shadow of the cliff, and let his hands drop down between his knees.

The look he had seen in his Padrona's eyes had made him feel terrible. His violent, faithful heart was tormented. He did not analyze—he only knew, he only

567

felt. And he suffered horribly. How had his Padrona been able to look at him like that?'

The moisture came thickly in his eyes now, and he no longer attempted to rub it away. He no longer thought of it.

Never had he imagined that his Padrona could look at him like that. Strong man though he was, he felt as a child might who is suddenly abandoned by its mother. He began to think now. He thought over all he had done to be faithful to his dead Padrone and to be faithful to the Padrona. During many, many years he had done all he could to be faithful to these two, the dead and the living. And at the end of this long service he received as a reward this glance of hatred.

Tears rolled down his sunburnt cheeks.

The injustice of it was like a barbed and poisoned arrow in his heart. He was not able to understand what his Padrona was feeling, how, by what emotional pilgrimage, she had reached that look of hatred which she had cast upon him. If she had not returned, if she had done some deed of violence in the house of Maddalena, he could perhaps have comprehended it. But that she should come back, that she should smile, make him sit facing her, talk about Maddalena as she had talked, and then—then look at him like that!

His *amour-propre*, his long fidelity, his deep affection —all were outraged.

Vere came down the steps and found him there.

"Gaspare!"

He got up hastily when he heard her voice, rubbed his eyes, and yawned.

"I was asleep, Signorina."

She looked at him intently, and he saw tears in her eyes.

"Gaspare, what is the matter with Madre?"

"Signorina?"

568

"Oh, what is the matter?" She came a step nearer to him. "Gaspare, I'm frightened! I'm frightened!"

She laid her hand on his arm.

"Why, Signorina? Have you seen the Padrona?"

"No. But—but—I've heard— What is it? What has happened? Where has Madre been all this time? Has she been in Naples?"

"Signorina, I don't think so."

"Where has she been?"

"I believe the Signora has been to Mergellina."

Vere began to tremble.

"What can have happened there? What can have happened?"

She trembled in every limb. Her face had become white.

"Signorina, Signorina! Are you ill?"

"No—I don't know what to do—what I ought to do. I'm afraid to speak to the servants—they are making the siesta. Gaspare, come with me, and tell me what we ought to do. But—never say to any one—never say —if you hear!"

"Signorina!"

He had caught her terror. His huge eyes looked awe-struck.

"Come with me, Gaspare!"

Making an obvious and great effort, she controlled her body, turned and went before him to the house. She walked softly, and he imitated her. They almost crept up-stairs till they reached the landing outside Hermione's bedroom door. There they stood for two or three minutes, listening.

"Come away, Gaspare!"

Vere had whispered with lips that scarcely moved.

When they were in Hermione's sitting-room she caught hold of both his hands. She was a mere child now, a child craving for help.

"Oh—Gaspare, what are we to do? Oh—I'm—I'm frightened! I can't bear it!"

The door of the room was open.

"Shut it!" she said. "Shut it, then we sha'n't—"

He shut it.

"What can it be? What can it be?"

She looked at him, followed his eyes. He had stared towards the writing-table, then at the floor near it. On the table lay a quantity of fragments of broken glass, and a silver photograph-frame bent, almost broken. On the floor was scattered a litter of card-board.

"She came in here! Madre was in here—"

She bent down to the carpet, picked up some of the bits of card-board, turned them over, looked at them. Then she began to tremble again.

"It's father's photograph!"

She was now utterly terrified.

"Oh, Gaspare! Oh, Gaspare!"

She began to sob.

"Hush, Signorina! Hush!"

He spoke almost sternly, bent down, collected the fragments of card-board from the floor, and put them into his pocket.

"Father's photograph! She was in here—she came in here to do that! And she loves that photograph. She loves it!"

"Hush, Signorina! Don't, Signorina—don't!"

"We must do something! We must—"

He made her sit down. He stood by her.

"What shall we do, Gaspare? What shall we do?"

She looked up at him, demanding counsel. She put out her hands again and touched his arm. His Padroncina—she at least still loved, still trusted him.

"Signorina," he said, "we can't do anything."

His voice was fatalistic.

"But—what is it? Is—is—"

A frightful question was trembling on her lips. She looked again at the fragments of card-board in her hand, at the broken frame on the table.

"Can Madre be—"

She stopped. Her terror was increasing. She remembered many small mysteries in the recent conduct of her mother, many moments when she had been surprised, or made vaguely uneasy, by words or acts of her mother. Monsieur Emile, too, he had wondered, and more than once. She knew that. And Gaspare—she was sure that he, also, had seen that change which now, abruptly, had thus terribly culminated. Once in the boat she had asked him what was the matter with her mother, and he had, almost angrily, denied that anything was the matter. But she had seen in his eyes that he was acting a part—that he wished to detach her observation from her mother.

Her trembling ceased. Her little fingers closed more tightly on his arm. Her eyes became imperious.

"Gaspare, you are to tell me. I can bear it. You know something about Madre."

"Signorina—"

"Do you think I'm a coward? I was frightened—I am frightened, but I'm not really a coward, Gaspare. I can bear it. What is it you know?"

"Signorina, we can't do anything."

"Is it— Does Monsieur Emile know what it is?"

He did not answer.

Suddenly she got up, went to the door, opened it, and listened. The horror came into her face again.

"I can't bear it," she said. "I—I shall have to go into the room."

"No, Signorina. You are not to go in."

"If the door isn't locked I must—"

"It is locked."

"You don't know. You can't know."

"I know it is locked, Signorina."

Vere put her hands to her eyes.

"It's too dreadful! I didn't know any one—I have never heard—"

Gaspare went to her and shut the door resolutely.

"You are not to listen, Signorina. You are not to listen."

He spoke no longer like a servant, but like a master.

Vere's hands had dropped.

"I am going to send for Monsieur Emile," she said.

"Va bene, Signorina."

She went quickly to the writing-table, sat down, hesitated. Her eyes were riveted upon the photograph-frame.

"How could she? How could she?" she said, in a choked voice.

Gaspare took the frame away reverently, and put it against his breast, inside his shirt.

"I can't go to Don Emilio, Signorina. I cannot leave you."

"No, Gaspare. Don't leave me! Don't leave me!"

She was the terrified child again.

"Perhaps we can find a fisherman, Signorina."

"Yes, but don't— Wait for me, Gaspare!"

"I am not going, Signorina."

With feverish haste she took a pen and a sheet of paper and wrote:

"DEAR MONSIEUR EMILE,—Please come to the island *at once*. Something terrible has happened. I don't know what it is. But Madre is— No, I can't put it. Oh, *do come*—please— please come! VERE.

"Come the *quickest* way."

When the paper was shut in an envelope and addressed she got up. Gaspare held out his hand.

"I will go and look for a fisherman, Signorina."

"But I must come with you. I must keep with you."

She held on to his arm.

"I'm not a coward. But I can't—I can't—"

"Sì, Signorina! Sì, Signorina!"

He took her hand and held it. They went to the door. When he put out his other hand to open it Vere shivered.

"If we can't do anything, let us go down quickly, Gaspare!"

"Sì, Signorina. We will go quickly."

He opened the door and they went out.

In the Pool of the Saint there was no boat. They went to the crest of the island and looked out over the sea. Not far off, between the island and Nisida, there was a boat. Gaspare put his hands to his mouth and hailed her with all his might. The two men in her heard, and came towards the shore.

A few minutes later, with money in their pockets, and set but cheerful faces, they were rowing with all their strength in the direction of Naples.

That afternoon Artois, wishing to distract his thoughts and quite unable to work, went up the hill to the Monastery of San Martino. He returned to the hotel towards sunset feeling weary and depressed, companionless, too, in this gay summer world. Although he had never been deeply attached to the Marchesino he had liked him, been amused by him, grown accustomed to him. He missed the "Toledo incarnate." And as he walked along the Marina he felt for a moment almost inclined to go away from Naples. But the people of the island! Could he leave them just now? Could he leave Hermione so near to the hands of Fate, those hands which were surely stretched out towards her, which might grasp her at any moment, even to-night, and alter her life forever? No, he knew he could not.

"There is a note for Monsieur!"

He took it from the hall porter.

A SPIRIT IN PRISON

"No, I'll walk up-stairs."

He had seen that the lift was not below, and did not wish to wait for its descent. Vere's writing was on the envelope he held; but Vere's writing distorted, frantic, tragic. He knew before he opened the envelope that it must contain some dreadful statement or some wild appeal; and he hurried to his room, almost feeling the pain and fear of the writer burn through the paper to his hand.

"DEAR MONSIEUR EMILE,—Please come to the island *at once*. Something terrible has happened. I don't know what it is. But Madre is— No, I can't put it. Oh, *do come*—please—please come! VERE.

"Come the *quickest* way."

"Something terrible has happened." He knew at once what it was. The walls of the cell in which he had enclosed his friend had crumbled away. The spirit which for so long had rested upon a lie had been torn from its repose, had been scourged to its feet to face the fierce light of truth. How would it face the truth?

"But Madre is— No, I can't put it."

That phrase struck a chill almost of horror to his soul. He stared at it for a moment trying to imagine—things. Then he tore the note up.

The quickest way to the island!

"I shall not be in to dinner to-night."

He was speaking to the waiter at the door of the Egyptian Room. A minute later he was in the Via Chiatamone at the back of the hotel waiting for the tram. He must go by Posilipo to the Trattoria del Giardinetto, walk down to the village below, and take a boat from there to the island. That was the quickest way. The tram-bell sounded. Was he glad? As he watched the tram gliding towards him he was conscious of an almost terrible reluctance—a reluctance surely of fear—to go that night to the island.

574

A SPIRIT IN PRISON

But he must go.

The sun was setting when he got down before the Trattoria del Giardinetto. Three soldiers were sitting at a table outside on the dusty road, clinking their glasses of marsala together, and singing, "Piange Rosina! La Mamma ci domanda." Their brown faces looked vivid with the careless happiness of youth. As Artois went down from the road into the tunnel their lusty voices died away:

> "Io ti voglio dare
> Un soldato Bersagliere,
> Io ti voglio dare
> Un soldato Bersagliere.
>
> Soldato Bersagliere
> Io non lo voglio—no!
> Io non lo voglio—no!"

Because his instinct was to walk slowly, to linger on the way, he walked very fast. The slanting light fell gently, delicately, over the opulent vineyards, where peasants were working in huge straw hats, over the still shining but now reposeful sea. In the sky there was a mystery of color, very pure, very fragile, like the mystery of color in a curving shell of the sea. The pomp and magnificence of sunset were in abeyance to-night, were laid aside. And the sun, like some spirit modestly radiant, slipped from this world of vineyards and of waters almost surreptitiously, yet shedding exquisite influences in his going.

And in the vineyards, as upon the dusty highroad, the people of the South were singing.

The sound of their warm voices, rising in the golden air towards the tender beauty of the virginal evening sky, moved Artois to a sudden longing for a universal brotherhood of happiness, for happy men on a happy earth, men knowing the truth and safe in their knowl-

575

edge. And he longed, too, just then to give happiness. A strongly generous emotion stirred him, and went from him, like one of the slanting rays of light from the sun, towards the island, towards his friend, Hermione. His reluctance, his sense of fear, were lessened, nearly died away. His quickness of movement was no longer a fight against, but a fulfilment of desire.

Once she had helped him. Once she had even, perhaps, saved him from death. She had put aside her own happiness. She had shown the divine self-sacrifice of woman.

And now, after long years, life brought to him an hour which would prove him, prove him and show how far he was worthy of the friendship which had been shed, generously as the sunshine over these vineyards of the South, upon him and his life.

He came down to the sea and met the fisherman, Giovanni, upon the sand.

"Row me quickly to the island, Giovanni!" he said.

"Sì, Signore."

He ran to get the boat.

The light began to fail over the sea. They cleared the tiny harbor and set out on their voyage.

"The Signora has been here to-day, Signore," said Giovanni.

"Sì? When did she come?"

"This morning, with Gaspare, to take the tram to Mergellina."

"She went to Mergellina?"

"Sì, Signore. And she was gone a very long time. Gaspare was back for her at half-past eleven, and she did not come till nearly three. Gaspare was in a state, I can tell you. I have known him—for years I have known him—and never have I seen him as he was to-day."

"And the Signora? When she came, did she look tired?"

576

A SPIRIT IN PRISON

"Signore, the Signora's face was like the face of one who has been looked on by the evil eye."

"Row quickly, Giovanni!"

"Sì, Signore."

The man talked no more.

When they came in sight of the island the last rays of the sun were striking upon the windows of the Casa del Mare.

The boat, urged by Giovanni's powerful arms, drew rapidly near to the land, and Artois, leaning forward with an instinct to help the rower, fixed his eyes upon these windows which, like swift jewels, focussed and gave back the light. While he watched them the sun sank. Its radiance was withdrawn. He saw no longer jewels, casements of magic, but only the windows of the familiar house; and then, presently, only the window of one room, Hermione's. His eyes were fixed on that as the boat drew nearer and nearer—were almost hypnotized by that. Where was Hermione? What was she doing? How was she? how would she be, now that—she knew? A terrible but immensely tender, immensely pitiful, curiosity took possession of him, held him fast, body and soul. She knew, and she was in that house!

The boat was close in now, but had not yet turned into the Pool of San Francesco. Artois kept his eyes upon the window for still a moment longer. He felt now, he knew, that Hermione was in the room beyond that window. As he gazed up from the sea he saw that the window was open. He saw behind the frame of it a white curtain stirring in the breeze. And then he saw something that chilled his blood, that seemed to drive it in an icy stream back to his heart, leaving his body for a moment numb.

He saw a figure come, with a wild, falling movement, to the window—a white, distorted face utterly strange to him looked out—a hand lifted in a frantic gesture.

577

The gesture was followed by a crash.

The green Venetian blind had fallen, hiding the window, hiding the stranger's face.

"Who was that at the window, Signore?" asked Giovanni, staring at Artois with round and startled eyes.

And Artois answered: "It is difficult to see, Giovanni, now that the sun has gone down. It is getting dark so quickly."

"Sì, Signore, it is getting dark."

CHAPTER XXXIX

THERE was no one at the foot of the cliff. Artois got out of the boat and stood for a moment, hesitating whether to keep Giovanni or to dismiss him.

"I can stay, Signore," said the man. "You will want some one to row you back."

"No, Giovanni. I can get Gaspare to put me ashore. You had better be off."

"Va bene, Signore," he replied, looking disappointed.

The Signora of the Casa del Mare was always very hospitable to such fishermen as she knew. Giovanni wanted to seek out Gaspare, to have a cigarette. But he obediently jumped into the boat and rowed off into the darkness, while Artois went up the steps towards the house.

A cold feeling of dread encompassed him. He still saw, imaginatively, that stranger at the window, that falling movement, that frantic gesture, the descending blind that brought to Hermione's bedroom a greater obscurity. And he remembered Hermione's face in the garden, half seen by him once in shadows, with surely a strange and terrible smile upon it—a smile that had made him wonder if he had ever really known her.

He came out on the plateau before the front door. The door was shut, but as he went to open it it was opened from within, and Gaspare stood before him in the twilight, with the dark passage for background.

Gaspare looked at Artois in silence.

"Gaspare," Artois said, "I came home from San

579

Martino. I found a note from the Signorina, begging me to come here at once."

"Lo so, Signore."

"I have come. What has—what is it? Where is the Signorina?"

Gaspare stood in the middle of the narrow doorway.

"The Signorina is in the garden."

"Waiting for me?"

"Sì, Signore."

"Very well."

He moved to enter the house; but Gaspare stood still where he was.

"Signore," he said.

Artois stopped at the door-sill.

"What is it?"

"What are you going to do here?"

At last Gaspare was frankly the watch-dog guarding the sacred house. His Padrona had cast upon him a look of hatred. Yet he was guarding the sacred house and her within it. Deep in the blood of him was the sense that, even hating him, she belonged to him and he to her.

And his Padroncina had trusted him, had clung to him that day.

"What are you going to do here?"

"If there is trouble here, I want to help."

"How can you help, Signore?"

"First tell me—there is great trouble?"

"Sì, Signore."

"And you know what it is? You know what caused it?"

"No one has told me."

"But you know what it is?"

"Sì, Signore."

"Does—the Signorina doesn't know?"

"No, Signore."

He paused, then added:

"The Signorina is not to know what it is."

"You do not think I shall tell her?"

"Signore, how can I tell what you will do here? How can I tell what you are here?"

For a moment Artois felt deeply wounded—wounded to the quick. He had not supposed it was possible for any one to hurt him so much with a few quiet words. Anger rose in him, an anger such as the furious attack of the Marchesino had never brought to the birth.

"You can say that!" he exclaimed. "You can say that, after Sicily!"

Gaspare's face changed, softened for an instant, then grew stern again.

"That was long ago, Signore. It was all different in Sicily!"

His eyes filled with tears, yet his face remained stern. But Artois was seized again, as when he walked in the golden air between the vineyards and heard the peasants singing, by an intense desire to bring happiness to the unhappy, especially and above all to one unhappy woman. To-night his intellect was subordinate to his heart, his pride of intellect was lost in feeling, in an emotion that the simplest might have understood and shared: the longing to be of use, to comfort, to pour balm into the terrible wound of one who had been his friend—such a friend as only a certain type of woman can be to a certain type of man.

"Gaspare," he said, "you and I—we helped the Signora once, we helped her in Sicily."

Gaspare looked away from him, and did not answer.

"Perhaps we can help her now. Perhaps only we can help her. Let me into the house, Gaspare. I shall do nothing here to make your Padrona sad."

Gaspare looked at him again, looked into his eyes, then

moved aside, giving room for him to enter. As soon as he was in the passage Gaspare shut the door.

"I am sorry, Signore; the lamp is not lighted."

Artois felt at once an unusual atmosphere in the house, an atmosphere not of confusion but of mystery, of secret curiosity, of brooding apprehension. At the foot of the servants' staircase he heard a remote sound of whispering, which emphasized the otherwise complete silence of this familiar dwelling, suddenly become unfamiliar to him—unfamiliar and almost dreadful.

"I had better go into the garden."

"Sì, Signore."

Gaspare looked down the servants' staircase and hissed sharply:

"Sh! S-s-sh!"

"The Signora—?" asked Artois, as Gaspare came to him softly.

"The Signora is always in her room. She is shut up in her room."

"I saw the Signora just now, at the window," Artois said, in an undervoice.

"You saw the Signora?"

Gaspare looked at him with sudden eagerness mingled with a flaming anxiety.

"From the boat. She came to the window and let down the blind."

Gaspare did not ask anything. They went on to the terrace above the sea.

"I will tell the Signorina you have come, Signore."

"Sha'n't I go down?"

"I had better go and tell her."

He spoke with conviction. Artois did not dispute his judgment. He went away, always softly. Artois stood still on the terrace. The twilight was spreading itself over the sea, like a veil dropping over a face. The house was dark behind him. In that darkness Hermione was hidden, the Hermione who was a stranger to him, the Hermione into whose heart and soul he was no longer allowed to look. Upon Monte Amato at evening she had, very simply, showed to him the truth of her great sorrow.

Now—he saw the face at the window, the falling blind. Between then and now—what a gulf fixed!

Vere came from the garden followed by Gaspare. Her eyes were wide with terror. The eyelids were red. She had been weeping. She almost ran to Artois, as a child runs to refuge. Never before had he felt so acutely the childishness that still lingered in this little Vere of the island—lingered unaffected, untouched by recent events. Thank God for that! In that moment the Marchesino was forgiven; and Artois—did he not perhaps also in that moment forgive himself?

"Oh, Monsieur Emile—I thought you wouldn't come!"

There was the open reproach of a child in her voice. She seized his hand.

"Has Gaspare told you?" She turned her head towards Gaspare. "Something terrible has happened to Madre. Monsieur Emile, do you know what it is?"

She was looking at him with an intense scrutiny.

"Gaspare is hiding something from me—"

Gaspare stood there and said nothing.

"—something that perhaps you know."

Gaspare looked at Artois, and Artois felt now that the watch-dog trusted him. He returned the Sicilian's glance, and Gaspare moved away, went to the rail of the terrace, and looked down over the sea.

"Do you know? Do you know anything—anything dreadful about Madre that you have never told me?"

"Vere, don't be frightened."

"Ah, but you haven't been here! You weren't here when—"

"What is it?"

Her terror infected him.

"Madre came back. She had been to Mergellina all alone. She was away such a long time. When she came back I was in my room. I didn't know. I didn't hear the boat. But my door was open, and presently I heard some one come up-stairs and go into the boudoir. It was Madre. I know her step. I know it was Madre!"

She reiterated her assertion, as if she anticipated that he was going to dispute it.

"She stayed in the boudoir only a very little while— only a few minutes. Oh, Monsieur Emile, but—"

"Vere! What do you mean? Did—what happened there—in the boudoir?"

He was reading from her face.

"She went—Madre went in there to—"

She stopped and swallowed.

"Madre took father's photograph—the one on the writing-table—and tore it to pieces. And the frame— that was all bent and nearly broken. Father's photograph, that she loves so much!"

Artois said nothing. At that moment it was as if he entered suddenly into Hermione's heart, and knew every feeling there.

"Monsieur Emile—is she—is Madre—ill?"

She began to tremble once more, as she had trembled when she came to fetch Gaspare from the nook of the cliff beside the Saint's Pool.

"Not as you mean, Vere."

"You are sure? You are certain?"

"Not in that way?"

"But then I heard Madre come out and go to her bedroom. I didn't hear whether she locked the door. I only heard it shut. But Gaspare says he knows it is locked. Two or three minutes after the door was shut I heard—I heard—"

"Don't be afraid. Tell me—if I ought to know."

A SPIRIT IN PRISON

Those words voiced a deep and delicate reluctance which was beginning to invade him. Yet he wished to help Vere, to release this child from the thrall of a terror which could only be conquered if it were expressed.

"Tell me," he added, slowly.

"I heard Madre—Monsieur Emile, it was hardly crying!"

"Don't. You needn't tell me any more."

"Gaspare heard it too. It went on for a long, long time. We — Gaspare made the servants keep downstairs. And then—then it stopped. And we have heard nothing ever since. And I—I have been waiting for you to come, because Madre cares for you."

Artois put his hand down quickly upon Vere's right hand.

"I am glad you sent for me, Vere. I am glad you think that. Come and sit down on the bench."

He drew her down beside him. He felt that he was with a child whom he must comfort. Gaspare stood always looking down over the rail of the terrace to the sea.

"Vere!"

"Yes, Monsieur Emile."

"Your mother is not ill, as you thought — feared. But—to-day—she has had, she must have had, a great shock."

"But at Mergellina?"

"Only that could account for what you have just told me."

"But I don't understand. She only went to Mergellina."

"Did you see her before she went there?"

"Yes."

"Was she as usual?"

"I don't think she was. I think Madre has been changing nearly all this summer. That is why I am so afraid. You know she has been changing."

585

He was silent. The difficulty of the situation was great. He did not know how to resolve it.

"You have seen the change, Monsieur Emile!"

He did not deny it. He did not know what to do or say. For of that change, although perhaps now he partly understood it, he could never speak to Vere or to any one.

"It has made me so unhappy," Vere said, with a break in her voice.

And he had said to himself: "Vere must be happy!" At that moment he and his intellect seemed to him less than a handful of dust.

"But this change of to-day is different," he said, slowly. "Your mother has had a dreadful shock."

"At Mergellina?"

"It must have been there."

"But what could it be? We scarcely ever go there. We don't know any one there—oh, except Ruffo."

Her eyes, keen and bright with youth, even though they had been crying, were fixed upon his face while she was speaking, and she saw a sudden conscious look in his eyes, a movement of his lips—he drew them sharply together, as if seized by a spasm.

"Ruffo!" she repeated. "Has it something to do with Ruffo?"

There was a profound perplexity in her face, but the fear in it was less.

"Something to do with Ruffo?" she repeated.

Suddenly she moved, she got up. And all the fear had come back to her face, with something added to it, something intensely personal.

"Do you mean—is Ruffo dead?" she whispered.

A voice rose up from the sea singing a sad little song. Vere turned towards the sea. All her body relaxed. The voice passed on. The sad little song passed under the cliff, to the Saint's Pool and the lee of the island.

"Ah, Monsieur Emile," she said, "why don't you tell me?"

She swayed. He put his arm quickly behind her.

"No, no! It's all right. That was Ruffo!"

And she smiled.

At that moment Artois longed to tell her the truth. To do so would surely be to do something that was beautiful. But he dared not—he had no right.

A bell rang in the house, loudly, persistently, tearing its silence. Gaspare turned angrily from the rail, with an expression of apprehension on his face.

Giulia was summoning the household to dinner.

"Perhaps—perhaps Madre will come down," Vere whispered.

Gaspare passed them and went into the house quickly. They knew he had gone to see if his Padrona was coming. Moved by a mutual instinct, they stayed where they were till he should come to them again.

For a long time they waited. He did not return.

"We had better go in, Vere. You must eat."

"I can't—unless she comes."

"You must try to eat."

He spoke to her as to a child.

"And perhaps—Gaspare may be with her, may be speaking with her. Let us go in."

They passed into the house, and went to the dining-room. The table was laid. The lamp was lit. Giulia stood by the sideboard looking anxious and subdued. She did not even smile when she saw Artois, who was her favorite.

"Where is Gaspare, Giulia?" said Artois.

"Up-stairs, Signore. He came in and ran up-stairs, and he has not come down. Ah!"—she raised her hands—"the evil eye has looked upon this house! When that girl Peppina—"

"Be quiet!" Artois said, sharply.

A SPIRIT IN PRISON

Giulia's round, black eyes filled with tears, and her mouth opened in surprise.

He put his hand kindly on her arm.

"Never mind, Giulia mia! But it is foolish to talk like that. There is no reason why evil should come upon the Casa del Mare. Here is Gaspare!"

At this moment he entered, looking tragic.

"Go away, Giulia!" he said to her, roughly.

"Ma—"

"Go away!"

He put her out of the room without ceremony, and shut the door.

"Signore!" he said to Artois, "I have been up to the Padrona's room. I have knocked on the door. I have spoken—"

"What did you say?"

"I did not say that you were here, Signore."

"Did you ask the Signora to come down?"

"I asked if she was coming down to dinner. I said the Signorina was waiting for her."

"Yes?"

"The Signora did not answer. There was no noise, and in the room there is no light!"

"Let me go!" Vere said, breathlessly.

She was moving towards the door when Artois stopped her authoritatively.

"No, Vere—wait!"

"But some one must—I'm afraid—"

"Wait, Vere!"

He turned once more to Gaspare.

"Did you try the door, Gaspare?"

"Signore, I did. After I had spoken several times and waited a long time, I tried the door softly. It is locked."

"You see!"

It was Vere speaking, still breathlessly.

A SPIRIT IN PRISON

"Let me go, Monsieur Emile. We can't let Madre stay like that, all alone in the dark. She must have food. We can't stay down here and leave her."

Artois hesitated. He thought of the stranger at the window, and he felt afraid. But he concealed his fear.

"Perhaps you had better go, Vere," he said, at length. "But if she does not answer, don't try the door. Don't knock. Just speak. You will find the best words."

"Yes. I'll try—I'll try."

Gaspare opened the door. Giulia was sobbing outside. Her pride and dignity were lacerated by Gaspare's action.

"Giulia, never mind! Don't cry! Gaspare didn't mean—"

Before she had finished speaking the servant passionately seized her hand and kissed it. Vere released her hand very gently and went slowly up the stairs.

The instinct of Artois was to follow her. He longed to follow her, but he denied himself, and sat down by the dinner-table, on which the zuppa di pesce was smoking under the lamp. Giulia, trying to stifle her sobs, went away down the kitchen stairs, and Gaspare stood near the door. He touched his face with his hands, opened and shut his lips, then thrust his hands into his pockets, and stared first at Artois then at the floor. His cheeks and his forehead looked hot, as if he had just finished some difficult physical act. Artois did not glance at him. In that moment both men, in their different ways, felt dreadfully, almost unbearably, self-conscious.

Presently Vere's step was heard again on the stairs, descending softly and slowly. She came in and went at once to Artois.

"Madre doesn't answer."

Artois got up.

"What ought we to do?"

A SPIRIT IN PRISON

Vere was whispering.

"Did you hear anything?"

"No."

Gaspare moved, took his hands violently out of his pockets, then thrust them in again.

Artois stood in silence. His face, generally so strong, so authoritative, showed his irresolution, and Vere, looking to him like a frightened child for guidance, felt her terror increase.

"Shall I go up again? I didn't knock. You told me not to. Shall I go and knock? Or shall Gaspare go again?"

She did not suggest that Artois should go himself. He noticed that, even in this moment of the confusion of his will.

"I think we had better leave her for a time," he said, at last.

As he spoke he made an effort, and recovered himself.

"We had better do nothing more. What can we do?"

He was looking at Gaspare.

Gaspare went out into the passage and called down the stairs.

"Giulia! Come up! The Signorina is going to dinner."

His defiant voice sounded startling in the silent house.

"We are to eat!"

"Yes, Vere. I shall stay. Presently your mother may come down. She feels that she must be alone. We have no right to try to force ourselves upon her."

"Do you think it is that? Are you telling me the truth? Are you?"

"If she does not come down presently I will go up. Don't be afraid. I will not leave you till she comes down."

Giulia returned, wiping her eyes. When he saw her Gaspare disappeared. They knew he had gone to wait outside his Padrona's door.

A SPIRIT IN PRISON

The dinner passed almost in silence. Artois ate, and made Vere eat. Vere sat in her mother's place, with her back to the door. Artois was facing her. Often his eyes travelled to the door. Often, too, Vere turned her head. And in the silence both were listening for a step that did not come: Vere with a feverish eagerness, Artois with a mingling of longing and of dread. For he knew he dreaded to see Hermione that night. He knew that it would be terrible to him to meet her eyes, to speak to her, to touch her hand. And yet he longed for her to come. For he was companioned by a great and growing fear, which he must hide. And that act of secrecy, undertaken for Vere's sake, seemed to increase the thing he hid, till the shadow it had been began to take form, to grow in stature, to become dominating, imperious.

Giulia put some fruit on the table. The meal was over, and there had been no sound outside upon the stairs.

"Monsieur Emile, what are you going to do?"

"Go to the drawing-room, Vere. I will go out and see whether there is any light in your mother's window."

She obeyed him silently and went away. Then he took his hat and went out upon the terrace.

Gaspare had said that Hermione's room was dark. Perhaps he had been mistaken. The key might have been so placed in the lock that he had been deceived. As Artois walked to a point from which he could see one of the windows of Hermione's bedroom, he knew that he longed to see a light there. If the window was dark the form of his fear would be more distinct. He reached the point and looked up. There was no light.

He stood there for some time gazing at that darkness. He thought of the bent photograph-frame, of the photograph that had been so loved torn into fragments, of the sound that was—hardly crying, and of the face he had seen for an instant as he drew near to the island. He ought to come to some decision, to take some action. Vere was depending upon him. But he felt as if he could do nothing. In answer to Vere's appeal he had hastened to the island. And now he was paralyzed, he was utterly useless.

He felt as if he dared not do anything. Hermione, in her grief, had suddenly passed from him into a darkness that was sacred. What right had he to try to share it?

And yet—if that great shape of fear were not the body of a lie, but of the truth?

Never before had he felt so impotent, so utterly unworthy of his manhood.

He moved away, turned, came back and stood once more beneath the window. Ought he to go up to Hermione's door, to knock, to speak, to insist on admittance? And if there was no reply?—what ought he to do then? Break down the door?

He went into the house. Vere was sitting in the drawing-room looking at the door. She sprang up.

"Is there a light in Madre's room?"

"No."

He saw, as he answered, that she caught his fear, that hers now had the same shape as his.

"Monsieur Emile, you—you don't think—?"

Her voice faltered, her bright eyes became changed, dim, seemed to sink into her head.

"You must go to her room. Go to Madre, Monsieur Emile. Go! speak to her! Make her answer! Make her! make her!"

She put her hands on him. She pushed him frantically.

He took her hands and held them tightly.

"I am going, Vere. Don't be frightened!"

"But you are frightened! You are frightened!"

"I will speak to your mother. I will beg her to answer."

"And if she doesn't answer?"

"I will get into the room."

He let go her hands and went towards the door. Just as he reached it there came from below in the house a loud, shrill cry. It was followed by an instant of silence, then by another cry, louder, nearer than before. And this time they could hear words:

"*La fattura della morte! La fattura della morte!*"

Running, stumbling feet sounded outside, and Peppina appeared at the door, her disfigured face convulsed with terror, her hand out-stretched.

"Look!" she cried, shrilly. "Look, Signorina! Look, Signore! *La fattura della morte! La fattura della morte!* It has been brought to the house to-night! It has been put in my room to-night!"

In her hand lay a green lemon pierced by many nails.

CHAPTER XL

"Monsieur Emile, what is it?" exclaimed Vere.

The frightened servants were gone, half coaxed and half scolded into silence by Artois. He had taken the lemon from Peppina, and it lay now in his hand.

"It is what the people of Naples call a death-charm."

"A death-charm?"

In her eyes superstition dawned.

"Why do they call it that?"

"Because it is supposed to bring death to any one—any enemy—near whom it is placed."

"Who can have put it in the house to-night?" Vere said. Her voice was low and trembling. "Who can have wished to bring death here to-night?"

"I don't know, Vere."

"And such a thing—could it bring death?"

"Vere! You can ask me!"

He spoke with an attempt at smiling irony, but his eyes held something of the awe, the cloudy apprehension that had gathered in hers.

"Where is your mind?" he added.

She answered: "Are you going to Madre's room, Monsieur Emile?"

He put the death-charm down quickly, as if it had burned his hand.

"I am going now. Gaspare!"

At this moment Gaspare came into the room with a face that was almost livid.

"Who is it that has brought a *fattura della morte* here?" he exclaimed.

A SPIRIT IN PRISON

His usually courageous eyes were full of superstitious fear.

"Signore, do you—"

He stopped. He had seen the death-charm lying on the little table covered with silver trifles. He approached it, made a sign of the cross, bent down his head and examined it closely, but did not touch it.

Artois and Vere watched him closely. He lifted up his head at last.

"I know who brought the *fattura della morte* here," he said, solemnly. "I know."

"Who?" said Vere.

"It was Ruffo."

"Ruffo!"

Vere reddened. "Ruffo! He loves our house, and he loves us!"

"It is Ruffo, Signorina. It is Ruffo. He brought it, and it is he that must take it away. Do not touch it, Signorina. Do not touch it, Signore. Leave it where it is till Ruffo comes, till Ruffo takes it away."

He again made the sign of the cross, and drew back from the death-charm with a sort of mysterious caution.

"Signore," he said to Artois, "I will go down to the Saint's Pool. I will find Ruffo. I will bring him here. I will make him come here."

He was going out when Artois put a hand on his shoulder.

"And the Padrona?"

"Signore, she is always there, in her room, in the dark."

"And you have heard nothing?"

"Signore, I have heard the Padrona moving."

The hand of Artois dropped down. He was invaded by a sense of relief that was almost overwhelming.

"You are certain?"

"Sì, Signore. The Padrona is walking up and down

595

the room. When Peppina screamed out I heard the Padrona move. And then I heard her walking up and down the room."

He looked again at the death-charm and went out. Vere stood for a moment. Then she, too, went suddenly away, and Artois heard her light footstep retreating from him towards the terrace.

He understood her silent and abrupt departure. His fear had been hers. His relief was hers, too, and she was moved to hide it. He was left alone with the death-charm.

He sat down by the table on which it lay among the bright toys of silver. Released from his great fear, released from his undertaking to force his way into the darkness of that room which had been silent, he seemed suddenly to regain his identity, to be put once more into possession of his normal character. He had gone out from it. He returned to it. The cloud of superstition, in which even he had been for a moment involved with Vere and with the servants, evaporated, and he was able to smile secretly at them and at himself. Yet while he smiled thus secretly, and while he looked at the lemon with its perforating nails, he realized his own smallness, helplessness, the smallness and the helplessness of every man, as he had never realized them before. And he realized also something, much, of what it would have meant to him, had the body of his fear been the body of a truth, not of a lie.

If death had really come into the Casa del Mare that night with the death-charm!

He stretched out his hand to the table, lifted the death-charm from among the silver ornaments, held it, kept it in his hand, which he laid upon his knee.

If Ruffo had carried death in his boy's hand over the sea to the island, had carried death to Hermione!

Artois tried to imagine that house without Hermione, his life without Hermione.

A SPIRIT IN PRISON

For a long time he sat, always holding the death-charm in his hand, always with his eyes fixed upon it, until at last in it, as in a magic mirror, among the scars of its burning, and among the nails that pierced it, as the woman who had fashioned it, and fired it, and muttered witch's words over it, longed to pierce the heart of her enemy, he saw scenes of the past, and shadowy, moving figures. He saw among the scars and among the nails Hermione and himself!

They were in Paris, at a table strewn with flowers. That was the first scene in the magic mirror of the *fattura della morte*, the scene in which they met for the first time. Hermione regarded him almost with timidity. And he looked at her doubtfully, because she had no beauty.

Then they were in another part of Paris, in his "Morocco slipper of a room," crammed with books, and dim with Oriental incense and tobacco smoke, his room red and yellow, tinted with the brilliant colors of the East. And he turned to her for sympathy, and he received it in full measure, pressed down and running over. He told her his thought, and he told her his feelings, his schemes, his struggles, his moments of exaltation, his depressions. Something, much indeed of him was hers, the egotistic part of a man that does really give, but that keeps back much, and that seeks much more than it gives. And what he sought she eagerly, generously gave, with both hands, never counting any cost. Always she was giving and always he was taking.

Then they were in London, in another room full of books. He stood by a fire, and she was seated with a bundle of letters in her lap. And his heart was full of something that was like anger, and of a dull and smouldering jealousy. And hers was full of a new and wonderful beauty, a piercing joy.

597

A SPIRIT IN PRISON

He sighed deeply. He stirred. He looked up for a moment and listened.

But all the house was silent. And again he bent over the death-charm.

He stood by a door. Outside was the hum of traffic, inside a narrow room. And now in the magic mirror a third figure showed itself, a figure of youth incarnate, brave, passionate, thrilling with the joy of life. He watched it, how coldly, although he felt its charm, the rays of fire that came from it, as sunbeams come from the sun! And apprehension stirred within him. And presently in the night, by ebony waters, and by strange and wandering lights, and under unquiet stars, he told Hermione something of his fear.

Africa—and the hovering flies, and the dreadful feeling that death's hands were creeping about his body and trying to lay hold of it! A very lonely creature lay there in the mirror, with the faint shadow of a palm-leaf shifting and swaying upon the ghastly whiteness of its face—himself, in the most desolate hour of his life. As he gazed he was transported to the City of the Mosques. The years rolled back. He felt again all, or nearly all, that he had felt then of helplessness, abandonment, despair. It was frightful to go out thus alone, to be extinguished in the burning heat of Africa, and laid in that arid soil, where the vipers slid through the hot crevices of the earth, and the scorpions bred in the long days of the summer. Now it was evening. He heard the call to prayer, that wailing, wonderful cry which saluted the sinking sun.

He remembered exactly how it had come into his ears through the half-opened window, the sensation of remoteness, of utter solitude, which it had conveyed to him. An Arab had passed under the window, singing in a withdrawn and drowsy voice a plaintive song of the East which had mingled with the call to prayer. And then he, Artois, being quite alone, had given way in his great pain and weakness. He remembered feeling the tears slipping over his cheeks, one following another, quickly, quickly. It had seemed as if they would never stop, as if there would always be tears to flow from those sources deep within his stricken body, his stricken soul.

He looked into the mirror. The door of the room was opened. A woman stood upon the threshold. The sick man turned upon his pillow. He gazed towards the woman. And his tears ceased. He was no longer alone. His friend had come from her garden of Paradise to draw him back to life.

In the magic mirror of the *fattura della morte* other scenes formed themselves, were clearly visible for a moment, then dispersed, dissolved—till scenes of the island came, till the last scene in the mirror dawned faintly before his eyes.

He saw a dark room, and a woman more desolate than he had been when he lay alone with the shadow of the palm-tree shifting on his face, and heard the call to prayer. He saw Hermione in her room in the Casa del Mare that night, after she knew.

Suddenly he put his hand to his eyes.

Those were the first tears his eyes had known since that evening in Africa years and years ago.

He laid the death-charm down once more among the silver toys. But he still looked at it as he sat back now in his chair, waiting for Gaspare's return.

He gazed at the symbol of death. And he began to think how strangely appropriate was its presence that night in the Casa del Mare, how almost more than strange had been its bringing there by Ruffo—if indeed Ruffo had brought it, as Gaspare declared. For the little green lemon represented a heart pierced. And Ruffo, all ignorantly and unconsciously, had pierced the heart of Hermione.

A SPIRIT IN PRISON

Artois knew nothing of what had happened that day at Mergellina, but he divined that it was Ruffo who, without words, had told Hermione the truth. It must have been Ruffo, in whom the dead man lived again. And, going beyond the innocent boy, deep into the shadows where lies so much of truth, Artois saw the murdered man stirring from his sleep, unable to rest because of the lie that had been coiled around his memory, making it what it should not be. Perhaps only the dead know the true, the sacred passion for justice. Perhaps only they are indifferent to everything save truth, they who know the greatest truth of all.

And Artois saw Maurice Delarey, the gay, the full-blooded youth, grown stern in the halls of death, unable to be at peace until she who had most loved him knew him at last as he had been in life.

As no one else would tell Hermione the truth, the dead man himself, speaking through his son, the fruit of his sin, had told her the truth that day. He, too, had been perhaps a spirit in prison, through all these years since his death.

Artois saw him in freedom.

And at that moment Artois felt that in the world there was only one thing that was perfectly beautiful, and that thing was absolute truth. Its knowledge must make Hermione greater.

But now she was hanging on her cross.

If he could only comfort her!

As she had come to him in Africa, he longed now to go to her. She had saved him from the death of the body. If only he could save her from another and more terrible death—the death of the spirit that believes and trusts in life!

He had been absorbed in thought and unconscious of time. Now he looked up, he was aware of things. He listened. Surely Gaspare had been away a long while. And Vere—where was she?

He had a strange desire to see Ruffo now. Something new and mystic had been born, or had for the first time made itself apparent, within him to-night. And he knew that to-night he would look at Ruffo as he had never looked at him before.

He got up and, leaving the death-charm lying on the table, went to the door. There he hesitated. Should he go to the terrace, to Vere? or should he go up-stairs to that dark room and try to speak to his friend? Or should he go out to the cliff, to seek Gaspare and Ruffo?

Ruffo drew him. He had to go to the cliff.

He went out by the front door. At first he thought of descending at once by the steps to the Pool of San Francesco. But he changed his mind and went instead to the bridge.

He looked over into the Pool.

It was a very clear night. San Francesco's light was burning brightly. Very sincerely it was burning beneath the blessing hands of the Saint. A ray of gold that came from it lay upon the darkness of the Pool, stealing through the night a little way, as if in an effort to touch the Casa del Mare.

In the Pool there was one boat. Artois saw no one by the sea's edge, heard no voices there, and he turned towards the crest of the island, to the seat where Vere so often went at night, and where Hermione, too, had often sought out Ruffo.

Gaspare and Ruffo were near it. Almost directly he saw their forms, relieved against the dimness but not deep darkness of the night, and heard their voices talking. As he went towards them Gaspare was speaking vehemently. He threw up one arm in a strong, even, and excited gesture, and was silent. Then Artois heard Ruffo say, in a voice that, though respectful and almost deprecatory, was yet firm like a man's:

A SPIRIT IN PRISON

"I cannot take it away, Gaspare. When I go home my mamma will ask me if I have put it in the house."

"Dio mio!" cried Gaspare. "But you have put it in the house! Is it not there—is it not there now to bring death upon the Signora, upon the Signorina, upon us all?"

"It was made for Peppina. My mamma made it only against Peppina, because she has brought evil into our house. It will hurt only Peppina! It will kill only Peppina!"

He spoke now with a vehemence and passion almost equal to Gaspare's. Artois stood still. They did not see him. They were absorbed in their conversation.

"It will not hurt the Signora or the Signorina. The *fattura della morte* — it is to harm Peppina. Has she not done us injury? Has she not taken my Patrigno from my mamma? Has she not made him mad? Is it not for her that he has been in prison, and that he has left my mamma without a soldo in the house? The Signora—she has been good to me and my mamma. It is she who sent my mamma money—twenty lire! I respect the Signora as I respect my mamma. Only to-day, only this very day she came to Mergellina, she came to see my mamma. And when she knew that my Patrigno was let out of prison, when I cried out at the door that he was coming, the Signora was so glad for us that she looked—she looked—Madre di Dio! she was all white, she was shaking—she was worse than my poor mamma. And when I came to her, and when I called out, 'Signora! Signora!' you should have seen! She opened her eyes! She gave me such a look! And then my Patrigno came in at the door, and the Signora—she went away. I was going to follow her, but she put out her hand—so, to make me stay—she wanted me to stay with my mamma. And she went down the stairs all trembling because my Patrigno was let out of prison.

602

Per dio! She has a good heart. She is an angel. For the Signora I would die. For the Signora I would do anything! I—you say I would kill the Signora! Would I kill my mamma? Would I kill the Madonna? La Bruna—would I kill her? To me the Signora is as my mamma! I respect the Signora as I respect my mamma. Ecco!"

"The *fattura della morte* will bring evil on the house, it will bring death into the house."

Gaspare spoke again, and his voice was dogged with superstition, but it was less vehement than before.

"Already—who knows what it has brought? Who knows what evil it has done? All the house is sad to-night, all the house is terrible to-night."

"It is Peppina who has looked on the house with the evil eye," said Ruffo. "It is Peppina who has brought trouble to the house."

There was a silence. Then Gaspare said:

"No, it is not Peppina."

As he spoke Artois saw him stretch out his hand, but gently, towards Ruffo.

"Who is it, then?" said Ruffo.

Moved by an irresistible impulse to interpose, Artois called out:

"Gaspare!"

He saw the two figures start.

"Gaspare!" he repeated, coming up to them.

"Signore! What is it? Has the Signora—"

"I have not heard her. I have not seen her."

"Then what is it, Signore?"

"Good-evening, Ruffo," Artois said, looking at the boy.

"Good-evening, Signore."

Ruffo took off his cap. He was going to put it back on his dark hair, when Artois held his arm.

"Wait a minute, Ruffo!"

The boy looked surprised, but met fearlessly the eyes that were gazing into his.

"Va bene, Ruffo."

Artois released his arm, and Ruffo put on his cap.

"I heard you talking of the *fattura della morte*," Artois said.

Ruffo reddened slightly.

"Sì, Signore."

"Your mother made it?"

Ruffo did not answer. Gaspare stood by, watching and listening with deep, half-suspicious attention.

"I heard you say so."

"Sì, Signore. My mamma made it."

"And told you to bring it to the island and put it in the house to-night?"

"Sì, Signore."

"Are you quite sure it was Peppina your mother wished to do evil?"

"Sì, Signore, quite sure. Peppina is a bad girl. She made my Patrigno mad. She brought trouble to our house."

"You love the Signora, don't you, Ruffo?"

His face changed and grew happier at once.

"Sì, Signore. I love the Signora and the Signorina."

He would not leave out Vere. Artois's heart warmed to him for that.

"Ruffo—"

While he had been on the crest of the island an idea had come to him. At first he had put it from him. Now, suddenly, he caressed it, he resolved to act on its prompting.

"Ruffo, the Signora is in the house."

"Sì, Signore."

"I don't think she is very well. I don't think she will leave the house to-night. Wouldn't you like to see her?"

"Signore, I always like to see the Signora."

"And I think she likes to see you. I know she does."

"Sì, Signore. The Signora is always glad when I come."

He spoke without conceit or vanity, with utterly sincere simplicity.

"Go to the house and ask to see her now—Gaspare will take you."

As he spoke he looked at Gaspare, and Gaspare understood.

"Come on, Ruffo!"

Gaspare's voice was rough, arbitrary, but the eyes that he turned on Ruffo were full of the almost melting gentleness that Hermione had seen in them sometimes and that she had always loved.

"Come on, Ruffino!"

He walked away quickly, almost sternly, towards the house. And Ruffo followed him.

CHAPTER XLI

ARTOIS did not go with them. Once again he was
governed by an imperious feeling that held him inactive,
the feeling that it was not for him to approach Hermione
—that others might draw near to her, but that he dared
not. The sensation distressed and almost humiliated
him. It came upon him like a punishment for sin, and
as a man accepts a punishment which he is conscious
of deserving Artois accepted it.

So now he waited alone on the crest of the island,
looking towards the Casa del Mare.

What would be the result of this strange and daring
embassy?

He was not long to be in doubt.

"Signore! Signore!"

Gaspare's voice was calling him from somewhere in
the darkness.

"Signore."

"I am coming."

There had been a thrill of emotion in the appeal sent
out to him. He hurried towards the house. He crossed
the bridge. When he was on it he heard the splash of
oars below him in the Pool, but he took no heed of it.
What were the fishermen to him to-night? Before the
house door he met Gaspare and Ruffo.

"What is it?"

"The Signora is not in her room, Signore."

"Not—? How do you know? Is the door open?"

"Sì, Signore. The Signora has gone! And the *fattura
della morte* has gone."

A SPIRIT IN PRISON

"The *fattura della morte* has gone!" repeated Ruffo.

The repetition of the words struck a chill to the heart of Artois. Again he was beset by superstition. He caught it from these children of the South, who stared at him now with their grave and cloudy eyes.

"Perhaps one of the servants—" he began.

"No, Signore. I have asked them. And they would not dare to touch it."

"The Signorina?"

He shook his head.

"She is in the garden. She has been there all the time. She does not know"—he lowered his voice almost to a whisper—"she does not know about the Signora and the *fattura della morte*."

"We must not let her know—"

He stopped. Suddenly his ears seemed full of the sound of plashing oars in water. Yet he heard nothing.

"Gaspare," he said, quickly, "have you looked everywhere for the Signora?"

"I have looked in the house, Signore. I have been on the terrace and to the Signorina in the garden. Then I came to tell you. I thought you should know about the Signora and the *fattura della morte*."

Artois felt that it was this fact of the disappearance of the death-charm which for the moment paralyzed Gaspare's activities. What stirring of ancient superstition was in the Sicilian's heart he did not know, but he knew that now his own time of action was come. No longer could he delegate to others the necessary deed. And with this knowledge his nature seemed to change. An ardor that was almost vehement with youth, and that was hard-fibred with manly strength and resolution, woke up in him.

Again his ears were full of the sound of oars in water.

"Ruffo," he said, "will you obey me?"

He laid his hand on the boy's shoulder.

"Sì, Signore."

"Go into the garden. Stay with the Signorina till I come."

"Sì, Signore."

"If it is a long time, if the Signorina is afraid, if she wants to do anything, you are to say that Don Emilio said she was not to be afraid, and that she was to wait."

"Sì, Signore."

The boy paused, looking steadily at Artois, then, seeing that he had finished, turned away and went softly into the house.

"Gaspare, come with me."

Gaspare said nothing, but followed him down to the foot of the cliff. One of the island boats was gone. When Gaspare saw that he ran to pull in the other. He held out his arm to help Artois into the boat, then took the oars, standing up and looking before him into the night.

"Row towards the village, Gaspare."

"Sì, Signore."

At that moment Gaspare understood much of what was in Artois's mind. He relied upon Artois. He trusted him—and this fact, of Gaspare's trust and reliance upon him, added now to the feeling of ardor that had risen up in Artois, gave him courage, helped to banish completely that punishing sensation which had condemned him to keep away from Hermione as one unworthy to approach her, to touch even the hem of her grief.

No need to tell Gaspare to row quickly. With all his strength he forced the boat along through the calm sea.

"Keep near the shore, Gaspare!"

"Sì, Signore."

Only the first quarter of the young moon was visible in the sky. It cast but a thin and distant glint of silver upon the waters. By the near shore the dimness of this hour was unbroken by any light, unstirred by any sound except the withdrawn and surreptitious murmur of the sea. The humped shapes of the low yellow rocks showed themselves faintly like shapes of beasts asleep. In the distance, lifted above the sea, two or three flames shone faintly. They were shed by lamps or candles set in the windows of the fishermen's cottages in the village.

Had Hermione gone to the village?

She might have left the island with some definite purpose, or moved by a blind impulse to get away and be alone. Artois could not tell. But she had taken the *fattura della morte*.

He wondered whether she knew its meaning, with what sinister intention it had been made. Something in the little worthless thing must have attracted her, have fascinated her, or she would not have taken it. In her distress of mind, in her desire for solitude, she would have hastened away and left it lying where it was.

Perhaps she had a purpose in leaving the island with the *fattura della morte*.

Her taking of it began to seem to Artois, as it had evidently seemed to Gaspare, a fact of profound significance. His imagination, working with an almost diseased rapidity and excitement, brought before him a series of scenes in which the death-charm figured as symbol. In one of these there were two women—Hermione and Maddalena.

Hermione might have set out on some wild quest to Mergellina. He remembered the face at the window, and knew that to-night everything was possible.

"Row quickly, Gaspare!"

Gaspare bent almost furiously to the oars. Then sharply he turned his head.

"What is it?"

"I can see the boat! I can see the Signora!"

A SPIRIT IN PRISON

The words struggled out on a long breath that made his broad chest heave. Instinctively Artois put his hands on the gunwale of the boat on either side of him, moving as if to stand up.

"Take care, Signore!"

"I'd forgotten——" He leaned forward, searching the night. "Where is the Signora?"

"There—in front! She is rowing to the village. No, she has turned."

He stopped rowing.

"The Signora has seen, or she has heard, and she is going in to shore."

"But there are only the rocks."

"The Signora is going in to the Palazzo of the Spirits."

"The Palazzo of the Spirits?" Artois repeated.

"Sì, Signore."

Gaspare turned and looked again into the darkness.

"I cannot see the Signora any more."

"Follow the Signora, Gaspare. If she has gone to the Palazzo of the Spirits row in there."

"Sì, Signore."

He drew the oars again strongly through the water.

Artois remembered a blinding storm that had crashed over a mountain village in Sicily long ago, a flash of lightning which had revealed to him the gaunt portal of a palace that seemed abandoned, a strip of black cloth, the words "*Lutto in famiglia.*" They had seemed to him prophetic words.

And now—?

In the darkness he saw another darkness, the strange and broken outline of the ruined palace by the sea, once, perhaps, the summer home of some wealthy Roman, now a mere shell visited in the lonely hours by the insatiate waves. Were Hermione and he to meet here? To-day he had thought of his friend as a spirit that had been long in prison. Now he came to the Palace of the

Spirits to face her truth with his. The Palace of the
Spirits! The name suggested the very nakedness of
truth. Well, let it be so, let the truth stand there
naked. Again, mingling with a certain awe, there rose
up in him a strong ardor, a courage that was vehement,
that longed at last to act. And it seemed to him suddenly that for many years, through all the years that
divided Hermione and him from the Sicilian life, they
had been held in leash, waiting for the moment of this
encounter. Now the leash slackened. They were being
freed. And for what?

Gaspare plunged his right oar into the sea alone.
The boat swung round obediently, heading for the shore.

One of the faint lights that gleamed in the village was
extinguished.

"Signore, the Signora has left the boat!"

"Sì?"

"Madonna! She has let it go! She has left it to the
sea!"

He backed water. A moment later the little boat in
which Vere loved to go out alone grated against theirs.

"Madonna! To leave the boat like that!" exclaimed
Gaspare, bending to catch the tow-rope. "The Signora
is not safe to-night. The Signora's saint will not look
on her to-night."

"Put me ashore, Gaspare."

"Sì, Signore."

The boat passed before the façade of the palace.

Artois knew the palace well by day. This was the
first time he had come to it by night. In daylight it
was a small and picturesque ruin washed by the laughing
sea, lonely but scarcely sad. Leaping from its dark and
crumbling walls the fisher-boys often plunged into the
depths below; or they lay upon the broad sills of the
gaping window-spaces to dry themselves in the sun.
Men came with rods and lines to fish from its deserted

apartments, through which, when rough weather was at hand, the screaming sea-birds flew. The waves played frivolously enough in its recesses. And their voices were heard against the slimy and defiant stones calling to each other merrily, as perhaps once the voices of revellers long dead called in the happy hours of a vanished vil-leggiatura.

But the night wrought on it, in it, and about it change. Its solitude then became desolation, the darkness of its stones a blackness that was tragic, its ruin more than a suggestion, the decisive picture of despair.

At its base was a line of half-discovered window-spaces, the lower parts of which had become long since the prey of the waves. Above it were more window-spaces, fully visible, and flanking a high doorway, once, no doubt, connected with a staircase, but now giving upon mid-air. Formerly there had been another floor, but this had fallen into decay and disappeared, with the exception of one small and narrow chamber situated immediately over the doorway. Isolated, for there was no means of approach to it, this chamber had something of the aspect of a low and sombre tower sluggishly lifting itself towards the sky. The palace was set upon rock and flanked by rocks. Round about it grass grew to the base of a high cliff at perhaps two hundred yards distance from it. And here and there grass and tufts of rank herbage pushed in its crevices, proclaiming the triumph of time to exulting winds and waters.

As Gaspare rowed in cautiously and gently to this deserted place, to which from the land no road, no foot-path led, he stared at the darkness of the palace with superstitious awe, then at the small, familiar boat, which followed in their wake because he held the tow-rope.

"Signore," he said, "I am afraid!"

"You—Gaspare!"

"I am afraid for the Signora. Why should she come

here all alone with the *fattura della morte?* I am afraid for the Signora."

The boat touched the edge of the rock to the right of the palace.

"And where has the Signora gone, Signore? I cannot see her, and I cannot hear her."

He lifted up his hand. They listened. But they heard only the sucking murmur of the sea against the rocks perforated with little holes, and in distant, abandoned chambers of the palace.

"Where has the Signora gone?" Gaspare repeated, in a whisper.

"I will find the Signora," said Artois.

He got up. Gaspare held his arm to assist him to the shore.

"Thank you."

He was on the rocks.

"Gaspare," he said, "wait here. Lie off the shore close by till I come back."

"Sì, Signore."

Artois hesitated, looking at Gaspare.

"I will persuade the Signora to come back with us," he said.

"Sì, Signore. You must persuade the poor Signora. The poor Signora is mad to-night. She gave me a look—" His eyes were clouded with moisture. "If the poor Signora had not been mad she could not have looked at me like that—at another, perhaps, but not at me."

It seemed as if at last his long reserve was breaking down. He put up his hand to his eyes.

"I did not think that my Padrona—"

He stopped. Artois remembered the face at the window. He grasped Gaspare's hand.

"The Signora does not understand," he said. "I will make the Signora understand."

"Sì, Signore, you must make the poor Signora understand."

Gaspare's hand held on to the hand of Artois, and in that clasp the immense reserve, that for so many years had divided, and united, these two men, seemed to melt like gold in a crucible of fire.

"I will make the Signora understand."

"And I will wait, Signore."

He pushed the boat off from the rocks. It floated away, with its sister boat, on the calm sea that kissed the palace walls. He gave his Padrona's fate into the hands of Artois. It was a tribute which had upon Artois a startling effect.

It was like a great resignation which conferred a great responsibility.

Always Gaspare had been very jealous, very proud of his position of authority as the confidential servant and protector of Hermione. And now, suddenly, and very simply, he seemed to acknowledge his helplessness with Hermione—to rely implicitly upon the power of Artois.

Vere, too, in her way had performed a kindred action. She had summoned "Monsieur Emile" in her great trouble. She had put herself in his hands. And he— he had striven to delegate to others the burden he was meant to bear. He had sent Vere to Hermione. He had sent Gaspare to her. He had even sent Ruffo to her. Now he must go himself. Vere, Gaspare, Ruffo— they were all looking to him. But Gaspare's eyes were most expressive, held more of demand for him than the eyes of the girl and boy. For the past was gathered in Gaspare, spoke to him in Gaspare's voice, looked at him from Gaspare's eyes, and in Gaspare's soul waited surely to know how it would be redeemed.

He turned from the sea and looked towards the cliff. Now he had the palace on his left hand. On his right, not far off, was a high bluff going almost sheer into the sea. Nevertheless, access to the village was possible by the strip of rocks beneath it. Had Hermione gone to the village by the rocks? If she had, Gaspare's keen eyes would surely have seen her. Artois looked at the blank wall of the palace. This extended a little way, then turned at right angles. Just beyond the angle, in its shadow, there was a low and narrow door-way. Artois moved along the wall, reached this door-way, stood without it, and listened.

The grass here grew right up to the stones of the ruin. He had come almost without noise. Before him he saw blackness, the blackness of a passage extending from the orifice of the doorway to an interior chamber of the palace. He heard the peculiar sound of moving water that is beset and covered in by barriers of stone, a hollow and pugnacious murmur, as of something so determined that it would be capable of striving through eternity, yet of something that was wistful and even sad.

For an instant he yielded his spirit to this sound of eternal striving. Then he said:

"Hermione!"

No one answered.

"Hermione!"

He raised his voice. He almost called the name.

Still there was no answer. Yet the silence seemed to tell him that she was near.

He did not call again. He waited a moment, then he stepped into the passage.

The room to which it led was the central room, or hall, of the palace—a vaulted chamber, high and narrow, opening to the sea at one end by the great doorway already mentioned, to the land beneath the cliff by a smaller doorway at the other. The faint light from without, penetrating through these facing doorways, showed to Artois a sort of lesser darkness, towards which he walked slowly, feeling his way along the wall. When he reached the hall he again stood still, trying to get accustomed to the strange and eerie obscurity, to pierce it with his eyes.

Now to his left, evidently within the building, and not far from where he stood, he heard almost loudly the striving of the sea. He heard the entering wave push through some narrow opening, search round the walls for egress, lift itself in a vain effort to emerge, fall back baffled, retreat, murmuring discontent, only to be succeeded by another eager wave. And this startling living noise of water filled him with a sensation of acute anxiety, almost of active fear.

"Hermione!" he said once more.

It seemed to him that the voice of the water drowned his voice, that it was growing louder, was filling the palace with an uproar that was angry.

"Hermione! Hermione!"

He strove to dominate that uproar.

Now, far off, through the seaward opening, he saw a streak of silver lying like a thread upon the darkness of the sea. And as he saw it, the voice of the waves within the palace seemed to sink suddenly away almost to silence. He did not know why, but the vision of that very distant radiance of the young and already setting moon seemed to restore to him abruptly the accuracy of his sense of hearing.

He again went forward a few steps, descending in the chamber towards the doorway by the worn remains of an almost effaced staircase. Reaching the bottom, he stood still once more. On either side of him he could faintly discern openings leading into other rooms. Perhaps Hermione, hearing him call, had retreated from him through one of them. A sort of horror of the situation came upon him, as he began thoroughly to realize the hatred, hatred of brain, of nerves, of heart, that was surely quivering in Hermione in this moment, that was driving her away into the darkness from sound and touch of life. Like a wounded animal she was creeping away from the hideous cruelty of men, creeping away from it and hating it. He remembered Gaspare's words about the look she had cast upon perhaps the most truly faithful of all her friends.

But—she did not know. And he, Artois, must tell her. He must make her see the exact truth of the years. He must win her back to reason.

Reason! As the word went through his mind it chilled him, like the passing of a thing coated with ice. He had been surely a reasonable man, and his reasonableness had led him to this hour. Suddenly he saw himself, as he had seen that palace door by lightning. He saw himself for an instant lit by a glare of fire. He looked, he stared upon himself.

And he shivered, as if he had drawn close to, as if he had stood by, a thing coated with ice.

And he dared to come here, to pursue such a woman as Hermione! He dared to think that he could have any power over her, that his ice could have any power over her fire! He dared to think that! For a moment all, and far more than all, his former feeling of unworthiness, of helplessness, of cowardice, rushed back upon him. Then, abruptly, there came upon him this thought —"Vere believes I have power over Hermione." And then followed the thought—"Gaspare believes that I have power over her." And the ice seemed to crack. He saw fissures in it. He saw it melting. He saw the "thing" it had covered appearing, being gradually revealed as—man.

"Vere believes in my power. Gaspare believes in my power. They are the nearest to Hermione. They know her best. Their instincts about her must be the strongest, the truest. Why do they believe in it? Why do they—why do they know—for they must, they do know, that I have this power, that I am the one to succeed where any one else would fail? Why have they left Hermione in my hands to-night?"

The ice was gone. The lightning flash lit up a man warm with the breath of life. From the gaunt door of the abandoned palace the strip of black cloth, the tragic words above it, dropped down and disappeared.

Suddenly Artois knew why Vere believed in his power, and why Gaspare believed in it—knew how their instincts had guided them, knew to what secret knowledge —perhaps not even consciously now their knowledge— they had travelled. And he remembered the words he had written in the book at Frisio's on the night of the storm:

"La conscience, c'est la quantité de science innée que nous avons en nous."

He had written those words hurriedly, irritably, merely because he had to write something, and they chanced —he knew not why—to come into his mind as he took hold of the pen. And it was on that night, surely, that his conscience—his innate knowledge—began to betray him. Or—no—it was on that night that he began to defy it, to deny it, to endeavor to cast it out.

For surely he must have known, he had known, what Vere and Gaspare innately knew. Surely his conscience had not slept while theirs had been awake.

He did not know. It seemed to him as if he had not time to decide this now. Very rapidly his mind had worked, rushing surely through corridors of knowledge to gain an inner room. He had only stood at the foot of the crumbling staircase two or three minutes before he moved again decisively, called again, decisively:

"Hermione! Hermione! I know you are here. I have come for you!"

A SPIRIT IN PRISON

He went to the right. On the left was the chamber which had been taken possession of by the sea. She could not have gone that way, unless—he thought of the *fattura della morte*, and for a moment the superstitious horror returned upon him. But he banished it. That could not be. His heart was flooded by conviction that cruelty has an end, that the most relentless fate fails at last in its pursuing, that the *fattura della morte*, if it brought death with it, brought a death that was not of the body, brought, perhaps, a beautiful death of something that had lived too long.

He banished fear, and he entered the chamber on the right. It was lit only by an opening looking to the sea. As he came into it he saw a tall thing—like a tall shadow—pass close to him and disappear. He saw that, and he heard the faint sound of material in movement.

There was then still another chamber on this side, and Hermione had passed into it. He followed her in silence, came to the doorway of it, looked, saw black darkness. There was no other opening either to sea or land. In it Hermione had found what she sought— absolute blackness.

But he had found her. Here she could not escape him.

He stood in the doorway. He remembered Vere's trust in him. He remembered Gaspare's trust. He remembered that Gaspare was waiting in the boat for him —for them. He remembered the words of Gaspare:

"You must make the poor Signora understand!"

That was what he had to do: to make Hermione understand. And that surely he could do. Surely he had the power to do it now.

For he himself understood.

40

CHAPTER XLII

"HERMIONE!"

Artois spoke to the void.

"Hermione, because I have followed you, because I have come here, don't think that I am claiming any right. Don't think that I imagine, because I am your— because I am—I mean that it has not been easy to me to come. It has not been—it is not a simple thing to me to break in upon—upon—"

He had begun to speak with determination. He had said the very first words with energy, almost with a warm eagerness, as of one hurrying on to vital speech. But suddenly the energy faltered, the eagerness failed, the ring of naturalness died out of the voice. It was as if a gust of cold air had blown out a flame. He paused. Then he said, in a low voice:

"You hate me for coming."

He stopped again. He stared at the void, at the blackness.

"You hate me for being here."

As he said the last words the blackness before him surely gathered itself together, took a form, the form of a wave, towered up as a gigantic wave towers, rolled upon him to overwhelm him. So acute was his sensation of being attacked, of being in peril, that his body was governed by it and instinctively shrank, trying to make itself small that it might oppose as little resistance as possible to the oncoming foe.

For it seemed to him that the wave of blackness was

620

the wave of Hermione's present hatred, that it came upon him, that it struck him, that it stunned and almost blinded him, then divided, rushing onwards he knew not where, unspent and unsatisfied.

He stood like a man startled and confused, striving to regain lost footing, to recover his normal condition.

"You hate me."

Had he spoken the words or merely thought them? He did not know. He was not conscious of speaking them, yet he seemed to hear them. He looked at the blackness. And again it surely moved. Again he surely saw it gathering itself together, and towering up as a wave towers.

His sensation was absolutely one of nightmare. And exactly as in a nightmare a man feels that he is no longer fully himself, has no longer the power to do any manly or effective thing, so Artois felt now.

It seemed to him that he was nothing, and yet that he was hated. He turned and looked behind him, moved by a fierce desire for relief. He had not the courage to persist in confronting that blackness which took a form, which came upon him, which would surely overwhelm him.

In the distance he saw a pallor, where the face of the night looked into the palace from the sea. And he heard the distant water. Still the little waves were entering the deserted chambers, only to seek an exit which they could never find. Their ceaseless determination was horrible to him, because it suggested to him the ceaseless determination of those other waves of black hatred, one following another, from some hidden centre of energy that was inexhaustible. As he listened the sound of the sea stole into his ears till his brain was full of it, till he felt as if into his brain, as into those deserted chambers, the waves were penetrating, the waves of the sea and those dark waves which gathered themselves together and flowed upon him from the void.

A SPIRIT IN PRISON

For a moment they possessed him. For a moment
he was the prey of these two oceans.

Then he made a violent effort, released himself, and
turned again to the chamber in which Hermione was
hidden. He faced the blackness. He was able to do
that now. But he was not able to go on speaking to
the woman who remained invisible, but whose influence
he was so painfully conscious of. He was not able to
speak to her because she was surely speaking to him,
was communicating to him not only her feeling towards
him, but also its reason, its basis, in that wordless language which is only used and comprehended by human
beings in moments of crisis and intense emotion. That
was what he felt, seemed to know.

He stood there, facing the blackness and listening,
while she seemed to be telling him her woman's reasons
for her present hatred of the man who had been for so
long a time her closest friend.

And these reasons were not only the reasons born of
a day's events, of the discovery of the lie on which her
spirit had been resting. She did not say—her heart did
not say only: "I hate you because you let me believe in
that which never existed except in my imagination—my
husband's complete love of me, complete faithfulness to
me. I hate you because you enclosed me in the prison
of a lie. I hate you because during all these years you
have been a witness of my devotion to an idol, a graven
image whose wooden grimace I mistook for the smile of
the god's happy messenger, because you have been a
witness of my cult for the memory of one who betrayed
my trust in him, who thought nothing of my gift to him,
who put another in the sanctuary that should have been
sacred to me, and who has poisoned the sources of the
holy streams that flow into and feed the soul of a good
woman."

If Hermione had silently told Artois reasons such as

these for hating him she would have roused him to battle with her, to defend himself with some real hope of holding his own, even of eventual conquest. But other reasons, too, did they not come from her, creeping out of her brain and heart and soul into his, reasons against which he had no weapons, against which he could make no defence?

He had claimed to understand the psychology of women. He had believed he comprehended women well, Hermione best of all women. But these reasons, creeping out of her into him, set a ring of illuminating fire about his misconception. They told him that though perhaps he had known one Hermione in his friend, there were other Hermiones in her whom he had never really known. Once in the garden of the island by night he had seen, or fancied he had seen, a strange smile upon her face that betokened a secret bitterness; and for a moment he had been confused, and had faltered in his speech, and had felt as if he were sitting with a stranger who was hostile to him, or, if not actually hostile, was almost cruelly critical of him. Now that stranger silently spoke to him, silently told him many things.

She told him—that which few men ever know—something of what women specially want, specially need in life. And the catalogue of these needs seemed to him to be also the catalogue of her reasons for hating him at this moment.

"Women need—I needed," she seemed to say, "not only a large and ample friendship, nobly condescending, a friendship like an announcement to citizens affixed to the wall of a market-place, and covering boldly all the principal circumstances and likely happenings of ordinary feminine life, but a friendship, an affection, very individual, very full of subtlety, not such as would suit, would fit comfortably women, but such as would suit, would fit comfortably, would fit beautifully one individual woman—me."

A SPIRIT IN PRISON

Ah, the "woman need" was flung away, like a stone thrown into the sea! It was the "I needed" that was held fast, that was shown to Artois now. And the "I" stood to Hermione for herself. But might it not have stood to the world for many a woman?

"I needed some one to whom I could be kind, for whom I could think, plan, hope, weave a fabric of ambitious dreams, look forward along the path that leads to glory. I needed some one for whom I could be unselfish, to whom I could often offer those small burnt sacrifices whose smoke women love to see ascending towards God, burnt sacrifices of small personal desires, small personal plans and intentions. I needed some one to need my encouragement, my admiration—frequently expressed—my perpetual sympathy hovering about him like a warm cloud of fragrant incense, my gentle criticism, leading him to efforts which would win from the world, and from me, more admiration of and wonder at his energy and genius. I needed some one to stir within me woman's soft passion for forgiveness, woman's delight in petting the child who has been naughty, but who puts the naughtiness aside and runs home to be good again. I needed some one to set upon a pedestal.

"These needs you fully satisfied.

"You gave me generously opportunities for kindness, for thoughtfulness, for impersonal ambition, for looking forward on your behalf, for unselfishness, for the sacrifice of my little personal desires, plans, and intentions, for encouragement of you, for admiration of your abilities, for sympathy—even for gentle criticism leading you to efforts which won from me eventually a greater respect for your powers and for secret forgiveness which ended in open petting. When I prepared the pedestal you were quite ready to mount it, and to remain upon it without any demonstration of fatigue.

"And so, many needs of mine you satisfied.

"But I had more needs, and far other needs, than these.

"I needed not only to make many gifts, to satisfy my passion for generosity, but to have many gifts, and gifts of a special nature, made in return to me. I needed to feel another often, if not perpetually and exclusively, intent on me. I needed to feel tenderness — watchful, quick, eager tenderness, not tenderness slow-footed and in blinkers—round about me.

"I needed a little blindness in my friend. That is true. But the blindness that I needed was not blindness to my little sacrifices, but blindness to my little faults.

"To a woman there is such a world of difference between the two! I longed for my friend to see the smoke ascending from my small burnt-offerings of self made for his sake. But I longed, too, for him not always to see with calm, clear eyes my petty failings, my minute vanities, my inconsistencies, my incongruities, my frequent lack of reasoning power and logical sequence, my gusts of occasional injustice—ending nearly always in a rain of undue benefits—my surely forgivable follies of sentiment, my irritabilities—how often due to physical causes which no man could ever understand!—my blunders of the head—of the heart I made but few, or none— my weak depressions, struggled against but not always conquered, my perhaps childish anxieties and apprehensions, my forebodings, not invariably well founded, my fleeting absurdities of temper, of temperament, of manner, or of word.

"But as definitely as my friend did not see my little sacrifices he saw my little faults, and he made me see that he saw them. Men are so free from the tender deceits that women are compact of.

"And as I needed blindness in some directions, in others I needed clear sight.

A SPIRIT IN PRISON

"I needed some one to see that my woman's heart was not only the heart of a happy mother, to whom God had given an almost perfect child, but also the heart of a lover—not of a *grande amoureuse*, perhaps, but of a lover who had been deprived of the love that is the complement of woman's, and who suffered perpetually in woman's peculiar and terrible way because of that deprivation.

"I needed an understanding of my sacred hunger, a comprehension of my desolation, a realization that my efforts to fill my time with work were as the efforts of a traveller in a forest to escape from the wolves whose voices he hears behind him. I needed the recognition of a simple truth—that the thing one is passionately eager to give is nearly always the thing one is passionately eager to receive, and that when I poured forth sympathy upon others I was longing to have it poured forth upon me. I gave because secretly I realized the hunger I was sharing. And often, having satisfied your hunger, I was left to starve, no longer in company, but entirely alone.

"I needed great things, perhaps, but I needed them expressed in little ways; and I needed little cares, little attentions, little thoughtfulnesses, little preventions, little, little, absurd kindnesses, tendernesses, recognitions, forgivenesses. Perhaps, indeed, even more than anything magnificent or great, I needed the so-called little things. It is not enough for a woman to know that a man would do for her something important, something even superb, if the occasion for it arose. Such an occasion probably never would arise—and she cannot wait. She wants to be shown at every moment that some one is thinking kindly of her, is making little, kind plots and plans for her, is wishing to ward off from her the chill winds, to keep from pricking her the thorns of the roses, to shut out from her the shadows of life and let in the sunbeams to her pathway.

A SPIRIT IN PRISON

"I needed the tender, passing touch to show me my secret grief was understood, and my inconsistency was pardoned. I needed the generous smile to prove to me that my greed for kindness, even when perhaps inopportune, was met in an ungrudging spirit. I needed now and then—I needed this sometimes terribly, more, perhaps, than any other thing—a sacrifice of self in my friend, in you, a sacrifice of some very small, very personal desire of yours, because it was not mine or because it was the opposite to mine. Never, never did my heart and my nature demand of yours any great sacrifice of self, such as mine could have made — such as mine once did make—for you. But it did demand, often— often it demanded some small sacrifice: the giving up of some trifle, the resignation of some advantage, perhaps, that your man's intellect gave you over my woman's intellect, the abandoning of some argumentative position, or the not taking of it, the sweet pretence—scarcely a sin against the Holy Ghost of truth!—that I was a tiny bit more persuasive, or more clear-sighted, or more happy in some contention, or more just in some decision, than perhaps I really was. I needed to be shown your affection for me, as I was ever ready, ever anxious, to show mine for you, in all the little ways that are the language of the heart and that fill a woman's life with music.

"All this I needed. My nature cried out for it as instinctively as the nature of man cries out for God. But all this I needed generally in vain. You were not always a niggard. You were ready sometimes to give in your way. But were you ever ready to give in mine when you saw — and sometimes you must have seen, sometimes you did see—what mine was? I longed always to give you all you wanted in the way you wanted it. But you gave when you wished and as you chose to give. I was often grateful. I was too often grate-

627

ful. I was unduly grateful. Because I was giving, I was always giving far more than I received.

"But all that time I had something. All that time I had a memory that I counted sacred. All that time, like an idiot child, I was clasping in my hand a farthing, which I believed, which I stated, to be a shining piece of gold.

"You knew what it was. You knew it was a farthing! You knew—you knew!

"And now that the hour has come when I know, too, can't you understand that I realize not only that that farthing is a farthing, but that all farthings are farthings? Can't you understand that I hate those who have given me farthings when my hands were stretched out for gold—my hands that were giving gold?

"Can't you understand? Can't you? Then I'll make you understand! I'll make you! I'll make you!"

Again the blackness gathered itself together, took a form, the form of a wave, towered up as a gigantic wave towers, rolled upon Artois to overwhelm him. He stood firm and received the shock. For he was beginning to understand. He was no longer confronting waves of hatred which were also waves of mystery.

He had thought that Hermione hated him, hated every one just then, because of what Ruffo had silently told her that day at Mergellina. But as he stood there in the dark at the door of that black chamber, hearing the distant murmur of the sea about the palace walls, there were borne in upon him, as if in words she told him, all the reasons for present hatred of him which preceded the great reason of that day; reasons for hatred which sprang, perhaps, which surely must spring, from other reasons of love.

His mind was exaggerating, as minds do when the heart is intensely moved, yet it discerned much truth. And it was very strange, but his now acute consciousness of a personal hatred coming to him from out of the darkness of this almost secret chamber, and of its complex causes, causes which nevertheless would surely never have produced the effect he felt but for the startling crisis of that day, this acute consciousness of a personal and fierce hatred bred suddenly in Artois a new sensation of something that was not hatred, that was the reverse of hatred. Vere had once compared him to a sleepy lion. The lion was now awake.

"Hermione," he said—and now his voice was strong and unfaltering—"I seem to have been listening to you all this time that I have been standing here. Surely I have been listening to you, hearing your thoughts. Don't you know it? Haven't you felt it? When I left the island, when I followed you, I thought I understood. I thought I understood what you were feeling, almost all that you were feeling. I know now how little I understood. I didn't realize how much there was to understand. You've been telling me. Haven't you, Hermione? Haven't you?"

He paused. But there was no answer.

"I am sure you have been telling me. We must get down to the truth at last. I thought—till now I have thought that I was more able to read the truth than most men. You must often have laughed—how you must have laughed—secretly at my pretensions. Only once—one night in the garden on the island—I think I saw you laughing. And even then I didn't understand. Mon Dieu!"

He was becoming fiercely concentrated now on what he was saying. He was losing all self-consciousness. He was even losing consciousness of the strange fact that he was addressing the void. It was as if he saw Hermione, so strongly did he feel her.

"Mon Dieu! It is as if I'd been blind all the time I have known you, blind to the truth of you and blinder still to my own truth. Perhaps I am blind now. I don't know. But, Hermione, I can see something. I do know something of you and of myself. I do know that even now there is a link between us. You want to deny it. You wouldn't acknowledge it. But it is there. We are not quite apart from each other. We can't be that. For there is something—there has always been something, since that night we met in Paris, at Madame Enthoven's''— he paused again, so vividly flashed the scene of that dinner in Paris upon his memory—"something to draw us together, something to hold us together, something strong. Don't deny it even now. Don't deny it. Can't I be of some help, even now? Don't say I am utterly useless because I have been so useless to you, so damnably useless in the past. I see all that, my wretched uselessness to you through all these years. I am seeing it now while I am speaking. All the time I'm seeing it. What you have deserved and what you have had!''

He stopped, then he said again:

"What you have deserved and what you have had from me! And from—it was so—it was the same long ago, not here. But till to-day you didn't know that. I was wrong. I must have been wrong, hideously wrong, but I didn't want you ever to know that. It isn't that I don't love truth. You know I do. But I thought that lie was right. And it is only lately, this summer, that I have had any doubts. But I was wrong. I must have been wrong. It was intended that you should know. God, perhaps, intended it.''

He thought he heard a movement. But he was not quite sure. For there was always the noise of the sea in the deserted chambers of the palace.

"It seems to me now as if I had always been deceived, mistaken, blind with you, about you. I thought you need never know. I was mad enough to think that.

A SPIRIT IN PRISON

But I was madder still, for I thought—I must have
thought—that you could not bear to know, that you
weren't strong enough to endure the knowledge. But"
—he was digging deep now, searching for absolute truth:
in this moment his natural passion for truth, in one direction repressed for many years deliberately and consciously, in other directions, perhaps, almost unconsciously frustrated, took entire possession of his being—
"but nothing should ever be allowed to stand in the
way of truth. I believe that. I know it. I must, I
will always act upon the knowledge from this moment.
Never mind if it is bitter, cruel. Perhaps it is sometimes put into the world because of that. I've been
a horrible *fainéant*, the last of *fainéants*. I protected
you from the truth. With Gaspare I managed to do it.
We never spoke of it—never. But I think each of us
understood. And we acted together for you in that.
And I—it has often seemed to me that it was a fine
thing to do, and that my motives in doing it were fine.
But sometimes I have wondered whether they weren't
selfish—whether, instead of protecting you, I wasn't
only protecting myself. For it was all my fault. It
all came about through me, through my weakness, my
cursed weakness, my cursed weakness and whining for
help." He grew scarlet in the dark, realizing how his
pride in his strength, his quiet assumption with Hermione that he was the stronger, must often have made
her marvel, or almost weep. "I called you away. I
called you to Africa. And if I hadn't it would all have
been different."

"No, it would all have been the same."

Artois started. Out of the darkness a voice, a low,
cold, inexorable voice had spoken—had spoken absolute truth, correcting his lie:

"It would all have been the same!"

The woman's unerring instinct had penetrated much

631

further than the man's. He had been feeling the shell;
she plucked out the kernel. He had been speaking of
the outward facts, of the actions of the body; she spoke
of the inward facts, of the actions of the soul. Her husband's sin against her was not his unfaithfulness, the unfaithfulness at the Fair, but the fact that all the time
he had been with her, all the time she had been giving
her whole self to him, all the time that she had been sur-
rounding him with her love, he had retained in his soul
the power to will to commit it. That he had been given
an opportunity to sin was immaterial. What was material was that he had been capable of sinning.

Artois saw his lie. And he stood there silent, rebuked,
waiting for the voice to speak again. But it did not
speak. And he felt as if Hermione were silently demanding that he should sound the deeper depths of truth,
he who had always proclaimed to her his love of truth.

"Perhaps—yes, it would have been the same," he
said. "But—but—" His intention was to say, "But
we should not have known it." He checked himself.
Even as they formed themselves in his mind the words
seemed bending like some wretched, flabby reed.

"It would have been the same. But that makes no
difference in my conduct. I was weak and called to
you. You were strong and came to me. How strong
you were! How strong it was of you to come!"

As if for the first time—and indeed it was for the first
time—he really and thoroughly comprehended her self-
sacrifice, the almost bizarre generosity of her implacably
unselfish nature. He measured the force of her love
and the greatness of her sacrifice, by the depth of her
disillusion; and he began to wonder, almost as a child
wonders at things, how he had been able during all
these years quite simply, with indeed the almost incredible simplicity of man, never to be shared by any
woman, to assume and to feel, when with Hermione,

that he was the dominant spirit of the two, that she was, very rightly and properly, and very happily for her, leaning comfortably upon his strength. And in his wonder he knew that the real dominance strikes its roots in the heart, not in the head.

"You were strong, then, and you were strong, you were wonderfully strong, when—afterwards. On Monte Amato—that evening—you were strong."

His mind went to that mountain summit. The eyes of his mind saw the evening calm on Etna, and then— something else, a small, fluttering fragment of white paper at his feet among the stones. And, as if her mind read his, she spoke again, still in that low, cold, and inexorable voice.

"That piece of paper you found—what was it?"

"Hermione—Hermione—it was part of a letter of yours written in Africa, telling him that we were coming to Sicily, the day we were coming."

"It was that!"

The voice had suddenly changed. It struggled with a sob. It sank away in a sob. The sin—that she could speak of with a sound of calm. But all the woman in her was stricken by the thought of her happy letter treated like that, hated, denied, destroyed, and thrown to the winds.

"My letter! my letter!"

"Hermione!"

His heart spoke in his voice, and he made a step forward in the darkness.

"Don't!"

The voice had changed again, had become sharp, almost cutting. Like the lash of a whip it fell upon him. And he stopped at once. It seemed to him as if she had cried out, "If you dare to give me your pity I shall kill you!"

And he felt as if just then, for such a reason, she would be capable of such an action.

"I will not—" He almost faltered. "I am not—coming."

Never before had he been so completely dominated by any person, or by any fate, or by anything at all.

There was again a silence. Then he said:

"You are strong. I know you will be strong now. You can't go against your nature. I ought to have realized that as I have not realized it. I ought to have trusted to your strength long ago."

If he had known how weak she felt while she listened to him, how her whole being was secretly entreating to be supported, to be taken hold of tenderly, and guarded and cared for like a child! But he was a man. And at one moment he understood her and at another he did not.

"Gaspare and I—we wished to spare you. And perhaps I wished to spare myself. I think I did. I am sure I did. I am sure that was partly my reason. I was secretly ashamed of my cowardice, my weakness in Africa; and when I knew—no, when I guessed, for it was only that—what my appeal to you had caused—all it had caused—"

He paused. He was thinking of Maurice's death, which must have been a murder, which he was certain had been a murder.

"I hadn't—"

But the compelling voice from the darkness interrupted him.

"All?" it said.

He hesitated. Had she read his mind again?

"All?"

"The misery," he answered, slowly. "The sorrow that has lain upon your life ever since."

"Did you mean that? Did you only mean that?"

"No."

"What did you mean?"

"I was thinking of his death," he replied.

He spoke very quietly. He was resolved to have no more subterfuges, whatever the coward or the tender friend, or—the something else that was more than the tender friend within him might prompt him to try to hide.

"I was thinking of his death."

"His death!"

Artois felt cold with apprehension, but he was determined to be sincere.

"I don't understand."

"Don't ask me any more, Hermione. I know nothing more."

"He was coming from the island. He slipped and fell into the sea."

"He fell into the sea."

There was a long silence between them, filled by the perpetual striving of the restless waves within the chambers of the palace. Then she said:

"Her father was on the island that night?"

"I think he was."

"Was it that? Was it that? Did Maurice make that atonement?"

Artois shuddered. Her voice was so strange, or sounded so strange in the dark. Did she wish to think, wish to be sure that her husband had been murdered? He heard the faint rustle of her dress. She had moved. Was she coming nearer? He heard her breathing, or thought he heard it. He longed to be certain. He longed to still the perpetual cry of the baffled sea.

"Then he was brave—at the last. I think he knew—I am sure he knew—when he went down to the sea. I am sure he knew—when he said good-bye."

Her voice was nearer o him. And again it had changed, utterly changed. And in the different sounds of her voice Artois seemed to see the different women who dwelt within her, to understand and to know them as he had never understood and known them before. This woman was pleading, as women will plead for a man they have once loved, so long as they have voices, so long as they have hearts.

"Then that last time he didn't—no, he didn't go to—her."

The voice was almost a whisper, and Artois knew that she was speaking for herself—that she was telling herself that her husband's last action had been—not to creep to the woman, but to stand up and face the man.

"Was it her father?"

The voice was still almost a whisper.

"I think it was."

"Maurice paid then—he paid!"

"Yes. I am sure he paid."

"Gaspare knew. Gaspare knew — that night. He was afraid. He knew—but he didn't tell me. He has never told me."

"He loved his master."

"Gaspare loved Maurice more than he loved me."

By the way she said that Artois knew that Gaspare was forgiven. And a sort of passion of love for woman's love welled up in his heart. At that moment he almost worshipped Hermione for being unable, even in that moment, not to love Gaspare because Gaspare had loved the dead man more than he loved her.

"But Gaspare loves you," he said.

"I don't believe in love. I don't want love any more."

Again the voice was transformed. It had become hollow and weary, without resonance, like the voice of some one very old. And Artois thought of Virgil's Grotto, of all they had said there, and of how the rock above them had broken into deep and sinister murmurings, as if to warn them, or rebuke.

And now, too, there were murmurings about them, but below them from the sea.

"Hermione, we must speak only the truth to-night."

"I am telling you the truth. You chose to follow me. You chose to hunt me—to hunt me when you knew it was necessary to me to be alone. It was brutal to do it. It was brutal. I had earned the right at least to one thing: I had earned the right to be alone. But you didn't care. You wouldn't respect my right. You hunted me as you might have hunted an animal. I tried to escape. I didn't go to the village. I turned in here. I hid here. But you saw me coming, and you chased me, and you caught me. I can't get away. You have driven me in here. And I can't get away from you. You won't even let me be alone."

"I dare not let you be alone to-night."

"Why not? What are you afraid of? What does it matter to you where I go or what I do? Don't say it matters! Don't dare to say that!"

Her voice was fierce now.

"It doesn't matter to anybody, except perhaps a little to Vere and a very little to Gaspare. It never has really mattered to anybody. I thought it did once to some one. I thought I knew it did. But I was wrong. It didn't. It never mattered."

As she spoke an immense, a terrific feeling of desolation poured over her, as if from above, coming down upon her in the dark. It was like a flood that stiffened into ice upon her, making her body and her soul numb for a moment.

"I've never mattered to any one."

She muttered the words to herself. As she did so Artois seemed again to be looking into the magic mirror of the *fattura della morte*, to see the pale man, across whose face the shadow of a palm-leaf shifted, turning on his bed towards a woman who stood by an open door.

A SPIRIT IN PRISON

"You have always mattered to me," he said.

As he spoke there was in his voice that peculiar ring of utter sincerity which can no more be simulated, or mistaken, than the ringing music of sterling gold. But perhaps she was not in a condition to hear rightly, or perhaps something within her chose to deny, had a lust for denial because denial hurt her.

"To you least of all," she said. "Only yourself has ever really mattered to you."

In a sentence she summed up the long catalogue that had been given to him by her silence.

His whole body felt as if it reddened. His skin tingled with a sort of physical anger. His mature pride that had grown always, as a strong man's natural pride does grow with the passing of the years, seemed to him instinctively to rush forward to return the blow that had been dealt it.

"That is not quite true," he said.

"It is true. I have always had copper and I have always wanted gold," she answered.

He controlled himself, to prove to himself that she lied, that he was not the eternal egoist she dubbed him. Sometimes he had been genuinely unselfish, sometimes —not often, perhaps, but sometimes—he had really sunk himself in her. She was not being quite just. But how could she be quite just to-night? And what did exact justice matter to-night? An almost reckless feeling overtook him, a desire to conquer at all costs in this struggle; to win her back, whether against her will or not, to her old self; to eliminate the shocking impression made upon her soul by the discovery of that day, to wipe it out utterly, to replace it with another; to revive within her that beautiful enthusiasm which had been as a light always shining for her and from her upon people and events and life; to make her understand, to prove to her that, after all allowance has been made for uncertainties and contradictions of fate, for the ironies, the paradoxes, the cruelties, the tragedies, and the despairs of existence, the great, broad fact emerges, that what the human being gives, in the long run the human being generally gets, and that she who persistently gives gold will surely at last receive it.

The thought of a lost Hermione struck to his heart a greater fear than had already that night the thought of a dead Hermione. And if she was changed she was lost.

The real, the beautiful Hermione—he must seize her, grip her, hold her fast before it was too late.

"Hermione," he said, "I think you saved me from death; I am sure you did. Did you save me only to hate me?"

She made no reply.

"Do you remember that evening when you came into my room at Kairouan all covered with dust from your journey across the plains? I do. I remember it as if it had happened an hour ago instead of nearly seventeen years. I remember the strange feeling I had when I turned my head and saw you, a feeling that you and Africa would fight for me and that you would conquer. It had seemed to me that Africa meant to have me and would have me. Unless you came I felt certain of that. And I had thought about it all as I lay there in the stifling heat, till I almost felt the feverish earth enclosing me. I had loved Africa, but Africa seemed to me terrible then. I thought of only Arabs, always Arabs, walking above me on the surface of the ground when I was buried. And the thought made me shudder with horror. As if it could have mattered! I was absurd! But one is often absurd when one is very ill. The child in one comes out then, I suppose. And I had wondered —how I had wondered!—whether there was any chance of your coming. I hadn't actually asked you to come. I hadn't dared to do that. But it was the same thing almost. I had let you know—I had let you know. And I saw you come into my room all covered with dust. You had come so quickly—at once. Perhaps—perhaps sometimes you have thought I had forgotten that evening. I may be an egoist. I expect most men are egoists. And perhaps I am the egoist you say I am. Often one doesn't know what one is. But I have never forgotten that day, and that you were covered with dust. It was that—the dust—which seemed to make me realize that you had not lost a moment in coming, that you hadn't hesitated a moment as to whether you would come or not. You looked as if—almost as if you had run all the way to be in time to save my life — my wretched life. And you saved it. Did you save me to hate me?''

He waited for her to speak. But still she was silent. He heard no sound of her at all, and for a moment he almost wondered whether she had discovered that the chamber had some second outlet, whether she had not escaped while he had been speaking. But he looked round and he saw only dense darkness. She must be there still, close to him, hearing everything he said, whether against her will or with it. He was being perfectly sincere, and he was feeling very deeply, with intensity. But out of his natural reserve now rose a fear —the fear that perhaps his voice, his speech, did not convey his sincerity to her. If she should mistake him! If she should fancy he was trying to play upon her emotions in order to win her away from some desperate resolve. He longed to make her see what he was feeling, feel what he was feeling, be him and herself for one moment. And now the darkness began to distract him. He wanted light. He wanted to see Hermione, to see which of the women in her faced him, which was listening to him.

"Hermione," he said, "I want you — I want — it's

hateful speaking like this, always in the darkness. Don't make me stay here. Don't make me feel all the time that I am holding you a prisoner. No, I can't—I won't bear that any more."

He moved suddenly from the doorway back into the room behind him, in which there was a very little, very faint light. There he waited.

Almost immediately the tall shadow which had disappeared into the darkness emerged from it, passed before him, and went into the central chamber of the palace. He followed it, and found Hermione standing by the great doorway that overlooked the sea. Hermione she was, no longer a shadow, but the definite darkness of a human form relieved against the clear but now moonless night. She was waiting. Surely she was waiting for him. She might have escaped, but she stayed. She was willing, then, to hear what he had to say, all he had to say.

He stood still at a little distance from her. But in this hall the sound of the sea which came from the chamber on the left was much more distinct and disturbing than in the chamber where she had hidden. And he came nearer to her, till he was very near, almost close to her.

"If you hated me for—once, when we were standing on the terrace, you said, 'Take care—or I shall hate you for keeping me in the dark.' If you hated me because of what I have done, with Gaspare, Hermione, I could bear it. I could bear it, because I think it would pass away. We did keep you in the dark. Now you know it. But you know our reason, and that it was a reason of very deep affection. And I think you would forgive us, I know you would forgive us in the end. But I understand it isn't only that—"

Suddenly he thought of Vere, of that perhaps dawning folly, so utterly dead now, so utterly dead that he

641

could no longer tell whether it had ever even sluggishly stirred with life. He thought of Vere, and of the poems, and of the secret of Peppina's revelation. And he wondered whether the record he seemed to read in the silence had been a true record, or whether his imagination and his intellect of a psychologist, alert even in this hour of intense emotion, had been deceiving him. Hermione had seemed to be speaking to him. But had he really been only impersonating her? Had it been really himself that had spoken to himself? As this question arose in his mind he longed to make Hermione speak. Then he could be sure of all. He must clear away all misconception. Yet, even now, how could he speak of that episode with Vere?

"You say you have always wanted gold, and that you have never been given gold—"

"Yes."

He saw the dark figure near him lift its head. And he felt that Hermione had come out of the darkness with the intention of speaking the truth of what she felt. If she could not have spoken she would have stayed in the inner chamber, or she would have escaped altogether from the palace when he moved from the doorway. He was sure that only if she spoke would she change. In her silence there was damnation for them both. But she meant to speak.

"I have been a fool. I see that now. But I think I have been suspecting it for some time—nearly all this summer."

He could hear by the sound of her voice that while she was speaking she was thinking deeply. Like him, she was in search of absolute truth.

"It is only this summer that I have begun to see why people—you—have often smiled at my enthusiasms. No wonder you smiled! No wonder you laughed at me secretly!"

642

A SPIRIT IN PRISON

Her voice was hard and bitter.

"I never laughed at you, never—either secretly or openly!" he said, with a heat almost of anger.

"Oh yes, you did, as a person who can see clearly might laugh at a short-sighted person tumbling over all the little obstacles on a road. I was always tumbling over things—always—and you must always have been laughing. I have been a fool. Instead of growing up, my heart has remained a child—till now. That's what it is. Children who have been kindly treated think the world is all kindness. Because my friends were good to me, the world was good to me, I got into the habit of believing that I was lovable, and of loving in return. And I trusted people. I always thought they were giving me what I was giving them. That has been my great folly, the folly I'm punished for. I have been a credulous fool. I have thought that because I gave a thing with all my heart it was—it must be—given back to me. And yet I was surprised—I could scarcely believe it—when—when—"

He knew she was thinking of her beautiful wonder when Maurice had said he loved her.

"I could scarcely believe it! But, because I was a fool, I got to believe it, and I have believed it till to-day—you have stood by, and watched me believing it, and laughed at me for believing it till to-day."

"Hermione!"

"Yes, you mayn't have meant to laugh, but you must have laughed. Your mind, your intellect must have laughed. Don't say they haven't. I wouldn't believe you. And I know your mind—at any rate, I know that. Not your heart! I shall never pretend—I shall never think again for a moment that I know anything—anything at all—about a man's heart. But I do know something about your mind. And I know the irony in it. What a subject I have presented to you all these

643

years for the exercise of your ironic faculty! You ought
to thank me! You ought to go on your knees and thank
me and bless me for that!"

"Hermione!"

"Just now you talked of my coming into your room
in Kairouan all covered with dust. You asked me if I
remembered it. Yes, I do. And I remember something
you don't—probably you don't—remember. There was
no looking-glass in your room."

She stopped.

"No looking-glass!" he repeated, wondering.

"No, there was no looking-glass. And I remember
when I came in I saw there wasn't, and I was glad.
Because I couldn't look at myself and see how dreadful
and dishevelled and hideous I was — how dirty even I
was. My impulse was to go to a glass. And then I was
glad I couldn't. And I looked at your face. And I
thought 'he doesn't care. He loves me, all dusty and
hideous and horrid, as I am.' And then I didn't care
either. I said to myself, 'I look an object, and I don't
mind a bit, because I see in his face that he loves me
for myself, because he sees my heart, and—'"

And suddenly in her voice there was a sharp, hissing
catch, and she stopped short. For a full minute she
was silent. And Artois did not speak. Nor did he
move.

"I felt then, perhaps for the first time, 'the outside
doesn't matter to real people.' I felt that. I felt, 'I'm
real, and he is real, and—and Maurice is real. And
though it is splendid to be beautiful, and beauty means
so much, yet it doesn't mean so much as I used to think.
Real people get beyond it. And when once they have
got beyond it then life begins.' I remember thinking
that, feeling that, and—just for a minute loving my own
ugliness. And then, suddenly, I wished there was a looking-glass in the room that I might stand before it and

see what an object I was, and then look into your face
and see that it didn't matter. And I even triumphed
in my ugliness. 'I have a husband who doesn't mind,'
I thought. 'And I have a friend who doesn't mind.
They love me, both of them, whatever I look like. It's
me—the woman inside—they love, because they know
I care, and how I care for them.' And that thought
made me feel as if I could do anything for Maurice and
anything for you; heroic things, or small, dreadful,
necessary things; as if I could be the servant of, or sacrifice my life easily for, those who loved me so splendidly,
who knew how to love so splendidly. And I was happy
then even in sacrificing my happiness with Maurice. And
I thanked God then for not having given me beauty.

"And I was a fool. But I didn't find it out. And
so I revelled in self-sacrifice. You don't know, you
could never understand, how I enjoyed doing the most
menial things for you in your illness. Often you thanked me, and often you seemed ashamed that I should do
such things. And the doctor—that little Frenchman—
apologized to me. And you both thought that doing
so much in the frightful heat would make me ill. And
I blessed the heat and the flies and everything that
made what I did for you more difficult to do. Because
the doing of what was more difficult, more trying, more
fatiguing needed more love. And my gratitude to you
for your loving friendship, and for needing me more
than any one else, wanted to be tried to the uttermost.
And I thought, too, 'When I go back to Maurice I shall
be worth a little more, I shall be a little bit finer, and
he'll feel it. He'll understand exactly what it was to
me to leave him so soon, to leave—to leave what I
thought of then as my Garden of Paradise. And he'll
love me more because I had the courage to leave it to
try and save my friend. He'll realize—he'll realize—'
But men don't. They don't want to. Or they can't.

A SPIRIT IN PRISON

I'm sure—I'm positive now that men think less of women who are ready to sacrifice themselves than of women who wish to make slaves of them. I see that now. It's the selfish women they admire, the women who take their own way and insist on having all they want, not the women who love to serve them—not slavishly, but out of love. A selfish woman they can understand; but a woman who gives up something very precious to her they don't understand. Maurice never understood my action in going to Africa. And you—I don't believe you ever understood it. You must have wondered at my coming as much as he did at my going. You were glad I came at the moment. Oh yes, you were glad. I know that. But afterwards you must have wondered; you did wonder. You thought it Quixotic, odd. You said to yourself, 'It was just like Hermione. How could she do it? How could she come to me if she really loved her husband?' And very likely my coming made you doubt my really loving Maurice. I am almost sure it did. I don't believe all these years you have ever understood what I felt about him, what his death meant to me, what life meant to me afterwards. I told —I tried to tell you in the cave—that day. But I don't think you really understood at all. And he—he didn't understand my love for him. But I suppose he didn't even want to. When I went away he simply forgot all about me. That was it. I wasn't there, and he forgot. I wasn't there, and another woman was there—and that was enough for him. And I dare say—now—it is enough for most men, perhaps for every man. And then I'd made another mistake. I was always making mistakes when my heart led me. And I'd made a mistake in thinking that real people get beyond looks, the outside—and that then life begins. They don't—at least real men don't. A woman may spend her heart's blood for a man through years, and for youthful charm

"'DELAREY LOVED YOU,' ARTOIS SAID, SUDDENLY, INTER-
RUPTING HER"

and a face that is pretty, for the mere look in a pair of
eyes or the curve of a mouth, he'll almost forget that
she's alive, even when she's there before him. He'll
take the other woman's part against her instinctively,
whichever is in the right. If both women do exactly
the same thing a man will find that the pretty woman
has performed a miracle and the ugly woman made some
preposterous mistake. That is how men are. That is
how you are, I suppose, and that was Maurice, too. He
forgot me for a peasant. But—she must have been pretty
once. And I was always ugly!"

"Delarey loved you," Artois said, suddenly, interrupting her in a strong, deep voice, a voice that rang
with true conviction.

"He never loved me. Perhaps he thought he did.
He must have thought so. And that first day—when
we were coming up the mountain-side—"

She stopped. She was seized; she was held fast in
the grip of a memory so intense, so poignant, that she
made, she could make, no effort to release herself. She
heard the drowsy wail of the Ceramella dropping down
the mountain - side in the radiant heat of noon. She
felt Maurice's warm hand. She remembered her words
about the woman's need to love—"I wanted, I needed
to love — do men ever feel that? Women do often,
nearyl always, I think." The Pastorale—it sounded in
her ears. Or was it the sea that sounded, the sea in the
abandoned chambers of the Palace of the Spirits? She
listened. No, it was the Pastorale, that antique, simple, holy tune, that for her must always be connected
with the thought of love, man's love for woman, and
the Bambino's love for all the creatures of God. It
flooded her heart, and beneath it sank down, like a
drowning thing, for a moment the frightful bitterness
that was alive in her heart to-night.

"Delarey loved you," Artois repeated. "He loved

you on the first day in Sicily, and he loved you on the last."

"And—and the days between?"

Her voice spoke falteringly. In her voice there was a sound of pleading that struck into the very depths of his heart. The real Hermione was in that sound, the loving woman who needed love, who deserved a love as deep as that which she had given, as that which she surely still had to give.

"He loved you always, but he loved you in his way."

"In his way!" she repeated, with a sort of infinite, hopeless sadness.

"Yes, Hermione, in his way. Oh, we all have our ways, all our different ways of loving. But I don't believe a human being ever existed who had no way at all. Delarey's way was different from your way, so different that, now you know the truth of him, perhaps you can't believe he ever loved you. But he did. He was young, and he was hot-blooded—he was really of the South. And the sun got hold of him. And he betrayed you. But he repented. That last day he was stricken, not by physical fear, but by a tremendous shame at what he had done to you, and perhaps, also, by fear lest you should ever know it. I sat with him by the wall, and I felt without at all fully understanding it the drama in his soul. But now I understand it. I'm sure I understand it. And I think the depth of a shame is very often the exact measure of the depth of a love. Perhaps, indeed, there is no more exact measure."

Again he thought of the episode with Vere, and of his determination always from henceforth to be absolutely sincere with himself and with those whom he really loved.

"I am sure there is no more exact measure. Hermione, it is very difficult, I think, to realize what any

648

human being is, to judge any one quite accurately. Some judge a nature by the distance it can sink, others by the distance it can rise. Which do you do? Do you judge Delarey by his act of faithlessness? And, if you do, how would you judge me?"

"You!"

There was a sound of wonder in her voice.

"Yes. You say I am an egoist. And this that I am saying will seem to you egoism. It is egoism, I suppose. But I want to know—I must know. How would you judge me? How do you judge me?"

She was silent.

"How are you judging me at this moment? Aren't you judging me by the distance I could fall, the distance, perhaps, you think I have fallen?"

He spoke slowly. He was delaying. For all the time he spoke he was secretly battling with his pride—and his pride was a strong fighter. But to-night his passion for sincerity, his instinct that for Hermione—and for him, too—salvation lay in their perfect, even in their cruel sincerity to themselves and to each other, was a strong fighter also. In it his pride met an antagonist that was worthy of it. And he went on:

"Are you judging me by this summer?"

He paused.

"Go on," she said.

He could not tell by her voice what she was feeling, thinking. Expression seemed to be withdrawn from it, perhaps deliberately.

"This summer something has come between us, a cloud has come between us. I scarcely know when I first noticed it, when it came. But I have felt it, and you have felt it."

"Yes."

"It might, perhaps, have arisen from the fact of my suspicion who Ruffo was, a suspicion that lately became a certainty. My suspicion, and latterly my knowledge, no doubt changed my manner—made me anxious, perhaps, uneasy, made me watchful, made me often seem very strange to you. That alone might have caused a difference in our relations. But I think there was something else."

"Yes, there was something else."

"And I think, I feel sure now, that it was something to do with Vere. I was, I became deeply interested in Vere—interested in a new way. She was growing up. She was passing from childhood into girlhood. She was developing swiftly. That development fascinated me. Of course I had always been very fond of Vere. But this summer she meant more to me than she had meant. One day—it was the day I came back to the island after my visit to Paris—"

"Yes?"

He looked at her, trying to read what she was feeling in her face, but it was too dark for him to discern it.

"Vere made a confession to me. She told me she was working secretly, that she was writing poems. I asked her to show them to me. She did so. I found some talent in them, enough for me to feel justified in telling her to continue. Once, Hermione, you consulted me. Then my advice was different."

"I know."

"The remembrance of this, and Vere's knowledge that you had suffered in not succeeding with work, prompted us to keep the matter of her attempts to write a secret for the time. It seems a trifle—all this, but looking back now I feel that we were quite wrong in not telling you."

"I found it out."

"You knew?"

"I went to Vere's room. The poems were on the table with your corrections. I read them."

"We ought to have told you."

"I oughtn't to have read them, but I did."

"A mother has the right—"

"Not a mother who has resigned her right to question her child. I had said to Vere, 'Keep your secrets.' So I had no right, and I did wrong in reading them."

He felt that she was instinctively trying to match his sincerity with hers, and that fact helped him to continue.

"The knowledge of this budding talent of Vere's made me take a new interest in her, made me wish very much—at least I thought, I believed it was that, Hermione—that no disturbing influence should come into her life. Isidoro Panacci came—through me. Peppina came—through you. Hermione, on the night when Vere and I went out alone together in the boat Vere learned the truth about Peppina and the life behind the shutter."

"I knew that, too."

"You knew it?"

"Yes. I suspected something. You led me to suspect it."

"I remember—"

"I questioned Peppina. I made her tell me."

He said nothing for a moment. Then, with an effort, he said:

"You knew we had kept those two things from you, Vere and I?"

"Vere and you—yes."

Now he understood almost all, or quite all, that had been strange to him in her recent conduct.

"Sometimes—have you almost hated us for keeping those two secrets?"

"I don't think I have ever hated Vere."

"But me?"

"Do you know why I told Vere she might read your books?"

"Why?"

"Because I thought they might make her feel differently towards you."

"Less—less kindly?"

"Yes."

She spoke very quietly, but he felt—he did not know why—that it had cost her very much to say what she had said.

"You wanted Vere to think badly of me!"

He was honoring her for the moral courage which enabled her to tell him. Yet he felt as if she had struck him. And so absolutely was he accustomed to delicate tenderness, and the most thoughtful, anxious kindness from her, that he suffered acutely and from a double distress. The thing itself was cruel and hurt him. But that Hermione had done it hurt him far more. He could hardly believe it. That by any road she could travel to such an action seemed incredible to him. He stood, realizing it. And the bitter sharpness of his suffering made him understand something. In all its fulness he understood what Hermione's tenderness had been in his life for many, many years. And then—his mind seemed to take another step. "Why does a woman do such a thing as this?" he asked himself. "Why does such a woman as Hermione do such a thing?" And he knew what her suffering must have been, and how her heart must have been storm-tossed, before it was driven to succumb to such an impulse.

And he came quite close to her. And he felt a strange, sudden nearness to her that was no nearness of body.

"Hermione," he said, "I could never judge your character by that action. Don't—don't judge mine by any cruelty of which I have been guilty during this summer. You have told me something that it was very difficult for you to tell. I have something to tell you. And it is—it is not easy to tell."

652

"Tell it me."

He looked at her. He was now quite close to her, and could see the outline of her face but not the expression in her eyes.

"My interest in Vere increased. I believed it to be an interest aroused in me by the discovery of this talent in her. I believed the new fondness I felt for her to be a very natural fondness, caused by her charming confidence in me. Our little secret drew us together. And I understand now, Hermione, that it seemed to set you apart from us. I believe I understand all now, all the circumstances that have seemed strange to me this summer. I wanted Vere's talent to develop naturally, unhindered, unaffected—I thought it was merely that —and I became exigent, I even became jealous of all outside interference. On the night we dined at Frisio's I felt strongly irritated at Panacci's interest in Vere. And there were other moments—"

He looked at her again. She stood perfectly still. Her head was slightly bent and she seemed to be looking at the ground.

"And then came the night of the Carmine. Hermione, after you and Vere had gone to bed Panacci and I had a quarrel. He attacked me violently. He told me—he told me that I was in love with Vere, and that you, and even—even that Gaspare knew it. At the moment I think I laughed at him. I thought his accusation ridiculous. But when he had gone—and afterwards—I examined myself. I tried to know myself. I spent hours in self-examination, cruel self-examination. I did not spare myself. Believe that, Hermione! Believe that!"

"I do believe it."

"And at the end I knew that it was not true. I was not, I had never been in love with Vere. When I thought of Vere and myself in such a relation my spirit

653

recoiled. Such a thing seemed to me monstrous. But though I knew that was not true, I knew also that I had been jealous of Vere, unjust to others because of Vere. I had been, perhaps, foolish, undignified. Perhaps —perhaps—for how can we be quite sure of ourselves, Hermione? how can we be certain of our own natures, our own conduct?—perhaps, if Panacci's coarse brutality had not waked up my whole being, I might have drifted on towards an affection for Vere that, in a man of my age, would have been absurd, have made me ridiculous in the eyes of others. I scarcely think so. But I want to be sincere. I would rather exaggerate than minimize my own shortcomings to you to-night. I scarcely believe it ever could have been so. But Panacci said it was so. And you—I don't know what you have thought—"

"What I have thought doesn't matter now."

She spoke very quietly, but not with bitterness. She knew Artois. And even in that moment of emotion, and of a sort of strange exhaustion following upon emotion, she knew, as no other living person could have known, the effort it must have cost him to speak as he had just spoken.

"That, at any rate, is the exact truth."

"I know it is."

"I have thought myself clear-sighted, Hermione. I have studied others. Just lately I have been forced to study myself. It is as if—it seems to me as if events had conspired against my own cross ignorance of myself, as if a resolve had been come to by the power that directs our destinies that I should know myself. I wish I dared to tell you more. I wish to-night I dared to tell you all that I have come to know. But I dare not, I dare not. You would not believe me. I could not even expect you to believe me."

He stopped. Perhaps he hoped for a word that would

deny his last observation. But it did not come to him. And he hesitated for what seemed to him a very long time, almost an eternity. He was beset by indecision, by an extraordinary deep modesty and consciousness of his own unworthiness that he had never before experienced, and also by a new and acute consciousness of the splendor of Hermione's nature, of the power of her heart, of the faithfulness and nobility of her temperament.

"All I can say, Hermione"—he at length went on speaking, and in his voice sounded that strange modesty, a modesty that made his voice seem to her almost like a voice of hesitating youth—"all that I dare to say to-night is this. I told you just now that we all have our different ways of loving. You have loved in your way. You have loved Delarey as your husband. And you have loved me as your friend. Delarey, as your husband, betrayed you. Only to-day you know it. I, as your friend—have I ever betrayed you? Do you believe —even now when you are ready to believe very much of evil—do you really believe that as a friend I could ever betray you?"

He moved, stood in front of her, lifted his hands and laid them on her shoulders.

"Do you believe that?"

"No."

"You have loved us in your way. He is dead. But I am here to love you always in my way. Perhaps my way seems to you such a poor way—it must, it must— that it is hardly worth anything at all. But perhaps, now that I know so much of myself—and of you"— there was a slight break in his voice—"and of you, I shall be able to find a different, a better way. I don't know. To-night I doubt myself. I feel as if I were so unworthy. But I may—I may be able to find a better way of loving you."

Quite unconsciously his two hands, which still rested upon her shoulders, began to lean heavily upon them, to press them, to grip them till she suffered a physical discomfort that almost amounted to pain.

"I shall seek a better way—I shall seek it. And the only thing I ask you to-night is—that you will not forbid me to seek it."

The pressure of his hands upon her shoulders was becoming almost unbearable. But she bore it. She bore it for she loved it. Perhaps that night no words could have quite convinced her of his desperate honesty of soul in that moment, perhaps no sound of his voice could have quite convinced her. But the unconsciously cruel pressure of his hands upon her convinced her absolutely. She felt as if it was his soul—the truth of his soul—which was grasping her—which was closing upon her. And she felt that only a thing that needed could grasp, could close like that.

And even in the midst of her chaos of misery and doubt she felt, she knew, that it was herself that was needed.

"I will not forbid you to seek it," she said.

He sighed deeply. His hands dropped down from her. They stood for a moment quite still. Then he said, in a low voice:

"You took the *fattura della morte?*"

"Yes," she answered. "It was in—in her room at Mergellina to-day."

"Have you got it still?"

"Yes."

She held out her right hand. He took the death-charm from her.

"She made it—the woman who wronged you made it to bring death into the Casa del Mare."

"Not to me?"

"No, to Peppina. Has it not brought another death?

or, at least, does it not typify another death to-night, the death of a great lie? I think it does. I look upon it as a symbol. But—but—?"

He looked at her. He was at the huge doorway of the palace. The sea murmured below him. Hermione understood and bent her head.

Then Artois threw the death-charm far away into the sea.

"Let me take you to the boat. Let me take you back to the island."

She did not answer him. But when he moved she followed him, till they came to the rocks and saw floating on the dim water the two white boats.

"Gaspare!"

"Vengo!"

That cry—what did it recall to Hermione? Gaspare's cry from the inlet beneath the Isle of the Sirens when he was bringing the body of Maurice from the sea. As she had trembled then, she began to tremble now. She felt exhausted, that she could bear no more, that she must rest, be guarded, cared for, protected, loved. The boat touched shore. Gaspare leaped out. He cast an eager, fiery look of scrutiny on his Padrona. She returned it. Then, suddenly, he seized her hand, bent down and kissed it.

She trembled more. He lifted his head, stared at her again. Then he took her up in his strong arms, as if she were a child, and carried her gently and carefully to the stern of the boat.

"Lei si riposi!" he whispered, as he set her down.

She shut her eyes, leaning back against the seat. She heard Artois get in, the boat pushed off, the plash of the oars. But she did not open her eyes, until presently an instinct told her there was something she must see. Then she looked.

The boat was passing under the blessing hand of San

Francesco, under the light of the Saint, which was burning calmly and brightly.

Hermione moved. She bent down to the water, the *acqua benedetta*. She sprinkled it over the boat and made the sign of the cross. When they reached the island Artois got out. As she came on shore he said to her :

"Hermione, I left the—the two children together in the garden. Do you think—will you go to them for a moment? Or—"

"I will go," she answered.

She was no longer trembling. She followed him up the steps, walking slowly but firmly. They came to the house door. Gaspare had kept close behind them. At the door Artois stopped. He felt as if to-night he ought to go no farther.

Hermione looked at him and passed into the house. Gaspare, seeing that Artois did not follow her, hesitated, but Artois said to him:

"Go, Gaspare, go with your Padrona."

Then Gaspare went in, down the passage, and out to the terrace.

Hermione was standing there.

"Do you think they are in the garden, Gaspare?" she said.

"Sì, Signora. Listen! I can hear them!"

He held up his hand. Not far away there was a sound of voices speaking together.

"Shall I go and tell them, Signora?"

After a moment Hermione said:

"Yes, Gaspare—go and tell them."

He went away, and she waited, leaning on the balustrade and looking down to the dim sea, from which only the night before Ruffo's voice had floated up to her, singing the song of Mergellina. Only the night before! And it seemed to her centuries ago.

A SPIRIT IN PRISON

"Madre!"

Vere spoke to her. Vere was beside her. But she gazed beyond her child to Ruffo, who stood with his cap in his hand and his eyes, full of gentleness, looking at her for recognition.

"Ruffo!" she said.

Vere moved to let Ruffo pass. He came up and stood before Hermione.

"Ruffo!" she said again.

It seemed that she was going to say more. They waited for her to say something more. But she did not speak. She stood quite still for a moment looking at the boy. Then she put one hand on his shoulder, bent down and touched his forehead with her lips.

And in that kiss the dead man was forgiven.

EPILOGUE

On a radiant day of September in the following year, from the little harbor of Mergellina a white boat with a green line put off. It was rowed by Gaspare, who wore his festa suit, and it contained two people, a man and a woman, who had that morning been quietly married.

Another boat preceded theirs, going towards the island, but it was so far ahead of them that they could only see it as a moving dot upon the shining sea, when they rounded the breakwater and set their course for the point of land where lies the Antico Giuseppone.

Gaspare rowed standing up, with his back towards Hermione and Artois and his great eyes staring steadily out to sea. He plied the oars mechanically. During the first few minutes of the voyage to the island his mind was far away. He was a boy in Sicily once more, waiting proudly upon his first, and indeed his only, Padrona in the Casa del Prete on Monte Amato. Then she was quite alone. He could see her sitting at evening upon the terrace with a book in her lap, gazing out across the ravine and the olive-covered mountain slopes to the waters that kissed the shore of the Sirens' Isle. He could see her, when night fell, going slowly up the steps into the lighted cottage, and turning on its threshold to wish him "Buon riposo."

Then there was an interval—and she came again. He was waiting at the station of Cattaro. Outside stood the little train of donkeys, decorated with flowers under his careful supervision. Upon Monte Amato, in the Casa del Prete, everything was in readiness for the arrival of the Padrona—and the Padrone. For this time his Padrona was not to be alone. And the train came in, thundering along by the sea, and he saw a brown, eager face looking out of a window—a face which at once had seemed familiar to him almost as if he had always known it in Sicily.

And the new and wonderful period of his boy's life began.

But it passed, and in the early morning he stood in the corner of the Campo Santo where Protestants were buried, and threw flowers from his father's terreno into an open grave.

And once more his Padrona was alone.

Far away from Sicily, from his "Paese," among the great woods of the Abetone he received for the first time into his untutored arms his Padroncina. His Padrone was gone from him forever. But once more, as he would have expressed it to a Sicilian comrade, they were "in three." And still another period began.

And now that period was ended.

As Gaspare rowed slowly on towards the island, in his simple and yet shrewd way he was pondering on life, on its irresistible movement, on its changes, its alternations of grief and joy, loneliness and companionship. He was silently reviewing the combined fates of his Padrona and himself.

Behind him for a long while there was silence. But when the boat was abreast of the sloping gardens of Posilipo Artois spoke at last.

"Hermione!" he said.

"Yes," she answered.

"Do you remember that evening when I met you on the sea?"

"After I had been to Frisio's? Yes, I remember it."

"You had been reading what I wrote in the wonderful book."

"And I was wondering why you had written it."

"I had no special reason. I thought of that saying. I had to write something, so I wrote that. I wonder — I wonder now why long ago my conscience did not tell me plainly something. I wonder it did not tell me plainly what you were in my life, all you were."

"Have I—have I really been much?"

"I never knew how much till I thought of you permanently changed towards me, till I thought of you living, but with your affection permanently withdrawn from me. That night—you know—?"

"Yes, I know."

"At first I was not sure—I was afraid for a moment about you. Vere and I were afraid, when your room was dark and we heard nothing. But even then I did not fully understand how much I needed you. I only understood that in the Palace of the Spirits, when— when you hated me—"

"I don't think I ever hated you."

"Hatred, you know, is the other side of love."

"Then perhaps I did. Yes—I did."

"How long my conscience was inactive, was useless to me! It needed a lesson, a terrible lesson. It needed a cruel blow to rouse it."

"And mine!" she answered, in a low voice.

"We shall make many mistakes, both of us," he said. "But I think, after that night, we can never for very long misunderstand each other. For that night we were sincere."

"Let us always be sincere."

"Sincerity is the rock on which one should build the house of life."

A SPIRIT IN PRISON

"Let us—you and I—let us build upon it our palace of the spirits."

Then they were silent again. They were silent until the boat passed the point, until in the distance the island appeared, even until the prow of the boat grated against the rock beneath the window of the Casa del Mare.

As Hermione got out Gaspare bent to kiss her hand.

"Benedicite!" he murmured.

And, as she pressed his hand with both of hers, she answered:

"Benedicite!"

That night, not very late, but when darkness had fallen over the sea, Hermione said to Vere:

"I am going out for a little, Vere."

"Yes, Madre."

The child put her arms round her mother and kissed her. Hermione tenderly returned the kiss, looked at Artois, and went out.

She made her way to the brow of the island, and stood still for a while, drinking in the soft wind that blew to her from Ischia. Then she descended to the bridge and looked down into the Pool of San Francesco.

The Saint's light was burning steadily. She watched it for a moment, and while she watched it she presently heard beneath her a boy's voice singing softly the song of Mergellina:

> "Oh, dolce luna bianca de l' estate
>   Mi fugge il sonno accanto a la marina;
>   Mi destan le dolcissime serate,
>   Gli occhi di Rosa e il mar di Mergellina."

The voice died away. There was a moment of silence.

A SPIRIT IN PRISON

She clasped the rail with her hands; she leaned down over the Pool.

"Buona notte, Ruffino!" she said, softly.

And the voice from the sea answered her:

"Buona notte, Signora.   Buona notte e buon riposo."

THE END

www.ingramcontent.com/pod-product-compliance
Lightning Source LLC
Chambersburg PA
CBHW020241030726
47499CB00001B/11